WITHDRAWN

THE TENTH AVATAR

by
GARY NAIMAN

© Copyright 2004, Gary Naiman
All Rights Reserved.

No part of this book may be reproduced, stored in
a retrieval system, or transmitted by any means,
electronic, mechanical, photocopying, recording,
or otherwise, without written permission
from the author.

ISBN: 1-59453-206-0

This is a work of fiction. Names, places, characters and incidents either are the product of the author's imagination or are used fictitiously, and any resemblance to any actual persons, living or dead, events, or locales is entirely coincidental.

Bookman Publishing & Marketing

Martinsville, Indiana
www.BookmanMarketing.com

Should the god's warriors fail and the forces of darkness prevail, the angered gods will unleash The Tenth Avatar to destroy the world and all its people in flames ....

Interpreted from The Vedas

1 | Kangchenjunga

In nine years of flying, Captain Matao Iimori had never faced a storm with this power. Since encountering the blizzard two hours ago, the FW 200C Condor had lost three thousand feet to fierce wind and ice, dropping it dangerously close to the world's most treacherous terrain. Blinded by snow, Iimori and his crew fought a desperate battle to hold the eastward heading that would lead them out of Tibet's turbulent weather into China where a squadron of Zeros waited to escort them to Nanking. There was only one problem. They weren't in Tibet....

Iimori rested his head against the black leather seat and stared at the snow striking the windshield. A sweet numbness crept through his arms and legs. His eyelids fluttered and began to close. Just a few minutes of blessed sleep. Not too much to ask.

He was about to nod off when something caught his eye. He glanced to his right and saw his co-pilot's head droop forward, his hands barely grasping the control wheel.

Iimori cursed under his breath and seized the wheel and throttles. "I'll take it, Fuchida."

"What?"

"I've got the plane."

Lieutenant Eiichi Fuchida slipped his hands off the co-pilot's wheel and slumped in his seat. He rubbed his forehead, trying to clear his head.

"She's too heavy. We need to de-ice again."

Fuchida didn't respond.

"Fuchida?"

"Something's wrong. Dizzy ...."

Iimori glanced at the blue lever beside his co-pilot's arm. He grimaced and flipped it on, sending a rush of oxygen into Fuchida's mask.

Fuchida shook his head and looked down at the lever. "I...must have bumped it with my elbow."

Iimori glared at his co-pilot. "You want me to recite that at your funeral! Snap out of it, Fuchida!"

Fuchida straightened up and took a deep breath of oxygen. "I'm sorry, Captain."

Iimori shook his head and pressed the throttles forward. He pulled back the wheel and felt the cockpit vibrate from the four surging Bramo engines. The defiant altimeter needle continued its downward slip.

The frustrated pilot leaned against the side window and squinted at the plane's left wing. Through the snow, he could see ominous ice patches on the engine cowlings, only inches from the motors. He glanced at his co-pilot. "What's the de-icer pressure?"

"Sixty percent."

"Use it."

"Captain?"

"Use it!"

Fuchida gripped a black lever on the floor beside his seat. He pushed it forward and watched a small pressure gauge drop from the rush of compressed air into inflatable rubber gaskets on the wings. It would only take a few seconds to know if the surging air was enough to dislodge the ice. He eased back in his seat and stared at the windshield. "Captain, maybe we should drop out of it."

Iimori's black eyes flared with anger. He yanked down his mask and vented two hours of frustration. "Every time I see a shadow, I think it's a mountain. If we drop any lower, we'll be part of Tibet. The only way out of this mess is up. Now pump that lever!"

Something struck the window beside Iimori's head. He turned away from his co-pilot and pressed his helmet against the glass. He flinched as a chunk of ice broke off the wing and disappeared into the whiteout. Another chunk peeled off the inboard cowling and flew past his face.

Seven thousand hours of flying had taught Matao Iimori to seize the moment. The gods look unfavorably at cowards. "I'm taking us up." He jammed the throttles forward, filling the cockpit with a deafening roar.

Fuchida stared in horror at the four surging rpm indicators.

Had the man next to him snapped? In a few seconds, those straining needles would collapse to zero. Unable to glide with its heavy cargo, the massive plane would plunge into Tibet's merciless foothills. Eighteen brave men were about to die because their crazed pilot decided to burn up four good engines for a few thousand feet of insurance.

Fuchida started to speak, but hesitated. Under the ancient code of *bushido* he must never question a superior officer, even unto death. He had already crossed the line and received a stern warning. Another act of defiance would not be forgiven. He clutched the de-icer lever while recalling the tiny gift inside his flight jacket. Let it go, Fuchida. Think of tomorrow. And home....

Tomorrow would be June 3, 1939. His son's first birthday. Tamiko would be waiting in front of Tokyo's Imperial Hotel with Fumumaro in her arms. Fighting back tears, he would step off the bus and embrace his little family amidst a sea of onrushing pedestrians.

He would reach into his flight jacket and pull out the small gold ring he'd purchased before leaving. With his wife's warm body pressed against him, he would stroke Fumumaro's black hair and place the ring in his son's tiny hand. Only a small gift, but the ring's engraved words would be an eternal reminder of his deepest love....

Always with you ....
Father

Before seeing his family, he would join his tired comrades at Yokosuka Naval Station. He would shake their hands and wish them good fortune in the hard days ahead. He would even shake Captain Iimori's hand.

The team would snap to attention for a final word from Major Tomonaga, their mission commander. The handsome young officer would step smartly down the line, pausing in front of each man to extend an opened hand in gratitude, his black eyes glistening with emotion.

With tears streaming down his face, Eiichi Fuchida would

clasp the major's hand while hearing the proud words that drive men to do the impossible.

"Mission accomplished, Lieutenant Fuchida. Well done...."

Fuchida felt the plane's nose surge upward. An invisible force pressed him against the leather seat. The cockpit vibrated from the roar of five thousand stampeding horses. His eyes focused on the rising altimeter needle. Seventeen thousand. Eighteen thousand. Eighteen five.

Yes, they were climbing. Fighting their way out of the storm. He could see blue sky breaking through the clouds. Sunlight flashed on his face. Only a few more seconds....

The cockpit shook from a loud thud. Stunned, Fuchida looked at his commander who was staring at the left wing.

"Smoke in number two!" Iimori feathered number two's throttle while scowling at the black smoke pouring from the left inboard engine. He pulled back the other throttles and pressed the wheel forward to level off, but the damage was done. The faltering engine showered the left wing with sparks.

Iimori tried to steady the pitching plane. A blast of heat struck his face. He leaned against the glass and saw flames spewing from the blackened engine. "Fire in number two!"

Fuchida gripped number two's extinguisher lever and began pumping a stream of retardant into the burning engine. He said a prayer and stared at the regurgitated foam spraying over the scorched wing. If the retardant failed, and the fuel tank ignited, he would never see his family again.

Overwhelmed by the retardant, the angry flames retreated into the sparking engine, disappearing in a wisp of black smoke. Seconds later, the smoke became a white vapor trail.

Fuchida lifted his trembling hand off the extinguisher lever and peered at the blackened engine. "I think it's out."

Iimori slumped in his seat and scanned the instruments. He had paid a dear price for a glimpse of heaven. Airspeed: one fifty and dropping. Altitude: eighteen five and dropping. Fuel: one half and dropping. With only three engines left, the plane's groundspeed had been reduced by one-fourth, cutting their effective range to fourteen hundred miles. Nanking was two thousand miles away.

Iimori pulled back the wheel and stared at the altimeter. No response. He pressed the throttles forward and tried again, but the needle continued its ominous fall. He glanced at the side window and shook his head. "I can't see the wing through this damn snow. How does it look on your side?"

Fuchida leaned to his right and squinted at the other wing. He fell back in his seat, his eyes fixed on the windshield. "Fresh ice, Captain."

Iimori clenched his fist and looked over his right shoulder. "Kigoshi, where are we?"

Second Lieutenant Tadao Kigoshi stared at the windshield, his hand clutching a pair of dividers.

Iimori glared at the petrified navigator. "Are you all right?"

"Yes, Captain."

"Then where the hell are we! Snap out of it, Kigoshi! I need a bearing!"

Shaken by the pilot's tirade, Kigoshi took a deep breath and leaned over his plotting table. He glanced at the compass and placed his dividers on the dimly lit map of Asia. It would be his twelfth attempt to plot their position since entering the monsoon two hours ago. The prior eleven efforts had proved futile, all indicating an ominous southward drift toward the towering Himalayas separating Tibet and Nepal. Impossible. They would have seen them by now. Unless—

Kigoshi put down the dividers and stared at the map. He rubbed his tired eyes and picked up the navigation wheel. The instruments were fluttering badly, but they were all he had. Winds from the northeast at ninety. Heading: due east at one ninety before losing engine. Effective groundspeed: one hundred five mph. Estimated angle of drift: thirty-five degrees southeast for two hours. Correction: Zero!

Kigoshi's eyes widened. The navigation wheel dropped out of his hand.

"Come on, Kigoshi! You think this plane runs on piss! The fuel's below fifty percent!"

Kigoshi picked up a pencil and scribbled the coordinates on a piece of paper. He leaned forward and touched the paper to

Iimori's flight jacket.
Iimori snatched the paper out of the young navigator's hand. "Three hundred fifteen degrees?"
"Yes, Captain."
"You want me to turn around and head northwest?"
Kigoshi swallowed hard and nodded.
"Are you mad?"
"Captain, we're in Nepal. Below the mountains. That's why we haven't hit anything."
"Nepal? Impossible, we couldn't make it over those peaks?"
Kigoshi clenched his fists. "We didn't. I think the storm sucked us into Nepal before we reached the Himalayas. They're above us now. Between us and China."
Iimori's jaw dropped. "Are you telling me we've been flying in Nepal for two hours? Below the Himalayas?"
"I think so, Captain. If the whiteout would break for a minute, I'd know for sure."
"Damn you, Kigoshi! What kind of navigator are you!" Iimori crushed the paper in his gloved hand and flung it at Kigoshi's face. "The hell with your coordinates. I'm correcting northeast. Replot a course for Nanking."
Iimori looked to his right and saw his co-pilot gaping at him with frozen eyes. "You better get the Major up here. And tell them we need more fuel."
Fuchida nodded and climbed out of the co-pilot's seat. He paused beside the shaken navigator and patted his shoulder before brushing past him to the cockpit door.
Kigoshi lowered his head. "I am sorry, Captain. I am dishonored before you."
Iimori gritted his teeth. He'd pleaded for a more experienced navigator, but was overridden by his mission commander because of Kigoshi's extensive geographic knowledge of Asia and Europe. So much for geographic knowledge. He took a calming breath and stared at the windshield. "Keep working your map, Lieutenant. And say a prayer for us."

* * *

Major Shinichiro Tomonaga put down his pencil and scanned the *Condor's* cramped passenger compartment. Across from him, Sergeant Mitsui had dropped off to sleep while the two German Jews used a small flashlight to play a game of gin rummy.

Tomonaga leaned back against the fuselage wall and studied the two parka-clad civilians. How strange they were. One minute playing cards like children, and the next poring through black notebooks filled with cryptic calculations. If it weren't for General Yasuda's strict orders to bring them back to Tokyo, he would have gladly left them in Norway. They were men without a country. Men trying to survive another day. Wars were better fought without such hapless creatures. Tomonaga jammed the journal into his pack and rested his head against the metal wall.

He was nearly asleep when a powerful jolt snapped him against his canvas restraining harness. He shook his head and saw Herr Kessler picking himself off the floor. Herr Stein lay beside him covered with scattered playing cards.

After ten hours of rugged flying, Tomonaga's patience had run out. He raised a clenched fist and shook it at them. "I told you to wear your harnesses! Now put them on!" He reached down for one of the playing cards and flipped it angrily at Stein.

The shaken Jew nodded and sat down. He didn't understand a word of Japanese, but Tomonaga's glaring eyes and menacing gestures more than made up for it. Stein picked up the flashlight and clipped on his seat harness while his friend gathered up the cards for a new game.

Tomonaga turned to Sergeant Mitsui who was rubbing a sore head. "Are you all right?"

"Yes, sir." Mitsui continued rubbing his tousled black hair.

"Better wear your helmet. It will keep that hard head from knocking a hole in the fuselage."

Mitsui smiled under his oxygen mask and slipped on the stained, brown-leather helmet. The protruding ear flaps and mask made him look like a baby elephant.

Tomonaga unclipped his harness and checked the blue oxygen bottle strapped to his belt. He'd done enough flying to know the violent jolt was caused by something internal. He grabbed an overhead strap and pulled himself up.

"Something wrong, sir?" Mitsui looked up at him with concerned eyes.

"Just stretching my legs, Sergeant. Get some sleep."

Tomonaga worked his way toward the metal door at the rear of the compartment. He lifted the restraining bolt and felt a rush of cold air against his face.

"Major Tomonaga!" Sergeant Morita's booming voice echoed through the *Condor's* cargo hold, sending a dozen Imperial Marines scrambling to their feet.

Tomonaga closed the bulkhead door and stared at the bowing marines. "How are we doing?"

Morita straightened up and mumbled through his mask. "We're well, sir."

Tomonaga jammed his fists against his hips. "Doesn't sound like it."

Morita's head snapped back. "WE'RE WELL, SIR!"

"That's better." Tomonaga slapped his arms against his parka and faked a shiver. "At least you won't spoil back here." He joined the marines in a good laugh and gestured for them to resume their card games.

Tomonaga squinted at the twin rows of canisters behind the crouched marines. "How are they holding up?"

"No problem, sir. I just checked the restraining straps. All secure."

Tomonaga eyed the canisters like a mother hen. "Did you feel that jolt?"

Morita nodded. "Sounded like an engine."

Tomonaga folded his arms and eased beside his sergeant. "I'm not worried with Iimori up there, but between you and me, I'll be glad when we clear this damn weather."

"The navigator?"

Tomonaga frowned under his mask. "Iimori was right. The kid is too light. I should have taken Genda."

Morita nodded and glanced at his watch. "Ten hours. I'm

starting to feel like a sardine. How long to Nanking?"

Tomonaga was about to reply when the bulkhead door swung open and Fuchida stepped into the cargo hold.

"Captain Iimori needs to speak with you, sir. He's asking for more fuel."

Tomonaga nodded and watched Fuchida disappear through the door.

"Trouble?"

"Just a briefing. It's been two hours since we hit the storm. Maybe we're coming out of it."

Morita glanced at his men. "We could use some good news."

"I'll see what I can do." Tomonaga lifted the door's restraining bolt. "Stay well, Sergeant. I'll try to get you some heat. We should land in twelve hours."

"Question, sir?"

"Yes?"

Morita leaned closer. "The men keep asking how much gold is in the canisters. They're placing bets. You know, thirty canisters at seventy-five pounds. That sort of thing."

Tomonaga nodded. "Sounds like a good way to pass the time."

"Tanaka thinks it's two million American." Morita looked down and waited for a reply.

Tomonaga leaned against him and whispered through his mask. "Tell Tanaka he's not close."

Morita's brown eyes lit up.

"Don't forget that fuel." Tomonaga patted Morita's shoulder and stepped through the door.

Morita watched the metal restraining bolt drop into place. He glanced at his watch. Twelve more hours and they'd be out of this sardine can. Twelve more hours....

He spun around and glared at the huddled marines. "What are you doing on your asses! This pig needs more fuel!"

The stunned marines jumped to their feet and snapped to attention. They watched the sergeant pick up a wrench and step to the line of metal drums strapped to the fuselage wall.

Morita unscrewed the first drum cap and jammed a rubber

hose into the opening. "The next one's yours, Tanaka. Left wing, got it?"

"Hai!" The marine nodded briskly.

Morita backed away and flipped on a pump connected to the right wing tank. "No smoking, gentlemen." He stared at the drum and listened to the gasoline gurgle through the hose.

Tomonaga stepped into the cockpit and rested a gloved hand on Iimori's shoulder. "How are we doing?"

"We have a problem, sir."

"Problem?"

Iimori hesitated. "The storm dragged us into Nepal. We're shut off from China."

Tomonaga stared at his pilot.

"It's my fault. Cut it too close. The damn monsoon snared us like a kite."

Tomonaga leaned forward and squinted at the snow blowing against the windshield. "Can we backtrack?"

Iimori shook his head.

"But we have plenty of fuel?"

Iimori gestured for Fuchida to take control of the plane. He leaned back in his seat and rubbed his tired eyes. "Backtracking means turning around and heading northwest to clear the mountains. Then turning east to get back on course. We'll waste five hours of fuel."

"Five?"

"At least."

Tomonaga pulled down his oxygen mask and stroked his stubbled chin. "What about flying back to Iran?"

"Too late. We passed our point-of-no-return an hour ago."

Tomonaga noticed the dead rpm gauge. "What happened?"

"Blew number two trying to climb out of this mess. It was the only way to escape the ice."

Tomonaga leaned toward the left window and peered at the snow blowing across the blackened wing. He caught a glimpse of the dead inboard propeller. "We're carrying a lot of ice?"

"Too much."

Tomonaga hesitated. "What do we do?"

"Head northeast. If we can find a pass into Tibet, we'll shake this damn storm and have a shot at one of the dirt strips near our lines. The Zero's will cover us until we get help."

"How close can we come?"

"Close enough. I'm not worried with the Zero's out there."

"What about the weather?"

"I think it's breaking up ahead."

Tomonaga gripped Iimori's shoulder and stared at the frozen windshield. "No one said it would be easy."

"No, sir."

Tomonaga slipped on his mask. "How far to the mountains?"

Iimori glanced back at his navigator who was poring over his charts. "Well, Kigoshi?"

"Hai!" The young second lieutenant jumped out of his seat and snapped to attention.

Tomonaga locked his black eyes on the fatigued navigator. "How does it look?"

Kigoshi struggled for words. "We should see the eastern Himalayas in a few minutes. Probably Kangchenjunga."

"Kang—"

"Kangchenjunga, sir. Twenty-eight thousand, but I think we can skirt it."

Tomonaga's eyes widened. "Twenty-eight?"

"Yes, sir."

Tomonaga fought his anger. "Quite a mess, Lieutenant."

"Yes, sir."

"Well, I'm sure you'll guide us through it."

Kigoshi didn't respond. His eyes were focused on the windshield.

Tomonaga turned and saw Iimori and Fuchida staring at the windshield. He leaned forward and noticed a wall of sunlit clouds emerging from the haze. "Good, we're coming out of it."

Iimori fell back in his seat and stared at his co-pilot. "How far do you make it?"

"I can't tell."

"Give me the damn wheel." Iimori seized control of the

plane and began easing its hundred eight foot wingspan into a steep left bank.

Tomonaga braced himself against the tilting cockpit. "What's wrong?"

"Mountain—dead ahead."

Tomonaga stared at the windshield in disbelief.

Iimori pressed the throttles forward and nodded at his co-pilot. "You better warn them back there. This damn wind is pushing me straight at it."

Fuchida couldn't move. His eyes were fixed on the monolith jutting through the broken clouds.

"Fuchida!"

Tomonaga gripped Iimori's shoulder. "I'll do it." He backed away from the stunned crew and turned for the cockpit door.

"Wait, sir!" Iimori looked back at his commander with desperate eyes. "Request permission to break radio silence for a distress call to our planes."

"But, Captain—"

"I'm sorry, sir."

Tomonaga glared at his pilot. "Do it." He turned and scrambled through the cockpit door.

Fuchida pulled out a small black book and began twisting the radio dials. "Our position, Kigoshi!"

Kigoshi scribbled the coordinates on a piece of paper and thrust it into the co-pilot's extended hand. He gripped the plotting table and gazed at the windshield. "God, I can almost touch it."

"Shut up!" Iimori turned the wheel to steepen the bank, but the stall-warning buzzer kicked on. He levelled off and stared at the wall of rock and ice stretching across the windshield. They were at least three thousand feet below the ridge crest. He gripped the wheel and listened to Fuchida bark out the distress call.

"Black Dragon calling Sanctuary. Time: eleven-twenty hours. Position: eighty-eight degrees east, twenty-seven degrees north. Heading: eighty-two degrees. In danger of crashing into north ridge of Kangchenjunga on Nepal-Sikkim border. Carrying thirty canisters of gold. If no further message received, assume Black Dragon down and send rescue force per Purple Code Nagumo. Repeat: Black Dragon calling Sanctuary...."

With seconds left, Iimori gritted his teeth and drew his last card. He pushed the wheel forward, sending the huge plane into a power dive. An invisible force pressed him against the seat. He could feel the blood rushing to his face. He looked down at the airspeed indicator. One fifty. One seventy. Two hundred. *Now!* He said a prayer and yanked the straining wheel against his stomach.

Tomonaga burst into the passenger compartment and grabbed an armful of blankets from under the seats.

"What's wrong, sir?" Mitsui started to get up.

"Stay down! Tighten your seat harnesses and press these against your faces!" Tomonaga flung the blankets at the three stunned passengers.

Kessler and Stein dropped their playing cards and gawked at him in panic.

"Do it!" Tomonaga staggered past them to the bulkhead door. He lifted the restraining bolt and rushed into the cargo hold as the plane surged upward from Iimori's desperate maneuver. "Morita!"

Sergeant Morita looked up and saw his commander's knees buckle from the plane's sudden climb. He tried to reach him, but the force pinned him to the floor.

"Brace yourselves!" Tomonaga kicked the door shut and clutched the bulkhead.

Iimori pressed the wheel against his stomach and glared at the windshield. He could hear Fuchida shouting the distress call above the engines. Behind him, Kigoshi dug his fingers into the plotting table while muttering a *Shinto* prayer.

He glanced at the altimeter. Twenty-one thousand. Twenty-one five. Twenty-two. They were going to make it!

The ridge of rock and ice rushed at his face. He pressed his back against the seat and screamed at the lumbering plane.

Gary Naiman

"Come on you German bitch! Only a hundred more—"

The windshield imploded as tons of ice and snow blasted into the cockpit, killing its three man crew instantly. Behind them, Sergeant Mitsui was crushed beneath the collapsing front bulkhead. Kessler and Stein cried out to their god before vaporizing in a fireball of exploding fuel.

Tomonaga was nearly to his feet when a tremendous force slammed him against the rear bulkhead. He felt the bulkhead give way to a blast of searing heat. His body catapulted into space. A chilled wind struck his face. He could see gray sky.

His right shoulder exploded in pain as his body skipped off the ice and cartwheeled into the air. He tried to cry out, but a crushing impact swept his breath away. Snow ripped across his face and chest. He caromed helplessly forward until his broken body came to rest in the deep snow.

He couldn't breathe. He rolled on his side and clawed at the snow covering his face. He began coughing, but the pain turned his coughs to agonizing cries.

Before blacking out, Tomonaga saw the *Condor's* decapitated tail section grind to a halt several hundred feet away. Beyond it, the snow-filled sky blazed with the plane's burning front section and wings. He closed his eyes and felt the snow striking his face. The air echoed with explosions, and the horrible cries of dying men. Then, there was only the wind....

An unmarked transport has crashed into a mountain on the Nepal-Sikkim border, its burning wreckage scattered across a twenty-three thousand foot ridge in a howling blizzard. A seemingly unnoticed event in a world preparing for war, but one far more important than imaginable for a few desperate men.

The gods had made their choices and taken positions in the clouds around Kangchenjunga. Four mortals would soon come to fight a battle that would determine the fate of mankind.

But we've gotten a bit ahead of ourselves. Ten years to be precise. Best to begin at a better time, in a better place . . . .

2 | *Valencia*

An hour had passed since Roberto set out along the banks of the Turia into the rich, green countryside above his native Valencia. His ears rang from last night's celebration and his head throbbed from too much *Rioja*.

God, it was hot. He wiped his brow and looked down at the splashing water. The river smelled so cool. Like an oasis in the desert. Enjoy it now, *hombre*. In a few weeks, the oppressive heat would reduce the Turia to a trickling stream. He yanked off his shirt and slipped down the rocky embankment into the swirling, blue-green water.

An invigorating chill swept through him as the mountain-fed current rushed over his face and body. He swam through the churning water and flipped on his back like a porpoise. The sky was so beautiful. The deepest of blues, and crystal-clear. He floated in space while recalling yesterday's celebration.

The *Festival of Juegos Florales* had been far more than a gala party for Roberto Hidalgo. With painters and writers pouring into Valencia to display their works, Roberto and his father had spent three agonizing months creating floats, galleries, and stages worthy of these sensitive *artistas*.

He smiled to himself while recalling Monsignor Diaz' stirring tribute to the Hidalgos before awarding them the Church's gold plaque for architectural excellence. But it was his father's emotional acceptance speech that won the day. The aging orator had them in tears when he raised his hands to the sun-drenched crowd and praised God for His greatest gift. *"España!"*

He closed his eyes and felt the cool water lap against his face. It was so refreshing. Like the soft breezes drifting across the plaza at last night's celebration. He heard the dancers' heels strutting against the pavement, their *castanets* clicking like a swarm of mating crickets. And the guitarists' *flamenco* chords pulsing through the crowd of handclapping Valencians. Driving them forward like shrieking banshees to clasp arms with their Andalusian brothers and sisters in a swirling rainbow of reds, yellows, blues, and greens. An orgy of love and camaraderie sorely missed in 1929 Spain.

He remembered the beautiful woman lying beside him in the darkness, her warm body pressed against him, her soft lips kissing him in the morning light. He'd never known a woman like Laura. So confident and outspoken, yet sensual and passionate in his arms. Always a step ahead, even when they danced the *paso doblé*. In only three months, he had fallen madly in love with her.

Roberto's bliss was interrupted when his buttocks grated against the rocks on the river's edge. Startled, he sat up in the water while a sunbathing frog blinked at him from a nearby rock. It was too hot to croak.

The Turia's unpredictable current had deposited him on the shore only a few feet from where he'd slipped into the river. So much for dreams, *hombre*. He stepped grudgingly out of the splashing water and snatched his shirt off a rock. It would only take a few minutes to reach the orange grove at the top of the hill.

"*Buenos dias,* Roberto!"

He spun around and saw Sancho waving at him from the field on his right. The laborer's white tunic and pants were streaked with perspiration from hours of digging in the midday sun. "*Hola,* Sancho! Are you mad, *obrero*? It's too hot to work today! Jump into the river, *amigo*! That sun will burn you to dried leather!"

Sancho smiled through parched lips. "I am already dried leather, Roberto! The land doesn't reward lazy men! And may I ask where you are going, son of Don Felipe Hidalgo? Perhaps into the shade of that orange grove for a little siesta? Perhaps you have tasted too much *Rioja* at yesterday's festival? Is that it, Roberto?" Sancho tipped his weatherbeaten sombrero toward the embarrassed young man while breaking into hysterical laughter.

Sancho knew him too well, as did the other laborers who farmed the rich soil of the *huertas* above Valencia. At twenty-eight, Roberto Hidalgo was living a magnificent dream. A handsome *caballero* with shining black hair and penetrating black eyes who easily won the hearts of lovely *mujeres* in the ancient Spanish city that was his home. At yesterday's festival, señoritas all but lined up for a tango with the wealthy son of Don Felipe Hidalgo, Valencia's foremost engineer and architect.

Roberto sighed and continued up the hill. If Sancho knew more, he might not be so envious. In a few years, Roberto's eyes would blur from endless blueprints and measurements. His back and legs would weaken from a thousand sleepless nights hunched over a drafting table. His hair would turn white from stressful deadlines and bidding wars. His heart would short circuit from the debilitating struggle to create structural art in a nation besieged with militant labor movements.

No, Sancho. Easier to rise with the sun and farm the soil, then quench your thirst with a jug of wine and beautiful woman under a starlit sky. Not such a bad life, *obrero*. Nothing is what it seems.

A warm breeze wafted across the cultivated plain, filling his nostrils with the heavenly scent of wildflowers and fresh oranges. He paused at the edge of the grove and looked east toward Valencia. The ancient city rose proudly from the Mediterranean Sea like a great, sprawling Atlantis, its medieval mosque towers silhouetted against the blue water and sky. God, he loved it here.

He crawled beneath the grove's sheltering branches and plucked a ripe orange from a nearby twig. He peeled away the fruit's taut skin and tore off a translucent crescent of orange meat. He bit into it, flooding his tongue with a burst of tart sweetness that made him moan with pleasure. He dug his fingers into the orange and jammed a second crescent of ambrosia into his mouth. Then a third.

With his thirst quenched by the sweet meat and citrus juices, he stretched out on his back and gazed at the latticework of branches and twigs crossing out the sun. He'd promised his father a blueprint of the *Miserere* renovation by this evening, but his eyes wouldn't stay open. His father would understand. He always understood....

Gary Naiman

* * *

Señor Hidalgo righted himself in the leather chair and blinked his eyes. The mantle clock was chiming five, but he didn't need a clock to know the time. The sun's late afternoon rays had reached the stone fireplace facing his desk, bringing to life the stunning portrait above the mantle.

He looked up at the beautiful woman staring down at him with soft, brown eyes. *"Buenos dias, mi amor.* You were in my dreams today."

They had met at the University of Madrid in 1896, a simple encounter while studying for exams on the grass beneath the great tower. Elena Montoya was a striking woman capable of melting any man with the slightest fix of her brown eyes, but it was her keen passion for living that drew him to her.

Raised by a stern militarist father, Felipe Hidalgo's obsession to succeed allowed little time for sensitive things, until the night he kissed her beneath the stars with the Mediterranean Sea lapping at his feet. From that moment, he knew this very special woman would be his shining beacon for life. He was devastated when she left him four years later.

Señor Hidalgo's lovely wife had been dead twenty-eight years, but he could still smell her sweet skin and taste her warm lips. Soon, they would reunite in a better world to walk along the sea and make love beneath the stars. Until then, he must be driven by two other passions. His work and his son.

He plucked the quill pen from its well and shuffled the papers. He was exhausted, but with only a week remaining to the Council presentation, there was no time for sleep.

"Señor, may I come in?"

Before he could answer, the study doors swung open and a petite woman stepped into the room clad in a silk white blouse and brightly flowered skirt.

"You must eat, señor. You are no longer a young man."

He shook his head. "I am not hungry."

"You must eat. We will not have any martyrs in this house." She stepped closer and planted herself beside him.

"Maybe some fruit and cheese."

"Fruit and cheese? You need warm food. Let me prepare

the *paella*. Then, you can get a good night's sleep and do twice as much work tomorrow."

"Sleep is out of the question."

"Martyr."

Startled, Señor Hidalgo put down the pen and looked at the attractive woman standing beside him. Maria had been his faithful companion for nearly thirty years. She was a young girl when his wife found her begging in the fields. Aside from delivering Roberto, Maria was the finest gift Elena Hidalgo gave her husband before she died.

"I am too tired to argue. Some *paella* then, but only a small bowl. And please find Roberto. I would like to eat with him."

"He should be here soon."

The Señor fixed his tired brown eyes on her. "It seems Roberto has become quite the lady's man."

Maria smiled and shrugged. "You have a very attractive son, like his father."

He ignored her compliment and looked down at the pile of sketches lying on the desk. "Roberto will need more than looks and charm to survive this cruel world. We'll eat in here so I can review his work."

"Yes, señor."

He broke into a warm smile and took her hand. "Too much loyalty, Maria. You should have found a good husband and bore him children instead of staying with this cranky old man."

She smiled and pushed back a wayward strand of black hair. "This is my home, señor. I am very happy here, but I would be happier if you would eat a good meal."

"Then I'll try to make you happy."

"Good, señor."

Señor Hidalgo waited for Maria to leave the room before slumping in the chair, his face twisted in pain. He reached down and probed the small, throbbing lump in his left side. A trickle of perspiration ran down his forehead. Dr. Vivar's words echoed in his ears from this morning's examination....

I'm sorry, Felipe.
Then, there is no hope?

Gary Naiman

There is always hope, but you should put things in order. The cancer is in your glands and is spreading quickly.
How long?
Perhaps a year.....

The Señor looked up at the portrait. He had planned to transfer the business to Roberto in five years, but that was no longer possible. The transition must begin now.

He wouldn't tell Roberto about the cancer. The days ahead would be hard enough without compounding them with a son's pity. At twenty-eight, Roberto Hidalgo must become a man, and the Señor must become more a father, and less a mother, to his beloved son.

Yes, they would discuss these things tonight. He ignored the pain and snatched the pen off the desk.

Roberto scrambled out of the grove and stared at the orange-streaked clouds above the sea. The air had cooled and a gentle breeze was blowing from the east. Behind him, the last rays of sunlight had disappeared behind the distant Meseta hills. Valencia was bathed in shadows, except for the Micalet's shining tower.

"Shit!" He bolted down the hillside toward the darkened city. Through the corner of his eye, he could see Sancho and his comrades, still laboring in the cooling twilight. Those poor creatures would till that soil until the last trace of daylight was gone. Incredible, considering they owned none of the land.

A full moon was rising over the great city when he ran across Viveros Park toward the wood and stucco home nestled beneath the conifer trees. He stopped at the wrought iron gate and swiped the perspiration off his face. Through the windows, he could see a light shining in his father's study. A candelabra flickered in the dining room. The night air hummed with a million passionate cicadas. He tucked in his shirt and rested a hand on the gate's metal latch.

Despite his best efforts, the unoiled gate screeched when he opened it. The alarm had been sounded. He crept up the cobblestone walk and edged toward the front door like a *torero* facing the bull at the moment of truth.

"Where have you been?"

So much for stealth. Maria was standing in the darkened doorway with hands on hips. "I fell asleep in the groves."

Maria shook her head. "Your father has been asking for you since five. He wanted to eat with you. Not very considerate, Roberto."

He stunned her with an embrace. "Maybe I should take a bath first?"

"Shame on you. You smell like the river." She forced back a smile and slapped him on the rear when he went by.

Refreshed by a bath and change of clothes, Roberto took a deep breath and gripped the twin, carved door handles leading to his father's study. He pushed the doors open and stepped into the dimly lit room. His father was writing feverishly at his desk.

"Good evening, Father."

The Señor flung his quill pen in the air and jumped back in his chair. "My God, Roberto! Do you want to give me a heart attack?"

Roberto raised his hands apologetically and eased into one of the chairs facing the desk. "I didn't know you were still working."

The Señor reached down and snatched the quill pen off the polished wood floor. "How can you say that? Do you think Don Alejandro and the Carlitas are sitting on their verandas eating grapes? They're killing themselves like me. Do you know why?"

Roberto held back a smile. "Because you taught them everything they know?"

The Señor nodded proudly while fumbling through the drawings on his desk. He lifted one of them next to the green-shaded desk lamp so his son could see it. "This is my sketch of the restored *Miserere*. It must blend perfectly with your blueprint."

"Yes."

The Señor studied the sketch for a moment, then looked at

his son. "We should compare them now. Where is the print?"

"Print?"

"Of the *Miserere*?"

Roberto looked down. "I'm afraid the festival got the best of me."

The Señor slipped off his reading glasses. "Are you telling me the print is not drafted?"

"I'm sorry. I was going to work on it today, but—"

"No excuses, Roberto!" The Señor jammed the quill pen into its inkwell. The skin beneath his thinning white hair flushed bright red. "You promised me it would be finished tonight. Don't you know a man is judged by his word?"

"Father, I—"

"Enough!"

Roberto stared at his father in stunned silence.

The Señor's face twisted in a frown. "When you were a child, you did frivolous things, and I laughed. For twenty-eight years, I have laughed. But no more. You are no longer a child, Roberto. You are a man with responsibilities. I don't want your meaningless apologies. I want that print!"

Roberto had not seen his father explode like this before. He stood up and gestured for the old man to calm down. "I'll draft it tonight. We can review it first thing in the morning. I'll work all night if necessary." He turned to leave the room, but the Señor's angry voice stopped him.

"Wait!"

Roberto turned to face the man he suddenly feared. "I don't think we should talk until you've had some sleep."

The Señor stood up and gestured toward the two leather chairs beneath the portrait. "There is something we need to discuss, and this is a good time."

Roberto shook his head and dropped into one of the chairs while his father walked across the room and sat facing him.

For a moment, Señor Hidalgo stared blankly at the portrait while searching for the right words. He sighed and looked at his son. "I'm fifty-nine, Roberto. This is work for a younger man."

Roberto looked at him in disbelief. "Nonsense. Your best

days are ahead. Don't worry so much. I'll finish the blueprint tonight and we'll modify it tomorrow. I'm sure you'll win the bid after what we did at the festival. Then, we can restore cathedrals and missions until my hair turns white like yours."

The Señor shook his head. "You don't understand. I'm tired, Roberto. Remember, I've had two responsibilities."

Roberto cracked a smile. "Your business and your son. You have done both well."

The Señor stared at him. "Have I?"

"How can you say that? No son could have a better father."

"Kind words, Roberto, but it's time to put them to the test."

"Test?"

The Señor looked down at his gnarled hands. "It's time for you to take over."

"Take over?"

"Yes."

Roberto ran his hand through his black hair. "Aren't we rushing things a bit? Maybe in a few years when I'm more prepared. Besides, what will you do? You're too young to give up your work. If you're tired, hire an assistant to do the leg work and drafting."

Señor Hidalgo watched his son fidget in the chair. Not a good sign from a young man who should be overjoyed at the chance to inherit Valencia's most honored architectural firm. "I don't need an assistant. I need a successor, and he's my son. It's time, Roberto. You've attended the best schools and trained with the finest architects in Spain, including myself. There is nothing you can't design and build from mind's eye. You have a wonderful gift, and it's time to use it."

Roberto wasn't listening. He was staring at the portrait above the fireplace. "She was so beautiful."

"What?" The Señor looked up at the portrait. "Oh…yes. I miss her more than you know. That's not easy to say after twenty-eight years, but it's true. Your mother has never left me because I see her every day."

"In the portrait?"

"And in you, my son." The old man rested his head against the leather seat. "Your mother enjoyed her short life to the fullest, and you are too much like her."

"Too much?"

The Señor slumped in his chair. "You're a free spirit, Roberto. A lover of life. You're not ready for what's coming."

"Coming?"

"I'm afraid we will have a new government soon. Do you know what that will mean for people like us?"

Roberto shrugged. "Probably nothing. We're not landholders like the *latifundistas* and textile barons. We provide a service everyone needs. Old buildings must be renovated, and new buildings designed. It doesn't matter who's in power. Communists, fascists, nationalists—they'll all need our services."

A look of shock swept across the Señor's face. "When you take over *Arquitectura Hidalgo,* Spain's political decay won't seem so slight. After working with me for ten years. I'm surprised you're so naive. Don't you realize our designs are meaningless unless they're built?"

"Of course I do." Roberto's face reddened.

"Have you noticed the way the laborers behave since these damn unions have grown so powerful?"

"They want land and money. What's wrong with that?"

"It's our land and money!" The Señor grimaced from a shooting pain in his side.

"Is something wrong?"

"Plenty is wrong, Roberto. The labor unions become more hostile each day. The new government will do anything to appease them. Don't you understand what a socialist government will mean?"

Roberto recalled Sancho laboring in the midday heat. "A better world perhaps."

Señor Hidalgo slammed his fist on the chair arm. "You won't speak so boldly when they begin draining the Hidalgo estate for their social programs."

Roberto shook his head. "I don't agree. It's time for Spain to care for its poor. It would be a breath of fresh air after so many years of greed."

The Señor glared at his son. "I'm sorry to hear this,

Roberto. Your road will be tougher than I thought."

"Certainly not because of a few *communistas* and *socialistas*? Hell, I prefer them over land barons and bankers."

"You're talking like a child."

"Impossible! Spain's children are too hungry to talk." Roberto's black eyes flickered with anger.

"What's wrong with you?"

"I'm not a child. Don't treat me like one."

Señor Hidalgo leaned back and sighed. "Listen to me, Roberto. Whatever your personal feelings, there are hard truths that must be faced. *Arquitectura Hidalgo* demands it."

Roberto glanced at the mantle clock. "It's late. I should start on that print." He patted the chair arm and stood up to leave.

"Wait."

"Yes?"

Señor Hidalgo stood up and stared at his son. "What you said about the *communistas* and *socialistas*...."

"Yes?"

"Never speak those words in this house again. We're Spaniards, Roberto. Patriots! There is no room for intruders and extremists in Spain. They are without honor and belong in the mud with the lizards."

Señor Hidalgo watched his son storm out of the room. He brushed away a tear and walked back to his desk.

3 | Corpus Christi

"Thank you, Don Alejandro." The Monsignor rose from his chair and nodded to the handsome, silver-haired architect standing at the easel.

"Are there any questions, Monsignor?"

Monsignor Diaz glanced at the six black-robed clerics seated to his left. "No, señor. You have been immaculately clear. God go with you."

Don Alejandro nodded politely and gestured for his aide to place their drawings and sealed bid on the table next to Don Carlita's. "My phone number is on a card inside the bid envelope. We are very anxious to begin the work."

"I understand."

The Monsignor waited for Don Alejandro and his aide to exit the meeting hall before nodding to the usher. "And now, we will welcome the final proposal from *Architectura Hidalgo*."

Roberto followed his father into the great hall where the Monsignor and priests were seated in a semicircle facing a table and easel. The setting reminded him of a painting he'd seen in Madrid entitled, *The Inquisition*.

Señor Hidalgo bowed to the Monsignor and stepped to the easel, followed by his son. He pulled a pointer from his leather portfolio and fixed his brown eyes on the seven judges while Roberto placed the first sketch on the easel and stepped quietly aside.

It only took a few moments for the cunning old man to snare them with his passionate oratory and imaginative drawings. Knowing his father's flare for dramatics, Roberto bit his lip and quietly flipped the sketches while waiting for the grand finale. He knew it was near when the Señor hesitated and stepped toward the seated clerics. His father always stepped forward when he was about to deliver the *coup de grace*.

The Señor clasped his hands and looked up at the stained glass window above the meeting hall. "It was on a day like this I saw the sketches appear in a beam of colored sunlight. I was praying for guidance beneath the stained glass windows of Valencia Cathedral."

The hall echoed with whispers from the shocked clergy.

"In that moment, I felt God's presence and knew He had chosen me to restore the Church of Corpus Christi—and the *Miserere*."

The Monsignor stood up. "You would restore the *Miserere*?"

Señor Hidalgo raised his eyes to the portrait of *The Virgin Mary* on the far wall. "I will restore the *Miserere* for nothing, in memory of my beloved wife who died giving birth to my only son. I miss her so...." He lowered his head and stepped off the podium amidst a burst of tearful applause.

When word of the Council's acceptance came that afternoon, Señor Hidalgo broke down and wept like a child. After consuming a bottle of wine and bowl of rabbit stew, he staggered up the winding staircase to his bedroom under the watchful eyes of Maria and his exhausted son.

Roberto was nearly out the front door when his father shouted down to him from the top of the stairs. "This is no time to celebrate! I'll expect a work plan and estimate for the *Miserere* by eight in the morning!"

Stunned, Roberto watched the old man disappear through the door of his bedroom. The transition of responsibility had begun.

The sun was setting behind the Meseta range when Roberto escorted Laura into the *Restaurante Flamenco* in Valencia's old quarter.

"Roberto!" Señor Adolfo Losas stepped between the linen-covered tables and extended a warm hand.

"Hello, my friend." Roberto clasped Losas' hand.

"It has been over a month. I thought you were angry with my food."

"Never, Adolfo. Your *paella* is the finest in Spain."

Adolfo stepped back and eyed the handsome couple. "And such a beautiful companion."

Laura smiled under her veil. "You are very kind, señor."

"But you look so sad, Roberto."

"Just tired. Nothing a bottle of wine won't cure."

Adolfo broke into a wide grin and winked at Laura. "I have a quiet table in the back. With candle or without, whatever you prefer."

Laura nodded politely.

He led them through the busy restaurant to a small rear table while deftly snatching a bottle of *Rioja* and two empty glasses from a passing waiter's tray. A bit off color perhaps, but Señor Losas didn't care. If not for the Hidalgo's extreme generosity in restoring his restaurant after last year's fire, Adolfo Losas would probably be back in Andalusia strutting an exhausting *flamenco* for a few flung coins.

They opted for no candle. With a guitarist strumming a soft medley of love songs, Roberto reached across the table and clasped her warm hands. "We should have gone to my apartment first."

Laura frowned and eyed the plate of veal on the table next to them. "I'm hungry, Roberto."

"I'm hungry too, *mi amor*—but not for food."

"You're too impatient." She pulled her hands away.

"But honest."

Laura removed her veil and took a sip of wine. She pushed the glass aside and stared at him with soft brown eyes. "We need to talk."

Roberto shrugged. "We can talk there."

"I'm serious, Roberto."

"So am I."

She sighed and shook her head. "Persistent young bull."

After assuring Adolfo their early exit had nothing to do with his food, they took a taxi to Roberto's apartment on Avenida Navarro Reverter. When he opened the door at the top of the stairs, the young Spaniard flinched from a sharp, acrid odor. "God, the developing solution."

"*Mi Dios*, Roberto. You'll kill us with your damn chemicals."

"Don't turn on the light. It might cause an explosion."

"*Mi Dios.*"

Roberto rushed to a table cluttered with brown bottles. He grasped a metal pan and carefully poured its milky contents into a funneled glass jug. He put down the pan and jammed a rubber stopper in the jug.

"That smell is disgusting." Laura groped across the dark room to its shuttered window. She swung open the shutters and took a breath of fresh air while studying the last glimmer of daylight above the rooftops across the street.

Roberto eased behind her and slipped his arms around her waist. "Better?"

"Except for that damn smell."

"It will be gone in a minute."

She sighed and leaned against him. "Can I ask you something?"

"Anything."

"Is your father ill?"

"Ill?"

"He looked so tired coming out of the church. I haven't seen him like that. He's always so full of passion and fire."

"Oh, he'll be fine after a good night's rest. We've both been working too hard." Roberto pressed his lips to her ear. "But never mind him. If it's passion and fire you want, try his son."

"Insatiable young bull." She removed her hat and dropped it on the chair beside the window. Her slender waist slipped through his hands as she turned to face him. "You eat too much squid, young Hidalgo. What will we ever do with you?"

"Do you know how much I love you?"

"I think you say that to all the *mujeres* you lure into this smelly den." She pressed her firm body against him and kissed him softly on the lips.

"Laura, I—"

"You talk too much." She pushed away from him and sat on the bed while shamelessly removing her blouse, skirt, and undergarments. Stretching naked on the bed, she rolled on her side and touched her fingers to her lips, gently blowing him a kiss. "Well, what are you waiting for, little boy? Or would you prefer a tense young virgin?"

Roberto's heart pounded against his ribs. He yanked off his clothes and slipped beside the beautiful woman lying on his bed. He took her in his arms and kissed her warm lips.

Her hand slipped between his legs. "I think you prefer older women." She laughed and dragged her tongue down his neck and chest—then lower.

"You're shameless. Thank God, you're so shameless."

"Do you like this, Roberto?" Her seductive voice drove him mad as her tongue darted between his legs.

They kissed each other's quivering bodies until the urge became unbearable. She dug her nails into his back and slipped beneath him. Her warm, moist lips pressed against his ear. "Now, Roberto, I want to feel you inside me."

He eased into her while uttering a soft moan. Their bodies swayed together in the cool darkness until the ecstasy exploded inside them. Clinging to each other, they gave themselves up in a moment of splendor only lovers can know....

Roberto glanced at the moonlight coming through the opened window. "I guess it's too late for dinner."

"I see your priorities have changed." Laura squeezed his hand.

"Maybe Adolfo will take pity on us before he closes for the night." Roberto tried to sit up, but Laura's soft arm pressed him back on the bed.

"I'm not hungry."

"But, you said—"

"Let's just talk."

Roberto put his arm around her and stared at the darkness. "What should we talk about?"

"I think your father is right."

Roberto's face twisted in a frown. "Please, not again. This is the third time you've brought that up today."

"I'm sorry, but someone has to make you understand that your father is trying to help you. It's not good to see the Hidalgos fighting."

Roberto looked away in frustration. "How many times do I have to tell you, there are no problems between us. He's just tired. He'll be fine after some rest. Then, he'll come to his senses and drop this crazy thing about retiring."

She leaned on her elbow and stared at his moonlit face. "It's not that simple. Your father isn't well."

"Are you *loco*? At dinner, the man ate like a horse and drank a bottle of wine. Now he snores in his bed like a bull. Oh, almost forgot. He's demanded a work plan by tomorrow morning. Does that sound like a sick man?"

She brushed back a strand of light-brown hair. "He loves you very much, Roberto. You owe him more than unkind words."

His face flushed. "Don't you think I know that? Now please drop it." He crawled out of the bed and pulled on his trousers.

"You think I'm enjoying this? It's for your own good, Roberto. You're no different than the rest of us. Spain is changing for the worst. We have to join hands. We have to be prepared."

"I'm prepared. And more than most. Hell, I'm even looking forward to it."

"You don't know what you're saying. The Church is warning everyone. The socialists have taken over. They'll destroy Spain."

His flush deepened. "What do you expect them to say? It will mean less *pesetas* for their swollen pockets. Think of it, Laura. A new republic. No more hypocrisy. Help for the poor. Medicine for the sick. Now that would be a godly thing. Who knows, I might even attend Mass again."

She fell back on the pillow and sighed. "I wouldn't say these things if I didn't care."

He sat on the bed and ran his hand along her bare leg. "Oh, if those priests could see you now."

She slapped his hand away. "Why can't you be serious?"

He shook his head. "Life is too short to worry so much. That's why we're in trouble. If you want to make things better, give each citizen a bottle of wine, a lover, and enough *pesetas* to get through the day. You'll see, it will be a happier world."

She frowned and stared at the ceiling. "Maybe for you, but I'll need more if we're to go on."

"Go on?"

She fixed her brown eyes on him. "Who are you, Roberto? Where are you going? You're like the river in summer. No direction. No purpose."

Roberto felt a tinge of anger. "You suddenly demand a lot, my darling."

"It's my life too."

Roberto brushed back his tousled hair and gazed at the opened window. "You're asking a lot of tough questions. Can I ask you one?"

"Anything."

"Why are you so interested in my future?"

"What?"

"Would you still love me if I was one of those poor laborers digging in the fields?"

"Damn you!" She jumped out of the bed and snatched her skirt off the chair. "You think I want your father's money?"

Roberto raised his hands apologetically. "Calm down, I was only joking."

"Joking? Don't you realize people have feelings? How can you say such a terrible thing to me?"

Roberto reached for her, but she backed away.

"Let me tell you something, young man. I'm tired of playing sex games with a child."

Roberto's face flushed. "Child?"

"I'd better go." She tucked in her blouse and snatched her purse off the chair.

"Wait. What's wrong with you?" Roberto stepped in front of her and blocked the door.

"A woman needs more than sweet words and tender kisses. We'll talk when you've grown up."

He tried to put his arm around her, but she pushed him away. "You're serious. You're really leaving."

"I'm very serious. I've thought about it for some time, but I wanted to be sure. It's not easy to walk away from someone you love."

"Because of a little argument?"

"It's more than that, Roberto. There are things a woman expects in a man. Important things like character and integrity." She brushed away a tear and reached for the door knob. "Please, let me go."

Roberto shook his head. "*Mi Dios*, I thought you were the one person who understood me."

"I do, Roberto, and it frightens me. There's another side to you. A dark side that reminds me of the *communistas*, and it's growing stronger."

Roberto glared at her. "First I'm a child. Then a *communista*. Anything else?"

"I'm sorry, Roberto."

"So am I." He stepped away from the door.

"You proud, foolish little boy." She kissed him on the cheek and walked out of the room.

He tried to sleep, but Laura's words echoed in his ears. How could he say such a cruel thing to her. Maybe she was right about taking life more seriously. Either way, he loved Laura too much to lose her over a stupid argument. He would talk to her tomorrow, and she would listen.

At four a.m. he sat up and flung his pillow at the wall. Something was eating at him and it was more than harsh words exchanged between lovers.

It had started last week, a growing restlessness he couldn't explain. He awoke in a cold sweat with his heart racing and hands trembling. A chilled draft swept across his face. He heard a faint voice whispering like a breeze through the trees. When he regained his senses, the voice was gone and the chill had become a rush of cool night air coming through the opened window.

Until now, he'd attributed the unexplained dream to three months of exhaustive work, but maybe it was time to see Dr. Vivar. There had to be a pill for such things.

He walked to the window and looked out at the dark buildings across the street. A baby's cry drifted through the still night air. Above the rooftops, he could see stars twinkling through the haze. The sun wouldn't be up for two hours, but he needed to walk now. He slipped on his shirt and pants, and shuffled down the steps to the deserted street.

A dank night mist had settled on Valencia, a strange occurrence for this time of year. He pulled up his shirt collar

Gary Naiman

and headed across the Plaza Porta de la Mar toward the Calle de la Paz and Great Cathedral. An invigorating climb up the Micalet's two hundred steps would provide an unobstructed view of the approaching Mediterranean sunrise, and set the stage for a better day.

He was nearly past the University when he spotted the Church of Corpus Christi nestled in the shadows on his left, its dark spire jutting into the night sky. He paused on the empty street and recalled his father's edict to deliver the *Miserere* work plan by eight a.m. The perfect distraction for a troubled mind.

It would only take an hour to survey the assembly and develop an estimate. Then, a quick trip to the market for a bouquet of fresh flowers and, who knows, he might even propose to his beautiful *amor* today. He smiled and walked up the steps to the church's weathered doors.

"Yes?" Padre Erneste Pizarro stepped into the candlelit vestibule.

"It's Roberto Hidalgo, Padre." Roberto dipped his hand into the fountain of holy water and crossed himself.

"*Mi Dios*, I can't believe my eyes. It's like seeing your father thirty years ago."

"I look that much like him?"

"Oh, yes. You're the mirror image of your father when he was your age." Pizarro stepped closer and adjusted his wire-rimmed glasses. He wasn't a young man, but his chiseled face, straight nose, and flashing brown eyes proudly declared his Valencian heritage.

"I feel strange in here."

"Strange?"

"It's been nearly three years since I stood in a church."

"Why have you stayed away so long?"

"I don't know, Padre. To be honest, I wouldn't be here now if it weren't for the restoration. I've come to inspect the *Miserere*."

"Ah, the *Miserere*." Pizarro smiled and gestured toward the chapel. "God works in strange ways, Roberto. Please, stay as long as you wish. Would you like me to show you the way?"

"How do you mean that, Padre?"
"Oh, I'm sorry. I meant—"
"Just a little joke. I'll be fine." Roberto patted the priest's arm and brushed past him into the softly lighted chapel. He genuflected and walked down the aisle while staring at the enormous painting of *The Last Supper* hanging above the altar.

At the completion of the Eucharist, the choir would break into the Fifty-first Psalm's *Miserere* while Ribalta's beautiful painting disappeared behind blue and black velvet drapes. With the choir's voices rising in an emotional tribute to Christ, the drapes would part, revealing a life-sized crucifix where the picture had stood. Overcome with emotion, the distraught congregation would praise God while falling on their knees weeping for their earthly sins. Not a bad performance for a few coins dropped in a donation bowl.

After personally reviewing the *Miserere*'s delicate assembly, Roberto's father had developed an estimate of the required upgrades and written them off as a minimal cost. Now, his son must prove him correct.

Roberto walked past the front pew toward the gold curtain at the left of the altar. He pushed through it and stepped into a darkened alcove. His hand groped the wall for a light switch.

A blinding flash stung his eyes as a dangling electric bulb lit up in front of his face. He cursed the sudden brilliance and squinted at the ninety-foot-high labyrinth of wheels, pulleys, and ropes that controlled the miraculous transformation.

It only took a few minutes to figure out the simple pulley system. He clutched the first wooden wheel with his left hand and unleashed its secured rope with his right while peeking through the curtain at the painting.

As the rotating wheel slid through his palm, two blue-velvet drapes closed over the great painting above the altar. A few turns of the wheel in the opposite direction returned the drapes to their original parted position.

The ritual with the second wheel was similar, only this time it was overlapping black-velvet drapes that slipped over the painting. No need for reconstructive surgery here, except perhaps a good cleaning of the heavy fabric.

The third wheel was more of a challenge for the young architect. Straining against the taut wheel, Roberto struggled to elevate Ribalta's huge painting into the darkness above the altar. With his arms cramping, he resecured the restraining rope after managing to lift the cumbersome painting only a few feet. Work must be done here. More pulleys to spread the weight and ease the task of making the painting vanish.

One to go. Roberto spit on his palms and wrapped the fourth rope around his waist. He gripped the control wheel with his left hand and began unleashing the rope with his right. It would only take a few seconds to free it from its restraining hook.

If only Roberto had asked Pizarro a few more questions, he would have realized two men worked the third wheel, while the fourth required three muscular clerics.

The rope snapped against his waist. Before he could react, a terrific force lifted him off the floor into the darkness above the screeching wheel. He clutched the rope with both hands and hung on for dear life. A loud crash echoed off the walls.

He was dangling ninety feet in the air. Everything was silent except the creaking rope. Regaining his senses, he crawled down the rope until his feet rested on the floor. He untangled the rope from his waist and pushed through the gold curtain. Better to have stayed up there.

He froze in horror. An eight foot crucifix had plunged into the altar, its thick restraining rope draped across it like a resting snake. Stunned, he stepped onto the altar and noticed a large crack where the crucifix had struck. The pulpit had been split in two. Thank God, Pizarro wasn't rehearsing a sermon.

He knelt down and ran his finger along the splintered gash in the wood. The entire altar would have to be replaced, and a new pulpit constructed. "Damn." He backed off the altar and stared at the fallen crucifix. If it had suffered any structural damage, the cost of replacement would be severe. Carpenters weren't cheap since joining the powerful UGT trade union.

He collapsed in the front pew, his eyes fixed on the crucifix. What a mess. All because of a silly lover's quarrel. How would he explain it to Pizzaro? Well, he wouldn't have to wait long. He heard a rustling sound and felt a warm hand on his shoulder.

"What happened, Roberto?"

"I'm sorry, Padre. I didn't know the crucifix was so heavy. I'm afraid it cracked the altar when it fell." He looked down and sighed. "This is my fault. I'll begin repairing it immediately."

The priest's hand grasped his shoulder. "Don't worry about the altar. It's only wood and can be fixed. I think we have a more serious problem."

"Padre?"

"Your soul, Roberto."

"My what?" He tried to turn around, but the priest's grip was like iron.

"It's time."

"Time?"

"To stop the pain."

"What?" Roberto tried to stand, but Pizarro's hand pressed him into the seat.

"Your road won't be easy. Look up, Roberto—into the darkness."

Something moved in the shadows above the altar. He gasped as images began to appear, like photographs emerging in a developing solution. His ears echoed with screams and wailing sirens. He saw women and children running through burning streets. Plumes of flame belched into a blackened sky. The air smelled from charred corpses.

"What's happening? Stop it!" He covered his face and begged for the heart-wrenching nightmare to end....

"Roberto?"

Roberto sat up and rubbed his forehead. Pizarro was looking down at him with concerned eyes. "I must have fallen asleep."

"Thank God, I thought you were injured. What happened?"

Roberto looked up in surprise. "I told you. The crucifix crashed into the altar when I untied the restraining rope."

"Told me? I just came back from the market. I've been

gone two hours."

Roberto stared at the priest in disbelief. "We talked. You sat behind me and we talked."

"It wasn't me, Roberto."

"Then, it was one of your aides."

"Aides? I have no aides. No one was here. I locked the doors so you wouldn't be disturbed." Pizarro stepped onto the damaged altar.

"Then, who was it? Someone playing a prank?"

Pizarro wasn't listening. He'd knelt beside the fallen crucifix. "Roberto, did you cut your hands?"

"My hands?"

Pizarro lowered his head.

"What is it?" Roberto stepped onto the altar and rested a hand on the priest's shoulder. A red fluid was dripping onto the altar from Christ's feet. Roberto reached down and dabbed the spreading crimson pool with his finger. It felt warm. He touched his finger to his lips and detected a taste of salt and iron.

"Padre?"

"Yes?"

"Is this part of *Miserere*?"

Pizarro shook his head. "You'd better leave, Roberto. I need to be alone. Please tell no one about this."

Roberto looked down at the widening pool of blood and felt a chill go up his spine. "What does it mean?"

"Please go, Roberto."

Roberto stumbled out of Corpus Christi and headed for his apartment. The early morning air was filled with pungent smells of fresh fruit and fish from the nearby market. He walked along the Calle de La Paz and bumped into a rush of students headed for their early morning classes at the University.

"Hey, watch it!"

He ignored their shouts and cut across the Plaza Porta de la Mar to Avenida Navarro Reverter, and his apartment.

He was about to unlock the door of his apartment when a rustling sound stopped him. He leaned against the door and peered into the shadows above the exposed roof beams. "Is someone there?"

"You will wear black."

He dropped to the floor and cowered against the door. "Who are you? Show yourself, dammit!"

There was no response. The rustling had stopped.

What was happening to him? He was coming apart. Get to Dr. Vivar now. He scrambled to his feet and bolted down the stairs.

But Vivar's pills didn't help. In the nights that followed, Roberto relived the nightmarish vision of death and destruction. Trembling in the darkness, he saw people running from burning buildings while diving aircraft cut them down with merciless machine gun fire. He heard their screams and saw bullets ripping up the ground in front of him. When he ran for cover, something bright flashed in front of his face. It was a small gold crucifix dangling from a chain around his neck.

The selection had begun. Soon, other screams would come from a desolate place across the world. Bloodcurdling cries from people ravaged by merciless men ...

4 | Karak

The thin air above the Deosai echoed with high-pitched whistles from marmots scurrying for their underground burrows. A horse and rider approached from the east, their silhouette swaying lazily through the windswept grass. They pulled a heavily burdened yak.

Karak blinked his tired eyes and scanned the distant yellow hills. They seemed no closer than when he left Skardu this morning. His father had warned him about the monotonous rocking. Easy to drift asleep on the Deosai, never to be heard from again. He tugged on the rein and slipped off his horse into the waist-high grass.

He reached into his pack and uncorked a goatskin of water while recalling his father's warning. *Three gulps—no more.* He savored the cool water and filled a small wooden bowl for his horse. A few decisive slurps and it was gone. Then it was the yak's turn. Each animal would get a second bowl before resuming the trek, but the rider only got one. It was summer on the Deosai and the highland streams were dry. To care for your animals was to care for yourself.

Karak stretched his arms toward the sky and scanned the horizon. Fifty miles behind him, Skardu's burnt-sienna hills reached toward the towering wall of ice that bore his name. The unconquerable Karakorum range, western extent of the Himalayas.

He smiled at a low hanging cloud and pretended to snatch the floating white fleece. How proud he felt today. His father had given him the finest birthday gifts imaginable, a strong horse and yak to carry him across the rugged Deosai. In a few hours, he would return from his first trading foray to the great bazaar at Skardu, no small feat for a young man traveling across the harshest terrain on earth.

After crossing fifty miles of desolate plateau at an altitude exceeding thirteen thousand feet, Karak Drasi had acquired everything his family and friends desired. Even the fur-lined boots for his sister. And there was still a tie of leftover wood strapped to his yak, proof he'd outbartered Skardu's most cunning merchants and traders.

A chilled breeze swept across the grass, whipping his father's prayer scarf against his face. He tucked the brown-checked cloth into his tunic and looked toward the mountains. The breeze had shifted and was blowing from the ice giants on the northeast horizon. Not a good sign. The shamans often warned that cold summer winds from the Karakorum meant approaching death, while warming winds from the southern valleys meant a long life.

Karak refreshed his animals a second time before tucking away the precious goatskin. He climbed on his horse and patted the steed's black neck while staring at the yellow hills. It would be a long day. He gave the yak's rope a good luck tug and pressed his heels into the horse's flanks.

Piercing cries of darting marmots filled the air as the three intruders continued their slow, westward trek across the rippling grasslands. The chilled breeze had become a cold, steady wind....

"*Ata! Ata!* Karak is home!"

Ghulam Drasi breathed a sigh of relief and placed his freshly polished climbing boots on the wool blanket. He stood up and turned to face the young girl who had barged into the hut.

"He's coming up the ridge, Father."

Ghulam embraced his trembling daughter. "Calm down, Nangi. You'll scare everyone to death."

"I'm so glad he's safe."

Ghulam felt his daughter relax in his arms. He slipped his hand under her chin and lifted her beautiful face toward him. "I'm surprised at you. Did you think I would send your brother out there unprepared?"

She broke into a smile and started for the door.

"Wait, Nangi."

"Yes?"

Ghulam nodded at her. "Remember, you are the daughter of Ghulam Drasi. You must always remain calm in front of our friends."

"Yes, Father." Nangi's black eyes danced with happiness. She turned and ran through the opened door.

A smile cracked Ghulam's lips. She was only sixteen, but someday his little "queen of the gods" would rule far more than a simple village in the hills of western Baltistan. He stroked his black beard and glanced at the polished climbing boots. One gift remained for his son. He slipped on his gray *choga* and stepped through the opened door.

The panicked villagers had gathered at the eastern edge of the village. Balti women in loose fitting bonnets clutched their babies while their confused husbands whispered to each other. They all stared at the cloaked rider approaching from the valley.

Ghulam straightened his shoulders and walked toward the alarmed villagers. "There is nothing to fear. It's Karak returning from Skardu."

The stunned villagers broke into shouts of anger. One of them threw up his hands and thrust them on his hips. "Your daughter scares us to death, Ghulam."

"Calm down, Rasul. She cries out for joy. Her brother has come home."

Rasul pointed a gnarled finger at Ghulam and glared at him with black eyes. "You may be *lambardar,* but that doesn't give you the right to act like a king. First, you entertain the *angrezi*. Then, you send out Nangi to panic us while we prepare our evening meals. It is wrong, I tell you."

Ghulam rested a hand on his friend's shoulder. Nangi has been scolded for acting so foolishly. She is very excited. Can you blame her?" He pointed to the approaching rider. "My son's horse and yak ride low with a full pack of tools and clothing. He has done well. Please rejoice with me. We have a new trader in our midst."

Ghulam turned to face the towering mountain in the western sky. He clapped his hands and gazed at the white summit. "Thank you, mother of the earth. You have guided my son's journey, and made an old man happy."

He glanced over his shoulder to see if his words had

worked. The villagers were staring at the peak in silence. He smiled to himself and turned away from the mountain. "Well, what are we waiting for?" He clapped his hands and watched Rasul and the others shuffle down the ridge toward his son.

He could barely contain himself. He straightened his *choga* and assumed a formal stance befitting his position as *lambardar*—the village leader. Karak's return must be handled with great ceremony.

He was nearly down the ridge when he saw Rasul break into hysterical laughter, followed by the others. He ran toward the commotion, his heart pounding against his ribs. His son slumped on the horse, his arm dangling at its side.

"What has happened?" He pushed through the roaring throng of shepherds and grasped Karak's limp arm. "My God."

Rasul shook with laughter. "He is fine, great leader. Can't you hear him snoring?"

"He's asleep?"

Rasul reached up and snatched the brown-checked cloth dangling from Karak's tunic. "Thank your prayer scarf his horse remembered the way home." Rasul fell on the ground and rolled from side to side in convulsive laughter while Ghulam stared at his snoring son.

Karak bit into a piece of white cheese and sipped the bowl of fresh goat's milk. He sighed with pleasure and felt a warm hand on his shoulder.

"You look so tired, my son. Maybe we should wait until morning to open the packs."

"I'm fine, Mother." Karak smiled and patted her hand.

"You should be fine after sleeping on your horse for fifty miles."

Karak winced from his father's piercing stare.

"Let him eat in peace!" Nangi stood up and glared at her father.

"Calm down, little one." Karak smiled at his young sister and put a finger to his lips, but she was too angry to listen.

"You have no right to talk to him that way. This was his first trek. You're not perfect. Should I tell him what happened while he was gone?"

"Enough!" Ghulam stood up and flung his empty bowl on the hide blanket while his daughter stared at him in shock. "Leave us. I want to be alone with my son."

"Does that include me?" Karak's mother put down the goatskin of milk and looked at her husband with tired eyes.

Ghulam hesitated. "I'm sorry, Diki. Please, I must talk with my son."

"Remember, you are both tired. It has been a hard day for us all." Diki smiled at him and gestured for Nangi to follow her.

Ghulam waited for his wife and daughter to leave the hut before sitting down. He reached for his clay pipe and began stoking it with stale tobacco.

Karak took a deep breath and spoke softly. "I was able to barter some wood for a fresh can of tobacco. It's pine-flavored with a touch of the *charas* weed. Your favorite."

Ghulam lit the pipe and smiled at his son. "I'm sure you did well at the bazaar. By the gods, I've taught you every trick I know."

"I'm sorry for falling asleep. It happened when I crossed the Chogu Chu. I was fine until then, but the trickling current made such a soothing sound. I saw the green pines on the hills and thought I was home."

"Thank the gods your horse didn't stray. If he had veered northeast toward the cool smell of the glaciers, you would have awakened in hostile country with an inviting pack of goods and an ancient single-shot rifle."

"It will never happen again."

Ghulam reached out and grasped his son's shoulder. "The mountains watch out for you, Karak. You're named for the mighty Karakorum. Your sister carries the spirit of Nanga Parbat—*Diamir*—Queen of the gods. I love you both more than my life." Ghulam's piercing eyes glistened through his rugged beard.

Karak patted his father's gnarled hand. "Then, you forgive me for falling asleep?"

Ghulam smiled. "I fell asleep many times at the Chogu

Chu."

"You?"

"That's why it is important to have a good horse to carry you home. But enough of this. Let's open your packs and see the treasures of Skardu." Ghulam laughed and slapped his son's shoulder.

Diki and Nangi stood dumbfounded when their two men burst from the hut with their arms draped around each other. Laughing like two drunkards, Ghulam and his son marched toward the bundled packs lying in a heap beside the campfire.

Ghulam squeezed his son's shoulder and whispered, "Soon, I'll have enough *rupees* to buy you a small caravan. There are great passes beyond Skardu, and you are destined to follow them, my son."

"*Rupees*? From where?"

"In time, you will know. Now, let's enjoy this wonderful evening." Ghulam spread his arms toward Nanga Parbat and cried out for the villagers to leave their huts and light the bonfires. It was time to open the packs and share the clothing, tools, and gifts from his son's journey.

And out they came, ceremoniously dressed in their finest pants, boots, tunics, and checkered cloaks. The men wore traditional peaked Balti hats, and their wives, loose fitting bonnets. Pine logs were stacked in two huge piles and struck with flints. Soon, roaring flames shot into the darkening sky above the Astor River Valley while Nanga Parbat blotted out the setting sun.

It was a night of laughter and joy for the family of Ghulam Drasi. Ignoring his fatigue, Ghulam's proud son entertained the villagers with contrived tales of battle against mythical cloud monsters and giant marmots. With the campfires burning brightly into the night sky, Karak distributed Skardu's wealth while the villagers applauded like excited children. So much happiness, so much love, and it was all about to end....

"Rasul!" Karak shuffled down the hillside toward the cloaked shepherd.

"So, you are finally awake, son of Ghulam Drasi. Your

friends tend to their woodcutting and animals while you sleep like a newborn baby." Rasul leaned against a rock and squinted at the wiry young man approaching him in the morning sunlight.

Karak reached into his tunic and extended a small gold box toward his father's best friend. "I was going to give you this last night, but I forgot."

Rasul took the box and studied it. "What is it?"

"Open it and find out."

Rasul rested his staff against the rock and pried open the box. "Ah, an amulet." He plucked the polished green stone from the box and held it up to the sunlight.

"It is jade and will bring you good luck. I bartered with a shaman to get it. I hope you like it."

Rasul stood up and smiled at Karak through his grizzled beard. "Thank you, young man. It's the finest gift I've ever received. I'll wear it in a small pouch around my neck, for good luck." He reached out and patted Karak's shoulder. "Walk with me."

They climbed down the hillside into a pasture near a winding stream called the Das Khirim Gah. After counting his grazing sheep, Rasul sat on the grass and gestured for Karak to join him.

"I'm glad you like your gift."

Rasul nodded and looked toward the Karakorum. "I'll use it to scare away the evil spirits in that cold wind. I don't like the smell of that wind."

Karak sniffed the air. "You mean, the smell of the glaciers?"

"No, young Drasi. I mean the smell of the *angrezi*."

"*Angrezi*?"

"Do you know your father had visitors while you were gone?"

"Visitors?"

"*Angrezi*. English pigs offering money for a *sirdar* to guide them up Nanga Parbat."

"Karak's face twisted in a scowl. "Did he shout them out of the village?"

Rasul shook his head. "He agreed to help them."

"What?"

Rasul grabbed his arm. "They are evil men. I watched them shake your father's hand. They kept glancing at your mother and sister with hungry eyes. I tried to warn him, but he wouldn't listen."

"But, you're his closest friend? He has always respected your words?"

Rasul looked down at the amulet. "He won't face the truth."

"Truth?"

"When he was a young man, Ghulam Drasi was known throughout the Deosai for his strength and courage. He would rise before the sun to cut down trees, then tend the sheep before going into the mountains to hunt game, and there was still enough left in him to drink and dance with your mother into the night." Rasul clutched the amulet. "Now, an old man lives with his dreams."

Karak sighed and looked at the grazing sheep.

"He agreed to meet them today at their camp in the Rupal Valley."

"Today?"

Rasul gripped his arm. "Stop him, Karak. You're the only one he'll listen to."

Karak's eyes widened.

"What is it?"

"His climbing boots are gone. He's already left!" Karak scrambled to his feet and charged up the hill. He was nearly to the village when he saw his sister running toward him.

"Karak!" Nangi ran to her brother and clutched his arm.

"What happened?"

"Mother wouldn't let me go with her. She told me to wait in the village."

"Where is she?"

"In the Rupal Valley. She's gone after Father."

Karak's face flushed. "The *angrezi's* camp?"

"You know?"

"By the gods, Nangi. Why didn't you tell me?"

She sobbed and began to cry. "He lied to us. He promised not to go with them. When we woke, he was gone. Why did he do that? We don't need the *angrezi's* filthy money."

Karak held his sister while recalling his father's promise to buy equipment and supplies for a caravan. It would be Ghulam Drasi's third gift of manhood for his son's twenty-first birthday.

"Did she go alone?"

"She was afraid to ask for help. The villagers are too angry. She didn't want you to know."

"My God. When did she leave?"

"I'm not sure."

"By the gods." Karak ran into their hut and grabbed his rifle and a pouch of powder and bullets. He burst out of the hut and tried to dodge his sister, but she grabbed his arm.

"I'm going with you."

"No, it's too dangerous. Go to Rasul. Tell him what happened." Karak pointed a hard finger at his sister. "I know that look in your eyes. Stay here, Nangi. I mean it."

"But—"

"Stay here!" He yanked his arm free and ran up the steep slope toward the ridge overlooking the Rupal Valley.

From the top of the ridge, Karak could see the fertile valley stretching toward the foothills below Nanga Parbat. He shaded his eyes and scanned the sunlit haze for a sign of life. Except for a few stray sheep, the thick yellow carpet looked deserted.

He was about to head south along the ridge when he noticed a column of smoke rising into the haze from the base of the foothills. It had to be the *angrezi's* camp. He took a deep breath and charged down the densely forested slope into the valley. Had he looked back, he would have spotted his sister climbing down the ridge behind him.

The Rupal Valley was blistering hot from the afternoon sun. There was no breeze. Karak stripped off his tunic and ran through the tall yellow grass toward the white smoke rising from the foothills. He clutched his rifle while recalling the first time his father led him into those foothills to hunt wild birds and game. He had learned so much from his father and mother, but most of all, they had taught him the meaning of love.

Karak was within a hundred yards of the *angrezi's* encampment when he heard a woman's agonizing screams. He crouched in the tall grass and edged closer. A man's rasping voice rose above the screams.

"Hold her down! That's it. My turn, dammit."

With his heart pounding, Karak pushed through the grass and stared in horror at the scene unfolding in front of him.

They'd stripped his mother naked and pinned her to the ground. One of the pigs had crawled on top of her while the other two watched with animal eyes.

"Hurry, dammit! I want her next." One of the two onlookers pulled down his pants and tried to drag the third man off her, but he was pushed away. When Diki screamed for mercy, her assailant raised his hand and slapped her senseless with all his might.

Karak stood up and gasped. His father was lying beside the fire, his face covered with blood. The old man clawed at the ground in a futile attempt to aid his ravaged wife.

"Bastards!" Trembling with rage, Karak aimed the rifle at the *angrezi* raping his mother.

"Watch it!" The two panicked *angrezi* dived into the tall grass as their comrade's head exploded in red spray from Karak's deadly bullet.

Karak ran to his mother's writhing body. He kicked away the dead man and tried to comfort her, but she was too hysterical to know who he was.

"Mother! My God."

He was lifting her in his arms when the two *angrezi* sprang from the bushes on his left. He grasped the rifle and tried to jam a bullet into the open chamber, but it slipped out of his sweating hand and rolled on the ground.

"Get him! Before he reloads!"

Karak reached for another bullet, but it was too late. The first *angrezi* slammed into him, sending the rifle flying into the dirt. When Karak tried to grab it, the second *angrezi* stomped on his hand with his boot, making him cry out in pain.

Karak felt a crushing weight on his back. He rolled over and swung wildly at the *angrezi* straddling him, but it was no use. Strong hands pinned his arms to the ground while the other *angrezi* pulled a knife from his belt.

"You killed our friend, you little shit. Now why did you go and do that? All we want is a little intimacy with the tasty lady. She's a bit old, but not a bad body, and plenty wild. I like that."

"She's my mother!" Karak broke free and took a wild swing at the grizzled face looking down at him. He lunged for the *angrezi's* throat and felt a terrific pain in his head.

His ears rang and the sky whirled overhead. They were pulling off his pants and pushing his face in the dirt. He felt a pain in his loins and heard a voice echoing in his ears.

"Forgot to tell you, chum. We like young boys too."

The nightmare continued while they sodomized him. When he tried to push them off, his head exploded in agony from the impact of the *angrezi's* rifle butt....

Everything was spinning. He heard a bloodcurdling scream. A familiar voice cried out to him.

"Help me, Karak!"

"Give me that bloody rock. She's clawing like a wildcat. Here, little one. This'll calm you down."

"Karak! Help—"

"Come on, let's strip her. Man, did we luck out. I thought we'd have to kill the old man and go back to the village for our jollies, but look at this. Two wild women stumble into our camp without us having to lift a finger."

"Look at the body on this one. And untouched too. Flip you for her. Heads, she's mine. I win! You get the old one."

"What about the old guy?"

"Hell with him."

"No, dammit. He gives me the bloody shivers the way he keeps clawing at the dirt. Cut his bloody throat and put him out of his misery."

"Hey, don't mess the girl up too bad. I want some of that before we kill her. There, old man. Now you can sleep. Might as well finish off the boy too."

Karak felt a sharp pain in his back as the *angrezi* shoved

the knife between his ribs. The last thing he heard was his mother's screams while the two men continued to ravage her and his sister....

Through the ringing darkness, he heard a clap of thunder and felt rain pelting his face. The black sky flashed with unearthly light. He tried to sit up, but a knifing pain stopped him. He collapsed on his side and stared at the darkness.

"Oh, God!" He could see them in the flashing light. Three glistening bodies sprawled in the mud only a few feet away, their eyes frozen in terror.

"No!" He tried to crawl toward them, but couldn't move. He buried his face in the mud as the sky exploded with thunder.

What was that taste? Blood! The rain had leeched the mud with his family's blood. To mingle with his own.

He heard footsteps sloshing through the mud. They were getting louder. Thank the gods, they'd come back to finish him.

"There—by the fire! Oh, God!"

Someone grasped his shoulder and turned him over.

"Karak, can you hear me? It's Rasul."

"Rasul?"

"What happened? My God, what happened?"

"Why...didn't...you...come?"

Rasul cradled Karak in his arms and stared at the mutilated bodies lying next to the abandoned campfire. His stunned eyes filled with tears as he tried to grasp what had happened. "Oh, Ghulam, why didn't you listen? Now I'll take this to my grave...." He broke down and wept while holding the last living Drasi.

They rigged a stretcher and carried him back to the village. In the days that followed, the wounded young man teetered between life and death while Rasul and his family fought to keep him alive.

In his delirium, Karak saw them lying naked on the flashing ground. Everything was still except the falling rain. Suddenly, his father reached out to him with his bloody hand while raising his voice to the heavens.

Gary Naiman

Vengeance, Karak! Vengeance!

He saw the villagers take them to the great mountain and light the torches. He heard the ancient chants and saw their glowing ashes swirl into the night sky above Nanga Parbat. Some ashes drifted west toward the great mountain. Others blew east toward the Karakorum before disappearing into the blackness.

Torn with guilt, Rasul sat alone at the nightly campfires. He clutched the amulet and listened to the delirious young man cry out to the spirits of his dead family, and he wept with each heart-wrenching scream.

For twelve sleepless nights, Rasul prayed for the spirits of his dear friends while begging the gods to spare the last living Drasi. His prayers were answered on the thirteenth night when Karak staggered out of Rasul's hut into a falling rain.

"Thank the gods." Rasul ran to him and grasped his arm.

"How long has it been?"

"Many days. We didn't think you would live after losing so much blood. The *angrezi's* knife barely missed your heart. Praise the gods, it's a miracle."

"My family?"

Rasul looked down. "They are with the gods."

Karak clenched his fists. "The *angrezi*?"

"They escaped."

"The one I killed?"

"Rasul looked at him in surprise. "Killed? We found no one."

"They must have dragged him away. They wanted to kill me so there would be no witness." He looked up at the flashing sky. "Were my mother and sister alive when you came?"

"What?"

"Were they alive?"

Rasul shook his head. "Why are you doing this? Let it go, Karak. It's over. They are with the gods."

"Gods?" Karak brushed back his soaked hair and glared at the old man. "Where were the gods when my sister begged for mercy? When they slashed my father's throat and raped my mother?"

"Rasul wiped his eyes. "We've notified the *Raj* in Skardu. They promised to—"

"They will do nothing. The *angrezi* own them." Karak turned toward his father's hut and started to walk away.

"Where are you going?"

"I'm leaving."

Rasul looked at him in shock. "You're what?"

"My father wanted me to build a caravan that would reach beyond Skardu. I'll take my horse and yak, and head northeast."

"But, you're not well. You need rest. There is nothing out there but death."

Karak looked toward the mountains. "I'll live, but I'd rather be dead."

"Don't do it, Karak. You're the last living Drasi. Stay here with your own kind. It would be your father's wish."

Karak lowered his head and sobbed. "She would have been a beautiful woman, my little queen of the gods."

"Karak, please—"

"Be well, Rasul. I won't forget you." He patted the old man's arm and shuffled toward his father's hut.

Karak left in the dark of night with rain pouring from the skies and chilled winds sweeping across the Deosai. He and his two animals would journey past the *Raj* at Skardu, and cross the desert into the foothills below the wall of glaciers separating Baltistan from China—toward his destiny at the roof of the world.

The gods were pleased. They had found their second warrior. They needed two more ....

5 | A New Path

Vivar leaned closer to the illuminated X-ray and traced the dark spot with his finger. He adjusted his glasses and placed a second X-ray beside the first.

"Well?" Señor Hidalgo slipped on his shirt and fumbled nervously with the buttons.

Vivar picked up a divider and measured the dark spot on the latest X-ray. He shook his head while pencilling the measurement in a black notebook.

"What is it?"

"A miracle. I've never seen such remission. The tumor has receded fourteen millimeters."

"Receded?" Señor Hidalgo stared at the brightly lit X-rays.

Vivar pulled off his glasses and smiled at his patient. "I'll not tempt fate, Felipe, but I can assure you a longer life than we expected three months ago. If the tumor remains in remission, there will be no need to operate." He waited for a reaction. "I don't understand. You should be overjoyed. We have witnessed a small miracle. God has granted you some extra time."

Señor Hidalgo slipped on his jacket and raincoat. "Thank you, Esteban."

"That's all you have to say?"

The Señor forced a smile. "I'm afraid it's a mixed blessing."

"Mixed?"

"How is my son?"

Vivar sighed and put down his glasses. "There is nothing wrong with him except fatigue."

"The pills do no good?"

"They help him sleep."

"Then, there is nothing you can do?"

Vivar grasped the old man's arm. "Roberto's problems are emotional. In three months, I have seen steady deterioration. He has lost weight and slumps around like a hurt animal. Something is eating at him."

The Señor lowered his head. "We haven't talked since he brought up the nonsense about the Church."

"Church?"

"I prefer not to discuss it."

"But, if you don't talk, how do you work together?"

"I write him letters, and he complies."

"*Mi Dios.*"

Señor Hidalgo looked at his friend. "I think he needs psychiatric care."

"No, Felipe. Roberto is full of crazy ideas, but he is quite normal. Talk with him. He needs a father's love."

"At twenty-nine?"

"At any age."

Señor Hidalgo patted the doctor's arm. "You're a good man, Esteban. I wish more were like you." He turned and walked out of the office.

A light drizzle was falling on Valencia. It was late October and there were predictions of unusually heavy rains along the Mediterranean coast. The Señor lifted his collar and climbed into a waiting taxi.

"Señor?" The driver smiled at him through the mirror.

"Please take me to the Church of Corpus Christi."

"Yes, señor."

Señor Hidalgo leaned back in his seat and pulled a folded newspaper out of his raincoat pocket. He flipped it open and stared at the headlines as the taxi pulled away from the curb. "*Mi Dios.*"

"Señor?"

"Look at this. The *peseta* has collapsed. Our currency is worthless, like the idiot running the government."

"You mean, Señor Rivera?"

"The fool was supposed to bring prosperity and order. Instead, he has alienated everyone." The Señor slapped the paper on the seat and stared out the rain-smeared window.

"Do you think we will have a new government, señor?"

"I dread the thought. Let me ask you, driver. Where are your sympathies?"

"With Spain, señor. We're at the church." The driver

guided the taxi through a deep puddle and pulled up to the curb in front of Corpus Christi.

Señor Hidalgo opened the taxi door and stepped into the falling rain. "Please wait, I'll only be a few minutes." He closed the taxi door and climbed the steps to Corpus Christi's renovated entrance doors.

The chapel smelled from fresh paint. The Señor crossed himself and walked down the aisle toward a kneeling priest. He crossed himself a second time and knelt beside his friend of thirty years.

Pizarro glanced at him and smiled. "Come to say a prayer for your dear wife, Felipe?"

"I've come to say one for Spain. I'm afraid we're in for a bad time."

"Have faith, Felipe. The Church will triumph over these radicals."

"It will take more than prayers to stop them. They have won the hearts of the laborers. Rivera should have clamped down on them when he had the chance. Now, it's too late." Señor Hidalgo frowned and looked up at the painting above the restored altar. "It's not politics that brought me here, Erneste. We need to discuss something."

"As you wish." Pizarro crossed himself and retreated up the aisle with his aging friend.

"Yes?" Pizarro stepped into the vestibule and clasped his hands.

"I have a taxi waiting, so I'll be brief. It concerns Roberto."

"Roberto?"

"You know he's been babbling about joining the clergy."

"He has discussed it with me."

"He told me you encouraged him to go through with it."

Pizarro looked into his friend's eyes. "When Roberto asked my advice, I told him to follow his heart."

"And that includes abandoning his responsibilities?" The Señor's face reddened.

Pizarro glanced down the aisle at the restored altar. "These things aren't easily explained. Perhaps God is calling him."

"God doesn't call weak men."

"How can you know that?"

Señor Hidalgo took a deep breath. "Listen to me, Erneste. Despite his limitations, my son was normal until he began restoring this church. Now, he cowers in the shadows like a hermit."

"Or a priest?"

"If you want to put it that way."

Pizarro's smile faded. "Roberto is going through a difficult time. I suggest you talk with him about these things. You have my promise not to intrude."

"I want you to intrude, dammit! I want you to talk him out of this insanity."

"I'm sorry, Felipe. This matter is between you and your son. Now please excuse me, I have to prepare for tonight's dinner at La Seo."

"And that's how you help a friend of thirty years?" Señor Hidalgo's eyes burned into the priest.

"I'll pray for both of you, Felipe. Good day." Pizarro turned and walked into the chapel.

Roberto clutched his chest and stared at the darkness in horror. The only sound was his labored breathing. He slid his hand across his chest where the bullets had struck, but there were no wounds. The diving aircraft was gone.

In three months, he hadn't slept a night without reliving the terrifying vision of men, women, and children running for their lives under a relentless hail of bullets. His nerves were shot. He was on the verge of breaking down.

Two hours had passed since he staggered up the steps to his apartment and collapsed on the bed. After working day and night on Corpus Christi's delicate *Miserere* pulley system, he had met his father's commitment to complete the restoration in time for Valencia's All Saint's Day celebration.

He sat up and wiped the sweat off his face. In the distance, the bells of the Micalet chimed seven. The All Saint's Eve dinner honoring Cardinal Saez would begin in less than an hour. Tomorrow, the Cardinal would conduct a special ceremony to consecrate Corpus Christi's restoration—proof the

Church remained strong in a nation seething with unrest.

Quickly showering and dressing, Roberto rushed out of his apartment and hailed a passing taxi. When he arrived at La Seo Cathedral, the honored guests were already seated at a large oak table beneath a wall of paintings in the great museum.

"Ah, my son has finally arrived. Please forgive him, Your Eminence. He has worked night and day on the restoration." Señor Hidalgo glared at Roberto while addressing the red-and-gold-cloaked official seated at the head of the table.

Roberto walked to the Cardinal and dropped on one knee. "I'm sorry, Your Eminence." He kissed the Cardinal's extended ring and felt a gentle hand touch his wet hair.

"God bless you, Roberto. Please, join your father."

Nodding humbly, Roberto took the empty seat beside his father. His eyes focused on the goblet of red wine in front of him.

"So, you embarrass me again."

His father's words were only a whisper, but they cut through him like a dagger. "I fell asleep."

"I'm not interested in your excuses. Did you finish the *Miserere?*"

Roberto clenched his fists and nodded.

The dinner was served quietly with occasional pleasantries exchanged between the Church Council and Roberto's father. It was past nine when Cardinal Saez finally rose from his carved wooden chair and extended his silver-and-gold goblet to the Señor. "We are very proud of your accomplishments, Señor Hidalgo. You have excelled in restoring the Church's sacred architecture to its deserved prominence." The Cardinal put down his goblet and eyed the small audience. "In these trying times, it is critical the Church's presence be felt more than ever. Thank you for contributing to that noble cause."

Roberto's father stood up and bowed to the Cardinal amidst a round of applause from the thirteen seated priests and officials. He straightened his royal-blue jacket and red sash while waiting for the Cardinal's gesture to begin speaking.

"Thank you for this wonderful honor, Your Eminence. I had no idea today would also bring me a personal miracle. I have just received word my cancer has gone into remission."

A deep hush fell over the audience as Cardinal Saez dropped into his chair in stunned silence. Roberto stared at his father while recalling Laura's prophetic words.

Señor Hidalgo took a deep breath and continued. "I wasn't going to speak of this tonight, but I feel it is a message from God to continue the Church's restoration effort throughout *España*. Your Eminence, I remain your humble servant and stand ready to assist you." The Señor slipped into his chair and lowered his head while accepting their standing applause.

"Father, I—"

"Not now, Roberto. Come to my home tonight."

"Your home?"

"We'll talk later, Roberto."

Señor Hidalgo's words overwhelmed the Council. Before closing the ceremony, Cardinal Saez extended his arms toward the Señor and assured him his message would not be forgotten. Blessing his fellow clergymen and guests, the Cardinal excused himself and proceeded into La Seo's historic chapel to pray beneath the legendary *Holy Grail*.

A light rain was falling when Roberto knocked on the door of his father's home. He could see the concerned look on Maria's face when she opened the door.

"He is very upset, Roberto. Maybe you shouldn't see him tonight?"

"This wasn't my idea." Roberto grasped her hand. "Why didn't you tell me?"

"He only told me today. I was devastated. He has always been so strong. Please be patient with him. He loves you so much."

Roberto nodded and walked down the dark hall toward the closed doors of his father's study. He leaned forward and pushed them open.

Señor Hidalgo was seated at the fireplace, staring at his wife's portrait. Roberto closed the doors and eased into the chair beside him. The dimly lit room was silent except for the crackling flames and ticking mantle clock.

Roberto leaned forward and spoke softly. "Why didn't you tell me?"

"I didn't want your pity."

"Pity?"

"I don't expect you to understand."

Roberto shook his head. "Are you feeling any pain?"

"No." Señor Hidalgo rested his head against the chair. "I asked you to come here because there is something you should know."

"Yes?"

"I have decided to remain head of *Architectura Hidalgo*. You'll not be taking over the business after all."

Roberto broke into a smile. "That's wonderful news. But you should go easy for awhile. Maybe take on that assistant."

"You're the only help I need."

"What?"

"Think of it, Roberto. You can continue your carefree life until I sell the business or die. The money will be yours to squander. Until then, I'll expect your loyalty."

Roberto's smile faded. "What are you saying?"

Señor Hidalgo glared at his son. "I visited Corpus Christi today."

"You saw Pizarro?"

Señor Hidalgo's face reddened. "I can tolerate your frivolous ways. I can even face the bitter truth that you're too weak to carry on my work. But I won't let you throw away twenty-nine years of struggle for a white collar and bible."

Roberto clenched his trembling fists. "You think I wanted this?"

"What?"

"You heard me. I'm coming apart!"

Señor Hidalgo stared at his son in shock. "What is it, Roberto? What's wrong?"

Roberto gripped the chair, his eyes fixed on the fire.

The Señor leaned forward and gripped his son's arm. "My God, this is my fault. We'll see a physician first thing in the morning."

"Physician? You mean, a psychiatrist?"

The Tenth Avatar

"Just for a consultation. It's the wise thing to do."

"Damn you." Roberto stood up in anger.

Señor Hidalgo fell back in the chair, his eyes fixed on his trembling son.

"What's wrong? Not frivolous enough for you? Is that it?"

"Calm down, Roberto. You're acting like a lunatic."

"Lunatic? Well, I'm not surprised after putting up with your stupid lectures for twenty-nine years."

"What?"

"I'm sick of your sermons. I don't want your damn money, your precious business, or your hypocritical friends. I need to get away from here before you kill the last thing I have."

Señor Hidalgo shook with anger. "Which is?"

"My love for you."

The Señor rose out of his chair. "You call this love? After I've sacrificed my life for you? How dare you!" He raised his hand and slapped it across his son's face. "I'll expect you at the ceremony. No excuses. Be there! Then, we'll find that doctor." He stormed out of the study while his son wiped his bleeding lip and stared at the portrait above the fireplace.

It was nearly eleven when Roberto walked past the *Marva Bar* on the way to his apartment. Hesitating, he heard the chords of a *flamenco* guitar and a sensual voice coming from inside. Maybe some warm music and wine would take away the bad taste in his mouth.

He pushed through the doors and stepped into the smoke-filled bar. Through the haze, a beautiful guitarist struck a final chord of ecstasy while crying out for the man she loved. The room erupted with cheers and applause. Gesturing to her accordionist, the young lady let out a passionate shriek and struck up a tango while young lovers rushed from their tables to dance the night away in the flickering candlelight.

This was the old, wonderful Spain Roberto loved so deeply. Warm bodies pressed against each other, moving as one to the tango's pulsing rhythm.

He eased to the bar and ordered a bottle of *Rioja*. He was well into his second glass when a tender hand grasped his arm.

Gary Naiman

"Roberto?" A beautiful face looked up at him in the soft candlelight.

"Laura?"

"It's been so long."

Roberto backed away, his eyes beaming. "You look wonderful." He reached behind the bar for an extra glass, but she grabbed his arm.

"Please, join us." She gestured toward a table in the corner.

Roberto noticed two uniformed men seated at the table. "Your brothers?"

She smiled and squeezed his arm. "Please, let me introduce you."

Roberto gulped down his wine and snatched the bottle. He forced a smile and followed her between the swaying dancers.

"Francisco, I'd like you to meet my friend, Roberto Hidalgo. He and his father are renowned throughout Valencia for their architectural restorations."

The portly officer stood up and extended his hand. "Pleasure to make your acquaintance, señor."

"Likewise." Roberto smiled and shook his hand.

"And this is Rafael, my fiancé."

Roberto's smile faded. He extended his hand to the handsome lieutenant who had risen from his seat. "Pleasure, señor."

"Please join us." The lieutenant waved toward a vacant chair.

"Thank you." Roberto sat down and placed his bottle on the table.

"How are you, Roberto?" Laura smiled nervously while lifting a glass of wine to her lips.

"Things are going well."

"And your father?"

"He's well. I just left him."

"Excuse me, señor. Is your father Don Felipe Hidalgo?" The portly officer smiled at him through the candlelight.

"Yes."

"He was honored tonight by Cardinal Saez?"

"Yes, for our restoration of Corpus Christi."

"It's an honor to meet you, señor. Your father is well respected among Spain's true patriots. You must be very proud."

"I am." Roberto picked up the bottle and filled their empty glasses with *Rioja*.

The portly officer nodded and sipped the red wine. "I'll be at Cardinal Saez's consecration ceremony in the morning. They've asked a few of us to attend in case the socialists try to disrupt things."

Roberto looked up in surprise. "I doubt there would be any trouble."

"Ah, my friend. Things have changed for the worst. With the government teetering, the months ahead could be very difficult."

Roberto sipped his wine and smiled at the officer. "Well, I'm sure the army will protect us from the socialists and anarchists."

"I detect a note of animosity in your voice."

Roberto turned to the young lieutenant who had finally spoken up. "Sorry, I'm just tired."

"I see." The lieutenant smiled and patted Laura's hand. "We should be going, my dear. We have an early morning and our plane leaves after the ceremony."

Roberto glanced at Laura. "So soon? Well, it's been a pleasure, Señor.... I'm sorry, I forgot your name."

"Lieutenant Campeador, at your service."

"Ah, named for a champion." Roberto stood up and shook the officer's hand. "Good night, Lieutenant. Best wishes to you both." He looked down at Laura and forced a smile. "Good night, Señorita Cortez. Wonderful to see you again." He clasped her hand and locked his black eyes on hers.

"Oh, forgive my rudeness." The portly officer stood up and extended his hand. "It's been a pleasure, Señor Hidalgo. I'll be in Morocco for awhile, but perhaps we can get together for dinner when I return. I'd like to hear your views on the political situation when we have more time to talk. I trust they are in line with your father's."

"I'll look forward to it, Señor—"

"Franco—Francisco Franco. God go with you."

Roberto slipped on his raincoat and picked up their check.

"No, señor. That's not necessary."

"Please, Señor Franco. I insist. You can pay next time. And in case our paths don't cross tomorrow, have a good flight to Morocco." He walked away and left them standing at the table.

Roberto pulled up his collar and stepped into the falling rain. From here, it was only a short walk to his apartment. He paused and sniffed the salt air while the rain trickled down his face. No hurry. It might be a long time before he smelled that air again.

"Roberto?"

He turned and saw Laura standing behind him.

"Are you ill, Roberto? You look so tired."

"I'm fine, and I see you have done well. Lieutenant Campeador seems very ambitious."

She clutched his arm. "Please listen, I only have a minute. When I saw you tonight, it reminded me of the wonderful times we had. I want you to know something."

Roberto touched a finger to her lips. "You were right about me. I'm not very strong. I wish you the very best." He kissed her gently on the lips. "Goodbye, Laura."

"Wait!" She watched him disappear into the falling rain.

Roberto eased across his darkened apartment to the shuttered window. He pushed it open and stared at the moon flashing between the clouds. The damp night air smelled sweet like her soft skin. He could still feel her long fingers clutching his arm. He closed his eyes and felt her warm lips and body pressing against him. A tender ache spread through his loins, making him sigh. He would always love her, and his beautiful Valencia.

The Micalet's belltower chimed midnight. In a few hours, the ceremony would begin at Corpus Christi. He would kneel with Valencia's clergy while his father received the Cardinal's blessing. The Señor would rise and gesture for his son to share the glory. Nodding, he would climb the steps toward his proud father while the crowd applauded and his lovely Laura gazed at him through moist eyes. How magnificent. How meaningless.

He reached into his shirt pocket and pulled out a folded letter. He could barely read it in the moonlight....

Señor Roberto Hidalgo,
We will be pleased to welcome you to the Seminary of Andalusia for a period of trial and reflection. We have received a warm letter of recommendation from Padre Erneste Pizarro at the Church of Corpus Christi. Padre Pizarro has expressed his deepest conviction that you have experienced a personal message from God to take up the cross. I assure you, we do not take this lightly. We await your arrival.
God bless you,
Padre Miguel Ordoña

Roberto stared at the leather traveling bag in the corner. The next few hours would be the hardest of his life.

Señor Hidalgo lifted his arms and glanced out the bedroom's lead-paned window. "The rain has stopped. It should be a beautiful morning."

"Yes, señor." Maria finished winding the red sash around his waist and backed away to admire her handiwork. "You have lost considerable weight. We need to put some meat on your bones."

The Señor slipped on his red tie and glanced at the grandfather clock in the corner. "*Mi Dios*, it's already past seven. Is my car here?"

"I'll check, señor."

The Señor snatched his speech from the nightstand and sat on the edge of the bed, his eyes focused on the classic scrawl.

There would be no further mention of the cancer. Only a fervent pledge to move forward with any new assignments the Church cared to grant. He broke into a wry smile. There would be many new assignments, not just in Valencia, but throughout Spain. Before he was done, *Architectura Hidalgo* would be revered throughout Europe.

"Señor?" Maria stepped into the bedroom and stared at the old man seated on the bed.

"The car is here?"

She hesitated. "Your son is downstairs and wishes to see you."

"Roberto?" The Señor stuffed the paper into his jacket and walked out of the room. When he reached the top of the stairs, he looked down and saw his son standing in the red-tiled foyer. He was holding a familiar leather bag.

Señor Hidalgo eased down the winding staircase. "What's wrong, Roberto?"

Roberto's voice trembled. "This is very hard."

"Hard?"

"I'm leaving."

"You're what?"

"I'm sorry, Father."

Señor Hidalgo grasped the staircase railing. "Where are you going?"

"To Andalusia."

"Andalusia?"

"I've been accepted into a seminary there—to prepare for the priesthood."

Señor Hidalgo sat on the stairs, trying to compose himself.

"They're willing to accept me for trial. I'll study under Padre Ordoña."

The old man slumped against the railing. "Roberto, I may have been a bit harsh, but this isn't the answer." He glanced at the leather bag. "We both need rest. After the ceremony, we'll spend the afternoon at the sea. We'll talk and listen to the waves."

Roberto rested a hand on his father's shoulder. "Don't blame yourself for this. It's not your doing."

The old man grasped his son's hand and looked up at him with frightened eyes. "We need to get you to a doctor. *Mi Dios*, why didn't I see this coming."

"Please stop." Roberto knelt down and embraced his father, his eyes full of tears.

For a moment, they clung to each other like two little boys.

Finally, the Señor pushed away from his son and stood up. "You don't know what you're doing. You won't last a week in a seminary. You're meant for the world, Roberto. Not a four-walled prison."

Roberto tried to speak, but his father raised his hand for silence. "Soon, we'll receive new orders from the Church. There will be much work to do. I need you, Roberto. You're the only one I can trust."

Roberto gripped the railing and stood up. "Please don't make this harder than it is."

"There is so much you don't know. The answers aren't out there. They're here, with me. We can find them together."

Roberto looked down. "I'm sorry."

The old man gripped his arm. "Think of your mother. Would she want this?"

"She would want me to find the truth."

"Truth? You call this finding the truth? Running away like a scared child?"

Roberto tried to embrace his father, but the old man pushed him away, his brown eyes suddenly filled with anger. "I warn you, Roberto. If you leave—it's forever."

Roberto lowered his head and picked up the bag. "Nothing lasts forever. Goodbye, Father." He turned and walked out the door. He was opening the front gate when Maria caught up with him.

"Don't do this, Roberto. It will kill him. He's built his life around you."

Roberto took her in his arms. "If I stay here, it will kill us both."

"That's not true. He loves you, Roberto."

A tear rolled down his cheek. "God, I'll miss this place."

"Then don't go. Stay here, where you're needed and loved."

Roberto hugged her and sobbed.

"We'll see Padre Pizarro. He can help you."

"He can't help me. He has problems of his own. Things you wouldn't understand."

"Then, we'll go to Dr. Vivar."

Roberto shook his head. "There is no pill for this."
Maria struggled for words. "You're tired. You need rest."
"It's more than that."
"More?"
"I need to find those people before it's too late."
She pushed away from him. "People? What people?"
"I see them in the night—in the fires. God, help them."
"*Mi Dios*, what are you saying?"
"Goodbye, Maria."
"No. You need help...." She collapsed against him.
He held her in his arms and broke down. "You're the only mother I've ever known. I'll never forget you." He kissed her on the cheek and pushed through the gate.
"Roberto!"
He walked across Viveros Park toward the Calle Cronista Revelles, and a waiting taxi. The air smelled sweet from fresh fruits and vegetables. Students rushed across the bridges toward their morning classes at the University. Below the bridges and tree-lined embankments, the Turia sloshed around Valencia's western perimeter like a rippling, silver snake. In the fields beyond the city, Sancho and the other laborers marched along the furrows, turning the earth with their crude hoes. It would soon be winter and the soil must be prepared for the spring planting. Above them on the hilltops, the exhausted orange groves had gone to sleep until spring.

Suddenly it was gone, fading into the distance in a plume of billowing white smoke. Roberto pressed his face against the dirt-smeared window and watched the Micalet drop out of sight as the train veered inland toward Granada.

6 | *Nanda Lal*

"By the gods, don't you see it?" Tundup pointed frantically at the haze.

"Keep moving, we don't have time for mirages. It's almost dark. The *dacoits* are waiting in the shadows to cut our throats." Karak dug his heels into the horse's flanks and glanced at the caravan of yaks trailing behind him.

Tundup cursed and mounted his horse. "Don't you see? We're near the sacred mountain. At the edge of the Ngari Highlands. We're too far north. There is no food here. We'll starve to death."

Karak glared at the hide-covered rider. "What are you saying?"

"We're lost."

"Lost? How can that be? You said we should head north?"

"I was wrong."

"By the gods, Tundup. What kind of guide are you? You talk like you've never climbed the high passes."

Tundup lowered his head. "I haven't."

"You what?" Karak jumped off his horse and seized Tundup's arm before the stunned Tibetan could react. "You lying scum. I paid you fifty *rupees* for this!" He clutched Tundup's wool coat and dragged him off his horse onto the rocky ground.

"Let go of me, madman!" Tundup struggled to break free, but Karak sat on his chest and pinned his arms.

"I'll ask you just once. Where are my fifty *rupees*?"

"You think I'm rich like a *rajah*? I used your *rupees* to buy food and gear for the trek. There are only five left. You can have them. They're inside my coat."

Tundup tried to pry his arms free, but Karak wouldn't allow it. He yanked off the nomad's wool hat and snatched one of his black coiled braids. Without hesitating, he pulled his razor-sharp *kukri* out of its leather sheath and sliced the two foot braid from Tundup's head.

"Stop! Are you mad!"

Karak dangled the severed braid in front of Tundup's face. "You'll grow this back, but not the next thing I cut off."

"No, wait! Your *rupees* are in a pouch inside my hat. Take your filthy money and go. And may the gods curse you."

Karak crawled off Tundup and dug through the wool inside the discarded hat. He ripped out a small hide pouch and counted the *rupees*. His face twisted in a scowl. "Only forty?"

Tundup stared at the severed braid lying in the dirt. "I spent ten *rupees* on clothes for my poor family."

"Liar."

"No, it's the truth. We have nothing. We're just trying to survive like you."

"Well, at least it sounds good." Karak jammed the wool hat on his head and mounted his horse. "I'll keep your hat as a reminder not to trust the *Drokpas*. I hope your head freezes into a block of ice when the sun sets. Goodbye, jackal." Karak dug his heels into the horse's flanks and headed southeast.

At sunset, Karak pitched a small tent and tended his animals. He used a few precious drops of water to cook a bowl of red rice and herbs over a smelly, yak dung campfire. The thick haze dissipated and the night sky filled with stars. He leaned against one of the packs and puffed on a crude, long-stemmed pipe. Everything was still except the distant wind. Suddenly, he heard a rustling sound in the darkness beyond the campfire.

"Go away, rabbit, or I'll have you on my plate." He smiled at the scurrying creature. After nearly two years roaming the vast highland frontier between India and Tibet, Karak Drasi could easily tell the difference between a darting rabbit and knife-wielding brigand. And god help the brigand who dared attack the bearded man seated at the fire.

This trek had led him farther from his homeland than any before. With his five yaks sagging from swollen packs of salt, red beans, barley, and corn, he would venture into Nepal's Dolpo country to barter for a plot of grazing land and some sheep. In a year or two, he'd take on some herdsmen and launch new caravans across the Himalaya's towering passes into Tibet and China—fulfilling his father's dream.

He snatched his long-barreled rifle and aimed it at the bright star in the eastern sky. Building a caravan meant acquiring new equipment and supplies, including better weapons than the ancient single-shot rifle in his hands. In the great markets, he could barter for food and supplies, but guns and gear required *rupees*. Lots of them.

He lowered the rifle and gazed at the smoldering pile of dung while recalling his treks into the mountains with his father. He had learned much from his father. Certainly enough to guide foreigners into the Karakorum and Central Himalaya. With the *angrezi* flocking to the great mountains in search of glory, it would be easy to offer his services as a *sirdar* or *shikari*. If an imposter like Tundup could pull it off, then certainly the son of Ghulam Drasi could accumulate a large sack of *rupees* escorting *angrezi* into the high passes and foothills. Good thoughts for a wayward soul passing a lonely night on the high Barkha plain.

His eyelids grew heavy as a pleasant numbness filled his brain. It had been days since he slept....

"Karak!"

His sister's screams echoed across the Rupal Valley while the angrezi stripped and raped her. Unable to move, he saw his ravaged mother crawling toward his abandoned rifle. She was reaching for it when one of the angrezi kicked it away.

"Look at that, Clive. The old gal's still kickin'. Come on old girl, there's still time for another roll in the clover."

The pig jumped on Karak's mother and raped her while shoving her face in the dirt. When he finished with her, he pulled out his knife and raised it over his head. "Ready, Clive?"

The other angrezi pulled his knife and pressed it against Nangi's quivering throat.

"On three then. One! Two!"

"No!" Karak sat up in the darkness and clutched his pounding chest. The only sound was the wind whistling through the distant ridges. The fire had gone out and it was very cold. He crawled into his small tent and huddled under a wool blanket, his rifle at his side.

This nightmare had been worse than the others. He saw them torture his mother and sister while his father lay dead beside the campfire. He pleaded for them to stop when they pulled their knives and slashed the throats of his loved ones. He listened to Nangi's stifled cry when the pig cut her throat and wiped the bloody knife blade on her exposed breasts. He saw her body convulse as she gasped her final breaths.

"Oh, God—no more." He pressed the rifle against his forehead and slid his hand down the barrel until his thumb rested on the trigger. His family was out there in the darkness. Calling him. Beckoning him home. A simple squeeze and he would be with them.

He slipped his thumb off the trigger and pushed the rifle away. It was too early to die. Promises must be kept. Earth's business must be done. He rolled on his back and stared at the darkness.

"There, on the ridge!" Kumar pointed at the sunlit horse and rider descending the rocky slope. "He carries a rifle."

"Calm down, you sound like a frightened little boy." Nanda Lal jammed his staff into the ground and leaned against it while studying the string of yaks trailing the horse and rider. "His animals strain from a heavy load. He must be a trader." Lal's black eyes lit up. "Maybe he has salt in those packs. We should greet him. He will need water."

"Where are you going? Take your rifle. He might be a brigand."

Nanda Lal ignored his brother's pleas. Using his staff for balance, he maneuvered up the steep slope with the grace of a mountain goat while eyeing the hide-covered packs strapped to the rider's yaks.

Karak slipped off his horse and spread his open hands in a gesture of peace. "*Salaam Alekwm.*"

"Peace be with you, traveler." Nanda Lal pressed his hands together and nodded in respect to the dust-covered man standing in front of him. "You have come a long way?"

"From Skardu and Leh, by way of Lake Drabye for salt."

"By the gods, you have traveled far." Lal smiled and glanced at the packs. "You carry salt?"

"As much as you need." Karak walked to the first yak and undid one of the straps. He dipped his hand into the open pack and pulled out a large chip of rock salt. He smiled and placed it in Lal's palm.

Lal licked the salt and smiled approvingly. "And what could a rich trader seek from my humble existence? As you can see, I am not a wealthy man." Lal lowered his head and swept his hand toward Kumar and the flock of grazing sheep.

Karak stroked his beard as if in deep thought. "Let me ask you, friend. Are you a happy man?"

Nanda Lal looked at Karak with puzzled eyes. "I am content."

Karak pulled off his wool hat and brushed back his shoulder-length black hair. "For two years, I have guided caravans across the plains of Skardu and Leh, through the Ngari Highland into the Chang Tang. Each time, I managed to save a few *rupees* to build my caravan. What you see is the result of my labor."

Nanda Lal glanced at the small yak caravan. "You have done well."

"Have I? Then why am I not a happy man?"

Lal scratched his head. "I am Nanda Lal Thapa. That nervous fool down there is my brother, Kumar. We're shepherds in need of salt and it seems you're looking for a place to rest. Come, we'll dine together and discuss our needs."

Karak nodded. "You are very kind to a weary traveler."

"How are you called?"

"Karak."

"You're Moslem?"

"I am a trader." Karak gestured for his host to lead the way down the slope.

Lamphuti stirred the pot of stewed rice and barley while eyeing the precious chunk of salt in Karak's outstretched palm.

"You are very generous, friend. My family thanks you." She took the salt and dropped it in the pot while nodding gratefully to her hide-cloaked guest.

Karak admired the colorful strings of turquoise and coral beads dangling from Lamphuti's bronze neck. "You're a beautiful woman. Your husband is a lucky man."

"You are very kind, sir. I think you're a charmer from across the mountains." Lamphuti smiled and continued to stir the stew while her chuckling guest strolled out of the hut.

"Drink with me." Nanda Lal extended a cup of freshly brewed tea and gestured for Karak to join him and Kumar at the campfire.

Karak pressed his palms together and nodded in gratitude. He was about to sit down when he noticed a pretty little girl peering at him from inside Nanda Lal's hut. Her face was round and bright, and she was clad in a homespun robe. He sat down and grasped the cup of tea, pretending not to see her. When the little one crept out of the hut, he focused his black eyes on her and winked.

Nanda Lal watched in amusement as the tiny girl broke into hysterical laughter and ran into the hut. "She is my daughter, Tsiring. I see you like children."

Karak sipped his tea and stared at the fire. "She reminds me of my sister in Baltistan. I loved to play games with her when she was a child."

"Your family is well?"

Karak sipped his tea. "My family is dead."

"Even your sister?"

"They're all dead."

Lal stared at the fire. "I'm sorry. Was it the plague?"

"A plague of sorts."

"I'm deeply sorry."

Karak nodded and sipped his tea.

"You're Balti?"

"I was raised in Baltistan, beneath Nanga Parbat."

"Parbat? I've heard of it. A monarch of the gods that lies to the north and west. I'm told it's unconquerable with sides so steep the snow cannot grip them. It must be a beautiful mountain."

"It is. My sister carried its name."

"You must be Moslem if you're from Baltistan."

Karak smiled and poked the fire with a stick. "There are many followers of Islam in Baltistan, but my father clung to the old ways."

"Old ways?"

"I believe in the living spirit of the mountains and sky."

"Ah, a shamanist. Then, you believe all things have life." Lal took a plate of spiced rice and barley from his wife, and passed it to his guest.

"I believe the spirits of my family have joined with the mountains. Someday, my spirit will follow them."

Nanda Lal nodded. "I understand. Tell me, friend. In your travels, have you prayed beneath the Crown Chakra?"

Karak looked into Lal's dark eyes. "Chakra? I've not heard that name. Is it a shrine?"

Kumar looked up in surprise. "But you must have seen it when you passed the great lake? It fills the northern sky."

"I remember seeing a large body of water, but no mountain. Unless—" Karak recalled Tundup's frantic reference to a phantom mountain rising through the haze.

Nanda Lal poured more tea into Karak's cup. "To reach our valley from the northeast, you must pass a great lake called Manasarovar. Beyond it lies the most sacred mountain on earth. We call it Kailas—The Crystal Shining—for it is the center of all things. The earthly presence of Mt. Meru."

"Meru?"

"The invisible source of the four sacred rivers. The center of life where *Shiva* resides."

Karak shook his head. "I'm not much for these things. The gods have little time for me."

A frown swept across Lal's face. "Hear me, friend. Kailas is the answer to all things. Perhaps you will find peace there."

"Peace?"

"From the pain of your lost family."

Karak looked into the flickering campfire. "You asked what I wanted in return for my salt."

"Yes?"

He sighed and looked up at the starlit sky. "I'm tired of wandering across empty plains with a chilled wind in my face, and listening to hungry wolves cry in the night. I long for a green valley with a small flock of sheep and a few yak pastured in the high ground. Can you help me?"

Nanda Lal stretched his arms and looked at the night sky. "The hour is late and my eyes are heavy. You can sleep in our hut."

Karak smiled and glanced at his caravan. "I'm afraid there is too much of the nomad in me for that. Thank you, but my tent will be fine. And thank you for feeding this weary traveler."

"I'll tell my wife you enjoyed her stew. Rest well, Karak. We'll trek many miles tomorrow."

"Trek?"

"To find your magic place." Nanda Lal and Kumar left their visitor sitting in front of the fading campfire....

In the days that followed, Nanda Lal led Karak and his small caravan along the Karnali River into Nepal's remote Humla Valley. There, beneath the mountain fortress known as the Himalaya, they traded with wool-clad Tibetan *Drokpas* desperate to exchange their goods before the winter snows blocked their return across the high passes to Tibet.

Following the Karnali south, they encountered vast forests of spruce, hemlock, and blue pine surrounded by winding ridges that reminded Karak of his home in Astor. He sniffed the crisp, scented air and recalled the first time his father led him into the forests to cut precious wood for their fires. It was a clean smell. A proud smell.

After trekking almost a week, they pitched camp on a high slope blanketed with fog.

Nanda Lal leaned back against a rock and watched the haze drift across the starlit sky. "Tomorrow, the weather will clear and we'll visit your new home."

"How can you be sure? For two days, I've seen nothing but fog."

"In time, you will learn to bless that fog. It hides the valley from the hungry eyes of thieves. Since I was a boy tending my father's flock, this valley has given food and shelter to our animals."

"Your father is alive?"

Lal shook his head. "He died many years ago, but his spirit lives in the valley."

Karak sprawled on his blanket and closed his eyes. "You make it sound like a paradise."

"No, it's just a beautiful valley where your yaks can graze in high pastures while your sheep gnaw at the grass below. Go to sleep, my friend. We have found your magic place." Nanda Lal closed his eyes and listened to a snow leopard's faint howl....

Karak shielded his eyes from the bright morning sunlight while staring in awe at the hills stretching before him.

"Those white specks are sheep. They graze along the banks of the river cutting through the valley. There are hundreds of them in the meadows." Nanda Lal swept his hand toward the northern horizon. "You think that blue haze is the sky? It's a wall of ice. The northern Himal rising into the heavens. And below it is a valley where your animals can graze in sheltered pastures, safe from the winter winds."

Karak shook his head. "I've never seen such beauty. It *is* a paradise."

Lal rested his hand on Karak's shoulder. "It's more than that, my friend. Welcome to your new home."

Karak's black eyes glistened with tears. "I wish my father was here."

"But he is. You told me his spirit lives in the mountains."

Karak grasped Lal's hand. "This is what I wanted. A quiet place to shepherd a flock and build a home."

"Then, I can have the salt?"

Karak smiled through his tears.

"Good, we have a bargain."

The sun was high in the northern sky when they finally reached the river basin. Lal waited for Karak to water his animals before leading him up a small knoll on the river bank. "I used to sit here with my father and talk about life. It's a good place."

Karak wiped his brow. "It reminds me of my home. I feel good here."

"Then, it's time for a decision. Soon, the winter snows will block the high passes to my village. If you stay here with your animals, it will be for the entire winter. There is no time to build a home. You will have to live in one of those caves." Lal pointed toward the shadows below the valley's southern ridge. "You're new to this country and have much to learn. Better you stay in my home for the winter. Your yaks will be safe here."

"But, how will I find them?"

"You can tag them with your colors. No one will disturb your markers. It's a mortal sin to poach from another's herd. In the spring, your yaks will carry unborn babies for your caravan. We'll come back and build a good home in the valley. Then, we'll gather your flock." Lal paused and scanned the sky. "You must decide now. Stay here for the winter or return with me. Those feather clouds will soon bring snow."

Karak looked toward the mountains. "Do the *angrezi* come here?"

"*Angrezi?*"

"I'm told they pay well for guides."

Lal picked up a stone and squeezed it. "We don't deal with them. They are like the jackal. When they come, we look the other way."

Karak smiled and gripped Lal's arm. "I've never known a true friend. If your family will have me, I'll be honored to stay with you through the winter."

"Good, let's mark your animals and get out of here while we can."

After marking the yaks with strips of brown-checkered cloth from his father's prayer scarf, Karak followed Nanda Lal into the high pastures above the valley where they said a brief prayer before releasing the fur-clad animals to graze beneath the Himal's sheltering ridges.

They followed the river back to Lal's home in Taklakot. A

week later, thick storm clouds boiled up from India. Ramming against the Himalayas, the black clouds blotted out the sun while dumping endless snow on the high passes.

With winter descending on Taklakot's eleven thousand foot plateau, Karak and Nanda Lal worked feverishly to store precious grains, rice, and firewood in a cave near the family's hut. While they toiled, Kumar led the sheep down the plateau's steep slopes to a sheltered pasture in the river basin.

For four long months, they cleared away snow, tended the animals, and prepared the meals while enduring the fierce blizzard winds raking Taklakot. In the evenings, they huddled around the hut's crude stone oven, exchanging tales of mountain spirits while Lamphuti hummed the ancient chants.

Karak had learned the art of woodcarving from his father. Using his knife and small blocks of wood, he spent long hours whittling tiny animals for Tsiring while the child stared at him with glistening black eyes.

He placed the small creatures in her hands and lifted her in his arms while whispering, "Your father should have named you Chandra, little one. Your face is like the full moon."

Hugging his neck, she fell asleep on his shoulder listening to the wind and snow buffet the stone hut.

At night, Karak sat in the soft firelight, staring at the family asleep across the room. With his eyes moist with tears, he recalled his own family, and happier times. Perhaps here, at the entrance to Nepal, he had finally found the peace he longed for.

It wasn't to be.

Lal looked up from the grinding wheel and saw his brother running toward him across the mud-soaked ground.

"*Angrezi!*"

Lal stared at his brother in shock.

Kumar bent over to catch his breath. "They stopped to talk with me in the valley. They speak our language. They're looking for a *sirdar* to guide them up Nanda Devi."

"Devi? Are they insane?"

"They asked me to spread the word. They're camped at the river."

"Did they tell you how much they will pay?" Karak stepped toward Kumar with a half-sharpened axe dangling from his hand.

"No, but I'm sure it's a fair sum. Their equipment and horses are top quality."

"Enough! They'll be gone tomorrow." Nanda Lal turned away and pressed his hatchet against the grinding wheel.

Nothing was said until they broke from their morning chores to eat the fresh stew Lamphuti had prepared. She grasped Karak's shoulder and placed a hot bowl of spiced rice and barley in his hands. "I know what you're thinking. Don't do it, Karak. These men have dirty hands. You don't want their soiled money."

Karak reached up and patted her hand. "It would only be a few weeks. If I can get a good price—"

"You're tempting the devil!" Lal stood up and glared at him. "Nanda Devi is sacred. It faces Kailas. Only pilgrims approach Devi."

Karak ignored his friend's tirade. "Then, I'll guide the *angrezi* away from the mountain."

"You expect them to pay for that trickery? Come to your senses, man. You don't need their filthy money."

Karak put down the bowl of stew. "There is no harm in talking to them. I'll be back before dinner." He stood up and started to walk away, but Lal seized his arm.

"I'm your friend. We've traded together. You've slept in my house and eaten my food. Don't my words deserve your respect?"

"I'll lead them away from here. Isn't that what you want?"

Karak tried to walk away, but Lal's grip was like iron. "Listen to me, Karak. I see great hatred in your heart. You try to cover it, but you can't. Don't go with these men. Come with me to Lake Manasarovar. An old man lives at the far end of the lake. He is a *yatri*, a pilgrim who has seen *Shiva*'s face. He can ease the pain in your soul. We'll leave tomorrow and be there in a few days." Lal released his grip and extended his open hand. "*Salaam Alekwm*."

Karak brushed past him and walked toward his horse. He

mounted the animal and eased next to Lal. "We'll visit this pilgrim after I guide the *angrezi* away from the mountain." He reached down and clasped his friend's hand. "*Salaam Alekwm.*"

"Wait!" Lal watched his friend ride across the mud-soaked ground toward the ridge leading to the valley.

Lamphuti grasped her husband's arm and gazed at the fading horse and rider. "What's wrong with him?"

"I'm afraid we have only seen one side of our friend. I don't think he'll be with us much longer." Lal lowered his head and walked toward the grinding wheel.

Karak tugged on the horse's rein and scanned the snow-patched valley stretching below him. The Karnali River wound into the haze, its swirling blue-green waters spilling over their banks from winter's first thaw. He leaned forward and studied the thin column of smoke rising from the river. It would take another hour to reach their camp. He pressed his heels against the horse's ribs and eased down the rocky slope.

The two *angrezi* were securing their tent when they spotted the horse and rider approaching from the haze. One of them dropped his gear and walked along the embankment toward the intruder.

"*Namaste.*" Karak raised his right hand and pulled on the rein.

The *angrezi* raised his right hand and smiled under his dark glasses and bush hat. He folded his arms and stared at Karak.

Karak slipped off his horse and walked toward him. He pressed his palms together and nodded politely. "Greetings, *sahib*. I was told you seek a guide for a trek up Nanda Devi."

The *angrezi* nodded. "That's right, chum. Do you know the mountain?"

"I was born here, *sahib*. I can climb it with my eyes shut."

"Can you now?" The second *angrezi* stood up and eased beside his comrade. He brushed off his white sweater and brown fatigue pants while staring at Karak. "Tell me, friend. How can we be sure you're not lying?"

At first, Karak thought it was his imagination. Something

jumped inside him when the second *angrezi* spoke.

"What's the matter, friend? Cat got your tongue?"

"I have no cats, *sahib*. But I can show you big cats in the caves to the west. I hunted there when I was young."

The second *angrezi* pulled off his bush hat and ran his fingers along the sweatband. "Why am I having trouble believing you? How much *baksheesh* would you expect for this little journey?"

Karak felt his face flush. His stomach churned from a rush of fear.

The second *angrezi* stepped closer. "You sick or something? Looks like you've got some kind of bug, the way you're shaking."

Karak clenched his trembling fists. "I'm sorry, *sahib*. A touch of malaria from my days in the jungle. Tell me how far you wish to go."

"Don't know. We'll trek into the foothills and decide then. They tell me the mountain's surrounded by other peaks."

"True, *sahib*, but there are passes between the summits that lead to Nanda Devi's eastern slope. From there, it will be your decision to go on."

The first *angrezi* pulled out a silver flask and gulped down something that made him wince. "Say, chum, are there any villages along the way?"

"A few, *sahib*, but they're difficult to find unless you know the way."

The *angrezi* took another gulp and stuffed the flask in his shirt pocket. "Any women in those villages?"

Karak felt his heart pounding. "Yes, *sahib*."

The *angrezi* wiped his mouth with the back of his hand and glanced at his friend. "What do you think? He seems pretty knowledgeable."

The second *angrezi* stared at Karak and stroked his stubbled beard. "How about twenty *rupees* for your trouble?"

Karak took a deep breath and fought to control himself. "Twenty *rupees* is fair—each way."

The *angrezi* scowled at him. "Are you daft? Twenty five total. That's my final offer."

Karak hesitated and looked up at the haze concealing the

mountains. "For thirty-five *rupees*, I'll take you to a village where the young girls are beautiful and untouched. You can stay there a few days while I explore a route up the mountain."

An evil grin spread across the second *angrezi's* face. He looked at his comrade and shrugged his shoulders. "Seems fair. What do you think?"

"Agreed. We'll pay you fifteen when we reach the village and the rest when we return. We can supply the gear and food."

Karak bowed and pressed his palms together.

"Good, we have a deal. Meet us here at sunrise."

"Yes, *sahib*." Karak turned and mounted his horse.

"One other thing."

"*Sahib?*"

"Where did you learn to speak such good English?"

"My father taught me, *sahib*."

Clive watched him ride into the haze. "He makes me nervous. I wonder if he's lying about those native girls."

"He better not be or we'll screw him instead." Roger walked back to the tent and picked up his hammer. "Think positive, old chum. Imagine, a village of sweet, untouched flesh just lying out there waiting for us. Remember that little cutie in Baltistan. Blast, was she a tigercat. I felt bad dragging that knife across her throat."

"Yeah. Her old lady wasn't bad either."

"Roger grasped a tent stake and slammed it with his hammer. "I don't know. Thirty-five *rupees* seems a lot."

"Yeah, guess it is. Maybe we should kill the bloody wog after we're done."

"Food for thought, old chum. Food for thought."

7 | Assignment North

The dark room flashed with lightning, followed by a clap of thunder. A damp wind swept against his face, rustling the papers on the table. He pushed out of the chair and staggered across the room to the opened window.

He could see the Sierra Nevada's peaks against the flickering sky. Another deluge was about to be unleashed on Andalusia's drenched valleys and towns, a fitting tribute to the turmoil raging through Spain.

He shut the window and staggered back to the table. Above him, the seminary's belltower chimed ten p.m. So much for Penance. Another nail in the coffin. He lit the candle and looked down at the opened journal lying on the table. Time for another depressing entry. He sat down and picked up the pen....

May 14, 1931:
Nineteen months have passed since the seminary opened its doors to me. When I first saw it on the hillside, it reminded me of a proud sanctuary where I could find the answer to the nightmare tearing at me. But I was wrong. After a year and a half of useless rituals, the nightmare is stronger than ever.
Today, I exploded at Brother Perez for cowering inside this sanctimonious prison while his nation begs for help. When Ordoña demanded an apology, I threw my bible at the altar and called him a hypocrite. I still see his green eyes burning into me when I challenged him to speak out against the Church....

Roberto closed the journal and collapsed in the chair. It was over. After wasting nineteen months in a self-imposed exile, it was time to return home. Time to rebuild his shattered life.

He looked down at the crucifix on his chest. What a fool he'd been. Pizarro's letter had cinched it. There was no miracle. No bleeding cross. He'd turned his back on the people who loved him because of a freak accident and some reddish-brown water dripping from a rusted chain. He'd thrown away everything because of a sick hallucination. A father's love, a woman's promise, an honorable life.

He slammed his fist on the table. His father was right. He needed help. It was time to go home and face the truth.

His thoughts were interrupted by a rap on the door.

"Roberto?"

He grimaced and pushed up from the table.

"Are you all right?" Ordoña stared at him from the dark corridor.

"I was writing a letter. I must have fallen asleep."

"You've missed Penance. You know that's serious."

"Yes."

Ordoña frowned and brushed past him to the window. He rested his hands on the sill and stared at the flashing sky. "We can't go on like this, Roberto."

"I know."

"We should talk in the morning."

"Why not now?"

Ordoña shook his head. "I've called a meeting in the assembly hall."

"Meeting?"

"The wolves are loose."

"Wolves?"

Ordoña grasped the crucifix on his chest. "The new government wastes no time. They just swept the national elections and already there is violence in the streets."

Roberto looked at the candle. "I'm not surprised. Madrid's been seething for months."

"Madrid? Brother Vega was in Granada this afternoon gathering supplies. There were gunshots and firebombs. Padre Varela was wounded."

"Granada?" Roberto looked at him in shock.

"We should prepare for the worst. I'm afraid the communists have taken over. We're all targets."

"But why? We're not politicians. Who would want to harm a bunch of hermits in a seminary?"

85

Ordoña spun around and glared at him. "Don't you understand? There are rumors of church burnings in Madrid and Valencia."

"Valencia?"

"Yes, even in your beautiful Valencia. Cardinal Saez has dispatched warnings to all cathedrals and missions. We could be attacked at any time. And you make light of it?"

Roberto stared at the burning candle. "What about the military? The Civil Guard?"

"Powerless. They're under that communist, Azaña. He's issued orders restraining them from taking action." Ordoña shook his head. "I'm afraid many innocent clerics will suffer before it's over."

Roberto sighed. "I'm sorry, I didn't know."

"Please come now. There is much to do, and little time. And you're still one of us." Ordoña brushed past him and disappeared through the door.

Roberto stared at the opened door. He was about to turn away when he noticed a crumpled paper lying on the floor. He reached down and picked up the unfinished letter.

For weeks, his letters had begun with the same soft words before being flung against the wall....

Father,

Nineteen months have passed since we said goodbye. I know how deeply my decision hurt you. My heart aches because of it. If you would answer my letter, I'm sure we could heal the past. If I can do anything to—

Roberto held the letter over the candle and watched it burst into flames. It would take more than sympathetic words to mend the wound between him and his father. The time had come for deeds. He dropped the charred letter in the candle tray.

He picked up his bible and started toward the door, but hesitated when a folded paper dropped out of the black book. It was the letter he'd received from Maria six months ago, his last contact with home. He bent down and picked it up while recalling her painful words.

In the letter, Maria described his father's rage when he realized his son would not be returning home. Cursing himself for betraying his dead wife, Señor Hidalgo lost all interest in his business while hungry competitors began usurping the Church's lucrative restoration offers.

When a concerned Padre Pizarro visited his friend's home, Señor Hidalgo lashed out at him, calling Pizarro a "Judas" for betraying their friendship. Blinded with anger, Señor Hidalgo cursed the priest out of his home.

In her final paragraph, Maria warned that the Señor had begun drinking excessively and appeared to be in some pain. Expressing her love for the young man she'd raised from a pup, she begged him to return home before it was too late.

Roberto squeezed the letter and stuffed it in the bible. Six months had passed since he received that letter. Six months without finding the words to respond. He pushed through the door and headed down the corridor.

Roberto took the last vacant seat at the semicircular oak table facing the portrait of Cardinal Saez. No words were spoken as the forty seated brothers focused their attention on the black-robed figure standing beneath the portrait. Above them, gusting winds whistled through a crack in the roof, causing the candles to flicker. The room's stone walls came alive with dancing shadows.

Ordoña held up a letter and scanned the congregation with piercing green eyes. "I won't dwell on the gravity of our situation since I've already met with each of you. Cardinal Saez's letter warns us to prepare for possible reprisals from militant *braceros* who have been led astray by the socialists and communists. As you know, shots have been fired and there are rumors of church burnings. We fear the new government will not lift a finger to help us."

Ordoña put down the Cardinal's letter and stared at the semicircle of young men seated in front of him. "Some of you have been here only a short time. You must therefore remain within these walls as guardians of the Church's property. For those of you who have been here longer, it's time to go into the countryside to help the sick and poor. We must regain the people's loyalty and save our nation from these Marxist invaders."

"Padre?" Roberto stood up in the shadows and waited for Ordoña to acknowledge him.

"Yes?"

"Are you quoting from the Cardinal's letter?"

"Why do you ask?"

"Because it would mean the Church has seen the light."

A rush of whispers swept through the hall.

Ordoña glared at Roberto. "Are you questioning the Church's motives?"

"I was, but this changes everything."

"Does it now." Ordoña brushed back his gray hair in a nervous gesture. "Then, you're ready to leave the security of these walls to face life's harsher side?"

Roberto nodded. "I've been waiting nineteen months for this moment. Even praying for it."

"I see." Ordoña nodded and reached for one of the brown envelopes stacked on the small table beside him. "Your prayer is answered, my son. You'll be assigned to Guernica."

The room shook from a clap of thunder.

"Guernica?"

"Yes, Roberto. You talk like a bold missionary. Let's see if you have the stomach for it." Ordoña extended the envelope to one of the brothers and nodded for him to pass it to the stunned young man in the shadows.

Roberto clenched his fists. He could feel the brothers' eyes burning into him. "I'll leave in the morning."

"No!" Ordoña shook with anger. "You'll leave tonight."

"But, the last bus left an hour ago."

"You can walk to Granada tonight and take the morning train. Walking is good for the soul. It cleanses the ego. Go with God, son of Don Felipe Hidalgo." Ordoña turned to the others and prepared to give them their assignments while Roberto stared at the brown envelope lying on the table.

It wasn't a night for man or beast. The steady rain had become a deluge, driven by gale force winds. Chains of lightning danced across the black sky, accompanied by deafening thunder. Swollen creeks spilled over their banks, sweeping away everything in their path.

Roberto raised his raincoat collar and looked up at the seminary's flashing belltower. Ordoña's harsh words rang in his ears. He reached into his pocket and clutched the brown envelope.

Guernica lay four hundred miles to the north in the province of Vizcaya, a rugged, mountainous region populated by Basque nationals. The Basque's cries for autonomy were well-known throughout Spain. Not the most friendly place to send a missionary.

He looked down the muddy road. It would take most of the night to reach Granada, if he didn't drown first. Tomorrow, he'd buy a ticket and board a train. But to where?

He noticed the battered signpost where the bus had dropped him off nineteen months ago. Nothing had changed since that day. The faded arrows still pointed south, east, north, and west. For too long, he had been like that signpost—wandering aimlessly down divergent roads. It was time to choose one road.

He felt a rush of anger. The Church didn't care about the poor. It was a political thing—a power thing. He had challenged them, and was about to become one of their sacrificial lambs.

He flinched from a bolt of lighting. The sky shook with thunder. Torrents of rain swept across the road.

Let the hypocrites find another fool. Priests like Ordoña should be the ones sent to Guernica. They had caused the problems with their self-righteous greed. The hell with them. The hell with them all.

With the hills flashing in unearthly light, Roberto gripped his leather bag and marched down the muddy road toward Granada. Behind him, the belltower clanged midnight. He would soon discover there was only one road, and it pointed north. A new day had begun....

8 | *The Angrezi*

Nanda Lal eased away from Lamphuti's warm body and sat up in the firelight, a deep frown etched on his face. The only sounds were his wife's and daughter's soft breathing. He looked down at Tsiring nestled beside his wife, her tiny hand clutching a small carved animal. Seven other carvings decorated the blanket beside her, each one a gift from her adopted big brother.

Lal pulled on his hide-covered boots while glaring at the empty blanket beside the stove. He snatched his woolen cloak off the floor and slipped through the door into the chilled darkness.

The eastern sky was brightening. Soon, the sun's rays would strike Nanda Devi and the western summits, turning them into blinding mirrors. He slipped on his cloak and walked across the frozen earth to the shed where his horse slept under a warm blanket. The animal didn't like being disturbed at this early hour, but it obediently anchored itself while Lal swung on its back and pressed his heels against its ribs.

At first, the gray horse was hesitant to climb the darkened ridge above their home, but Lal was in no mood for delays. He dug his heels into the horse's ribs and prodded the snorting animal up the rocky slope until they crossed the ridge crest and began the steep descent to the valley, and his brother's camp.

Kumar leaned on his shepherding staff and waved to the familiar figure approaching him on horseback. He could see the urgency on his brother's face.

"You saw him?" Lal looked down from the horse's back.

"I tried to talk him out of it, but he wouldn't listen."

"How long ago?"

"It's too late, my brother."

Lal started to pull away, but Kumar snatched the horse's mane.

"Let go, fool! He's my friend."

"And mine too." Kumar extended a remnant of the brown-

The Tenth Avatar

checked cloth Karak had used to mark his yaks in the Karnali Valley. "He gave me this."

Lal took the cloth from his brother's hand and stared at it.

"He thanked you for being his friend, and warned you not to follow him. When I tried to stop him, he smiled and asked that you care for his yaks, for they now belong to you."

Lal looked at his brother in shock. "But that was his dream—to settle here in peace?"

"I'm afraid the gods have chosen a different road for our friend. For some men, there is no peace."

Lal clutched the torn cloth and gazed at Devi's sunlit peak.

The *angrezi* were breaking camp when they spotted the lone rider coming toward them along the river bank. Clive dropped his pack and rested his hands on his hips. "What took you so long, chum?"

"I am sorry, *sahib*. There were goodbyes to be said."

"Goodbyes? Hell, you'll only be gone a few weeks?"

"Forgive me, *sahib*." Karak slipped off his horse and stared at the two khaki-clad Englishmen.

Clive brushed back his blond hair and studied the bearded man standing in front of him. "What do you think, Roger? Are thirty-five *rupees* too much for this bloke?"

Roger folded his arms and eyed Karak's horse from under the brim of his bush hat. "That animal looks pretty old. Will he hold up?"

"He is very smart, *sahib*. He can prowl the upper slopes like a snow tiger."

Roger scratched his stubbled face. "Thirty *rupees*."

"Thirty?"

"Take it or leave it."

"But, you said—"

"Ten when we reach the mountain. The rest when we return."

Karak lowered his head. "I have no choice. It would be a disgrace to return to my family empty-handed."

"Good, then let's be on our way." Clive picked up his pack and walked toward his horse.

Gary Naiman

Karak was about to climb on his horse when Roger blocked him and pointed a stern finger at his nose. "I don't know what's bugging me, but I don't like you. If you so much as breathe funny, I'll cut your balls off. Got me?"

Karak lowered his head and nodded.

"Damn wogs. Can't trust any of 'em." Roger spit at the ground and walked away.

They rode along the river bank until they reached the foothills, then veered southwest into a narrow gorge lined with steep ridges. At high noon, they stopped to water the horses and refresh themselves in a mountain stream winding through the bottom of the gorge. Roger and Clive were dousing themselves with cold water when Karak broke the news.

"We must leave the horses here until we return."

"What?" Roger sat back on his haunches and wiped the water off his face.

Karak nodded toward the gorge's western wall. "The horses can't go on. From here, we must climb on foot."

Roger stood up and pointed a menacing finger at Karak. "I warned you, dammit."

"I am sorry, *sahib*. This is the only way to reach Nanda Devi."

"And the village with the young girls?" Clive glared at him with water dripping down his face.

"Yes, *sahib*. We can reach the village in two days. The horses will be safe in one of the caves. I'll leave them food and water, and place stakes at the entrance to stop the wolves and black bears."

Roger picked up his bush hat and slapped it against his thigh. "What about your great horse? You said he could climb like a snow tiger?"

"That was before you cut my fee, *sahib*."

"What!"

"Just joking, *sahib*." Karak walked away from the stunned Englishman.

After spending the next two hours securing a cave for the horses, Karak balanced the backpacks and replenished the goatskins with water from the stream. He climbed to the cave and reached between the protective barrier of razor-sharp spikes to pat his horse on the nose.

"What the hell are you doing?" Roger climbed toward him, followed by Clive.

Karak smiled at the two grumbling Englishmen and gestured for them to follow him up the ridge.

At first, the *angrezi* insisted their newfound guide stay between them, but they soon fell behind after weakening from the agonizing climb. Slowing his pace, Karak eased their minds by reassuring them this was the fastest route to the hidden village at the base of Nanda Devi—and its untouched maidens.

At sunset, they camped in a cave below the crest of the ridge. The exhausted *angrezi* were smokers, and not in the best of shape. After lighting a campfire of brush and wood lugged up from the forest below, Karak prepared a meal of boiled rice and barley which he dished into small bowls sprinkled with herbs from his leather pouch. The *angrezi* devoured the food like hungry jackals, leaving nothing but empty bowls and a depleted cooking pot.

"Sorry, old chap. You're more used to this climbing than we are. Here's some chocolate, if you like." Roger reached into his pack and started to pull out a chocolate bar, but Karak gestured for him not to bother.

"Don't like our chocolate, eh? Well, we'll eat it ourselves. Here you go, Clive. Have some dessert." Roger broke the bar in two and handed a piece to his friend while shrugging his shoulders. A few shots of rum, and they were out cold.

Karak awakened them in the morning with two more bowls of the spiced concoction and some tea. After breaking camp, the threesome climbed to the ridge crest and rested while waiting for the thick haze to clear.

"There, *sahib*. You can almost see the village from here." Karak pointed into the haze while Clive tried to figure out what he was looking at.

"Blast, Karmak. I can't see a bloody thing."

"That's Karak, *sahib*."

"Never mind that. Where's the bloody mountain?"

"In front of you, *sahib*. Don't you see it?"

"I don't see anything but bloody haze."

"You're looking too closely, *sahib*. Open your mind and let your eyes feel its presence."

Clive stepped back in awe. The western sky had become an immense wall of blue ice with two opposing summits. "That's Nanda Devi? Blast, there's no way I'll climb that monster."

"It is your decision, *sahib*. It will take several days to reach the summit. The air is very thin near the top. We can go as high as you wish."

"Forget it, Karmak. The village will do."

Karak noticed the sick smile on Clive's ruddy face. "That's Karak, *sahib*. A wise decision."

"Well, now what?"

"It will take two days to reach the village. We must descend the western side of the ridge to the valley and trek through the grasslands to the foothills."

"Well, let's get on with it. What the hell are we waiting for?" Clive tugged at his backpack and gestured for Karak to lead the way.

The sun was setting behind Nanda Devi's towering summits when they finally camped in one of the caves at the far end of the valley. Karak pitched a small tent outside the cave while explaining he would stand watch in case the cave belonged to a roaming bear or leopard. Not the most comforting words with the valley and foothills deep in Nanda Devi's shadows.

The *angrezi* lit a campfire and broke out two bottles of rum. After stuffing themselves with more of Karak's spiced concoction, they guzzled the potent brown rum and began exchanging slobbering tales of past conquests. It was nearly midnight when Roger called out to Karak. "Hey, Klakik, or whatever you're called. Come join us by the fire."

Karak scowled and jammed his sharpened *kukri* into its sheath. He crawled into the small cave and sat cross-legged next to the fire while Roger shoved a cup of rum in his hands. "Relax, old man. Have a shot of good old English rum."

Roger watched Karak sip the rum, then broke out laughing when he winced and began choking. "Gotta watch that stuff,

The Tenth Avatar

old chap. It's the real thing. Not that crap you guys drink over here."

"Karak put down the cup and stared at the fire. "I'm not a drinker, *sahib*. There is a saying among my people that it's death to have a clouded mind above the clouds."

"But the clouds are up there, Kloric." Clive slid next to Karak and draped an arm across his shoulders. "So, tell me more about this village. You know, the young women."

Karak was about to speak when Roger let out a groan and clutched his stomach.

"You should watch that liquor, *sahib*. The altitude is very tricky. Even here, we are four of your kilometers above the jungle.

Roger grimaced and waved his hand in disgust. "Hell, it's not the altitude. I drank more on Nanga Parbat."

Karak's eyes widened. "You climbed the queen of the gods?"

"Well, maybe halfway. We were—"

Clive interrupted his friend before he could finish. "Enough of that business, Roger. You know we shouldn't talk about 'times gone by' in front of others." He glared at his friend and tried to change the subject. "So, Kloric, about these untouched women. When do we see this great sight?"

Karak forced a smile. "I'm afraid you will never get my name correct, *sahib*. You surprise me."

Clive slid his arm off Karak's shoulders and leaned back against the cave wall. "And why is that, old chum?"

"Never mind that crap. My goddamn stomach's on fire!" Roger clutched his stomach and doubled up against the cave wall. "What the hell's wrong with me?"

Clive grabbed Karak's wool cloak and nodded toward his ailing friend. "What's wrong with him?" He watched Karak slide next to Roger and place a hand on his glistening forehead.

"Well?"

"Your friend is burning up with fever, *sahib*. I think he is dying."

"What?" Clive lunged for his rifle and aimed it at Karak's heart. "What the hell did you do to him?"

Karak shrugged his shoulders. "I poisoned him, *sahib*."

"You what?"

"I poisoned him, *sahib*. He'll be dead in a few minutes, but first there will be great pain."

"You're joking."

"No, *sahib*. I'm deadly serious."

"Scum!" Clive lifted the rifle and squeezed the trigger, but the weapon only clicked.

"I'm afraid there are no bullets in your rifle, *sahib*. I removed them when you and your friend fell asleep from the alcohol in your flask. Don't you know it's death to have a clouded mind above the clouds?"

Clive stared at his friend writhing in agony against the cave wall. His eyes darted to the packs where the machete's handle protruded from its sheath. He took a deep breath and lunged for it.

Clive yanked the silver blade out of its sheath and waved it menacingly at Karak. "Idiot—why didn't you try to stop me? Now I'm gonna cut you in two."

"I didn't stop you for the same reason I didn't poison you, *sahib*."

"What?"

"It's time to collect an old debt, *sahib*. I want you to die with a knife in your hand." Karak reached into his belt and pulled out the *kukri*. "This knife was my father's. Do you know how long I've had it, *sahib*?"

Clive clutched the machete while shaking his moaning comrade's foot. "Snap out of it, Roger. This bloke's insane."

Roger looked up at his friend and tried to speak, but instead made a gurgling sound as black blood spewed out of his mouth onto the cave floor.

"I'm waiting for an answer, *sahib*. How long have I had this knife?" Karak kicked the flaming coals at Clive and glared at him.

"How the hell should I know, wog?"

"I took this knife from the blood-soaked ground after you butchered my family. Do you remember that day, *sahib*? In the Rupal Valley below Nanga Parbat?"

Clive's face twisted in horror. "You! But you should be dead? I stuck in the knife myself?"

"I am dead, *sahib*. You're looking at a ghost."

"Bastard! I'll kill—"

Karak lunged across the campfire like a snow leopard, slashing at Clive's wrist before the Englishman could swing the machete.

The stunned *angrezi* yelped as the *kukri* cut deep into his wrist, forcing him to drop the machete. In desperation, he reached out and clutched Karak's throat with his other hand while screaming for his convulsing friend to help him.

Karak felt Clive's fingers dig into his windpipe. The pig cursed him and groped for the fallen machete with his bloody hand.

Clive had the machete in his fingers when Karak slashed viciously at the hand clutching his neck. Clive let out a terrifying scream as the razor-sharp blade severed his hand at the wrist. He pulled back in horror, his eyes staring at the bleeding stump.

Karak ripped the severed hand off his throat and threw it in the fire. "You won't need this one either, *sahib*." He slashed at Clive's remaining hand as it grasped the machete.

"My hands! You cut off my bloody hands! For God's sake, Roger! Help me!" Clive looked down at Roger's motionless body lying against the cave wall, his eyes frozen in contorted horror.

Karak grabbed the hysterical *angrezi*'s blond hair and dragged him through the cave entrance. He slammed him on his back and pressed the *kukri* against his throat. "I'm afraid there is no village with vulnerable women, *sahib*. Not like the one you visited three years ago in Astor. Remember how my mother and sister screamed while you raped them?"

"No, please! You people aren't supposed to take lives. It's against your religion. You're supposed to forgive your enemies."

Karak pulled on Clive's hair until he screamed in agony. "I do forgive you, *sahib*. And to prove it, I'll cut out your diseased heart so you're pure again."

"No! In the name of God!"

"Remember how they screamed when you slashed their throats? And how I pleaded for mercy when you stuck the knife in my back? Now you scream, *sahib*. I like that sound. Scream, *sahib*. Scream!"

"No!"

Karak raised the *kukri* and plunged it deep into Clive's chest. The hysterical *angrezi* convulsed in agony, his terrified blue eyes frozen on his executioner. When his eyes finally closed, Karak sliced through muscle and bone until the animal's heart was exposed in a geyser of red spray. Digging his hand into the chest cavity, he ripped the dripping muscle out of the *angrezi* and carried it into the darkness where he held it up to the moon above Nanda Devi.

"Vengeance, Father! Vengeance!"

9 | Granada

Roberto wiped his sweating face and looked down the deserted road. From the angle of his shadow, it was high noon.

He'd been walking through ankle-deep mud for seven hours. Granada couldn't be more than a few miles away. He could still catch an afternoon train and reach Valencia tonight. He took an exhausted breath and stumbled toward a vine-covered stump.

He plunked down on the stump and began scraping the mud off his boots with a stick. Hesitating, he noticed his reflection in a small puddle beside his foot. He bent down and studied the mud-spattered face peering up at him from the rippling puddle.

The handsome *torero* was gone, replaced by tired eyes, matted black hair, and a stubbled beard. He dropped the stick and looked down the muddy road. It would be a painful homecoming.

His hand slipped into his raincoat pocket and pulled out the apple he'd plucked off a tree this morning. It was a far cry from a Valencia orange, but this wasn't Valencia. He bit into the overripened fruit and tried to grasp the past twelve hours....

He'd spent the night in an abandoned barn after a nearby lightning strike convinced him to delay his trek to Granada until the storm passed. Collapsing on a bed of wet straw, he quickly dropped into exhausted sleep below the barn's badly leaking roof.

He was awakened in the middle of the night by a strange rumble. The rain had stopped, but he could still hear the roof dripping in the cold darkness. The rumble grew louder, accompanied by a metallic clanking sound.

He ran out of the barn and spotted a column of motorized vehicles sloshing past him on the mud-drenched road. The clanking came from two armored cars at the head of the column. The moon broke through the clouds, revealing a cluster of glistening helmets inside one of the trucks.

The rumble subsided as the vehicles faded into the night

like a line of swiftly moving rodents. He felt a sudden chill. They were headed southwest toward Granada.

He climbed a hill looking for flashes that might indicate trouble, but saw nothing. The air was still except for an occasional roll of thunder over the Sierra Nevadas. With sunrise still an hour away, he mustered his courage and headed down the muddy road toward Granada. It wasn't a pleasant journey.

In the early morning light, he walked past a village floating in mud and sewage. Without plumbing facilities, the townspeople were forced to bury their wastes. Unfortunately, the drenching rains had leeched the bacteria-carrying spoilage into the gray mud surrounding their primitive shacks. The smell was unbearable.

Moving on, he reached a second village of thatched huts rising from the ubiquitous gray soup. He looked up in horror at the surrounding ashen slopes and saw people living inside whitewashed cave dwellings, their only escape from the wind, rain, and mud.

A rag-clothed girl stood in the doorway of the nearest hut munching a piece of soiled bread. Her exhausted mother stirred a boiling cauldron in the shadows behind her. The tired woman reached into a basket and flung a few turnips and greens into the bubbling water while stirring the concoction with a wooden ladle. The little girl waved at him and went inside.

He bent over and clutched his knees, the nausea churning inside him. Could this be Spain? People living in caves like prehistoric men and women? Families forced to share their meager huts with livestock and disease-carrying vermin? All this within a few miles of the Seminary of Andalusia and its self-righteous occupants? God damn their souls to hell. And his for being one of them....

Roberto was jarred from his thoughts by the sound of a racing motor. He stood up and watched a large black automobile splash past him. The small red-and-gold flag whipping from its antenna indicated it carried government personnel. He frowned and dropped the half-eaten apple.

He was about to start down the road when the vehicle skidded to a halt and backed toward him. A young Civil Guardsman swung open the rear passenger door and stared at him through dark-green sunglasses. "*Buenos dias*, Padre."

Startled, Roberto nodded at the black-shirted guardsman. "*Buenos dias.*"

"You have business in Granada?"

"Just passing through. I've been reassigned from the Seminary of Andalusia."

The guardsman forced a smile. "You'll be taking a train?"

"Yes."

"We'll be glad to give you a lift. The roads aren't safe for clerics these days." The guardsman gestured for Roberto to climb inside.

"You're very kind, sir. Thank you." Roberto scraped the mud off his boots and stepped into the car.

The handsome guardsman removed his tri-cornered, black leather hat and placed it on his lap, revealing a crop of neatly-combed black hair. "Looks like you've had a rough walk?"

Roberto nodded.

"May I ask your destination?"

Roberto braced himself against the bouncing car and gazed out the mud-smeared window.

"Padre?"

"Oh, I'm sorry."

"Your destination?"

"Valencia."

The guardsman flashed a nervous smile. "Beautiful city. I've only visited it once, but it's permanently etched in my memory. Have you ever been there?"

"I was born there. It's my home."

"Ah, how good for you." The guardsman looked away. "I was born in Madrid. Can't say I miss it these days."

Roberto nodded. "I've heard things are bad there."

The guardsman frowned. "Things are bad everywhere, Padre. The communists are carrying out open attacks against churches and priests. Only today, the pigs burned the Convent of Trinitarian Nuns in Madrid."

Roberto shook his head. "Can't you stop them?"

"The Minister of War has ordered us to stand down. If we disobey orders, we'll be court-martialed."

"Maybe Cardinal Saez will intervene."

A sneer crept across the guardsman's face. "He already has. The Cardinal issued a pastoral letter condemning the new government. He's urging all Catholics to stand firm against the enemies of Jesus Christ. I've heard he'll be expelled soon."

"Expelled?"

"So much for the Church, eh Padre?" The guardsman glanced out the window. "We're coming into Granada. We can drop you near the station. I wouldn't linger. The union pickets are all over the city. We've been ordered to let them have their way."

Roberto looked out the window at the red-walled Alhambra Palace rising proudly on a hill above the city. He was about to turn away when he noticed four plumes of black smoke drifting into the sky above the city's northeast quarter.

"Damn insurgents." The guardsman leaned over the driver's shoulder.

"What is it?"

"I'm not sure. My men have orders not to retaliate if fired upon. Damn Azaña. Damn him to hell. Doesn't the fool understand?"

"Understand?"

The guardsman leaned back in the seat and slipped off his sunglasses, revealing two piercing brown eyes. "If we don't put down these mobs, things will boil over."

"You mean—revolution?"

The guardsman stiffened. "That will never happen. The army will never permit it."

"I don't understand."

"Pray you never have to, Padre. It will be the end of us all."

Nothing further was said until the car screeched to a halt at the Elvira Gate.

"Sorry to drop you here, but we have work to do." The guardsman pushed open the door and stepped out of the car.

Roberto followed him and extended his hand. "Thank you,

officer—"

The guardsman stepped back and flipped on his tri-cornered hat. "Names aren't important. Just say a prayer for the Good Samaritan who pulled you out of the mud." He nodded toward the bustling intersection in front of them. "The train station is three blocks up that street to the left. Walk briskly, Padre. Good luck." He climbed back in the car and gestured for the driver to proceed.

Roberto watched the car disappear around a corner while the guardsman's warning echoed in his ears. He picked up his leather bag and walked across the busy intersection amidst a clatter of car horns and hissing buses. Pedestrians jostled past him while rushing to their places of business. It felt good to be back in civilization.

He'd walked a block when a newspaper vendor caught his eye. The brown-bereted old man held a paper above his head while shouting its headlines to a throng of shocked Granadians.

"Terrorists on the loose! Cities burning! Guard helpless!"

Roberto edged closer to the flapping newspaper and its terrifying black headline. He stared in disbelief at photographs of cathedrals afire in Madrid and Seville. A woman standing next to him gasped and began to cry.

He stepped back and scanned the street. Everything seemed normal except for the shouting vendor. Were things really this bad or was the press just trying to sell more papers? A few wayward fires shouldn't throw a nation into panic. But what about those plumes of smoke?

He looked up at a clock on one of the buildings. Only twelve forty. With trains leaving all day, another hour wouldn't matter. He could still reach Valencia tonight. He turned and headed down the Gran Via Colon toward the city's center. Twenty minutes later, he wished he hadn't.

Once gala Granada no longer echoed with laughter and the strains of *flamenco* guitars. In only a few months, the city had become a tense cauldron of vengeful union picketers, bitter landowners, starving immigrants, and frustrated Civil Guardsmen.

Roberto was within two blocks of the Royal Cathedral

when a line of picketers brushed passed him carrying placards condemning Spain's corrupt Church. He heard their whispers and felt their burning stares. Suddenly, one of them grabbed his arm and glared at him with drunken eyes. "Filthy church bastard. You call yourself a priest?"

Roberto froze in horror. "I'm not a priest."

"Lying coward! You're just like the rest." The picketer made a menacing move toward him, but one of his comrades yanked him away.

"Not here, Pedro. Too many guardsmen." The two picketers ducked into the crowd.

Roberto leaned against the lamp post and tried to control his racing heart. The guardsman's word's rang in his ears. *Walk briskly, Padre.*

He turned and retreated uptown toward the train station. Moving quickly, he brushed past faceless pedestrians while clutching the traveling bag in his right hand. When he reached the intersection, a rush of panic swept through him.

My God, what am I doing here? They think I'm a priest. I'd better get out of this black suit before someone sticks a knife in my back. Incredible, I just abandoned the Church and some fanatic's going to make me a martyr.

He bolted across the intersection and raced up a narrow street toward the station. Unfortunately, it was the wrong street.

A half hour later, he paused in the middle of a park and put down his bag. He remembered seeing a sign for *Jardine del Republica*. But where was the station? Damn, he should have asked someone directions. They couldn't all be assassins.

"Hey, Priest!"

He turned and saw a brown-suited man with a low-brimmed hat walking across the grass toward him. A half dozen shabbily-dressed picketers followed close behind.

The stranger halted and peered at Roberto with menacing black eyes. He was shorter than Roberto, but his scarred cheek and stocky build more than compensated for his lack of height. "What's in the bag, Priest?"

Roberto glanced over the stranger's shoulder and recognized the drunk who had confronted him on the street.

"What's wrong, Priest? Can't you talk?"

"I'm not a priest."

"Funny, you look like a priest in those black clothes."

The drunk stepped forward and glared at Roberto. "Hey, Miguel. Maybe he's a Civil Guardsman."

The stranger frowned and flicked up his hat brim. "No, Pedro. I think he's a priest. Look at the way he trembles. All priests tremble these days."

Roberto noticed the picketers edging closer. A bead of sweat trickled down his face.

The stranger stepped toward Roberto and stuck out his chest. "I am Miguel Pedroza of the Union General de Trabajadores. Perhaps you would like to join us?"

"Join?"

"You have to stand for something, Priest. Since you have no courage, the least you can do is donate your money to the UGT brotherhood."

"I have no money."

"Bullshit, all you priests are loaded."

Roberto felt his heart jump. The picketers had surrounded him. He heard thunder and looked up at the clouded sky. It had begun to rain.

Pedroza reached out and touched Roberto's traveling bag. "What's in here? Maybe a stray gold coin or two?" He tried to grab the bag, but Roberto yanked it away. "There's nothing in my bag but books and clothing."

The drunk swiped at Roberto's raincoat. "Maybe he's got some money inside those black clothes?"

Pedroza's frown became an ugly sneer. "Yeah, I bet he's loaded with gold coins from his friends in the Church. Let's see what's inside that coat." Pedroza reached out, but Roberto slapped his hand away. "I said it's only books and clothing! Now let me—"

"Search him!" Pedroza backed away while two picketers seized Roberto's arms.

"Let me go, dammit!"

Pedroza stepped forward and pointed a finger at Roberto's nose. "What kind of talk is that? A man of the cloth cursing his brothers. We'll let you go after we collect our dues. Welcome to the UGT, Padre. Strip the bastard!"

Roberto felt a sharp pain in back of his knees. Powerful arms slammed him to the ground. A dirty hand dug into his jacket and clutched the crucifix hanging from his neck.

"Well, would you look at that. The priest is loaded with gold." The hand yanked at the gold cross, snapping its chain.

"Animal!" Roberto freed an arm and lunged for the cross, but the picketer slapped his hand away. Roberto's side exploded in pain from a sharp kick to the ribs. When he tried to roll over, someone slammed their fist into his jaw, knocking him senseless.

His head was spinning. Someone jumped on his chest and began pummeling his face with punches. It was Pedroza. Roberto yanked his arms free and tried to block the blows.

Something stirred inside him. He saw the black planes diving at helpless women and children. He heard their screams and felt the bullets tearing up the ground in front of him, and he heard the voice cry out from the shadows...

Fight them, Roberto. Fight them!

Roberto lashed out with his right fist, catching Pedroza square on the jaw. He heard a loud groan and saw the union boss sprawled on the ground beside him. He sat up and stared at the unconscious thug through his swollen eyes.

"Did you see that? He knocked out Miguel. What kind of priest are you? Now we're gonna really get rough!"

Roberto felt hands tearing at his shirt. Punches landed on his face and chest. He rolled on his stomach and covered his head with his hands. Someone struck him in the back with one of the placards. His ears were ringing. Everything was going black.

"What the hell are you doing!"

A voice cried out through the darkness. Roberto felt the picketer's hands pull away as they stepped back from his crumpled body.

"Are you all right, friend?" Someone grabbed his shoulder

and turned him over. "God, he's a priest! Are you all insane!"

Roberto looked up in stunned silence. A young man in a gray suit was standing between him and the picketers, his fists clenched.

Pedroza shook away the cobwebs and scrambled to his feet. "I'm sorry, Señor Lorca. We didn't know he's a priest."

"The hell you didn't." The incensed young man brushed back his black hair and glared at the picketers. "What have we become? Is this all we fought for? To steal like thieves? To beat up a helpless priest?"

Roberto struggled to his knees and tried to clear his throbbing head. He spotted the gold crucifix lying in the rain-soaked grass and picked it up. For a moment, there was only the sound of rain striking the leaves.

Pedroza waved for the picketers to disband. When they were out of earshot, he wiped the blood off his lip and scowled at the young man. "You go too far, Señor Lorca. For eight years, these corrupt pigs have horded their wealth behind Rivera's government. Now, when we have a chance to even things, you turn on us. That's dangerous, my friend, even for you."

The young man stepped into Pedroza's face. "Are you threatening me?"

"Good day, señor." Pedroza turned and stormed across the park.

Roberto staggered to his feet with a little help from his rescuer. He wiped the blood off his face and looked at the handsome, clean-shaven face staring at him. "He called you Lorca."

The young man nodded and extended a handkerchief. "Federico Garcia Lorca, at your service, Padre. I'd offer you some wine, but I know you only partake during the Eucharist."

Roberto looked at him in shock. "When things were simpler, nothing made me happier than lying on a beach with a bottle of *Rioja* and the beautiful *Gypsy Ballads* of Federico Garcia Lorca. I am honored, señor. Please, let me buy you that glass of wine." He took a step and fell down.

Lorca grabbed Roberto's arm and helped him up. "I know a

good cafe near here, but you'd better lean on me."

They stumbled across the park to the Gran Via Colon, then walked a block to the nearest cafe.

La Castanet was known for its dry Andalusian. They took a table by the window and ordered two glasses of the light, fragrant wine, and a wet towel for Roberto's swollen eyes.

Lorca smiled and raised his glass. "God Almighty, I think we still have a chance. I just saved Spain's only drinking priest."

Roberto smiled through his cut lip and took a stinging sip of wine. He pushed the glass aside and buried his aching head in his arms while trying to regain his senses. When he looked up, Lorca was staring at the passing pedestrians, a deep frown on his face.

Lorca sipped his wine. "My heart aches, Padre. Spain's noble experiment fails."

"The new government?"

Lorca slumped in his chair. "Zamora's a stooge the Republicans put in place to appease the Rightists. He can't be trusted."

"You know this?"

Lorca smirked. "If we're lucky, Azaña will become prime minister and push Zamora into a closet. Then we'll have a chance."

"Azaña? The pig who turns his back on helpless priests?"

"You're wrong, Padre. Azaña is a good man, a true Loyalist with the political skill to see us through this mess. We need him. The Rightists are already packing the government with insurgents. It will take a strong hand to keep them in line." Lorca gulped down his wine. "I'm afraid we're in for a bad time."

Roberto stared at him. "You saved my life back there. What can I do to repay you?"

Lorca shook his head. "Don't worry about such things. You would do it for me, right?"

Roberto nodded.

"Enough said." Lorca snapped his fingers at the waiter. "So, where's your church?"

"I have none."

Lorca's eyes widened. "How can a priest have no church?"

Roberto looked down at his wine. "I'm not a priest."

Lorca threw up his arms. "I think I'll write a play about the priest I rescued in Republic Park. I'll call it *Revelations*. Will you please explain all this to me?"

"I spent two years in a seminary. Last night, I was reassigned to a godforsaken town in Vizcaya. It's their way of punishing me for asking the wrong questions."

Lorca stared at Roberto. "Vizcaya? Lots of problems up there." He snatched a fresh glass of wine from the waiter's tray. "What are you going to do?"

"I'm going back to my home in Valencia."

"You're leaving the Church?"

Roberto gulped down his wine and reached for a fresh glass. "I was on my way to the train station when Pedroza and his apes attacked me."

"Hmmm—this must be very hard for you."

Roberto shook his head. "I've wasted two years of my life. My father hates me. The woman I love is gone. I'll probably be excommunicated, and I just got the shit beat out of me. Yes, I'd say it's been a bit hard."

Lorca bit his tongue to avoid laughing. The Andalusian was taking effect. He leaned back in his chair and sipped his wine. "Well, since you're not a priest, I guess I can call you Roberto."

Roberto lifted his glass of wine and gulped it down. "Señor Lorca, you can call me anything you wish."

Lorca smiled and grasped Roberto's arm. "Please, call me Federico."

Roberto nodded and pressed the wet towel against his left eye. "I should be going. I can still catch a late afternoon train."

"You're welcome to stay at my home. You can take the early morning express."

"A tempting offer, my friend, but I need to see my father while I still have the courage."

"Problems?"

Roberto nodded. "Big ones. It's going to be hard to face

him. He might even shoot me."

Lorca smiled and flipped a wad of *pesetas* on the table. "Come—we'll take a taxi to the station."

Roberto rubbed his forehead. Was this really happening? Was he really sitting in a Granada cafe discussing the world with Spain's foremost writer and poet? Or was he lying unconscious in the mud from too many punches to the head? He felt Lorca's hand on his shoulder.

"Come, Roberto. Before you pass out."

They hailed a taxi and headed crosstown toward the train station. They were almost there when Lorca glanced at his watch and snapped his fingers in anger.

"What's wrong?"

"We need to take a little detour. I forgot my friend. We were supposed to meet for drinks an hour ago. I hope you don't mind."

Roberto nodded and rested his head against the seat while Lorca instructed the driver to stop at the *Granadine Inn*. When their taxi pulled up to the curb, Roberto was nearly asleep.

"Come on, I'll buy you another glass." Lorca tugged at Roberto's arm until he crawled out of the taxi, dragging his bag behind him.

The inn looked more like a hotel with its spacious tiled lobby and ornate paintings. Roberto took off his soiled raincoat and ducked into a restroom for some emergency surgery on his torn jacket and shirt. After a few quick stitches with the needle and thread in his bag, he dunked his head in a wash basin and splashed cold water on his face and neck.

He was almost feeling human when he toweled off and looked in the mirror. His cheeks and forehead were a mass of abrasions. Both eyes were blackened. Add the fat lip, and he resembled a boxer who had just taken the beating of his life. He took a deep breath and stepped out of the restroom.

Lorca was standing at the entrance to the bar, his eyes fixed on a man seated in the corner. The man's clothes seemed out of place for an inn like the *Granadine*. Bright reds, browns and greens, and a polka dot bandana that made him look like a gypsy.

Roberto edged beside Lorca. "Is he a dancer?"

Lorca broke out laughing. "*Buenos dias*, Pablo!"

The shocked patrons looked up from their drinks as the stranger stood up and spread his arms. "Garcia, you pig! Where the hell have you been?"

The two men embraced while the crowd stared at them.

Lorca waved at Roberto. "Come join us for a drink, Priest!" He roared while the stunned patrons stared at Roberto. "Look, I've found a drinking priest! He's one of us, dammit! One of us!" Lorca grabbed a bottle of wine off the table and guzzled it.

Adding embarrassment to his day in hell, Roberto eased to the table and sat beside the two men.

Lorca gestured for a fresh bottle and began an incessant conversation with his friend. Suddenly, he leaned back in his chair and lifted his wine glass. "Pablo, join me in a toast to my new friend."

Pablo lifted his glass and smiled. "Any friend of Federico's is a friend of mine." He flung the wine into his mouth and gulped it down.

Lorca tried to copy Pablo's deft maneuver, but most of the wine splashed on his face and shirt. He ignored the mess and gestured toward Roberto. "My poor friend is leaving the clergy. Too bad, we need men like Roberto these days."

Pablo looked at Roberto with deep-set black eyes. "Are you a priest?"

"He's not a priest, but he'd make a damn good one." Lorca wrapped his arm around Roberto's sore shoulders, making him wince. "Still in pain, eh? Well, this will cure you." Lorca picked up the bottle and refilled Roberto's glass, leaving a puddle of wine on the table.

Pablo ignored him and continued staring at Roberto. "Tell me, friend, why are you leaving the Church?"

Lorca leaned between them and frowned. "They want to send him to Vizcaya. Can you beat that? I guess my friend rubbed some papal feathers the wrong way."

Pablo leaned closer. "Is that true?"

Roberto shook his head. "That's part of it. There's a lot more."

"I see. Where in Vizcaya?"

"A town called Guernica."

Pablo's eyes lit up. "Shit, there's a lot of trouble up there. The damn government keeps making promises to the Basques it can't keep. One of these days, the damn province will blow up in Spain's face."

Roberto looked into the man's piercing black eyes. "You've been there?"

"I visit Guernica and Bilboa from time to time. I have a small place across the Pyrenees—in Biarritz. Too bad you're caught in such a mess. I think you'd like it up there. It's beautiful country. The Bay of Biscay is breathtaking from the hills. Say, if you change your mind, ask for my friend Sebastian. He's a frustrated artist like me. When I go up there, we camp on the beach and drink and paint for days."

Roberto smiled and finished his wine. "I need to be on my way."

"You live here?"

"No, I'm taking a train to Valencia."

"Your home?"

Roberto nodded and stood up to leave. He glanced down at Lorca who was swaying in his chair. "I'll never forget this day. From gray mud to red wine. How does that book open?"

Pablo smiled. "The best of times, the worst of times. Something like that."

"Please tell Señor Lorca he will always be my friend. After I settle things in Valencia, I'll write to him."

Pablo stood up and extended his hand. "Forgive me for staring. You have such an interesting face. So intense. Even pained."

Roberto clasped Pablo's hand. "It's from all the punches."

"Please, I'm not joking. I can see it in your eyes. Magnificent black eyes. They seem to gaze into another world."

Roberto suddenly felt uncomfortable. He pulled his hand away.

"I'm sorry, señor. I get carried away by interesting eyes. You don't suppose I can entice you to remain here a few days to capture that pain on canvas."

Roberto looked at him in surprise. "You want to paint me?"

"Oh yes—even more than I want to get laid. Can't we work this out?"

"I'm flattered, señor, but I have to go. Maybe another time."

Pablo picked up his glass and lifted it to Roberto. "I'll look forward to it. We can split the profits. Good day, Señor—"

"Hidalgo—Roberto Hidalgo."

"A noble name." Pablo gulped down his wine. "Be well, Roberto Hidalgo."

Roberto turned and walked out of the bar. He was about to leave the hotel when an attractive young woman grabbed his arm. "Forgive me, Padre, but could you get me Señor Picasso's autograph?"

Roberto's jaw dropped.

"You didn't know?"

Roberto staggered past the young woman and hailed a taxi. His head was spinning. Picasso? Lorca? It couldn't be. He must be lying dead in that park.

"Where to, Padre?" The driver peered at him from inside the taxi.

Roberto opened the passenger door and paused. A crowd of angry picketers was marching down the Gran Via Colon toward the Royal Cathedral. He crawled into the taxi and shut the door. It was indeed the best of times, and worst of times.

"Padre?"

"Please take me to the train station."

As the taxi sped away from the curb, Roberto leaned back in the seat and slipped his hand into the weatherbeaten traveling bag. He probed behind its torn liner and pulled out one of the five gold sovereigns he'd stashed there two years ago. The gold disk was worth enough devalued *pesetas* to fill his bag. "Are the banks still open?"

"Until five."

"We better stop at one unless you have lots of paper."

"The bank it is, Padre. But they're in worse shape than my purse."

The taxi driver waited while Roberto argued with the bank manager for a fair exchange. The banks were in financial ruin, and gold coin was a frightening sight. Twenty minutes later, Roberto climbed into the taxi with his bag full of *pesetas*.

It was nearly six when Roberto stepped into Granada's ornate train station. The tiled interior resembled a mosque except for the rushing passengers and ticket windows. Roberto walked across the concourse and paused in front of the rotating schedule board. The board showed one train remaining to Valencia, and it didn't leave until midnight.

"Damn." Roberto collapsed on a bench and grimaced from a pair of sore ribs. He placed the leather bag between his feet and closed his swollen eyes. When he opened them, the clock on the wall read seven p.m.

He glanced at the row of phone booths across the concourse. It wouldn't be easy to dial that number, but it had to be done. He stood up and walked to the ticket counter.

"Good evening, Padre. Where are we going tonight?" The blue-uniformed ticket agent smiled at him.

"One way to Valencia."

"Beautiful city. Twelve hundred *pesetas* please."

Roberto reached into his pocket and pulled out a wad of bills. He placed them on the counter and began counting.

"Save your energy, Padre. It's worthless scrip." The agent opened a drawer and scraped the wad of crumpled paper into it. He stamped a ticket and handed it to Roberto. "Have a pleasant trip. And say a prayer for us."

Before leaving the counter, Roberto exchanged a second wad of *pesetas* for some coins. He stuffed the coins into his raincoat pocket and walked across the station's red-tiled floor to one of the vacant telephone booths.

After dropping a dozen coins in the slot, he placed the bell-shaped handset against his ear and leaned toward the funneled speaker. "Valencia, operator. Viveros-six-three-nine-nine."

He took a deep breath and listened to the ringing phone. Maria was probably serving his father a fresh rabbit stew and bottle of *Rioja*. After dinner, the Señor would return to his study for an evening of work and a few moments by the fire.

He'd be asleep by midnight.
"Hidalgo residence."
"Maria?"
He heard a gasp. "Maria, are you there?"
"Mi Dios. Is it you, Roberto?"
"It's good to hear your voice. It's been too long."
"Where are you?"
"Granada. I'm at the station. I'm coming home."
"Thank God. We thought you didn't get Padre Pizarro's message?"
Roberto hesitated. "Message? What message?"
"He phoned Padre Cortez at the Church of St. John in Granada. Padre Cortez promised to deliver the message to your seminary in the hills. It was the only way to reach you."
Roberto felt a chill go through him. "What's wrong, Maria?"
"You don't know?"
"What is it?"
"My God." She sobbed and forced out the words. *"Your father is dying. It's cancer."*
He couldn't speak. His body slumped against the booth.
"Please hurry, Roberto. He keeps calling to you in the dark. Dr. Vivar can do nothing. It's only a matter of hours."
Roberto felt his stomach churning. "I'll be there in the morning. The train arrives at five."
"Oh, Roberto. We didn't know. It came on so fast."
"I'll be there soon." Roberto placed the handset on the cradle and stared at the black phone.

10 | *The Old One*

A full moon had risen over Nanda Devi, its bright yellow disk floating in the chilled darkness. The air was still. It was a quiet time. A peaceful time.

He dropped against a rock and rubbed his cramped arms and legs. His exhausted body begged for sleep. It had taken most of the day to reach the seventeen thousand foot ridge crest. Another few hours wouldn't matter. Better to rest and hike down to the horses at sunrise.

He built a fire and boiled some rice and tea which he devoured like a hungry animal. Satisfied by the warm food, he stretched out on the rocks and studied the twin moonlit peaks jutting into the night sky. His eyelids grew heavy and began to close....

A deep, guttural howl snapped his eyes open. He sat up and heard a second howl echo off the rocks. It was coming from the valley.

He'd placed the *angrezi*'s remains outside the cave for his wolf brothers. By cutting out their diseased hearts, he'd ensured the *angrezi*'s evil spirits would not infect the proud animals. By now, the wolves had dragged the carcasses to their hungry cubs. The howls came from the pack's leader thanking his host for a delicious meal.

He looked down at the darkened valley and said a prayer for his wolf brothers. His bitter enemies were dead. Vengeance was taken. He fell back on the blanket and closed his eyes. His last conscious thought was a prayer that the heart-wrenching nightmare was finally over....

He heard her screaming in the darkness.
"Oh, God! They killed Mother and Father!"
"Where are you, Nangi? I can't see you."
"On the mountain."
"Mountain? What mountain?"
"Help me, Karak! They're coming after me!"
"No, Nangi. They're dead. I killed them."

"They're hurting me! Help me!"
"No. They're dead. You're all dead!"

He opened his eyes and saw Nanda Devi peering down at him, its moonlit summits glistening with ice. He sat up and wiped the sweat off his face while trying to control his racing heart.

Why was she afraid? The *angrezi* were dead. Vengeance was taken. Her spirit was free to join their mother and father in eternal peace. Why didn't she know? He clenched his fists and glared at the glowing summits. It would be a long, sleepless night on the ridge below Nanda Devi.

At sunrise, he trekked down the ridge toward the cave where he'd left the horses. With Nangi's panicked voice still ringing in his ears, he looked eastward at the cloud-covered passes leading to Nepal.

It was time for a painful decision. It would only take a few days to rejoin Nanda Lal, Lamphuti, Tsiring, and Kumar in the meadows below Taklakot. His friends would never know the *angrezi*'s fate because he would tell them the heathens had abandoned him below Nanda Devi.

With the *angrezi* quickly forgotten, he and Nanda Lal would trek along the Karnali River into the Nepali highlands where his yaks grazed beneath the Himalayan wall. There, he would fulfil his dream of building a caravan while living out his life in peace.

Yes, it was a wonderful dream, but it would never happen. With blood on his hands, he could no longer remain in this foreign land. Other *angrezi* would come looking for their missing comrades, accompanied by the Indian police. In time, the white satans would hang him and his friends for sheltering a murderer. His death meant nothing, but seeing Nanda Lal and his family suffer at the hands of heathens would be his worst nightmare.

He looked northwest toward Baltistan and the Karakorum, and he remembered the pain on Rasul's face the night he left him standing in the rain. It would be difficult to return to that place of bitter memories, but it was the right thing to do.

He closed his eyes and sniffed the fresh ice of the Karakorum. After two lonely years, it was time to go home. The son of Ghulam Drasi would be welcomed by his people. Working with Rasul, he would build a great caravan and travel to the bazaars of Skardu and Leh. In time, Rasul's village would prosper because the son of Ghulam Drasi had returned.

Comforted by thoughts of old friends, he sipped some water and headed down the ridge toward the horses that would carry him home.

At high noon, he froze in horror. The stakes had been torn out of the ground like kindling. An animal's agonizing cry echoed from the cave.

He slipped the rifle off his shoulder and fumbled for a bullet. The pouch was full of stones. The *angrezi* had taken no chances. He flung the rifle at the ground and grasped the *kukri* in his belt. He raised his pack in front of his face and crept into the dark cave, his hand clutching the *kukri*. It was time to face the devil.

Through the darkness, a large black bear clawed at the blood-soaked body of his horse. In a final act of defiance, the fatally wounded animal lifted its head and cried out as the bear swiped its razor-sharp claws across the exposed neck. Lurching in agony, the dying horse fell back on the cave floor and gasped its last breath, its glazed eyes staring at Karak.

He tried to contain himself, but the sight was devastating. First his family—now this. He bit his lip to stifle a scream of anguish, but the bear already smelled him. The crouching animal lifted its head and spun around. It was too late to run. The snarling bear reared up on its hind legs and let out a deafening roar.

Karak backed against the cave wall and watched the ominous black hulk waddle toward him, its forelegs raised to strike. A second deafening roar echoed through the cave. He could feel the bear's hot breath on his face. It slashed at him, ripping the pack out of his hand.

He dived to the cave floor and heard the razor-sharp claws screech across the rocks above his head. His heart pounded against his ribs. *One chance. Strike!*

He lunged upward and drove the knife deep into the bear's exposed chest. The bear howled in pain and swept its massive forearm against him, flinging him against the rock wall.

He huddled against the rocks, waiting for the animal to finish him with those deadly claws. His left side throbbed from the bear's ferocious blow, but there was no fear in his heart. To die fighting a black bear was to die with honor. He gripped the bloodstained *kukri* and stared at the darkness, listening for the last sound he would hear on this earth. The roar of an enraged bear.

But there was no roar. The wounded bear grasped its chest and backed away. It turned and crawled out of the cave into the sunlight.

Karak was too shaken to move. He slouched against the cave wall, waiting for the crazed animal to return. When nothing happened, his eyes turned to the dead horse lying beside him, and he began to cry.

His father had given him the horse on his twenty-first birthday. He recalled the long day spent breaking the wild animal that continually bucked him into the tall grass. And the coarse feel of its mane when he grabbed a clump of hair and swung on its back for another try.

He remembered crossing the rugged Deosai plain to Skardu and Leh. And their treks across northern India into the Ngari and Chang Tang highlands. And eastward into Nepal with its towering Himalaya.

Karak reached down and patted the animal's blood-soaked head. "I'll miss you, friend." He bent down and kissed the glazed eye, then gently brushed it closed.

Before moving on, he piled sticks and dried brush into the cave, and lit a funeral pyre. Chanting ancient shamanist hymns, he wished his friend's spirit a swift journey into the mountains—to live forever with the spirits of his dead family.

Karak searched for the *angrezi*'s horses, but they'd disappeared into thin air. He gave up when he heard his wolf brothers howling in the night. Their cubs would grow strong from all the fresh meat.

He discarded the *angrezi's* useless packs and boots, choosing instead to live like his shamanist ancestors. Subsisting on plants, berries, and small game, he turned away from Nepal and trekked north across the Ngari's windswept tundra toward the beautiful lake he remembered passing with his useless guide, Tundup. Challenged by rifle-carrying *Drokpas* leading their yak caravans south toward Taklakot, Karak's greeting was always the same. Clad in rags, he would lean on his wooden staff and stare at the threatening *Drokpas* while softly muttering, "*Namaste*, my friends. I am a *yatri*."

The startled *Drokpas* would lower their rifles and break into smiles while offering him cheese and rancid butter-tea which he consumed like a famished animal. Before moving on, the *Drokpas* would gather around him exclaiming, "*Namaste, yatri*. Go in peace and pray for our spirits at Kang Rampoche. *Om Mani Padme Hum*."

Karak would press his hands together in the universal gesture of peace, then move on while waving to them with his rag-covered arm. His father had taught him well. When trekking on foreign soil, wear the rags of a pilgrim and you will be treated kindly.

But what was "Kang Rampoche?" Karak had travelled the region long enough to know the Drokpa's cryptic words meant "precious jewel of glacial snow." But what was it? Spirit or reality? The answer came on the fourth day when he approached the lake known as Manasarovar.

He sat on a hill and ate a piece of stale bread while studying the cobalt-blue lake stretching before him. Strange, the way the horizon shimmered above the lake—like invisible spirits dancing on the water.

Karak's tired eyes widened. He stood up and stared at the lake in disbelief. An ivory mountain shuddered in the haze. Was it real or a mirage? He recalled Tundup pointing into the northern haze. Yes, he'd found it. Kang Rampoche. Nanda Lal's "Crystal Shining." They were one and the same. He shuffled down the hill toward the lake and glowing mountain.

He was nearly to the shore when a soft voice called out to

him.

"*Namaste, yatri.* May I join you?"

Karak spun around and saw an old beggar smiling at him from the shore. The beggar was clothed in rags and bowed by age, looking like he would topple over if not for the wooden staff in his hands. His braided hair was snow-white and very long, hanging below his rag-covered shoulders like a horse's mane. Below his frayed robe, a pair of blistered feet protruded from worn leather sandals. Not a pretty sight, but the old man's hypnotic voice and overpowering eyes more than compensated for his impoverished appearance.

"I'm sorry, old one. My journey will be too hard for you."

"Where are you going?"

"Across the Karakorum—to Baltistan."

The old man looked at Karak with puzzled eyes. "Baltistan? Forgive me, friend. I thought you were trekking to the Crown Chakra to perform the *kora.*" The old man lifted his trembling right arm and gestured toward the mysterious mountain beyond the lake.

"Why would I want to go there?"

The old man shook his head. "I'm sorry. I thought you were a pilgrim."

"Pilgrim? I'm just a lonesome traveler going home. Tell me, old one. Why is that mountain so important to you?"

The old man smiled and sat cross-legged on the bare ground. "Join me and I'll answer your question." He gestured for Karak to sit beside him.

"Another time." Karak glanced nervously toward the setting sun.

"I see you're anxious to return to your home." The old man gestured a second time. "Only for a moment. Please, join me."

Karak started to turn away, but hesitated. The old man's colorless eyes were like the magic crystals he'd seen in the great market at Skardu. He sighed and sat beside him.

The old man stared at the shimmering mountain as if in a trance. A gust of chilled wind rippled across the water and brushed their faces.

"What is it?"

"Kailas—the Crystal Shining. Center of the earth where the four holy rivers spring to give life and death. Where *Shiva* sleeps."

Karak gazed at the faint white peak rising into the northern sky. "Is it a mountain or a mirage?"

"Kailas is everything, Karak. Spirit, earth, sky—even you and me. Kailas is worshipped by all Hindus and Buddhists for it is the earthly presence of Mount Meru, invisible center of the universe."

Karak scrambled to his feet and backed away from the old man. "How do you know my name?"

"Your tortured spirit cries out for help, and mine answers. Don't be afraid. There is no evil here. Join me on my *kora* and find the answer you seek."

Karak pushed back his long black hair. "Answer? I seek no answer?"

The old man's albino eyes burned into him. "Your dead sister cries out to you in the night. She is lost, like you."

Karak clenched his fists and glared at the old man. "What kind of black magic is this?"

"You're headed the wrong way, my son. Come with me to the Crystal Shining, and know the truth."

Karak looked into the old man's eyes and felt a calming breeze sweep across his face. A sudden peace radiated through him.

"Look at the mountain, my son."

Karak followed the old man's eyes as they turned toward the mountain. "It looks like a temple."

"It is a temple. A stepped glacier spills down from the summit. Many believe those steps lead to *Moksha* and *Nirvana*. That Kailas is the Stairway to Heaven."

Karak frowned and shook his head. "I should be moving on."

"You still don't understand. Is your heart so darkened, you're afraid of the light?"

"How can you know my heart?"

"Her name was Nangi."

Karak stepped back in shock. "Who are you?"

"Just a lonely pilgrim." The old man leaned on his staff and stood up. "Come with me and make an old man happy." He turned away and shuffled along the shore.

With the sun dropping behind Nanda Devi, it was too late to hug the foothills leading toward Baltistan. His wolf brothers would soon begin the night hunt, their fond memories shortened by hunger. And that wounded bear might be waiting in the shadows to take revenge. After wandering the highlands for two years, the son of Ghulam Drasi could certainly afford a quiet night with a lonely old beggar. Karak picked up his wooden staff and followed the old man along the shore.

They camped on the lake's north shore. Karak offered the old man some stale cheese and bread, knowing the pilgrim would not accept the meat of a killed animal. With darkness closing on the lake, they lit a small fire and brewed some tea while the last rays of sunlight turned the surrounding hills orange, then blood red.

The old man sipped his tea and looked north. "Tomorrow, we will begin the *kora*."

"What?"

"Sleep well, my son. There will be no nightmares tonight."

11 | A Father's Love

The slow-moving train cleared the Sierra Nevada's rugged foothills while veering northeast toward the moonlit plains of Murcia and Alicante. After a brief stop at Alcira, it began a gradual descent toward the coast on the final leg of its midnight journey.

Roberto pressed his face against the window and squinted at the darkness for a chance glimpse of an old friend. He was about to give up when the hills parted, revealing the Gulf of Valencia glistening like a silver mirror beneath the full moon.

In a few hours, the sun would rise from the Mediterranean Sea to awaken the sleeping fishing villages and farms along Spain's fertile gold coast. Refreshed after a warm sleep beside their loved ones, Sancho and his fellow laborers would kiss their wives and children, and march into the fields with hoes draped over their shoulders. An army of *obreros* farming land they still did not own.

Along the coast, booted fishermen would guide their wooden trawlers into the Mediterranean's churning waters for a healthy catch of shrimp, squid, marlin, and eel. At the nearby seaport of El Grao, dock workers would tug on hemp ropes, lifting nets of crated wine, oranges, and olive oil onto steamers bound for the world's ports. And above it all, jutting into the morning sky, Valencia's belltowers would ring in a new day.

Roberto leaned back in the seat and closed his eyes. He was nearly asleep when his nostrils flinched from a heavenly aroma drifting through the partially-opened window. He leaned against the glass and spotted rows of orange trees flashing past him in the moonlight. The air smelled so sweet.

He looked up at the moon and felt a tear roll down his cheek. He was home. Thank God, he was home.

His melancholy was shattered when the compartment door slid open and a blue-uniformed young man dropped into the seat across from him. The young man pulled off his blue garrison cap and folded it in his lap.

Roberto nodded politely and rested his head against the

seat.

"Are you a priest?"

"Pardon?"

"Are you a man of God?"

"I'm studying for the priesthood."

"Difficult time to be traveling, wouldn't you say?" The young man stared at Roberto with shining black eyes.

Roberto looked away. "It's a difficult time for everyone."

The young man nodded approvingly. "Then, you're for putting an end to this anarchy?"

"Who isn't?" Roberto forced a smile while wishing the young man would go away.

"You have business in Valencia?"

"My father isn't well."

"You're from Valencia?"

Roberto nodded. "I've been studying at a seminary near Granada."

"I see. Have you been away long?"

"Over a year."

The young man leaned forward. "Do you know Valencia has become a bastion of the Republican-Communist conspiracy?"

Roberto sat up and glared at the young man. "Tell me, citizen. Which group do you represent?"

"Why, the *Falange*, of course. Several of us just returned from training with *Il Duce's* army in Italy." The young man stroked his short black hair and leaned closer to Roberto. "Let me tell you, citizen. We were deeply impressed with the progress Italy has made since throwing out the communists and jews. In time, the new order will purge the same lice and vermin from Spain. Then, we can join arms with our brothers in Germany and Italy to form a better world."

Roberto slumped in his seat and listened to the train's clacking wheels.

"Well, don't you agree?"

"Perhaps, but what role will you play?"

"Role?"

"Where will you fit in?"

The young man looked at him with startled eyes. "At the forefront, of course."

Roberto shook his head. "Impossible."

"What?"

"It will be impossible for a young Spaniard with black eyes, black hair, and olive skin to survive in a blond, blue-eyed world. I'm surprised you haven't noticed."

"How dare you!" The young man glared at Roberto.

"Sorry, but your arrogance and uniform won't be enough. When the purge comes, I'm afraid you'll be one of its victims." Roberto turned away and gazed out the window. "Forget this nonsense and find a warm *mujere*."

"Swine!" Trembling with anger, the young man stormed out of the compartment leaving Roberto alone with his thoughts and some badly needed sleep.

When Roberto awoke, the compartment was bathed in bright sunlight. He sat up and took a breath of fresh Mediterranean air. Through the window, he saw palm groves surrounding a small town above the sea. It was Elche, only a stone's throw from Valencia.

He blinked from a flash of reflected sunlight. A polished dome gleamed in the sun. He leaned against the window and saw the Micalet's ancient tower rising above the Torres de Serranos gate.

As the train approached the great fortress city, Valencia's classic buildings came into view above the ancient walls. He could see the Museo de Bellas Artes and Palace, Great Cathedral, Silk Exchange, and Church of Santa Catalina with its six-sided bell tower.

He stared at the old buildings through tear-filled eyes while recalling the music and laughter of better times. The warmth of Laura's body pressing against him. His father's rough hand stroking his hair. The groves of ripe oranges. Oh, yes—the groves.

"Valencia!" The conductor's booming voice filled the compartment as the train ground to a halt. After nineteen painful months, Roberto Hidalgo was home. But the greatest pain was to come.

The taxi ride from Valencia's classic rail station was not what Roberto envisioned. The morning crowds appeared subdued. There were no smiles or conversation. Only strained, angry faces.

A man in a shabby brown uniform strolled along the sidewalk carrying a dark placard. Painted on the placard was a harsh, shadowed face with penetrating cold eyes and a bony finger pressed against pursed lips. The implication was clear. Trust no one.

When they drove past the University, Roberto noticed two men arguing beside a poster of Jose´ Antonio Primo de Rivera, son of the dictator who had ruled Spain before the Second Republic forced him out of office. In the poster, Rivera was dressed in the same blue uniform the young man had worn on the train. His right arm was extended in a fascist salute.

One of the men grabbed the poster and ripped it off the brick wall while the other reeled in shock. As the taxi veered around a corner, Roberto heard two distinct pops echo off the buildings. "Did you hear that, driver?"

The driver shook his head and pulled the taxi to the curb. "We're here, Padre."

Roberto paid the driver while glancing nervously through the rear window. He slid out of the taxi and hurried up Corpus Christi's front steps to the carved oak doors. He gripped the door handles and hesitated. Two years ago, he had opened these same doors and walked into a nightmare. He took a deep breath and swung them open.

The dark chapel was deserted. In the shadows, he could see the blue and black velvet curtains cloaking Ribalta's great painting. To the left of the painting, his trained eyes detected the shadow of the rope leading to the massive crucifix hidden above the altar.

"Roberto?"

A firm hand grasped his shoulder. He spun around and saw Pizarro staring at him from the aisle.

"*Mi Dios*, are you all right?"

"I'm sorry, Padre. For a moment, I thought—"

Pizarro grasped his arms. "Look at you, Roberto. Have you

been in a fight?"
"Roberto forced a smile. "It's a long story."
"I can't believe my eyes. Where is the young *torero* who left me two years ago?" Pizarro leaned forward and embraced him.
Roberto patted the old man's shoulder. "How is he?"
"I found out about the cancer last week. I hadn't visited him since he threw me out."
"How bad is it?"
Pizarro looked down. "Very bad. The doctor is with him now."
"Is he conscious?"
"Sometimes. You better hurry, Roberto. I'll be there soon."
"Roberto clutched the crucifix on his chest. "You gave me this, remember?"
"Best thing I ever did."
Roberto lowered his head and walked out of the chapel.
He walked across town to the Puente del Real Bridge where he paused to look down at the Turia's rushing waters. The river was high from the spring storms. In some spots, it had washed over the concrete banks and flooded the adjoining streets.
He leaned over the bridge railing and stared at the churning waters. Even the river seemed full of rage today. He stayed there a moment gazing at the water before pushing away from the railing and heading across the bridge.
He was halfway across Viveros Park when he stopped in front of the tree where he'd carved his initials many years ago. He traced his fingers across the thick bark and looked toward the cluster of conifer trees at the far edge of the park. How many times he'd run across that grass to the beautiful home beneath those trees. He took a deep breath and headed toward them.
He unlatched the gate and edged up the cobblestone path to the oak door containing his father's crest. Hidalgo was a proud name for it marked a *caballero*—a gentleman. He stared at the crest and lifted the metal knocker.
For an instant, Maria didn't recognize the disheveled cleric standing on the cobblestones. She tilted her head and stepped

into the light for a closer look.

"Yes, it's me."

"Roberto! Thank God." She collapsed in his arms and sobbed.

"I'm so sorry." He broke down and embraced the only mother he'd ever known.

They clung to each other until Maria pushed away from him and wiped her eyes. "You didn't cause this, Roberto. It's God's work. Don't blame yourself."

Roberto looked through the opened door. "Is he awake?"

She patted his hand and led him across the red-tiled foyer to the foot of the stairs.

Roberto grasped the bannister and looked up the stairs at the shadows. "Do you think he'll recognize me?"

"If not you, who? You're his life, Roberto."

He sighed and followed her up the stairs.

When Roberto stepped into the bedroom, he reeled in shock. His father was lying on the bed beneath a red quilt. The old man's arms were skin and bone. His bearded face was pale and drawn. His eyes were closed and his mouth was partially open.

Roberto staggered to the bedside and felt Dr. Vivar grab his arm. "Be strong, Roberto. He slips in and out of consciousness. I'm afraid we don't have much time."

Roberto sat in the chair next to the bed. Fighting back tears, he grasped his father's hand and held it against his cheek. He closed his eyes and listened to the old man's strained breathing, and he remembered their happy nights together in this room. Nights spent talking, studying, dreaming. Warm nights. Precious nights.

He gathered himself and leaned forward. "I'm home, Father."

At first, there was no response. Suddenly, the old man's hand twitched and his face turned toward his son. "Roberto?"

Roberto squeezed his father's hand and smiled through his tears.

"I thought you'd forgotten."

"Forgotten?"

The old man's eyes widened. "The banquet. The Cardinal will be there. I need you to flip the sketches."

Roberto leaned closer. "I didn't forget. I'll be there. At your side. We'll dazzle them."

The old man smiled through his parched lips. "I knew you'd come home. Nothing can stop us now."

Roberto kissed his father's hand and looked into the old man's bloodshot eyes. "I'm sorry, Father. I'm so sorry...." He buried his face in the quilt and broke down.

His father's hand stroked his hair. It was so soothing. So comforting. Like a gentle wave washing away the pain. He was safe again. A child again.

"I was wrong, Roberto."

Roberto looked up and saw his father staring at him.

"You're meant for great things—wondrous things. I saw it in my sleep. A voice spoke to me."

"Voice?"

"It was so soft, like a summer breeze."

Dr. Vivar rushed to the bedside and grasped the old man's wrist.

"I saw him, Roberto. Standing in the bright light."

Roberto looked up at Vivar, but the physician could only shake his head.

"I tried to look at his face, but the light blinded me."

Roberto tried to speak, but the words wouldn't come. He lowered his head and waited for the end.

The old man clutched his son's crucifix. "Stop them, Roberto. Before it's too late. Before he comes."

"Who, Father?"

"His name is *Kalki*. You don't want to see his face. No one wants to see his face." The old man looked toward the window. "Do you see the light? It's so beautiful. So...."

Roberto felt his father's hand go limp. The old man's eyes closed. Vivar felt for a pulse and lowered his head. "He's gone, Roberto."

Roberto kissed his father's hand and rested it on the blanket. He heard Maria sobbing behind him. "Maria, is Padre Pizarro here?"

"He's coming, Roberto. He's coming...."

Roberto grasped the crucifix. "God, forgive me." He raised his hand and made the sign of the cross, and he began to pray....

Don Felipe Hidalgo was buried next to his wife on a hillside overlooking the Cami de la Mar, a quiet rural road lined with olive trees. From there, they could watch the sea and feel the warm sun on their faces, and be together again.

After the funeral, Roberto drove to the sea with Maria and Padre Pizarro. They walked along the shore and talked about happier times. Some tears were shed. Some laughter too. It was a good day, a healing day.

The sun was dropping behind the Meseta hills when Roberto took Maria's hand. "Will you be well?"

She smiled and squeezed his hand. "Your father was generous. I've saved it all."

He held her in his arms. "That house is too big for such a tiny lady. You should find a special man to make you happy."

She reached up and kissed him on the cheek. "I'll be fine. But what about you? What will you do? Where will you go?"

He gestured toward the car. "It's getting dark. We can talk later."

He walked her back to the car and helped her inside, then patted her arm and walked down the beach toward the lonely figure standing on the shore.

"It's so beautiful." Pizarro stared at the orange-tinted clouds above the sea.

Roberto crouched down and scooped a handful of sand. "I've always loved this time of year. Everything so fresh and clean."

"You'll be going back to Granada?"

"No, I've been assigned to a mission in Vizcaya."

Pizarro spun around. "Vizcaya? *Mi Dios*, there's trouble up there. Who's idea was this?"

Roberto watched the sand pour through his fingers. "There is something you should know."

"Yes?"

"Before this happened, I wasn't going to Vizcaya. I was

coming home."

Pizarro looked at him in shock. "You were leaving the Church?"

Roberto shook his head. "Everything seemed so clear before I picked up that phone. Now—" He hesitated and looked at the sea.

"I don't understand?"

"I spent yesterday going through my father's books with Señor Valdez. Except for the house and possessions, there is nothing left."

"What? How can that be? He was a wealthy man?"

Roberto forced a smile. "Large, unexplained withdrawals over the past year. Maybe he gave it back to the Church. He always feared the gates of heaven closing on him. He probably wanted to increase his chances."

"*Mi Dios.*"

Roberto reached into his coat pocket and pulled out Ordoña's sealed brown letter. "Don't tell Maria. It's best she not know. That way, she won't worry when Valdez sells the home. She has plenty of money, and I asked him to watch out for her. I only hope she finds a good man. She deserves a happy life."

"But, what about you? If you're right about your father's estate, you're penniless?"

Roberto cracked a grin. "Strange words coming from a priest. I thought you'd be overjoyed."

"Please, Roberto. I was your father's friend. I don't want to see his son hurting."

"Oh, don't worry about me." Roberto ripped open Ordoña's letter and read it. "It seems one Padre Segurra has need of my assistance in Guernica. I can catch an evening train and be there tomorrow. If Ordoña contacts you from Granada, tell him the Church's loyal servant is on his way to Basque country."

"Then, you're not giving up?"

Roberto shook his head. "I just need to pick up my bag and I'll be on my way."

"God bless you, Roberto."

"Save your blessings for Spain, Padre. I'll be all right. If things don't work out, I'll become a carpenter or something. Jesus was a carpenter, wasn't he?"

Pizarro grasped Roberto's arm. "Maybe I should speak to Ordoña. There are plenty of needs in Spain's other provinces."

Roberto forced a smile. "A friend told me Guernica lies in beautiful country. Maybe I'll like it up there."

Pizarro shook his head. "You know how to reach me."

Roberto smiled. "Strange how little things can change a person's life. All this because of a bad dream and some rusted water dripping on an altar."

Pizarro lowered his head and walked toward the car.

Valencia's station swarmed with travelers rushing to catch the evening train to Madrid. Roberto bought a ticket and led his two friends onto the steamy rail platform. Embracing Maria, he promised to visit her in the fall for a picnic by the sea. She kissed him and gave him a familiar slap on the rear when he turned to walk away, then covered her mouth in embarrassment when a nun glared at her. She'd forgotten his priestly garments.

Roberto stepped onto the rear passenger car's platform and looked down at Pizarro. "Be well, Padre."

"*Mi Dios*, I almost forgot." The priest reached into his coat pocket and pulled out a white envelope. "When I visited your father last week, he was delirious and thought I was you. He gave me this."

"What is it?"

"I don't know." Pizarro handed the envelope to Roberto and watched him stuff it in his bag.

"I'll read it on the train. Goodbye, Padre." Roberto reached down and grasped Pizarro's hand as the train lurched and began to move.

The priest's eyes filled with tears. "There is something else, Roberto. Something you should know."

"Better hurry, Padre, or you'll be on your way to Madrid."

Pizarro looked up at him and forced out the words. "Forgive me, Roberto."

"For what?"

"Lying to you."

"Lying?"

"The blood on the crucifix wasn't rust. I had it checked after you left the church. It was true blood, but like none ever seen. I was afraid for you, so I made up the story about the rust."

"The blood was real?"

"It was more than real. It contained all blood types. Do you know what I'm saying? It was universal. The blood of all men."

Roberto felt Pizarro's hand slip away. He watched him fade into the steam as the words rang in his ears.

12 | The Crystal Shining

They awoke in chilled darkness and headed north toward the mountain, using the moon to light their way. The haze had dissipated and the sky was filled with stars.

Karak kept glancing at Kailas' moonlit face. Eons of thawing and refreezing had molded a pattern of ice ridges which resembled steps rising into the glowing clouds. An ivory staircase to heaven.

As the morning sky brightened, the mountain took on an orange, then yellow hue. Suddenly, the peak burst into a blinding beam of reflected sunlight. When Karak uncovered his eyes, the peak had faded into the morning haze.

After a brief rest, the Old One led Karak up a steep hill beyond the lake. Hiking over the crest, they descended into a valley of dense yellow grass and waded through the rustling straw like two men fording a stream.

The sun was high in the sky when they cleared the valley and paused at the entrance to a narrow pass. Karak wiped the sweat off his face and eyed the shadowed entrance. "It smells like a bear's cave."

The Old One ignored Karak and sank on his knees. He reached into his ragged clothes and pulled out a string of prayer beads while mumbling an ancient chant.

"What is it?"

The Old One gripped his staff and pulled himself up. "Follow me and say nothing." He gestured toward the pass and shuffled through the dark entrance.

"Wait!" Karak shook his head in frustration and followed the Old One into the pass.

The narrow passage was filled with dank, cold air that smelled like decayed waste. There was no sunlight inside the towering black walls. It reminded Karak of the maze he'd seen in the market at Skardu, except this time he was the rat.

"How far to the other side?"

The Old One raised his arm. "Say nothing. Keep walking and don't look back."

Karak shook his head and jammed his hands inside his ragged clothes in an effort to stay warm. Twice, he caught himself glancing over his shoulder at the shadows. He had the strangest feeling they were being followed.

When they cleared the pass, the sun was dropping toward Kailas. Startled by the brightness, Karak blinked his eyes and squinted at the green meadow stretching before them. "Where are we?"

The Old One sat on the ground and pulled out his prayer beads. "We're in the Valley of Death."

"The what?"

"We've walked through the Portal of Death. We're dead."

Karak glared at him. "I'm not in the mood for games."

The Old One shrugged his feeble shoulders. "To be reborn, one must first die. We will circle the mountain until we reach the valley on the other side. There, we will be reborn."

"Circle the mountain? Are you mad?"

"The Old One fingered his prayer beads. "There can be no turning back from the *kora*. We're dead and must be reborn." He pulled himself up and shuffled away while Karak stared at him in stunned silence.

With the sun setting behind Kailas, they walked across grasslands teaming with marmots and wild hares that reminded Karak of the Deosai plain. As the mountain's shadow closed over them, Karak nearly tripped over a pilgrim lying prone on the ground. When he tried to help the pilgrim to his feet, the Old One yanked him away while whispering he must not disrupt the pilgrim's *gyang chatsel*, which he later explained was their way of marking progress around the great mountain before taking sleep.

At dusk, they descended into a green valley bristling with flowering buds. When they were deep in the valley, the Old One dropped his staff and sat down. "We'll rest here tonight."

Karak dug into his rags and pulled out some stale bread and cheese.

"Eat nothing."

"I'm hungry."

The Old One grasped Karak's shoulder and pointed into the

darkness. "Look closely and tell me what you see."

At first, Karak saw nothing. Suddenly, a light flickered through the blackness. Then another. He gazed at the sea of flickering lights.

"They are pilgrims. It is time for the *kora*. You're on sacred ground." The Old One frowned. "Don't eat."

Karak stuffed the bread back in his clothes. "We have a good moon. Why not keep going?"

"Be patient. Time doesn't matter here." The Old One struck a flint to some sticks of wood and lit a campfire. "See, now we're one of them." He warmed his hands over the smoldering fire and sipped some water from the flask strapped to his shoulder. "Tomorrow, you will continue alone."

"Alone?"

"I'm going to the prayer wall at the far end of the valley. For thirteen days and nights, I will fast beneath the great mountain to honor my thirteen *koras*."

Karak looked at the Old One in disbelief. "You've circled the mountain thirteen times?"

"Only after thirteen *koras* can one approach the sacred mountain. After my fast, I'll climb the great glacier to see the face of heaven." The Old One glared at Karak. "You must not follow me. Do you understand?"

Karak stood up in anger. "You expect me to sit here for thirteen days while you crawl up a glacier? I'm turning back."

"You can't go back. Continue the *kora* and find the answer you seek. To gaze on Kailas is to behold the answer to all things. I'll meet you at the north face in thirteen days."

When Karak awoke the next morning, the Old One was gone. He cursed himself and marched north. Enough time had been wasted on this insane diversion. When he reached the north face, he'd break the circle and head northwest toward the Ngari plain, and home.

Driven by an obsession to escape the mountain, he raced across thick grasslands blooming with scented wildflowers and herbs. Along the way, he passed kneeling pilgrims muttering ancient chants while deftly fingering their prayer beads. He'd learned not to interrupt them.

In the evenings, he heard faint sounds of rushing water, perhaps from one of the four rivers the Old One had mentioned. He climbed the hills and scanned the moonlit valleys for a glint of reflected water, but saw nothing. Frustrated by the invisible rivers, he lay beside the campfire and gazed at the stars until his eyes finally closed.

On the fifth day, he caught his first glimpse of Kailas' north face shining through the haze. The stepped glacial snow had been replaced by a rugged wall of granite flecked with patches of ice. If the south face led to heaven, the north face must lead to hell.

He was about to move on when he noticed a pass leading to the foothills below the mountain. It couldn't be more than a mile away. His eyes focused on the narrow entrance. After stumbling over pilgrims for five days, he owed himself a closer look. No better time than now. He'd never travel this way again. In a few weeks, it would all be a fleeting memory. He kicked the ground and headed across the meadow toward the mountain.

He was within a hundred feet of the entrance when he spotted what appeared to be a prayer wall carved in the rocks. He moved closer and eyed the ancient writings while recalling the Old One's warning not to approach the mountain.

He edged beside the prayer wall and ran his fingers across the ancient symbols. They felt cold. He stepped back and looked up at the mountain. It seemed so close. He could almost touch it. He patted the prayer wall and marched into the pass. It would take longer than he expected.

At sunset, he stumbled out of the pass and collapsed on a rock-covered slope. The mountain's huge shadow swept over him, sending a chill up his spine. The only sound was his labored breathing. Above him, the summit glowed yellow against the darkening sky. A shooting star flared over the peak. It was the last thing he remembered before falling into exhausted sleep....

He sat up and squinted at the fog. Voices cried out to him, but he couldn't see their faces.

"Karak."
He rolled over and scrambled for his kukri.
"Don't be afraid."
He clutched the knife and looked up in horror. The Old One stepped out of the fog and extended his arms. His rags were gone, replaced by an ivory robe.
"What happened to you?"
"I have wonderful news. I have seen your sister."
"What?"
"Come with me." The Old One retreated into the fog while gesturing for him to follow.

Karak clenched his fists and followed the Old One onto the granite. When he tried to step up, his sandaled feet slipped and he crashed on the rocks.

"Use my staff!" The Old One extended his wooden staff and watched him snatch it. "That's it—climb!"

Karak jammed the staff against the granite and pulled himself up. He stepped up and felt the ice bite into his sandals.

"Don't plant your feet! They'll freeze to the ice." The Old One headed up the ice-covered rock while his exhausted companion struggled to keep his balance.

They were nearly to the summit when Karak collapsed on the rocks.

The Old One dropped on his knees and extended a bare arm toward his beaten companion. "Take my hand."

Karak looked up and gasped. "I'm finished."

"Take it!"

Karak reached for the Old One's hand, but nearly slipped off the ice.

"Again!"

Karak glared at the bony hand hovering above his head. He ignored the cramping pain and lunged for the Old One's wrist.

"That's it. Hang on."

Karak felt a powerful force lift him off the ice. He looked down and saw his feet dangling in space. He was like a bird caught in a powerful wind. He tried to look up, but the light blinded him.

"Don't look at it. I promised Him you wouldn't look at it."

He looked down and saw a granite ledge jutting through the fog. Powerful hands lowered him to the frozen rock. He tried to stand, but was too weak. He could hardly breathe. His face was covered with flecks of ice.

A hand reached through the chilled fog and touched his face. It was so cold, like frozen granite.

"Oh, my brother. You feel so warm."

"My God." He reached up and clasped the trembling hand.

"Your face is so warm. But I feel tears? Why are you crying?"

He sobbed and forced out the words. *"Are you with Mother and Father?"*

Her hand pulled away. *"How can you ask that? You know they're dead."*

"But, Nangi. You're—" Karak felt a strong hand grasp his shoulder.

"Say nothing. She can't face the pain."

Karak looked up and saw the Old One standing in the light. *"You brought me here for this?"*

The Old One glared at him. *"I brought you here to know the truth. Your sister is trapped between life and death. In time, she'll accept her fate and enter Samsara with your mother and father. Until then, her spirit cowers on a mountain where she fled to escape her attackers."*

"But, she has done nothing wrong? Why is she suffering?"

"You are not ready for these things. But know this. Find the mountain where she hides and you will free her soul, and your own."

Karak squinted at the light. *"Are you mad? There are hundreds of mountains?"*

"Her spirit will draw you like a magnet."

Karak was about to speak when a cold shadow brushed across his face. *"What was that?"*

"You've stirred Him with your questions. It is time for you to leave. This mountain is His home."

"Whose home?"

"My home, Karak." The Old One stepped onto the ledge

The Tenth Avatar

and looked eastward with colorless eyes. "These mountains are the guideposts. Guardians of the sacred balance where Heaven meets the Earth. Here, all things and people are one spirit. Your climb is over, Karak Drasi. You have touched Moksha."

With those words, the Old One spread his arms toward Tibet and disappeared into the light....

When Karak awoke, he was lying on the rocky slope facing the mountain. From the sun's angle, it was late morning. He rubbed his eyes and looked around for the Old One, but he was gone.

He climbed the slope for a better look at Kailas' haze-covered summit. Everything was still except for a gentle mist rolling across the mountain's north face.

It couldn't have been a dream. He still felt the heavenly light on his forehead when the Old One spoke to him. His face still tingled from Nangi's cold fingers.

He turned away from the mountain and looked northwest across the great Ngari plain toward Baltistan. Behind him, the mighty Himalayan ice wall guarded Nepal like an enormous white fortress. Which way, Karak? Which way?

He crawled down the rocks and headed west. It would take several days to complete the *kora*. Time enough to choose a path....

13 | Guernica

An hour had passed since the train pulled out of Madrid's Atocha Station on its northward run to Burgos and Bilboa. After clearing the city's perimeter, it began a grueling climb into the rugged foothills below the Guadarrama Mountains, a journey that would take most of the night because of the steep, winding grades.

Roberto rested his head against the seat and studied the red sky above the mountains. The last rays of sunlight were striking the foothills below Monte Abantos. Above him, the Escorial's spired domes and fortress walls stood proudly on a plateau overlooking Madrid, a fitting tribute to Spain's forgotten monarchy and the world it once dominated.

He watched the Escorial's ivory and gold Pantheon of Monarchs drift past his window until it disappeared in the train's smoke trail. When he was a child, his father brought him to the great palace to view the relics of four centuries of Spanish royalty, and to introduce him to the world's richest architecture. The hours they spent walking the Pantheon's marble corridors would never be forgotten, not because of the magnificent gold statues, or ornate mosque domes and royal crypts, but because of his father's firm grip and reassuring words.

In his thirty years on earth, Roberto had never felt an emptiness like this. He had lost his closest friend. The warm, firm hand was gone. He was truly alone.

He frowned and turned away from the darkening window. If not for a wrenching twist of fate two years ago, he might be inside the Escorial at this moment, restoring its marble tombs and arches, instead of heading north toward a Basque town with a name he couldn't remember.

Pizzaro's words echoed in his ears. The blood was real, unlike any ever seen. He looked down at his fingers and recalled the blood's salty taste when he touched it to his lips. Was it a sick prank? Miracle? Or something else? Something evil, like the nightmare still haunting him. He closed his eyes and listened to the clicking wheels.

Oh, to be swimming in the Mediterranean under a rich blue sky. No pain or sorrow. No screaming mobs. No unexplained miracles. Only the water lapping at his face while he floated in the warm afternoon sun.

He thought of Laura, her soft lips caressing him in the darkness, her warm body pressed against him when he gave himself up to her, the sweet scent of her skin when they drifted into deep sleep with the moonlight streaming through his apartment window.

He recalled the last night he saw her standing in the rain outside the *Marva Bar*. He should have taken her in his arms at that moment, but he was too stupid to know what he had. Fool! He'd walked away while Lieutenant Campeador stood by like a waiting vulture. By now, she had probably married the handsome officer and bore him two children.

But what if she hadn't? What if she was still a single woman living in Valencia. He could catch a morning train in Burgos and be home by tomorrow night. It wouldn't be hard to find her. He was no longer a wealthy man, but that shouldn't matter. He sank in the seat. Who was he kidding? It mattered. It had always mattered.

He was nearly asleep when the compartment door slid open and a sharp voice snapped his eyes open.

"Ticket please."

He looked up and saw a blue-uniformed conductor standing in the doorway with a silver punch in his hand.

"Sorry to disturb you, Padre." The portly official reached out with his other hand.

Roberto sat up and pulled the yellow ticket out of his jacket pocket. When he handed it to the conductor, he noticed a small red-gold-and-purple flag in the man's lapel. Proud symbol of the Second Republic.

The conductor studied the ticket and forced back a yawn. "I see your destination is Guernica."

Roberto shrugged his shoulders. "I've been assigned there."

"Have you now." The conductor punched the ticket and handed it to him.

"You know the town?"

The conductor nodded.

"What's it like?"

The conductor stared at him with bloodshot, green eyes. "See if you can be reassigned."

"Reassigned?"

"It's a bubbling stew up there. One day, the whole place will boil over." The conductor started to turn away and hesitated. "Oh, almost forgot. They don't like outsiders, especially if they're from the Church. They think you're spies sent in by the Monarchists and Carlists."

"I'm sorry I asked."

The conductor shrugged. "It's a beautiful place if you're Basque or Asturian. A little cold and damp in the evenings, but you'll spend most of your nights inside. You see, it's not wise for outsiders to walk Guernica's streets at night, especially if they're priests. God be with you, Padre." He tipped his cap and exited the compartment.

Roberto leaned back and sighed. His tired mind couldn't take anymore. He closed his eyes and dropped off to sleep.

When he awoke, the train was straining up a steep grade. Refreshed, he leaned against the window and saw the Guadarrama's snow-capped peaks silhouetted against the moonlit sky. It was a beautiful spring night in the mountains of central Spain, and he needed fresh air. He slipped out of the compartment and headed for the car's rear platform.

The view was breathtaking. With the train slowed by the steep grade, he could see Madrid's faint lights far to the south. A full moon flashed between the peaks, flooding the surrounding pine forests with soft, silver light.

He grasped the railing and took a deep breath of chilled night air. Madrid's lights flickered a final time, and disappeared into the darkness.

It was time to face the truth. He loved Valencia more than his life, but turning back in disgrace wasn't the answer. He would go to Guernica and look up this Padre Segurra at his mission on the river Mundaca. After a few days of trial, he would make his decision.

With the Church finally waking to its responsibilities, things might be different. There might be a real purpose in sending him up there. From the sound of Ordoña's letter, Segurra had lost control of the situation. Young blood was needed to restore the Basque's confidence in the Church. Maybe this was the answer to Corpus Christi and his terrible nightmares. Maybe his chance had finally come.

He sighed and looked up at the stars. And if not? France lay on the other side of the Pyrenees, and his friend, Jacques Dupont. He'd maintained correspondence with Jacques since graduating from the University of Madrid seven years ago. In that time, Jacques had built a successful architectural practice in Paris. There would always be a place for him there.

He shook his head and smiled. Interesting choice. Martyrdom in Basque country, or wine in Paris.

He was startled by a sudden rattling as the train rolled across a wooden trestle. Below him, water splashed in a moonlit gorge. A deer stood on the rocky bank, its nose dipped in the cold stream. God, it was beautiful up here. Another world. A better world. He took a final breath of crisp night air and opened the door to go inside.

"Oh, excuse me, Padre."

Roberto stepped back and stared at the beautiful woman standing in the doorway.

She pushed back her long black hair and smiled. "I wanted to get some air. It's so confining with all those snoring men."

Roberto peered down the dimly lit aisle at the rows of drooped heads. "I see what you mean. It's beautiful out here. A little cold, but it feels good."

She brushed past him and stepped onto the platform. "Won't you join me?"

Roberto flashed a polite smile through his stubbled beard. "I was just going back to my compartment."

Her eyes lit up. "You have a private compartment?"

"I was fortunate. Someone cancelled at the last minute."

"Lucky you." She grasped the rail and looked up at the moon. "You're right about it being beautiful. A smart person would jump off this train and stay up here."

After two years of celibacy, Roberto was not about to walk away from a beautiful señorita with a stunning figure and jet black hair streaming in the wind. He shut the door and eased beside her. "My name is Roberto. I'm studying for the priesthood."

She smiled at him with flashing white teeth. "I'm Ana. Pleasure to meet you, Roberto."

"Are you traveling alone?"

She frowned and looked away.

"I'm sorry, it's not my business."

"I'm going to Oviedo—in Asturias. My husband is visiting family there."

Roberto sensed a strain in her voice. "You're from Asturias?"

"I was born in Cadiz. My husband is Asturian. Until last month, we were living with the *braceros* in the south."

"So far apart. How did you meet?"

She shook her head. "It's not important. We'd hoped to make a new life in Sevilla or Granada. When the new government promised land to the people, we thought they were sincere. We were wrong."

Roberto reached down and lifted her shawl over her bare shoulders. "You'll get sick in this cold. This isn't southern Spain."

She smiled and leaned against him. "And where are you from, Roberto?"

"Valencia."

"Such a beautiful place. Are you studying for the priesthood there?"

"No, I've been assigned to a mission in Basque country."

She looked at him in shock. "*Mi Dios*. That's not a good place for visiting clergy."

Roberto nodded. "So I've been told. It seems we're both headed in strange directions." He hesitated and looked out at the mountains. "I hope you don't take this wrong, but I have an empty seat in my compartment. If you'd like, I'd be happy to give it to you."

She broke into a smile. "What took you so long? I haven't

slept in days." She brushed past him and pulled open the metal door. "Well, which one is it?" She laughed and swept her hand toward the compartments at the far end of the car.

When they entered his compartment, Ana wasted no time stretching out on the seat. She watched him sit across from her with folded hands. "You may not be a priest, but you just led me to heaven."

"Heaven?"

"A warm bed and good night's sleep. Rest well, Roberto." She rolled on her side and flicked the shawl over her bare shoulders.

"I have some cheese and wine in my bag."

She poked her head out of the shawl and smiled at him with tired eyes. "Wine, eh? Good night, señor."

Roberto broke into a sheepish smile. "Goodnight, señora."

He snatched his raincoat off the overhead rack and draped it over her while wondering if her Asturian husband knew how lucky he was. Her olive skin and pouting lips reminded him of Laura, but that was where the comparison ended. There was a depth to her Laura never had. A sensitivity he couldn't explain. He smiled and returned to his seat.

He couldn't take his eyes off her. In a few hours, she'd catch a train to Oviedo while he proceeded to Guernica. They'd shake hands politely and say a brief goodbye. She might even kiss him on the cheek for being so kind to a lonely traveller.

He rested his head against the seat. The train was picking up speed. They'd crossed the last grade and were descending the foothills toward Burgos. It felt good to be with a woman again.

He fell into a deep sleep and dreamt she was sitting beside him. He felt her hand brush his hair. She kissed him on the lips and whispered softly in his ear.

"Thank you, Roberto. You're not a priest, so I feel no shame. I think we'll meet again. Maybe in Guernica when you've taken your vows. On that day, I'll ask you to hear my confession. Goodbye, my handsome friend. I won't forget you."

He felt her slip something in his hand. The last thing he

remembered was the compartment door sliding open and the train grinding to a stop.

When he awoke, the compartment was empty and the conductor was strolling through the car shouting, "Bilboa!"

He rubbed his eyes and looked out the window at a row of green hills rising through the white mist. Beyond the hills, a line of reddish-brown peaks jutted into the blue morning sky.

His raincoat was lying on the empty seat across from him. She had probably gotten off the train in Burgos. He sat up and brushed back his hair. At least she could have said goodbye.

He started to get up and noticed a folded piece of paper on the floor beside his foot. He picked it up and opened it. The scrawled words were simple and direct....

Roberto...
Thank you for lifting my spirits. I see Spain still lives in the body of a warm, young man. You'll make a fine priest. God knows, we need you. Until we meet again ....
Ana

He crumpled the note and smiled. It wasn't a dream. The note had fallen out of his hand while he slept. They would meet again.

"Bilboa!" The conductor's voice rang out a second time.

Through the window, plumes of brown and yellow smoke rose from factories along a river. Beyond the smudged mills, rows of brick buildings and tenements stretched across a haze-covered valley toward a line of forested hills.

As the train rumbled into Bilboa's dark station, Roberto noticed a large red flag with green and white crosses draped on a stone arch above the tracks. It sent a chill through him.

He stood up and slipped on his raincoat. It smelled good— like a woman. He was about to pick up his bag when a different smell made him wince. It reminded him of his developer solution.

Sulfur. It was coming from the mills. He slid open the compartment door and stepped into the crowded aisle. Some of the passengers had placed handkerchiefs over their noses. What

The Tenth Avatar

a stench. So much for touring the Basque capital. Maybe Guernica would smell better. He clutched his bag and followed the line of weary passengers out of the rail car.

The concourse was jammed with citizens rushing to their jobs. He brushed past a prosperous-looking man in a brown tailored suit. A uniformed valet carried the gentleman's leather suitcase and valise. The moustached gentleman smiled and tipped his hat before disappearing into the crowd.

Others didn't look so prosperous. Burly men with rugged faces, dressed in black, brown, and gray work clothes, some of them wearing black berets, most of them carrying black lunch pails.

He saw women dressed in black with red, green, and yellow shawls draped over their shoulders. And smiling, blond-haired children walking beside their mothers, the sun streaming down on their fair-skinned faces from the skylight. And hanging protectively above them all, an enormous red-green-and-white flag warned visitors this was not Spain.

He paused at the schedule board and eyed the departures. The next train to Guernica would leave on track four at seven a.m., thirty minutes from now. He reached into his jacket pocket and grasped the ticket. On his map, Guernica was only fifteen miles away.

He scanned the concourse and spotted a busy portal with a black and white sign reading *QUATRO*. People were already filing through it, so he'd better hurry. He took a nervous breath and headed across the concourse. He was nearly to the portal when a loud voice stopped him.

"Hey, Priest!"

He turned and saw three Basque laborers staring at him from the concourse. They were clad in black work clothes and appeared to be mill workers. Two of them carried lunch pails, but the third held a vivid placard of a broad-shouldered militiaman forcing an ugly Civil Guardsman to drop his blood-smeared sword. Written across the violent scene in bold, red letters were the words....

Against military brutality! The invincible strength of the proletariat!

"Hey, Priest, are you deaf?"

Roberto ignored the Basque and started toward the portal, but one of them cut him off.

"You're not just deaf. You're dumb too. Read my lips, Priest. No foreigners are allowed in Guernica." The worker reached out and snatched Roberto's jacket collar.

Enough! He'd been through too much to take this shit from an anarchist. He wasn't going to be a martyr.

"Mariano, give me a hand with this pig. He's the biggest priest I've seen in—"

Roberto's left fist caught the stunned Basque flush on the jaw. Dazed, the Basque staggered back and shook his head. "Bastard! Now you're gonna pay." He charged into a solid right cross that dropped him like a sack of wheat.

"What the hell! What kind of priest are you?" The Basque with the placard rushed at Roberto, but his friend grabbed him.

"Wait, Mariano!"

"Let me go, idiot. I'll carve the pig to shreds." The Basque reached into his pants and pulled out a knife.

"You're the idiot." His friend pointed at two leather-capped Civil Guardsmen rushing toward them with pistols unholstered.

The Basque stepped back and glared at Roberto while his friend helped their injured comrade to his feet. "I'll see you again, Priest." He turned and ran across the concourse with his two shaken comrades.

The lead guardsman raced to Roberto's side and pushed back the gathering crowd. "Are you all right, Padre?"

Roberto nodded and stepped back from an angry spectator.

The guardsman drew his pistol and took a menacing step toward the shouting heckler. "You shouldn't be here, Padre. And neither should we."

Two red-bereted Basque militiamen burst through the crowd and glared at Roberto and the two guardsmen. One of them stepped forward and jammed his fists against his hips while eyeing the drawn pistol. "Are you crazy? What do you think you're doing?"

The guardsman slipped his pistol into its holster and gestured toward Roberto. "This priest was being attacked by anarchists. We won't tolerate such things."

The militiaman shook his head. "You and that priest have no business here. We're a free state and have no dealings with Spain."

The guardsman glanced at the angry crowd. "We were passing through when we saw the trouble. Our only interest is to escort this man to safety."

"Where are you bound?"

"Oviedo."

The militiaman scowled and scratched his stubbled beard. "You won't be welcome there either. You should go back to Madrid with the rest of your secret police. You're playing with fire." The crowd broke into angry cheers as the proud militiaman stuck out his chest and soaked up the glory.

"Our orders are to proceed to Oviedo, and that is where we'll go. Now if you and your friends will step aside, we'll be on our way." The guardsman grabbed Roberto's arm and started to pull him away.

"No!" Roberto yanked his arm free while the guardsman looked at him in shock. "I've been ordered to report to Padre Arronategui at the Church of San Juan." He reached into his jacket pocket and handed Ordoña's letter to the stunned militiaman.

The militiaman read it and passed it to his comrade. "Call Arronategui and get confirmation."

The second militiaman nodded and ran toward a wall phone at the far end of the concourse while his comrade stared at the man dressed in black.

Angered by Roberto's refusal, the lead guardsman pressed against him and whispered in harsh tones. "You ask us to risk our lives for this? Do you know what you're doing?"

Roberto looked down. "I'm sorry. You should be on your way."

"Fool. When you step on that train, you'll be committing suicide. Come with us and we'll vouch for you with the Church. I don't want your blood on my hands."

"I'm sorry. Like you, I have my orders."

The militiaman folded his arms and glanced at the schedule board. "If I were you, Priest, I'd listen to the guardsman. You're not welcome here. A train leaves for Madrid in one hour. If you're smart, you'll be on it."

"If I was smart, I'd be an architect."

"What?"

Roberto shook his head and looked away.

Five minutes later, the second militiaman ran across the concourse and gestured for his comrade to step aside. After a brief conference, the first militiaman approached Roberto and handed him Ordoña's letter. "It seems you're telling the truth. Padre Arronategui questioned why you're late."

"I had to make a stop in Valencia."

"Valencia? You should have stayed there." The frustrated militiaman shook his head. "Remember, I warned you. The train to Guernica leaves in five minutes."

Roberto nodded and turned toward the two guardsmen. "I'm very sorry about this."

"So are we." The enraged guardsmen turned away and headed toward the portal marked *UNO*, and their train to Oviedo.

The train ride to Guernica was uneventful except for a few menacing stares from the seated Basque passengers. Roberto ignored them and pulled out his bible. Tough to kill a priest reading his bible.

When he opened the bible, Ana's folded note dropped in his lap. He unfolded the small paper and reread her soft words.

He was about to stuff the note in his bible when a strange thought struck him. If she was going to Oviedo, why get off in Burgos when she could have stayed with him in that comfortable compartment and caught a train in Bilboa?

He closed the bible and stared at the passing hills. Maybe it was him. She seemed a little nervous when he offered her the wine. Hell, who could blame her? He frowned at the battered reflection in the glass. He looked more like a thug than a priest with that unkempt beard, blackened eye, bruised cheek, and split lip. My God, how times had changed.

He rested his head against the seat and noticed an old woman glaring at him. She was missing a few front teeth, but her mumbled curses were quite clear. The words weren't pretty. He turned toward the window and pretended she wasn't there.

The small train cleared Bilboa's factory haze and snaked eastward through green and brown hills. As it approached Guernica, the rugged hills gave way to pastures sprinkled with black-faced sheep and colorfully attired shepherds. Beyond the pastures, a line of rocky foothills stretched toward the towering Pyrenees Mountains.

To the north, a churning gray river wound through a forest before fading into the fog. He pulled out his map and studied it. It must be the Mundaca, flowing downstream toward the Bay of Biscay.

He folded the map and smiled. The sea was on the other side of that forest, waiting for him like an old friend. There must be a path. Maybe even a road. Nothing to it, just follow the river to the sea.

As the train veered north, he saw Guernica emerging from the haze. The first thing that struck him was a long, two-story brick building on the town's western boundary. Smoke poured from a tall stack adjacent to the building. So much for clean air.

Except for a few church steeples, Guernica resembled Bilboa. It was smaller of course, perhaps a few hundred brick and stone buildings clustered along the river. Twin plumes of smoke drifted from stacks on the town's east and west side. He frowned and looked away. Picasso should have told him about the smoke.

"Guernika!" The conductor's gravel voice boomed through the passenger car as people snatched their belongings and lined up at the exit.

Roberto took his place in line and felt someone tug his sleeve. He turned and saw a young woman staring at him. She was dressed in black with a red shawl draped over her head and shoulders. An empty market basket dangled from her hand.

"Yes?"

She smiled at him with a pretty round face. "Are you from Bilboa, Padre?"

"I'm from Valencia."

Her face twisted in anger. "Valencia? What are you doing here? Are you crazy?"

Shaken by her sudden anger, Roberto turned away and followed the crowd through the exit door. He could feel their eyes burning into him as he walked beneath the crossed Basque flags leading into the station's small concourse.

The station emptied quickly, leaving him standing alone near a ticket window. He scanned the concourse and spotted an old man in a weathered brown uniform leaning against the wall beneath the crossed flags. A rifle rested against the man's hip while he fumbled for a cigaret. Roberto took a deep breath and strolled toward him. "Excuse me."

The disheveled guard lit the cigaret and looked at Roberto with bloodshot eyes. "Yeah?"

"Maybe you can help me. I'm trying to locate Padre Arronategui at the Church of San Juan." Roberto pulled out Ordoña's letter and extended it with a trembling hand.

The guard snatched the letter and frowned. "You're assigned here?"

"Yes."

The guard scanned the letter and handed it back to Roberto. "You better come with me."

"Where are we going?"

"Just follow me." The guard slung the rifle over his shoulder and nodded toward the exit.

The morning sky was filled with low, drifting clouds that reminded Roberto of Valencia in the spring. The air was cold and a stiff breeze gusted between the buildings. From the look of the wet street and sidewalks, it had rained overnight. The street was nearly deserted except for a few passers-by. Their long wool jackets and boots made them look out of place in the town. They should be in the hills tending their sheep.

Roberto pulled up his raincoat collar and noticed a building across the street with a sign reading *Julian Hotel*. "Nice hotel."

"Never mind that. The church is this way."

They passed a jai alai fronton and restaurant, the *Arrien*. Roberto recalled trying his hand at the game while attending the University of Madrid. The damn leather ball nearly killed him when it ricocheted off the playing wall and hit him in the head. An inhuman game if there ever was one.

They walked past a block of tenement buildings with washed clothes dangling from lines strung between the windows. When they turned the corner, Roberto detected a familiar sweet odor. "That smells like candy?"

The guard shrugged his shoulders. "It should. It's from the candy factory."

"You have a candy factory?"

The guard turned and glared at Roberto. "I'm not a tour guide, and I'm not enjoying this. Take a look around you."

Roberto didn't have to. Since leaving the station, he was painfully aware of the bitter glances and whispers coming from the milling citizens. Not one smile. Only pure hatred. He felt like a leper. "Are we near the church?"

"Around the corner." The guard nodded toward a white steeple jutting above the tenements.

The guard led Roberto through the church's wooden doors and told him to wait in the vestibule. Roberto crossed himself and sat on a bench beside a fountain of holy water. It was a small vestibule, but solidly constructed of gray mortar and stone. A portrait of *The Last Supper* filled the far wall. Above the chapel entrance, two small Basque flags declared church and state were one and the same in Guernica.

Roberto heard footsteps echoing from a dark corridor on his left. The guard stepped out of the shadows, followed by a stocky priest with gray hair and a stern-looking face.

"You're Roberto Hidalgo?"

Roberto stood up and nodded politely.

"I'm Padre Arronategui. Your papers please."

"Papers?"

"The letter from Padre Ordoña." The priest's tone was rude and impatient.

Roberto fumbled for the letter and handed it to the black-cassocked priest.

"Why are you so late?"
"I had business in Valencia."
"That's your home?"
"Yes."
Arronategui looked at the guard. "Wait here."
The guard nodded and sat on the bench.
"Come with me." The priest gestured for Roberto to follow him down the corridor.
They stepped into a small office that appeared to be part of a living quarter. Arronategui gestured for Roberto to sit across from him at a desk strewn with papers. "Care for some wine?"
Roberto nodded.
Arronategui reached for a decanter and poured two glasses of milky-white wine. He handed one to Roberto and sat down behind the desk. "Can I ask you a question?"
"Yes."
"Why are you here?"
Roberto shrugged. "I was assigned here."
"Why not Valencia or Madrid?"
"It was the Church's decision, not mine."
Arronategui's face reddened. "Do you know Segurra?"
"Padre Segurra? I've never met him."
"He's very ill. I suspect they want to replace him with you."
Roberto put down his wine. "Where is he?"
"At his mission, about a mile from here."
"Outside the city?"
Arronategui glared at his guest. "There are many things you don't know. Let me enlighten you." He gulped down his wine and pushed it aside. "Vizcaya belongs to the Basques, not Spain. Whatever you've been told, the Spanish Church has no business here. We're an independent nation with our own priests and government. And we're fed up with papal stooges being sent here to spy on us. Am I clear?"
Roberto was stunned by the priest's words.
Arronategui leaned forward. "Am I clear, young Hidalgo?"
Roberto's face flushed. He tried to restrain himself, but it was no use. "You are very clear. As I told you, this wasn't my

idea. The thought of going to a small province with balloon-headed people disgusts me."

Arronategui's frown turned to a sneer. "How dare you."

Roberto jumped out of the chair. "And how dare you! I just came from my father's funeral. It was hard enough climbing on that train—but to be accused of being a spy by a pig-headed old man. That's where I draw the line. I'll report back to Granada immediately." He picked up his bag and turned to leave.

"Wait a minute, you fool!" Arronategui sat back in his chair, his fists clenched. "I don't care about you, your father, Segurra, or the damn Spanish Church. I didn't assign you here, but at least we have one thing in common."

"Yes?"

"Neither of us wants you here. The guard will escort you to Segurra's mission or the rail station—whichever you prefer. Either way, we'll not see each other again." Arronategui reached for the decanter and poured himself another glass of the fruity white wine.

Roberto stormed past the stunned guard and bolted out of the church.

"Hey, where do you think you're going?" The guard chased him into the street and grabbed his arm. "Did you hear me? Where are you going?"

Roberto dropped his bag and stared at the small crowd of Basques gathered on the street corner. They reminded him of a pack of wolves waiting for their wounded prey to fall.

"Well, Priest?" The guard lit a cigaret and glanced nervously at the crowd.

Roberto had never felt anger like this. He recalled Ordoña's biting words the night he left the seminary. There was no place for dissenters in the Spanish Church. In the old days, they'd deal with him through the Inquisition. Today, things were more sophisticated. Just send the rebel on a hopeless assignment into hostile territory, and let nature take its course.

"Come on, I don't have all day."

With his father's estate in shambles, going back to Valencia meant certain disgrace. If he disobeyed his papal order to remain in Guernica, he'd be branded a coward by the powerful Spanish Church. Even Pizarro couldn't help him. Honoring his order meant exile and possible death at the hands of Basque nationalists. He was staring down three roads that led to disgrace, excommunication, and death. Pick one, señor.

He took a deep breath and looked at the guard. "Take me to the mission."

The guard shrugged and flicked away his cigaret. "Bad choice."

They walked through the mumbling crowd and headed past a stone building with *Town Hall* carved on the wooden arch above the door. A large flag whipped in the breeze above their heads, this one displaying a gnarled tree. They passed a town square filled with children playing soccer. A group of women chatted beside a fountain while their men played cards. A guitarist strummed a Basque folk tune. It reminded him of Valencia.

Roberto detected the sound of rushing water. They passed the candy factory and headed down a narrow road toward a paved bridge supported by metal beams. He could see the river splashing against its rocky banks. "Is that the Mundaca?"

The guard looked at him in surprise. "How do you know that?'

"I did some reading on the train."

The guard smirked and gestured for Roberto to sit on a rock while he lit another cigaret. He took a puff and flicked the match into the river. "You came here on the Madrid train?"

Roberto nodded and bit into a piece of cheese from his bag.

"What time did you reach Bilboa?"

"Time?"

The annoyed guard tapped his watch.

"Early this morning. Maybe six."

The guard puffed his cigaret and looked at the bridge. "You were lucky. The train behind you was blown up outside Burgos."

"Blown up?"

"Dynamited by anarchists—or so they say. I heard it on the radio."

"My God. How bad?"

The guard shrugged his shoulders. "They didn't say. I don't expect they will."

"Why?"

"The train was packed with Civil Guardsmen headed for Oviedo. Don't want to start a panic in Madrid. Not with the damn government on its last legs." The guard flicked his cigaret into the river. "Well, let's get going. Segurra's mission is just up the road."

Roberto didn't hear him. He was staring at the churning river.

14 | Segurra

It didn't look like a mission. The crude structure on the hillside resembled a cottage with its gray stone walls, brown shuttered windows, and red tiled roof.

The guard stopped and turned toward Roberto. "Segurra's probably asleep. Don't see him much since the attack."

"Attack?"

The guard tapped his chest.

"He had a heart attack?"

"Bad one. Before his heart gave out, he'd chop a stack of wood and lug it up the hill without blinking an eye. Now, the poor old fart can't even lift an axe."

Roberto looked up at the mission. "Who leads the Mass?"

The guard spit at the ground. "He gets by. Besides—no one prays here except the sick and dying, and they only come because they can't make it to town. We don't hold it against them, but you'll never see a healthy Basque step into a Spanish church."

"Spanish? But Vizcaya is part of Spain?"

"In a pig's ass." The guard's face reddened. "We're a free state and have been since Ferdinand and Isabella swore it at the sacred oak six hundred years ago. Hell, even your new government honors our *fueros*."

"You make it sound like a separate country?"

The guard sneered at him. "Now you're getting it. Hey, you're pretty smart."

Roberto bit his lip and decided to change the subject. "How does he survive?"

The guard scratched his beard. "Arronategui and the other priests let him in town on market day. I used to take him there, but since he got sick I've been doing the shopping for him."

"That's good of you."

"Hell, I take it out of his monthly allowance from the Church. Not much, just a few *pesetas*." The guard paused and looked up the hill. "I guess you'll take care of his food and supplies from now on. Remember, you're only allowed in town on Monday. That's market day. If you need anything, it has to wait until Monday—got it?"

"What if something happens to him?"

The guard shrugged. "Already has. Two heart attacks. The last one nearly finished the poor bastard. A herder found him sprawled on the altar before Sunday Mass. Good thing Montero was sober."

"Montero?"

"The Doc."

Roberto stared at the guard in horror. "How can you people do this? The man's done you no harm."

The guard spit at the ground. "It's not us. It's your own Church. Hell, we've been pretty decent to the old fart. Don't believe that shit about us killing priests and nuns. You won't find more god-fearing Catholics than us. It's just we don't trust pious pigs who screw their own people. And now, they send you up here to protect their precious mission because the old guy's dying. They don't care about him. Or you either!"

The guard waved his hand in disgust. "Hell, I need a drink. See you on Monday. I'll be at the bridge at noon." He turned and walked down the road toward the river.

Roberto sighed and looked up at the mission. The air was still except for a tinkling bell coming from a blackfaced sheep grazing beside the road. He scanned the surrounding hills for its owner, but saw no one.

He looked east toward the Pyrenees. Ten years ago, he'd crossed those mountains with his friends from the University. Time to do it again. It would only take a few days to reach Biarritz. Then, a phone call to Jacques Dupont, and his new life would begin.

A raindrop struck his face. Then another. He looked up and saw a line of dark clouds closing from the north. Lightning flickered over the mountains, followed by the rumble of thunder. It was spring and high crossings were dangerous. "Damn." He picked up his bag and trudged up the rocky hillside toward the mission. Paris would have to wait another day.

The cross on the roof was decaying from dry rot. He ran his

fingers along the door and peeled off a chip of brittle wood. Not a good sign. The mission was suffering from neglect.

He looked down the road toward the bridge and candy factory. Through the mist, San Juan's white steeple jutted above the red tenements. Beyond it, the ugly brick stack spewed black smoke over the town. A convent's stone tower rose above the trees on a hillside beyond the town, its cross silhouetted against the darkening sky. It reminded him of the seminary. The guard's harsh words echoed in his ears. This *was* another country.

He rapped on the door and waited for a response. Nothing. He lifted the latch and stepped into the mission.

He was standing in a barren chapel that reminded him of the abandoned Catholic school he'd seen in the hills outside Granada. Instead of pews, five rows of wood benches faced a simple altar. The ornate gold crucifix on the wall was definitely out of place.

Rain blew into the room from two opened windows on his left. He dropped his bag and closed the shutters, barely leaving enough light to see.

"Padre Segurra?" He waited for an answer, but only heard the rain pattering on the tile roof. He walked down the narrow aisle and sat on the front bench, his eyes fixed on the gold crucifix.

"Who are you?"

He froze. That voice. It sounded like—

"Let me see you."

He stood up and scanned the deserted chapel. The voice seemed to be coming from behind the altar. He moved closer and spotted a door in the shadows. He edged toward it and pushed it open.

He was standing in a small, dark room. A desk and chair were positioned against a shuttered window to allow the occupant to look out while he worked.

"Open the window so I can see you."

His heart nearly jumped through his chest. The voice was coming from the shadows on his right. He rushed to the window and pushed open the shutter, flooding the room with silver light.

"Please, come closer."

He turned and saw an old man lying on a bed. The man wore a black cassock and appeared to be in some pain. His right hand clutched the small gold crucifix on his chest. His face was pale and drawn.

Roberto eased next to the bed. "Padre Segurra?"

"Yes?"

"I'm Roberto Hidalgo. I was ordered here to assist you."

The old man looked up at Roberto with confused brown eyes. "You're a priest?"

"I'm from the Seminary of Andalusia—near Granada. I was ordered here by Padre Ordoña. The Church is very concerned."

Segurra smiled through his parched lips. "You've come a long way. There's some fresh soup on the stove in that alcove behind you. And a bottle of *Madeira*, if you care to indulge."

Roberto helped Segurra to a small table in the alcove. After sitting him down, he ladled some warm soup into a bowl and poured a glass of wine. By the time he sat across from his host, he'd nearly consumed them both.

Segurra brushed back his thinning white hair. "You're welcome to finish the soup. And have more wine."

"I'm fine." Roberto pushed the bowl aside and rested his arms on the table. "The guard who brought me here said you nearly died."

Segurra smiled. "I'm fifty-nine. Life is short." He looked down at the crucifix. "Funny, how things turn out. Twenty-three years ago, Luis almost killed me. Now he cares for me like a baby."

"The guard's name is Luis?"

The priest nodded. "He tries to act tough, but he has a good heart, like the rest of them."

Roberto shook his head. "Forgive me, Padre, but they've not exactly welcomed you with open arms. They treat you like a leper. My God, you can't even go into town to worship."

Segurra frowned. "Why should I want to worship there? This is a house of God. On this hillside, it stands taller than any

Basque church in Guernica or Bilboa."

"But, you have no congregation? You're shut off from the people?"

"So skeptical. That's not good for a future priest. The Guernicans are free to worship where they wish. I can't blame them for wanting to stay with their own kind."

Roberto looked down at his empty wine glass. "Why would the Church send a missionary into a hostile province when the missionary doesn't believe in his cause?"

Segurra shook his head. "You have much to learn. We're men of God, not holy crusaders."

Roberto felt a tinge of anger. "The Basques think we're spies."

"That's because the Church wants us to be spies. The Church is political. I'm not. That's why I've been forgotten."

Roberto looked into the old man's brown eyes. "Is that why they sent me here?"

"What do you mean?"

Roberto stroked his stubbled chin. "I spoke out against them."

"You what?"

"I called them hypocrites."

Segurra's shoulders slumped. "There's a pump outside the window. I could use some water."

Roberto nodded and grabbed a clay jug off the table. He walked to the window and reached for the pump's rusted handle. A few strokes and fresh water was gushing into the jug from the pump's spout. He returned to the table and poured the priest a cup.

Segurra sipped the water and stared at his young guest. "Maybe I can intercede with Cardinal Saez."

Roberto's eyes widened. "You know the Cardinal?"

"Oh, yes. We spent many years together at the Great Cathedral in Toledo during our training. We used to joke about becoming famous missionaries in far-off lands." Segurra grimaced. "It didn't quite work out that way. He ended up Spain's most powerful cleric, and I ended up in Guernica."

Roberto looked out the window at the falling rain. "And

now, there are two of us."

"I'm afraid so, young man." The old man gulped down the water. "Like you, I spoke out when I saw laborers starving in the fields while their rich land bosses stuffed themselves with mutton. Saez warned me to shut up, but I was too much a zealot for that. I shouted until the walls shook." Segurra nodded at the jug and watched Roberto refill his cup. "My brothers called me a heretic. Everyone ignored me. You know, the silent treatment."

"And that's why they sent you here?"

"Not quite. Saez intervened a final time and calmed things down. He warned me it was my last chance." Segurra lowered his head. "I should have listened to him."

"You spoke out again?"

"Worse than that. I saw a laborer beaten for stealing some bread for his dying wife. I couldn't stand it any longer."

"Yes?"

"I wrote the Vatican."

"You wrote the Pope?"

"I accused him of surrounding himself with pharisees."

Roberto stared at the old man.

"A month later, Saez notified me that my services were needed in Vizcaya. I left on the evening train and never saw him again." Segurra's eyes glistened with tears. "Twenty-three years have passed since that day. I would like to see Toledo before I die."

"Why haven't you gone back?"

"If I'm seen outside Guernica, I'll be excommunicated for abandoning my post. It was ordered by the Pope."

"God."

Segurra sipped his water. "Don't blame the Basques for my exile. As you can see, it's otherwise."

Roberto stood up and walked to the window. "Do you know what has happened since the new government took power?"

"Only through rumors."

Roberto glanced out the window at the falling rain. "It seems your friend Saez is about to be exiled. The Second

Republic doesn't care for his rebellious views."

Segurra's jaw dropped. "Pedro exiled?"

"Ironic, isn't it. Couldn't happen to a nicer man."

Segurra's face reddened beneath his thinning white hair. "How can you say that? A priest can't seek revenge." The old man tried to stand, but couldn't make it. He collapsed in the chair, gasping for breath.

Roberto helped Segurra back to the bed and sat beside him. He grasped the ailing priest's hand and spoke softly. "I'm sorry, Padre. I wish they were all like you."

Segurra looked up at him with tired eyes. "What are you going to do?"

Roberto hesitated. "I'm not as strong as you. Tomorrow, I'm going over the mountains."

The old man grimaced. "Don't do it, my son. We all suffer in life, but to abandon God is to abandon the world to come."

"Sorry, I'm not ready for those things."

Segurra clutched the crucifix on his chest. "Will you do something for me?"

"If I can."

"Tomorrow is Sunday. I'm too weak to lead the Mass. Will you conduct it for me?"

"Me?"

"You're trained in the Blessed Sacraments?"

"Yes—but I'm not a priest."

Segurra's brown eyes filled with tears. "Be one tomorrow. At least you'll know what you're giving up. And you'll make an old man happy."

Roberto pulled his hand away. "But, you have no congregation?"

"Who told you that?"

"The guard."

Segurra broke into a weak smile. "How would Luis know? He never attends Mass."

Roberto leaned forward. "People come?"

Segurra nodded. "Each week more come. Shepherds, migrants—even their families. Last week, there were so many, some stood outside in the rain."

Roberto stared at Segurra in disbelief. "The guard said no healthy Basque would step into a Spanish church."

"He's right."

"What?"

"This is God's church, Roberto. Not Spain's. We're God's messengers, not *conquistadors*. People don't care about political regimes. They only want to pray in peace. I'm giving them that." The old man's eyes lit up. "You want passion? This is my passion. Do this one thing for me. It's all I ask. Keep the flame burning in Guernica."

Roberto spent the rest of the day doing badly needed chores while preparing the mission for the Mass. Even if the old man was wrong, the least he could do was humor him.

The preparation was surprisingly simple after those long rehearsals at the seminary. He finished before ten and decided to get a breath of night air before stretching out on one of the benches.

The rain had stopped and a quarter moon was breaking through the clouds. Lightning still flickered over the Pyrenees, but the storm appeared to be withdrawing. The air was crisp and a light breeze drifted across the hillside. Through the darkness, he heard the swollen Mundaca splashing against its banks. The town was dead silent.

He sat on a rock and looked up at the moon. Almost two weeks had passed without a recurrence of the nightmare. Maybe it was finally over. A smile cracked his lips. Maybe his father had put an end to it.

Tomorrow, he would say goodbye to Segurra and head across the mountains. From the look of the sky, there was a good chance the weather would hold out until he reached France. By the time Luis came looking for him on Monday, he'd be long gone.

He reached into his pocket and pulled out the letter he'd scrawled earlier that evening. He'd ask Segurra to send it to Granada. The words were simple and direct....

Padre Ordoña,
Thank you for your challenge, but I'm afraid I must

decline. Perhaps I'll try another time when the Church has purged itself of hypocrites and cowards.
   Your unfaithful, enlightened servant,
   Roberto Hidalgo

He stuffed the letter in his pocket and stepped inside the mission.

Roberto was awakened by voices coming from outside the mission. At first, he thought it might be a passing shepherd and his flock, but the approaching footsteps quickly changed his mind.

He rolled off the bench and staggered to the window. Easing open the shutter, he was stunned to see a crowd of people standing on the hillside in the bright morning sunlight. From the look of their worn clothes, they appeared to be shepherds.

For a moment, they eyed him and said nothing. Finally, one of them stepped forward and placed his hands on his hips. The tall, stocky man wore black boots, blue work pants, and a faded brown shirt under a yellow, fleece vest. His thick blond hair streamed back over his ears. He stared at Roberto with deep-set blue eyes. "Who the hell are you?"

Roberto backed away from the window and walked to the door. He opened it and looked down at the threatening man and his small army. "My name is Roberto. Padre Segurra asked me to lead the Mass."

The man reared back his head. "Now why would he do that?"

"He's not well."

A black-haired man eased beside the first and began conversing with him. He wasn't as tall as his comrade, but his stocky build and rugged face weren't to be ignored. He patted his friend's shoulder and stepped toward Roberto. "Are you a priest?"

Roberto flinched. "I'm passing through on a pilgrimage to France. I offered to conduct the Mass for Padre Segurra. After that, I'll be moving on."

The young man folded his arms and studied Roberto with green eyes. "You said your name was?"

"Roberto."

"From?"

"Southern Spain."

The young man shook his head. "Why don't I believe you?"

Roberto shrugged. "You don't have to. After Mass, I'll be on my way and you'll never see me again."

The young man looked down and kicked the ground.

"Please—come in. I wish there was more room. Some of you will have to stand at the windows. I'm sorry—I didn't expect so many." Roberto stepped back and gestured toward the mission.

The young man looked up and nodded. "You win, pilgrim. But I still don't believe you." He looked back at the crowd and nodded for them to follow him into the mission.

"Padre?"

Segurra opened his eyes and looked up at the trembling young man standing beside the bed. "What's wrong, Roberto?"

"You were serious. There must be forty people out there."

"You didn't believe me?"

"I thought maybe a few sick and elderly, but this is a full congregation."

Segurra smiled. "Is the Eucharist prepared?"

Roberto nodded nervously.

"Good—then conduct the Mass. I'll say a prayer for you." He closed his eyes and turned away.

"But—" Roberto glanced at the cassock and vestments hanging from the hook beside the door. Segurra wasn't going to let him off that hook. He took a deep breath and slipped them on.

Segurra's vestments felt heavier than the garb he'd worn during training at the seminary. Or maybe it was the weight of the moment. He looked down at the sleeping priest and slipped through the door into the chapel.

They were jammed shoulder to shoulder in the pews. The

men had removed their caps and placed them on their laps. The women wore black and red scarfs. At least half of them carried bibles.

Roberto stepped onto the altar and rested his hands on the small lectern. He looked out at the filled chapel and felt his heart pounding. To his right, another dozen people stared at him through the unshuttered windows.

His guts were churning. He didn't know whether to laugh or cry. Except for that fateful morning at Corpus Christi, this was the strangest moment of his life. He placed the bible on the lectern and lowered his head. "Let us pray...."

The Mass took exactly one hour. He read from the *Holy Scriptures* and lit incense to purify the altar. He blessed the bread and wine, and watched the people file from their seats to kneel before him. He blessed them while they tasted the sacred flesh and blood of Christ, and he watched them return to their seats while their comrades filed into the mission to take their turn.

When it was over, he resumed his position at the lectern and looked down at them. He would never forget their faces, or this moment on the altar. He had tasted the Church's power, and it scared him to death.

He leaned forward and spoke softly. "I've enjoyed this time with you. Can I ask you a question?"

"You can ask me." The blond-haired man stood up and stared at Roberto with those deep-set eyes.

"Are you from the town?"

"I'm Augustin." The blond-haired man gestured toward the shorter man seated on his left. "This is my brother, Gorka. We're herders from a village near Guernica."

"And your friends?"

Augustin shrugged. "We come from everywhere. Fishermen, like Ixidro." He nodded toward an old man with a leather face and white beard seated in the front row. "Laborers, like Juan." He gestured toward a brown-jacketed man on his right. "And miners, like Julio." He turned and pointed to a handsome, black-haired man in the back row.

Roberto stiffened. She was sitting beside the man called

Julio. He couldn't believe his eyes. He stared at her and forced a nervous smile.

"Does that answer your question?"

"What?"

"Your question."

Roberto blinked and looked at Augustin. "When I came here, the guard told me no Basques step into a Spanish church."

"Spanish?" Augustin reared back his head and glared at Roberto. "This hill belongs to the Basques, and so does this mission."

Roberto hesitated and looked down at his bible. He lifted his head and forced a smile. "And so it should. I'm glad you invited me here today. I hope we'll meet again."

Augustin's glare became a scowl.

Roberto wiped a drop of perspiration off his face. "Can I ask you one more question?"

"Yeah?"

"Why do you worship here instead of the churches in town?"

Augustin shrugged his shoulders. "Never thought about it. Probably because it's closer to our sheep." He looked at a young, blond-haired woman seated in the last row. "Hey, Francesca. What do you think?"

She stood up and smiled at Roberto. "This is my first time. It sounded so pretty in the hills. Too bad you're leaving, Padre. I've never seen such a handsome priest. If you would stay, I might come again."

The room exploded with laughter while Roberto tried to conceal his red face. He backed away from the lectern and raised his hands. "Thank you. Please come back next week. I'm sure Padre Segurra will be better by then. God bless you." He stepped off the podium and walked toward the departing crowd.

"No sermon, Padre?"

He turned and saw Ana smiling at him. She gestured toward the tall, young man standing at her side. "Padre, this is my husband, Julio."

"Pleased to meet you, Padre." The black-haired young man extended his hand and smiled. "I see you've already met my wife."

Roberto nodded and shook Julio's hand. "I didn't expect to see Ana again. And of all places, here."

Julio's smile faded. "Things happen that way, Padre. But look at you. Ordained in only two days. *Mi Dios*, you must have powerful friends."

Roberto lowered his head. "Then—you know?"

"Of course. Wives tell their husbands everything."

"Please, I'll be gone by this afternoon and—"

Ana broke out laughing and grabbed Roberto's arm. "Don't do this to him. Your secret is safe with us, Roberto. Besides, it was a beautiful ceremony."

Roberto shook his head. "I feel like an imposter."

"We're all imposters, Roberto." Ana glanced at the crowd filing out of the chapel. "They tell me Padre Segurra is very ill. Maybe you should stay awhile. This is no time for us to be without a priest."

Roberto started to speak, but Julio cut him off. "Ana is right. We got out of Oviedo just in time. The damn Civil Guard is calling everyone a Marxist. Arrests, torture—even worse. They're out of control. The government won't lift a finger to stop them. Next, they'll send in the damn military."

"Military?"

Julio's black eyes flashed with anger. "The pigs are ready to invade because a few drunken kids blew up a train and torched a couple buildings. You've got to expect some unrest in times like this."

"Ana told me you're Asturian."

Julio glared at his wife. "What else did she tell you?"

"Nothing." Roberto hesitated. "Will you go back?"

Julio frowned. "In time. But when I do, my hands won't be empty."

Ana stepped toward her husband, but he brushed her away. "And I won't be alone. The Basques open their doors to us because they see what is happening. Our freedom is their freedom. The bell tolls for us all. In the end, we'll stand together."

Ana placed her hand over her husband's mouth and smiled. "*Mi Dios*, Julio. You're shouting like a raving madman. Calm down before you scare our friend away. We want him to stay, remember?"

Roberto stared at her and recalled the guard's words at the bridge. Terrorists blowing up a train full of Civil Guardsmen. Lord knows how many killed. And the man facing him calls it an act of drunken kids? Was life so cheap up here?

Julio took a deep breath and brushed back his hair. "Sorry—I'm a little worked up. I've been running for months. First Oviedo, then Cadiz and Seville." He trained his black eyes on Roberto. "I'm tired of running."

"That's quite enough, *mi amor*." Ana stepped back and glared at her husband.

Julio ignored her and grasped Roberto's arm. "Hard times are coming. Many will die. We'll need a priest more than ever."

Roberto shook his head. "I don't understand. If the Basques are your friends, why not worship in town with Arronategui?"

"You ask too many questions." Julio stepped to the door and nodded to Augustin and his brother. "Come in here for a minute."

Augustin flicked away his cigaret and stepped into the mission, followed by Gorka.

"Our friend wants to know why we aren't with Arronategui. Better he hear the answer from a Basque."

Augustin turned to Roberto. "You ask too many questions."

"Sorry."

"Our priests want us to stay out of this mess—to ignore our friends in Asturias and Catalonia. They think wearing blinders will protect us when the military decides to step in. They think the new government will honor the *fueros*—our independent rights."

"Why shouldn't it?"

Augustin glared at him. "If the military steps in, you can kiss the new government goodbye. There will be no Republic. You think Zamora and Azaña can stand up to the army?

They'll be crushed like flowers—and us along with them."

Roberto couldn't speak. He remembered the Civil Guardsman's warning outside Granada.

Gorka stepped toward Roberto, a sneer on his face. "Enough talk. If you're going to France—go. Otherwise, stay here and be our priest. We don't ask twice."

"I thought you didn't trust me?"

Gorka folded his arms. "I don't. I know about Valencia and Granada. And your outbursts against the Church. If it was my doing, you'd be gone already." He hesitated and looked down. "Picasso tells us you're a good man—so we listen."

Roberto stared at him in shock. "Picasso contacted you?"

"And others. Some of them might surprise you. Remember, there are many like us—even in your precious Valencia." Gorka glanced at his brother. "Enough talk. There are sheep to be sheared." He turned and walked out of the mission, followed by the others.

Roberto watched them hike down the hill to the road. When they reached the bridge, they turned into the forest, and disappeared.

He spent the next hour sitting on the rock outside the mission. The warm spring breeze felt good against his face. He could smell the pines on the surrounding hills, and the fresh grass growing in the meadow across the road. The air carried a faint aroma of burnt sugar from the candy factory. A church bell chimed in the distance.

He stood up and walked into the mission. Beams of sunlight radiated through the opened windows, striking the crucifix above the altar. He dropped into the rear pew, his eyes staring at the reflected gold light.

A few days had rattled his soul. He had lost his dearest friend, but found a beloved memory that would never die. He was penniless, but had gained the freedom to find a new life. Beaten senseless in Granada, he'd been rescued and befriended by Spain's greatest writer. And now, instead of exile, rebellious Basques and Asturians offered him a new, unexpected road.

He glared at the cross. The Church would regret the day they sent him here. Before he was done, all Vizcaya would stand with him. He would be more than a thorn in the Church's side. He would be a dagger.

And if he was wrong, there were always the Pyrenees—and Jacques Dupont.

He stepped into the rectory and eased beside the bed. "Padre?"

Segurra blinked his eyes and looked up at him.

"I have news."

"News?"

"We had a good Mass. I met them all."

"There were many?"

"Just like you said. It was a beautiful morning."

The priest smiled at him through glazed eyes. "I'm happy for you, Roberto. At least you have this moment."

Roberto reached down and grasped Segurra's shoulder. "How do you feel?"

"Tired. I've never been so tired."

"Maybe I should stay awhile."

"Stay?"

"It's going to take some time before you're strong enough to stand in front of that unruly mob. France can wait. I'll stay until you're back on your feet."

Segurra's eyes brightened. "Stay as long as you wish. You're welcome here, my son."

Roberto patted the priest's arm and walked to the window. He looked down at the pump handle and noticed a raven peering up at him with gleaming black eyes. When he reached for it, the black bird flapped its wings and darted away.

"Can I ask you a question, Roberto?"

"Yes."

"How did it feel standing on the altar?"

"I'm not sure."

"Would you do it again?"

"Again?"

Segurra clutched the crucifix. "It's intoxicating. The more you do it, the more you want it."

Roberto looked out at Guernica. "Speak for yourself, Padre. I prefer a quiet walk by the sea. Besides, I'm the last person to lead a flock of lost souls into the light."

"So skeptical, my young priest."

"I'm not a priest."

"Soon, Roberto—soon." Segurra gasped and clutched his throat.

Roberto ran to the bed and placed his hand on the priest's chest. "I'll get the doctor."

Segurra grimaced. "I had such a beautiful dream. A white horse darted through the clouds, its wings glistening like polished ivory. I saw its rider. His name...was...*Kalki*...."

"Padre!"

Segurra's glazed eyes stared at the ceiling.

Augustin lit a cigaret and looked out at the Bay of Biscay. Behind him, Gorka and Juan dragged the last crate out of the cave.

The setting sun had turned the clouds dull-orange. It would probably rain tomorrow. Best to leave now to allow plenty of time for the return trip from Oviedo. With a little luck, they'd be back before sunrise. A quick dip in the river, and they'd still have time to herd their livestock to market.

"That's it. Fifteen crates. They probably don't work." Gorka shuffled beside his brother while wiping his hands with a rag.

"Did you gas up the truck?"

"Loaded and ready to go."

"I hope the damn ammo stays dry." Augustin flicked his cigaret in the sand and headed up the beach, followed by his brother.

When he reached the truck, Augustin noticed Julio and Ana stuffing their backpacks with red sticks. He eased next to Julio and crouched down. "What's the word?"

"The midnight train is carrying twenty guardsmen. The pigs are trying to sneak in without being noticed. This should wake them up."

"Who are you taking?"

"Me."

Augustin stood up and glared at his brother. "You?"

Gorka shrugged. "I'm going with them."

"Are you nuts? You've got a wife and kid. What if something happens?"

Gorka nodded toward Julio and Ana. "What about them?"

"It's different. They have no children. Besides, they're crazier than us."

"Speak for yourself." Gorka patted his brother's arm and picked up one of the packs. Julio had stuffed it with enough dynamite to blow the train to kingdom come.

"Listen to me, dammit."

"Sorry, big brother. Time to join the fight." Gorka slung the pack over his shoulder and shuffled through the sand toward an old man standing beside a second, weatherbeaten truck. Julio and Ana were about to join him when Augustin stepped in their path.

"What?" Julio adjusted his pack.

"You know what. That's my brother crawling into that truck. If things get hot, don't let him go in—understood?"

Julio smiled and gripped his friend's shoulder. "Piece of cake. He'll be fine." He started to turn away.

"Wait—there's one more thing."

"Yeah?"

"What about the cleric?"

Julio shrugged. "From what I've seen, he's the perfect fit. Disillusioned. Lonely. Trying to be a man. You know the type."

Augustin looked at Ana. "What about you?"

She brushed back her hair. "I'm against it. He's too unstable. We're asking for trouble."

Augustin smiled. "Maybe you can keep him in line."

She frowned and looked out at the sea. "Let him go, Augustin."

Julio tugged at his pack. "Enough talk. If he tries to leave, Luis has orders to kill him and dump his body in the river."

Ana looked at her husband in shock.

"Surprised? Hell, he's not even a priest. Just another young stud you won't get a chance to play with."

"Bastard!" She tried to slap him, but he grabbed her wrist.

"Come on—we've got work to do. Good luck, Augustin. Tell Corrella my heart is with him and the others."

Augustin frowned and climbed into the first truck with Juan and Ixidro. He gunned the engine and plowed through the sand toward the forest road leading to Guernica. From there, they would pick up the main road to Bilboa—and Oviedo.

When they drove past the second truck, Augustin leaned out the window and shouted at his brother. "Hey, Gorka! Don't take one in the back or you'll blow up half of Spain!"

15 | Connecticut

Karen groped for the cigaret pack on the nightstand and felt it crinkle in her hand. She flicked the lighter and placed a fresh cigaret between her lips.

A relaxing sensation swept through her as the nicotine swirled into her lungs. She exhaled and leaned back against the pillow, her hand resting on her bare stomach. The only sounds were Jim's soft breathing and the clock chiming in the hall. She took another drag and stared at the darkness while softly exhaling the smoke.

Six o'clock? She crushed the cigaret in an ashtray and crawled out of bed. Her hand fumbled for the robe on the floor. She slipped it on and staggered across the bedroom to the partially-draped window.

Frozen rain was falling through the street lamps outside their apartment building. She frowned and looked down at the glazed sidewalk. When would this damn weather end? Things were depressing enough without having to contend with another New England ice storm. She yanked the drape shut and stormed into the living room.

She collapsed on the couch and let out a frustrated sigh while staring at the rain-spattered window. In another hour, they'd turn into his parent's driveway for the big introduction. His parents, dammit! Was he crazy?

They'd only known each other a few months and he was already taking her home to meet mom and dad. Come on, Miss Vostok. Even a slut like you knows what that means. First, the traditional family get-together. Then, a few weeks hanging around with mom, enriched with increasingly warm embraces from dear ol' dad. Finally, the big night when Jim pulls out the engagement ring and says the magic words.

It wasn't too late to cut the cord. Just slip on your clothes and leave him a note. Then, a few days of lying low to build up courage, and the proverbial cold shoulder to finish him off. That was the right thing to do. The noble thing. She leaned against the cushion and closed her eyes.

She'd met Jim at a New Year's Eve party thrown by Charlotte Manning, a wealthy acquaintance whom Karen appeared to worship, but actually despised. In the past three years, Karen Vostok had become quite proficient at the game of ladder-climbing. Fact is, you have to kiss someone's ass if you're going to follow them up the ladder. No problem. After twenty five years in hell, Miss Vostok had kissed about everything that moved, so another ass didn't matter much in depression-ravaged 1931.

Funny how the tenacious Miss Vostok suddenly became ill when Charlotte introduced her to Jim Halberton. Actually, it was more like a swoon than the flu—but it worked. Karen's charming knight in shining armor whisked her away from the madding crowd while offering to take her to a hospital, but of course she refused. When Jim asked where she lived, the cunning Miss Vostok explained that her roommate was throwing a party, suggesting they go to his place instead.

When they reached Jim's apartment, the dizziness conveniently returned and she collapsed on his soft blue couch. The closest Karen came to real illness that night was her shock when the gallant Mr. Halberton fed her some soup, tucked her away on the couch, and retired to his bedroom for a good night's sleep.

She couldn't believe it. The first guy who didn't try to jump her bones, and from the look of things, he was rich. *Enough analysis, Miss Vostock. We're in a goddamned depression.* She sprung off the couch and headed for the bedroom. No way was the charming Mr. Halberton getting away so easily.

Jim tried to speak when she climbed under the covers and pressed her naked body against him, but Karen buried her warm lips on his before he could get out the first word. The poor guy never had a chance. Karen's long black hair, blue eyes, and movie star face were too much for any man to resist. Throw in a five-foot-nine perfect figure, and the experience to use it, and it was only a matter of seconds before the virile young man succumbed. A few well-placed passionate licks and whispers, and they were off to the races.

The love storm continued for weeks while the

overwhelmed young man tried to screw his lovely Karen to death. But there were surprising rules to their passion play. When Jim began cutting classes to rendezvous with her for afternoon delights, Karen put her foot down and warned she would cut him off if he didn't graduate with honors. Strange code of ethics for the crafty lady from Scranton, PA, but education was the one thing Karen valued above all else—especially when it meant a ticket out of hell. In a few weeks, she'd graduate from a local arts college with a degree in journalism—her one true love. Interesting coincidence that Jim majored in journalism at Yale.

Everything was going well until last week when he mentioned something about meeting his parents. She should have squelched it then, but she was too caught up in her books to pay attention. Between waitressing, attending classes, and studying for finals, she could barely keep her eyes open. Damn, why didn't she pay more attention? Now it was too late.

"What are you doing in here?"

She looked up in surprise. "My God, are you trying to give me a heart attack?"

"Sorry." He leaned over the couch and kissed her gently on the forehead. "It's ten-after-six. We'd better get moving. First impression, you know."

She nodded and stood up. It wasn't the first impression that worried her. What if they were all out to dinner one night and some rich old fart strolled up to the table and gave her a big wet one for old times sake?

"Come on, honey. The shower's nice and hot."

She crushed the empty cigaret pack and flung it at the wall. So much for nobility.

The ride from New Haven to Cheshire was more like a bobsled run. Jim's Packard skidded from one side of the glazed country road to the other. By the time they pulled into the driveway of his parent's home, Karen's hand was numb from squeezing the door handle.

"Not too bad. Only ten minutes late."

She watched him walk past the hood of the car to her door.

He looked so innocent with his auburn hair glistening in the headlights and that nervous smile on his face. She looked down at her gloved hands. *God, what have I done.*

The Halberton's home looked like a Rockwell painting—a beautiful two-storied white colonial with green-shuttered windows and a gray, sloped roof. They were nearly to the front steps when the door swung open and a balding, middle-aged man beamed down at them with blue eyes.

"I was getting worried."

Jim smiled at his father and helped Karen up the salt-covered steps. When they reached the door, Mr. Halberton embraced his son like he hadn't seen him in ten years. *Careful, Miss Vostok. They're very close.*

"Karen?" An attractive, charcoal-haired lady in a blue cashmere sweater, yellow scarf, and gray skirt smiled at her from a spiral staircase across the white-marble foyer. The chic woman glided toward her and extended a hand.

Karen slipped off her glove and grasped Mrs. Halberton's hand. "Karen Vostok. I'm very pleased to meet you, Mrs. Halberton."

"Jim's bragged so much about you. I can see why."

"Thank you. That's very kind."

"Vostok—is that Polish?"

"My father was Russian."

"And your mother?"

"Lithuanian."

"They've passed away?"

Karen nodded.

"I'm so sorry. It must be difficult without a mom and dad."

"It has its moments."

Francine Halberton smiled and embraced her son. "You had me worried with all this snow."

"We're fine, Mother. And hungry too." Jim sniffed the air. "Smells like Gisele whipped up something for the gods."

"Wouldn't want to disappoint you. Well—let's break open some wine." Mrs. Halberton took her son's arm and nodded for Karen to follow them.

Karen felt a warm hand on her shoulder. "Pleasure to meet

you, Karen."

"Mr. Halberton, I've heard so much about you."

"If it's from Jim, I know it's good." He smiled and extended his elbow. "Hope you don't mind an old man's company."

She smiled and leaned against him. "Jim should have told me he has such a handsome father. Where did you get those blue eyes?"

"Good English stock with a touch of Saxon blood. But we can talk later. You must be starved. Hope you like lamb." He took her arm and led her into the candlelit dining room behind his babbling wife and son.

The meal was served by an elderly French maid named Gisele. Karen had dined in better places, but never with more elegance and warmth. A chilled *Chablis* accompanied blue-china bowls of chicken consommé, followed by a crisp endive salad, and hearty portions of roast lamb, potatoes, mint jelly, and baby peas. Add the warm apple cobbler with melted cheddar cheese, and it was obvious the Halbertons were putting their best foot forward.

Karen spoke very little during dinner, except for an occasional "yes," "no," or "really." Few words were spoken by anyone except Mrs. Halberton who completely dominated the conversation. At one point, Karen almost broke out laughing when her hostess appeared to speak while inhaling.

After dinner, they adjourned to the living room for more small talk and coffee. The conversation began with kudos for Jim's upcoming graduation, and best wishes for Karen's approaching finals at New Haven Fine Arts College. When Mrs. Halberton launched into a dissertation on her volunteer work at the local hospital, Karen noticed Mr. Halberton toying nervously with his pipe as if something were bothering him. She smiled politely and pretended to listen to Mrs. Halberton's boring monologue.

The grandfather clock in the foyer was chiming ten when Edmund Halberton finally stood up and smiled at Karen. "Care to join me for a nightcap?"

She looked up in surprise. "Delighted."

"Hey, what about me?" Jim started to get up.

"Stay here and talk with your mother. We'll only be a few minutes. I want to give Karen the grand tour." Mr. Halberton wrapped his arm around Karen and led her across the living room to a pair of closed double doors. He swung them open and gestured for her to go inside.

The study looked like a military museum with its paneled-oak walls plastered with war photographs, battle ribbons, plaques, maps, and newspaper clippings. Mr. Halberton closed the doors and walked to a small bar beside the fireplace. "Care for a brandy?"

"A small one, thank you." Karen walked along the wall squinting at the dirt-smeared faces staring at her from the sepia prints. She was fascinated by the photographs of doughboys in the trenches.

"So, you're majoring in journalism." Mr. Halberton smiled and handed her a snifter of brandy."

"Yes, I love it. Can I ask how you collected all these photographs. They're breathtaking."

Mr. Halberton shrugged. "I took them."

"You were a war photographer?"

"Combat photographer with the American Expeditionary Force that went over in 1917."

Karen's eyes lit up. "I'm stunned. Jim never told me."

Mr. Halberton smiled and sipped his brandy. "Like all young men, my son looks to the future. I'm afraid the Great War doesn't mean much these days. Actually, I've forgotten most of it myself. If it weren't for these photographs and clippings, it would probably be a faint memory."

"You were on the front lines?"

He gulped down his brandy and smiled. "Every battle from Argonne to Belleau Wood." He pointed to a blow-up above the mantle. "Hell, that's me talking to Blackjack Pershing."

Her jaw dropped. "This is incredible."

"Try this one." He walked to the desk and held up a gold-framed photo of two men in cowboy hats and khakis who appeared to be shaking hands.

"That's not TR?"

The Tenth Avatar

He looked at her in surprise. "Very good, Karen. Not many would catch that."

"Who's the young man?"

"Hell, that snot-nosed kid is me shaking hands with TR just before we climbed that damned hill."

Karen looked at him in disbelief. "You mean, San Juan Hill?"

He nodded. "Damn near got my head blown off that day. Best picture in the bunch, if you ask me."

"I had no idea, Mr. Halberton. These pictures are stunning."

"Well, from what Jim tells me, you're pretty stunning too. Please, sit down." He gestured toward the two leather chairs facing the fireplace. "Care for more brandy?"

"I'm fine, thank you. But what about Mrs. Halberton and your son?"

"Oh, they're fine. It's good for them to have some time alone. Jim doesn't stop by much since he met you." He poured a brandy and picked a black folder off the desk. "Please, I'd like to talk a few minutes."

She nodded and sat down.

"Jim tells me you're from Scranton, Pennsylvania. Good people in Scranton. Good, hardworking folk." He sat across from her and sipped his brandy. "Was your dad a miner?"

"No, he worked in the mills." She hesitated. "You have a lovely home, Mr. Halberton. I'm afraid mine was more humble."

"I understand. Nothing to be ashamed of. Hell, I started in a Brooklyn slum." He gulped down his brandy and leaned back in the leather chair. "So, what are you going to do after graduation?"

She sipped her brandy and put it down on the cocktail table. "I'm not sure. I have a friend who promised me an interview in Hartford, but I'm skeptical."

"I'd be too. This damned mess is getting worse. Before long, you'll see newspapers closing their doors along with the rest of the country." He frowned and reached for the bottle of brandy. "I'm afraid you'll need real pull to get that cub reporter's job."

She sighed. "People still have to eat. I'll waitress and do odd jobs until things get better. I've survived for twenty five years. Another year or two won't matter."

He leaned forward and fixed his blue eyes on her. "I wish it was that simple. This damn thing's gonna last for years."

"You think it's that bad?"

"It's worse than that. Years of screwing up don't get fixed overnight. The only thing that'll pull us out of this mess is another war. I'll be too damn old to cover it, but maybe my son can pick up the ball."

She broke into a smile. "Now I know why Jim keeps dreaming about an overseas assignment."

Mr. Halberton frowned. "In time, Jim will make a fine editor. Better others do the dirty work." He chugged the fresh brandy and set it down. "How would you like some help?"

"Help?"

"Since I retired to writing books, I've pretty much lost contact with my buddies in New York, but I think they'll lend an ear to an old war chum."

She felt her heart pounding. "If you're offering to help me, I'd be eternally grateful."

"Good, I'll start making calls tomorrow. Just don't mess up those final exams."

Karen couldn't believe her ears. She stood up and walked over to him. "I don't know what to say. You don't know what this means to me." She reached down to grasp his shoulder, but he brushed her arm away.

"You better hear the rest." He gestured for her to sit down.

"What's wrong?"

"Please—sit down."

She eased back to her chair.

He leaned forward and took a deep breath. "I want you to listen very closely. I'm not going to repeat this. Frankly—I find it distasteful."

"Distasteful?"

He stroked his thinning white hair. "As you've probably noticed, my son is very important to me."

She nodded and forced a smile.

"I've devoted my life to him. He's all I have besides my wife and memories of 'days gone by.' It would be a shame if anything ruined his future." He hesitated and cleared his throat.

Her puzzled look became a frown. "You mean—me?"

"Understand what I'm saying, Karen. I have nothing against you. In fact, I admire a person who crawls out of the mud to make something of themselves."

"Mud?"

He ignored her and went on. "It's just that Jim will be measured by his integrity. One day, he'll run a major newspaper. That means jealous enemies and public scrutiny." He looked down and sighed. "I don't want him carrying any baggage."

Her face flushed. "What are you saying?"

"I'm prepared to help your career, but there's a price. I don't care how you do it, but I want this thing ended between you and my son."

"Ended?"

"Yes."

"I should be going." She stood up to leave.

"Please—I'm almost finished."

She glared at him. "You expect me to drop the man I love because his parents don't approve?"

"That's exactly what I expect."

"How dare you."

"Oh—I dare, Miss Vostok. And if I were you, I'd consider the alternative." He picked up the black folder and handed it to her.

"What is this?"

"Open it."

She flipped open the cover and froze in shock.

"That picture was taken last year during a police raid in Hartford. I believe that's you stepping out of the paddy wagon."

"How did you get this?"

"By accident. Last month, I was having lunch with a friend who works at the *Hartford Courant*. He asked about Jim and I mentioned your name. I guess it triggered something in his memory because he checked the archives and sent me that picture. It's from a headline in last year's *Courant*. I didn't know for sure until tonight. You're wearing less makeup, but that is you, isn't it, Miss Vostok?"

She collapsed in the chair and gazed at the photograph.

"There's a copy of the news story clipped to it, if you'd like to read it. I believe it includes your name."

She shook her head.

"Drink?"

"I'd better be going."

He nodded and looked her in the eye. "Then—we have an agreement?"

"I don't know."

"For God's sake, Karen. Do you think I went looking for this? If it fell into my hands that easily, imagine what a professional investigator could scrape up after you're married. Do you want to put Jim through that? And your children?"

She stood up and placed the folder on the table. "Good night, Mr. Halberton. It's been enlightening."

He stood up and gestured to the folder. "Please don't force me to use this. I will, you know."

"Oh—I believe you."

"Nothing will be said until I hear from you. Goodnight, Karen." He walked her to the study doors and pushed them open.

When they rejoined Jim and his mother, Karen managed to deflect Jim's barrage of questions by admonishing him for not telling her about his dad's exciting past. After a few minutes of polite conversation and forced smiles, Karen apologized for feeling a little under the weather. Taking the hint, Mr. Halberton stood up and thanked her for coming while his wife gave her the customary mother-in-law embrace. Karen's intuition told her Jim's mother didn't know the dark secret inside that folder in the study.

The rain had stopped when they stepped into the frigid night air. Mr. Halberton extended a polite hand and smiled. "I'm glad we had this chance to talk. Hope to see you soon."

"Likewise." She stepped back and watched Jim embrace his father.

The ride back to Jim's apartment was pure hell. He barraged her with questions about the closed door, *tête-á-tête* with his dad. When she tried to evade his questions, he pressed even harder. On the verge of blowing up, she finally warned him to shut up because she felt sick to her stomach.

When they climbed into bed, she turned away and pretended to be sick, but it didn't work.

"What's wrong?"

"I feel awful."

"Don't play games. I know something happened in there."

"What?"

"Please...."

She sighed and pressed against him. "Let's talk tomorrow."

"No—we'll talk now."

She rolled on her back and looked up at him. "Your parents are wonderful. That's the problem."

"Problem?"

"I didn't think things would go this far. I'm not ready for this. Dating was fine, but we're on a one-way train to the wedding chapel."

He shrugged. "So, we'll take it easy for awhile. It's not a problem."

"I'm afraid it is. I don't want to hurt you. And I don't want to hurt them."

"How can anyone get hurt? Hell, I'm in love with you."

She brushed away a tear. "I know. That's why this is so hard."

"Hard?"

"We've only been together a few months. You don't even know me."

He took her in his arms. "I know enough. You're everything I want."

She pushed him away. "You're talking like a child. Life's not that simple."

"So, we'll wait. It's no big deal."

She took a deep breath and looked into his green eyes. "It is a big deal. I need to get away. To think things through. I'm leaving tomorrow."

"You're what?"

"It's for the best. You'll see. In a few weeks, I'll be a fading memory."

He looked at her in shock. "I don't believe this. What did he say to you? What did he do to you?"

"Nothing, dammit. This is my decision."

"But why?"

She swallowed hard. "I don't love you."

He clutched her arm. "You're lying. It's him, isn't it? Quit lying to me, dammit!"

"I didn't know until tonight. When I saw you with your mom and dad, I knew it wouldn't work."

"Damn him. He caused this. What did he say? Tell me the truth, goddammit!"

"He didn't say anything. Your dad's a wonderful man. You should spend every day with him. It's great to have a caring father." She looked away and sobbed.

"You're my life, Karen. Don't do this to me." He took her in his arms and kissed her passionately. She didn't resist. Maybe a good fuck would get him through the night.

They made love until he couldn't go on. He fell asleep in her arms while she stroked his hair and relived bitter memories. When he awoke the next morning, she was gone. No note. No flower. Nothing.

Jim spent the next few weeks struggling through finals and graduation while searching for her, but she'd vanished into thin air. Had he looked harder, he would have found her at the YWCA in New York City, shedding a few tears while preparing for her new job at the *New York Times*. It would take a little longer to finish school this way, but transferring her credits into Columbia was worth the effort—especially with Edmund Halberton pulling the strings. As for Jim—he didn't know how lucky he was.

16 | Exiled

The air smelled from pine and moist earth. There was no daylight, only dark-green shadows broken by sunbeams penetrating the dense canopy of leaves.

Roberto pulled out his canteen and gulped some water. He stuffed the canteen in his belt and looked down at the gray river splashing against its banks. Droplets of water sprayed against his face. He closed his eyes and felt its power—and for a moment—he was home.

It had taken longer to hike through the forest than he expected. With the sun dropping to the west, he would only have a short time on the beach before turning back to the mission—but it was worth it. He hadn't faced the sea since leaving Valencia. Time to see an old friend again.

It was September 11, 1931. Four months had passed since he buried Segurra on the hillside below the mission. After pleading with the Church for a decent burial in Segurra's native Toledo, his letters and telegrams had been answered with a communiqué instructing him to remain at the mission until a suitable replacement could be found. There was no mention of Segurra. No expression of sadness. It was as if the priest never existed.

He stared at the swirling water and recalled the morning he laid his friend to rest. With a cold rain falling on the hillside, Augustin and the others gathered around the wood coffin to pay tribute to the simple, caring priest who only wanted to make the world better.

Following the eulogy, they lowered Segurra's coffin into a grave and shovelled fresh earth over it while Roberto gave a final blessing. When it was done, Gorka and Ixidro helped him plant a wooden cross etched with nine simple words....

Padre Ferdinand Segurra,
Gone to find a better place....

Roberto flinched as a raven brushed past his face and

landed on a nearby branch. He stared at the shiny black creature picking its feathers with its sharp beak. Could this be the same bird that had given him the evil eye when he reached for it on the pump handle four months ago? He leaned toward it and smiled. "Hello, friend. Surprised to see me? Well, that makes two of us."

The bird flapped its wings and darted away. It looked so free as it rose through the treetops into the afternoon sky. Oh, to be able to spread your wings and fly.

For four long months, he'd gazed eastward at the rugged Pyrenees while asking himself why he was still here. No need to climb the mountains. Just stuff your meager belongings into your traveling bag and follow the shoreline to Biarritz. Who knows, with a little persuasion some fisherman might give you a ride in his boat.

When Gorka and the others convinced him to stay, he thought it would be a new beginning. Instead, he was exiled in a mission on a rocky hillside overlooking a town that denied his existence. Except for his weekly trek to the market with Luis, and an occasional wave from a passing shepherd, his only contact with the Basques came during Sunday Mass.

The congregation had burgeoned to seventy, most of whom stood outside the windows. Last week, he tried moving the ceremony to the hillside, but the damn birds began eating the holy bread amidst a chorus of hysterical laughter.

Following Mass, the congregation of shepherds and laborers dispersed quickly, returning to their homes in the town and countryside. Some of them disappeared into the forest beside the river. When he asked to join them, the message was the always the same. "Maybe next week when we're not so busy." They were hiding something, and it was time to find out what it was.

The breeze was picking up. He heard waves rushing against a shore. Only a few more yards. He ran across the carpet of pine needles toward the bright light coming through the trees.

There! Between the trees! The Bay of Biscay stretched across the horizon like a sparkling turquoise mirror, its gentle waves washing over the sand. He kicked off his shoes and ran down the beach with them dangling in his hands. Through the spray, he could see fishing boats plodding eastward toward their anchorages in Getaria and San Sebastian—and beyond that, Biarritz. Oh, to have a wad of *pesetas* and *francs* in his pocket. The casinos along the coast were supposed to be breathtaking. And the women—

He caught himself. What kind of priest thinks such evil thoughts? He broke out laughing and spread his arms to the sea. "Hell, I'm no priest. I'm an imposter!"

He stripped off his shirt and plunged into the warm surf. Unfortunately, his inactivity had turned his arms and legs to rubber. When he tried to swim out against the current, he ended up on the shore gasping for breath.

Damn. Only his thirty-first birthday and he was a physical wreck. No excuse for that. From now on, he'd swim every day.

"Roberto?"

Startled, he turned and saw Ana staring down at him from a slope above the beach.

"You're not supposed to be here."

"What?"

She walked down the slope toward him. "It's not safe to come here alone. We told you that."

He smiled and shrugged his shoulders. "I love the sea. It's part of me."

She hesitated and looked out at the bay. "Yes, it's very beautiful. And now that you've seen it, please go back. The others are coming up the beach behind me. If they see you—"

He squinted into the haze and spotted a group of men walking toward them. They appeared to be carrying long boxes or crates of some kind.

She reached up and stroked his wet beard. "Please, Roberto. Do this for me. And shave off that stubble. Your face is too handsome to be buried under a black beard."

He frowned and picked up his canteen. "It's time to quit playing games, Ana. I didn't come here to be stuck on a hill. Tell that to your husband and friends." He turned and walked up the beach toward the forest.

Julio dropped his crate and ran along the beach toward her.

"Who the hell was that?"

She looked down and said nothing.

"Damn!"

"What's wrong?" Augustin shuffled toward them.

"Roberto paid us a visit."

"What?"

Julio brushed back his hair. "I don't like it. Maybe he is a spy."

Augustin glared at the tracks leading into the forest. "Then, he's a dead one."

"The hell he is!" A one-armed man in a wool vest charged toward them.

"Stay out of this, Sebastian. Just because Picasso says he's okay doesn't mean he is."

Sebastian spit out his cigaret and stepped into Augustin's face. "Are you trying to start something?"

Augustin looked down at the old man scowling at him. He broke into a smile and stuffed a fresh cigaret into Sebastian's mouth. "You shouldn't waste a good cigaret, *compañero*. Tobacco's hard to come by these days." He stepped back and glanced at the fading sun. "Let's get these crates in the cave. We'll talk about our friend tonight." He turned and walked away.

Julio started after him, but Ana grabbed his arm. "What are you going to do to him?"

"You heard Augustin. We'll figure it out tonight." He tried to turn away, but she wouldn't let go.

"It's not that simple. He may not be a priest, but he is a man of God, and a decent one too."

"So?"

She glared at him and forced out the words. "If anything happens to him, we're finished."

Julio yanked his arm free. "Hell, we're already finished." He walked away and left her staring at him with tears in her eyes.

He watched them lug the crates up the slope. They pulled away driftwood and brush, exposing a cave entrance. Ixidro,

Julio, and Gorka dragged the crates inside. When they were done, they covered the entrance and followed the others into the forest.

Augustin was about to join them when he hesitated and lit a cigaret. For a moment, he just stood there looking out at the sea. He shook his head and flicked the butt in the sand, and he was gone.

Roberto scrambled up the slope and yanked away the driftwood. He crouched in the dim light and followed the dark tunnel a few feet before giving up. Without a flashlight or torch, it was impossible to go on.

He remembered reading that eighteenth century pirates used the caves along the Bay of Biscay to store their treasures. It didn't take a genius to guess the treasure in this one. He'd seen enough crated weapons to know rifles were in those boxes.

But how many? And for what purpose? He frowned and squinted at the darkness. If he only had a match.

He was crawling out of the cave when he noticed a crumpled piece of paper sticking out of the sand. He snatched it up and detected an odor of gun oil. He peeled open the paper and gazed at the words. They were printed in Russian. He stuffed the paper in his pocket and bolted out of the cave.

San Juan's bell was chiming eight p.m. when Augustin and his followers filed into the town hall and took seats around the small stage in the center. By the time their lookouts closed the doors, a hundred Basques and Asturians had jammed into the archaic meeting hall, many of them standing along the walls.

Arronategui and the other priests had warned against congregating like this. The town had even received a stern communiqué from José Antonio Aguirre, President of the Basque Republic, directing that no provocative actions be taken against the Civil Guardsmen in neighboring Asturias....

Citizens!
Every possible effort must be put forth to maintain the tenuous democratic rights granted by the Second Republic to

Gary Naiman

their Basque brothers in Vizcaya....
  José Antonio Aguirre

But the tide was turning against passive tolerance. While Aguirre deluded himself that all was well, Civil Guardsmen continued venting their anger on the rebellious miners in neighboring Asturias. Each day, more Basques threw down their olive branches and picked up rifles as rumors spread of guardsmen crossing their border in pursuit of communist-inspired terrorists. Ironic the rifles were Soviet. It was only a matter of time.

Sebastian leaned close to the black radio and slowly turned its dial while the hall grew silent. He glanced at the two men guarding the door and turned up the volume, filling the hall with whining static. "Here it comes." He leaned back in the chair and listened to a crackling voice break through the static.

Augustin patted his brother's shoulder. "Sounds like you're a celebrity. You blew that damn car to bits."

Gorka shrugged. "Easy as shearing a sheep. The fools didn't leave someone behind to watch their car when they started down the street after Ana. She's the one who deserves the credit. Hell, you should have seen their faces when it blew into the sky. First no car. Then no Ana. They were really shook. That's one fine looking woman, I tell you."

Augustin put a finger to his lips and glanced at Ixidro who was writing down instructions from the coded broadcast. "You getting all this?"

Ixidro nodded and kept writing. "Big convoy coming through Vitoria on Wednesday. Maybe fifty guardsmen in covered livestock trucks. Shit, I'd like to pick them off with a thirty calibre from one of the rooftops. It'd be a duck shoot."

"Can't do that." Julio rested a hand on Ixidro's shoulder. "That's what they want. Then, they can pour the whole goddamn army in here. No—we'll bury some sticks in the road outside the town and blow them to hell." He smiled at Gorka. "How about it, señor? Ready for some real fireworks?"

Gorka nodded while his brother glared at Julio.

"That's it." Sebastian flicked off the shortwave radio and

nodded for Juan and Pedro to carry it back to its hiding place in the cellar. He pushed out of his chair and scanned the crowd until he spotted Augustin. "Well?"

Augustin looked up at the old man staring down at him from the stage. He frowned and stepped on the stage while Sebastian took his seat with the others. The room fell silent.

Augustin took a deep breath and looked out at the crowd. "I'm sorry about this. I should have known our guest wouldn't stay put long. He's too ambitious for his own good. It's my fault. I should have sent him away weeks ago."

"So, what do we do?" Julio edged beside the stage and looked up at his friend.

Augustin tried to force out the words. "This isn't easy. Killing a priest is more than a sin. It's a curse."

"Hell, he's no priest. He's a fake." Julio jumped on the stage while his wife stared at him in shock. "I'll do it myself, if it bothers you. He won't feel anything. Just a quick pop and it'll be over."

"In the face or back of the head?"

The room filled with stunned whispers as everyone turned toward the figure standing at the opened door.

Julio squinted at the door. "How the hell did you get in here?"

Roberto shrugged his shoulders and closed the door. "I followed everyone else. I guess your men had a little too much wine at dinner." He brushed past the two stunned guards and walked down the aisle toward the stage.

"You have no right to be here."

Roberto ignored him and placed the crumpled paper on the stage. "I think this belongs to you. It must have dropped out of one of the crates."

Julio bent down and picked up the paper.

"I believe it says you received fifty rifles in this shipment. I took a year of Russian at the university. Still remember enough for a weak translation. Not very smart to leave that lying in the sand."

Julio crushed the paper in his hand. "Why did you come here?"

"To stop you from committing suicide. I think that's my job as your priest." Roberto climbed on the stage. "But it seems you plan to kill me, señor. So, answer my question. Will the bullet come from behind or will I get to see you place the pistol against my forehead?"

Julio glared at him.

"I only ask one favor. If you're going to kill me, do it now. In front of your people." He turned toward the stunned congregation. "And after I'm dead, ask yourselves what makes you any better than those soldiers butchering your friends in Oviedo."

"Damn you! I've had enough of your pious bullshit!" Julio charged at Roberto and took a wild swing at his head, but as others had already learned, the innocent looking man in black had also studied boxing at the University of Madrid.

The first punch broke Julio's nose. The second gushed the air out of him. The final left-right combination dropped him like a rock as the screaming crowd rushed the stage.

Augustin looked down at his unconscious friend and sneered at Roberto. "Okay, imposter. Try me." He started toward Roberto and froze as a gunshot echoed off the walls. "What the hell?" He looked down and saw Sebastian pointing a smoking pistol at the ceiling. "What the hell's wrong with you?"

Sebastian lowered the pistol. "The enemy's out there, remember?"

Augustin clenched his fists. "I think he's standing right here."

"That's not true!" Roberto looked down at the angry crowd. "Wait, dammit! I have a right to be heard! You owe me that much!"

"Shut up, imposter! Take him!" A burly fisherman charged the stage, but hesitated when Augustin waved him back.

Augustin helped Julio to his feet. "Okay, imposter. Have your say. But be quick about it." He stepped off the stage, dragging his semiconscious friend with him.

Roberto looked out at the hostile crowd. "I came here to help you. If you're looking for spies, don't waste your time on me." He hesitated and scanned their angry faces. "I went to the sea to keep from going crazy in that mission—not to spy on you. When you asked me to stay here as your priest, I didn't expect to be stuffed on a hillside. One exile is enough, thank you."

"Kill him, dammit!"

"Shut up and sit down!" Augustin glared at the stunned heckler.

"If I could turn back the clock, I would have stayed in Valencia—but it's too late. I've lost everything. If I hadn't made enemies in the Church, I would have received my priesthood and lived comfortably in Granada or Toledo—or even Valencia. But the Church is too vengeful to allow one of its own to step out of line. That's why they condemned me here."

"Get to the point." Gorka stood up and folded his arms.

"I was assigned here to help Segurra. It was the Church's way of punishing me for speaking out."

"You challenged the Church?" Francesca stood up and looked at him with puzzled eyes.

"More than once. If you don't believe me, ask your leaders. They seem to know everything about me. Isn't that right, Augustin?" He looked down at Augustin and waited for a response, but the blond-haired Basque didn't bat an eyelash.

"I was ready to cross into France when you stopped me. I can't explain why, but I decided to stay. Maybe it was because of what happened in Valencia. Hell, maybe I am insane. I've committed every possible sin. Even false Ordainment. I'll probably go to hell for it."

He paused and looked down at his trembling hands. "I've had some problems that made me leave home. I've been running ever since. Well—I'm sick of running. This time, I decided to stand and fight. And I'm glad I did. If I can stop you from killing yourselves, maybe my life will be worth something."

"It's not worth much now!" The fisherman stood up and pointed a menacing finger at Roberto.

"Enough!" Augustin jumped on the stage and glared at

Roberto. "You think we want this? Are you too stupid to see what's happening? They're going to invade and you expect us to greet them with flowers? Hell no. We'll fight to the last man, woman, and child if we have to. But we'll stay free!"

The room exploded with cheers, but Roberto stood his ground. "You think this is a game? You're playing with fire. Listen to your president. Put down your weapons before it's too late."

Ixidro stood up and shook his fist at Roberto. "Idiot. You think we're alone? We have the Russians at our side."

"Russians? You think they care what happens to you? They just want a piece of Spain to continue their revolution."

Augustin glared at Roberto. "Enough talk. Let me ask you, imposter. What should we do with someone we can't trust?"

Roberto shook his head. "That's the wrong question. What should you do with someone you can trust? If I was a spy, do you think I'd be standing here now? Hell, I'd be in Oviedo spilling my guts to the Civil Guard."

Gorka jumped on the stage. "You said it yourself, Roberto. You're here because you're crazy. Can we trust a crazy man?"

"Put it to a vote, dammit!" Sebastian stepped forward and threw his pistol on the stage. "Or isn't this a democracy any more?"

Augustin looked down at the old man. "Fair enough, *compañero*. Hey, Luis!"

"Yeah?" The grizzled guard stepped away from the wall.

"Take this madman for a walk until we're done. And watch his hands. He fights pretty good for a martyr."

Luis looked up at Roberto with his grizzled face. "Come on, you're holding up the meeting."

Roberto sighed and looked at Augustin. "So, it's in the back of the head after all."

"Get out of here."

Roberto felt something tap his ankle. He looked down and saw Luis gesturing toward the door with his rifle. He scanned the crowd a final time, then stepped off the stage and walked down the aisle, followed by his executioner.

A full moon was shining on Guernica when they exited the

town hall. They turned left and walked past the *Arrien Restaurant* and jai alai fronton. At the *Bank of Vizcaya*, they veered right toward the *Astra-Unceta* munitions factory, its black smokestack silhouetted against the moonlit sky.

They were passing an archaic building called *Casa del Juntas* when Roberto felt Luis nudge him with the rifle barrel.

"Hold it, I want to show you something."

A cold chill shot through him. The time had come.

"Open that gate." Luis pointed to an iron gate next to the building. He waited for Roberto to lift the latch, and gestured for him to go inside.

They walked down a narrow path along the side of the building and entered a small, moonlit courtyard.

Luis gestured toward a tree stump surrounded by stone benches. "Well, what do you think?"

"Think?"

"About our tree?"

Roberto stepped closer. "You mean, that stump?"

Luis frowned. "It was more than a stump before Napoleon's pigs cut it down. You should see the painting inside the Carmelite Convent. Hell, it's even on our flag. A beautiful oak tree, six hundred years old." He pointed to the stump. "Ferdinand and Isabella knelt right there when they pledged our independence. This tree is magic, I tell you. Who knows, it might even save your life tonight." He laughed and sat on one of the benches.

Roberto walked to the stump and touched it. "It looks like fresh shoots are coming through the bark."

"What?" Luis stood up and walked next to him. He leaned his rifle against the stump and ran his fingers along the green sprouts breaking through the decayed wood.

"What's wrong?" Roberto edged toward the rifle.

"It can't be. The tree's been dead a hundred years. I was here yesterday. There was nothing." He backed away and stared at the tree with concerned eyes.

Roberto snatched the rifle and pointed it at him. "I think you forgot this."

Luis waved his arm in disgust. "Don't waste your time. The

damn thing doesn't shoot."

"What?" Roberto cocked the bolt and saw it was empty. "But, I thought—"

"I was going to kill you? Hell, you are crazy. No one's going to kill you. Augustin's just trying to figure out what to do with you. We did the same thing with Segurra when he came here. Even if you were a spy, we wouldn't kill you. We're not mad like the Asturian. We'd just send you away. We don't kill priests, even if they're fakes. We'd burn in hell for that."

Roberto lowered the rifle and collapsed on the bench. "Then, why are they voting?"

"I told you. To decide what to do with you. Say, that was a pretty good speech back there. I bet they ask you to stay."

"I don't believe this is happening."

Luis walked to the bench and sat beside him. "Yeah, it's pretty strange."

"What?"

"The way that stump is growing. It's a bad omen." Luis shook his head and stared at the moonlit stump.

17 | On Aconcagua

Bonaventure lunged upward and drove his axe into the ice. He gasped for breath and clung to the sleet-covered handle while bracing against the blasts of frigid wind ripping at the sixty degree slope.

Akaal had begged him to return to camp three with the others, but he was too hardheaded to listen. In less than two hours, the prevailing winds had shifted from east to west, sucking the Pacific's moisture-laden air into the Andes. Perfect conditions for a blizzard at twenty-three thousand.

Señor Calabra's stinging words echoed in his ears. In a crisis, Bonaventure's first responsibility was his team's safety. Instead, he'd abandoned Calabra and his two Argentine brothers at twenty thousand feet for an insane rush to the top.

He squinted at the blowing snow and recalled opening Calabra's letter four months ago. A simple offer to lead a small expedition to the top of Aconcagua, tallest peak in the western hemisphere, for the tidy sum of five hundred English pounds. The perfect challenge for the mountaineer who had conquered Ecuador's Chimborazo, Peru's Hauscaran, France's Mont Blanc, Africa's Kilimanjaro, Alaska's McKinley, Switzerland's Matterhorn, Finsteraarhorn, and Eiger—and a dozen other peaks throughout the world.

And he'd climbed them all with flare and care. In fourteen years, Julian Bonaventure had attacked the great summits with a boldness and savagery unheard of in his profession, yet he'd never lost a climber to the mountains.

When the Royal Society rejected his petition for membership, he spit in their faces for calling him reckless and undisciplined. Hypocrites! Liars! Unless you were born a blueblood, no act of courage or stamina would permit entrance to their hallowed hall.

The Royal Society's rejection was more than a crushing disappointment for the man who had risen from poverty to become the very best. It was an act of war. Since that painful day five years ago, Julian Bonaventure had conducted a personal vendetta against the Society, disgracing them at every opportunity.

He always seemed a step ahead of them. When the Society's exhausted climbers staggered onto a targeted summit, their spirits were shattered by Bonaventure's blue and orange pennant flapping in the wind. And there was always that same cutting note clipped to the pennant's wire staff....

Sorry old chaps!
Maybe next time ....
Bonaventure

When one of their climbers protested Bonaventure's reckless infringements in *The London Times*, the enraged mountaineer gave him a taste of his famed savagery, decking him in front of the Royal Hall while his stunned cronies looked on.

When the bobbies hauled him away, the inebriated mountaineer shouted at the jeering Society members, calling them spineless worms. It cost him a night in jail, but that was nothing for the man who had tasted far worse.

His thoughts were shattered by a fierce gust of wind. He pressed against the blizzard-swept wall while recalling his final angry exchange with Calabra....

"*You gave it your best shot, old man. Good show.*"
"*Where do you think you're going, Señor Bonaventure?*"
"*To the top. Wish me luck.*"
"*Are you crazy? This is my expedition. I'm the sponsor, not you. If you leave us now, we'll die up here. What kind of mountaineer abandons his team for personal gain?*"
"*Calm down, old man. You're in good hands with Akaal. Blast, he's climbed mountains that make this one look like a rock pile. He's a Gurkha, señor. Heart of a lion.*"

Bonaventure recalled winking at Akaal, but only receiving a scowl in return.

Señor Calabra was a good and decent man, but he also was stupid. In time, the wealthy Argentine would realize he and his two friends had reached their limit. There was no reason to be ashamed. They'd given their best effort before pulling in their ropes. But to curse a fellow climber for trying to reach the top—well, that was crossing the line. He gritted his teeth and recalled their parting words....

"Damn you! If I was younger, I'd punch you in the nose."
"Well—you're not, so get a hold of yourself."
"Judas!"
"Listen to me, man. You're part of a mountaineering team. There's no ego. Only good wishes for the ones who go on."
"You expect my good wishes?"
"If you were going on, I'd give you mine."
"Then here they are. I hope you rot up there, Señor Bonaventure. Do you hear me? I hope you die up there!"

Bonaventure freed the axe and swung it at the ice above his head. He pulled himself up and pressed against the slope.

An unsettling thought struck him. Maybe Calabra was right. Instead of retreating when he saw the snow clouds building to the west, he'd charged up the treacherous Horcones Glacier and scaled the two thousand foot ice wall leading to the north ridge and summit—all to approximate the harsh conditions of the Himalaya.

Following the climb, he'd cross the Pacific and Indian Oceans to Calcutta, then proceed by train to New Delhi where he'd rendezvous with the Morel expedition for his first crack at the majestic Himalaya—and another five hundred pounds. Yes—maybe it was personal gain. Well—so be it.

He clenched the axe handle and recalled Calabra's final tirade when Akaal led the incensed Argentines down the slope to camp three....

"The money was for a successful climb, señor. Abandoning your team means failure. Expect no money. You're climbing the mountain for nothing!"

Bonaventure slid up his leather snow goggles and rubbed his face. Without the five hundred pounds, his Swiss chalet would be repossessed by the banks within a week—and his promise to Hans Furgler would be broken.

A bolt of lightning flashed through the whiteout, followed by a deafening clap of thunder. He tightened his grip and heard an ominous roar. With no sheltering rocks, he could only press against the ice and hope for the best.

The roar became deafening. He glanced left and saw tons of dislodged snow plummet into the whiteout. A huge chunk of ice ricocheted off the wall within inches of his face.

He spit out a mouthful of snow and heard a dull, cracking sound. The ice shuddered against him. He could see fractures spreading in all directions. The wall was giving way!

Enough of this crap. What kind of mountaineer are you? Forget the bloody wind. Quit cowering against this goddamn wall and climb!

He yanked down his snow goggles and squinted at the whiteout.

There! He could barely see it flashing through the haze. The summit! A white fortress rising above the storm.

A blast of wind slammed into him, nearly blowing him off the wall. The mountain was fighting back like a violated woman. He freed the axe and raised it over his shoulder. "Mine, dammit! You're mine!" He sprung upward and plunged the axe into the ice.

Twenty feet to the ridge crest. He tried to lift his arm, but it felt like rubber. Cramping pain surged through his back and legs. *Screw it! Keep going! Fifteen feet! Ten!*

He scrambled onto the snow-covered crest and felt the ice vibrate under him. *Move! Before the whole bloody crest gives way.*

He tried to stand, but his legs and arms wouldn't respond. He tried again and collapsed on his side. The ice in front of his face was cracking.

What a way to bow out. All because he was too proud to listen to his friend. He was going to die up here while those bloody hypocrites in London broke out the champagne. No, dammit! He wouldn't give them that.

He jammed the axe's shaft into the ice and pulled himself up. *Higher! Above the storm!* He kicked his boots into the crest and leaned into the howling wind.

"Bonaventure!"

He slumped against the axe. Had his mind snapped?

"Bonaventure! Can you hear me!"

He tried to yell, but the wind swept his breath away. He reached into his pack and yanked out the flare gun. "Here! I'm here!"

He cocked the trigger and aimed the pistol at the blizzard. The gun lurched as a green flare exploded in the whiteout, showering him with sparks.

Through the blowing snow, he saw a gloved hand fumble for a grip on the ice. He staggered toward the specter and dropped on his knees. He seized his friend's wrist and dragged him over the crest. "What the hell are you doing here?"

Akaal pulled back his black fur hood and lifted his snow goggles. "Can't let you have all the glory."

Bonaventure slid up his goggles. "What about Calabra?"

"They're safe at camp three, but mad as hell."

"Three? Impossible, you couldn't cover that ground in four hours."

Akaal shrugged.

"Dammit, man. Those idiots are too stupid to be left alone. They'll panic and try to go down. That's certain death."

Akaal stood up and anchored himself against the wind. "They won't be alone. We'll be with them. I told them you were coming down with me."

Bonaventure grunted and stood up. "In your bloody dreams. I'm only two hours from the top."

"Top? Are you insane? You can't make it."

"I'll dig a snow cave and sit it out until the storm blows through. Piece of cake. Now get down there and stay with those fools."

Akaal glared at his friend. "You'll freeze to death up here. In another hour, the escape route will be blocked."

"So be it. Give me your axe."

"What?"

"Give me your bloody axe!" Bonaventure snatched Akaal's axe out of his belt and started up the crest.

"Wait—you'll never make it!"

Bonaventure ignored him and headed up the slope.

"Listen to me, dammit! Señor Calabra promised to give us

the money if you returned with me."

Bonaventure stopped and looked down at his friend. "Tell that fat pig to wire-transfer the money to Switzerland or you'll leave him and his two stupid friends on the mountain."

"What?"

"You heard me. Get it in writing. See you soon, old chum." Bonaventure clutched the two axes and glared the summit. Only a thousand feet to go....

18 | Reinosa

"Easy, Esmeralda. Nothing to be afraid of." Augustin eyed the trembling animal and edged closer.

"She's going to bolt." Roberto stared at the sheep's gleaming black eyes.

"Calm down. She's not looking at you. I'm the one she's worried about." Augustin rested a hand on the sheep's trembling back. "Steady, old girl. Just want some of that thick fleece for winter. Only take a minute."

Esmeralda tried to run, but Augustin was too quick. He lunged forward and snatched her off the ground like a sack of wheat. Before the bleating sheep could react, he flung her on her side and twirled a rope around her back legs while holding her down with his other hand.

"See—nothing to it." He picked up the shears and began snipping off the thick, yellow-white fleece.

"Do they ever get used to it?"

"Hell—how would you like it if Gorka cut off your hair while I held you down?"

Roberto nodded and sat on a rock while his friend clipped the petrified animal. He leaned back on his hands and took a breath of warm, summer air. A breeze had picked up, filling the meadow with tufts of floating pollen.

Almost a year had passed since they came to him in the dark courtyard of the Sacred Oak to announce he was free to stay or move on—as he wished. When he gawked at them in shock, Gorka and his wife, Alazne, broke out laughing and invited him to dinner at their home in the neighboring hamlet of Marquina. From imminent death to a dinner invitation. Interesting way to celebrate your thirty-first birthday.

"That's it, my dear." Augustin untied the ewe's legs and watched her spring past Roberto into the meadow.

"She looks naked without her fleece."

Augustin pushed back his matted blond hair. "She'll be fine. Esmeralda grows fleece faster than any other sheep. She's the only one I can clip this late in the summer. With winter so close, the others would freeze to death without their coats, but Ezzie's special."

"Special?"

"It's the wine."

"Wine?"

"I give her a shot of *txakolina* every night. Makes her fleece grow like weeds."

Roberto leaned forward. "You're serious?"

"Hell, yeah. It won't work on the other sheep cause they get drunk. But old Ezzie can hold her liquor."

Roberto bit his lip.

"Well, are you ready?" Augustin extended the shears and nodded toward one of the sheep.

"Me?"

"Must learn shearing if you're gonna be one of us. Come on, I'll help you hold her down."

"But, you said they'd freeze to death?"

"Just a few snips. For practice. Come on." Augustin stood up and walked across the meadow toward the grazing sheep.

Roberto frowned and pushed himself off the rock. Why couldn't these people ever relax. They definitely were a breed unto themselves. No true Spaniard would drive himself like this on such a beautiful day. He picked up the shears and followed his open-shirted friend across the meadow.

They'd managed to tackle one of the scurrying animals and were about to apply the shears when Augustin stopped and looked toward the town.

"What is it?"

Augustin focused his blue eyes on the bridge. "Something's up."

Roberto glanced over his shoulder while trying to hold down the straining sheep. Sebastian was shouting at them from the bridge. Roberto couldn't understand what he was saying, but the fiercely waving arm meant something was wrong.

"Come on." Augustin let go of the sheep and scrambled to his feet, leaving Roberto to wrestle the panicked animal.

"Wait—what should I do?"

"Let her go and come on!" Augustin ran down the road

toward Sebastian.

Roberto released the sheep's legs and learned the most important lesson in shearing. Always turn away. The bleating animal kicked him in the groin and bolted across the meadow. The walk to town would be a slow, painful one.

When Roberto stumbled into the jammed town hall, he was startled to see Arronategui seated in the front row with two other clerics. There were no empty seats, so Roberto limped along the wall and stood next to Gorka and Alazne.

"What happened?" Gorka nodded at Roberto's limp.

"A sheep kicked me."

Gorka smiled and glanced at the hoof print on Roberto's pants. "Learning to shear, eh? Bet you won't make that mistake again."

Roberto grimaced and looked up at the stage where Sebastian was fumbling with the radio. "What's going on?"

"Trouble." Gorka touched a finger to his lips while the room filled with whining static.

Roberto wiped his brow and noticed Gorka's young daughter, Linda, standing beside her mother. He gave her a wink and watched her break into a shy smile while darting behind Alazne's skirt.

A warm feeling surged through him. If he had married Laura, they would have a child like Linda by now. He sighed and looked up at the stage. The radio static had given way to the far-off strains of a tango. It reminded him of Valencia, and better times.

"Here it comes." Sebastian leaned back in the chair and turned up the volume. It was August 11, 1932....

"We interrupt this program for a special news bulletin. Citizens! This is Radio Madrid. We are relieved to announce the treacherous coup attempt by subversive army officers has been crushed by troops loyal to the Second Republic."

Arronategui and the two clerics stood up and broke into applause while nodding for the congregation to join in—but no one responded. Embarrassed, they sat down and listened to the rest of the message....

"*General Sanjurjo has been placed under house arrest in Seville with his accomplices. We repeat that the coup attempt has been crushed. At this moment, forces loyal to the government are being deployed to remaining hotspots in Extremadura, Catalonia, and Asturias. You are advised to remain in your homes until the last of the traitors has been arrested. God bless you and long live the Second Republic!*"

Sebastian leaned forward and lowered the volume. "That's it."

The room surged with whispers as Arronategui stood up and stepped onto the stage. He scanned the crowd and began speaking in a loud voice. "It is critical you follow the instructions on the radio and remain in your homes or places of business until the all clear is given."

He paused and studied the defiant faces peering up at him. "You think I don't know what's going on? You can thank God I'm one of you. You're playing Russian Roulette—and you know what I mean!"

He caught himself and lowered his voice. "Listen to me, friends. We're like an island in a storm. Please don't get involved in the dark activities across the border. That's the excuse the military is waiting for. They'll pour troops in here like they did in Oviedo. You know what that will mean? The end of our *fueros*—our sacred independence. Do you want to end up like those poor souls in Asturias?"

He dabbed his brow with a handkerchief. "In time, the violence will end. Until then, our only hope is to remain neutral. Are you with me?"

They lowered their heads and remained silent.

Arronategui's face twisted in a frown. "I'll take that as a 'yes'. I'm holding a special Mass tonight for our friends in Oviedo. Anyone wishing to attend is welcome. God be with you." He stepped off the stage and headed for the door, followed by the two clerics.

He was about to exit the hall when he stopped and pointed

a menacing finger at Roberto. "How dare you pose as one of us!"

Roberto looked at him in shock.

"You know what I mean. Holding Mass like you're a priest. Have you no shame? Are you that desperate for self-worth? God have mercy on your soul." He glared at Roberto and stormed out of the hall.

Roberto felt Alazne grasp his trembling arm.

"He's just upset. Let it be."

"Who does he think he is—Jesus Christ?" He started after the departing priest, but she tugged on his arm.

"Please, Roberto. There are more important things to deal with today."

Augustin stepped on the stage and looked down at Luis who was standing at the door. "Are they gone?"

Luis glanced out the door and nodded.

Augustin stuffed his shirt in his pants and took a slow, deep breath. "Men like Arronategui and Aguirre mean well. In their minds, we'll be safe if we don't get involved." He hesitated and looked down at Julio. "Are they right?"

Julio jumped on the stage and stood beside his friend. He stepped forward and scanned the congregation, his eyes filled with anger. "If Arronategui was right, my friends in Oviedo wouldn't be crying out for help. We were given promises too—and we believed them. Work hard and don't make trouble. The mine owners and government will take care of you." He glared down at Roberto. "We were fools! The pigs tricked us! We trusted them and they turned us into slaves! To mine cheap coal for their fat wallets! When we woke up, it was too late!"

A dozen men and women stood up and began shouting and shaking their fists.

"And you're next! They'll promise anything to get your ports and iron ore. Then, they'll take your homes and livestock. And rape your women! And when they're done with you, they'll put a bullet in your head and shove you in a grave of wet earth. I know these things. I've lived these things!"

Roberto looked around and saw everyone coming to their feet. The room echoed with shouts and stinging epithets.

Julio raised his fist in the air. "Our only chance is to fight them. Asturians and Basques can't be stopped if we stand together. The Russians are with us. We have guns and dynamite. We'll stop the pigs before they reach Oviedo. We'll blow up their trucks and gun them down. This time, they'll know we mean business. The hell with Arronategui! Are you with me?"

The cheering crowd rushed the stage, their fists shaking in the air.

"Wait! You don't know what you're doing!" Roberto tried to reach the stage, but he was pushed back by the angered citizens. He tried again, but Gorka pulled him away.

"There's nothing you can do, Roberto. It's better you leave." Gorka's strong hands pulled him toward the door.

"Listen to me, man. You can't fight that kind of power. If you attack that convoy, they'll cross the border and hunt you down like animals. Arronategui's right. This isn't the way."

"Stay out of it, Roberto." Gorka shoved him outside and slammed the door in his face. Roberto tried to open it, but it was locked from the inside. He backed away from the door and saw Francesca and two laborers staring at him from across the street.

"What's wrong, Roberto? Why did they do that?"

He lowered his head and walked down the front steps. He didn't need to be inside to know what was happening. Sebastian had switched the radio to the daily shortwave broadcast of troop movements. The idiots were going to attack the truck caravans approaching Oviedo.

He walked past the restaurant and bank, then turned north on Mugica Road until he found himself standing in front of the *Casa del Juntas*. In another two weeks, Basque deputies would flock here from throughout Vizcaya to set the province's agenda for the coming year—if they were still alive. He pushed through the iron gate and walked up the stone path toward the courtyard, and its ancient oak.

A fresh cluster of green shoots fought to break through the stump's gnarled bark. The shoots he spotted last year had died off, but there was definite life in the remains of the old tree.

He sat on one of the stone benches and gazed at the stump while recalling Luis' warning about the unexplained shoots. A smile cracked his lips. "Too much wine, Luis. You need to get laid. You all need to get laid."

A flock of birds darted across the blue sky. They were headed east toward the Pyrenees. He watched them disappear behind the roof tops.

He should have left when he had the chance. Last month, he finally telephoned Dupont in Paris, only to discover the young architect had sold his practice for a better opportunity in South America. If he had joined Dupont last year, he would be with his wealthy friend now, beginning a new life in Argentina, instead of sitting in a courtyard with a gray-brown tree stump while a bunch of lunatics committed suicide.

He reached down and scooped a handful of dirt. It felt cold and wet, like the grave Julio described in his tirade. He clenched the dirt and recalled the vision in Corpus Christi. People dying. Planes diving from the sky. And that voice challenging him to stop the pain.

"Roberto?"

He flung the dirt at the ground and spun around. "What are you doing here?"

Ana eased beside him. Her eyes were red, like she'd been crying. "Sebastian tried to stop them, but they won't listen. They're going to kill themselves."

He looked down at the spilled dirt.

"A convoy of guardsmen is headed for Oviedo. They're going to blow it up. They think it's a game. They're like children playing at war."

"I'll talk to Augustin. He'll listen to reason."

She sat beside him and rubbed her forehead. "What's happening to us, Roberto? We're no better than those pigs torturing the people in Oviedo."

He reached down and scooped another handful of dirt. "It's Julio. He's full of hate. I see it in his eyes—eating at him like a cancer."

"I caused this."

"What?"

She wiped away a tear. "Do you remember that night on the train?"

"Every moment."

"I promised to give my confession after you became a priest."

"I'm not a priest."

"You're the only one I can trust."

He felt the dirt pour out of his hand.

"When Gorka and Alazne found us in the fields, I was almost dead."

"Please, I'd rather not—"

"I was bleeding while Julio cursed me and my unborn son."

Roberto looked at her in shock.

"It was God's punishment."

"Punishment?"

"Before coming here, we lived in Cadiz. Julio had moved there to escape the turmoil in his homeland. He was trying to find jobs for his family. He'd promised them a better life in the south. It was very hard for him when news of the atrocities began leaking out of Oviedo."

"You met there?"

"We were introduced by a friend in Cadiz. I fell in love with Julio that day. He was so strong. I had no one."

"Your parents are dead?"

"I never knew my parents. My sister raised me."

"Roberto wiped the dirt off his hand. "She's in Cadiz?"

"In a grave. She died from fever three years ago."

He stared at her, unable to speak.

"After we married, Julio took a job as a dockworker. I became a seamstress in a Cadiz textile mill. Things were looking up until he began asking questions about jobs for his family. The labor bosses panicked. We didn't know it, but they had a secret agreement with the industrialists and landowners."

"Agreement?"

"They were taking union dues from our pay and splitting the money with the shipbuilders and *latifundistas*. They didn't want outside labor flooding into Cadiz because it would cause trouble with the locals. No need for disruption when you're making lots of money."

Roberto clenched his fist and recalled the fight with Pedroza. "What about the new reforms?"

"Reforms? The so-called reforms gave the unions the perfect excuse to throw us out. We lost our jobs when the UGT promised not to hire workers from outside Cadiz. After slaving on the docks for a year, Julio was replaced because he wasn't a native of Cadiz."

"But the reforms are meant to protect local *braceros*—land laborers—not dock workers?"

"I don't know these things. All I know is Julio asked for an explanation and was thrown out of the union office. When he threatened to rally his comrades in a strike, the union boss exploded and called in thugs." She paused and wiped her eyes. "I found Julio bleeding in the street near the dock. The next day, I lost my job in the textile mill."

"You? But you were from Cadiz?"

"Marriage has its drawbacks, Roberto. My husband is Asturian."

Roberto looked down at his clenched fist.

"When we went to the Monsignor for help, he told us to go back to our own kind. He didn't lift a finger to help us. I guess he was getting some of that money too. That's why Julio is so bitter toward the Church." She paused and rubbed her forehead.

Roberto handed her his canteen and watched her take a few swallows. She gave it back to him and looked down at the handkerchief in her hand.

"Now the hard part." She took a deep breath. "The union boss told our landlord we had no money. When Julio pleaded with him to give us a few days, the pig laughed and threw us out in the street."

"God."

"With winter coming, we headed north into Sevilla looking for work. We had no money, and Oviedo was five hundred miles away." She hesitated and wiped her eyes. "We had to beg for food. That's when I—" She sobbed and pressed her trembling fist against her mouth.

"Maybe we should stop."

She shook her head and forced out the words. "We'd spend our nights in the fields or a barn. I'd wait until Julio fell asleep before sneaking into the towns and offering my body to the local *caciques* and their *latifundista* bosses. They'd take me into their inns and have their way with me. Sometimes they'd pay me. Other times, they'd spit on me and throw me in the street without a *peseta*." She wiped her eyes. "But we survived, Roberto—we survived."

He looked away and fought the anger. His problems were nothing compared to this.

"When I became pregnant, I told Julio it was his child, but he knew better. He didn't say anything until that night in the fields when I lost the baby." She clenched her fists. "He went crazy. He called me a whore and left me lying there with Gorka and Alazne trying to stop the bleeding. I wanted to die. Oh, God—how I wanted to die." She broke down and collapsed against him.

He held her in his arms and tried to comfort her. "You had no choice. Don't blame yourself for trying to survive."

"There is always a choice."

"Come on—I'm tired of looking at that stump." He helped her up and felt her warm body press against him.

"Take care of yourself, Roberto. You mean so much to me." She reached up and kissed him on the lips. Before he could speak, she was gone.

He frowned and looked at the stump. "And I wanted to be a priest...."

Roberto was headed into the forest when he heard Sebastian's battered truck rattling toward him on the dirt road. The olive-gray contraption skidded to a stop in a cloud of dust.

"Where are you going, *amigo*?"

Roberto swiped at the swirling dust and walked toward the bearded face peering down at him from the driver's cab. "To talk them out of killing themselves."

"It's too late. They're gone."

"What?"

"I was going after them when I saw you. I could use your help."

Roberto stepped closer. "How bad is it?"

"Worse than I thought. I picked up another message after they left. The convoy's being covered by fighter aircraft. They'll be scouting the road ahead of the trucks. If they spot Julio and the others—"

"God." Roberto ran around the truck and climbed into the seat beside the old man. "When did they leave?"

"An hour ago. They're headed for the road leading out of Reinosa."

"In Santander?"

"Si. Three troop convoys are closing on Oviedo from the west, south, and east. Julio's team is assigned to attack the one coming from the east."

Roberto clung to the door while Sebastian shifted into reverse and spun the truck around in a cloud of dust. The old man jammed the gearshift knob forward and skidded across the Renteria Bridge, nearly hitting a passing shepherd.

"Hey, Sebastian! What the hell's wrong with you!"

Sebastian ignored the screaming shepherd and sped past the candy factory and fire station. "This is my fault, Roberto. I should have shot out their tires."

"Calm down. Do you want me to drive?"

"What's wrong, don't trust a one-armed man?" Sebastian gunned the engine and skidded past the munitions factory onto the paved road winding westward into the Cantabrian Mountains.

"These other two teams, are they Asturian or Basque?"

"Asturian, with a few advisers from—"

"The Soviet Union?"

"Never mind that." Sebastian gripped the wheel and sped into the shadows of the mountains. It would take at least two hours to catch up with Julio and the others.

The sun was dropping toward the hills when Sebastian slammed on the brakes and pulled off the road in a screeching cloud of dust.

"What is it?"

"Shut up and listen."

Roberto heard an ominous drone. He stuck his head out the window and scanned the low-hanging clouds.

"Shit." Sebastian gunned the engine, throwing Roberto against the seat. They bounced across the rocky ground and skidded to a stop under a cluster of pine trees.

Sebastian shut off the engine and squinted through the mud-smeared windshield. "Come on." He jumped out of the truck and ran up the rocky hillside with Roberto trailing behind him. They were nearly to the top when Roberto heard the whine.

"Get down!" Sebastian pushed him into a clump of bushes as the ground shook from two powerful explosions.

Roberto spit out a mouthful of dirt and looked at the sky. "Did he see us?"

"We'd be dead if he did."

Roberto pushed away from Sebastian and scrambled to the hill crest. At first, he was blinded by the setting sun. He shaded his eyes and saw black smoke rising from a clump of pines across the road. He was about to stand when a double-winged aircraft roared over his head and swooped down at the burning trees, raking them with machine gun fire.

The pines lit up with a blinding orange flash and the ground shook from a shattering explosion. He buried his face in his arms. Debris was falling everywhere.

Sebastian crawled next to him and gripped his shirt. "Stay down! He hit the dynamite!"

Roberto squinted at the burning forest and saw five men charging out of the smoke.

"Fools!" Sebastian looked down at his panicked friends. He stood up and fired his pistol in the air, then began waving it frantically above his head. "Here, Augustin! On the hill!"

Roberto saw Augustin gesture for the others to follow him up the hill. He could see Ixidro and Juan trailing behind Augustin, followed by Julio and Gorka. They were nearly to the crest when the plane dived out of the sun, its lethal machine guns spouting flame.

Julio and Augustin dived behind the rocks as the hillside

erupted with twin lines of impacting bullets. Juan cried out and clutched his chest, then fell flat on his face. Ixidro let out an agonizing scream and dropped on his side, clutching his shattered leg.

Roberto gagged from the choking smoke and dust drifting over the hill crest. Fighting to see, he stood up on his knees and saw Julio lifting Ixidro's broken body in his arms. Sebastian had run down the hill and was kneeling beside Juan. Behind them, Augustin raced down the hill toward his brother's writhing body.

He looked up and saw the plane circling for another deadly pass. Through the smoke, he could see Augustin dragging his brother up the hill. He gasped when he saw blood gushing from Gorka's mouth. His ears filled with a sickening whine as the plane began its strafing run. He clenched his fists—and he heard the voice....

The pain, Roberto. Stop the pain ....

With his heart pounding against his ribs, Roberto scrambled over the crest and charged down the hill toward Augustin and his wounded brother. He heard the rat-a-tat and saw orange bursts flashing through the propeller.

"Get out of here!" Augustin tried to push him away.

"No—keep going!" Roberto dropped on his knees and picked up one of the dynamite sticks protruding from Gorka's discarded pack. He snatched Gorka's pistol off the ground and shot at the fuse, sending orange sparks flying in all directions. *One chance, torero. One chance.*

He stood up and saw the line of impacting bullets rip toward him. His ears rang from ricocheting bullets. He could see the pilot's black leather helmet behind the propeller. The plane was coming right at him!

He flung the dynamite stick in the air and dived at the rocks. A terrific concussion slammed into him, followed by the sound of a sputtering engine. He rolled on his back and saw the smoking plane struggle for altitude as it limped into the clouds.

He heard men cheering. Sebastian and Julio were running

toward him. Strong hands picked him up and dragged him over the crest. His ears rang. Everything was moving in slow motion. He remembered seeing Sebastian's dirt-smeared face before blacking out....

"Roberto?"
He opened his eyes and saw Ana looking down at him.
"Thank God."
"Where am I?"
"In Marquina." She reached down and placed a fresh cloth on his forehead.
"What happened?"
"They brought you here yesterday. I was so worried."
He looked up at the ceiling and remembered the diving plane. "Where are the others?"
"They're well. You should rest now."
He clutched her wrist. "Where are they, Ana?"
She hesitated and looked down. "They—"
"How are you feeling?" Julio barged into the room and brushed her aside.
Roberto squinted at the handsome face looking down at him. "How are the others?"
"Fine, thanks to you." Julio glanced at his wife. "You were very brave out there, *amigo*. Foolish, but brave. I like that in a man."
Roberto frowned and looked away. "I need to sleep."
Julio patted his shoulder. "We can talk later. I'll be outside if you need me." He whispered something to his wife and left the room.
"Are you in pain?"
He turned toward her and smiled. "Just tired. I'm glad Segurra isn't here to see this. Who ever heard of a priest attacking a plane?"
She smiled and grasped his hand. "Go to sleep. I'll be here with you."
He closed his eyes and felt the room slip away....

He heard waves crashing against the rocks. A stiff breeze

blew against his face. He opened his eyes and blinked at the bright sun.

He was standing on a hillside overlooking the sea. Rows of whitecapped waves surged toward the rocky shoreline. Behind him, reddish-brown slopes were covered with rows of orange and olive trees. He could see ripening Valencias protruding from the jagged branches.

He was about to head up the slope when he noticed a woman standing on the beach. She wore a royal-blue riding dress and waist-jacket. Her black, flamenco hat and yellow parasol seemed out of place in modern Spain. Yet, there was something strangely familiar about her.

He walked down the hillside and eased beside her. "Excuse me, señorita. Have we met before?"

She turned and smiled beneath her veil. "You might say that."

"Pardon?"

She lifted the veil and trained her brown eyes on him. "Hello, Roberto."

"My God." *He was staring at the most beautiful woman he'd ever seen—the woman in the portrait above his father's fireplace. He backed away and struggled for words.*

"Why are you afraid? There is nothing to fear. I just wanted to see you this one time—my handsome son."

"It can't be." *He dropped on his knees.*

Her soft hand stroked his hair. "I'm sorry we never had this chance together. I've missed you more than you could know. When they gave me the choice of living without you, I chose death." *She reached under his chin and lifted his face.* "I'm so glad, Roberto. You're meant for great things. In time, you will know the truth— and we'll be together. Goodbye, my son."

"No—you can't leave now. Not after all this time. There is so much I want to tell you."

"I'll never forget you, Roberto. Your father and I will always be at your side. Remember, Roberto. I'll always be with you."

"Mother!"

She turned and disappeared into the mist....

He opened his eyes and saw a small lamp burning on the table beside his bed. A woman's soft breathing came from the shadows in the corner. He sat up and saw Ana asleep in a chair. It reminded him of the night on the train. For a moment, he sat there looking at her. She was so beautiful in the soft light—like the woman in his dream.

He slipped out of the bed and staggered past her into the dark hallway. When he reached the living room, he saw Julio sprawled on a couch, his hand clutching an empty bottle of wine. From the looks of him, their little conversation would have to wait until morning. Better a man be sober when he's called an ass.

He squinted at the darkness. Voices were coming from outside the house. It sounded like someone was crying. He edged toward the front door and noticed it was partially open. He pushed through it and steadied himself against the jamb.

Augustin was sitting on the front step with his arms around Alazne and Linda. The child was crying.

"What's wrong?"

"Roberto!" Alazne looked up at him with tear-filled eyes.

He stepped forward, but a rush of dizziness stopped him. He reached out blindly and felt Augustin's strong arms grab him. When his head cleared, he was sitting on the steps beside Augustin. Alazne and her daughter were gone.

"You have a concussion. It will take a few days for the dizziness to go away."

He rubbed his forehead and looked at the moonlit hills. "Why were they crying?"

Augustin picked up a stone and grasped it in his palm. "When I met you, I thought you were a coward and a fool. I was only half right."

"Why were they crying, Augustin?"

Augustin clenched the stone. "I think you know."

"God—no."

"He died in my arms in the back of the truck. My little warrior." Augustin fought the tears, but it was no use. He broke down and wept like a child.

Roberto wanted to cry, but he couldn't. He leaned against his friend and stared at the hills.

"Juan's dead. Ixidro made it, but he'll never walk again. And my brother's wife and child will never laugh again." He glared at the hills. "They killed my brother, Roberto. They'll pay for that. Oh—how they'll pay." He stood up and stormed across the moonlit pasture toward the hills.

"Augustin—wait!"

"See, Roberto. I warned you. Asturias is just the beginning. We're next."

Roberto spun around and saw Julio leaning against the opened door.

"It took some time for Augustin to know the truth, but now he is with us. And you too, *compañero*. Welcome to the revolution."

Fighting his dizziness, Roberto stood up and glared at the drunk swaying in the doorway. "What's wrong with you? What kind of demon has you in its teeth? For God's sake, don't go any further with this."

Julio cracked a bitter smile. "Spoken like a true priest. I was right. We need you more than ever. You know—to show us the way when we go astray. Hey—listen to me. I made a rhyme." He staggered next to Roberto and grabbed his arm. "Come on, citizen. You need rest. Quite a pair, eh. A drunken revolutionary and a dizzy imposter."

Before Roberto passed out on the bed, he heard Ana arguing with her husband. The air cracked with a loud slap, followed by a slamming door. He felt her hands on his chest. Her warm cheek pressed against his—and he heard her crying.

In the months to come, Roberto would be torn between the inviting mountains to the east and his love for Spain. His pleas for reason would fall on deaf ears while the light of freedom flickered—and died.

With the nation ravaged by riots, famine, and financial collapse, the Second Republic would feel increased pressure from the Church and military to put a stop to the growing insurrection.

But the fragmented government would be unable to step up to the greatest challenge in Spain's history. Instead of unifying the people, misguided bureaucrats would pour gasoline on the fires of revolution. Powerful rightist organizations like José Maria Gil Roble's CEDA would battle the socialist-led PSOE worker's party in a feverish struggle to control the Cortes—Spain's parliamentary assembly.

New names would rise up to lead the disillusioned masses. Men like Alejandro Lerroux and his corrupt Radical Party, or José Calvo Sotelo and his monarchist *Renovacian Espanola*. Instead of bringing unity, these militant factions would polarize Spain and breed even more dangerous reactionary groups like the fascist *Falange*, under Primo de Rivera. And the green-shirted *Requetes*, Republican Assault Guards, Civil Guards, and anarchist-inspired militias.

In the end, the only names that mattered would be Generals Mola and Varela, Colonel Yagué, and the man Roberto toasted at Laura's table that fateful evening in Valencia, so long ago.

The seeds were sewn and the devil walked the earth. It was time to reap the whirlwind....

19 | New York Magic

It didn't look like a sheep shelter with its flagstone terrace and brightly colored umbrellas. Hard to believe an 1870 stone barn could become Manhattan's latest swank restaurant.

Karen peered through the bay window at the flowered banquet table. A red carpet ran along the floor to the seat of honor at the table's center. The mayor's chair had been positioned to allow him an unobstructed view of the beautiful mural of Manhattan on the far wall.

She sniffed the air and detected an odor of freshly cooked veal and garlic. Too bad her name wasn't on the guest list. She hadn't tasted good meat in three years.

She stepped back from the window and studied the thick green foliage framing the restaurant. Nice touch. A taste of country dining nestled beneath the trees of Central Park. An afternoon escape for those fortunate executives who had dodged the bullet five years ago when the market collapsed. And they should celebrate. After all, they were the survivors. The others were either on skid row or pushing up daisies from thirty-story swan dives off Wall Street's towering skyscrapers.

Karen aimed her camera at the flock of dignitaries waiting for Mayor La Guardia to exit his horse drawn carriage. She looked through the eyepiece while nervously adjusting the focus knob. *Come on, Mr. Mayor. Let's get this over with. I'm hungry.*

The crowd broke into cheers as the portly, top-hatted mayor stepped down from the carriage and eyed New York's latest restaurant.

Karen took a deep breath and slipped her finger on the shutter switch. She could hear the other cameras rattling while their operators jockeyed for position. She peered through the eyepiece and framed the picture. *Steady, Miss Vostok. Just a step back and—*

Her heel struck something, sending her sprawling backwards. She looked up and saw the camera fly out of her hands. Her back and head slammed against the ground along with the expensive camera.

She couldn't breathe. The bright sky flashed with stars. She shook her head and blinked at a blue-uniformed policeman bending over her. Her ears rang with hysterical laughter, but that wasn't the worst sound. Shutters were clicking.

"Are you all right, ma'am?"

She sat up and rubbed her head. "What happened?"

"Gotta watch those rocks. You went down like a clown doing a pratfall."

She gave the cop a dirty look and plucked a dead leaf out of her hair. "Where's my camera?"

The cop pointed at the sidewalk. "Looks like you broke the lens. Hope the *Times* insures its equipment. Kind of tough these days with all the bankruptcies."

She seized the camera and detached its shattered lens. "Damn!" She flung the broken lens against a tree while the photographers clicked away. She didn't need to look at them to know their subject.

Mayor La Guardia and his entourage had entered the *Tavern on the Green* for a brief lunch and dedication ceremony. Karen's assignment was to get a close-up shot of the mayor's grand entrance while her senior associate, Stan Jacobs, joined other reporters inside the restaurant for a round of interviews and free gourmet lunch. At-a-boy, Stan. Not bad for the middle of a depression.

The cop helped her up and watched her brush the leaves off her dress. "Sorry, ma'am. Maybe you can catch a shot of him when he comes out." He tipped his cap and walked away while the crowd of snickering photographers lowered their cameras.

For a moment, Karen stared at the disabled camera like a little girl who has just broken her favorite toy. She stuffed the black contraption into her worn handbag and turned to face the crowd. "Anyone want another shot? Next time I'll show more leg." She glared at the stunned photogs and pushed through them.

How could she be so clumsy? After three years training with Rudd Franklin and Stan Jacobs, this should have been a snap. Instead, she was about to lose her job for blowing a front page photograph of New York's powerful new mayor. And to seal her fate, tomorrow's newspapers would carry photographs of the *New York Time's* ace photographer falling on her ass while Mayor Fiorello La Guardia christened Manhattan's newest restaurant. So much for dreams of grandeur, Miss Vostok.

She slung the heavy handbag over her shoulder and marched up Central Park's West Drive toward The Lake. Along the way, she saw a homeless drunk sleeping under a tree. Her stomach wrenched. In a few hours, Frank Gerramino would slap a pink slip in her hand and she'd join that poor, hapless soul under the tree.

It only took ten minutes to reach The Lake. She plunked down on a bench near the skate house and slumped against the creaking wood. The sun was breaking through the late-morning clouds. It felt warm on her face.

A robin landed on the grass and looked up at her. The robin poked the grass and flew away. Hell, even the birds were hungry.

She looked out at the lake and spotted a kid's sailboat bobbing in the current. Nice picture with the sun reflecting on the water. Too bad it wouldn't save her job.

She yanked her handbag open and stared at the broken camera. In a few minutes, Stan Jacobs would come running up the path shouting her name. When he heard the bad news, he'd probably throw up in the lake. This wasn't his fault, but she was his responsibility—and everyone tread on thin ice these days. A chill went through her. *God, please don't let anything happen to Stan. Not with a wife and three kids.*

She sighed and stared at the sailboat fighting the current. She was a lot like that little boat. For three tough years, Karen Vostok had managed to stay afloat in the midst of the nation's worst depression. With the *Time's* staff dropping like flies, she fought to keep her job by working around the clock to take whatever menial work was offered. When angry employees stormed out of the Times Building after being told they must take pay cuts and assist the night shift on the printing presses, Karen bought a pair of overalls and marched into the press room that same night because she remembered Edmund Halberton's prophetic words that the worst was yet to come.

For three agonizing years, she struggled through sleepless nights of ear-shattering machinery and splattered ink, followed by exhaustive days of field work with her camera. Except for the barest essentials, everything she earned went to her evening journalism classes at Columbia University. Driven by a relentless passion to succeed, she pushed herself to the edge of sanity—but she survived while those poor, naive souls who had stormed out of the Times Building three years ago begged for food on Forty-second Street while their starving children cried.

A gust of cool wind brushed against her face. She pushed back her hair and recalled the sound of the camera crashing on the ground. Had she come this far to fail because of a protruding rock and broken lens? After three years of getting by without sleep to learn everything she could about the newspaper business, was she going to end up in the streets because of a blown photograph? And what about the other twenty five years in hell? Were they for nothing?

She yanked the camera out of her bag and placed it on her lap. After staring at it for a moment, she reached into the bag and dug through her junk until she felt a small box at the bottom. Thank God, she hadn't forgotten. Rudd had taught her to be prepared for the worst—and that meant carrying a spare lens.

She popped open the box and pulled out the precious black cylinder. *God—please let it fit.* She twisted the lens on the shutter and smiled. A few peeks through the eyepiece and some knob-twisting assured her there was no other damage except a bent shutter brace.

She stood up and focused the camera on the sailboat and its young red-haired skipper running along the shore. The boy was clad in a navy-blue sailor suit and white shoes. An elderly couple watched proudly from a nearby bench. From the look of their tailored clothing, they must be his wealthy grandparents. *Great life, kid. Enjoy.*

She watched the boy kneel down and reach for the boat. He grasped it in his hand and lifted it out of the shimmering water.

How touching. She clicked the shutter and broke into a smile. *Excellent shot, Miss Vostok. Front page stuff all the way. Hell, no—I'm not done yet.*

She stuffed the camera in her bag and slung the bag over her shoulder. The mayor would be leaving soon. There was still time for an exit photo. Same setting as when he came in. Catch him pausing on the steps. Who the hell would know the difference? She took a final glance at the lake and shuffled down West Drive.

When she approached the restaurant, she noticed the photographers had retreated to the wood benches along West Drive. Some of them munched sandwiches while glancing nervously at the Tavern's horseshoe-shaped driveway. The carriage driver was standing in front of the entrance, feeding his horse a bag of oats.

She edged up to the Tavern's bay window and tried to get a glimpse of the mayor, but her view was obstructed by drawn maroon drapes. Too bad. From here, she could get a great shot of La Guardia stuffing his face with veal while half of New York starved in the streets. No wonder they'd kept photographers out of the restaurant.

She leaned against a tree and looked up at the sun flickering through the branches. A stiff breeze had picked up from the east. It would probably rain tonight. She closed her tired eyes and listened to the rustling leaves—and she heard a voice shouting in the darkness....

You stupid bitch! I told you to get whiskey, not bourbon! You can't even read, you good for nothing little whore! If your mother was alive, I'd walk out of here tomorrow! You're goddamn lucky I'm willing to put up with you, you little tramp! Now go to bed before I use my strap on you! I'll be in later....

She shuddered and looked down at her clenched fists. A bead of perspiration trickled down her forehead. She brushed it away and fixed her blue eyes on the restaurant entrance.

What was she afraid of? Nothing could be worse than that awful memory. She took a deep breath and marched through the door.

"Excuse me, ma'am. You can't go in there." A maroon-uniformed doorman stepped in her path.

"But my uncle promised me a photo?"

"Uncle?"

"Mayor La Guardia, stupid. I'm his niece. Didn't they tell you?" She watched him glance over his shoulder and gesture toward the *maitre d'*. He was off balance. Now or never, Miss Vostok. She rushed past him into the restaurant.

"Hey, where are you going?"

She ignored him and bolted for the banquet table.

"Stop her! She's not cleared!"

Two burly security men seized her arms while a dozen shocked bureaucrats and reporters jumped out of their seats.

"How about a photo, Mr. Mayor?" She couldn't believe her words. She was shouting at the little man seated at the center of the table. "Come on, Mr. Mayor. It'll only take a minute."

"Let's go, lady. You've had your fun." The two guards confiscated the camera and dragged her away from the table while La Guardia stood up and glared at Stan Jacobs and the other stunned reporters.

She struggled against the two powerful men, but it was no use. If she had any aces left, it was time to pull them.

They were nearly to the door when she jerked her head back and shouted at the top of her lungs. "A photo's not much to ask for a little discretion! You know—Tammany Hall and Mr. Cardolani!"

Strong hands pushed her out the door into the arms of a waiting cop—the same one who had helped her a few minutes ago.

"Now why did you go and do that, ma'am? Now I have to take you in for threatening a city official." The cop yanked away her handbag and handcuffed her, then whisked her toward a waiting patrol car.

She was too tired to resist. She looked down at her cuffed hands while the mysterious name echoed in her ears. *Cardolani? Where the hell did he come from?*

Suddenly it struck her. She had seen his name in an old

Herald article while doing some research at Columbia's library a few months ago. When La Guardia broke up Tammany Hall, he promised to purge the city's longstanding corruption, but rumors persisted that he'd cut a secret deal with a union boss named Cardolani. The implications were clear. Posing as a reformist, La Guardia was actually a puppet of an opportunistic crime family that had infiltrated New York's labor unions.

When La Guardia and William Norris successfully sponsored the pro-union, *Norris-La Guardia Bill* in 1932, the Cardolani story faded beneath a tidal wave of favorable headlines describing La Guardia's push to unseat Jimmy Walker as mayor. Surprising, given it made such good copy. The controversial story was probably untrue, but its sensationalism would have sold lots of papers. Not very smart.

"Watch your head, ma'am." The cop shoved her into the backseat and shut the door. Minutes later, they were racing down Tenth Avenue toward the Forty-second Street Precinct Station in Hell's Kitchen, only three long blocks from Karen's desk in the austere Times Building.

She collapsed in the seat and peered out the window at the pedestrians and cars. In the distance, St. Patrick's chimed high noon. Hard to top this, Miss Vostok. A pink slip and jail on the same day....

"What the hell happened?"

Karen sat up and rubbed her eyes. Stan Jacobs was peering at her through the cell bars.

"Well?"

"I screwed up."

He pushed back his brown hat and scratched his balding head. "Yeah, you might say that. What got into you? You want to cost us our jobs?"

She stood up and stepped over a sleeping drunk. "Does Gerramino know?"

Stan nodded and stepped aside while a guard stuck a key in the lock and opened the cell door.

"I can go?"

"Come on, I'll buy you a coffee." Stan gestured nervously

toward the metal security door leading to the precinct's front desk.

She grabbed her coat and started to walk out of the cell, then hesitated and looked down at the cot. "First good sleep I've had this year."

"Will you come on before they change their minds?" He grabbed her arm and dragged her down the corridor.

They walked across town and stopped at a small coffee shop next to the Paramount Building on Seventh and Broadway. Nothing was said until she began sipping her coffee.

Stan leaned forward and glared at her. "How could you mess up like that?"

She put down the coffee and sighed. "I can't believe it either. What should I do? I'll do anything, Stan."

"Forget it, lady. You've done enough."

"You mean that scene in the restaurant?"

Stan's face reddened. "How could you do that to me? It was my turn to interview him, dammit. When he found out you were with the *Times*, he gave me the brush off."

"Oh, Stan. I'm sorry."

He raised his hand for silence. "Forget the sad eyes and start thinking what you're gonna tell Gerramino. Coming back without a picture is one thing, but blowing an interview with the mayor—hell, that's pretty serious."

She slumped in the chair and stared at her coffee. "How's he taking it?"

"He threw me out of his office when I told him. He damn near foamed at the mouth." Stan pushed away his coffee and dropped two dimes on the table. "Well—no sense dragging it out." He stood up and nodded toward the door. The desperate look on his face made her cringe.

The trek to Gerramino's office felt like the last mile. With car horns blaring around them, they crossed bustling Seventh Avenue and stopped in front of the renowned, wedge-shaped building housing the *New York Time's* publishing offices. The belt of white electric bulbs girding the facade was silent now, but at any moment it could come alive with the latest rolling headlines, visible for blocks along the "Great White Way."

Under Adolph Och's astute leadership, the *New York Times* had become America's greatest newspaper. But there were problems. Pink slips fluttered down from Och's executive office like tiny death warrants. If one landed on your shoulder, the next stop was the street. Karen shuddered and pushed through the swinging glass doors into the crowded lobby. Gerramino was probably signing hers now.

They rode the packed elevator to the second floor and stepped into a cavernous room filled with cluttered desks, overflowing wire wastebaskets, and stressed-out reporters hunched over their clicking typewriters.

"Hey, Karen, where have you been?"

She forced a smile and patted Danny Mallory on the shoulder. "Checking out the Forty-second Street Precinct."

"Huh?"

She gave him a hug. With that brown sweater and flaming red hair, Danny was the stereotype of all copy boys. Too bad he was targeted for the next round of pink slips. She'd overheard it in a conversation between Gerramino and Stan, but she didn't have the heart to tell him. Who knows, in a few minutes they might walk out together.

"You're first." Stan pointed to the frosted glass door on her left.

"You're not coming?"

He took off his hat and flipped it on his desk. "Good luck."

She frowned and headed up the aisle toward the last row of desks, and nearly went down for the second time today when she tripped over a wire wastebasket. She kicked the wastebasket and stormed toward her desk while the stunned reporters looked on.

She yanked off her coat and draped it on the desk. The handbag felt lighter. She pulled it open and noticed the camera was gone. "Hey Stan, they got my camera!"

Stan shook his head and pointed to the frosted glass door. "First thing he wanted to see."

"Great." She straightened her disheveled skirt and blouse while scanning the room for a friendly face. They'd all gone back to their typing. "Yeah—just great." She straightened up and marched down the aisle toward the frosted glass door.

It was always a bit eerie walking down that aisle. Many of the desks had been vacant for months. The two dozen reporters and office personnel who had survived kept their heads down while trying to look as busy as possible. None of them said a word when she walked by, but she knew what they were thinking. Who could blame them? It was bad luck to talk to the latest victim. It might rub off.

She waited for the secretary's nod while eyeing the black letters on the frosted glass....

Frank Gerramino
Editor-in-Chief

Frank Gerramino had run the show for almost twenty years. He was Adolph Och's selection from day one, and the best there was. In recent months, Karen had been allowed to sit in on some of his meetings because of her excellent photos of street people and Manhattan's seamier side. She'd heard he had a vicious temper. Time to get a firsthand look.

"He's ready, Miss Vostok."

She took a deep breath and opened the door.

Gerramino was sitting behind a stack of proofs, tearing into them with his blue pencil. The blinds were raised on the bay window behind his desk, presenting a sweeping view of Times Square. Karen squinted at the bright light and saw dust floating in the sunbeams. Gerramino looked like an angel sitting in those dusty sunbeams—*The Angel of Death*.

He jiggled his hand nervously in the air without looking up. "Shut the door and sit down."

She closed the door and slipped into one of the wood chairs facing his desk. Sighing softly, she folded her hands in her lap and stared at the most powerful newspaper editor in the world. She'd almost relaxed when he looked up and slammed his pencil on the desk, causing her to jump halfway out of the chair.

"You really blew it, lady. What do you think I should do

about it?"

She tried to remain calm, but her voice broke. "I'm sorry, Mr. Gerramino. If you would just give me another chance—"

"You think I'm Santa Claus?" He pointed angrily at the bay window behind him. "There are lots of good people down there begging for your job. I bet they won't screw up."

She felt a surge of anger, but managed to suppress it. "In three years, I've never made a mistake like that. I know I blew it, but it will never happen again. Please, Mr. Gerramino. This is my life."

"You have a funny way of showing it, Miss Vostok." He plunked the damaged camera on the desk. "You think these lenses grow on trees? We're in the middle of a depression."

"Take it out of my pay. I'll make it up. Whatever it takes."

He rocked back in the black leather chair and stroked his kinked charcoal hair. His gray vest was open, revealing an unbuttoned collar and loosened red tie. There was no paunch. His eyes and mouth were etched with worry lines, giving him a pained look.

He reached into a drawer and pulled out a brown pipe and pouch of tobacco. Swiveling the chair toward the window, he stuffed a plug of tobacco into the pipe and struck a match while she trembled behind him. He placed the pipe in his mouth and took a few calming puffs. "You don't think I owe you anything?"

"Sir?"

"I did my little favor for Ed Halberton three years ago. The rest was up to you."

She nodded and lowered her head. "Yes, sir."

"I could fire you right now without giving it a second thought."

She looked down at her clenched fists and felt the blood rush to her face. Three years of agony for this? Enough! He was starting to sound like dear old dad. Better starving to death than sitting here like a deer on a spit. "Mr. Gerramino, are you going to fire me?"

"I'm considering it."

"Then do it, goddammit. But quit boring me with your

arrogant mouth."

He whirled around and yanked the pipe out of his mouth. "What did you say?"

"You're the editor. I shouldn't have to repeat it." She started to get up.

"Wait a minute. I didn't excuse you."

"Shove it!" She leaped out of the chair and turned to leave.

"Wait, dammit! I'm not going to fire you...."

Her trembling hand froze on the doorknob.

"Please—sit down."

She turned around in shock and saw him standing behind the desk with a smile on his face.

"I like a good argument, Miss Vostok. It makes my day." He gestured toward the empty chair and watched her stumble into it.

"That's better." Gerramino walked to the window and looked out at Times Square while she stared at him in disbelief.

For a moment, he said nothing while puffing on his pipe and looking down at the Square. When he finally spoke, the anger was gone. "I love this time of year. Sunlight on the buildings. White clouds floating over the city. Steam rising from the streets. People rushing back and forth to survive. A nation struggling to get back on its feet. You can feel it from up here. Know what I mean?"

She stood up and pretended to look past him. "Yes, sir."

He took a final drag on the pipe and turned to face her. At five-foot-nine, Frank Gerramino wasn't an imposing man, but his rugged voice and piercing black eyes more than made up for it. "I've been studying your file. You've been through a lot."

She looked down and nodded.

"Me too. Grew up just a few blocks from here. Hell's Kitchen." He paused and glanced at the open folder on his desk. "You're from Scranton?"

"Yes."

"Tough place, Scranton. Good, hardworking people. Was your dad a miner?"

"My dad was a bastard."

"I see. Well, it's not my business." He placed the pipe in

the ashtray. "It took a lot of guts to stand up to me. I like people with guts. They make good reporters. But they've gotta have talent too. Know what I mean?"

"I think so."

He rested his hands on the desk and leaned forward. "What about you, Miss Vostok? Would you make a good reporter?"

"Sir?" She looked up in surprise.

"You're a hell of a good cameraman. I've studied your work. I think it's time to find out what else you can do. What do you think?"

Her eyes brightened. "You mean, as a reporter?"

"Gotta start some time. I just have one question."

She wiped away a tear. "Yes?"

"How did you pull it off?"

"Sir?"

"The mayor's office called an hour ago. It seems La Guardia wants you to stop by for an interview. Six sharp. How did you do it?"

She stared at him with blank eyes.

"Well?"

She shook her head. "I guess La Guardia likes feisty women too."

Gerramino let out a nervous laugh and pointed his finger at her. "I'm giving you a ten dollar raise, but that lens comes out of it. Fair enough?"

"Plenty fair. Thank you."

He sat down and picked up his pencil. "Get out of here. I've got work to do."

Stan and Danny were leaning against her desk when she staggered out of Gerramino's office. Stan straightened up and stared at her with concerned eyes. "How did it go?"

"What?"

Stan reached out and grabbed her arm. "You okay?"

She was too dazed to speak. She remembered Danny patting her shoulder when she picked up her coat and bag. After that, everything was a blur until an onrushing pedestrian slammed into her on Broadway.

"Hey, lady! Watch where you're going!"

"What? Oh, sorry." She looked around, but he'd vanished into the crowd. She heard St. Patrick's chiming four p.m. above the blaring car horns. Just enough time for a shower and change of clothes. She brushed back her hair and headed down Broadway.

When she reached Forty-first, she hesitated and looked around in confusion. Where the hell did she live? She squinted down Forty-first, trying to clear her exhausted head. She spotted the National Theatre's marquee just past Seventh Avenue. *That's it, dummy. To the right!*

She raced down Forty-first and ran up the steps of her apartment building across the street from the theatre. Pausing in the vestibule, she fumbled through her handbag and pulled out a small purse.

Buck fifty. Just enough for a sandwich and round trip subway to City Hall. The stop at the Public Library would have to be on foot. She'd need a good hour in there before heading to City Hall. It would be the most important hour of her twenty-eight year life.

She leaned against the vestibule wall and closed her tired eyes. Just a quick nap. Not too much to ask. Her head relaxed against the wall.

She was nearly asleep when the name, *Cardolani,* flashed through her mind. Sleep tomorrow, Miss Vostok. Too much at stake now. She pushed through the door and trudged up the steps to her third floor apartment.

City Hall was located a mile north of the Battery in a triangular park on Manhattan's east side. After spending an hour at the Public Library, Karen hopped the jammed IRT down Broadway to Chambers Street, and City Hall Park.

The church bells were chiming six when she ran up the steps of New York's most important building, a dignified two-story marble structure with massive arched windows and a domed tower rising between its ornate wings. She was in too much of a hurry to admire the sculpture of *Lady Justice* atop the tower.

She stopped at the reception desk inside the rotunda,

identifying herself to a matronly lady who smiled and picked up a phone. The circular walls echoed with footsteps and laughter from well-dressed bureaucrats fleeing the building for the day. Karen watched them file out the door, carrying their leather briefcases. Next stop, the nearest swank bar.

She felt a surge of anger. Those leeches were ready to party while their constituents starved in the streets. Oh—to nail them all.

"The Mayor's assistant is coming down to see you, Miss Vostok. He'll be here in a minute."

She looked down at the receptionist in surprise. "Isn't the Mayor here?"

The receptionist shrugged and picked up a pencil.

"Miss Vostok?"

Karen turned and saw a blue-suited man with blond hair standing on one of the curved marble staircases. He shuffled down the stairs and walked toward her with his hand extended.

"I'm Mr. Smith. The Mayor asked me to drive you to his favorite restaurant. Easier to talk there."

She forced a smile and gestured toward the door. "Lead the way, Mr. Smith."

They took a chauffeured limo to *Guffanti's,* a small Italian restaurant on Seventh Avenue. She became a little edgy when the limo swerved into an alley next to the restaurant.

Mr. Smith pointed to a side door and smiled. "We've arranged a quiet meal. Hope you don't mind?"

She returned the smile and followed him out of the limo.

The door led into a dark hallway with a drawn checkered curtain on the right. Smith opened the curtain and motioned for her to step inside. She smiled nervously and walked into a small, candlelit dining room with four gingham-covered tables, obviously reserved for private meetings.

"Good to see you again, Miss Vostok." Mayor La Guardia stood up from the rear table and extended his hand. He was wearing a dark-blue business suit and vest.

"The pleasure's mine, Mr. Mayor." She shook his hand and noticed a gray-suited gentleman with a black moustache and slicked-back hair standing off to the side. The room wasn't well-lit, but she recognized the rugged face from the photograph at the library. "Hello, Mr. Cardolani." She reached out and clasped his hand.

"Miss Vostok." He nodded politely.

"Please, join us." La Guardia gestured toward an empty chair and waited for her to sit down.

Cardolani sat next to La Guardia and extended an opened cigaret case. "I'm impressed, Miss Vostok. I didn't think I was that easily recognized."

She smiled and plucked out a cigaret. "I saw your photograph in a news clipping at the library."

"Library?"

"That's right."

"I'll be damned. How did that happen?"

"It's in the newspaper archives. It won't last much longer. The paper's already yellowing." She placed the cigaret between her lips and leaned toward him while he flicked his lighter.

"You're very attractive, Miss Vostok."

She leaned back and took a slow drag. "Thank you. Well—what can I do for you gentlemen?"

La Guardia leaned forward and glanced nervously at his friend. "I'll be brief. Sorry about what happened today, but you had no business barging in like that."

"Agreed." She puffed on the cigaret and blew smoke at the ceiling.

La Guardia glared at her. "What did you mean by that crack about my friend?"

She placed the cigaret in an ash tray. "I thought you might want to work together—that's all."

His face flushed. "Let's not talk in riddles, Miss Vostok. What do you want?"

She nodded and folded her hands on the table. "You ran on a platform to clean up corruption. You'll need a good reporter to pull it off. Good publicity, and all that."

La Guardia leaned back in his chair and glanced at Cardolani. "So, you want to be in on the action. Is that it, Miss Vostok?"

"That's it."

He stroked his chin with his knuckle. "You're asking a lot. What are you offering?"

She trained her blue eyes on him. "My loyalty, and some damn good press coverage."

He shrugged his shoulders. "I already have good press coverage. What makes you so special?"

"Well, for one thing, I'll be too busy with all those exclusives to do any more research on your friend." She reached for the cigaret, but Cardolani grabbed her wrist.

"You're plenty smart, Miss Vostok. I hope you're smart enough to stay out of trouble. It's dangerous out there. People get hurt. Even reporters."

She pried his fingers loose. "I understand, Mr. Cardolani."

A white-shirted waiter brushed through the curtain and placed a bottle of freshly-opened wine on the table. When he tried to pour it, Cardolani waved him off and picked up the bottle. "Let's drink to it." He poured the red wine and glared at her with dark brown eyes.

They spent the next few minutes sipping wine and exchanging pleasantries. She sensed their little meeting was over when the mayor glanced at his watch and pushed away his glass.

"It's been a long day, Miss Vostok. I like to sleep on this sort of thing. You'll get my answer in the next few days."

She nodded and started to get up.

"One question, Miss Vostok." Cardolani placed his hand on hers.

"Yes?" Her voice broke. She could feel her knees trembling under her skirt. In another second, she'd pee her pants.

"What do you think about labor unions?"

"Unions?"

"That's what I said."

"I love them. I think we need one at the *Times*."

"Really? So, you're sympathetic to labor's cause?"

"Absolutely. Hell, I'd belong myself if we had a union."

His hand slipped away. "Good night, Miss Vostok. Mr. Smith will give you a ride back to Times Square."

"No need. I can hop the subway."

Cardolani fixed his brown eyes on hers. "We insist, Miss Vostok. It's too dangerous for an attractive young woman to walk the streets at night. Too many things can happen to her."

She felt a cold draft on her face. Mr. Smith had pulled open the curtain and was standing over their table.

"Car's ready, Miss Vostok."

She sighed and walked out of the restaurant, followed by her escort. When they reached the purring limo, Smith's chauffeur opened the passenger door.

"Really, Mr. Smith, I can take the subway."

"We prefer it this way." Smith nudged her into the back seat and sat beside her. She felt her heart pounding as the chauffeur closed the door.

Smith pulled out a cigaret and lit it. "Did you and the Mayor have a good conversation?"

"I think it went well."

"Good." He took a deep drag and blew the smoke out the cracked window. "I've worked with Mayor La Guardia since last year. Mr. Cardolani and I are very close friends. You might say we came up together. I'm sure you know how hard it is to reach the top."

She felt a sudden chill. The chauffeur had taken his place behind the wheel, but the limo wasn't moving.

"Sometimes we have to bend a little to reach our goal. Know what I mean?" Smith leaned forward just enough to reveal a black thirty-eight revolver inside his coat.

"Miss Vostok?"

"Yes?"

"Please answer my question."

"Oh—about bending a little? Hell—that's what I'm trying to do. You know—survive like everyone else."

"One more question."

"Sure."

"Are you holding back on us?"

"Holding back?"

"Waiting to spring something on us."

She gulped and looked him in the eye. "You think I'm

crazy?"

"I don't know. Are you?"

Her eyes widened as he reached into his coat and grasped the concealed revolver. No time for well-chosen words. Just blurt out your best shot.

"Consider this, Mr. Smith. If I'm good enough to get this far, won't I serve you better as a living asset than a dead liability?"

He leaned back in the seat and dragged his empty hand out of his coat. "Joe?"

"Yeah, boss?" The burly chauffeur glanced over his shoulder.

"Take us to Times Square. I've changed my mind. The East River's too cold this time of year."

The limo pulled out of the alley while Karen stared blankly at Joe's thick neck. Quite a day, Miss Vostok. And it wasn't over.

She breathed a sigh of relief when the limo pulled up to the Times Building and Joe stepped out to open her door.

"This is where you get off, Miss Vostok." Smith nodded at the open door.

She smiled nervously and crawled out of the back seat. Before Joe shut the door, she peeked inside at Smith who was lighting a cigaret. "Then, I'll hear from you?"

"Goodnight, Miss Vostok." He took a puff and turned away while the door slammed shut.

She watched the black limo speed away from the curb into the sea of red lights on Seventh and Broadway. Above her, the *Time's* marquee flashed with news of the latest dust storm in Oklahoma.

She was dead-tired, but it would only take a few minutes to brief Gerramino on her meeting with the mayor. She wouldn't mention Cardolani. Just tell him the mayor wanted to clear the air about the unfortunate incident this morning. No sense blurting out anything about future exclusives since nothing had been promised. Besides, Cardolani might have second thoughts and she might end up in the East River.

She pushed through the glass doors and strolled past Andy,

the security guard.

"Anything wrong, Miss Vostok?"

"No, Andy. Is Mr. Gerramino still here?"

Andy chuckled. "You know he never leaves before eleven. He's usually walking out when you're coming in to work the presses." He leaned over the desk and eyed her dressy clothes. "Hey—no presses tonight?"

"Good question." She shuddered and walked to the elevators. She pressed "Two" and backed away while the door on her left slid open.

At first, they just blinked at each other in disbelief. Gerramino pushed the handsome young man out of the elevator and stepped beside him. "I take it you know each other."

The young man removed his low-brimmed hat and stared at her. "Is it really you?"

She stepped back and nodded.

Gerramino scratched his head. "What are you doing here, Miss Vostok?"

"What? Oh—sorry. I wanted to brief you on my meeting with the Mayor."

"Hell, that can wait until tomorrow. Mr. Halberton and I were just going out for a nightcap. Care to join us?"

She reached out and grasped Jim's arm. "I can't believe it's you."

"I just got in from London."

"London?"

"I'm with *Reuters*."

"*Reuters*?"

"Come on, we can talk over drinks." Gerramino seized their arms and led them across the lobby toward the swinging doors.

Gerramino hailed a taxi and ushered them into it. They were nearly to Fifty-second Street when he broke the question. "So, how do you know each other?"

Jim smiled at her. "We met when I was at Yale. Haven't seen each other in—how long has it been?"

She smiled and leaned against him while Gerramino quickly put two and two together.

The Tenth Avatar

"Hell—it's none of my business. You know, I just promoted Miss Vostok to reporter. She's been with us for three years. Best damned photographer I ever saw. Glad we got her." Gerramino reached across Jim and patted her on the knee while she looked at him in shock.

In that brief moment, Karen Vostok knew her life was about to change. Whatever fate had taken over, she could feel its power pulsing through her. From the filth of a coal mining town and abuses too terrible to recall, she had climbed out of the mud to sit in a taxicab with the world's most powerful newspaper editor while the Great White Way lit up the night with a magnificent brilliance.

They hopped out of the taxi and followed Gerramino into the *Onyx Club*. The popular nightclub was packed, but Gerramino had no problem getting them a comfortable table overlooking the dance floor and bandstand. After ordering drinks, he stunned them by standing up and excusing himself.

"What's wrong?" Karen looked up at him in surprise.

"Nothing. Just remembered I have an early morning meeting. Jim, I hope you'll forgive me."

Jim stood up and shook his hand. "No problem. I'll see you tomorrow at two."

"You got it. We'll eat in my office. I'd like to wrap this up before you head back." Gerramino patted Karen's shoulder. "Don't keep my friend up too late. We've got some important business to do. Have a good evening, folks." He gave them a mock salute and faded into the darkened nightclub. On the bandstand, a Harlem jazz group had broken into some serious rhythm and blues.

"Interesting man."

She smiled and looked down at her drink while fumbling for something to say.

Jim pushed his drink away and leaned across the table. "It's good to see you."

She raised her head until their eyes met. "When I saw you in that elevator, I thought I'd lost it. I'm still shaking."

He slipped his hand into hers. "You look tired."

"I'll be all right."

"Sure?"

Gary Naiman

She squeezed his hand and smiled.

"Then, come on. You always were my favorite partner." He nodded toward the couples flooding the polished blue floor.

They stepped between the darkened tables and mingled with young lovers swaying to the sad melody of a woman who has lost her man. He took her in his arms and felt her warm body relax against him as the music carried them away.

"Sounds like you're doing well?"

She smiled and looked up at him. "I'm getting by."

"Any boyfriends?"

"Oh yeah. Lots."

"I'm not surprised. With your looks, they're probably lined up at your door."

"The only males at my door are hungry cats. I haven't been out in three years."

He gave her a skeptical look. "Sure those aren't two-legged cats?"

The band broke into a swing medley as the *Onyx Club* came to life. He stepped back and grasped her waist. "How about it, Miss Vostok? Want to have some fun?"

Her eyes brightened.

"Well, are you up to it?"

"I can try."

With the walls echoing with jazz, she pirouetted under his raised arm and spun away. Snapping back on her heels, she clung to his extended hands while doing a "sugar push" with a set of hips that had the boys on the sidelines drooling on their ties.

She was exhausted, but the rhythmic beat was overpowering. After three years of bitter memories, it was time to relive those magnificent nights when they danced until the sun came up. And made love. And dreamed. Yes—it was time to smile again. To dance again. And could they dance.

The other couples gave way as the two whirling dervishes tore up the floor with steps that made the stunned onlookers gasp for breath. One fool tried to cut in and caught a mouthful of Karen's streaming black hair as she whirled by. He took the hint and retreated into the clapping crowd.

With drums pounding, they danced their hearts out until she spun into his waiting arms amidst an explosion of cheers and whistles. Exhausted, the two exhibitionists staggered off the floor while the band leader nodded his approval and changed the tempo to a slow one.

But that was just the beginning. They left the *Onyx Club* in time to catch Cab Callaway's midnight show at the *Cotton Club* on Broadway and Forty-eighth. From there, they moved on to the *Versaille* on Fiftieth where they danced under the rotating crystal globe like two teenagers in a marathon.

With the depression raging, clubs like the *Onyx, Kit Kat, Versailles*, and *Famous Door* had become sanctuaries from the pain sweeping the nation. And it wasn't only the elite that flocked to these fortresses of happiness. For many, this was a final chance to spend a night in paradise before the shadows of despair closed over them like those dust clouds in Oklahoma. Eat, drink, and be merry because tomorrow you might be lying in an alley with your starving brothers and sisters. There was no hope—so live each moment like it was the last.

At three in the morning, Jim pushed away from her and scanned the *Versaille's* dimly lit dance floor. Many had left, but a few hearty souls still swayed to the soft, melodic sounds of a muted trumpet and rustling drum.

"Karen?"

"Hmmm?"

"I think you fell asleep on the last one. Come on, I'll take you home."

"No, I'm fine." She pressed her head against his chest and continued to sway in his arms.

"Let's sit down for a minute."

"Just hold me and feel the music."

He kissed her softly on the forehead. "There's something I need to ask you."

"Ask?"

He sighed and held her close. "I'll be back in a month. Can I see you again?"

She looked up at him with tired eyes. "How's your dad?"

"What?"

"Your dad, how is he?" She felt him tense in her arms.

"We haven't talked in three years."

"You were right, we better sit down." She grabbed his arm and led him back to the table.

She took a deep breath and looked him in the eye. "What happened?"

"It's not important."

"It is to me."

Jim reached for his scotch and gulped it down. "I had it out with him the day after you left. I don't know what he told you in that study, but it turned you to ice."

She grasped his hand. "For God's sake, Jim. He's your father. He loves you. God—you don't know how lucky you are."

"Lucky?" He pulled away from her. "He thinks I'm crazy for wanting to be a foreign correspondent. Had it all planned for me at *The Herald*. Right up the ladder to assistant editor. Eventually, the top job. Well, I'm not like Gerramino, Hessler, or any of those power-mad Napoleons. I belong in the field with the wind on my face, not sitting behind a desk firing people while my stomach churns with ulcers."

"Jim, please."

"It took some time, but I finally figured it out. He's afraid his son might make a name for himself and steal his glory. Until he understands that, we have nothing to say to each other."

She clutched his sleeve. "That's not true. Have you ever looked at those photos in his study. He risked his life for every one of them. Don't you see? He's afraid for you. Don't blame a father for loving his son."

"How can you defend him? What did he ever do for you?"

She leaned back and recalled Gerramino's prophetic words. He owed nothing to Edmund Halberton. And neither did she. Karen Vostok had earned her day in the sun, and no dirty photograph would ruin it.

"Listen to me, Karen. We've gone our separate ways since that night. We can go on like that forever—if that's what you want. I didn't plan on this happening, but I'm glad it did.

Whatever you want is fine with me, but you're gonna listen this one time. I love you, Karen. I'll always love you. Nothing will change that."

She looked into his eyes and felt a tear trickle down her cheek. His face was strained, but that boyish look was still there. She looked down and brushed away the tear. "You're right about it being late. We should be on our way."

"If that's what you want."

He was about to get up when she reached out and kissed him passionately on the lips. "You can see me anytime, Mr. Halberton. But we still have tonight."

"What?"

She rested her hand on his leg. "Quit feeling sorry for yourself and take me to bed."

"Karen, I—"

"Please don't say anything. Just kiss me."

They took a cab to the Astor Hotel and went up to his room. It felt so good making love in the soft darkness, their warm bodies intertwined while crying out words of passion only lovers can know. Dawn was breaking over New York when they finally collapsed in each other's arms. They would sleep until noon.

That afternoon, Jim accepted Gerramino's offer to join the *New York Time's* European bureau, much to the chagrin of Franz Hessler, *Reuter's* chief editor. Though friends, Hessler and Gerramino were bitter rivals when it came to international news circulation. Stealing Hessler's best foreign correspondent would turn their rivalry into a blood feud.

As for Karen, Gerramino chewed her out for being late to work, then patted her on the back while explaining La Guardia had called to offer her exclusive coverage of imminent arrests involving embezzlers in New York's garbage collection department.

As the months passed, Karen Vostok become famous for her uncanny breaking news stories, each one timed to make it impossible for the competition to cut in. Bitter reporters speculated she'd made a Faustian pact with the mayor. With the *Time's* circulation soaring through her vivid accounts of La

Guardia's relentless war on corruption, terrifying headlines began creeping onto the revered newspaper's front page....

Hindenburg Dead! Chancellor Hitler to Succeed Him

Spanish Government Struggles Through Another Recall Election

Violence and Death in Northern Spain!

They all carried the same byline....

**From the New York Time's European Desk ....
J. J. Halberton**

With their success growing, Karen saw Jim whenever possible, often for only a few hours. Occasionally, he managed a free weekend for an escape to the Berkshires, and some light hiking and heavy lovemaking. Life was good. Nothing mattered but their passion for work—and each other.

If there was any sadness in that wonderful time, it came on New Years Day in 1935 when Karen noticed an obscure "obit" about an *ex-Time's* reporter named Stanley Jacobs who had hung himself while his starving family slept in a dilapidated rooming house on Bowery Street. It seems Mr. Jacobs had been fired from the *Times* nine months earlier for alleged incompetence. The *Time's* chief editor, Frank Gerramino, had no comment except a sad regret.

Power can be intoxicating. We easily forget our friends. The day after her promotion, Karen heard Stan had resigned during a heated argument with Gerramino. She knew better, but never lifted a finger to help him. Too risky to stick her neck out when things were going so well. She would put in a good word for him when the time was right—but that time never came.

The gods were satisfied. They had found their third warrior....

20 | The Wager

"Man down!"

Aloka spun around and saw Dorje and Jawa hunched over their comrade beside the stream. "What's wrong with him?"

"He's burning up!"

"Damn." Aloka ran across the pale grass and knelt beside the unconscious porter. He felt the man's flushed face and looked at Dorje. "Just a touch of fever. He'll be all right."

"Are you mad? If we don't get him back to Dharan, he'll be dead in a few days."

Aloka shook his head. "We can't stop now. I've given my word."

"The hell with your word. Tell the English we have no choice."

Aloka glared at his brother with seething brown eyes. "Easy for you to say. You don't have to feel his whip."

"You're the lead guide. It's your responsibility. Now get on with it." Dorje nodded toward the khaki-uniformed man peering down at them from the rocks.

Lieutenant Caruthers slipped off his cap and smoothed back his glistening blond hair while watching his guide trudge toward him. "What's wrong, old chap? Another one of your men sick?"

Aloka stopped in front of the Englishman and forced a weak smile through his dirt-smeared face.

"Well?"

Aloka forced out the words. "I'm afraid we must turn back."

"Turn back?" Caruthers let out a nervous laugh and slapped his swagger stick against his leg. "Not funny, old chap. I'm in no mood for jokes today."

"I'm not joking, *sahib*. We can't go on."

Caruthers pressed the swagger stick against Aloka's bare arm. "Are you daft? We're only eight days from the mountain. No bloody way are we turning back."

Aloka stepped back from the menacing stick. "It's malaria, *sahib*. Kami's the fourth one down since we left Dharan. We should have worn nets and long pants when we crossed the Terai."

"Nonsense. You're acting like an old woman."

"I'm sorry, *sahib*."

"Blast, two porters should be enough. Come on, we're wasting time."

Aloka shook his head. "They won't go on."

"What?"

"I'm sorry, *sahib*. They won't go on—and neither should we."

Caruthers flung his swagger stick against the rocks. "Listen to me, you disgusting little toad!"

"What is it, Lieutenant?" A second man in military khakis and sergeant stripes stepped around a boulder and pulled up his pants.

"It seems our brave guide has caught something."

"Malaria?"

"No, just a bad case of cowardice."

Aloka flung his pack on the ground. "I am not a coward, *sahib*! I can't help it if they're scared."

"Then, we'll go up without them."

"That would be suicide, *sahib*. Kangchenjunga is more than a mountain. We won't have a chance without skilled porters. I am sorry, *sahib*. I will go no further."

"You'll what?" Caruthers made a threatening move toward the Indian, but his sergeant restrained him. "Damn you, Akola."

"Aloka, *sahib*."

"Listen to me, you stupid wog. If we don't reach the bloody north ridge in two weeks, I'll be out three months pay. I bet the whole bloody officer's club you'd take my picture up there, and you're not going to mess it up."

"But, *sahib*. They—"

"This is your fault, dammit! Now pick up your bloody pack and lead the way. I want to be in Chirawa by tomorrow morning." Caruthers snatched his swagger stick off the ground and slapped it against his leg.

Aloka lowered his head and walked to the stream where the porters were tending their ailing comrade. He knelt beside his brother. "The fools want to go on without you."

Dorje glanced at the two Englishmen and shrugged his shoulders. "Then, give them back their *rupees* and return with us to Dharan. Look at the good side. In a few days, we'll be rid of them. The mountain will see to it."

Aloka glared at his brother. "Has the malaria affected you too? If anything happens to the *angrezi*, their comrades will whip the skin off our backs. I've had enough of their beatings to last a lifetime."

Dorje reached into his pack and pulled out a small canvas purse. "Give these *rupees* back to the *angrezi*. Our lives are worth more than their filthy money." He slapped the canvas purse into his brother's hand and walked away.

Aloka gripped the purse and watched his brother and Jawa prepare a makeshift stretcher for their feverish comrade. "You're going to leave me with these madmen?"

Dorje looked up at his brother. "Not if you're smart and return with us."

"Damn you, Dorje. What kind of brother are you?"

"A wise one."

Aloka clenched his fists and let out a final tirade. "I warn you, this will not be forgotten. When you look up after stuffing your face with rice in Dharan, something wet will strike your forehead. It will be me pissing in your eye from the top of the north face!" Aloka snatched Kami's pack off the ground and headed toward the waiting Englishmen.

"Fool!" Dorje grabbed his half of the stretcher.

With Aloka glaring at them, the two porters lifted their ailing comrade and began a trek across the Tamur Valley toward Dhoban, Hille, and the Siwalik foothills leading to Dharan.

The following afternoon, Aloka and the two Englishmen reached Chirawa, a small village nestled beneath a cirque of fifty foot boulders.

Gary Naiman

Aloka hadn't slept the night before. At one point, he'd considered abandoning the two Englishmen under cover of darkness, but quickly reconsidered when Sergeant Forsham gave him the evil eye. No way were they going to let him out of their sight.

Moving on from Chirawa, they proceeded north toward the line of white citadels rising into the clouds.

"Which one's Kangchenjunga?" Caruthers jabbed his swagger stick under his armpit and lifted a pair of black binoculars to his eyes.

"The summits to your left are Makalu and Everest, *sahib*. Kangchenjunga is to the right."

Caruthers shook his head. "Blast, I see three summits to the right. Which one's the big K?"

"Kangchenjunga has five summits, *sahib*. You can't see the other two from here. Each one protects the gods' treasures. There is gold peak, silver peak, grain, gems, and books."

"What kind of gibberish is that? I didn't ask for a history lesson. Just tell me which one we're going to climb."

"None of them, *sahib*."

Caruthers jammed the binoculars into their leather case. "You still don't understand, do you, Akola?"

"Aloka, *sahib*."

"Now listen very closely because I won't explain again. You don't have a choice! Gold, silver, grain, whatever! We're climbing that bloody mountain whether you like it or not!"

"Please listen, *sahib*. Your friends played an evil trick on you when they made that wager."

"Trick?"

"Kangchenjunga has never been climbed, *sahib*. It rises twenty-eight thousand feet into the clouds. Many experienced mountaineers have perished on its slopes. It's an angry mountain, *sahib*. It dislikes being violated."

Caruthers broke into hysterical laughter. "You expect me to believe that rot? You talk like it's some kind of god instead of a pile of rocks."

"I'm sorry, *sahib*. Your fellow officers tricked you. They do that to all the new officers assigned to Dharan. Ask your sergeant if you don't believe me."

"Shut up, you imbecile! That's quite enough!" Caruthers flicked his swagger stick in front of Aloka's nose.

"I'm trying to help you, *sahib*. Come to your senses and turn back. We're entering sacred ground. You must not go further. If you—"

Aloka's words were cut off by the stinging crack of Caruther's swagger stick across his cheek. "I said that's enough! Now lead the way!"

Aloka rubbed his burning cheek and put on his pack. No further words were spoken as they proceeded around a stone wall containing strange cryptic engravings.

For two days, they hiked past stone *mani* walls and sacred rock piles called *chortens*, moving ever closer to the great white monster looming above them on the northeast horizon.

Passing through Ghunsa, they encountered stonewalled houses surrounded by tattered prayer flags flapping spiritual wishes in the valley's brisk winds. With frightened villagers staring at them from the security of their houses, Caruthers posed for a photo beneath a weatherbeaten Buddhist monastery that appeared deserted.

Moving on, they pitched camp in a lush meadow where Caruthers posed for photos beside a waterfall while Aloka prepared a bubbling stew of curried barley and vegetables.

Sergeant Forsham had become noticeably quiet since losing the porters. Any questions directed at him were answered with clipped one-word responses. But there was more to his silence than met the eye. Now it was Forsham who looked away when Aloka stared at him across the campfire, and they both knew why.

Forsham was Aloka's last hope. If Aloka could unnerve the sergeant enough to force a confession, the threesome might still have time to turn back before the deadly confrontation with the gods.

The next two days were spent walking across grass-covered moraine while frightened women and children gawked at the two fair-skinned English soldiers.

"Who are they, Akola? They don't look like the beggars we

saw in Ghunsa and Chirawa?"

"They're Tibetan, *sahib*. They're waiting for their husbands to return from trading in Sikkim."

"Maybe I can ease their loneliness." Caruthers smiled at one of the robust women."

"That would be unwise, Lieutenant."

The sergeant's firm voice stunned Caruthers. He looked at him in surprise. "Aren't you a bit out of place, Sergeant?"

"I'm sorry, Lieutenant, but with a bloody war brewing in Asia, we don't need to create an international incident by violating some Tibetan princess."

"I was joking, Sergeant. Loosen up, man."

"I'm sorry, Lieutenant."

"I was beginning to think you'd lost your voice."

"Just tired, Lieutenant."

Caruther's anger faded. "Tell me, Sergeant. How long have you been stationed out here?"

"Two years."

"Ever long for a woman?"

"What do you think?"

"I take that to mean 'yes'. Well—you're not the only one, so don't be so bloody critical."

"Yes, Lieutenant."

Caruthers nodded and patted Forsham's shoulder. "Two years, eh? Well—stick with me and I'll take you out of this hellhole when I get promoted. I could use a man like you. A man who speaks his mind, but knows when to stop."

"Yes, Lieutenant."

"Come on, let's get this bloody hike over with."

An hour later, Aloka pointed toward an enormous white wall barely visible through the haze. "The Kangchenjunga Glacier, *sahib*. From here, we turn east and follow the glacier twelve miles to the base of the mountain."

"Are you telling me that bloody thing is twelve miles long?"

"Yes, *sahib*."

Caruthers pushed up the brim of his cap and rubbed his forehead. "What the hell's wrong with me? I feel dizzy."

Aloka forced back a sneer. "It's the altitude, *sahib*. We've been moving steadily upward since we left the Tamur Valley."

Caruthers sat on a rock and stroked his aching forehead. "How high are we?"

"Almost seventeen thousand."

"Impossible, we haven't even reached the mountain."

"The altitude is deceptive, *sahib*. Even the valleys are high. When we reach Pangpema, we'll only be eleven thousand feet from the top of Kangchenjunga."

"Hell—that's two miles."

Aloka restrained his anger. "Look at the good side, *sahib*. We've already climbed three miles. Think of it. Only two miles to go. A brave man like you should have no trouble becoming the first man to reach Kangchenjunga's summit. Just a few killer avalanches and blizzards stand between you and a winning bet." Aloka smirked at the lieutenant and pointed to a clearing. "We'll camp here tonight. You must rest for tomorrow's trek."

Caruthers rubbed the back of his neck and stared at the flickering fire.

"Feeling better, Lieutenant?"

"My head feels like a balloon."

"This should help." Forsham extended a warm cup of tea to his commanding officer.

"My bloody watch stopped. What time is it?"

"Almost one."

"Where's the wog?"

"Asleep in his tent."

Caruthers gulped down the warm tea and staggered to his feet. "That's quite a view."

"That it is, Lieutenant." Forsham eased beside Caruthers and studied the moonlit peaks in the eastern sky. "We're north of the mountain."

"North? We've passed it?"

"Not exactly. We're circling to the north ridge. That's the best side for a climb."

The Lieutenant took a slow breath. "Walk with me,

Sergeant."

Forsham nodded and followed Caruthers away from their encampment. When they were out of Aloka's earshot, Caruthers stopped and turned to face his sergeant. He scratched his stubbled chin and spoke softly. "What do you know about all this?"

"Lieutenant?"

"About the bet. Are they really putting me on?"

Forsham frowned beneath his black eyebrows.

"Go on, Sergeant. Spit it out."

"In my two years at Dharan, you're the third new officer they've pulled it on. Rather cruel if you ask me?"

Caruther's face reddened. "Why didn't you tell me, dammit?"

"I'm sorry, Lieutenant. It's not my place to get involved in officer's matters. There's no way a sergeant can win that battle. Frankly, I didn't think you'd fall for it. You seemed smarter than the others."

Caruthers glared at the sergeant. "Did you take the other officers to the mountain?"

"Yes."

"How far did they go?"

"They gave up when we reached Pangpema. That's when Aloka spilled the beans."

"He's in on it?"

Forsham forced a weak smile. "He's just a scared wog afraid of losing his soul. Don't be too hard on him, Lieutenant. His kind always gets the short end."

Caruthers shook his head in anger. "Blast, Sergeant. You must really enjoy making me look like a blooming idiot."

"May I speak freely, Lieutenant?"

"Go on."

"I despise it."

"You what?"

"I hate coming here. I did some climbing before joining up. Even had friends in the 1930 expedition that tried to assault that devil."

"Kangchenjunga?"

Forsham nodded. "They were nearly wiped out by an avalanche on the north face. One of them told me the whole bloody ice wall collapsed on them. Think of it, Lieutenant. One thousand feet of ice breaking off a mountain while you're standing helpless at twenty thousand."

Caruthers ignored him and sat on a rock. He pulled out a cigaret and lit it while gazing at the shimmering peaks.

"Excuse me, Lieutenant. This isn't a good place. The men in the 1930 expedition were luckier than your two predecessors."

"The two officers?"

"Carrier and Smith."

Caruthers shrugged. "They were killed on maneuvers outside Dharan."

"Yes—and each one died shortly after returning from their trek to Kangchenjunga. Major Camp wrote it off to malfunctioning explosives, but Aloka has another explanation."

Caruthers gestured for Forsham to sit beside him. "Go on."

"The Hindus and Tibetans worship Kangchenjunga as a sort of guardian spirit. They believe it's the home of a fierce, protecting god. Remember the statue we saw in Ghunsa?"

"The ugly red chap on the white horse?"

"That's him—and it was a lion. Aloka's ready to bust a gut because he thinks we'll be punished for violating the mountain's sacred ground—like the others."

Caruthers frowned and puffed his cigaret. "You don't believe that poppycock?"

"If I did, I wouldn't be here." Forsham pulled out a cigaret and lit it. "As a matter of fact, I'm about to win you a goodly sum of money."

Caruthers leaned back and eyed Forsham. "Not funny, Sergeant. From the sound of things, I'm about to lose three month's pay and a lot of respect."

"Not necessarily." Forsham puffed his cigaret. "Were you serious about taking me out with you?"

Caruthers nodded. "Before you let me down."

"What if I make it up with interest?"

"What do you mean?"

Forsham leaned back against the rocks. "It goes like this. When the officers demanded that I accompany you on the trek, I held out until the fools promised me a one-tenth share. I insisted it was only fair since I was doing all the dirty work."

Caruthers flicked his swagger stick at the ground. "Get to it, Sergeant."

"I wrote down the bet and made the fools sign it. It's in my pack."

"So?"

"Excuse me, Lieutenant. You officers are really dense."

"What?" Caruthers stiffened.

"The blokes signed a paper saying all you have to do is climb Kangchenjunga. Don't you get it?"

Caruthers stood up and straightened his jacket. "What the hell are you trying to say?"

"All you need to do is *climb* Kangchenjunga. You know—put your feet on it and take a few strides up the rocks. With Aloka as your witness, and a photograph of you standing a hundred feet up the north face, you'll pull out the paper and show it to the bloody idiots while they fork out three week's pay times five officers. Quite a haul if you ask me."

Caruthers scratched his head in astonishment. "Are you telling me they signed something that says I win without climbing the mountain?"

"Exactly."

Caruther's eyes brightened. "Let me see the paper."

"When we get back to camp. I'd better let Aloka in on it before he splits a gut." Forsham stood up and flicked away his cigaret.

"Wait a minute, Sergeant." Caruthers rubbed his chin with the back of his hand. "What about your one-tenth share? You expect me to believe you gave it up? That's a lot of money out here."

Forsham broke into a grin. "Before we left, I bet a dozen regulars a month's pay you'd win. The fools bought it. I guess they're all stupid in Dharan."

Caruthers burst into laughter and slapped the sergeant's boot. "I knew I was right about you. We'll stick together from now on."

"Just get me out of Dharan, Lieutenant. Come on, we'd better get some sleep."

"One thing. Sergeant."

"Yes?"

"Don't tell Akola about this. I don't trust him. Let the wog suffer."

The next day, they reached a sprawling yellow grassland at the edge of the great glacier. Aloka shaded his eyes and scanned the glacier. "We're only a few hours from Pangpema, *sahib*. We'll camp there tonight and approach the mountain tomorrow."

"Get on with it then." Caruthers gestured toward the mountain with his swagger stick.

"Hold it." Sergeant Forsham dropped his cigaret and pulled out his binoculars.

"What is it?"

"Someone's coming toward us from that tall grass."

Caruthers stepped back and unbuttoned his holster. "Is he alone?"

"Looks like it." Forsham focused his binoculars on the lone figure wading through the grass.

Aloka shaded his eyes and studied the approaching stranger. "He appears to be a *dhami* or *yatri, sahib*."

"A what?"

"A shaman or pilgrim."

"How can you tell?"

"He wears a *chuba* and walks with a shepherd's staff. His hair is very long and covers his shoulders."

The stranger was within a few paces of them when he stopped and trained his black eyes on Aloka. He placed his staff on the ground and pressed his finger tips together. "*Namaste*"

Aloka placed his palms together and nodded. "*Namaste, muzzafer*. Do you speak Hindustani?"

The stranger smiled. "I speak many languages."

"Good—then we'll speak Hindustani so my two friends

Gary Naiman

won't understand."

"As you wish." The stranger glanced at the two Englishmen.

"Are you a pilgrim journeying to the great mountain?"

"Great mountain?"

"There—above the haze." Aloka gestured toward Kangchenjunga.

The stranger cupped his hand over his eyes and stared at the white peaks. "Tell me, friend. Is that the last mountain?"

Aloka forced a smile while trying to understand the stranger's question. "Yes—before entering Sikkim. Then, there are others."

The stranger glanced at the two English soldiers. "You come from Dharan?"

"Ah—then you know the area?"

"I've heard Dharan is an *angrezi* training camp."

"Yes—for our Gurkha brothers who serve the English."

"Brothers serving *angrezi*?"

Aloka shuddered. "From your dress, you appear a holy man."

"I'm searching for someone."

"I see."

The stranger shook his head. "I have come many miles to find this place."

"Will you pray on Kangchenjunga?"

The pilgrim picked up his staff and leaned against it while studying the white giant filling the eastern horizon, "Is that the mountain's name?"

"Yes. The ancient texts say it was given its name by Lha-Tsan Ch'enbo, a *lama* who brought the living Buddha to Sikkim."

"It's a beautiful mountain, but I feel great anger spilling from its peak."

Aloka nodded. "It's the home of a warrior spirit that guards the surrounding valleys."

"Have you seen him?"

"No, but the villagers have. He wears a red cloak and silver armor. The villagers worship him for good harvests and flowing water."

The stranger glared at Caruthers and Forsham. "Does this warrior spirit protect the villagers from the *angrezi*?"

Aloka frowned. "They forced me to bring them here. I wish they were dead."

Caruthers brushed past Aloka and extended his hand to the stranger. "Allow me to introduce myself. Lieutenant John Caruthers of His Royal Majesty's Dharan Regiment. My sergeant and I are trekking to Kangchenjunga on a reconnaissance."

The stranger nodded.

"Tell me, sir. Do you speak English?"

"I understand your words."

"He is on a pilgrimage to Kangchenjunga, *sahib*."

"Shut up, Akola. I've already surmised that." Caruthers smiled at the stranger and gestured toward the mountain. "Perhaps you'd like to camp with us tonight. Then we can go to the mountain together."

The stranger ignored the lieutenant and focused his black eyes on Gold Peak. "Yes—I can feel you. After so many mountains—I've found you."

"What? I'm sorry, I don't understand that language." Caruthers stared impatiently at the stranger.

The stranger smiled and looked at Caruthers. "I'm sorry, Lieutenant. Your offer is very kind. I would be honored to share your camp."

They reached Pangpema at sunset. After finishing a dinner of curried rice and vegetables, Caruthers waited for Aloka and Forsham to retire before sitting down beside the stranger.

"Nothing like a good warm fire on a cold night." Caruthers stretched his hands toward the crackling flames.

The stranger smiled and stared at the fire.

"Care for a cigaret?"

"No, thank you."

"I say, old chap. Is that a knife in your sash?"

"It is. One has to eat along the road."

"You mean—wild animals?"

"And other things."

Caruthers frowned. "Well—it's none of my business, but it seems a bit unusual for a pilgrim to carry a knife and eat meat."

"I am not a pilgrim."

"But Akola said—"

"Your guide is imagining things."

"I'll be damned." Caruthers glanced at the two tents where Aloka and Forsham were snoring. He leaned toward the stranger and whispered, "I don't trust either of those blokes. The sergeant would sell his mother to get out of Dharan, and Akola will do anything to prevent me from stepping on his precious mountain."

The stranger looked up in surprise. "You're going to climb the mountain?"

"You might say that. The plan is to crawl a hundred feet up the northwest face and take a photograph. Not very exciting if you ask me."

"But the mountain is sacred?" The stranger's eyes danced with anger.

"Now see here, friend. I've been pretty lenient until now because I thought we could work something out. But if that's your attitude—"

"What do you mean, 'work something out'?"

Caruthers grabbed a stick and poked the campfire's glowing embers. "Frankly, I'd like to climb a bit higher, but I need someone who's skilled."

The stranger shook his head. "May I ask you a question, Lieutenant?"

"Go ahead."

"Why do you wish to give up your life to a mountain of ice?"

Caruthers jabbed the coals. "I don't. That's why I need someone with the skill and courage to guide me up there."

"How high would you like to go?"

Caruthers glared at him with ice-blue eyes. "I'm better than those fools in Dharan. I want to climb that damn mountain and pose for a picture on the summit. It would make history."

"I see."

The Tenth Avatar

Caruthers grabbed the stranger's ragged sleeve. "You're laughing at me, aren't you? Listen to me, you fool. Someday, I'll lead a great army while those slobs rot in Dharan with that decrepit excuse for a sergeant."

The stranger snared Caruther's wrist and pulled his hand away.

"Say, you're pretty strong for a beggar."

"You were tearing my sleeve. These are my only clothes."

Caruthers let out a nervous laugh. "So tell me, how many mountains have you climbed?"

The stranger ignored him and sniffed the air. "The wind blows from the mountain."

Caruther's patience had run out. "Listen to me, you beggar. I'm an officer in the King's army and you're nothing but a mystic in rags. Now answer my question, dammit!"

The stranger smiled at Caruthers. "In my travels east, I've been *sirdar* to several expeditions up the great mountains. I'm well schooled in the climbing arts."

Caruthers nodded and lit another cigaret. "Excellent. Tomorrow you'll take me up Kangchenjunga."

The stranger glared at Caruthers. "I warn you, Lieutenant. Wake your two friends and leave this place now."

Caruthers flung his cigaret at the fire. "How dare you threaten me! I have a good mind to whip the daylights out of you! You're taking me up that mountain whether you like it or not!"

The stranger's eyes softened. "As you wish, *sahib*." He bowed his head.

Caruthers stood up and slapped his swagger stick against his leg. "That's better. In the morning then." He turned and headed for his tent.

The morning sun was still behind the eastern peaks when Caruthers felt someone nudge his foot.

"Come, *sahib*, we should leave before the sun rises." The stranger stared at him through the parted tent flap.

Caruthers sat up and rubbed his eyes. "Are the others awake?"

"No, *sahib*. I thought you didn't trust them. If we leave now, we can avoid them."

Caruthers brushed back his blond hair. "We don't need them?"

"No, *sahib*. They'll just slow us down. If we go now, we'll reach the mountain by sunset." The stranger nodded at the camera sticking out of Caruther's pack. "Excellent picture, standing on the northwest face at sunset."

Caruthers grinned. "You're right. I'll pin a note to the sergeant's tent. When do you think we'll be back?"

"Your friends should be prepared to wait several days. But you're their commanding officer? What do you care?"

Caruther's slapped his leg. "Right again. Say, old chap. Do you have a name?"

The stranger bowed his head. "I am Karak, *sahib*—at your service."

"Interesting name. Give me a few minutes to pack."

"No need, *sahib*. I've packed everything we need except your camera and personal belongings."

"Excellent, Karak—excellent."

Caruthers scribbled a note instructing Forsham and Aloka to wait for him until he returned. He pinned it to Forsham's tent and accidentally kicked the sergeant's boot when he stepped away. He held his breath and stared at the motionless boot, waiting for Forsham to barge out of the tent in a frenzy. He was relieved when nothing happened.

They'd gone a half mile when Karak stopped and muttered something.

"What is it?"

"I forgot to pack the extra rope."

"We have enough rope."

"You never have enough rope, *sahib*."

Caruthers slapped his leg with the swagger stick. "Then go back and get it, dammit. But hurry, the sun's coming up." Caruthers watched his newly appointed guide shuffle down the hill toward the camp. "And don't try anything cute or I'll have you hunted down and flogged!"

When Karak reached the camp, he stopped at Forsham's

tent and eyed the protruding boot. An ugly sneer crept across his face as he nudged the boot with his sandal. He kicked it and stepped toward Aloka's tent.

It only took a minute to drag Aloka's lifeless body into Forsham's tent. He carefully positioned the two corpses and knelt down to admire his handiwork.

Forsham's glazed eyes were frozen on Aloka's. Each man's left hand gripped the other's throat while their right hands clutched knives buried deep in the other's gut.

It had been easy to slay them while they slept. Except for a few muffled gasps, Forsham and his Indian slave died quietly while their sleeping lieutenant dreamed of grandeur.

When their intertwined bodies were discovered, it would appear the two had become embroiled in a fierce argument that turned deadly while their commanding officer was off exploring the mountain.

Karak ripped Caruther's note off the tent flap and crumpled it in his fist. He scooped up his pack and headed across the meadow.

The sun was setting on Kangchenjunga's northwest face when Karak and Lieutenant Caruthers dragged their exhausted bodies onto a narrow ledge above the glacier. Three days had passed since they'd crept out of camp and headed up the great mountain. In that time, they'd crossed a treacherous moraine of crushed rock and ice, climbing steadily upward toward the great wall. The tall grass was gone, replaced by a windswept tundra of frozen earth and boulders. Equipped with only rope and pitons, they belayed themselves to the rocks and began a merciless ascent up the forty-five degree wall leading to the mountain's north ridge.

Caruthers mopped the chilled sweat off his forehead while fighting to catch his breath in the thin air. "How far have we gone?"

Karak glanced at the wall of ice poking into the tinted clouds. "We're four thousand feet below the ridge. From there, it's another mile to the summit."

"You mean, we've only climbed a thousand feet in three

days?"

"Yes, *sahib*."

"We should be doing better than that. What kind of guide are you?"

Karak shrugged his shoulders. "What's your hurry, *sahib*? There is nothing up there but death."

Caruthers ripped open his anorak. "I can't breathe, dammit. You'll have to take my picture here. We've gone far enough."

Karak wasn't listening. His eyes had focused on the snow-covered peak flashing through the clouds.

Caruthers yanked out his camera and thrust it at Karak. "Here—take the bloody picture before it's too dark. We're going down."

Karak's eyes filled with tears as the peak faded behind the clouds.

"What the hell's wrong with you?"

"Oh, God." Karak lowered his head and sobbed.

"That's it, you damn beggar. I've had it with you!" Caruthers pulled out his revolver and jammed it against Karak's forehead. "Take the bloody picture or I'll blow your head off!"

Karak raised his head and stared at the barrel. "I'm sorry, *sahib*. The thin air has affected me."

Caruthers lowered the revolver. "Some bloody climber you turned out to be. Take the bloody picture and let's get off this bloody mountain."

"Yes, *sahib*." Karak grasped the camera and stood up. "There, *sahib*. You can stand on the ledge with the peak jutting into the sky above you. A stunning picture."

Caruthers holstered the revolver and smoothed back his blond hair. He adjusted his dark glasses and struck a pose with his red anorak flapping in the wind.

"Excellent, *sahib*. But you should look up at the peak. It will add stature to the photograph."

Caruthers nodded and turned his face toward Gold Peak. In the distance, the mountain rumbled from an avalanche. "How's this?"

"Magnificent, *sahib*. Perhaps just a bit higher."

"Enough! Take the bloody picture before I faint in this damn air." Caruthers looked higher, exposing his bare throat.

"Hold it, *sahib*. May you always remember this moment."

In one lightning motion, Karak dropped the camera and swept his knife from its sheath, slicing Caruther's throat from ear to ear. No one would ever harm his sister again.

21 | *The Portrait*

The miner grasped Roberto's torn sleeve and looked up at him with desperate, bloodshot eyes. "Bless me, Padre."

"Stay calm, friend. Try to stay calm." Roberto lifted the man's head and pressed a ladle of water against his parched lips.

"Is he swallowing any of it?"

Roberto frowned and eased the man's head down on the blanket. "I don't think he has the strength."

Dr. Montero shook his head. "Just like the rest."

"For God's sake, where's Arronategui?"

"He'll be here soon."

Roberto's face flushed. "What kind of priest is he? Doesn't he know people are dying?"

Montero grasped the wounded man's wrist and pried his hand off Roberto's bloodstained sleeve. "Never mind Arronategui. That woman in the corner is asking for a priest. She doesn't have much time."

"I can't leave this man now."

"He's dead, Roberto."

Roberto looked down at the coal miner's frozen eyes. "My God."

Montero brushed the miner's eyes closed and stared at the moaning bodies lying on the stone floor. "I can mend broken bones, but there is no cure for this. Crushed spirits. Shattered dreams. Dead loved ones. These people have nothing to live for."

Roberto's head was spinning. His stomach wrenched from the rancid smell of death. Fighting back nausea, he brushed past Montero and ran through the bodies toward the arched doors at the front of the chapel. He barged through them and collapsed on the convent's stone steps while trying to clear his whirling head.

For six months, he had comforted an unending stream of men, women, and children staggering into Guernica from the Cantabrian Mountains. All had escaped tortures more horrible than could be imagined.

Without adequate medical facilities, the Guernicans had been forced to convert the Carmelite Convent into an emergency first-aid station. Nuns became nurses. Butchers donned surgeon's gowns, performing brutal operations under the painful guidance of Ferdinand Montero, the town's only doctor. Shepherds and fishermen donated their blood in a futile effort to keep the poor creatures alive. And Roberto spent six agonizing months cradling broken bodies in his arms while praying for their ravaged souls. But where in the name of God were the priests?

He gulped the cool morning air and looked west toward the Cantabrian Mountains. For weeks, he'd listened to accounts of horror beyond those mountains that put the Inquisition to shame.

In Oviedo, anyone remotely associated with the October 1934 coal miner uprising had been dragged from their homes and imprisoned in General Yagué's dungeons where his sadistic torturers vented their wrath on them. No Asturian was safe from Yagué's brutality—all because the miners had finally rebelled against the fat industrialists that ruled them like slaves.

Instead of intervening, the Second Republic looked away while its frightened reformists rationalized the suppression as a necessary act of defense against the communists and anarchists infiltrating Spain's northern province of Asturias.

But the real infiltration had occurred within the Second Republic itself. Overrun by extreme rightist organizations like the CEDA, Spain's once-promising liberal government was forced to consider any act of defiance a threat to national security that must be put down with maximum force.

And who could blame them? With Spain besieged by violent strikes and worker revolts, and unemployment soaring to twenty percent, Prime Minister Azaña was forced to step down when the 1933 elections placed Alejandro Lerroux and his powerful Radical Party in power. The man Garcia Lorca revered as Spain's last hope for democracy was cast aside by a nation on the brink of anarchy—while its frustrated military watched, and waited.

But the change in government did no good. With suppression turning to repression, the workers became even more militant. In December 1933, new waves of anarchist-incited labor riots broke out in Rioja, Catalonia, Aragon, and Andalusia. When the Civil Guard tried to respond, they were overrun by thousands of crazed laborers who had forgotten the meaning of fear. Armed with Soviet-supplied rifles and grenades, the incensed laborers constructed makeshift barricades and shot it out with the Guard in street battles reminiscent of the French Revolution.

With the terror spreading to Barcelona, Madrid, and Roberto's precious Valencia, Spain's panicked upper classes turned to militant demagogues like José´ Calvo Sotelo, new head of the CEDA. Upon taking over the powerful rightist organization, Sotelo immediately handed over the CEDA's massive treasury to General Emilio Mola for a pledge of military protection. It was exactly the funding Mola needed to launch the most heinous plot in Spain's history.

The unrest reached the boiling point in October 1934 when Asturia's oppressed miners picked up rifles and marched against their masters. With street fighting breaking out in the cities, and cries of communist revolution filling the air, Madrid's teetering government could no longer stand idly by. Yagué's army was ordered to Asturia to crush the uprising. On that tragic day, Spain died.

"What are you doing here?"

Roberto looked up in shock at the scowling face of Padre Arronategui. The priest was leading a half-dozen clerics carrying medical packs.

"Well, are you deaf?"

Roberto forced a tired smile. "I was waiting for you."

"Get out of my way."

Roberto stood up as Arronategui brushed past him, followed by the mumbling clerics. "I'm glad you came, Padre. There are so many calling for you."

Arronategui glared at him. "I never want to see your face again." He yanked open the convent doors and went inside with the others.

Roberto clenched his trembling fists and fought the anger churning inside him. He looked out at Guernica's steeples and smoke stacks silhouetted against the brightening eastern sky. He could barely keep his eyes open. He staggered down the steps and headed across the lawn toward the convent's iron gate. The town was only a short distance down the hill.

Strange combination, a convent and munitions factory only a few hundred yards apart. Roberto stopped in front of the *Astra-Unceta* Works and looked up at the smoke drifting from its red brick stack. Inside, young Markel Uranga and his brother Nikola were working around the clock with a dozen other men—packing bullets to kill people.

The adjoining militia barracks looked deserted. The fools were probably in Bilboa picking up more smuggled arms for their arsenal. Before long, they would start shooting at the Civil Guardsmen massed on the border, and all hell would break loose.

Roberto rubbed his tired eyes and sat down against the barracks' wall. From here, he could see the convent's stone tower rising above the trees on the hillside. He rested his head against the wall and felt his body relaxing. As his eyes closed, a strange thought struck him. Maybe when the fools returned with their smuggled rifles, he'd lead them to that convent on the hill for a little glimpse of their future. Maybe that would stop them from committing suicide....

"Roberto?"

He opened his eyes and saw Sebastian's stubbled face peering down at him. The old man wore a black beret and brown poncho. A gray canvas bag hung from his shoulder.

"Catching a few winks, eh?"

Roberto stood up and brushed the dust off his worn black pants. From the look of the bright sky, he'd slept for hours.

"I'm going to the sea. Want to come along?"

Roberto rubbed his tired eyes. In his four years in Guernica, he'd learned that Sebastian only painted by the sea in times of trouble. "What is it, *compañero*?"

Sebastian smiled through his yellow teeth. "It's time for an old man to drink with his friend."

Roberto stared at him. "You won't tell me what's wrong?"

"Maybe after the first bottle of *txakolina*. Well—what's it gonna be? I need to catch the afternoon light." Sebastian gestured toward the rusted truck parked across the road.

Roberto rubbed the back of his neck. "I'm pretty tired, *amigo*."

Sebastian glanced at Roberto's bloodstained sleeve. "Another night in the convent?"

Roberto nodded.

"All the more reason to drink by the sea. Nothing like a bottle of *txakolina* to erase bad memories."

Roberto recalled those sad eyes in the convent. "It'll take more than a bottle of wine to forget what I've seen."

Sebastian shrugged his shoulders. "No problem, I have five."

Roberto pushed back his disheveled hair. He hated *txakolina*, but it was better than nothing. "Give me a couple hours."

"Couple hours? Hell, we can drive there in twenty minutes."

"I need to do something first."

Sebastian frowned. "Meet me on the beach, a half mile east of the caves. And don't disappoint me or I'll shoot you."

Roberto patted his friend's shoulder and walked away. He was nearly to the bank when the truck roared past him with Sebastian hanging out the window.

"Be there! I mean it!" The truck skidded around the corner, nearly hitting Francesca and two other women carrying blankets and food.

Francesca dropped her pack and shook an angry fist at the truck. "Damn you, old man! Someone should take that disgusting hunk of metal away from you!"

She yanked her pack off the curb and stormed across the street, followed by the two women. "That friend of yours is a madman. You shouldn't associate with him."

Roberto smiled. "He'll calm down after he drinks and paints a little."

"He's a menace."

"He has his moments."

Her face softened. "Are you coming from the convent?"

Roberto nodded.

"We're taking these supplies there."

"Good, they need everything we can give."

She glanced at the two women standing beside her. "Anita and Carmella have never seen war. Do you think they should stay outside?"

Roberto glanced at the two trembling women. "Maybe it's for the best."

Francesca eased closer. "Is it very bad?"

"It's bad."

She grasped his arm. "You look so tired, Roberto. You should sleep. You need to be strong for tomorrow's Mass."

"Strong?"

She looked down and sighed.

"What's wrong?"

"You should talk to Augustin. He's at the town hall with the others. God be with you, Roberto." She nodded for Anita and Carmella to follow her.

He watched them walk past the munitions factory and disappear into the trees below the convent. What did she mean? And why was Sebastian going to the sea?

Almost three years had passed since the skirmish in the hills outside Reinosa. Things had remained quiet since that tragic afternoon, largely due to President Aguirre's persistent negotiations with the crumbling Second Republic. At home, Aguirre had overcome impassioned cries for rebellion by convincing his people that pacifism was the only way to protect their sacred guarantee of independence. His fervent pleas had kept the wolves at bay for three tumultuous years—but nothing lasts forever.

Roberto turned down Mugica Road and headed for the town hall. He passed the butcher shop and waved at Juan Alegria and his wife, Josefina, busily slamming their meat cleavers into a flank of fresh beef. Josefina looked up and managed a weak smile. She knew where he was coming from.

When he reached the fountain at the center of town, he heard a commotion coming from the town hall. He turned left at the *Arrien*—and froze.

Augustin and a dozen men were climbing into a brown truck parked in front of the town hall. A small crowd of women had gathered around them shouting words of encouragement. Instead of shepherd's clothes, Augustin and his comrades were dressed in brown militia fatigues and boots. Each wore a black beret. Each carried a bandoleer and rifle.

One of the men appeared to be an outsider. He wore a brown officer's cap with a red star on the crown. A rifle and bandoleer were slung across his chest.

"Augustin, wait!" Roberto ran up to his friend and grasped his arm.

"Stay out of this, Roberto. We have business to do."

"What's going on?"

Augustin nodded toward the Cantabrian Mountains. "They're in Vizcaya."

"Who?"

"We just got word from Asturias that a brigade of guardsmen crossed the border looking for escapees from Oviedo. They're already in Portugalete."

"The Guard's in Vizcaya?"

Augustin's eyes flared with anger. "They've gone too far. They're gonna pay." He opened the driver's door and started to climb into the truck, but Roberto pulled him back. "You can't go out there. They have planes, remember?"

Augustin looked down at him and smiled. "We're not alone. You'll see. God be with you, friend. Go tend my sheep until I get back." He pushed Roberto away and climbed into the truck.

They were pulling away when Roberto heard Julio's voice echo off the buildings. "Augustin! Wait for me!" With his unbuttoned shirt dangling out of his trousers, Julio snatched a rifle and bandoleer from the open crates and ran toward the moving truck.

Augustin stuck his head out the window and tried to wave him off, but it was no use. The determined Asturian jumped into the back of the truck and crawled into the waiting arms of his comrades while Augustin screamed at him. "Stay behind, idiot! You know the rules! One of us has to stay behind!"

Julio ignored him and crawled under the canvas with the others as the truck sped away.

"Fools!"

A familiar voice rang out from the crowd. Roberto turned and saw Ana walking toward him. One of the women spit at the ground when she went by. Another muttered a curse and stormed away, followed by the others. Their husbands were on that truck and no whore was going to call them fools.

Ana eased beside him and watched the truck disappear around the corner. "I tried to stop him. God knows I tried."

"It's no use. They're more lost than those sheep in the hills."

"Sheep don't pick up rifles."

They watched the truck turn onto the cinder road leading to Bilboa. It made a grinding sound as Augustin pressed the clutch and jammed it into second gear. Seconds later, it faded into the haze.

Ana lowered her head. "Who's going to tell Alazne? She thinks Augustin is tending the sheep."

"My God. First Gorka—now this."

"You should tell her, Roberto."

"Me?"

"You're our priest."

"The hell I am."

She looked up in shock.

"This isn't my Spain. People killing each other. Hatred everywhere. I don't belong here."

She gripped his arm. "What are you saying?"

"I'm getting out."

"You're what?"

"I'm sorry, Ana. It takes a strong man to be a priest. A man stronger than me."

"No—" She collapsed against him. "Don't do this. You're

all I have."

Her words echoed in his ears. He felt her warmth. "You have a husband."

"I have no one."

He lifted her chin and looked into her brown eyes. He wanted to say something noble and reassuring, but different words came out. "I'm going to the sea to drink with Sebastian. Will you come with me?"

"What?"

"I don't want to spend my last day in Spain drinking with an old man." He waited for an answer, but she said nothing. "I'll be at the bridge in half an hour. If you're not there, I'll understand." He brushed his hand across her cheek and walked away.

Roberto stepped out of the post office and felt a stiff breeze on his face. The streets were deserted except for a few people going about their chores. A Basque flag flapped overhead. The morning clouds had dissipated and the sky was bright blue.

He walked past the fire station where Juan Silliaco was polishing the town's only fire engine, a dilapidated pumper from the early 1920's. Juan stood up and gestured toward the shining piece of junk. "Hey, Roberto! What do you think?"

He managed a feeble smile and continued on his way while clinging to the crumpled letter in his hand. The news he feared had come. Pizarro's previous letter had warned of trouble, but this one spelled it out.

He passed the *Julian Hotel* and rail station. The air smelled from burnt sugar. Two girls coming off their shift at the candy factory called out to him, but he didn't hear them. His eyes were focused on the Renteria Bridge.

She was standing on the bridge looking down at the rushing water. Her jet black hair rustled against the red shawl draped over her bare shoulders. He stared at her and recalled the night they met on the train—and he finally knew the answer to the question that had plagued him for four long years. It wasn't the Basque's sanctimonious pleas for spiritual guidance that had kept him in this desolate place—or his love of Spain. It was simpler than that—and it was standing on that bridge.

She turned and looked at him with those flashing brown eyes. "Are you all right?"

"A little tired. Come on, Sebastian promised to shoot me if I didn't get there in time." He stuffed the letter in his shirt pocket and took her hand. The sea was four miles away.

They followed the river through the dense forest of pines and hanging moss. Above them, the afternoon sun flickered through the canopy of branches. When they reached the Ria Guernica estuary, the scent of pine needles gave way to the smell of salt air. They heard waves and saw the white beach flashing through the trees. They kicked off their shoes and ran across the warm sand, and for a moment forgot the chaos erupting around them.

"It's about time! What took you so long?" Sebastian waved to them from the beach. He was standing at an easel jammed in the sand. Another man stood at a second easel, dabbing the canvas with his brush.

Ana nudged Roberto's arm. "Do you know him?"

Roberto shrugged and shuffled toward the two painters. He was nearly on top of them when the second man poked his brush into a jar of colored water and turned to face him. He wore a blue-striped jersey, brown slacks, and pair of leather sandals. A red bandana was wrapped tightly around his bald head. He walked toward Roberto and extended his hand. "So—we meet again."

Roberto froze in shock. "Señor Picasso?"

"In the flesh, my friend."

Ana gasped and stepped away. "He is Picasso?"

"Oh, yes." Roberto clasped the artist's hand.

Picasso gripped Roberto's shoulder and studied him with piercing black eyes. "I see you've aged a bit, young Hidalgo. That's good. It will add depth to my portrait."

"Portrait?"

Picasso gestured toward the easel. "We have enough light for three hours. If you can tolerate me, we'll finish by sunset."

Roberto looked at Sebastian. "Was this your idea?"

The old man smiled. "It's my gift to you, Roberto. Wars

come and go. People live and die. But my friend's art will last forever—and so will you."

"And who are you, lovely lady?" Picasso took Ana's hand and kissed it.

"My name is Ana. I'm honored, señor." She stared at him in disbelief.

"I'm the one who should be honored. I've never seen such beauty. No doubt you're Roberto's long lost sister." He winked at Roberto and broke out laughing. "Please, Ana. Have some wine while I paint your friend. I've waited four long years for this chance."

Picasso took her arm and led her to a blanket spread on the sand. He poured her a glass of wine while glancing at Roberto. "Tough being a priest, eh, my friend?"

"I'm not a priest."

"I can see why." Picasso smiled and looked down at Ana. "But enough of this idle talk. There is work to be done."

The artist shuffled to his easel and began rubbing a charcoal stick against a piece of stone. He paused and looked at Roberto. "Well?"

Roberto reached into Sebastian's bag and pulled out a bottle of *txakolina*. He popped the cork and took a long swig. "What do you want me to do?"

Picasso grinned and gestured toward the sand with his charcoal. "Just lie there and look at the sea. I'm the one who has to do the work."

Roberto sighed and stretched out on the warm sand facing Picasso. He leaned on his elbow and took another swig of wine. "God, that sun feels good."

"Like Valencia perhaps?" Picasso leaned forward and swept the charcoal boldly across the canvas.

"How is Federico?"

"He is well, but I think he should leave Andalusia."

"Leave?" Roberto started to sit up but Picasso motioned for him to remain still.

"Federico loves Spain more than his life. He won't stand by while the landowners and Carlists try to return to the old ways. His writings and plays have become too controversial. That can be dangerous—even for Spain's greatest writer."

Roberto wiped a trickle of sweat off his forehead. "I haven't written him in months. I wish he were here with you."

"It would be a good thing. A chance for him to get away from politics." Picasso put down the charcoal and picked up a handful of silver pigment tubes. He squeezed them onto a palette and dabbed them with his brush. He glanced at Roberto and stroked the canvas. "Your eyes are troubled. They remind me of the mud pools in Santamamine Cave. Clear and serene until you drop a pebble into the water. The mud swirls to the surface in shades of black, brown, and gold. If you look hard enough, the colors paint a picture before fading away." Picasso frowned and backed away from the canvas.

"What is it, Pablo?" Sebastian stepped toward the canvas, but Picasso waved him back.

"I've never felt this before." Picasso stared at Roberto's sweating face and dabbed the brush into the pigments on the palette. "Do you feel it, Roberto?"

"What?"

"The pain inside you. I see it in your eyes."

"Pain?" Roberto started to get up.

"No—stay there." Picasso's face twisted in an ugly sneer as he thrust the brush at the canvas.

Roberto stared at the artist. Through the corner of his eye, he saw Sebastian easing toward the blanket where Ana was sitting. The only sounds were Picasso's labored breathing and the waves lapping at the shore.

The sun was setting behind the Cantabrian Mountains when Picasso finally backed away from the canvas. His face and jersey were streaked with brown, black, and gray pigments. He turned away from the painting and wiped his sweating face with his forearm.

Sebastian scrambled to his feet and yanked a bottle of wine out of his bag. He shuffled beside his motionless friend and popped the cork. "Finished, eh? Hey, Roberto, come have a look at—"

Sebastian's words jammed in his throat.

"What is it? What's wrong?" Ana stood up and walked

beside him. "*Mi Dios.*" She backed away and covered her mouth.

"Quit playing games. I can't be that ugly." Roberto lifted his cramped body off the sand. "Time for the moment of truth." He stepped around the easel and peered at the canvas in disbelief.

He was staring at a woman's distorted face. Her mouth was frozen in a scream. Her terrified eyes looked up at the sky. A dead child hung from her arms. Behind her, a horse reared its head in agony. Blood poured from a huge gash in its side. Instead of skin, the horse was plastered with scorched newspapers. A bull stood nearby, its horns dripping blood. And there were other faces. Strained, twisted faces looking up in terror. They reminded him of the dying man in the convent. A tapestry of white and gray ghosts floating on a black and brown scorched canvas.

Picasso looked down at his paint-smeared hands. "I'm sorry, Roberto. If you want, I'll destroy it."

Roberto shook his head and looked out at the sea. "It's what you saw."

"Come on, we still have two bottles left. Let's drink and forget this silliness." Sebastian reached into his pack and yanked out a bottle of wine.

Picasso sighed and glanced at a fishing boat moored in the shallows off the beach. "I should be going. I promised a lady drinks in Biarritz tonight. Mustn't disappoint her." He walked to the easel and swept the loose brushes and pigments into his pack. He was about to fold the easel when he paused and looked at the painting. "Well, Roberto?"

"Keep it, señor. Something to remember me by."

"As you wish." Picasso rolled up the painting and slipped it into a leather tube. He walked to Ana and took her hand. "An interesting day. If you're ever in Paris, look me up. I'd love to paint you."

"I'd be honored, señor."

He turned and extended his hand to Roberto. "When I get to Paris, I'll phone Federico and tell him you're well. I won't mention the painting. Write to him, Roberto. Make him leave

Spain."

Roberto clasped Picasso's hand. "Go with God, señor."

"Goodbye, my friend. I won't forget you." The artist slung his pack over his shoulder and headed down the beach toward a small rowboat resting on the sand.

Sebastian edged beside Roberto. "I'll just be a minute. I don't think we'll see each other again."

"He's not coming back?"

Sebastian frowned. "The Rightists are cracking down on artists and writers. That's why Federico should get out." He patted Roberto's arm and headed down the beach after his friend.

They watched Picasso row the small boat to the waiting fishing trawler where two men helped him aboard. Sebastian stood on the shore waving farewell to his friend as the trawler slipped away from its mooring and chugged eastward along the coastline. When it was out of sight, he wiped his eyes and marched up the beach toward them. "Well—I guess we should be going."

Ana grasped Roberto's arm. "We've decided to stay awhile. Hope you don't mind."

"Mind?" Sebastian fidgeted with his poncho. "Of course not. It should be a beautiful night for a walk back to town."

They helped Sebastian load his truck. He was climbing into the driver's seat when Ana reached up and kissed him on his stubbled cheek. "If they were all like you, *hombre*, it would be a better world."

"Ha! You talk like I'm a saint." He gunned the engine and gestured for her to step back. The truck wheeled around and screeched down the dirt road toward Guernica.

Roberto swiped at the fumes. "You were right about him. They don't come any better. I wonder how he lost that arm."

"In the Great War. An artillery shell exploded in his trench. He was the only one who survived."

"I'm glad he did." Roberto looked out at the Bay of Biscay. The darkening sky was streaked with orange clouds from the setting sun. "I haven't seen a sunset like this in years. It reminds me of home."

"Then, let's enjoy it." She gestured toward the blanket where a bottle of *txakolina* lay on its side with two glasses.

Roberto looked at the blanket and smiled. "It seems our friend is trying to complicate things."

"I'm afraid they're already complicated." She reached up and kissed him softly on the lips.

"What are you doing?"

"Saying goodbye to a dear friend." She looked up at him and smiled. "There's only one problem. Somewhere along the way, I fell in love with him."

He stared at her, unable to speak. Her warm body pressed against him. In another few seconds, it would be too late to stop.

This was wrong. He was a man of God and she was a married woman. They were in enough trouble without adding this. *Don't do it, man. Leave her now. Leave them all. Cross those mountains.*

Who was he kidding? He took her in his arms and kissed her while her body ground against him. Forget the nightmares and miracles. Forget the holy crusades. If Spain wanted to commit suicide, let it. If the Church didn't care, why should he?

They dropped on the blanket and clung to each other with the waves lapping at their feet. He felt her naked body slide against him. Her warm lips and tongue drove him mad. Everything he ever wanted was in his arms. He ripped off his clothes and made love to her while a blood-red moon crept over the Pyrenees, and lit up the sea....

The tide was washing over them when they gasped their last breath of pleasure and collapsed on the soaked blanket. The full moon had turned bright yellow and climbed into the night sky above the sea.

Roberto leaned over and kissed her softly. "I've never felt this close to anyone."

She stroked his wet hair and smiled. "We better move higher before we drown."

They put on their clothes and climbed onto the rocks

overlooking the sea. Roberto leaned against a boulder and filled their glasses with wine. "You know, I'm getting used to this stuff."

Ana nestled against him. "What time do you think it is?"

"Close to midnight. We should be getting back."

She frowned and looked out at the flickering water. "Why are you leaving when we need you most?"

He gulped down the wine and rested his head against the boulder. "I have a close friend in Valencia. We've stayed in contact since I left four years ago. Last week, he sent me a letter warning the Church was planning to replace me."

"What?"

"There's more. Arronategui wired Madrid that I'm stirring up trouble."

She straightened up and stared at him. "Do you know what you're saying?"

"My friend in Valencia is a priest. We've known each other since I was a child. I trust him with my life." He poured a glass of wine and gulped it down. "I knew they'd try to disgrace me. They've hated me since the day I told them off. But the letter I received today increased the stakes."

"Letter?"

"It seems I've made some serious enemies. Padre Segurra warned me it would happen. The Church has concocted a story that my father died a rich man and left me his money. They've convinced Madrid the money belongs to the Church."

"What money?"

"Good question. They claim millions of *pesetas* were advanced to my father for work he never fulfilled. They're coming up here to arrest me for embezzling Church funds."

"*Mi Dios*, Roberto. Is any of it true?"

He frowned and looked up at the stars. "I wish it was. Since Madrid shut off my monthly entitlement, I don't have enough money to buy an egg. My father died a penniless man. He's lying in a simple grave above the Mediterranean Sea."

"Can't your friend help you?"

"They'd arrest him for aiding an enemy of the state. I'll never let that happen." He slumped against the boulder. "These things are my doing. I destroy everything I touch. I won't hurt anyone else. If I don't leave now, you'll all pay for my weakness."

"But—where will you go? The Church is very powerful. They'll hunt you down like an animal?"

"I'm not sure. I'll head into the mountains and see where they take me."

"My God, Roberto."

He put his arm around her and looked up at the moon. "Remember the night we met on the train? How bright the moon was? Everything so clear and fresh?"

"We should have jumped off that train and stayed up there." She pressed against him. "God, I don't want tonight to end."

He kissed her softly on the lips. "Come on—we'll take a long, slow walk in the woods."

"Take me with you."

"What?"

"I want to go with you."

"Are you crazy? In a few days, I'll be a hunted man."

"I don't care. I'd rather sleep in a cave with you than spend another day in this godforsaken country." She locked her brown eyes on him. "There's nothing here but hatred and death."

He stood up and extended his hand. "They'll be back soon. You should be waiting for them."

She rose into his arms and kissed him while praying time would stand still—but time stops for no one.

Lieutenant Guevera stretched his arms and looked up at the brightening sky. "Are you awake, Sergeant?"

"Yes, Lieutenant." Sergeant Cortez scrambled to his feet and straightened his tricornerio hat.

"Give me some light." Guevera reached inside his tunic and pulled out a map while his sergeant fumbled for the flashlight. He unfolded the map on the rocky ground and popped open a small pocket compass.

It took a few seconds to align the map with the compass.

Guevera knelt down and tapped the map with his finger. "We've skirted Bilboa. The sea's a mile to our left and Guernica's ten miles dead ahead. We'll be there by late afternoon."

"Guernica?"

"We need to make a stop there."

Cortez glanced nervously at the forest stretching in front of them. "But why? We've already found seven bodies. None of the escapees made it through the mountains. Hell, they were half-dead when they crossed the border."

Guevera stood up and stretched his aching back. "We're not going to Guernica to hunt down escapees. I have orders to arrest a communist posing as a priest. We're to bring him back to Oviedo for transport to Madrid."

"Priest?" Cortez rubbed the back of his neck. "Lieutenant, we only have fifty men and twenty rounds. We're deep in Basque country. If we march into Guernica, we'll be asking for big trouble."

Guevera nodded. "We have our orders. Assemble the men—we're moving out."

Cortez saluted and headed down the slope toward their camp.

"And, Sergeant...."

Cortez turned and looked up at his commanding officer.

"Don't worry so much. You think I'd take us in here without cover?"

Cortez forced a nervous smile under his black moustache and continued down the slope.

They moved out at dawn—fifty uniformed Civil Guardsmen with obsolete Enfield rifles slung over their shoulders. Their only other weapons were Lieutenant Guevera's thirty-eight calibre revolver and the flare kit dangling from Cortez's belt.

The July sun beat down on their snakelike column as it wound through the forested valleys toward Guernica. The guardsmen's sunburned faces glistened from the oppressive humidity. Ignoring protocol, they unbuttoned their heavy black tunics and poured water on their faces from the leather canteens strapped to their belts. They were young and brave, but greener than the trees around them.

They'd marched three hours when Lieutenant Guevera finally raised his hand. "We'll rest here twenty minutes."

Cortez turned toward the tired, sunburned faces and pointed to a cluster of rocks on his right. "Twenty minutes! Stay alert!" He watched them stumble into the rocks.

Guevera pulled out his map and scanned the surrounding hills. "We're making good time. Two more hours should do it."

"Cigaret, Lieutenant?" Cortez extended a blue pack of cigarets to his commander.

"French, eh? Thank you, Sergeant. I could use a bottle of wine and a good woman too." He smiled and stuck a cigaret between his parched lips while Cortez struck a match and lit it for him.

Guevera puffed the cigaret and studied the black-uniformed men sprawled against the rocks. "How are they holding up?"

"They're fine, but I haven't told them where we're going."

Guevera nodded. "I'll speak to them before we move out. They're so damn young." He puffed nervously on the cigaret. "God, I miss my wife and son."

"How long since you've seen them, Lieutenant?"

"Too long. The army promised me a transfer back to Madrid if I pull this off. It means a lot to me."

Cortez nodded and lit a cigaret.

"What about you, Sergeant? Any family?"

Cortez took a long drag and leaned against a boulder. "No one, Lieutenant. All I've ever known is the army."

"You were a regular?"

"In Franco's Moroccan Legion before they shipped me back to Spain. They said I was too old to be a regular, so they stuck me in the Guard." Cortez winced. "Sorry, Lieutenant."

Guevera smiled. "Must be lonely."

"It has its moments, but—" Cortez straightened up and flicked away his cigaret.

"What is it?"

"I'm not sure. Something flashed on that hill."

Guevera dropped his cigaret and scanned the surrounding

hills. "Tell the men to form up. We're only four miles from Guernica. Let's get in there and get the hell—"

Cortez reeled in shock as the rocks echoed with a rifle crack.

Guevera clutched his throat and stiffened. He stared at the sergeant with stunned eyes.

"Lieutenant!" Cortez watched his commander collapse on the ground, blood spurting from an ugly hole in his neck.

The air exploded with gunfire. A bullet ricocheted off the boulder next to Cortez's head. He dived on the ground and looked back at his stunned men. Many of them had abandoned their rifles and crawled under the rocks.

"No, idiots! Pick up your rifles! Scatter and prepare to return—" A terrific force slammed into Cortez's back. His shoulder exploded in paralyzing pain. He clutched his chest and felt blood oozing through his tunic. The bullet had struck bone and splintered into his lung.

Fighting the pain, Cortez crawled into the rocks and began waving frantically at his panicked men. "Here! Rally around me!"

At first, no one moved under the hail of incoming fire. Suddenly, two guardsmen grabbed their rifles and bolted for their wounded sergeant. Two more tried to follow, but only one made it. The other took a bullet in the chest and straightened up while a second round caught him between the eyes. He gazed into space and toppled forward like a piece of wood.

But they kept coming—crawling toward their screaming sergeant while bullets rained down on them. When one fell, a comrade would grab his uniform and drag him toward the rocks until he made it or dropped from a bullet in the head.

Cortez seized a discarded rifle and stared in horror at the massacre taking place around him. Only twenty-three guardsmen had survived. The others were scattered across the rocks with blood pouring from their heads and chests. And still the bullets rained down on them—tearing into their lifeless bodies while their comrades watched in horror.

Cortez stuck his tricornerio hat on the barrel of his rifle and waved it above his head. "For God's sake, stop shooting!

They're just kids! They don't mean any harm! Let us go and we'll—"

He pressed his face against the rock as a hail of bullets shredded his hat and ripped the rifle out of his hand.

One of the wounded guardsmen shook his fist at the hills and began shouting curses. Then another. The air was filled with epithets as the incensed young men fired back at their executioners.

"Sergeant!"

Cortez dropped on his belly and looked in horror at the clearing beyond the rocks. Lieutenant Guevera was crawling toward him, his face covered with blood.

"Give me your hand, Lieutenant!"

The lieutenant shook his head and gasped. "The time."

"What?"

"The time, dammit!"

Cortez glanced at his watch and stared at the pitiful creature lying in front of him. "Fourteen fifty."

"At fifteen hundred…shoot…the flares."

"Flares?"

"Do it! And tell…my wife…." Lieutenant Rafael Guevera gasped his last breath as the ground erupted with impacting bullets. His body convulsed and fell still.

"My God. Bastards. Fucking bastards!" Cortez fought the pain in his chest and opened fire on the hills.

"We've got them! Finish them!" Augustin climbed on the hill crest and emptied his rifle on the cluster of black uniforms huddled in the rocks below. "This is for my brother, you sons of bitches!"

"Get down, Augustin! You've got the sky at your back!" Julio waved at his friend, but the towering blond Basque was too full of hate to listen. After three years living with the pain of his brother's death, he was finally striking back at the wolves that wanted to destroy his home.

"Idiot!" Julio climbed next to his friend and opened fire on the guardsmen. Across the valley, others stood up and raised their rifles in victory while their comrades emptied round after round on their outnumbered enemy.

Cortez crouched behind the rocks and reached into his ammo pack for the last of his bullets. Many of his comrades had pulled ammo from the dead while crying like babies. But they kept shooting at the silhouettes on the hilltops. Brave young men too full of anger to be afraid any longer.

"Sergeant—they're coming!"

Cortez looked at the blood-smeared face crying out to him. The young man was pointing to the hills where the Basques had begun their descent into the valley. Cortez had seen this before in Oviedo, except it was Yagué's military that had closed ranks on the wounded miners and blasted away at them until they were a mass of red pulp.

Cortez glanced at his watch. Fifteen hundred hours. The lieutenant's final order echoed in his ears. Only a few seconds left. The Basques were almost on top of them. He yanked the flare gun out of his belt and shoved in a red cartridge. Follow orders, dammit. Even if they made no sense.

He raised the flare gun and hesitated. A drone was coming from the sky. He looked up and saw the Basques frozen on the hillside, their heads straining upward.

One of the guardsmen pointed to a line of twin-winged fighters climbing out of the sun. He raised his arms and began cheering. "They're ours! Thank God, they're ours!"

Cortez squeezed the trigger and felt the gun recoil in his hand. The flare rocketed skyward and exploded in a shower of hissing red sparks. He uncocked the pistol and jammed in a second cartridge.

"Fall back!" Julio turned and scrambled up the hill as the air filled with a deadly whine. The hunter had become the hunted. He glared at the Russian advisor cowering in the rocks above him. "Where are your planes? Where are your fucking planes?"

The panicked Russian scampered over the hill crest and disappeared. The promised Russian fighters were nowhere in sight.

"Fucking pig!" Julio emptied his rifle on the rocks where the Russian had stood. He charged after him as the slope erupted with impacting bullets.

"Down, Julio! Get down!" Augustin dived behind a rock and felt the bullets rip into the ground beside him. His left ankle exploded in pain as one of the thirty calibre rounds found its mark. He clutched his leg and felt the ground shake under him. The hillside across the valley erupted with impacting bombs. He saw four men staggering through the thick black smoke. They were on fire.

Julio reloaded his rifle and stared at the line of planes rising into the blue sky. They were almost out of sight when the lead plane rolled over and plunged into a power dive. It was coming straight at him, the wind screaming through its wings. "Kill the bastards! Blow them out of the sky!" He gestured for his comrades to fire on the diving planes, but they were gone.

"Get down!" Augustin crawled beside his friend and shoved a final bullet in his rifle. His ears filled with a deafening whine as the plane opened fire.

Julio dropped on one knee and patted Augustin's shoulder. "So it begins, my friend. So it begins...." He raised his rifle to the sky and squeezed the trigger as bullets ripped into the ground around them. He fell backward, his bloody hand clutching his chest.

The black shadow roared over them revealing a second aircraft spouting flame from its wings. Augustin felt the bullets thud into the ground around him. Deadly, thirty calibre projectiles tore into his chest and stomach. Everything was going black.

He heard the bombs whistling toward him—and he uttered his last words. "We should have brought Roberto. No one...shoots down planes...like our priest...."

The hillside disintegrated in smoke and flames. The Civil War would not begin for another eleven months, but Julio's final words had sealed Spain's coffin. "So it begins, my friend. So it begins...."

22 | My Best Friend

Karen placed the black purse and gloves on the foyer table. Behind her, the clock on the living room mantle had come to life with a chiming rendition of *Hail Britannia*. She slipped an envelope into the purse and listened to the clock emit nine melodic pings.

She turned away from the table and stepped into the living room where the clock had completed its ritual and resumed a fresh countdown to the next performance. The only sounds were the ticking clock and sleet pattering against the window.

It looked more like a study than a living room. An oak bookcase spanned the twenty foot wall on her left, its shelves packed with books on every subject known to man. All had been read.

On her right, a writing desk and blue-velvet sofa faced a large bay window with a sweeping view of the East River, Welfare Island, and the Queensboro Bridge. She glanced at the window and frowned. Not much of a view today with that "nor'easter" blowing in from the Atlantic.

A *Blue Boy* reproduction hung above the red brick fireplace in front of her. Two brown leather chairs had been angled to face the fireplace and painting. A leather ottoman was centered between them to provide a shared footrest on those cold nights when a warm fire felt so good against chilled feet. Each chair had its own reading table with books and papers stacked to allow just enough space for a drink. A floor lamp was positioned behind the chairs to provide ample light when reviewing "glossies" and news copy.

She shuddered and felt a tear roll down her cheek. So many precious moments had been spent in this room. She could feel his presence. His warm body pressing against her. His lips caressing her neck. His soft moans of pleasure when he gave himself to her in the darkness.

She heard the faint hum of cars on the bridge, barely audible above the pattering sleet. How many times they'd listened to that vibrant, confident hum while drifting to sleep on the sofa, their eyes fixed on the stars twinkling above the river. It all seemed so close, yet so far away.

She blinked and looked out the window. The storm had broken and sleet thudded against the glass. It was New Year's Day, 1937, and the weather was particularly severe—a fitting tribute to this eighth year of the Great Depression.

She walked around the sofa and peered at the low-hanging clouds sweeping across Welfare Island. To her left, the Queensboro Bridge was surprisingly busy for a holiday—a hopeful sign people still fought to survive the nation's worst crisis since the Civil War. But it all meant nothing today.

She dropped on the sofa and rested her head against the cushion. Maybe it was all a bad dream. Maybe when she awoke, he'd be looking down at her with those dark-green eyes. Yes—that was it. Just a few minutes of forgiving sleep and all would be well again. She closed her eyes and listened to the sleet....

"Hey, don't fall asleep on me now."

She blinked her tired eyes. The grandfather clock in the corner was chiming eleven p.m.

"Wake up, Sleeping Beauty. We've got things to talk about."

She sat up and saw him jabbing a poker at the fireplace. "What's wrong?"

He glanced at her and smiled. "Don't want to freeze to death. It's below zero out there."

She looked out the chalet's frost-covered window. A full moon had risen above the mountains and flooded the snow with soft blue light.

"Most beautiful night I've ever seen. Snowcapped peaks. Star-filled sky. Everything glowing. Too much for words." He picked up a fresh log and flipped it on the grate.

"You're crazy." She fell back on the couch and closed her eyes. After a day of crawling around Pike's Peak in full pack, Karen Vostok was in no mood for midnight chats.

A beautiful numbing sensation crept through her. She was nearly asleep when he kissed her on the lips.

"God, I love you."

She lifted her aching arm and patted his shoulder. "Please, honey. I'm not going anywhere. We'll fuck in the morning."

"No—we've gotta talk now. It's really important. We're leaving tomorrow."

It took a few seconds for his words to sink in. "Leaving?"

"Yup."

She pushed him away. "What are you talking about? We've still got three days?"

"Wish we did." He stood up and walked to the small wood stove in the corner. "I made some coffee. Want a cup?"

She grunted and stretched her sore back. After three years of intimacy, she'd learned Jim Halberton was the hardest-headed person on God's earth—except for her.

"Here you go, Miss Vostok. Two lumps and a dash of cream, just the way you like it."

She took the cup of coffee and gave him the evil eye. "Are you all right?"

"Never felt better."

She sipped the warm coffee and placed it on the cocktail table. "You're sure?"

He nodded and sat on the couch. "Mind if I put my feet up?" He swung his stocking-covered feet across her extended legs and jammed them between her hip and the cushion. "Ah, heaven."

She shook her head and pushed back a wayward strand of black hair. "So tell me, what's so important to wake your girl friend from the dead?"

The smile faded from his face. His green eyes flashed beneath the thick mop of auburn hair. "I found the story of the century."

"Huh?"

"Oh yeah, it's the big one."

"That's it—we're taking you down to the doctor. The thin air's wiped out your brain." She started to crawl off the couch, but he grabbed her ankle.

"Calm down, honey. Just sip your coffee and listen."

"I'm not in the mood for this, Jim. I'm damn tired."

"Please—I'll give you the short version." He sipped his coffee and watched her relax against the cushions. "Do you know why I hired Carlton Ames?"

She sighed impatiently. "Because he's the perfect 'yes man'."

He frowned. "Come on, you can do better than that."

She shrugged. "To let him do all the work so you can spend more time with me."

"Ha! If that was the reason, I'd spend the extra time sitting on my ass in the *Time's* lobby waiting for an audience with the 'queen of sleaze'."

"What?"

He nodded defiantly. "Be honest, Karen. You love that job more than anything—including me."

"You've got a lot of nerve. I've always made time for you. And what's this queen of sleaze crap?"

He raised his hands. "Don't get mad. I'm no better. Hell—we finally take our first real vacation and I'm cutting it short."

"Queen of sleaze? How dare you." She leaned against the cushion and sipped her coffee. Enough acting, Miss Vostok. He was right and she knew it. It was November, 1936. Nearly three years had passed since that fateful meeting in the *Time's* lobby. In that time, they'd sacrificed everything for their careers. Except for brief escapes to her Sutton Place apartment, they'd never stopped to smell the roses.

And the roses smelled so damn good. In three years, Karen Vostok had become the *New York Time's* top reporter with a string of exposés that had the city's politicians reeling from West 193rd to Battery Place. Like Faust, she'd kept her pact with La Guardia, and he'd kept his promise. Everyone was happy—even Mr. Cardolani whose powerful trash collection union had gained a permanent foothold in New York's five boroughs.

Not so bad. People needed unions in these hellacious times. Unfortunately, some innocents had suffered. Like most politicians, the mayor had become ruthless in destroying his opponents—even if his slandered victims did nothing wrong. But who was Karen Vostok to question the accuracy of the mayor's leads. Innocents are often sacrificed in the struggle for the greater good.

Yes—the three years had been most rewarding. While others starved in the streets, the *Time's* attractive reporter vacated her small, one room flat on West Forty-first for a spacious retreat overlooking the East River. From her new uptown suite in Sutton Place's prestigious "Ark" apartments, she maintained a weekly liaison with La Guardia while planning her next earth-shattering story.

He squeezed her foot. "Are you ready to listen?"

"What?"

"To my story."

"Go on."

"I hired Carlton Ames so I could live my dream."

"Dream?"

"You know. To get out in the field—where the action is."

She straightened up and looked him in the eyes. "What are you saying? You're not rummaging around Europe looking for trouble?"

"Afraid so."

"Are you crazy?"

"Might be."

Her face flushed. "That's not funny. You can get killed. For God's sake, Jim. I'm no correspondent, but anyone can see what's happening over there."

"Asia too. That's why it's important to get out the truth. The people here are so caught up in the damn depression, they're wearing blinders. By the time they snap out of it, Europe will be under that paperhanger's boots. And guess who's next?"

She pulled her feet away from him and sat on the edge of the couch. "Does Gerramino know?"

"You kidding? He'd fire me on the spot."

She stroked her forehead. "How long has this been going on?"

"Since I hired Ames. I promised him a big promotion if he kept his mouth shut. Guess what he said?"

"Oh, Jim. What the hell's wrong with you?" She stood up

and walked to the window.

"Calm down, it's almost over."

"Over? Sounds like it just started."

He crawled off the couch and eased beside her. "I'm serious, honey. After this story, I'm chucking the whole international thing and coming home." He slipped his arm around her waist. "Three years out there is enough. It's time to settle down and raise a family, don't you think?"

She pulled his hand away. "You're right about it being a beautiful night. Why did you have to ruin it?"

"Hell, Karen. I'm not asking you to give up anything. After my story breaks, Gerramino will welcome me home like a long lost brother. He'll give me a big promotion and fat desk overlooking Times Square, and I'll be content cause I'll have you."

"Oh, really? Aren't you taking a lot for granted, Mr. Halberton?"

"You know I didn't mean it that way."

She shook her head. "So, what's this great story?"

He hesitated and looked out at the snow. "A few months ago, I made contact with an operative working for the English."

"Operative? You mean spy?"

"I guess you could call him that. I met him by accident at a Nazi rally in Berlin."

She spun around and stared at him. "You were in Berlin?"

"In the flesh. Got the royal treatment too. Good publicity and all that. Gotta tell you, the *Führer* was really at his best that day. I never believed that garbage about him studying Wagner until I saw him in action. Hell, he almost had me in tears when he started trembling and rolling those eyes."

"You saw Hitler?"

"Hell, I shook his hand. Got a private audience. Even an autographed photo. Good thing I took German at Yale."

"My God."

"You know what struck me most? It wasn't his words. It was that damn shrieking voice and shaking fist. And those crazed eyes sweeping across us like a hungry wolf. Magnificent, even if he is nuts."

She stared at him in disbelief. "You don't know what you're doing. That crew's a bunch of lunatics. You can't play games with them."

He locked his green eyes on her. "Don't think I can pull it off, eh? Well, you're wrong. My father isn't the only one who knows how to snare a big story. This one's mine, dammit. Biggest story of the twentieth century."

She walked back to the couch and sat down, her eyes staring at the log burning in the fireplace. "I didn't know how much you envied your father—until now."

His face reddened. "What are you talking about? I'm doing this because I love it."

"Doing what? Trying to kill yourself?"

He walked back to the couch and sat beside her. "I may be a little wild, but I'm not suicidal. This whole thing will be over in a few weeks and I'll be on my way home with a valise full of goodies that'll make Gerramino drop his teeth."

"You are crazy. And I'm crazy for putting up with you."

His eyes lit up. "I'm telling you, honey. It's the story of a lifetime—and it's still unfolding. I thought it ended in Europe, but it goes further. It's the whole world, dammit. If my man in Berlin delivers the goods he promised, I'll blow the lid off the Third Reich and wake up everyone before it's too late. Hell— you're a reporter, and a damn good one. What would you do?"

She shook her head. "I don't know."

"The hell you don't. If you were in my shoes, you'd chase this story until you dropped."

She pushed back her hair and looked him in the eye. "Why did you wait so long to tell me?"

"Things didn't heat up until last month. Hell, we only see each other every six weeks. I wasn't holding out on you. I love you too much for that."

She felt her eyes well up with tears. At moments like this, he reminded her of a little boy, an irresistible little boy with auburn hair and dark-green eyes. "I don't want to lose you, Jim. Not after putting up with you for three years."

"You mean that?"

"Idiot. You think I'd be up here if I didn't care?"

He leaned over and kissed her on the cheek. "Then it's time for the next part. Damn, I've got a lot of ground to cover tonight."

"Wait a minute. What about the story?"

He shrugged. "That's all I can tell you until I get back."

"What? You woke me for that?"

"No—for this." He grasped her hand and slipped a small, blue-velvet box in her palm.

"What are you doing?"

He took a deep breath. "I'm asking you to marry me. I think it's time, don't you?"

She stared at the box, unable to speak.

"There's a justice of the peace in Pike's Peak. He opens for business at nine. I'm leaving for London the day after tomorrow. Won't be back until Christmas. How about making a lonely traveler happy?"

She opened the box and stared at a flickering diamond ring.

"I bought it in Switzerland. Cost me two month's salary. Hope you like it."

"My God."

"They had this great clock that plays *Hail Britannia*. Maybe I'll pick it up next week. You know, for the mantle. It'll go well with the painting."

She wiped away a tear.

"I love you, Karen. So say 'yes', dammit."

She hesitated and looked down at the ring. "I think we should wait. Maybe when you come back."

His shoulders dropped. "Why wait?"

"I didn't expect this. I need some time to think."

"Three years isn't enough?"

"It's not that."

He looked into her eyes. "It's my dad, isn't it?"

"Your dad?"

"Be honest."

She grasped his hand. "I am being honest. This is strictly between us. You want the truth, so here it is." She paused and looked down at the box. "I've never been able to keep anything good. Can't explain why. All I know is everything I touch dies.

That's why I've gotten used to being alone. It's gonna be hard to change that." She lifted his hand to her lips and kissed it. "But if anyone can do it, it's you."

He looked down and sighed. "Looks like I struck out."

She leaned over and kissed him. "You've still got one strike left."

"Don't give up?"

She sobbed and took him in her arms. "You better not. You came mighty close tonight." She pulled him down and slipped under him. The grandfather clock was chiming midnight....

She opened her eyes and stared at the sleet-spattered window. Someone was ringing the entrance buzzer. She pushed off the sofa and staggered across the living room to the intercom in the foyer.

"Yes?"

"It's Frank."

"Frank? I must have dozed off." She rested her head against the intercom.

"Want me to come up?"

"No—I'll be down in a minute." She turned away from the intercom and stepped back into the living room.

She hesitated and stared at the mantle clock. Still nine? She walked closer and noticed the pendulum wasn't moving. When she opened the case and tried to wind it, there was no resistance. The spring had broken.

An uneasiness swept through her. She turned and gazed at the room. It seemed different somehow. Empty. Without warmth. Even the colors had faded. Like a dying memory.

Her stomach churned. She walked into the foyer and slipped on her coat and hat. She snatched her purse and gloves off the table. A glance in the mirror and she was out the door.

When she stepped off the elevator, Frank Gerramino was standing in the lobby with an umbrella in his hand. He eased beside her and spoke softly. "Are you all right?"

She nodded and took his arm. "Let's get this over with."

They pushed through the doors and stepped into the cold, damp wind. A black limo was parked in front of the apartment with its motor running. A uniformed chauffeur stood next to the opened rear passenger door, his gloved hand on the handle. He nodded and tipped his hat when they ducked inside.

She watched the chauffeur climb into the driver's seat in front of her. The only sounds were the car's heater and sleet glancing off the window.

"It's icing up pretty fast, but we should make it on time." Gerramino patted her gloved hand and leaned back in the seat as they pulled away from the curb.

The limo turned right on First Avenue and headed north. It turned right on 161st and picked up Boston Road through the Bronx until it intercepted Highway One and sped north toward New Rochelle and Connecticut.

They were sloshing through New Haven when Karen put down the crinkled letter. She must have read it a dozen times in the past twenty-four hours. Easy enough when you can't sleep. She glanced at Frank who had dozed off beside her. This was probably the most painful drive he'd ever taken, but Frank Gerramino could handle it. Anyone raised in Hell's Kitchen knew how to deal with pain.

She rubbed the steamed window with her gloved fist and peered at the barren trees. The storm had let up and the sky was brightening. A green "Wallingford" sign flashed into view, its arrow pointing left. She felt the limo slow down and ease to a stop.

They turned left and sped down a narrow country road lined with spruce trees and snow-patched fields. After driving a short distance, they pulled into a driveway filled with black limousines. Their limo eased into the line and waited while a uniformed attendant opened an iron gate and directed the procession of cars through it. The sign on the gate was unmistakable....

Pleasant Haven Cemetery

Karen fumbled with the letter and flipped to the final page. She read it for the thirteenth time....

Well—guess that's it, my darling. Just one more night in Paris and I'll wrap this thing up. Then, it's across the Channel for a few days with ol' Carlton, and I'll be home for Christmas.

Can't wait to see the look on Gerramino's face when I break the news. There's enough stuff in my valise for a year's worth of headlines.

Gotta tell you, honey, I'm scared to death about the next twenty-four hours. Things have gone so damn well. Guess you gotta expect some nerves when you're this close to a huge story.

Hope you like the little book. Wish I could tell you more. I've said too much already, but I want you to know what's keeping me from you.

Don't forget to wind the new mantle clock for good luck. Hope it works. See you soon.

All my love,
Jim

"We're here, ma'am."

Karen looked up and saw the chauffeur standing at the opened door with an umbrella in his hand.

"Ready, Karen?" Frank Gerramino patted her wrist.

She took a deep breath and stuffed the tear-stained letter into her purse. When she stepped out of the limousine, she saw a line of familiar faces climbing out of the other limousines parked along the cemetery's cinder road. Raising umbrellas, they shuffled across the wet snow toward a tented gravesite covered with freshly cut flowers.

"Wait here." Frank patted her shoulder and walked toward the gravesite where five men were standing beside a parked hearse.

Karen clutched the chauffeur's umbrella and watched Frank and the other men slide a black coffin out of the hearse's opened rear door. Carefully positioning the coffin on their shoulders, the six men walked to the gravesite and placed the coffin on the platform that would lower it to its final resting place.

Everything seemed frozen in time. The drizzle pattering

against the opened umbrellas. Distant thunder. Silver light shining on sombre faces. The damp, biting cold.

The chauffeur leaned against her. "Are you all right, ma'am?"

She clenched her fists and nodded. Through the corner of her eye, she noticed Jim's parents step out of the limo behind the hearse. Without shedding a glance in her direction, Edmund Halberton wrapped his arm tightly around his grief-stricken wife and staggered toward the congregation.

The ceremony only lasted ten minutes. Frank delivered a brief, touching eulogy, paying tribute to "a fine young man who gave his life so others may know the truth." He closed the speech by unveiling a bronze plaque that would hang in the *Time's* lobby as a reminder of Jim Halberton's ultimate sacrifice to keep his nation informed.

After a brief moment of silence, Reverend Claremont recited the Twenty-third Psalm and gestured for the coffin to be lowered into the grave. When it was done, each person came forward and dropped a rose into the darkness while saying goodbye to the friend they respected and loved. College chums, neighbors, Carlton Ames and the London staff—all were here to say goodbye to the young man who had taught them to dream.

Francine Halberton came forward, but broke down in her husband's arms. Fighting back tears, Mr. Halberton plucked the rose from her hand and staggered forward until he was standing at the edge of the grave. He lowered his head and dropped two roses on the coffin—and he bid farewell to the son who had been his life.

Karen waited until the last of the procession departed before coming forward. She knelt at the edge of the grave and kissed a yellow rose, then dropped it gently on the coffin. There were no tears. Just a soft, "Goodbye, my best friend."

She knelt beside the grave for almost an hour, listening to the frozen rain patter on the tent's canvas roof. It reminded her of the rain pattering on the window the last night they clung to each other and dreamed of a better tomorrow.

That evening, Edmund Halberton thanked Dr. Wallace and watched him walk to his car in the falling snow. He closed the front door and looked at the dimly lit staircase leading to his wife's bedroom.

By now, Dr. Wallace's powerful sedative had numbed Francine Halberton's terrible pain. Maybe tonight, there would be no sobs of anguish when she tried to cope with the emptiness tearing at her soul. After nine months of pain, and twenty-nine years of love, her only child had been snatched from her arms in the blink of an eye, his life snuffed out in a fatal auto accident on a lonely highway near Paris.

Mr. Halberton walked across the darkened living room and climbed the steps to his study. He pushed through the doors and walked toward the cluster of framed pictures on his desk. He lifted one of them in his hand and stared at the young face looking up at him. Six years had passed since that picture was taken. Six long years. They hadn't talked since that day. Now it was too late.

He clutched the picture and staggered across the study to one of the leather chairs facing the fireplace. He dropped in the chair and stared blankly at the dying fire.

A father's dream had been shattered by a freak accident across the sea. There would be no inheritor. No namesake. No grandchildren would sprout like twigs from the family tree to carry on the Halberton name.

He rested his head against the cushion and recalled the horrible days in the trenches when waves of impassioned American boys sacrificed their incomplete lives to drive the Kaiser into oblivion. Many brave young men died in those trenches, and many families died with them. As a war correspondent, he felt like he knew them all. Now his son was with them. God rest his soul. God rest all their souls. He broke down and wept while his son's picture slipped out of his hand and crashed on the stone floor....

The doorbell? He wiped away his tears and glanced at the clock on the mantle. It was nearly midnight. He must have dozed off. He gathered himself and pushed out of the chair.

"Karen?" He stepped back in shock.

"Can I come in?"

"Of course." He stepped aside and watched her brush past him into the foyer.

"I'm sorry for coming so late."

He nodded and closed the door. "Let me take your coat. We can talk in the study." He hung her black raincoat on a hook and led her across the living room.

He closed the study's double doors and gestured toward the twin leather chairs. "I'll start a fire."

"Please, not on my account. I'll only be a few minutes."

He shrugged. "It's no trouble. I'll probably spend the night here."

"How's Mrs. Halberton?"

"Sedated. Otherwise, I'm sure she'd want to see you." He knelt down and pushed some kindling under a log on the hearth. "Would you like a drink?"

"No, thank you." She sat on one of the leather chairs.

He struck a match to the kindling and backed away while brushing off his hands. "There—it'll just take a minute."

He was pouring a stiff scotch when he saw her pick Jim's picture off the floor. "Hard to believe that was taken six years ago. Seems like yesterday."

"The glass is broken."

"Oh—I must've dropped it when I dozed off. I'll fix it tomorrow."

Karen leaned forward and gazed at the fire. "I have a car waiting, so I'll be brief."

Mr. Halberton chugged his scotch and sat across from her. "You're not staying for the Yale ceremony?"

She shook her head.

"Well—no reason you should. You didn't know any of his close friends. They're different from your crowd."

Karen clenched her fists. "I know how you feel about me, so I won't mince words. I'm very sorry for your loss, Mr. Halberton. In case you're interested, I loved him too."

He stared at the burning log.

She reached into her purse and pulled out the envelope. "This was your son's last letter to me. I thought you'd want to read it."

Startled, Mr. Halberton eyed the envelope and took it from her hand. He slipped out the three-page letter and flipped on his reading glasses. The only sound was the crackling flames.

"What is this?" His eyes flashed with anger.

"Jim wrote that letter ten days ago—the night before they killed him."

Mr. Halberton sat up and clutched the letter. "My God, what was he trying to do?"

She sighed and looked at the fire. "I'm not sure. He said it was the biggest story of the century. I didn't believe him, but I do now."

He dropped the letter on the cocktail table. "Did Frank Gerramino know about this?"

She shook her head. "Jim made me promise not to tell him."

"Damn you. How could you do this?"

"What?"

"You killed him, dammit. You killed my son. Goddamn your soul to hell!" He clenched his fists and glared at her.

She stared at him in shock. "You don't know what you're saying? You can't mean that?" She reached out to comfort him, but he pushed her hand away.

"Get out of my house, Miss Vostok. I never want to see you again."

She dug her fingers into the chair arm. Her face was red hot. He'd accused her of killing his son. Tell him the truth, dammit! Edmund Halberton had killed his son with the same warped self-righteousness he was showing now. Tell him, dammit! Don't let him get away with it again.

She stood up and snatched the letter off the table.

"Where are you going with that letter?"

"I'm sorry for your pain, Mr. Halberton. I came here to give you this, but you don't deserve it."

"What?" He stiffened in the chair, his tear-filled eyes burning with rage.

"You won't see me again, but there's one thing you should know. My name isn't Vostok. It's Karen Halberton."

"What?"

"Your son loved me, Mr. Halberton. And I loved him—far more than you could know. We were married on Thanksgiving day." She stared at his stunned face. "Goodnight, Mr. Halberton. No need to see me to the door. I know the way out."

She walked down the front steps and headed for the black limousine purring softly at the end of the driveway. The chauffeur spotted her and stepped out of the limo to open the door.

Before getting in, she paused and looked back at the green-shuttered colonial. A small light was burning in one of the upstairs windows. She squinted through the snowflakes and saw a woman staring down at her. Instinctively, she raised her hand and waved to the elderly woman. There was no response. She took a deep breath and looked at the night sky. A full moon was breaking through the clouds. Tomorrow would be a better day.

23 | Nightmare Lived

"Damn peasants! Get out of the way!" Lieutenant Colonel Wolfram von Richthofen jammed his foot on the Mercedes accelerator pedal, sending shocked pedestrians scrambling for their lives on the narrow street in front of him.

"That should wake them up!" Lieutenant Hans Asmus gripped his officer's cap and hung on for dear life as his commander skidded the Mercedes around a tight corner, nearly decapitating an elderly couple scurrying for safety.

Richthofen ignored his bootlicking aide and slammed on the brakes in front of the Burgos Town Hall. He shut off the ignition and climbed out of the mud-spattered Mercedes.

A leather-jacketed officer flicked away his cigaret and snapped to attention. "Good evening, Colonel."

"Good evening, Major Fuchs." Richthofen returned his wing commander's salute and brushed past him into the town hall. "Be quick, men. I dislike being late." He charged up the stairs, followed by his two panting subordinates.

Richthofen paused at the paneled door at the top of the stairs. He removed his black officer's cap and slipped it under his arm while Lieutenant Asmus opened the door, revealing a brightly lit conference room. The clock on the wall read six twenty-nine.

"Good evening, Lieutenant Colonel Richthofen." An elderly Spanish officer rose from his chair at the head of a large oak conference table. He was joined by a multi-uniformed array of Spanish and Italian officers seated to either side.

"Colonel Vigon. Gentlemen...." Richthofen nodded and took his place at the table while his two men remained at the door.

"Please—be seated." Colonel Vigon spread his arms and resumed his seat, followed by Richthofen and the others. All officer's caps were placed on the table, brims pointed outward.

Richthofen's eyes darted around the table. "And where is General Mola this evening?"

"Unavailable." Vigon smiled nervously.

"You have authority to act on his behalf?"

Vigon nodded and glanced around the table. "Unless there is an objection."

"None here." Richthofen shrugged.

"Good—we can proceed." Vigon gestured for an orderly to spread the latest battle maps on the table.

The officers spent the next half hour bickering over the opposing red and blue arrows sketched across the maps. None of them appeared surprised by Mola's sudden departure to the stagnated northern front.

After promising a swift victory over the Basques, Mola's fifty-thousand-man army had ground to a frustrating halt in northern Spain's rugged terrain, unable to advance due to poor roads, dynamited bridges, lethal land mines, and crippling tank traps. While expressing concern for their commander's safety, Mola's Carlist and Falangist officers quietly hoped a stray bullet would soon end his life. Perhaps it would come from the rifle of a Basque militiaman perched on a hilltop above Vitoria, or from the pistol of an Asturian anarchist stealing into Burgos under cover of night. Who knows, it might even come from General Franco himself. The culprit didn't matter, as long as the bullet found its mark and put an end to their incompetent leader.

After distinguishing himself with a brilliant military coup at the war's outbreak nine months ago, General Emilio Mola had fallen flat on his face in a futile attempt to overrun Madrid from the north, a decisive stroke that would have brought the bloody war to a swift end.

With Spain's Republican government on the verge of collapse, Mola's northern army was poised to invade the capital when his ally, General Franco, unexpectedly diverted his converging southern army west toward Toledo in a reckless effort to rescue Colonel José Moscardo and a thirteen-hundred-man garrison from certain annihilation inside the ancient Alcazar fortress. Franco's rugged Moorish army pulled off the daring rescue while Mola watched through glazed eyes.

For his glorious victory, Franco was appointed Head of State and Commander-in-Chief of all Nationalist forces. The news from Madrid wasn't as glorious. Instead of pressing his assault, Mola dug in while Soviet arms flowed into the beleaguered capital. When the indecisive general finally launched a second assault, his forces met stiff resistance and were driven back to the Guadarrama Mountains.

Reinforced with Soviet training and weapons, Madrid's Loyalists spit in Mola's eye and prepared for a long siege. A calculated betrayal had elevated Francisco Franco to ultimate power, and disgraced his friend.

As Commander-in-Chief, Franco wasted no time ordering Mola to abandon his futile Madrid campaign in favor of a northward thrust to crush the remaining Asturian, Basque, and Catalan resistance. Madrid was symbolic, but Spain's industrial wealth lay in its northern factories and shipyards. Once the north was taken, Franco would control Spain's destiny.

But General Mola erred again by underestimating the power of hatred. With the towns of Irun and San Sebastian captured, and the Basque's supply lines shut off at the Pyrenees, Mola elected to march on Vizcaya, the Basque's final stronghold. Expecting an easy victory against the province's ragged militia, Mola's fifty thousand man army hit a stone wall.

Freed from their prisons by the desperate Republican government, thousands of Asturian miners picked up communist-supplied rifles and joined their Basque brothers in a staunch defense against Mola and his hated insurgent army. A similar scenario unfolded in Barcelona where thousands of liberated prisoners took up weapons and stormed the military that had tortured and killed their families.

Mola blundered by not recognizing the fierce courage of these poorly-armed, undisciplined militia. Outmanned and outgunned, the rabble threw themselves against him with one purpose. They weren't fighting for Spain or the Republic. They were fighting for their homelands in Asturias, Euskadia, and Catalonia. Instead of collapsing under Mola's onslaught, the incensed citizens fought to the death while clawing at every inch of their native soil.

Bogged down by the determined rebels, Mola's besieged

army was forced to dig in below Vitoria while its frustrated commander conducted fruitless meetings in his Burgos headquarters, trying to find a way to break the iron ring of Basques and Asturians defending their homeland. And while Mola floundered, a seething General Franco focused his binoculars on fortress Madrid, unable to press forward until his incompetent general completed his mission in the north.

"So—where does this leave us?" Colonel Vigon leaned back in his chair and studied the officers poring over the maps.

"If I may speak, Colonel." Richthofen capitalized on his fluent Spanish to get the chief-of-staff's attention.

"Of course."

Richthofen waited for the others to resume their seats. Rising slowly to his feet, he straightened his jacket and snatched one of the pointers from the table. "As I see it, we've marched into a Basque trap." He eyed each of the stunned officers.

Vigon adjusted his glasses and glanced nervously at the maps. "I don't understand."

"It's frighteningly simple." Richthofen traced the pointer along the line of red crosses marking the Basque army's grudging retreat toward Bilboa. "They fight a skirmish, then withdraw a few hundred yards to fight again. But first, they blow up another bridge. Tough crossing those swollen rivers in the spring, isn't it?" Richthofen rested the pointer on the map and stared at the officers with steel blue eyes.

One of the Spanish officers stood up and leaned over the map. He looked at Richthofen and frowned. "You're not implying a band of rabble can defeat us?"

"No. We'll beat them eventually, but when our depleted regiments turn back to Madrid, they'll find a powerful, unified Republican army waiting. By chasing these peasants up here, we've given the Second Republic precious time to arm itself with Soviet weapons and planes. That's why General Franco is so concerned." Richthofen looked around the room. "Don't you see? This wallowing in Burgos gives the enemy valuable time. General Franco can't take Madrid without our help. Every day the Republicans hold the capital, they become stronger. And we grow weaker in these damn mountains fighting a bunch of sheep herders."

Vigon stroked his chin and looked at the maps. "You make it sound hopeless."

Richthofen cracked a Prussian smile. "Far from it, Colonel. If we act now, we can crush the Basques and dispatch a reinforced army to Madrid within two months. General Franco will be pleased with our decisive action."

Vigon shrugged his shoulders. "But how?"

"Turn the enemy's strategy against him." Richthofen picked up the pointer and held it over the map. "I've studied their movements carefully. They continue to withdraw toward Bilboa using these three roads." He tapped the map three times. "Notice something, gentlemen." He watched the officers rise out of their chairs and lean over the map. "All three roads converge on a small bridge—here." He tapped the pointer on a yellow circle. "The Renteria Bridge—over the Mundaca River—just southeast of—excuse me, Colonel—how is that town pronounced?"

Vigon eyed the dot inside the circle. "Guernica."

"Thank you. One well-designed air strike can knock out that bridge and freeze their retreat. If it's coordinated with determined assaults from the south and east, we'll trap the pigs outside Guernica and crush them before they can join their comrades in Bilboa. When the Basques see what we have done, they'll give up in fear. It will break their spirit, gentlemen. We'll march through them like a hot knife through butter."

The room fell silent as each of the officers studied the yellow circle. Finally, the Italian air-unit commander spoke up. "Who would lead such an attack?"

Richthofen straightened his shoulders. "I would be proud to use the Condor Legion. We have the latest aircraft at our disposal. It would be an excellent trial for our new Heinkels and Messerschmitts. I could launch forty aircraft in the morning."

"But—a plan must be drawn? There must be preparations?"

Richthofen broke into a wry smile. "I've already done that."

The stunned Italian glanced nervously at the map. "Is the town defended?"

"I don't care if it is."

The Italian frowned. "May I remind you that our air attack on Bilboa was a shambles. The Russian Chato fighters clobbered us."

Richthofen's drawn face hardened. "There is risk in everything, sir. My attack will be swift and unexpected. We'll be gone before they know what hit them." He rested the pointer on the map and picked up his cap. "We have talked enough. It's time to act. I'll await your decision." He turned and nodded for his wing commander and aide to follow him out of the room.

They were nearly to the Mercedes when Major Fuchs addressed his commander. "Your orders, Colonel?"

Richthofen opened a small gold case and pulled out a cigaret. He placed it between his lips and waited for Lieutenant Asmus to light it. "Beautiful night, Major Fuchs."

"Yes, Colonel." His wing commander smiled and looked up at the stars.

Richthofen puffed nervously on the cigaret. "Use Moreau to lead the attack. This is work for a butcher. It's time to show these idiots how it's done."

Lieutenant Asmus looked at his commander in surprise. "You think they'll approve?"

"They damn well better or I'll bomb them too." Richthofen puffed on the cigaret and looked up at the stars. "I wish my cousin were alive. We'd climb into his Fokker triplane and strafe the bastards ourselves." He flicked the cigaret into the street. "Come on, Lieutenant. I have work to do. I lied about the plan. It will take me half the night to draw one up." He climbed into the Mercedes and turned on the ignition....

A dense, night fog had fallen on Guernica. There was no movement. No sound except the faint clinking of sheep bells in the hills. The town seemed peaceful and secure, its black steeples jutting through the white blanket of fog.

What a lie. To the east, the night sky flickered with bursts of yellow accompanied by dull, staccato thuds. Instead of flowers, the air carried an ominous odor of cordite from skirmishes against the advancing Nationalist forces.

Roberto slipped his arm around her waist. "They're closer tonight."

"It's the fog. Everything seems closer in the fog."

He frowned and opened the mission door. The chapel was pitch black. He switched on a flashlight and led her past the altar to the rectory.

"I'll make some coffee." She walked to the wood stove in the corner.

"There isn't any. Just some tea in that tin." Roberto lit the kerosene lamp on the table and watched the room come alive with flickering shadows.

"I wish we had some brandy."

"Brandy? We're lucky to have water."

She sighed and struck a match. "I prefer brandy just now."

He sat at the table and looked down at his bloodstained hands. "I learned how to remove a bullet today. Not too hard. Just ignore the screams and dig it out."

Ana scooped some tea into a strainer and immersed it in a small kettle. "You probably saved his life."

"He died ten minutes later. He was just a boy."

She backed away from the stove and rested a hand on his shoulder. "Don't blame yourself. There was nothing you could do. Without morphine, most of them go into shock and die."

Roberto wasn't listening. He stood up and staggered through the door. When he reached the rear of the mission, he stuck his head under the pump and grasped the rusted handle.

The cold water sent chills down his neck and back. He turned his face toward the spout and felt the refreshing water splash against his nose and mouth. It reminded him of the warm summer day so many years ago when he plunged into the Turia's rushing waters. He was about to step away when he felt her press against him.

"Me too." She lowered her blouse and positioned her head under the pump.

He pumped the handle and ran his free hand along her bare

neck and shoulders while the cold water spurted over her. When she was done, she stepped away and pushed back her soaked hair. He could see her breasts heaving against the wet blouse.

"More?" He nodded toward the handle.

"You're all I want tonight." She pressed against him and buried her lips on his.

He dug his hands under her linen blouse and felt her hips grind against him. "Oh, Ana."

"Love me, Roberto. Forget the damn war and love me."

He swept her in his arms and carried her inside the mission. A bit sacrilegious perhaps, but no disrespect was meant. Hopefully, God wouldn't mind. After all, love was Spain's only hope.

They slipped under the covers and kissed each other's naked bodies. She tasted so sweet. He loved her so much. He rolled on his back and felt her on top of him. Her wet hair dragged across his face. Her lips found his. He could feel her heart pounding against him. It was good to be a man again. Good to love again. They gave themselves to each other in the soft light while the teakettle whistled a lonely tune....

He was awakened by a sharp rap on the door.

"Roberto?"

He crawled out of the bed and slipped on his pants, taking care not to awaken the beautiful woman asleep beneath the covers. He pushed through the door and saw Sebastian staring at him from the dark chapel.

"I take it you're not alone."

Roberto stepped into the chapel and closed the door. "What time is it?"

"Past midnight. I only have a minute."

"What's wrong?"

"Captain Sanchez has called an emergency meeting in the town hall. It sounds like we're gearing up for the big one. The last trucks left for the front an hour ago. The sky's on fire. I think Mola's making his move."

Roberto brushed past him and walked to the window. He

swung open the shutters and gazed at the flickering horizon. The thuds had grown louder. "Do you want me to come with you?"

"Hell, no. We have enough trouble keeping Arronategui off our backs without throwing you in his face. One look at you and he'll start screaming for your arrest." Sebastian shook his head. "You know, he's still trying to get the Church to replace you? I think he's lost his mind. He doesn't want to face the truth. The damn fool thinks he and the Church are one big happy family. He thinks he can run across the bridge and greet Mola's Carlists with a handful of roses. Hell, they'll cut him down before he can say 'Viva Mola'. The idiot doesn't know it, but he's their enemy—just like us."

Roberto turned toward his friend. "Can we stop them?"

Sebastian frowned. "If Mola comes at us with all he has, the jackal will be in Guernica within a week. After that, our last chance will be the iron ring around Bilboa." He stood up and eased next to Roberto. "That's why I'm here."

"What?"

"It's time for you and that charming young lady on the other side of the door to get the hell out of here."

Roberto shook his head. "It's a little late for that, don't you think? Besides, she'll never leave."

Sebastian looked at the door. "She still blames herself for his death?"

"For all their deaths. I've tried to make her forget, but it's no use."

"Get her out of here, Roberto. There are enough martyrs in Guernica."

"Maybe you should talk to her."

Sebastian patted his friend's arm. "In the morning. Until then, take this." He reached into his pocket and handed Roberto a folded paper. "It's a map that will get you past Mola's lines to France. And for God's sake, don't wait too long. It's your ticket out of this mess." He turned for the door.

"Sebastian?"

"Yeah?"

"What about you?"

The old man smiled through his grizzled beard. "I've seen men die, Roberto. A thousand in a few minutes. And the sky on fire like tonight. When this mess is over, they'll blame Franco and his insurgents—but I'll know better. We did this, Roberto. We put our country to death." He paused and wiped his eyes. "Hell, I'm not afraid to die. I'll just grab my paints and go to the sea. But you and Ana are still young. You can make a difference. In time, Spain will be free again and you'll return to bring back the old ways. I think your father would want that."

Roberto looked down and nodded.

"Go with God, my young friend." He turned and walked out the door.

Roberto watched the old man disappear into the darkness below the mission. To the east, the Pyrenees flashed from volleys of artillery fire. Once his symbol of escape to a better world, those mountains would soon swarm with advancing enemy troops.

He flipped open Sebastian's scribbled map and studied the penciled line. If his friend was right, they must leave tomorrow before Mola's approaching troops cut off their escape route. It would be a dangerous crossing, with death lurking behind every rock, but it was their only chance.

Remaining in Guernica meant imprisonment, torture, and death. Escape by sea was impossible due to the Italian naval blockade. Retreating west toward Portugal was futile since the Nationalists sealed its border. Everything to the south was in enemy hands. There was only one shot, and it was east across the Pyrenees to France.

He pushed away from the window and collapsed in the front pew, his eyes fixed on the darkened altar. Two years had passed since Julio and Augustin met their deaths in the hills above Bilboa. Since that day, no Mass had been performed on that altar. Without leaders, the people had drifted back to Arronategui and his Church of San Juan.

He stared at the gold crucifix above the altar. Sebastian was right. It was time to go. No sense staying where you're not wanted. The Guernicans had made their choice. Let Arronategui deal with Mola's army when it marched across the

Renteria Bridge.

But what about Spain? What about the short, portly officer he toasted in the *Marva Bar* eight years ago? Francisco Franco Bahamonde was about to become the world's newest dictator, taking his place beside the crazed house painter in Germany, and strutting little general in Italy.

Roberto felt his jaw tighten. Too bad he and *El Caudillo* never managed to have that dinner together. He would have strangled the little pig with his bare hands.

He leaned forward and clenched his fists. What had happened to them? There was no right or wrong—only bitter chaos. Basque and Asturian industrialists scorned the starving refugees flooding their steel mills and mines with cheap labor. Basques, Marxists, Anarchists, and two million peasants were stamped "reds." Falangists, Carlists, Monarchists, and Catholic conservatives were marked "fascists." Yet, these supposedly unified factions fought among themselves like animals thrown in the same cage. Spain was consumed with hatred and violence. Brother killed brother. Sister killed sister. And while the hemorrhaging continued, Italian and German insurgents flooded across Spain's borders to test their latest weaponry against the USSR's pro-Republican "advisors." There were more foreigners fighting the damn war than Spanish.

Roberto brushed back his wet hair. He should have left for France that night on the beach. She would have gone with him and never known her husband's terrible fate. Instead, he led her back to town to await Julio and Augustin's return. She would tell her husband the truth, and he would let her go.

But Ana never had that chance. Julio's remains were brought back in a canvas bag along with Augustin's and the others. None of them survived the government's relentless bombings. Ironic that Basques and Asturians now allied themselves with the same Spanish government that took their comrades lives two years ago. No, it wasn't ironic. It was sick. They were all so damned sick.

"Roberto?"

He looked up in surprise. Ana was standing in the doorway wrapped in a blanket.

"I heard voices."

"Sebastian paid us a visit."

"Sebastian? In the middle of the night?"

"He gave me a map. He says we should leave."

"Leave?" She sat beside him. "Is he crazy? What about Montero and the hospital? We can't walk out on him?"

"The Nationalists are making their move. They'll be here in a few days. I was lucky two years ago, but this is different. It's more than me now. It's you too."

She reached up and stroked his hair. "We'll be all right. Our men are good fighters. They'll stop Mola and Solchaga like they did in Vitoria."

He pulled her hand away. "Sebastian knows what's coming. You think that bombing in Durango was an accident? The planes killed two hundred innocent people. Mola's desperate. He's thrown away the rules. And we're right in his path."

She looked at the altar. "We'll stop them. God is on our side."

"God doesn't care what happens here. If he did, we wouldn't be sweating in that convent with those mutilated bodies."

She looked at him in shock. "Get a hold of yourself, Roberto. You need sleep. Come back to bed."

"Bed? You think we'll be safe in bed? Listen to me, Ana. Your husband is gone and nothing will bring him back. It wasn't your fault he killed himself. Two years is long enough to mourn the dead."

"Damn you." She stood up and glared at him.

"Then damn me. But you're leaving tomorrow whether you like it or not."

She stormed into the rectory. He heard her slipping on her clothes. Seconds later, she brushed past him headed for the door.

"Where are you going?"

"Back to the convent where I'm needed. Get some rest, Roberto. We'll talk tomorrow." She walked out the door and faded into the darkness.

The hours passed slowly. At five a.m., the distant guns fell silent. He could hear Segurra's wall clock ticking in the darkness. Strange, how quiet it had become. No night birds. No breeze. Just that ticking clock.

At six thirty, the first rays of sunlight burst through the brown haze. He staggered out of the mission and soaked his head under the pump's spout. When he was done, he walked onto the rocky hillside and stared at the sun's obscured disk. The air stunk from cordite. Everything was still, like the calm before a storm. He took a nervous breath and walked into the mission.

He'd spent the night going through Segurra's personal belongings. What he needed had been stuffed into the worn leather valise dragged from under the bed. After so many years, the valise was in good shape except for its torn liner and a few scuff marks. His father had given him the bag on his eighteenth birthday when he left home for college in Madrid. It was the only thing remaining from his father. His only other possessions were the bible and gold crucifix Pizarro had given him when he entered the clergy eight years ago.

The wall clock chimed seven. He sat on the bed and recalled the day he left Pizarro and Maria standing on the train platform. Pizarro's final words echoed in his ears....

Universal! The blood of all men!

An uneasiness swept through him. He remembered the darkness of Corpus Christi. The firm hand on his shoulder. The soft voice. The taste of salt and iron. He shook his head and climbed off the bed.

He was about to pack his bible in the valise when a folded paper dropped out of it. He bent down and picked it off the floor. There was no need to open it. He'd memorized the words.

Despite warnings from his friends, Garcia Lorca had chosen to remain in his native Granada when the war broke out. Hated by the Rightists for his liberal views, he was arrested for treason on August 16, 1936. Three days later, he was shot with a batch of "reds" and buried in an olive grove near the gushing spring he loved so dearly.

Roberto clutched the paper and looked out the window at Guernica. Lorca's words were as fresh in his mind as the day he read them a year ago. A simple poem, sent by one friend to another....

THE POLICE
by
Federico Garcia Lorca
With their souls of patent leather they come down the road.
Hunched and nocturnal, where they breathe they impose,
silence of dark rubber and fear of fine sand....

Roberto stuffed the paper in his bible while recalling the day his friend saved his life in Granada. Another good man was gone. Another nail driven into Spain's coffin. He dropped the bible in the traveling bag and walked out of the room.

It was Monday, April 26, 1937. The wind had shifted and the sky was clearing over Guernica. The perfect setting for market day. The hell with the war raging at Vizcaya's borders. People had come from as far as Lequieto to bargain, drink, and sing.

Roberto crossed the bridge and walked past the candy factory toward the town plaza and market. It would only take a few minutes to reach the Carmelite Convent at the far edge of town. By now, Ana had reflected on his words with a cooler head. Hopefully, she'd confided in Dr. Montero.

He recalled Montero's valiant struggle to save the hapless, broken bodies in that convent on the hill. If anyone symbolized Spain's tragedy, it was Ferdinand Montero. The frustrated physician would clear out of here in a heartbeat if not for his Hippocratic oath. And he wasn't the only one. For weeks, Basque families had packed their possessions with their wagons and livestock in case the lookouts sounded the alarm. With Guernica only twelve miles from the front, they must move quickly to reach Bilboa's protective ring of trenches and bunkers.

Mola and Solchaga might overrun defenseless Guernica, but thirty thousand determined Basque militia waited in trenches at the outskirts of Bilboa, armed to the teeth with rifles, machine guns, mortars, and artillery. If the fools tried to march on them, it would be a war of annihilation with women and children joining their men in a fight to the death. Mola's cowardly insurgents would quickly cave and retreat to Burgos.

Roberto walked past the train station. Across the street, Juan Cristobar and his brother were standing on a scaffold slapping a fresh coat of paint on the *Julian Hotel's* weathered sign. Roberto smiled at them, but they pretended not to see him. He turned away and proceeded up the narrow street.

The plaza was jammed with noisy vendors and shoppers—a churning throng of reds, blues, blacks, and browns—their burnt faces glistening in the morning sun. The air was thick with the smell of fresh fruits and vegetables.

A cow looked up at him and mooed. Its owner sat on a stool milking it while his young son looked on with fascinated eyes.

A guitarist strolled past the fountain strumming a folk ballad. He was followed by an old woman selling straw hats.

A young man placed a wild rose in his girlfriend's blond hair. She backed away and spun around like a Parisienne model while he admired his handiwork. They embraced and walked away laughing. It reminded Roberto of the holiday festival in Valencia—when he danced with Laura and drank *Rioja* wine.

He walked across the plaza and headed for the *Casa del Juntas*. A few polite nods were offered from familiar faces in the crowd, but they quickly looked away when he went by. Since Augustin's death, the townspeople had turned a cold shoulder to the imposter on the hillside above Guernica. Arronategui had made sure of that. If he couldn't have the scoundrel arrested and deported to Madrid for trial, he could at least isolate him and his whore from Guernica's God-fearing Catholics. In time, the Church would answer his pleas to have the traitor removed. Unfortunately for Arronategui, the monarchist Church didn't care much for Basques these days—

including their priests.

"Roberto!"

He turned and saw Francesca running toward him, her face filled with concern. She grabbed his arm and nodded toward the iron gate next to the parliament building. "The tree, Roberto. Please...."

He followed her through the gate into the courtyard behind the building.

"There." She pointed a trembling finger at the stump. Two enormous green shoots had sprouted into the air. Fresh leaves had burst through the buds.

He eased toward the stump and reached for the leaves.

"No—don't touch them. It's the work of the devil."

"Devil?"

She collapsed on the bench. "Don't you see? The tree was dead and now it lives. It's a bad omen. Bad for us all."

He smiled and sat beside her. "I think it's a good omen when a sleeping tree comes to life. It's a rebirth, Francesca. A new hope."

She looked at him with puzzled eyes. "I went to the meeting last night. They told us to be ready to leave at any time. Does that sound like hope?"

Roberto hesitated. "We have to be prepared."

"Prepared? This is my home, Roberto. My family's home. We can't desert our flocks. Our fishermen can't abandon their boats. We have nothing else."

"I'm sorry, Francesca. If there was anything I could do—"

"There is." She pushed away from him. "Leave Guernica now."

He looked at her in shock.

"Arronategui doesn't speak for us all. We've watched you care for the wounded—and comfort them when they died. That's what a priest should do." She grasped his hand. "You're very special to us, Roberto. We don't want you to die."

He shook his head. "I won't go without Ana."

"Then, take her with you."

"She's too full of guilt."

Francesca squeezed his hand. "She'll go because she loves

you. Please, Roberto. Time is short. I feel it in my bones."

He put his arm around her. "Maybe we should all go."

She forced a smile. "I'm going to miss you—my most handsome priest."

"I'm no priest, Francesca."

"You are to me, *torero*." She leaned over and kissed him on the cheek. "Goodbye, my handsome priest." She stood up and walked down the path to the iron gate.

He sat on the bench studying the shoots until the sun's rays made him turn away. It was high noon. Music and laughter echoed from the plaza. The wine had done its job. He stood up and walked to the stump.

He plucked a leaf off one of the shoots and rubbed it between his thumb and forefinger. It felt cool and firm, its veins thick with sap. Soon, other shoots would sprout from the ancient stump, weaving a latticework only God can make.

The Tree of Guernica had risen from the ashes. No dictator could kill it. No army could crush its fighting spirit. In the end, its people would triumph. He turned and walked out of the courtyard.

He headed up Mugica Road toward the deserted *Astra-Unceta* arms factory. The final truckload of arms and ammunition had pulled out last night, headed for the front. The factory's equipment and gunpowder had gone the other way, trucked to Bilboa for use by its beleaguered defenders.

The adjoining militia barracks had been converted to a field hospital to handle the spillover from the convent. More likely, it would serve as a mortuary until the bodies could be buried. Not a pretty sight in a town housing a jai alai fronton and candy factory.

He walked past the deserted factory and headed up the hill toward the convent. When he reached the front gate, he saw Ana and three nuns carrying a covered stretcher toward the graveyard. He pushed through the gate and ran up to her. "I'll take it."

Startled, she stepped back and watched him grab the stretcher handle. She pushed back her hair and stared at him through bloodshot eyes. She could barely stand.

"Wait for me on the steps." He gripped the stretcher and followed the nuns into the graveyard.

They laid the dead soldier to rest in a freshly dug grave. Roberto bowed his head and listened to Sister Montaña recite a prayer for a young man who would never know life's tapestry. She stepped to the edge of the grave and dropped a rose on the wrapped body. After a brief silence, she backed away while the grave digger picked up his shovel and went about his work.

Ana was sitting on the steps when he returned, her face buried in her arms. He sat down and put his arm around her.

"I went to my husband's grave this morning. Alazne was there with Linda, laying fresh flowers on Gorka's grave. When I tried to comfort her, she pushed me away and called me a whore."

"God."

"I'll never forget her black eyes burning into me."

"It's not her fault. She's overwhelmed with grief. Trying to find an answer like everyone else. God help her."

Four nuns brushed past them carrying another shrouded stretcher to the graveyard. Montero was wasting no time clearing space for the next wave of wounded. The determined physician would continue his tireless struggle until a Nationalist soldier burst into the convent and put a bullet in his head.

She rested her head against his chest. He held her close and listened to the wind rustle through the trees....

The convent's bell was chiming four when Ana shook his arm. He rubbed his eyes and looked up at her.

"I bought some fresh fruits and vegetables. They're at my home. We'll need them for the climb."

His eyes widened.

She bent down and kissed him. "I'll meet you at the bridge in half an hour."

"I'll be there. God knows, I'll be there." He held her in his arms and felt her warm lips on his.

He watched her walk through the gate and disappear into the trees. Sebastian's words rang in his ears. Someday, they would return to bring back the old ways—and make his father proud. He climbed the steps and pushed through the oak doors.

The convent echoed with the groans of dying men. Montero was leaning against the far wall, his arms hanging at his sides. Roberto eased beside him and rested a hand on his shoulder.

"Roberto? I thought you'd be gone by now?"

"I came to say goodbye."

Montero smiled and rested his head against the wall. "Is Ana going with you?"

"If she doesn't change her mind."

"I'm glad."

Roberto grasped the old man's arm. "Maybe you should pull out too. They'll need you in Bilboa."

"In time." Montero looked at Roberto through bloodshot eyes. "Go with God, my friend. Make them know the truth. What you see here is just the beginning. If it's not stopped, we'll all burn in hell."

"Stay well, physician." Roberto patted Montero's arm and walked out of the convent. When he reached the front gate, he hesitated and looked back at the graveyard—and he felt the words well up from his gut. "I'll come back, Augustin. Someday—we'll all come back. Goodbye—friend." He pushed through the iron gate and headed down the tree-covered slope toward the town.

He was nearly to the arm's factory when the bell began clanging. He looked up and saw two nuns standing on the convent's roof, their winged hats silhouetted against the bright sky. One of them rang a hand bell while pointing frantically toward the south.

He cupped his hands to his mouth and shouted, "What is it?"

"Avion!"

He turned and saw something flicker in the blue sky. A faint hum filled the air. He shaded his eyes and squinted over the roof tops.

Planes—closing from the south in multiple "V" formations, the sun gleaming on their wings.

The bells of Santa Maria Church began peeling, followed

by the Church of San Juan. The air was filled with ringing bells and a steady, pulsating drone.

Planes from the south? Veering northwest? Bilboa was only fifteen miles away. The planes would be over the great city in minutes!

He ran down Mugica Road into the crowded plaza. Everyone was looking skyward at the arrow-shaped formations. "We've got to warn Bilboa!"

One of the vendors glared at him. "Calm down. The Russian fighters will clobber them before they cross the hills."

"Fool!" Roberto brushed past him and ran for the post office. If the telegraph was working, he might get off a message to Bilboa before it was too late.

"Where are you going?"

Roberto felt a strong hand grip his arm. Arronategui was glaring at him with fire in his eyes. "We've got to warn them."

"We've already done that, fool. You think we're stupid? Now get out of town before I have you carried out."

Roberto yanked his arm away. "You fat, ignorant pig!"

"What did you call me?"

"You spineless pig! I'm sick of you and your goddamned church! You're the hypocrites who caused this mess!"

Arronategui stepped back in shock. "You curse a man of God? An imposter curses a priest? How dare you! I'll have you shot for this!"

"Go to hell!" Roberto lunged at the stunned priest.

What was happening? A brilliant orange flash lit up the street. A blast of hot air slammed into him, sending him sprawling backward along the ground. His ears rang from a deafening explosion. Everything was shaking. Dazed, he sat up and saw Arronategui running for his church. People were screaming and running in all directions.

Where was the train station? And post office? Thick black smoke and flames billowed into the sky where they had stood. And that sound? A sickening whine ringing in his ears? He looked up and saw four twin-engined planes diving toward him. The blood froze in his veins. Their target wasn't Bilboa.

He stared at the sky and remembered the vision at Corpus

Christi. The black planes diving at the town. The screams. The explosions. The death. "My God. Guernica. It was Guernica!"

A twin-engined plane roared over his head. He scrambled to his feet and started running down the street toward the bridge, but a blinding flash stopped him in his tracks. He dropped on his face and covered his head as a deafening explosion rocked the ground. A hot blast of air surged over him. Debris was falling everywhere. He couldn't breathe. The air was black with choking smoke.

He peered through the smoke and flames. The *Julian Hotel's* facade had been blown away. Smoldering bodies lay scattered in the rubble, many of them decapitated. Four stories of exposed rooms sagged from the bomb's awesome force. Behind him, hysterical men, women, and children ran for their homes. There were no shelters. Stacked sandbags were useless against this power.

A second plane roared over his head. The ground shook from two explosions as the jai alai fronton blew to bits sending chunks of concrete flying in all directions. He covered his head and pressed his face against the street. These weren't soldiers? This wasn't the front? What kind of animal would do this to helpless people?

"Roberto!"

He looked toward the fire station and saw Juan Silliaco and three men trying to drag a lifeless body from the rubble of the post office. "Get out of there, Juan! It's no use!"

A line of bombs ripped across the buildings behind him sending plumes of black smoke and flame into the air. Screaming women and children ran from the burning buildings. Another line of bombs tore into the apartments surrounding the plaza, crumbling them like mud castles.

He stood up and fought to regain his senses. *The bridge! Head for the bridge!* He staggered through the rubble and ran for the river. He was nearly to the candy factory when three aircraft roared over the trees leaving a trail of floating silver objects in their wake.

He dived into the rubble and covered up as the candy factory erupted in flames. The air filled with agonizing screams as girls ran from the burning building, their clothes and hair on fire. Some of them dived into the river. Others staggered in circles until they dropped like burning dolls.

One of the girls saw him and pleaded for help. God, it was Francesca! He charged out of the rubble and tried to smother the flames with his bare hands, but it was too late. He crawled away from her smoldering body and clenched his burned hands.

A wave of planes roared over the plaza, dumping silver death on the tenements and homes. A wounded peasant tried to herd his cows past the Bank of Vizcaya. He was blown to bits along with the animals when a bomb scored a direct hit on the bank.

A string of bombs crashed through a line of roofs on the south side of the plaza, blowing the buildings off their foundations. Flames spouted from shattered bedroom and living room windows. The air filled with bloodcurdling screams as burning women and children hurdled through the flames onto the street below. The sky was on fire. Guernica had become a furnace.

His head was spinning. He couldn't breathe. He staggered past the flaming candy factory toward the river. An hysterical woman ran past him, her clothes on fire. He could smell her burning flesh. She threw herself into the water and vanished in a pillar of steam.

He dropped on his knees and peered through the smoke. The bridge was intact! Untouched by the falling bombs. And there was something else. It was deserted.

He froze in horror. Had she run into the fields with the others? Or was she still back there, trapped in those flames?

The ground shook from two devastating explosions. Santa Maria's steeple rose into the sky like a pillar of fire, then toppled into the smoke and flames.

Unable to move, Roberto squinted down the smoke-filled street leading to the plaza. He said a prayer and turned away from the river toward the raging inferno.

The town plaza was a cauldron of fire. Corpses of humans and animals lay strewn around the fountain. To his right, a dozen people huddled against a makeshift shelter of sandbags. A dazed woman stretched her trembling hands to the sky. A family ran from one of the burning buildings on his left, their clothes smoldering from the intense heat. A panicked donkey galloped across his path, followed by a pig and some chickens. A horse lay dying in the street, a huge gash in its side. The air was filled with scorched paper.

"Ana!" He dropped on his knees and gagged on the choking black smoke.

"Help me!"

He spun around and squinted through the swirling blackness. Someone was kneeling on Mugica Road, maybe fifty yards away. He stumbled through the thick smoke and dropped beside him.

It was Arronategui, weeping uncontrollably in the center of the debris-filled street. Behind him, his precious Church of San Juan was engulfed in flames.

Arronategui looked up at Roberto and screamed through his burned lips. "Why did they do this? I'm a man of God! A man of the cloth!"

"Come on, you can't stay here. The steeple's going to collapse." Roberto grabbed Arronategui's arm, but the crazed priest yanked it away.

"It was you! You caused this! You're the devil!"

Roberto lunged for his arm, but Arronategui crawled into the smoke.

"Roberto!"

He turned toward the plaza and saw her running toward him, her body framed by the burning buildings. A beam of sunlight broke through the smoke, lighting her blackened face. Her left arm was covered with blood. Her shredded blouse and skirt smoldered from falling cinders.

"Ana!" He jumped to his feet and ran toward her as the sky filled with an ominous whine. A black, twin-engined plane burst through the smoke, its wing guns blazing.

"Get down! For God's sake, get down!" He charged into her, driving her to the pavement as bullets tore across the plaza. Chips of dislodged tar and concrete flew into the air as the deadly projectiles chewed up the street and ricocheted off the stone fountain. He clung to her as the plane swept over them and climbed into the smoke-filled sky. In the distance, he heard the deadly rat-a-tat of planes diving on the helpless families fleeing into the hills.

He looked down Mugica Road. The Astra-Unceta's smokestack was still erect amidst the smoke and flames. Beyond it, the convent's gray belltower rose defiantly on the hillside. If they could reach the hill below the convent, the trees would conceal them from the attacking planes.

He heard the plane circling for another strafing run. *Now or never, torero. A few hundred yards. Your only chance.*

He grabbed her arm. "Come on. We've got to—"

She hung limp against him. He rolled her over and gasped. Blood poured from two bullet holes in her chest. He ripped open her blouse and tried to stop the bleeding with his palm, but it was no use. "God!"

He stood up and lifted her in his arms. Dr. Montero was his only hope. With flames lapping at him from the burning buildings, he stumbled down Mugica road toward the Carmelite Convent.

He couldn't see. Tears streamed down his face. He tried to walk faster, but his exhausted legs wouldn't respond. He was nearly to the arms factory when he felt her hand touch his cheek. He sank to his knees, his arms cradling her. "We're going to make it. We're almost to the convent."

She opened her eyes and looked up at him. A smile broke through her burned lips. "Be brave, my love. Save yourself. I'll always be with you." She tried to touch his face, but her hand slipped away. "I love you, Roberto. My brave...handsome...priest...." Her eyes locked on him.

"No! Ana!"

The air filled with a deadly whine. The black, twin-engined aircraft burst through the smoke and opened fire on the plaza. It was diving straight at him.

He cradled her lifeless body in his arms and rose to his feet. "Murderer! God damn your soul to hell! I'll get you! So help me, God! I'll get you!"

Flames spouted from its wings. The street disintegrated in front of him from impacting bullets. He could see the helmeted pilot peering at him through the windshield. Chunks of concrete nicked his face as the twin lines of bullets straddled him. He heard the plane's roar above his head. And it was gone.

The hours following the bombing were a blur. He carried her blood-soaked body to the graveyard next to the convent. With darkness falling on the burning city, he held her in his arms and wept for the woman who had taught him the meaning of love.

He buried her in a shallow grave beside the others, and prayed God would give her peace....

He climbed into the northern hills and veered east toward the river. It was nearly midnight when he dived into the Mundaca's rushing waters. He barely made it across. He crawled up the embankment and collapsed on a bed of pine needles. He was asleep in seconds.

When he awoke, the sunlit forest was blanketed with thick, acrid smoke. He could see the fires burning through the trees. By now, rescue workers were entering Guernica from the neighboring towns and villages. They wouldn't have much time to drag away the wounded and dead. The eastern slopes rocked with artillery fire. Mola's army was only a few miles away.

He ran along the forest road leading to the bridge. Along the way, he passed families huddled against the trees, their blank faces staring at him from the shadows. He stopped and tried to talk to an old woman, but she didn't respond. He bent down and touched her cold forehead. She was dead.

When he reached the meadow east of the bridge, he froze in horror. Hundreds of bodies were sprawled on the grass, many with their eyes fixed on the sky. Shepherds lay huddled against their sheep. Fathers clutched their wives and children. All of them were dead.

His stomach heaved. He collapsed on his knees and

vomited uncontrollably. If this wasn't hell, it would do.

Mustering his strength, he stood up and stumbled across the meadow. He tried not to look down at them, but it was impossible. His foot brushed against a tiny hand protruding from a blanket. A single bullet had penetrated the infant's brown swaddling cloth. The baby's frozen hand clutched a tuft of grass.

Sobbing, he looked up at the mission standing unscathed on the rocky hillside. The planes had missed it. It was perhaps the last remaining building in Guernica.

He started up the hill and hesitated. A man was lying face-down on the rocks below the mission, a sack of broken paint bottles scattered at his side.

He climbed the hill and knelt beside the motionless body, his hand resting on the man's bloody shirt. "You should have gone to the sea, *amigo*. Now I have to dig another grave." He buried his face against Sebastian and wept for a dying nation.

He left under cover of darkness, using a flashlight to guide his way. He headed into the eastern hills toward the artillery fire. It would take a week to reach France—if he reached France.

He lasted three hours before collapsing against a boulder. There was no moon, only stars twinkling through the drifting smoke. He rested his head against the valise and fell into exhausted sleep.

He awoke to bright sunlight streaming down on his face from the nearby peaks. The artillery fire had stopped. Everything was still. He chewed on a piece of bread and checked the map.

He was about to move on when he heard an ominous sound echo off the rocks. He dropped on his knees and cowered behind the boulder. The crunching boots grew louder, accompanied by a clanking sound that reminded him of the rain-swept night outside Granada six years ago.

The clanking sound became a roar as a tank burst through the brush and roared past him, followed by a column of brown-uniformed soldiers. Petrified, he pressed his face against the boulder and listened to them shout at one another.

One of them described his wife in Pamplona. Someone laughed and offered to pay her a visit if he got out first. The rocks echoed with laughter. Another talked about his sister in Burgos. She was dating a German officer in the Condor Legion. One of the men cursed him. There was no laughter.

He leaned forward and caught a glimpse of their glistening faces. They looked so young, like children playing at war with baggy uniforms and toy rifles slung over their shoulders. Except for the red-arrow patches on their shoulders, they were no different than those young men lying in the convent above Guernica. He clung to the boulder and watched them fade into the haze....

The following day, he entered a narrow pass winding north toward the sea. His legs and arms ached from the steady, upward slope. By late afternoon, he was climbing through dense fog. Droplets of moisture mingled with the sweat on his face. He could smell the salt air.

Exhausted, he collapsed against a rock and pulled out his last piece of bread. He stared at the white chunk of bread and felt a rush of panic. Water was no problem with the swollen streams, but how long could he last without food? He devoured the bread and gulped down some water from his canteen.

That night, things grew desperate. He'd reached a three thousand foot ridge overlooking the fog-shrouded Bay of Biscay. The sun had dropped behind a wall of approaching storm clouds. Lightning flashed above the sea. The mountains shook with thunder.

With hunger chewing at his insides, and frozen rain stinging his face, he crawled into a small cave and huddled against the rocks. He ripped open the valise and dug out his torn raincoat in a futile effort to stay warm. Exhausted, he curled in a ball and fell into deep sleep....

"Hello, Roberto."

He sat up in horror. Lorca was standing at the cave's entrance, his brown eyes glaring at him, his body riddled with bullets.

"No—you're dead!"

"Don't be afraid. There is no death. Only light and shadow. Come—walk with me." Lorca smiled and retreated into the darkness.

"Wait!" Roberto scrambled to the entrance and froze. Something was standing in the driving rain. He blinked his eyes in disbelief. A white horse stood on the rocks, its hooded rider peering down at him. "Who are you?"

The rider leaned toward him. "We've met before. Don't you remember?"

That voice. It couldn't be.

"Stop the pain, mortal. Time is very short."

"Who are you, dammit?" Roberto rushed at the cloaked rider, but the horse backed away.

"Stay back, mortal. You don't want to see my face. Your world doesn't want to see my face. I am Kalki."

Roberto collapsed on the rocks. A red beam of light pulsed from the rider's hood. He felt its searing heat.

"Your alchemists have gone too far. They have unleashed the forbidden sun. The floodgates are opened. The anti-gods walk the earth. THAT WILL NOT BE ALLOWED!"

The rider raised up on the white horse and rose into the flashing sky....

Roberto's eyes snapped open. Bright sunlight streamed into the cave. He sat up and tried to collect his senses. The piercing voice rang in his ears.

He grabbed the canteen and splashed water on his face. His stomach ached from hunger. He dug into the valise and groped for a scrap of food—anything to keep him alive. He'd eat the damn leather if he had to.

His fingers seized something soft. He pulled out a chunk of bread and stared at it in shock. How could he have missed it? It must have wedged behind the torn liner. He stuffed the bread in his mouth and wolfed it down like a starving animal. Quenching his thirst with water from the canteen, he collapsed against the cave wall and gazed at the sunlit floor. He was asleep in seconds.

When he awoke, the gnawing hunger was gone. He crawled

through the entrance and stood up in the warm sunlight.

The sky was crystal clear and the Bay of Biscay stretched below him like a turquoise mirror, interrupted only by whitecaps rushing against the rocky shore. He could see San Sebastian, its jewel-like harbor glistening in the afternoon sun. To the east, the mountains began a gradual descent to Biarritz.

Artillery thuds echoed from the western hills. The sky above Guernica was thick with brown and black smoke.

There was no time to lose. He was entrenched in hostile territory with twenty painful miles remaining to the French border. He must dodge Nationalist patrols all the way—an almost impossible task.

He reached into his shirt pocket and clutched Sebastian's torn map. *Twenty miles, hombre. Twenty miles....*

He scrambled into the cave and grabbed his battered valise. He was about to close it when he noticed a yellowed envelope protruding from the torn liner. His name was scrawled across the face.

He lifted the envelope out of its hiding place and held it toward the light. Carefully tearing away one end, he pulled out a sheet of crinkled paper and gently unfolded it. He could barely read the faded script...

May 7, 1931
My Son,
When you read this letter, I'll be dead. Two years have passed since we last saw each other. They have been sad years. I have regretted every moment of them.

There can be no peace for a father who loses his son. No way to recapture precious moments from a happier time. In these final words, I ask that you know my sorrow and forgive me for hurting you.

It's too late to erase the past, but in these final hours, I'll try to brighten the future. Excepting my home, and the sum I am leaving to my dear Maria for her unflinching loyalty through these difficult years, I bequeath to my son, Roberto Hidalgo, all my wealth which has been transferred to the Bank of Zurich, in the hope that he will use it to carry on my good

name while following his dream—wherever it may lead.
God go with you, my son.
Your Loving Father,
Don Felipe Hidalgo
(zero-three-five-nine-one)

Roberto stared blankly at the letter. How could this be? Could six years pass without him knowing the truth? What kind of madness was this?

He slumped against the cave wall while struggling to recall his final moments at the train station in Valencia. He remembered Pizarro handing him an envelope and muttering something about his father. In his anguish, he must have jammed the envelope into the valise with enough force to bury it inside the torn liner.

His face flushed with anger. He crumpled the letter in his hand. He could still feel Ana's lifeless body dangling from his arms when he carried her to the graveyard. No money on God's earth would bring her back from the dead. Or bring back Sebastian and Augustin. Or save Francesca when she burned to death in front of him. Or breathe life into that infant lying beside its mother in the meadow. They were gone—and so was Spain.

He jammed the letter into his pocket. It would take four days to reach the border. Maybe his hate would keep him alive until then.

Roberto Hidalgo was dead. He died in the flames of Guernica on a spring night in 1937. In his place stood a hardened man driven by two passions. To find the answer to an apparition called Kalki. And to destroy the black-winged devil that took away the last thing he loved....

24 | China

Frank Gerramino put down the typed letter and looked up in shock. "Is this some kind of joke?"

"I'm afraid not."

"Then, what the hell's wrong?"

"I'm sorry, Frank."

"Sorry?" Gerramino leaned forward and glared at her. "Have you lost your mind? The best damn reporter in New York is gonna throw away five years of sweat and blood? Are you nuts?"

She looked down at her folded hands. "I can't do it anymore."

"Do what?"

"Destroy people's lives."

Gerramino glanced at the newspaper lying beside her resignation letter. "Because of Farley?"

"And others."

"Come on, Karen. Farley was suicidal. He would've done himself in regardless of your story. Hell, he deserved it. The creep embezzled thirty thousand bucks from the welfare fund."

She stroked her forehead. "He was set up. You know it, and I know it. That's the way La Guardia works. If someone gets in his way, they end up smeared across the headlines. And guess who does the dirty work." She reached across the desk and picked up the newspaper. "The best part of the story is on page two. Farley left a wife and baby. What about them, Frank? What about them?"

Gerramino took the newspaper out of her hand and placed it on the desk. "You're just tired. Take a week off. Go down to Miami and lie in the sun."

She looked at him with pleading eyes. "God, I wish it was that simple. I'd be on a train today. No, Frank—it's time to let someone else do this job."

He threw up his hands. "Just like that? You walk out on me just like that?"

"There are lots of starving reporters out there—remember?

Gary Naiman

Any of them can do my job. The only problem will be replacing them every few years. That's when it catches up to you. When you can't look in the mirror anymore."

Gerramino picked up his worn brown pipe and dipped it in a pouch of tobacco. "Snap out of it, dammit. It's not character assassination to turn the floodlights on a bunch of vermin sucking the blood out of seven million starving people. Exposing the scum makes the next guy think twice before he crosses the line. A few innocent people are bound to get hurt along the way. But think of the thousands you help. For God's sake, don't throw everything away because some suicidal jerk blew his brains out."

She forced a smile. "You always were the great orator, Mr. Gerramino. I'll miss you."

"Miss, hell! I'm not going to accept this resignation until you give me a good reason. So far, you're striking out." Gerramino chomped on his pipe and lit it with violent puffs. "It's money, isn't it?"

"Are you kidding? I'm already making more than I'm worth."

"I'll be the judge of that. Tell you what. Starting Monday, I'm giving you a twenty five percent raise with a bonus to match—for all your good work in the past five years."

"Are you going to listen to me? If it were money, I'd stay here."

"Then, what is it? And get off that burn out crap."

Karen stood up and walked around the mahogany desk to the bay window overlooking Time's Square. "That sleet's really coming down. Looks like an early winter."

"Yeah—real nostalgic if you have a job."

She nodded at the paper lying on the desk. "It wasn't easy writing that letter."

"Then, let's throw it away before you make the biggest mistake of your life."

"I can't do that, Frank."

Gerramino turned toward her and slipped off his wire-rimmed glasses. "I think you owe me more than a piece of paper and some one-liners."

The Tenth Avatar

She eased back to the chair and sat down. She had just walked through forbidden territory and gotten away with it. No one infringed on the sacred space between Frank Gerramino's desk and that bay window—no one, except Karen Halberton.

"Want a drink?"

"Thanks." She watched him reach into a side drawer and lift out a bottle of scotch and two glasses.

"Sorry, I'm too lazy to get ice. Besides, it ruins the bouquet." He poured two stiff shots and handed her one of the crystal glasses. "Cheers." He gulped down the scotch and set the glass aside. So much for bouquet.

She sipped the scotch and rested the glass on her lap. "You're right about me owing you. If it wasn't for you, I'd probably be selling my body out there in the rain."

"Hell, you would've made it somehow. Your kind always does. I knew people like you in the 'Kitchen'. Knock 'em down and they bounce right back in your face like one of those toy punching bags. Never could figure it out. It's gotta have something to do with hate."

"Maybe so." She gulped down the scotch and placed the empty glass on the desk. "Sure you want to hear this?"

"Go ahead."

She took a deep breath. "I need to finish what Jim started."

Gerramino shrugged. "You want overseas duty? Hell, give me two months to set it up and you can work with Carlton in London. All I'll ask is an occasional trip back here. You know—to keep an eye on the domestic stuff. That way, it'll justify the extra salary and bonus."

She frowned. "I know what you're trying to do, but you've gotta understand. I don't want to work behind a desk. I want to pick up where my husband left off. In the field, before they killed him."

Gerramino stared at her with black eyes. "Well, thanks for clearing that up. Now I know you're nuts."

"Maybe, but there's something you don't know. Something that's eaten at me for two years."

"Yeah?"

"She fixed her blue eyes on him. "I knew about Jim's story

a month before he died. And how dangerous it was. I could've stopped him, but I didn't."

Gerramino stroked his graying hair. "You're a reporter. What else could you do?"

She leaned closer. "Don't you see, Frank? I killed him."

Gerramino sank in his chair. "You didn't kill him. He killed himself because of his father."

"What?"

"You think I'm stupid? Jim wanted to show up the old man. He was doing all right until he got impatient. That mistake's done in many a good soul."

"Maybe so—but I could've stopped him."

Gerramino hesitated. "If anyone's responsible for Jim's death—it's me."

"You?"

He reached into a side drawer and pulled out a manila folder. "I've never shown this to anyone." He handed her the folder and watched her fumble through the loose telegrams.

"What is this?"

"I knew about your husband's little escapade from day one."

She stared at him in shock. "And you didn't stop him?"

Gerramino poured himself another scotch. "I came mighty close. Even rehearsed my little tirade. When I found out he was in Berlin, I placed a call to his London hotel and left an urgent message. He finally got back to me the next day with a phony story about the hotel screwing up his messages." Gerramino pinched his finger and thumb together. "I came that close to firing him over the phone."

"But—you didn't."

Gerramino gulped down the scotch. "When a reporter's in the field, it's hard to pull them back. Jim was green as hell, but he made up for it with smarts and guts. That's why I hired him away from *Reuters*."

He placed the empty glass on the desk. "I was enraged when he lied to me, but I didn't want to lose him. He was so close, I decided to let him take the shot. If he pulled it off, I'd have an excuse not to fire him. I could live with that because the story always comes first."

Gerramino's eyes glazed over. "That weak moment cost your husband his life. I'm sorry, Karen. It's eaten at me too."

For a moment, neither of them spoke. The only sound was the steam hissing in the radiator.

Gerramino broke the unsettled silence. He slipped on his glasses and scanned her resignation letter. "So, what's this mysterious new job?"

She looked at the sleet splattering against the window. "It's with *Reuters*."

It took a few seconds for her words to sink in. Gerramino's face reddened into a deep scowl. "*Reuters?*"

"I promised Franz Hessler a decision by tomorrow."

"Hessler? That sonofabitch!" Gerramino slammed his fist on the desk. "I don't believe this. The bastard's trying to get even for Jim. So help me, I'll strangle that little slime with my bare hands." He stood up and barged to the window, nearly knocking over the leather chair.

"Frank, I—"

He whirled around and pointed a menacing finger at her. "It's Swensen, isn't it? I should've known Hessler would send in one of his stooges to pull it off. What an asshole I've been. Never suspecting what they were up to. I should've known something was wrong when you started dating that blond Adonis."

Karen glared at him. "Just a goddamn minute. I'm not dating Eric. We're friends. He doesn't know what's going on. I met Hessler through him, but that's where it ends. The rest is my doing."

"Oh, sure. With a little prodding from that arrogant slime." Gerramino leaned against the desk. "Don't you see what Hessler's doing? By stealing you away from me, he squares things. He doesn't give a damn about you. You'll rot in some rat-infested country."

"You don't think much of me, do you?"

"You're wrong about that. If I didn't care, I wouldn't be busting a gut in front of you." He paused and lowered his voice. "Don't do it, Karen. If you want to leave, I'll call Bart

Rawlings at the *Tribune*. He'll hire you before I finish making the offer. But for Christ's sake, don't go with that scum in London."

She folded her hands and watched him yank his leather chair back into place. He sat down and stared at her like an angry father. God, how she wished he was her father.

"Well?"

"You're wrong about Jim's story. My husband was onto something. He was just denting the surface when they stuffed that gallon of liquor into him and drove his car into a tree."

Gerramino shook his head. "You mean that crap about September 1939?" He leaned forward and rested his arms on the desk. "You're a good reporter, Karen. You know what it takes to print a story. Without corroborating evidence, it's pure speculation. Jim came close to tasting what it's all about, but that's not good enough. Now, it's too late. The story's lost its punch. If Hitler invades Europe next September, it won't surprise anyone except that idiot Chamberlain. First, the damn paperhanger repatriated the Rhineland. Then, he snared Austria. Last week, he marched into Czechoslovakia with a bunch of scared peasants throwing flowers at his feet. It's only a matter of time before he goes too far. Give it up, Karen. The suspense is gone."

"It's gone because you didn't publish Jim's story two years ago."

"How could I? Without proof, we would've been roasted by our competitors, not to mention our own government. In case you haven't noticed, I like my job."

She shook her head. "There was no follow-up. You let Carlton run with it. That was like tossing it in a waste basket."

Gerramino's neck reddened. "I'm sorry, there was no story."

"Hessler thinks there is. He promised me a shot at it after I do some work for him."

"And you believed him? Goddammit, Karen. He'll say anything to get you. He's a goddamned liar."

"Well—you wanted reasons. I've given you a couple of good ones." She stood up and extended her hand. "Goodbye,

Frank."

He looked at her in disbelief. "Do you know what you're saying?"

"Yes."

He frowned and looked down at the resignation. "One favor?"

"If I can."

He rose to his feet and clasped her hand. "Sleep on it. Let's meet tomorrow at noon. If you still want to leave, I won't interfere."

She nodded and forced a smile. "Still friends?"

"Always."

She brushed away a tear and walked out of the office.

He waited until the door closed before punching the intercom. "Louise, call the *Cunard Line*. I need to reach Eric Swensen before he docks in New York. He's on the *Queen Mary*."

Gerramino heard a church bell clanging in the distance. He took his finger off the intercom and stepped to the window.

Nine a.m. Those soaked pedestrians should be rushing to their jobs instead of milling around like cattle. Hell, what jobs? In a few minutes, those beaten souls would line up at the nearest soup kitchen where one of their brethren would dish out a tin of watered-down stew and a hard slice of bread. Just enough to get them through another day.

Gerramino pulled off his wire-rimmed glasses and rubbed his eyes. He'd witnessed the same daily ritual for nine years— and it was getting worse. Like every other city, once-proud New York had become a refugee camp for the nation's growing army of poor. Riots were breaking out in the streets. Babies were starving. Families were broken.

A tear rolled down his cheek. He looked up at the gray sky and muttered, "Wake up, America. God, what's happened to us?"

Karen's eyes snapped open. The entrance buzzer? She sat up and glanced at her watch. It was past ten.

She squinted through the steamed bay window. The rain

had stopped and a half-moon was breaking through the clouds above the East River.

The buzzer rang again. She stood up and shuffled around the sofa to the intercom in the foyer. "Yes?"

"It's Eric."

"Eric? You're not supposed to get in until tomorrow?"

"Well—I'm here."

She hesitated and glanced at the opened bedroom door.

"Are you gonna let me freeze to death out here?"

"Sorry." She pushed the button and stepped back in anger. What the hell did he want at this hour?

She closed the bedroom door and paused at the mirror in the foyer. Her eyes dropped to the copy of *Gone With The Wind* on the table. She smiled and pinched her cheeks. Scarlett O'Hara had nothing on her. But where the hell was Rhett Butler? She straightened her blouse and waited for the unwelcome knock.

"Good evening, Miss Halberton." The handsome six-footer pulled off his Alpine hat and smiled at her.

"Come in." She stepped back from the door and felt his wet coat brush against her. "You smell good. What is it?"

He shrugged. "Me."

"Arrogant Swede." She took his coat and gestured toward the sofa. Gerramino was right about him being an Adonis with that lean build and tousled blond hair. Add the handsome, boyish face and Eric Swensen had it all. Too bad she wasn't interested.

He sat on the sofa and looked at the flashing moon. "Looks like an early winter."

"You came up here to tell me that?"

He smiled and leaned back on the couch. "Got a drink for a weary traveler?"

She poured a bourbon and handed it to him. "So—how's London these days?"

His smile faded. "Sounds like you'll know soon enough."

"What?"

"Please, Karen. I'm too tired to play games. I called my boss an hour ago. He was plenty mad."

She sat next to him and forced a smile. "He should be. It's the middle of the night back there."

He chugged the bourbon. "Want to know why I called him? I'll give you a hint. It's why I'm here."

She folded her hands in her lap and looked down. "I get the drift. How did you find out?"

"It's not important. From the sound of things, I would've known by tomorrow." He sat up and placed the empty glass on the table. "It's China, isn't it?"

"That's my business."

He locked his Nordic blue eyes on her. "Are you nuts? Do you know how many reporters have turned it down? Do you have any idea what you're stepping into?"

She snatched his glass off the table and walked to the bar. "I've been briefed."

"By who—Hessler? It's suicide, Karen. The chances of getting to Vasquez are one in a thousand. Even if you manage to reach him, the Japanese will never let you out of there."

She turned and stared at him. "What was that name?"

"Name? You mean—Vasquez?" He shook his head in disbelief. "Hell—hasn't anyone told you the truth?"

She smiled nervously and refilled his glass. "I thought you might do that." She walked back to the couch and sat beside him.

"I don't believe this."

She handed him the fresh bourbon. "I was going to call you tomorrow. I respect you, Eric. You're the best. Europe, Asia—you've seen it all. I don't trust Hessler either. I knew you'd give me the straight scoop."

He sipped the bourbon and glared at her. "Nice speech, except it doesn't make sense. Hessler told me you've already accepted."

"That's not true. I wanted to talk to you first." She looked at him with those soft, blue eyes.

"You're something, Miss Halberton. You expect me to believe that bull?" He leaned back against the cushion and gazed at the window. "Nice view, with the moon shining down like that."

"Yes—very nice."

He looked down at his drink. "How much do you know?"

"Not much, except it's a story that could wake us up. If someone can get out of there with pictures and accounts of the brutality, it might shake the pacifists out of their tree. Sounds pretty important, don't you think?"

"Yeah, especially when you're chasing a Pulitzer. Only problem is the award will be placed on your coffin."

She looked down. "That's all I know."

Eric stared at the moon. "You'll be flown to Honolulu on the *China Clipper*. After a four hour layover, you'll island-hop to Manila in the Philippines. You'll spend three days there undergoing intensive briefings on Chinese geography, diplomatic rules of conduct, identification techniques, and emergency measures."

Karen lit a cigaret and leaned back on the sofa. "Go on."

"Identification techniques are the most important part of the briefings. They include passwords for validating key contacts, and methods of spotting Japanese agents that might be tailing you. Throw in some emergency escape measures, and they'll increase your chances to fifty-fifty."

Karen puffed the cigaret and placed it in an ashtray. "If you're trying to scare me, it's working."

"I'm telling you the truth."

"How come you know so much about it?"

Eric shook his head. "Hessler tried to recruit me before he nabbed you. I turned him down when I found out the Japanese were onto us."

Karen snatched the cigaret and took another puff. "Why are the Japanese so worked up? It's no secret they're raping half of China."

Eric sat up and glared at her. "That, my dear, is exactly why you shouldn't be given this assignment."

"I resent that. I asked a civil question."

"God, Karen."

"What's wrong?"

"Plenty."

She puffed the cigaret. "Franz mentioned a missionary who

has photographs of atrocities against the citizens of Nanking and Shanghai. Is that Vasquez?"

He nodded.

"So I get in there, meet with him, and get the hell out. Sure there's some risk, but it'll be worth it. When those photos hit the front page, they'll give us a good slap in the face."

Eric gulped down the bourbon. "If that's all there was, you might have a chance." He took a deep breath and looked her in the eyes. "I'm gonna tell you something that could finish me."

"I understand."

He put the empty glass on the table. "Father Antonio Vasquez has saved hundreds of Chinese civilians by smuggling them through Japanese lines."

She nodded. "Franz didn't mention his name, but he told me about his humanitarian work."

"Did he tell you Vasquez is a spy?"

"What?"

"Vasquez is a British Intelligence operative. A missionary who volunteered his services to the English after the Japanese invaded China. Since then, he's traded vital information to the Brits for food and supplies. That's how he cares for the refugees."

Karen stared at him. "What kind of information?"

Eric hesitated. "If a war starts, we'll face an enemy more powerful than any in history. In Europe, it'll be Hitler. In Asia, the Japanese. Our one chance will be to keep them apart. They know it, and we know it. If their armies link up through Asia and Europe—we better learn Japanese and German."

"You mean—we could lose?"

"We would lose."

Karen's eyes lit up.

"The Japanese are in China for more than bloodlust. Their armies are pressing southwest toward northern India. And Nazi agents posing as mountaineers are crawling around the Himalayas trying to find a route that could link them up. If they're successful, they'll open an eight thousand mile supply line and defend it with everything they have—and they have plenty. It'll be the world's biggest nightmare since Attila-the-

Hun."

"What about the missionary?"

"Vasquez has gathered vital information from the refugees. The Brits are sweating bullets trying to correlate his findings with possible weak spots in the Himalayan wall."

"Weak spots?"

"Passes and low lying valleys the Japanese could cross undetected. With the damn mountains and heavy weather in that region, it's impossible to track an advancing force from the air. If the Japanese and Germans find that magic passage, nothing will stop them. That's why the Brits are relying on Vasquez's information."

Karen shook her head. "You know this is pretty hard to take."

"Believe it! And believe this. Until a few weeks ago, Vasquez was able to radio his reports to British agents in India. Since then—nothing. The Brits think the Japanese picked up his signal and he had to go silent. The Japanese are close to nabbing him. He's not gonna make it."

Karen snuffed out the cigaret. "Then—it's not about atrocities."

"Never was. That stuff's been coming out of Nanking for months, but no one cares. No story there, except some raised eyebrows. It'll take more than pictures of mutilated bodies to shake things up over here. People are too worried about their next meal to care about the rest of the world. Sorry, but that's the way it is."

"Then, why send me in?"

"Desperation."

"Huh?"

"Before he went off the air, Vasquez radioed India he'd discovered something called 'NI'. I guess it shook them up pretty bad."

Her eyes widened. "NI?"

"Something's up. I don't know what it is, but two British agents have blown their cover trying to find him. They're probably dead by now. Getting to Nanking is like crossing a minefield." He shook his head. "The Brits are pulling out all their aces. Some genius even came up with an idea a reporter might get through. You know, some naive soul who doesn't know the full story. Ideally, an ambitious type trying to make a name for herself." He paused and watched for a reaction, but there was none. "They're betting the Japs will let the reporter lead them to Vasquez. Then, they'll try a last minute rescue."

"In the heart of China?"

"Desperation, remember? It's their only shot."

"Sounds suicidal."

"They prefer 'sticky'. It has a better ring."

She rubbed her forehead. "That's it?"

He nodded.

"Well—that's quite a story."

"It's more than that. You said it yourself. Suicide."

She leaned over and kissed him on the cheek. "We're both tired. Call me in the morning."

"Don't do it, Karen."

She stood up and brushed back her hair. "Come on, handsome. I'll walk you to the door."

She kissed him goodnight and locked the door. It was nearly midnight. Better get some sleep, Miss Halberton. Tomorrow would be quite a day.

She turned off the living room light and pushed through the bedroom door. The luggage on the bed was almost packed. She could finish in the morning.

She slid the two bags off the bed and set the alarm for four. It would be hard falling asleep, but she had to try. She slipped off her clothes and climbed under the covers. She didn't know it, but she would never sleep in that bed again.

At eleven a.m., Eric stormed through the *Time's* lobby and rushed into one of the waiting elevators. He stepped off on "Two" and weaved through the bustling newsroom until he was standing at Frank Gerramino's frosted glass door.

"Go right in, Mr. Swensen."

He nodded to the secretary and turned the knob.

Gerramino was standing at the window, his hands clasped behind his back. "The letter's on the desk."

Eric walked to the desk and picked up the opened letter. He read the words and sank into a chair.

"It was taped to my door when I got in this morning."

"Did you try to reach Franz?"

"I have a call in to him."

Eric shook his head and placed the letter on the desk. "I saw her last night. God knows, I tried to talk her out of it."

Gerramino unclasped his hands and turned around, his black eyes trained on the shaken foreign correspondent. "You're not lying to me?"

"I didn't know."

Gerramino's head snapped to the side as the intercom went off. He reached across the desk and pushed the button.

"Mr. Hessler's on the line, sir."

"Put him through." Gerramino sat down and placed his hand on the phone. He gestured for Eric to pick up a second phone on the conference table in the corner. "Hello, Franz. It's been too long."

"Much too long, my friend. So, what's up?"

"Quit playing games, Franz. You know why I'm calling. I want you to stop this thing."

Hessler hesitated before speaking. The only sound was the transatlantic phone static. *"Sorry, my friend. Even if I wanted to, it's too late. She's undercover now. You know the rules."*

Gerramino gripped the phone. "What the hell are you doing? She's too green. You're sending her into a death trap."

"Like her husband? Is that what you're trying to say?"

Gerramino's face reddened. He was about to launch into a tirade when Eric cut him off.

"Franz, this is Eric."

"Eric? What are you doing there?"

"Trying to save a young woman's life. Listen to me, Franz. This isn't the way to get even. You can call this thing off now. Do it, Franz. For me."

The phone filled with static. They could hear Hessler's labored breathing on the other end.

"Sorry, the story's too important. She knows the risk. I wish my other reporters had her guts."

Eric's face flushed. "You bastard."

"Watch it, young man. I suggest you get out of there and go back to work. We all have our jobs—including Miss Halberton. She's in good hands. Remember, there are interested parties involved."

"On both sides, dammit!"

Hessler sighed. *"I have an important dinner engagement. We can pick this up another time. If that's all you have—"*

"You sonofabitch!" Gerramino screamed into the mouthpiece. "If you don't call her back, I'll rip your heart out!"

Hessler laughed. *"Take a pill, Frank. Good talking with you. Auf Wiedersehen."* The phone clicked and went dead.

Gerramino slammed the receiver on the hook and stared at Eric.

"What are we gonna do?"

Gerramino sank in the chair. "It's her decision."

Eric placed the receiver on the hook. "I'll resign, dammit."

"No—that would really shut the door." Gerramino picked up the letter. "You better get back to work. Thanks for stopping by."

"We've got to do something."

Gerramino rose from the chair and extended his hand. "I'll figure it out. Keep in touch." He shook Eric's hand and watched him disappear through the frosted glass door.

Gerramino leaned on the desk and listened to the steam hiss in the radiator. He reached down and opened the side drawer. "Well—that's that." He slipped Karen's letter into the manila folder.

He straightened up and stepped to the window. Beams of sunlight lit up his face. He looked down at Time's Square and forced out the words. "Godspeed, Miss Halberton. Godspeed...."

"Care for a drink?"

Karen looked up at the attractive stewardess and smiled. "A martini, thank you."

"Straight up, or on the rocks?"

"Whatever."

"First flight?"

"No—just a little nervous."

"I'll make you a double." The stewardess smiled and headed up the aisle.

Karen stuffed the pile of notes into her briefcase and leaned back against the cushioned seat. She glanced at her watch. Two hours had passed since the *DC-3* took off from Newark's Metropolitan Airport. It would take sixteen more to reach San Francisco. After a night's layover, she'd board Pan Am's *China Clipper* for the grueling, sixty hour hopscotch to Manila.

She closed her eyes and listened to the *DC-3's* humming engines. She could still see the empty newsroom sprawled in front of her when she stepped off the elevator at five thirty this morning.

It only took a few minutes to clear her desk and tape the envelope to Frank's office door. It contained a simple note with one typed line....

I'm sorry, Frank.
Goodbye....

She recalled hesitating at the elevator and looking back at the white envelope stuck on the frosted glass. It would only take a second to remove it. Then—a quick call to Franz Hessler in London, and *Reuters* would be a fading memory. She'd almost changed her mind when that horrid voice filled her ears....

You stupid bitch! I told you to get whiskey, not bourbon! You can't even read, you good-for-nothing little whore! If your mother was alive, I'd walk out of here tomorrow! You're goddamn lucky I'm willing to put up with you, you little tramp! Now go up to bed before I use my strap on you. I'll be in later....

"Here you go, ma'am. Dry, with a twist." The stewardess placed the martini next to her and smiled. "We'll serve lunch in an hour. Enjoy the flight."

She smiled and watched the stewardess disappear through the maroon curtain. Across the aisle, a well-dressed executive looked up from his paperwork and nodded politely. She returned the kindness and resumed her forward-facing position.

The martini tasted like fruit of the gods. She leaned back in the seat and studied the passing clouds. Not bad, Miss Halberton. Sipping your favorite drink at ten thousand feet. Beats starving at the YWCA. Only problem is you just gave up the job of a lifetime for a plane trip to the unknown.

She fumbled through her briefcase and grasped a black notebook. No need to pull it out. After two years, she'd memorized the contents.

Jim had sent her the notebook with his final letter—for "safekeeping." It read like a journal, with each entry carefully dated and printed with findings from his field work. Most of the entries appeared valueless and full of conjecture. Leads that dissipated. Mistaken assumptions. Passages filled with uncertainty and self-criticism. More like a foreign correspondent's training manual than anything of importance.

After plodding through thirty pages of Jim's frustrating rhetoric, it was the final page that shook her. The writing was barely legible, as if he was under great stress. Strange, after focusing on Hitler's Germany, he would suddenly turn his attention to Japan and the Far East.

Until last night, she'd considered those final entries a collection of indecipherable gibberish. Names without meaning—like "Nishina," "Noguchi," and "Stein." References to "alchemy" and "gold." All of it reading like a child's fantasy. Until Eric dropped those two letters."

She closed the briefcase and placed it on the floor while recalling Jim's final exhortation that "NI" was the key to "the Norway mission" and "a top-secret flight across the Middle East and Asia." He was so upbeat about the "revelation" and "greatest story of the century."

She felt her eyelids growing heavy. The vibrating engines and stiff martini were taking effect. There were so many questions, and so few answers. Better to sleep on it. Her head relaxed against the cushion....

Gary Naiman

    Had Karen stayed awake, she might have noticed the oriental gentleman seated across the aisle in row three. Mr. Hasagawa had picked up her trail from an accomplice when she arrived at Newark's Metropolitan Airport three hours earlier. He would stay with her until she boarded the *China Clipper* in San Francisco, at which time Mr. Akagi would take over. In the Philippines, Mr. Nomo would join her until she landed in Shanghai. From there, the jaws would begin to close.

    Her last conscious thought was the jade statuette she had seen while walking through the Metropolitan Museum's *Far Eastern Exhibit* last Sunday. Strange, she would recollect such a nebulous work of art at a time like this, yet the statuette had intrigued her from the moment she laid eyes on it. A winged horse and hooded rider descending to earth to cleanse its evil. The final incarnation of the Hindu God, *Vishnu*. The Tenth Avatar, known only as *Kalki*....

25 | *Eammon*

HITLER OCCUPIES CZECHOSLOVAKIA!
Thousands of troops flood Sudetenland after Chamberlain signs pact with Führer

Eammon lowered the newspaper and stared at the guests rushing through the *Hotel Bern's* lobby. Had Chamberlain lost his mind? He might as well climb into a coffin and let the *Führer* nail it shut. Someone should put a bullet in both their heads before it was too late.

He slipped off his reading glasses and glanced at the wooden clock above the hotel's reception desk. Almost two p.m. In another minute, the damn yellow bird would pop out of the clock and begin its unnerving ritual. Maybe this time he'd climb up there and strangle it.

He closed the newspaper and flipped it on the cocktail table. Enough bad news for today. This morning's telegram had been no different than the others. The same frustrating words....

White Lion:

Status quo....

Lion Tamer

What were they waiting for? Didn't the fools know delays were dangerous? Gotta keep moving, dammit. Either give the "go ahead" or bring him home. This was no way to run a ship.

He flinched from two loud "cuckoos." The bird burst through the clock's twin doors, its ugly head bobbing at him. He cursed it and looked away. If hell was boredom, this was hell.

Maybe a stroll around Bern would help. He'd taken so many in the past two weeks, he could probably do it blindfolded. He stuffed his reading glasses into a breast pocket and started to get up.

He hesitated and slipped back in his chair while studying a

well-dressed gentleman seated on a white couch across the bustling lobby. From the look of the man's charcoal hair, he appeared middle-aged, perhaps in his late forties. He was engrossed in a newspaper.

Eammon's eyes lit up. A bright object flickered beneath the man's jacket. He leaned forward to make sure. Yes—a small gold crucifix and chain rested on the man's chest, just below his protruding white collar

Could this be the one? The timing wasn't good, but no matter. After three futile tries, things were getting desperate. Quit wasting time. Give it a shot and hope for the best.

Sensing Eammon's interest, the priest looked up and smiled. Eammon nodded and returned the smile. He pushed out of the chair and walked across the red-carpeted lobby to the seated gentleman. "Sorry for staring like that. It's always good to see a fellow clergyman."

The priest glanced at Eammon's crucifix. "I see we have something in common."

Eammon extended his hand. "Father Eammon Collins of Saint Timothy's Parish in Belfast."

The priest stood up and shook Eammon's hand. "Pleasure, Father. Padre Roberto Santiago of the Church of Saint Tome in Toledo."

"Ah—from Spain. If you prefer, I speak the native language."

"No need." Santiago gestured toward the empty couch. "Please, sit down. Great view of the river from here."

Eammon smiled and sat on the couch while his new acquaintance placed his newspaper on the cocktail table and sat beside him.

"What brings you to Bern, Father Collins?"

"Please, call me Eammon. I'm vacationing here until my request for transfer is approved."

"Transfer?"

"Yes, and I'm afraid it's gotten to me. I'm a bundle of nerves." Eammon gestured to a passing waiter. "Some wine?"

"Thank you."

"A dry Swiss?"

"Fine."

Eammon chuckled. "I expected you to ask for a *Rioja* or *Alicante*."

"Tempting, but since I left Spain, I've tried to cultivate a taste for other wines."

"I see. When in Rome, do as a Roman. Two glasses of your finest *Rhone*, please." Eammon watched the waiter stroll across the plush red carpet toward the bar.

Santiago locked his black eyes on Eammon. "Tell me about your transfer."

Eammon's smile faded.

"Is something wrong?"

"I'm a little anxious."

"About the approval?"

Eammon nodded. "This assignment means a lot to me. I've studied the Far East for years. Now, I have a chance to take over a mission there."

"In Asia?"

"In eastern Nepal, near the Sikkim border." Eammon paused while the waiter set down their drinks.

"Sounds fascinating, but isn't there some danger?"

"You mean, the Japanese? I don't think so. They're two thousand miles from the Himalayas."

"What about the locals? I've heard they don't welcome outsiders."

Eammon shrugged. "That's part of being a missionary, isn't it." He reached for his glass and lifted it to the Spaniard. "To a better world."

Santiago smiled and clinked his glass against Eammon's. "A peaceful world." He winced from the tart wine and put down the glass. "You said you'll be taking over the mission. Are you replacing someone?"

Eammon sipped his wine and rested it on his lap. "I'm the first one going in. That's why it's so exciting."

"You'll be alone?"

Eammon nodded. "I'll occupy a deserted Buddhist monastery at the foot of the eastern Himalayas. The local government granted us permission after some serious negotiations. You know...." Eammon rubbed his forefinger and thumb together.

"They took money?"

"More than that. We gave them guarantees no attempt would be made to impose Christianity on the people. In return, the Church has a new outpost in the Far East."

"Outpost?"

"It's a bit complicated." Eammon drank his wine and placed the empty glass on the table. "This talk is too sombre for such a beautiful day."

"I'm sorry, I didn't mean to pry."

Eammon smiled and looked out at the river. "That sun on the water reminds me of Ireland."

"You have family there?"

Eammon shook his head. "My parents are dead. I have no brothers or sisters."

"I'm sorry."

"Don't be. I have friends all over the world. The secret is to keep in touch. A telegram each day shows them I care. That's the answer to loneliness."

Santiago smiled. "It's good to meet an optimist."

"We're men of God, my friend. You know—eternal optimists." Eammon signed the waiter's receipt. "Say—if you'd like some exercise, I could use the company."

The Spaniard's eyes brightened. "I'd love it. I arrived on the train this morning and my legs feel like lead."

"You came from Spain?"

"Zurich. I left Spain months ago." Santiago stood up and gestured toward the hotel entrance. "Well—whenever you're ready."

"Aren't you going to finish your wine?"

Santiago looked down at the half-filled glass of *Rhone*. "Enough of Rome and the Romans. I should have ordered the *Rioja*."

The two clergymen broke into laughter and strolled out of the hotel into the Swiss capital's bustling streets.

After stopping at the post office to send a telegram, Eammon led his companion on an exhaustive trek around

Bern's moat-like perimeter. Walking briskly along the Aare River's tree-lined banks, the two priests passed rows of red and white buildings resembling fortress battlements.

Eammon was well-versed in European history. Pointing out the University and Swiss National Parliament, he launched into a lengthy explanation of Switzerland's complex political system while his fading companion struggled to keep pace. When Santiago raised his hand and plunked down on a bench beside the river, Eammon apologized profusely for not noticing his depleted condition.

"Just a little winded. I'll be fine in a minute." The Spaniard leaned back on the red bench and took a deep breath.

"Maybe we should go back to the hotel."

"No—I'm all right." Santiago mopped his perspiring brow. "My God, Eammon. You're in incredible condition for—"

"A man of some years?" Eammon smiled and smoothed back his thinning white hair. "Maybe a touch of arthritis here and there, but I've been taking plenty of exercise since I heard about Asia. Must get ready for those mountains."

"The mission is in the mountains?"

Eammon sat beside him. "Yes, and quite high. Three miles above sea level."

"*Mi dios.*"

"Oh—it'll take some time to get acclimated, but I'll manage. That's why I decided to take my sabbatical in Switzerland."

"You came here to climb?"

The Irishman nodded. "Might as well do some hiking to ease the stress of waiting. That way, I'll be ready for Nepal."

"Is there a chance they won't approve the transfer?"

Eammon glared at him. "Must be positive, remember?"

The Spaniard nodded. "I'm sure everything will work out. So—when are you hiking into the mountains?"

"Tomorrow morning. I'm taking a train to Zermatt in the Pennine Alps. From there, it's on foot to the Matterhorn."

"Matterhorn? That's fourteen thousand feet?"

Eammon chuckled. "I won't come near that."

"*Mi dios*, you must be quite a climber."

"Hardly." Eammon stood up and patted Santiago's shoulder. "Sure you don't want to go back to the hotel?"

"I'm enjoying this too much." Santiago pointed to the large dam rising above the city. "Is there a way to the top?"

"If you don't mind the grade."

The Spaniard pushed off the bench. "I love hiking. I'm just a little out of shape."

Eammon smiled and led the way while breaking into a lecture on Bern's founding in 1191, and its displacement of Zurich as Switzerland's capital in 1848.

When they reached the hydroelectric power station at the top of the dam, Eammon stepped to the railing and looked out at the sea of red roofs. "I can see our hotel. We've come a long way."

Santiago staggered to the railing. "Thank God, the rest is downhill."

The Irishman smiled and turned to face him. "Well—we've talked enough about Bern and myself. What brought you to Switzerland?"

"Me?"

"You."

Santiago hesitated and looked out at the rooftops.

"The Civil War, eh? Was it very bad for you?"

"It's too soon to look back."

"Sounds like you had a rough time."

"I had my moments."

"Did you lose friends?"

"We all lost friends?"

Eammon looked down at the Aare's splashing water. "What are you going to do?"

"I'm not sure. Probably stay here until I'm reassigned."

"Back to Spain?"

Santiago shook his head. "That depends on Spain."

Eammon leaned against the railing. "I have an idea. How would you like to take a little trek into the Alps?"

Santiago's face brightened. "You're serious?"

"Absolutely. I could use the company. I think you'd enjoy it. What do you say?"

"I'd love to, but—"

"Good, we'll meet in the lobby tomorrow morning at six. Come on, I'm starving. Dinner's on me." Eammon turned and headed down the steep road while the Spaniard gawked at him in stunned silence.

"Well, what are you waiting for?"

Santiago broke into a grin and marched down the road with his new friend.

After a jovial dinner in the hotel's restaurant, Santiago excused himself and returned to his room for some frantic packing. His climbing boots were battered from crossing the Pyrenees, but they would do. He threw some clothes into his leather valise and collapsed on the bed. He was asleep in seconds.

He'd acquired the false identity from a forger in Paris. The fake passport and identification cards cost a tidy sum, but a quick wire-transfer from the Bank of Zurich more than covered it.

Until recently, Paris and Bern had given him the obscurity needed to avoid detection by the Church's relentless agents. Unfortunately, that changed last week when he received Pizarro's letter warning him to be on the alert.

He was shocked to learn that his father's attorney, Señor Valdez, had been arrested and tortured by the *Falange*. Unable to withstand the pain, Valdez disclosed that Don Felipe Hidalgo had transferred an enormous sum of gold to a secret account in Zurich before he died.

It was only a matter of time before the Nazi-trained agents discovered Roberto Hidalgo had not died in the fires of Guernica. A few coins placed in the right hands, and they would acquire the secret five-digit code to his father's Zurich account. Once they detected his large money transfers to Paris and Bern, the jaws would quickly close on Padre Roberto Santiago of the Church of St. Tome.

Eammon was about to take his nightly stroll through fog-shrouded Bern when the desk clerk stopped him. A telegram had been received from London. He tipped the clerk and stuffed the flimsy envelope into his raincoat.

He walked along the river and listened to the current splash against the banks. Pausing under a street lamp, he peeled open the envelope and unfolded the telegram. He cursed while fumbling for his reading glasses. It was no fun growing old....

White Lion:
Agree with your method of dealing with stranger. Possible candidate, but proceed with extreme caution. Checking contacts in Spain for verification of his identity. If possible, send photo to assist search. If he's hostile, will use Gideon to handle unpleasantries. If not, Gideon will direct him to Calcutta for final decision. Next communication...two days in Zermatt.
Good luck,
Lion Tamer

Eammon pulled out his lighter and burned the telegram. He hadn't expected this. Santiago seemed so perfect. Maybe too perfect.

A drop of rain struck his glasses. A light drizzle had begun falling. He slipped off his wire glasses and returned them to his breast pocket. Best to sleep on it. Risk came with the job. As always, it was a question of judgement.

He stepped away from the street lamp and faded into the fog.

Before catching the morning train to Zermatt, Eammon led his dazed traveling companion on a mad dash to the post office to fire off a last-minute telegram. When Eammon handed the scribbled message to the clerk, Roberto heard him mention Bombay. He was about to speak when he caught himself. Best not to pry. The fewer questions asked, the fewer returned.

Roberto handed the clerk an envelope and paid the required postage. The envelope was addressed to the Bank of Zurich and contained a request to wire a five thousand franc "letter of credit" to the Inn at Zermatt, in Roberto Santiago's name.

Instead of using his signature, Roberto had coded the letter with the scripted digits, *Zero-Three-Five-Nine-One*. The new encryption scheme had been enacted by the Swiss Parliament to protect funds transferred by Jews trapped in Nazi Germany. Ironic the new code was being used by a Catholic to escape similar tyranny in his native Spain.

The two priests hopped a taxi to the train station, barely catching the *Zermatt Express* as it rolled out of Bern. They'd hardly settled in their compartment when Eammon dug into his traveling bag and pulled out a map of Switzerland. He spread the map on his lap and nodded for Roberto to sit beside him.

"From here, we'll rail south to Lake Thun for a brief stop. Too bad we won't have time for a photograph. They say it's beautiful in the fall."

Roberto stiffened. "You have a camera?"

"Of course. With my fading memory, photographs are very important. My heavens, man. Don't tell me you're afraid of a photograph? What are you, some kind of spy?" Eammon let out a burst of laughter and continued. "From Thun, we'll rail across the Bernese Alps to the Pennines. If we're lucky, we'll catch a glimpse of Finsteraarhorn."

"Finster—"

"A beautiful peak in the Bernese Alps—almost as high as the Matterhorn."

"Sounds striking." Roberto leaned back in the seat and stared at the green pastures rolling by. He rested his head against the cushion and felt his eyelids grow heavy. It was such a beautiful morning. He drifted into deep sleep....

He was crawling through choking, black smoke. His hands burned from the smoldering rubble. He tried to stand, but an exploding bomb sent him sprawling across the ground. The air echoed with screams. He squinted through the drifting smoke and saw charred bodies lying in the town square.

"Roberto!"

She was running toward him, her blouse smeared with blood.

"Ana!" *He scrambled to his feet and ran toward her as the*

air filled with a sickening whine. A black, twin-engined aircraft burst through the smoke, its wing guns spouting flame.

"Get down!" He slammed into her as the ground erupted with exploding rounds. He buried his face against her and felt the plane roar over his head.

"Come on, before it dives again." He tried to help her up, but she hung limp in his arms. He looked down at her face and froze. She was staring at him with glazed, lifeless eyes.

"No!" He swept her into his arms and staggered through the smoke. He could see the Carmelite Convent on top of the hill. If he could reach Dr. Montero, there was still a chance.

He was almost to the trees when the plane dived through the smoke and opened fire.

Twin lines of impacting bullets ripped toward him. He looked up and saw the pilot glaring at him from the windshield.

"Bastard! You'll burn in hell for this! I'll make you pay! So help me, God! I'll make you pay!"

"Roberto!"

He blinked his eyes and saw Eammon staring down at him.

"Are you all right?"

He rubbed his forehead. "I must have been dreaming."

"Dreaming? My God, man. You were trembling like someone having a heart attack. Look at you. You're soaked." Eammon extended his handkerchief.

Roberto mopped his face and glanced out the window. "Where are we?"

"Near the Rhone River and Pennine Alps. We left Lake Thun an hour ago. But never mind that, how do you feel?"

Roberto took a deep breath and looked down at the damp handkerchief. "I'm all right. Just a bad dream."

"You call that a dream? You should see a doctor."

"Already have."

"And?"

"He told me to grin and bear it."

"Some doctor." Eammon dropped into the seat across from him. "You called out a woman's name. Ana, I think."

Roberto sighed. "We were very close. I lost her in the

bombing."

"In Toledo?"

Roberto looked out the window at the majestic white peaks filling the western horizon. "When do we reach Zermatt?"

"Soon." Eammon leaned back and folded his arms, his face twisted in a frown.

After checking into the Inn at Zermatt, Roberto bought Eammon lunch while trying to ignore the incident on the train. The remainder of the day was spent renting hiking equipment and getting acclimated.

At dusk, the two men ate a light dinner and took a stroll along the scenic deck overlooking Zermatt's snow-covered slopes. They were watching a skier make his final run when Eammon broke the silence. "You know—it's important fellow trekkers communicate freely and openly."

"And?"

"That nightmare on the train is really bothering me."

Roberto frowned and gripped the railing. "My God, you're persistent."

"Sorry, but as a fellow trekker—and priest—I'd like to know what's eating at you."

Roberto leaned forward and rested his forearms on the wood railing. He looked into the shadows and spoke softly. "Ten years ago, I had a vision that made an eight foot crucifix bleed. Since then, I've lost my father and the woman I loved. I've seen innocent people burned to death in their homes. I've seen a summer day turn to hell—and a meadow become a graveyard. I've been beaten within an inch of my life—and shot at by strafing planes. I should be dead, but this damned creature keeps visiting me in my dreams—taunting me to go on. Other than that, life's been pretty good." Roberto turned toward Eammon. "Does that answer your question?"

"I'm sorry."

"I'll see you at sunrise." Roberto pushed away from the railing and walked into the inn.

A light snow was falling on the Pennine Alps when they set

out for the Matterhorn. Eammon took the lead and pointed into the gray haze. "The mountain's eight miles from here. That wall of rock on our right is Hornli Ridge. We'll follow it to the glacier."

"Then what?"

"Depends on us. We'll climb as high as we can. They say the view's incredible from the top of the glacier." Eammon gestured toward the ridge and moved out. He'd failed to mention the exquisite view came with a price. After trekking steadily upward for six hours, the two priests collapsed on a rock and stared in awe at the white glacier rising into the haze.

Eammon pulled out his map and traced their route with his finger while munching a piece of chocolate. "This must be the Furgg Glacier. According to the map, it rises two thousand feet before converging with the mountain. From there, it's another five thousand feet to the summit."

Roberto scratched his head. "I thought the Matterhorn was fourteen thousand?"

"It is. We're at seven thousand."

"Well—that explains it."

"What?"

"Why I can't breathe."

Eammon smiled and stuffed the map in his pack. "I guess we've overdone it."

"I guess we have."

"Tell you what. Let's climb another hour and camp on that ledge." He pointed to a buttress of protruding ice. "The weather should clear overnight. Tomorrow morning, we'll hike to the top of the glacier and take some pictures. If we leave at noon, we should reach the inn by sunset. Fair enough?"

Roberto nodded and followed his friend up the jagged ice.

At eight thousand feet, they pitched their tents on the buttress. No words were spoken as the two exhausted men ate some biscuits and guzzled their canteens of water.

Praying he wouldn't dream, Roberto stretched out in his small tent and listened to the snow rustle against the canvas roof....

* * *

"Roberto!"

Roberto sat up and blinked at the sunlight streaming into his tent.

"Wake up, man. You've got to see this."

He took a breath of cold air and crawled out of the tent. Eammon was standing a few feet away, his gleaming sunglasses focused on the western sky.

"Put on your glasses."

Roberto turned around and winced from a blinding flash.

"Put on your glasses, man! The sun's reflecting off the ice."

Roberto slipped on his sunglasses and looked to the west. An enormous, cathedral-like mountain towered above him, its glistening white peak jutting into the blue sky. The mountain's massive ridges extended toward him like two embracing arms.

Eammon rested a hand on Roberto's shoulder. "Now you know why I want this assignment."

"Unbelievable."

Eammon patted his shoulder. "It's getting late. We're a thousand feet from the top of the glacier." Eammon picked up his pack and headed up the glacier while his friend stared at the Matterhorn.

They spent the morning exploring the glacier and snapping pictures. Roberto couldn't take his eyes off the mountain. He'd never seen anything so beautiful. He could feel the white colossus pulling at him—urging him to climb higher. It was intoxicating.

At high noon, they folded their tents and headed down the glacier. It had been a magnificent day—one Roberto would never forget. He kept pausing to look back at the peak until Eammon finally grabbed his arm.

"We have to pick up the pace. Heavy weather's coming and we're still five miles from the inn. And I'm starving." Eammon tugged at his pack and led his friend down the glacier toward a warm fire and meal.

The two exhausted priests staggered into the Zermatt's lobby at dusk. Fighting the urge to sleep, they agreed to meet in the restaurant for an early dinner.

After a warm bath and change of clothes, Roberto mustered his strength and headed down the oak staircase to the lobby. He pushed through a crowd of inebriated skiers and walked past the stone fireplace leading into the restaurant.

"Collins? I'm sorry, Father. I have no reservation in that name."

Roberto scanned the small restaurant. "Maybe he fell asleep."

The *maitre d'* smiled. "Would you like to be seated?"

"I'll be back in a minute."

Roberto walked out of the restaurant and headed for the house phone. He was about to call Eammon's room when he spotted him standing on the deck outside the lobby, still wearing his hiking clothes.

Roberto pushed through the door into the chilled night air. "What are you doing out here?"

Eammon turned and held up an opened letter. "News."

"Your transfer?"

"Approved."

"Oh, Eammon." Roberto rushed toward him and clasped his hand.

Eammon smiled and patted his shoulder.

"Come on—we should celebrate."

"In a minute." The Irishman stuffed the paper in his pocket and leaned back against the railing. "I've been thinking about you."

"Me?"

"The way you kept staring at the mountain today." He locked his green eyes on Roberto. "I could use your help up there. To keep the peace, and all that."

Roberto looked at him in shock. "You want me to go with you?"

"Seems like good idea."

"But—I'd be excess baggage. Besides—I'm Spanish. We're warm-blooded creatures. I'd freeze to death up there. *Mi dios*, I'm freezing now."

"I'm serious, Roberto. Don't you see? I'm offering you a new life. A new beginning."

Roberto shook his head.

"What's wrong?"

"I'm not ready to give up this one. There's still a chance Franco will lose. I want to be there when it happens. To spit in his face."

"You can't mean that?"

"There is still a chance. If Madrid can hang on—"

"My God, Roberto. You read the papers. Forget Spain. Start worrying about Poland and France."

Roberto raised his hand for silence. "Let's break open some wine." He walked inside and left Eammon standing in the darkness.

The morning train ride to Bern was uneventful. When they stopped at Lake Thun, Eammon stepped off the train to stretch his legs.

It only took a minute to duck into the post office with the roll of film. He'd enclosed a note requesting a follow-up by their agent in Calcutta. That should provide enough time to verify his traveling companion's identity. If there were any revelations about Roberto Santiago, he needed to know them before leaving India for Nepal.

Before re-boarding the train, Eammon pulled out the telegram he'd received in Zermatt last night. It contained an unexpected warning....

White Lion:
This is last communication until you reach Bombay. We have reason to believe hunters are on your trail...and closing.
Beware White Lion. Your new acquaintance may be one of them. Leave now!
Lion Tamer

Eammon crumpled the telegram in his fist and climbed back on the train. When he reached their compartment, Roberto was asleep. He sat across from him and felt the train lurch forward.

Gary Naiman

Time for a decision, Mr. Collins. Was the man sleeping across from you a sheep—or a wolf in sheep's clothing? Should it end here?

He reached into his pocket and grasped the fountain pen. It would only take a second. A quick jab under the left ear. Not so much as a whimper.

He felt his hand slip off the pen. If his instincts were right, Roberto was the perfect recruit. The Spaniard had been through hell, and it showed. Eammon had seen others like him. Lost souls struggling to keep their sanity in a world gone mad. It might take a little time, but his friend would come around. After all, he was being offered a chance to find that better world he so desperately needed.

Eammon looked out at the mountains. Finsteraarhorn was blanketed with snow clouds. It was October 4, 1938, and the winter storms would soon begin. Your move, Father Collins.

At three p.m., their taxi pulled up to the curb in front of the *Hotel Bern*. Roberto was about to step out when Eammon grabbed his arm. "This is where we say goodbye."

"What?"

"I'm catching a train to Paris in an hour."

"You're leaving?"

Eammon nodded.

"*Mi dios*, at least have a drink with me."

"Another time. I'm sorry, Roberto. These things happen quickly."

"How long will you be in Belfast?"

"I'm not going to Belfast."

Roberto's jaw dropped. "You're going straight to India?"

"Yes."

"But—what about your parish? Don't you have to put things in order?"

"That's been taken care of."

Roberto stared at him in disbelief. "My God, Eammon. India's halfway around the world. Give yourself a chance to rest. You're not a young man."

Eammon patted his friend's shoulder. "Think of it, Roberto.

A chance to carry the cross to an ancient land. To spread Christ's word where it's never been heard. Sounds like something worth living for, don't you think?"

Roberto frowned. "The battle should be fought here, not in some *Shangri-la*."

Eammon smiled and extended his hand. "Until we meet again?"

Roberto sighed and shook his friend's hand. When he pulled his hand away, a folded paper was stuck in it.

"In case you change your mind."

Roberto shook his head. He stepped out of the taxi and took his bag from the driver.

The taxi pulled away from the curb and disappeared around the corner. A light snow was falling on Bern.

Roberto didn't unfold Eammon's letter until that evening. He didn't know it, but the words would change his life...

Roberto,
In case you reconsider, I can be reached through Father Gideon at Gloria Church in Bombay. I'll tell him to keep a candle burning in the window.
I can't explain why, but our meeting seemed so fateful. We're different in so many ways, yet we seem driven by a dream of a better world. I think we'll meet again— at the roof of the world. Until then....
Eammon

Roberto left Bern the following day. He hadn't forgotten Pizarro's ominous letter. After two years of walking in shadows, he had learned the importance of movement. Lingering meant detection and arrest.

It was raining when his train pulled into Paris' Gare de Lyon station. He moved quickly through the bustling concourse and hailed a taxi while glancing at the passing cars.

"Good evening, mon Pere."

Roberto forced a nervous smile. "Rue Cherbourg, nombre quarante-cinq."

"Oui, mon Pere."

When the taxi pulled away from the curb, Roberto noticed a man in a trench coat step into the car behind them. Nothing unusual for rush hour on a Paris workday. There were hundreds like him—except for one thing. The man tugged nervously at his hat brim before disappearing into the waiting car.

Roberto felt his heart pounding. He had seen the man before—this morning in the *Hotel Bern's* lobby. He wouldn't have noticed him if it weren't for that nervous, tugging hand.

"Terrible weather, mon Pere." The driver peered at him through the rear-view mirror.

"Yes—terrible." Roberto stared at the driver with glazed eyes. He didn't need to look out the rear window to know they were being followed. "I've changed my mind, driver. Take me back to the station."

"Mon Pere?"

"The station, dammit! I think we're being followed. I'll pay you fifty francs if you lose him."

"Oui, mon Pere." The driver shrugged his shoulders and veered onto Boulevard St. Marcel, nearly hitting a line of crossing pedestrians. Pressing the accelerator, he cut between two trucks and skidded down a side street while his passenger clung to the door handle. "We'll be there in a minute, mon Pere."

Roberto felt a trickle of sweat on his forehead. He'd seen the man in the *Hotel Bern's* lobby before boarding the bus to the train station. The man was arguing with a young clerk at the front desk. He recalled the clerk handing the man a yellow card while stuffing something into his pocket that resembled a wad of Swiss francs. The card came from the *Hotel Bern's* guest file. If it was Roberto Santiago's, it contained all his room charges, including the fee for processing his letter of credit from the Bank of Zurich.

There was only one explanation. The *Falange* had broken into his Zurich account and traced his latest withdrawal to the *Hotel Bern*. They had closed the circle. The final piece had fallen into place. The bribed desk clerk must have pointed him out when he boarded the bus. They had found Roberto Hidalgo.

He took a nervous breath and looked out the rain-smeared

window. Gare de Lyon station was coming up on the right. He must move quickly—before they recovered. He jumped out of the taxi and paid the driver.

"Mon Pere, you gave me a hundred francs?"

He ignored the shouting driver and ran into the terminal. It was seven forty-five. A train left for Milan in fifteen minutes.

He pushed his way to the ticket window and pulled out a wad of francs. "One ticket to Milan." He watched the agent inspect his passport and check the photograph.

"You're fortunate, mon Pere. We're almost full." The agent stamped his passport and inserted the ticket. "Have a pleasant trip." He slid the precious documents across the counter into Roberto's waiting hand.

Only five minutes left. Roberto ran through the crowded concourse, carrying the worn leather valise that had been at his side for so many years. He never looked back.

He managed some broken sleep on the train, awakening every few minutes to scan the rows of seated passengers. Any of them might be a *Falange* agent waiting for a chance to pump him full of drugs and smuggle him back to Spain.

A frightening thought struck him. Had he imagined all this? Had his mind finally snapped? Had Corpus Christi and Guernica finally taken their toll? Was he running from phantoms that didn't exist? He closed his eyes and listened to the man snoring beside him.

When he awoke, the sky was brightening. He could see rolling countryside dotted with farms. He glanced at his watch. Five a.m. The train would reach Milan within the hour.

No time to lose. He would take a taxi to the nearest hotel. On the way, he would stop at a post office and mail a letter to Zurich requesting a funds transfer to Milan. If it worked, he would leave for crowded Rome that same day. If not, he still had enough money to reach the nearest airport and catch a plane to London. It was his only chance.

His thoughts were interrupted by the sound of screeching metal. The train shuddered and slowed down. Something was wrong. This couldn't be Milan.

Gary Naiman

He leaned across the snoring man and peered out the window, but only saw trees. He fell back in his seat and glanced at the elderly woman seated across the aisle. Her face was frozen in terror. She clutched the hand of the man seated beside her.

The train ground to a stop beside a forest. For a moment, there was only the sound of hissing steam and people whispering to each other.

Voices were coming from outside the window. He leaned over and squinted into the drifting steam.

The voices grew louder. He heard a grating sound, like boots crunching through loose gravel. He'd heard that sound before—in the Pyrenees.

Two men burst through the steam and walked past the window. They wore black trench coats with military caps trimmed in green.

The rear door swung open and the two trench-coated men stepped into the car, followed by three others dressed in black uniforms and boots. The conductor wasn't in sight.

After eyeing the filled car, the two trench-coated men began checking identification cards and interrogating the frightened passengers.

Roberto glanced across the aisle and saw the old woman staring at him, her brown eyes wide with panic. She shook her head and muttered two barely distinguishable words. "Black shirts."

"Your papers please."

Roberto looked up and saw a scarred face glaring down at him beneath the black military cap. He reached into his jacket and handed the officer his passport.

"You're Spanish?"

Roberto nodded.

"Your sympathies?"

Roberto didn't need an explanation. He'd been asked the question before. He returned the glare with his own. "That should be obvious."

The officer didn't even blink. "You have business in Milan?"

"I'm seeking funds for our cause."

The officer placed his hand on the seat back and bent close to Roberto's face. Roberto could smell the nicotine on his breath. "And what cause is that?"

"The Generalissimo, of course. Our men trained here, remember?"

The officer nodded and straightened up. "Good luck, Padre. I'm sure *Il Duce'* will be sympathetic to the Spanish Church. We're all working toward the same goal." He handed the passport to Roberto. "Stay well."

Roberto rested his head against the seat and tried to control his racing heart. When he heard the passenger door close, he sat up and scanned the aisle.

Ashen faces stared blankly into space. At least a dozen passengers were gone, including the elderly couple that had sat across from him. The man seated on his right was no longer snoring. He gazed into space, his green eyes frozen with terror.

The train lurched forward and began to pick up speed. Roberto stared at the two empty seats across the aisle. Where were they? He lunged across the aisle and dropped into the empty seat beside the window.

He could see them through the steam. A line of passengers being herded into the woods like cattle. He spotted one of the black-uniformed militiamen eyeing them as they went by. The man held their passports and appeared to be checking off names.

Roberto looked back in horror. The elderly couple was standing next to the militiaman. The woman's hands were locked in prayer. Her husband's head bled from a gash above the left temple. They vanished into the smoke.

Roberto collapsed in the seat, his eyes staring into space. How could he stand by while innocent people were arrested and beaten? What had he become? Was he any better than those men in black trench coats?

Roberto was stunned when the Bank of Milan issued him a large sum of *lira* from a letter of credit received from the Bank of Zurich.

Gary Naiman

His account was still intact. The *Falange* may have bought some vital information, but the Bank of Zurich apparently drew a hard line when it came to relinquishing funds to foreign governments. The pigs must have been furious.

After a brief stay in Rome, he spent the next four months at a small mission in Krakow, Poland. He'd met Father Banco on the train between Milan and Rome. Banco was a shaken priest on the verge of collapse from threats of retribution for his sympathetic treatment of Jewish refugees. Banco welcomed Roberto's company and offered him a spare room at his mission in Krakow.

With rumors of violence rampant in the streets, Roberto tried to console the unstable priest. He was successful until the morning of March 3, 1939, when he awoke to find a scribbled note advising him to get out of Poland before it was too late—as Father Banco had done while he slept.

That night, a roving band of thugs shot and killed the town's banker and his family while they slept in their beds. Torching the banker's house, the brown-shirted terrorists roamed Krakow's dark streets, screaming obscenities and breaking store windows. The outnumbered police didn't lift a finger to stop them.

The brown shirts stormed the mission and battered down its front doors. Shouting "Jew Lover!" they flung torched bottles into the chapel—but no one was inside. Roberto Hidalgo, alias Santiago, had crawled out a rear window and disappeared into the night.

The final straw was broken on April 3, 1939, when a radio broadcast crushed Roberto's last ray of hope for his beloved Spain. Seated in the lobby of an Athen's hotel, he listened to the crackling voice of Julian Besteiro, the British-backed Foreign Minister who had finally convinced Madrid's besieged defenders to lay down their arms to Generalissimo Franco's overwhelming forces...

"Madrilenos!
The moment has arrived for avoiding further bloodshed.
Let us all be calm and serene, at present, accepting the

surrender of Madrid as the best means of salvation. Viva España!"

Roberto stared at the brown radio while recalling the cool shade of the orange groves above Valencia. How sweet the air smelled that summer's day. Now it was gone—stamped out by the fat little general he should have strangled that night in the *Marva Bar*.

After defending Spain's flame of freedom for two years, four months, and twenty-one days, Madrid's beaten patriots had finally laid down their arms. These were the gallant men and women his trembling father spoke of that night in the study ten years ago. Without them, the devil now reigned supreme in the personnage of Señor Francisco Franco Bahamonde—*El Caudillo*—new dictator of Spain.

That afternoon, Padre Roberto Santiago withdrew several thousand English pounds from the Bank of Athens, along with a stack of gold certificates. Clutching Eammon's note, he left Europe forever.

26 | Bombay

Something was out there. A strip of land, barely visible in the thick fog. He blinked his eyes and prayed it wasn't a mirage. After three weeks in gut-wrenching seas, he was at the end of his rope.

The ship's horn let out a deafening blast. He could see a curved peninsula stretching toward him like a giant claw. It had to be Colaba Point. He gripped the railing and took a slow, deep breath. Thank God, the turbulent voyage was almost over.

Since departing Istanbul a month ago, Roberto had learned a painful lesson. His passionate love for the sea wasn't shared by his stomach. Surviving on liquids and crackers, he'd spent the last thirty days heaving his guts into four oceans. His only relief came three weeks ago when the *Mephistopheles* passed through the Suez Canal's calm waters, only to resume her pitching voyage in the Red Sea.

Unable to muster the strength to leave his compartment, he huddled against his toilet while praying for the rolling swells to subside. But things only grew worse when the tramp steamer left the Gulf of Aden and plowed into the storm-swept Arabian Sea.

If not for the kindness of Sir Geoffrey Wells, a fellow passenger who plucked him from the railing during one of his violent upchucks, Roberto might have died from dehydration. But then again, what good Christian wouldn't come to the aid of a priest?

"How are we feeling today, Father?"

The gruff voice startled him. He turned and saw Sir Geoffrey limping across the *Mephistopheles'* weathered deck with his gnarled brown cane in hand. Dressed in a white cotton suit and cloak, the portly old man extended a friendly hand while smiling through his neatly-groomed, silver moustache. "Hang on, Father. In another hour, you'll be standing on firm ground."

Roberto patted his stomach. "Actually, I feel quite human. To be blunt, I could eat a cow."

"Ha! Unwise to partake of bovine in this part of the world. Sacred, and all that. But if you're serious about wanting some solid food, allow me to treat you to a fine cut of roast mutton at the Taj."

"Taj?"

"Oh, I almost forgot. You've never visited Bombay. Delightful city. And the Taj's bar and restaurant are world-renowned." Sir Geoffrey rested his elbows on the railing and squinted at the approaching strip of land. "Ah—you can smell Crawford's Market from here. I bet they just finished laying out the fresh fruits and vegetables. Look—there's Saint Thomas's steeple." Sir Geoffrey pointed toward a distant tower barely visible in the dissipating fog. "We're coming around Colaba Point. That's the old lighthouse."

Roberto nodded and squinted at the fog. Sir Geoffrey was having too much fun to spoil it by confessing he saw nothing.

The steamer veered northeast around Colaba point and headed into Bombay's great harbor. Acting more like an excited child than an English aristocrat, Sir Geoffrey seized Roberto's arm and pointed to an enormous yellow arch off the port bow. "There it is, Father. The Gateway of India. Symbol of His Majesty's presence."

"Impressive."

"It was built to commemorate King George's visit in...."

Roberto wasn't listening. His eyes had focused on the life preserver hanging from the bridge's railing. He stared at the black *Mephistopheles* stamped on the white doughnut.

When he boarded in Istanbul, he remembered questioning why they would name a ship after the devil. Now he knew.

He agreed to join Sir Geoffrey for lunch at the "Taj" and excused himself for some last-minute packing.

His small cabin stunk from the four-week battle with seasickness. He opened the porthole and felt a welcome rush of fresh air. The sun was breaking through the fog, its rays striking the water.

He reached into his jacket pocket and grasped Eammon's tattered letter. In the past six months, he must have read it a thousand times. It was like a magnet, pulling him steadily eastward.

He noticed his reflection in the porthole's glass window. It wasn't the face of a thirty-eight-year-old man. The pale skin was drawn tight over the cheekbones. The black hair was streaked with gray. The eyes and mouth were creased with wrinkles. A scar ran down the forehead, terminating at the left eyebrow. It had come from a chip of shattered concrete in Guernica's town square.

He looked down at his scarred hands. He could still feel her warm body in his arms when he carried her through the rubble. The hot ashes burned his flesh. His eyes stung from the acrid, black smoke. He heard the aircraft's deadly whine as it dived on the square and opened fire.

He looked at the glass and shuddered. His face had twisted into an ugly scowl. His black eyes glistened with anger. A bead of sweat trickled down his forehead.

He stepped to the wash basin and splashed some cold water on his face. Something clinked against the metal basin. It was the gold crucifix dangling from his neck. He looked down at it and sighed.

Harsh times require harsh acts. If not for his black vestments and forged identity, he'd probably be rotting in a Madrid prison, waiting to join his friends in Spain's blood-soaked earth. Dictators look unkindly at defiant citizens, particularly when they flee their mother country with large sums of money.

By now, the *Falange* had discovered his Zurich account was empty from massive withdrawals to Milan, Athens, and Istanbul. It would take some time to detect his escape on the *Mephistopheles*, but once they picked up his trail, they'd come after him like hungry wolves. If he could keep them off balance long enough to reach the mountains north of India, they'd never find him.

He turned away from the mirror and stepped to the black trunk in the corner. It was strapped to a metal pipe for protection against the stormy seas. He ran his fingers along the thick padlock and steel-riveted surface. Only thirteen hundred miles to go. Thirteen hundred miles....

The Tenth Avatar

His thoughts were interrupted by a knock on the door. "Yes?"

"Officer Aldrich."

Roberto opened the cabin door and stared at the ship's third mate. "Thank you for coming."

The white-uniformed officer removed his cap and placed it under his arm. "I'm sorry, Father. I only have a minute. We'll be docking soon and the Captain needs me on the bridge."

Roberto nodded and swung the door open. "Can you ensure my trunk reaches Thirty-four, West Oval Maidan?"

Aldrich stroked his sandy hair. "Father?"

Roberto pulled out his billfold and reached inside the leather flap. "Will twenty pounds be sufficient?" He extended two ten pound notes.

Aldrich's eyes lit up as he took the money from Roberto's hand. He stepped into the cabin and studied the two-by-four-foot trunk. "Thirty-four, West Oval Maidan. No problem, Father. I'll see to it personally."

"The landlord is on the first floor. His name is Gombu. Give him my name and he'll show you to my apartment."

"Have a pleasant journey, Father." Aldrich tipped his hat and started to walk away.

"Mr. Aldrich."

"Yes, Father?"

"Please be careful. The trunk is rather heavy."

Aldrich smiled. "No problem, Father. Artifacts for a church?"

"Yes, and rather fragile. Good day, sir." Roberto watched the young officer disappear up the ladder leading to the bridge. He paused for a final look at the trunk, then picked up his leather valise and walked out of the cabin.

The ship's horn let out a deafening blast as the captain brought the *Mephistopheles* hard-a-port to line up with the massive yellow arch known as the Gateway of India.

Roberto stepped to the railing where a small crowd of passengers watched a tugboat ease alongside the ancient steamer. A cluster of fishing boats darted past the *Mephistopheles'* bow. Beneath the arch, a uniformed-band broke into strains of *Hail Brittania* while a crowd of cheering spectators waved at friends and loved ones on the approaching black steamer.

The horn emitted a second blast as the ship's engines shifted to "DEAD SLOW." A flock of sea gulls flew over the bow and veered toward the hills beyond the city. The strip of land had become a sprawling city of white colonial estates, quaint steeples, and bustling streets. All of it carefully architected to conceal dilapidated slums, primitive markets, and an army of beggars. This was Bombay, shining symbol of England's rule over India, its twin peninsulas jutting into the Arabian sea like an embracing claw.

The Taj's gold grandfather clock was chiming high noon when Roberto stepped into the hotel's plush lobby. Unlike its namesake, five hundred miles away, this Taj Mahal honored Victoria's reign with royal violet carpeting, gold-fluted ceilings, and ivory pillars.

"Father Santiago!" Sir Geoffrey limped nervously toward Roberto with his cane in hand. "I'd almost given up on you."

"I'm so sorry. I took a taxi to my flat and made the mistake of letting him go. I had to walk back through the crowds. I've never seen so many people."

"Ah, my friend. You're in Bombay, and it's lunch hour."

Roberto wiped the perspiration off his brow. "You'll have to forgive me. I'm soaked. It's a steam bath out there."

Sir Geoffrey broke into a hearty laugh and gestured toward the pillared portal leading into the restaurant. "A glass of wine and some warm food should make you feel better."

Roberto soon discovered the Taj was a haven for disembarking British citizens. With the docks swarming with moaning beggars, the Taj's magnificent restaurant offered arriving passengers a chance to escape Bombay's oppressive humidity while relaxing under banks of whirling electric ceiling fans. Here, they could reminisce about merry old England while sipping gin and tonics, and stuffing themselves with a hearty meal.

After swigging down two iced gin and tonics, Sir Geoffrey

ordered a bottle of *Madeira* in deference to his Spanish guest, not realizing the wine was Portuguese. Roberto smiled and sipped the fruity wine while his boisterous host ordered a third gin—and both their lunches.

"Are the accomodations to your liking?"

"Very nice, thank you. I appreciate your help."

Sir Geoffrey nodded and glanced around the dining room. "Never can be too careful when traveling in the Far East. Gombu's an honest wog. Hard to find that over here." He watched the waiter place his drink on the table. "So tell me, Father. How long will you be staying in Bombay?"

"I'm not sure. I'm to look up a priest at Gloria Church, and go from there."

Sir Geoffrey put down his drink and stroked his wet moustache. "Sounds a bit mysterious."

"A little."

"Have you been reassigned by the Church?"

"Reassigned?"

Sir Geoffrey shrugged his shoulders. "Because of the trouble in Spain."

Roberto frowned. "The decision to leave Spain was mine."

"I see. Now you do have me intrigued. Why would a man of the cloth leave his native country when it needs him most?"

Roberto's ears pricked up. Too many questions. Maybe it was the old man's innocent drinking, but he'd learned to keep his guard up. "You know—I've never seen such magnificent fans. Were they imported?"

"What?"

"The ceiling fans. They're magnificent."

"Oh, yes—quite. But my question, Father. Why did you leave Spain?"

"Adventure, I suppose. Probably the same spirit that moved you to travel to India."

Sir Geoffrey frowned. "I assure you, my reason for coming here isn't adventure. My son and his family will arrive from New Delhi next week. I'm taking them back to England."

"Back?"

"Blast, I never would have brought them here if I'd known

Sir Chamberlain would succeed with Hitler."

Roberto's eyes widened. "You brought them here for safety?"

"Of course. With that megalomaniac marching into the Rhineland and Austria, I feared the worst. And I wasn't alone. These damn new aeroplanes make the Channel useless for defense. My God, bombs could fall on London. It happened once before, you know. In the big one. Bloody frightening too." Sir Geoffrey paused and stared into space.

"Are you all right?"

"The thought of bombs falling on our homes. Frightening, I tell you."

"I understand."

Sir Geoffrey gestured for the waiter to bring him another gin.

"Why didn't you leave England?"

Sir Geoffrey looked up in shock. "I'm surprised at you, Father. A priest from war-ravaged Spain should know that answer. I would never abandon my country in time of need. Which makes me wonder why you did."

Roberto nodded toward the silver serving cart being wheeled toward them. "I believe our lunch has arrived."

"Lunch? Oh—yes."

The next half hour was spent engaging in polite conversation while the two men hurriedly consumed chilled garden salads and healthy portions of roast mutton, scalloped potatoes, and Yorkshire pudding.

Sir Geoffrey leaned back in his Victorian chair and stroked his silver moustache. "Excellent meal."

"Indeed."

"Feel better?"

"Like a new man."

Sir Geoffrey pulled a silver watch out of his vest pocket and flipped it open. "I say, the bloody cricket match begins in fifteen minutes. I have to dash to the sports club. Care to join me?"

Roberto folded his napkin. "Sorry, I have to meet someone."

"Oh yes—your friend at Gloria Church. Well—I guess it's goodbye then. Sorry to see it end so quickly. Perhaps we'll cross paths again." Sir Geoffrey placed his napkin on the table and started to get up.

"Please." Roberto gestured for him to remain seated.

"Yes?"

"Before we go our separate ways, I'd like to answer your question about Spain."

Sir Geoffrey frowned. "It's not important."

"It is to me." Roberto looked his host in the eye. "The Civil War tore my country apart, and me with it."

"I should be going." Sir Geoffrey started to get up, but Roberto seized his arm. "What are you doing?"

"I'm answering your question, señor." Roberto leaned forward. "I didn't run away. I stayed in Spain until there was no hope left. Until everyone and everything I loved was dead."

Sir Geoffrey pulled his arm away. "That's enough, sir. You're talking nonsense."

Roberto's face grew hot. He rose to his feet and glared at his host. "You still don't understand. Let me put it this way. God is dead in Spain, and it's only the beginning. The world will burn in hell because it turned its back on Spain."

"That's quite enough!" Sir Geoffrey stood up and grabbed his cane.

"I'm sorry, but you haven't seen what I've seen. You can't fight the devil, Sir Geoffrey. I've lost too many friends who tried."

"And God bless them for it!" Sir Geoffrey's face turned beet red.

"Please listen. You've been so kind. Let me return the favor."

"Get to the point." Sir Geoffrey glared at Roberto.

"Is your wife in England?"

"My wife died two years ago."

"I'm sorry. Then, you have no one in England?"

"It's not your business."

Roberto reached out and grasped the old man's wrist. "Don't go back there. Stay here with your son. I don't know why, but I see your death in England."

"Damn you!" Sir Geoffrey turned away and limped out of the restaurant amidst a rush of shocked whispers.

Roberto left the Taj and spent a few minutes milling through the crowds along Apollo Blunder dock. He stopped below the Gateway of India and gazed across Bombay's boat-filled harbor toward mainland India.

It was early May and a stiff, humid breeze was blowing at his back. Sir Geoffrey had warned the monsoon would be particularly severe this year.

A chill swept through him. What was he doing here? He'd come five thousand miles to escape prison and death, but to what end? To join an aging missionary on a pile of ice and rock? To live in obscurity while Generalissimo Franco ground his heels into Spain? Would that be his epitaph?

He took a deep breath. It was too late for remorse. Too late to bring back the dead. Better to live an obscure missionary than die in a Spanish prison. And if that didn't work—there was always the four hundred pounds of gold in his trunk. Just sit it out in the mountains until the world regained its senses. If the past ten years had taught him anything, it was that there is always another day. He frowned and headed for the row of taxis in front of the Taj.

"Please take me to Gloria Church. I believe it's near Victoria Gardens."

"Yes, Father. Sit back and I'll have you there in no time."

The driver was obviously looking for a large fare. After a few minutes of pointing out landmarks like Flora Fountain, Rajabal Tower, and Victoria Terminus rail station, it was apparent they were taking the scenic route.

Roberto glanced at his watch and leaned forward. "It's urgent I get to Gloria Church. Don't worry about money. I'll make it worth your while."

"Yes, Father."

The car's tires squealed as the driver veered onto Sir J. J. Road, nearly wiping out a family crossing the intersection. They sped through central Bombay's slums and headed north on "Sir J. J." while Roberto stared at the hordes of beggars huddled against the tenements. He slumped in the seat while recalling his painful trek through the hills outside Granada. "God, there are so many poor."

"Yes, Father. They are the unclean ones."

"Unclean?"

"The forgotten ones. The untouchables. Lowest of low. For them, there is no hope." The taxi screeched to a stop. "We're here, Father."

Gloria Church stood proudly at the entrance to Victoria Gardens and the old museums. The stately church looked like it had been transplanted from England.

Roberto paid the driver his promised tip and asked him to wait. He stepped out of the taxi and hurried up the church's stone steps to the teak doors.

It took a minute for his eyes to adjust to the darkened vestibule. He eased across the stone floor and stepped into the chapel.

The altar was bathed in colored sunlight from two stained glass windows on the right. The setting reminded him of Valencia Cathedral the day his father delivered his impassioned speech to the Council.

He started down the aisle and hesitated. A black-robed priest knelt at the altar, his head bowed in prayer. Roberto walked down the aisle and knelt beside him. "Father Gideon?"

"Yes?"

"I'm Father Santiago."

The elderly priest looked up in surprise. "Indeed. I'd given up on you, Father. Eammon told me you'd follow him in a month."

Roberto shrugged. "I'm afraid he's more optimistic than me."

"Considerably. We can talk in the rectory." Gideon crossed himself and backed away from the altar.

Gideon was a slightly built man who appeared well into his sixties. Though not completely bald, he'd chosen to shave his head, accentuating a pair of pointed, devilish ears. But it was Gideon's hazel eyes and breathless voice that captured Roberto's attention. Several times during their conversation,

Roberto had to blink to clear his head. Gideon's voice and eyes were mesmerizing.

"Eammon spoke highly of you, Father Santiago. I'm sure he'll be overjoyed to see you after spending six months with Sherpas, Gurkhas, and the like."

Roberto forced a smile. There was something sinister in Gideon's voice—a hostility that made him uneasy. "Have you heard from Eammon?"

"I received a letter two months ago. He sounded well, but kept asking about his lost friend from Spain. I understand you're from Toledo."

"Yes, the Church of Saint Tome."

Gideon's hazel eyes locked on Roberto. "Funny, I thought you'd be an older man."

Roberto felt a sudden chill. "It sounds like you've done some research."

"I'm afraid it's necessary these days. The Church has many enemies. The devil takes many forms."

Roberto nodded. "Perhaps you've confused me with Padre Santana. Our names are often mixed up."

"No matter, let's get down to business." Gideon snatched a pen out of its inkwell. "Where are you staying?"

"West Oval Maidan."

"The address?"

Roberto hesitated. "Thirty-four."

Gideon scribbled the address on a piece of paper. "I'll arrange for a car to pick you up tomorrow evening at five. A train leaves for Calcutta at six. If you like, I'll pick up your ticket in advance. You can pay the driver at the station."

Roberto leaned back in his chair. "Tomorrow?"

"Best to move quickly. The monsoon is coming. You'll be crossing lowland jungles. The rivers and swamps are very treacherous during the rains." Gideon stuck the pen in its inkwell. "Your driver will give you the name of your contact in Calcutta."

"What about the leg from Calcutta to Nepal?"

"Your contact in Calcutta will take care of that."

Roberto frowned. "You make it sound so mysterious."

"Sorry, we've learned to be cautious about divulging the whereabouts of our missionaries."

Roberto glanced at his watch. "Well—I should be going. I have a taxi waiting." He stood up and extended his hand. "Thank you for your help, Father Gideon."

Gideon stood up and shook Roberto's hand. "Sorry to be so abrupt. Give Eammon my regards. Good luck."

Roberto was nearly out of the room when he heard a familiar crackling sound. "Is that a radio?"

Gideon's face flushed. "I was just getting ready to tune in the British Isles when you arrived. Only way to keep up with what's happening back there."

Roberto nodded. "It must be very powerful to pick up their signal."

Gideon shrugged. "Not really. It just depends on the time and weather. It helps pass the hours." He gestured toward the door. "You should be going. You'll need a good night's sleep. It's almost two days to Calcutta, and the trains aren't very comfortable."

As Roberto followed Gideon out of the rectory, he noticed a partially-opened door across the darkened corridor. The door was cracked just enough to catch a glimpse of an amber dial, and a familiar object silhouetted against its glowing face.

Gideon walked across the vestibule and pushed open the teak doors. He winced from the sudden daylight. "God be with you, Father."

"And with you, Father. Maybe when we meet again, you'll be able to transmit as well as receive."

Gideon smiled nervously. "I'm afraid that will never happen. Too expensive for my meager allowance." He nodded toward the waiting taxi. "Your driver looks eager to get started. You must have promised him a large tip."

Roberto smiled and walked down the steps.

That night, Roberto lay awake listening to the motor traffic on Oval Maidan. Unable to sleep in the oppressive heat, he crawled out of bed and rummaged through his traveling bag until his hand snatched the bottle of *Bordeaux* he'd purchased in France. He pried off the cork and poured himself a glass of the maroon liquid, then plunked down in a rattan chair facing the opened window.

Something was wrong. If it was so important to beat the monsoon, why wait until tomorrow evening? After leaving Gideon, he'd checked the departure schedules at Victoria Terminus. Trains left for Calcutta every hour, twenty hours a day.

He gulped down the wine. In ten years, he'd seen enough radios to spot the difference between a receiver and transmitter. Gideon had lied. The object in front of that amber dial was a microphone.

"Dammit!" He slammed the glass on the table, shattering it in his hand. Wincing in pain, he yanked his bleeding hand away and wrapped it with a handkerchief.

There was only one answer. Gideon was with them. By now, he'd alerted the *Falange* to the priest named Santiago. They would be in that car tomorrow evening when it pulled up to Thirty-four, West Oval Maidan—and he'd be on his way back to Spain.

He stared at the black trunk in the corner. A trickle of sweat rolled down his forehead. He glanced at his watch. Ten p.m. There was still time.

He burst out of his apartment and rushed down the stairs to the landlord's door. "Gombu! Wake up, dammit!"

The stunned Indian opened the door, clad in a robe and nightcap. "What is it, Father?"

"I need to leave for Calcutta tonight."

"Tonight?"

"I'll pay you whatever it takes."

"But, it's impossible to get tickets now."

Roberto grabbed Gombu's arm. "Sir Geoffrey said you're the best. Now get me on that midnight train or I'll tell him you're useless."

Gombu stepped back in shock. "I'll try, Father. But it will cost a great deal."

"Do it!" Roberto pulled out his wallet and handed the Indian a fifty pound note.

A half hour later, Gombu appeared at Roberto's door with two red-uniformed porters. "We must hurry, Father."

"Well—get on with it." Roberto nodded toward the trunk and watched the porters lug it down the steps toward a waiting carriage. He scanned the small apartment a final time and spotted the opened bottle of *Bordeaux* on the table. "I'll need you tonight." He popped in the cork and stuffed the bottle in his traveling bag.

The porters loaded the trunk on the carriage and jumped aboard. One of them picked up a buggy whip and cracked it over the horse's ears. The black carriage pulled away from the curb into the night traffic.

Gombu hailed a taxi and yanked open the door. He bowed and extended a yellow ticket. "Hurry, Father."

"I was wrong. You are the best." Roberto snatched the ticket and handed the Indian a fifty pound note. He patted Gombu's shoulder and climbed into the taxi.

"May Shiva watch over you, Father." Gombu closed the door and watched the taxi speed away from the curb. He shook his head and stuffed the note in his pocket.

Roberto untied the bloody handkerchief and inspected the cut on his palm. It should be his worst problem. He leaned back in the seat and closed his eyes. He could still see the amber dial glowing in the darkness, the ominous microphone silhouetted against it.

How much had they paid Gideon to betray him? Certainly more than a few pieces of silver. Judas goats didn't come cheap these days. He rested his head against the seat and felt the warm breeze on his face.

A frightening thought struck him. What about Eammon? If Gideon was with them, then Eammon must be too. No—it wasn't true. Eammon and those mountains were his last hope. He had nothing left. It was too late to turn back. Get to the mountains and hope for the best.

Ten minutes later, the black-and-yellow taxi screeched to a stop behind a line of emptying cabs. It was nearly midnight, but the brightly lit street swarmed with passengers dressed in colorful *sari's* and cottons. It seemed as though the whole world had been dumped on the street in front of him.

"Victoria Terminus, *sahib*."

Roberto paid the driver and crawled out of the cab. Across the street, Victoria Terminus' ornate facade towered above the crowd like an enormous brown fortress, its spotlighted domes and spires stretching into the night sky. His ears rang with chimes from the station's Roman-numeraled clock. It was eleven.

Desperate to catch their trains, hordes of shouting passengers pressed forward toward the narrow, wrought iron gate leading into the concourse. Even the beggars had crawled away from the unruly mob.

Roberto was about to join the crushing mass of humanity when a deep voice called out to him.

"Father!"

Roberto felt his heart jump as a blue-and-yellow-turbaned policeman grabbed his shoulder. *My God, they have me! I'm finished!*

"Sorry, Father—you're standing off the curb. You could be seriously injured." The Indian guided Roberto onto the curb and stepped back with hands on hips.

"I'm sorry. A bit disoriented, I guess."

"This is no place for that, Father. Good evening." The uniformed Indian nodded politely and strolled away, leaving Roberto standing next to a signpost with his heart pounding through his chest.

Roberto clutched his bag and raced across the street. Panic swept through him. He began pushing through the crowd with total abandon.

"Hey—watch where you're going, idiot!"

Roberto felt a strong hand grab his arm and push him out of the way like he was a feather. A tall, lean Englishman flashed past him with a large bag slung over his shoulder. "I'm sorry, sir. I didn't mean to bump you."

The Englishman glared at him with ice blue eyes. His thick, black hair was matted against his glistening forehead, and his stubbled face showed the strain of hard times.

"Why are you looking at me that way? I said I was sorry?"

Angered by Roberto's feeble apology, the stranger started toward him, but he was intercepted by a stocky Indian with even blacker hair who pushed him aside while gesturing frantically for Roberto to move on.

Roberto clenched his fists and turned toward the wrought iron gate. After ten years in hell, he was tired of backing down. At thirty-eight, Roberto Hidalgo was a bitter man. The sweet smell of oranges had been replaced by the nauseating stench of unwashed humanity fighting to get on a train bound for the world's poorest city.

27 | Bonaventure

Akaal relaxed his grip on Bonaventure's arm. "Are you all right?"

"Never mind me, dammit. That bloke needs some manners."

"I think he was a priest."

"I don't care if he was the bloody Pope. He should watch where he's going."

"He meant no harm."

Bonaventure mumbled a curse and snatched his pack off the concrete. "Come on, let's get out of this bloody zoo." He turned toward the exit gate and bumped into a well-dressed Englishman coming the other way.

"Watch where you're going, idiot!" The angered Englishman waved his cane menacingly in the air.

"That's it!" Bonaventure slammed his pack on the concrete and spun around with clenched fists.

The stunned Englishman lowered his cane and backed away. He was looking into the eyes of a wild animal. No fear, just an ominous glare coming from the khaki-clad man in front of him. "Sorry, old chap. I didn't realize you were one of us."

"I'm not one of you."

"I see. Well—no harm intended." The Englishman tipped his hat and walked away.

"You were speaking about manners?" Akaal looked down to stop from laughing.

"Come on, before I get us arrested." Bonaventure slung his pack over his shoulder and marched through the exit gate with Akaal on his heels. He spotted a line of waiting carriages and pushed toward them amidst a blare of angry car horns and shouting travelers.

"Where are we going?"

"To the nearest bar." Bonaventure heaved his pack into a carriage and hopped aboard. He leaned forward and tapped the turbaned driver on the shoulder. "You speak English?"

The driver frowned and shrugged his shoulders.

"Tell him to take us to the nearest cheap bar." Bonaventure brushed back his matted black hair and watched his friend climb into the carriage.

With a full moon lighting the way, the weatherbeaten carriage rolled past Victoria Dock while its two exhausted passengers gazed at the lights of Bombay Harbor.

Bonaventure glanced at the four-legged creature clopping along the road in front of them. "That blasted horse looks more tired than me."

"He is old. It happens to the best of us." Akaal pulled out a small tobacco pouch and wad of cigaret papers. "Smoke?"

"Might as well. Looks like I won't be climbing for awhile."

"Things will work out." Akaal licked the rolled cigaret and handed it to his friend while the driver looked back in shock.

"What's wrong with him?"

"We're not supposed to share my spit. We're of different color."

"Bull." Bonaventure jammed the cigaret in his mouth and pulled out a small gold lighter. He flicked it open and lit the cigaret while the driver turned away in disgust.

"You're very tense tonight."

"Am I now." Bonaventure looked down at the cigaret lighter. "You know, I bought this bloody thing in Zurich ten years ago. Now I can't afford the bloody alcohol to fuel it. It's supposed to be solid gold. Maybe it'll bring in a few pounds at a decent pawn shop."

Bonaventure slipped the lighter into his sweat-stained shirt pocket and took a deep drag of the brown cigaret. The carriage was approaching a row of dilapidated shanties. One of them had a weathered "BAR" sign hanging over its slatted front door.

Bonaventure nudged Akaal. "Looks like Piccadilly Circus."

"Lovely."

With the carriage still moving, Bonaventure hopped out and snatched his pack off the seat. "Don't pay him yet. We don't know if the bloody dive is open."

Akaal climbed out and dropped five *rupees* into the driver's opened palm. "He needs the money more than us."

"He's probably loaded."

Akaal watched the carriage turn back toward Victoria Terminus. "The drivers are so poor, they use their carriages to sleep. They have no homes."

"Hell, neither do we. At least he has a place. Come on, let's get drunk."

The dimly lit bar was deserted except for a rugged-looking bartender wiping some glasses with a dirty towel. From the sound of the sea chanty coming from his beard-covered lips, he was a fellow Englishman.

"Hi, mate." Bonaventure leaned against the makeshift wood bar, nearly toppling it over.

The red-bearded bartender turned around and glared at Bonaventure with bloodshot eyes. "Looking for trouble, are we?"

Bonaventure raised his open palms. "You've got me wrong, mate. I'm just a fellow countryman who wants a bottle of your best English whiskey."

"Oh yeah? Show me your money."

Bonaventure pulled out a half pound note and placed it on the bar. "Hope this is enough, cause it's all I've got."

The bartender eyed the paper and snatched a dusty brown bottle off the shelf. He wiped it with his dirty towel and placed it on the counter. "My finest." He swept his hand across the counter and stuffed the note in his shirt pocket. "Need a glass?"

"Two."

The bartender placed two shot glasses beside the bottle. "Waiting for someone, eh?"

"The other glass is for my friend."

The bartender glanced at Akaal. "Him?"

"Him."

"I'll be damned." The bartender rubbed his mouth with the back of his hand and staggered back to his dirty glasses.

Bonaventure ignored the bartender's slur and snatched the bottle and glasses off the counter. He sat at one of the empty tables and uncorked the bottle. "Whiskey, my ass. Smells more like rubbing alcohol and shoe polish." He poured a shot and stared at the smelly brown liquid. "Oh, well...." He took a deep breath and chugged it down.

Akaal sat down and pushed the second glass toward his friend. "Where will you go?"

Bonaventure scowled from the whiskey and poured Akaal a shot. "Don't know."

"You should think about it."

Bonaventure poured another shot and gulped it down. He winced and put down his empty glass. "I'm too tired to think."

"I don't want to leave you like this."

"Who are you, my bloody wet nurse?"

Akaal locked his black eyes on Bonaventure. "I'm your friend."

Bonaventure pushed the bottle aside and leaned across the table. He smiled and rested a hand on Akaal's wrist. "My Lord, you're dark-skinned. I never noticed how dark you are."

"And your skin is like the snow. Even in the sunlight, you never turn red. I think you're made of ice."

Bonaventure reached out and grabbed a clump of Akaal's shiny black hair. "You know—I never had a friend until I stumbled across you in that pub. You are my friend, aren't you?"

Akaal smiled and clutched Bonaventure's wrist. "For life. Now let's get out of this foul-smelling cave and find a place to sleep." Akaal snatched the shot of whiskey and gulped it down.

"Not bad—eh?"

"It tastes like yak piss, but I've had worse."

The two men spent the next hour staggering past deserted Crawford Market and the bazaars until they reached Marine Drive on the Back Bay. They headed west and followed the curved waterside highway until they shuffled onto Chowpatty Beach, below Malabar Hill.

"Looks like we're not alone." Bonaventure stared at the mass of snoring humanity strewn across the moonlit beach.

"Beggars. They have no home, so they sleep here."

"Well—then this is where we belong." Bonaventure swigged down the last of the cheap whiskey and dropped the empty bottle in the sand. He grabbed Akaal's arm and trudged across the beach, looking for a vacant spot. A distant belltower chimed two a.m. It was the last sound he heard before passing out beside a sleeping beggar.

They'd met in London seven years ago. As chief guide to His Majesty's Royal Infantry Brigade in Dharan, India, Akaal had been ordered to accompany Dharan's commanding officer to England on a mission to gain funding for a specially-trained force of mountain troops.

Despite the Defense Ministry's contention that the Himalayas provided a natural barrier against attack from the north, Major "Josh" Camp argued vehemently that a properly-trained Japanese force could gain a towering foothold in Nepal by scaling certain high passes in the Himalayas. Once achieved, Camp warned that India would be laid bare to invasion from the north by thousands of battle-hardened Japanese troops, crippling England's presence in the Far East through the massacre of thousands of overwhelmed soldiers and civilians.

Embarrassed by the Ministry's stern rejection, Camp lashed out at Akaal for his inadequate support during the hearings. While Akaal insisted it was not his place to interrupt his superiors during high level discussions, Camp's assertion was indeed correct. No native Nepali wanted English troops crawling through their sacred mountains—no matter what the cause. The Himalayas belonged to the gods. To make war in the mountains was to make war on the gods—and that would end the world.

Angered by Akaal's betrayal, Camp abandoned him in London and returned to Dharan in a fit of rage, but not before warning the Gurkha that he would be stripped of rank upon his return to India.

Bonaventure had returned to his native London from a successful ascent of Mount Chimborazo in Ecuador. Eager to get the chill out of his bones, he strolled into his favorite pub near Piccadilly Circus just in time to see Akaal defending himself against three cockney drunks who resented dark-skinned wogs sharing their drinking space.

The young Gurkha was handling himself pretty well until he turned his back on the bartender and caught a brickbat on the head.

When Bonaventure tried to come to the unconscious Gurkha's aid, the bartender called him a wog lover and took a wild swing at him with the brickbat. Most unwise. When the melee ended, Bonaventure had laid out the three men with the brickbat he'd taken from the bartender after flattening him with a vicious left hook.

That night, the two battered mountaineers exchanged war stories in an English jail while munching on stale biscuits. By the time they were released the next morning, Bonaventure had gained a deep respect for the stocky, five-foot-six-inch Gurkha who had climbed the great snow peaks between Nepal and Tibet.

To Akaal, Bonaventure was a stranger sent by the gods to rescue him from harm's way. In Akaal's world, nothing carried greater respect than a fellow human being's act of compassion.

Abandoned by Major Camp, Akaal spent the next few days recovering from his concussion in Bonaventure's London flat. In that time, Akaal's respect for Bonaventure grew even stronger when he learned his boisterous host had risen from less than humble beginnings to become one of the finest mountaineers on the globe.

Born in 1900 to an English mother abandoned by her Italian merchant marine lover, Julian Bonaventure spent his childhood begging in London's streets while his impoverished mother gave herself to any man willing to provide them with enough money to survive another day.

When his mother succumbed to influenza in 1908, the rag-covered boy was placed in an orphanage where he was left to the mercy of the vermin-infested institution's perverted staff. He managed to escape four years later, but the damage was done. The embittered youth bore scars that would never heal.

Bonaventure's early manhood was spent groveling for food in London's Whitechapel district. When that didn't work, he resorted to pickpocketing and card-marking. Running from shouting bobbies, the exhausted youth would dart into the nearest alley, only to suffer a fierce beating at the hands of desperate street thugs bent on stealing his daily earnings.

With his body aching from countless pummelings, Bonaventure's only refuge came at night when he lifted a bottle of rum from the local distillery and climbed onto Whitechapel's slippery roof tops. Anchoring himself against a chimney, the bitter young man drowned his pain with booze while gazing at the fog-shrouded moon. When his eyes finally closed, he dreamt of a mountaineer standing tall on an ivory peak, the sun on his face, the world at his feet—and for a moment, he was free.

Bonaventure's fate changed in 1918 when he was arrested while attempting to pickpocket a visiting Swiss national in a London pub. As it turned out, Hans Furgler was preparing to return to his native Switzerland with the body of his dead son who had been killed in the air war over France.

Seeing the dirt-smeared face glaring at him from behind Bathgate's prison bars, Furgler suddenly realized fate had dealt him a chance to sooth the deep pain in his heart. Instead of bringing charges against Bonaventure, he offered to adopt the young street tough despite vehement protests from the judge who gave up in frustration after uttering a final warning....

"Once a wolf—always a wolf."

Jumping at the chance to escape his eighteen years in hell, Bonaventure accompanied his newfound guardian to Switzerland, and a small chalet nestled in the Bernese Alps below a fourteen thousand foot mountain known as Jungfrau.

In their first weeks together, Hans tried desperately to undo the harm done by years of beatings and abuse, but nothing seemed to work. Finally resorting to physical discipline, Hans quickly learned the judge was right. Beating a wild animal only makes it more defiant.

With winter closing on the Alps, Bonaventure cursed the old man and fled into the mountains like a wolf cub running from its captor. Instead of chasing him, Hans decided to let the animal run wild until hunger and exhaustion forced it to return.

And Bonaventure did return, driven back by the merciless Alpine winds and snow. He said nothing while gorging himself on hot stew and tea, but Hans knew what he was thinking. It was only a matter of time before his wild animal would attempt another escape into the deadly, snowpacked mountains.

But the escape never came. Instead of punishing the youth, Hans dragged him out of bed the following morning and led him into the chilled air with a climbing rope and equipment in hand. Holding out the coiled rope, Hans declared it was time for Bonaventure to learn the art of mountaineering. "If you're going to escape, for God's sake do it with style." He thrust the rope into Bonaventure's hands and led him into the rocky terrain below Jungfrau's ice-coated south face.

When they were well inside the mountain's imposing shadow, Hans gripped Bonaventure's arm and declared, "When you climb this mountain, you'll be a man. Until then, you're nothing but a boy."

Bonaventure cursed Hans that day, but the old man's words struck a nerve. Under the aging mountaineer's watchful eyes, Bonaventure learned the crucial skills of belay and rappel while his hands bled from exhaustive struggles up the mountain's impregnable wall.

When the blizzards came, and wiser people huddled in the warmth of their chalets, Bonaventure clung to Jungfrau's ice-covered slopes while his adopted father shouted at him from the haze.

"Do you want to die down there! Climb, dammit! Before the mountain dumps a load of snow on your head!"

A year later, Julian Bonaventure scrambled onto Jungfrau's snow-covered summit while his stern taskmaster screamed at him from the ledge below.

"See, Julian! You're a man now! You've conquered the world!"

Bonaventure rose to his feet and looked out at the great white peaks filling the horizon. His dream had been fulfilled. He'd climbed through the haze of Whitechapel's rooftops to become a mountaineer—the sun on his face—the world at his feet. With tears streaming down his cheeks, he raised his clenched fists and shouted at the clouds. "Free, dammit! Free!"

"Julian!"

Bonaventure looked down in horror. Hans was lying on the ledge, his gloved hands clutching his chest. He raced down the summit and knelt beside the old man.

Hans dug at his throat. "Can't breathe...."

"We'll get you down. I'll rig a stretcher."

"Too late...."

"Don't talk like that. You're not gonna die on me." Bonaventure tried to help him up, but the old man collapsed in his arms.

"I'm so proud of you, Julian. You conquered a mountain...and you conquered yourself. I love you, Julian. My son...." Han's blue eyes locked on the summit.

Bonaventure stared at the limp body in his arms. He checked for a pulse, but there was none. The only sound was the wind whistling through Jungfrau's summit.

On January 3, 1920, Julian Bonaventure buried his adopted father in the ice at thirteen thousand. He planted his blue and orange pennant next to the makeshift grave, and remained at his father's side through the long, frigid night.

When the first rays of sunlight struck Jungfrau's ivory summit, Bonaventure eased over the ledge and said goodbye to the man who had made him free—and for the first time in his life, he cried.

That moment on Jungfrau lit a fire inside Bonaventure that would never die. In the years that followed, he assaulted the Alps with a ferocity never seen before. One by one, they fell to his blue and orange victory pennant. From the Matterhorn to the Eiger. From Finsteraarhorn to Mont Blanc.

His Alpine conquests only whetted his appetite for greater challenges. Travelling to the Americas, he humbled Shasta, Whitney, McKinley and Rainier. Then on to South America to conquer the Huascaran in Peru, and Chimborazo in Ecuador.

His friendship with Akaal came at the perfect time. With the situation still tenuous in Dharan, Akaal joined his comrade on an expedition to Africa where they raced up legendary Kilimanjaro. Then, with funding from a wealthy Argentine businessman named Calabra, they scaled mighty Aconcagua in a raging blizzard while the incensed Argentine cursed them from below.

In twelve years of record-breaking ascents, Bonaventure gained a reputation for tenacity and courage unheard of in the journals of mountaineering. Yet, to the prestigious Royal Society in his native England, he remained a reckless fool unworthy of recognition.

But Bonaventure knew the true reason for their snubbing. Born in the streets, he'd intruded on a skill reserved for the elite. Men like him must never set foot in the Society's hallowed hall, or defile its peaks. In time, he would disappear in an avalanche or blizzard. The name "Bonaventure" would become a fleeting memory—and things would be proper again.

But the Society's rejection backfired. Incensed by their hypocritical self-righteousness, Bonaventure stole their glory. Monitoring their plans, he and Akaal beat their climbers up every targeted mountain, leaving only a note and his hated blue and orange pennant to greet their infuriated leaders when they scrambled onto the summit.

In 1934, Bonaventure's string of conquests reached the Far East. With Akaal reinstated in Dharan by its new commanding officer, the two climbers trekked into Northern India and began offering their services to lucrative mountaineering expeditions pouring in from Europe.

They were an unbeatable combination. Bonaventure's fierce tenacity blended perfectly with Akaal's endurance and knowledge. Undaunted by the weather and extreme altitudes, the two mountaineers led their teams steadily upward toward the roof of the world. Twenty-thousand—twenty-two—twenty-three—and still they pressed higher. Conquest followed conquest as they approached the mighty one. The five ledges of great snow—Kangchenjunga.

Driven by his fierce hatred of the rich, and a lifelong passion to climb above Whitechapel's slums, Julian Bonaventure turned his back on the world and reached for the stars. Until last month, when it all came tumbling down....

Bonaventure sat up and rubbed his aching forehead. The sky had brightened just enough to reveal a deserted beach.

Gary Naiman

Where were the beggars? They'd vanished into thin air?

He brushed the sand out of his hair and looked down at his empty lap. Where was she? Where was the beautiful Indian princess? And the flower-draped barge? And blue lake? He frowned and looked down at the canvas bag lying beside him. Damn—he'd made love to a bloody duffle bag.

He reached out and shook Akaal's wrist. When nothing happened, he leaned over and shouted at the top of his lungs. "Corporal Dawa—front and center!"

"Sir!" Akaal sat up and saluted while Bonaventure broke into hysterical laughter.

The Gurkha rubbed his eyes and brushed the sand out of his hair. "Not funny."

"Sorry, mate, but your snoring was so loud it drove the bloody beggars off the beach." He patted Akaal's shoulder and stood up. "Blast, I'm hungry." He stretched his arms and studied a line of fishing boats headed past Colaba Point.

"I have a few pounds left. We can buy some fresh fish and vegetables at the market."

"Anything but rice. I never want to see another bowl of rice."

"Rice is the staff of life."

"I'd rather be dead."

Bonaventure crouched down and scooped a handful of sand through his fingers. He sighed and looked out at the harbor. "I guess you'll be leaving soon."

"Very soon."

"Can't you get out of it?"

"Don't want to. The money's too good. My brothers and sisters depend on me for *rupees*."

"Hell, you could make a better living offering your services to mountaineers. You're about the best I've seen."

Akaal pulled out his cigaret kit and rolled two fresh ones. "I'm afraid times have changed. With war coming, the climbers will stay home."

Bonaventure took one of the cigarets and lit it. "You think the Japanese will declare war?"

"They already have, but the world looks away while their

armies rape China and march toward India."

"Hell, they're not strong enough to make it over the mountains. And why bother? Nothing over here but a bunch of bloody snobs and beggars."

Akaal lit his cigaret and took a deep drag. "I don't know about snobs and beggars, but the Japanese must be stopped before they reach my home."

Bonaventure looked at him in surprise. "You'd fight beside the Brits after the way that idiot Camp treated you? After he embarrassed you in front of your men?"

Akaal smiled. "I have no great love for your people, but I'll do anything to protect my home."

Bonaventure puffed his cigaret and stared at his friend. "Answer a question, old chum."

"If I can."

"Why did you come all the way to Bombay if you planned to stay in Nepal?"

Akaal stood up and brushed the sand off his khaki shirt and pants. "I was concerned about you. I know how much it hurt you to lose your home. I was afraid you might do something rash."

"Like kill myself?" Bonaventure flicked his cigaret in the sand. "Don't worry about me, old chum. Too much bloody hate for that." He stood up and slung his duffel bag over his shoulder. "Come on, let's get some food."

Akaal glanced at the rising sun and followed his friend across Chowpatty Beach toward bustling Bombay and some freshly caught fish at Crawford's Market.

In a few hours, Akaal would board the afternoon train to Calcutta, then proceed north to Siliguri on the *Darjeeling Mail*. From there, he would trek west into Nepal and his family's village, where he would embrace his loved ones and settle down for a two week rest before rejoining the Royal Army in Dharan.

They arrived at Victoria Terminus late that afternoon. Bonaventure watched Akaal count his small wad of pound notes. "Hope I left you enough money to make it back."

"Barely. But what about you?"

"I have enough to get by until I find work."

"But, I thought—"

"I lied."

"You have money?"

Bonaventure smiled. "I can loan you some if you need it."

"No—but you should have told me."

Bonaventure looked down and fumbled for words. "Hell of a boring ride, if you ask me."

"Quite boring."

"Well—guess it's goodbye then." Bonaventure reached out and clasped his friend's hand.

"You'll be all right?"

"I'll be fine. And for God's sake, don't get shot by some lunatic recruit."

"You can always reach me through the telegraph link." Akaal clutched Bonaventure's wrist. "Goodbye—friend." He turned and faded into the mass of humanity pushing through the station's main entrance.

Bonaventure stared at the milling crowd and dipped his hand into an empty pocket. "Oh well—ashes to ashes." He heaved a sigh and walked toward a prosperous looking European who had made the careless mistake of slinging his jacket over his shoulder with a fat wallet protruding from the inside pocket.

28 | Nevo

Roberto blinked at the sunlight flooding the passenger compartment. Across from him, the plump Indian lady and her son had been replaced by a meek looking man in a dark-blue suit and straw hat.

"Good morning, Father." The handsome Indian smiled and removed his hat, revealing a crop of neatly brushed black hair.

Roberto nodded politely and glanced at his watch in astonishment. Seven forty-five? Nearly twelve hours had passed since he dropped off to sleep on the rocking train. He sat up and rubbed his stiff neck.

"You must like our trains. You have slept since I boarded last night in Jabalpur. I was becoming a bit worried about you."

Surprised at the Indian's crisp English, Roberto smiled and uncorked the canteen of water he'd purchased in Bombay. He extended it to the Indian.

"Thank you, Father, but we're forbidden to drink from the same vessel as a foreigner. Nothing personal, you understand."

Roberto nodded and took a long swig of water. He rested his head against the worn leather seat and looked out the window at the flashing marshlands.

Thirty hours had passed since the *Eastern Express* pulled out of Bombay on its tedious journey across India's dry plains and eroded brown hills. Skirting the Ghats, a low-lying mountain range on India's west coast, the Express plodded eastward across parched yellow grasslands where impoverished farmers tilled the hardened soil in hopes their seedlings of millet, wheat, and cotton would take root in the approaching monsoon.

The slow-moving train followed the Narmada River northeast toward the legendary Ganges, bypassing the Deccan and Chota Nagpur highlands before veering southeast toward the fertile marshlands leading to Calcutta.

Picking up speed, the black steam engine and its string of maroon-and-yellow passenger cars raced across an unending chain of earthen dams spanning silver marshes. In a few weeks, the entire landscape would become an enormous flood plain.

"Are you a missionary?"

The Indian's question startled him. "I'm trying to reach a fellow missionary in Nepal. I've been assigned to assist him."

"Nepal?" The Indian frowned. "Difficult journey. Have you arranged transport into the sacred kingdom?"

"Not yet."

"You know—passage into Nepal is not easy." The Indian waited for a response, but none came. "Even if one is fortunate to gain entrance, the terrain is extremely taxing and dangerous."

"I'll work out the details in Calcutta. I've come too far to worry about it." Roberto sighed and stared out the window.

"Perhaps I can help."

"You?"

The Indian pulled a small white card out of his shirt pocket and extended it to Roberto. "Allow me to introduce myself. I am Sonam Chandola."

Roberto took the embossed card from the Indian's hand. "Your card reads 'Nevo'?"

"My business name, Father. In all humility, I must admit to being rather well-known throughout India, and even into Nepal and Sikkim."

"I see."

"I can provide whatever you need—guides, porters, supplies—anything. Why—for the right price, I'll even ask the gods to light your way."

Roberto flashed a polite smile while pondering Nevo's words "If we came to terms, how long would it take to reach my destination?"

"Which is?"

Roberto slumped in the seat. "I don't know."

"You don't know where it is?"

"No."

Nevo's eyes widened. "Now that's refreshing. It might cost a bit more under those conditions."

Roberto looked up in surprise. "You could find it?"

Nevo smiled. "All things are possible for the right sum. Do

you know the name of the missionary?"

"Collins—Father Eammon Collins."

Nevo's black eyes flashed. "It wouldn't be too difficult. I'd have you there in a few days." He smiled and folded his hands. "For a fee, of course."

"Of course."

Nevo's smile faded. "May I ask you something?"

"Yes?"

"Are you aware Nepal is quite turbulent?"

"Turbulent?"

"Foreigners are most unwelcome there."

Roberto nodded. "I'd pay you well for transport to my colleague's mission."

"Despite the risk?"

Roberto nodded.

"Good—then we have an arrangement."

"If the price is right."

"It will be a fair price." Nevo glanced out the window. "Ah—I can see Howrah Bridge and the rail station. We're coming into Calcutta. Do you have transport to your hotel?"

Roberto frowned. "I don't have a hotel."

"You have not made reservations?"

"No."

"Hmmm. Without reservations, getting a decent hotel room in Calcutta is almost as difficult as entering Nepal."

Roberto shook his head in frustration.

"Let me try to help. Perhaps I can find you a room."

Roberto's eyes brightened. "Thank you, Mr. Nevo. I'll be happy to pay for that too."

Nevo chuckled. "No need, Father. I am not a poor man. Besides, a few days in Calcutta will give you some time to think things over."

"You mean, about going on?"

"Perhaps."

When Roberto stepped off the train, he was struck in the face by a smothering blast of heat and humidity, the likes of which he'd never experienced. In a matter of minutes, his black shirt and jacket were soaked with perspiration. He grasped his leather traveling bag and staggered into the baggage line while fighting a wave of dizziness.

A hand grasped his arm. "Please, Father. Allow me to fetch your baggage."

He turned and saw Nevo staring at him with penetrating black eyes. "Thank you, but I can handle it."

"Don't you trust me?"

Roberto mopped his sweating brow. "I'm sorry, but—"

Those were the last words he remembered before awakening in the back seat of an automobile. He tried to sit up, but fell back from the dizziness.

"You must go slowly, Father. Calcutta's heat is most trying before the monsoon."

"Mr. Nevo—is that you?"

"Yes, Father."

"Where am I?"

"In my car. We're on the Howrah bridge crossing the Hooghly River. That's Calcutta on the other side."

Roberto sat up and glanced over the driver's shoulder at the sprawling city. On his left, the muddy Hooghly was packed with barges and steamers fighting for dock space. Throngs of half-naked Indians waded along the river's polluted shore.

"It's a good thing I managed to stop your head from striking the floor. Concrete is not good for the skull."

Roberto rubbed his forehead. "The last thing I remember was the damned heat."

"Please—have some water."

Roberto reached out and took a cup of cold water from Nevo. He hesitated and forced a weak smile. "I assume this hasn't touched your lips."

Nevo smiled and watched Roberto swig down the cool liquid. When the Indian reached for the empty cup, Roberto grasped his small, dark wrist. "Thank you, Mr. Nevo."

Nevo patted Roberto's hand. "You'll be happy to know your trunk will be waiting for you when we arrive at the *Great Eastern Hotel*. I hope you don't mind, but I took the liberty of removing the baggage ticket from your wallet when you fainted. I assure you nothing has been disturbed."

Roberto slipped his hand off Nevo's wrist and leaned back in the seat. "Hotel? You said it was impossible to get a room?"

Nevo glanced at his grinning driver. "We were lucky, Father. I managed to get you a vacancy overlooking Dalhousie Square."

Roberto rested his hand on the small gold crucifix lying on his chest. "I don't know how to repay you."

"Oh, I'll think of something. Perhaps we could have dinner tonight and discuss your trek to Nepal. I assume you're comfortable with my assistance?"

Roberto nodded. "We'll settle the terms at dinner."

"Excellent." Nevo glanced out the window. "Can I ask you one more question?"

"Yes?"

"I'm curious why a missionary would want to venture into the Himalayas when his services are so badly needed here in Calcutta."

"Things are that bad?"

Nevo shook his head. "They're worse than that, Father. Calcutta is the world's melting pot of despair. Look, they even flock to the doors of the *Great Eastern* for help."

Roberto glanced out the window and got his first bitter taste of Calcutta. As their automobile screeched to a stop in front of the *Great Eastern's* pillared entrance, it was besieged by a crowd of ragged beggars pushing for a cooler spot in the shadows beneath the covered patio. "My God, why doesn't someone help them?"

"Difficult question, Father. Perhaps tonight we'll take a walk in the streets to find the answer." Nevo stepped out of the car and gestured for Roberto to follow him. "Please move quickly, Father, or they'll tear your pants when you walk through them." He waited for Roberto to step out of the car and led him toward the *Great Eastern's* arched entrance.

Roberto's hotel room was a welcome escape from Calcutta's oppressive heat and humidity. Equipped with a ceiling fan and balcony, the spacious room was beautifully furnished with pastel blue carpeting, canary-yellow walls, white linen draperies, and an exotic bamboo desk and chair. A rainbow of freshly cut flowers protruded from a black vase on the night stand beside the canopy bed.

On the wall opposite the bed hung a large portrait of Warren Hastings, Calcutta's first Governor General. Hasting's erect figure glared down at the bed, his hands clasped in front of him.

As promised, Roberto's bulky trunk had been lugged up the hotel's rear stairs by two exhausted porters and placed neatly in the corner next to the slatted closet door. The trunk's thick padlock was intact and its black, steel-riveted surface looked none the worse for wear after its six-thousand-mile sea and rail journey.

Roberto removed his drenched clothing and filled the bathroom's cast iron tub with cold water. He was about to step into the refreshing bath when he glanced through the opened door at the inviting canopy bed. As if drawn by a powerful magnet, he stumbled naked across the bedroom and collapsed on the cool, white linen bedspread like a baby returning to its mother's womb. The bath would have to wait.

They'd agreed to rendezvous in the lobby at seven. Refreshed after a long nap and cooling bath, Father Roberto Santiago walked down the Great Eastern's spiral staircase into a gathering of prosperous looking gentlemen and ladies sipping cocktails beneath the lobby's whirring ceiling fans.

Roberto exchanged smiles with a lovely English lady and eased toward a red-and-gold Victorian chair near the hotel's entrance. He sat down and gestured to a white-jacketed Indian who approached him with a linen towel folded across his extended forearm.

"Care for a drink, Father?"

"A lemonade, thank you."

Roberto spent the next twenty minutes sipping a cool lemonade while glancing nervously at the ornate black-and-gold grandfather clock beneath the staircase.

It was nearly seven thirty when Nevo rushed into the lobby. "Forgive me, I was caught in a financial negotiation with an

The Tenth Avatar

old friend."

Roberto stood up and clasped Nevo's extended hand. "Everything went well?"

"Extremely. Come—I have a great place for dinner."

Roberto followed Nevo out of the lobby into the steaming dark street. He'd only walked a few feet when a flash of lightning stopped him in his tracks.

"The gods prepare us for the monsoon."

Roberto looked up at the flashing sky. "I thought it didn't come until June?"

"It doesn't. This is just the first warning. It won't rain for several days."

Roberto wasn't listening. Another flash lit up the dark street in front of him, filling his eyes with horror. The flickering sidewalk was moving, its rustling shadows creeping toward him like a devilish apparition.

"*Paise, Barasahib! Paise!*"

A hideous mass of broken humanity crawled toward him, their palms cupped upward and their voices moaning a discordant hymn that curdled his blood.

"Keep moving, Father. You're not ready for this." Nevo clutched Roberto's arm and pulled him away from the horrible sight.

They rushed across Dalhousie Square amidst a disorienting mass of onrushing pedestrians, hissing buses, honking automobiles, scurrying buggies, swaying livestock, and screaming street vendors. Roberto's stomach churned from the sickening smell of stale vegetables and decayed waste. He leaned against a lamp post and felt his stomach wrench.

"*Paise, Barasahib! Paise!*"

Someone clutched his jacket. Roberto looked down in horror at a legless beggar trying to snatch his crucifix.

"We'd better take a buggy, Father. I'm afraid your trinkets are too much for these desperate souls."

Nevo hailed an empty buggy and helped his shaken friend into the worn leather seat. He climbed in beside him and shouted instructions in Hindustani while the young driver grasped the buggy's two protruding wooden handles and lifted them to waist height.

As the two-wheeled conveyance rolled down the jammed street, Roberto gazed in bewilderment at the faces crying out to him from the darkness. "What are they saying?"

"Most ask for money. Some beg for food. A few curse you for abandoning them to the gutter."

"Me?" Roberto felt a deep pain well up inside him. "What did I do?"

"Nothing. That's the problem, you see."

"This is wrong. We should do something."

"There is nothing you can do, Father. There are too many of them."

"I can't stand it, dammit!" Roberto tried to climb out of the buggy, but Nevo pushed him back in the seat with a surprising show of strength.

"There is plenty of time for compassion. I assure you Calcutta's beggars will still be here after we've had our talk."

The hand-drawn buggy veered onto Chowringhee Street where Nevo quickly paid the driver and escorted Roberto to a waiting taxicab. "Please hurry before those creeping shadows catch up with us. The beggars are very angry tonight. It must be the lightning and thunder."

"They're afraid of the lightning?"

"They know the monsoon is near. When the rains come, many will drown in the streets."

Roberto ducked into the taxi and collapsed in the seat while trying to control his wrenching stomach. The taxi plodded through Chowringee's dense crowds while Roberto stared in horror at the tragic souls crying out to him from the pavement. Crippled men, women, and children rushed toward the taxi with empty wooden cups, their hollow eyes burning into him like the horrible faces in Picasso's painting.

A groaning mother charged out of the darkness with a naked child in her hands. She thrust the child at Roberto's face while staring at him with terrified eyes. "*Dal, Brahman. Dal!*" It didn't take a translator to know the desperate woman was pleading for rice. Roberto gasped and looked away. The poor creature didn't realize her baby was dead.

When the taxi turned onto Park Street, a new sound echoed off the filthy tenement buildings—a rhythmic tapping that quickly grew to deafening proportions.

"What is it?"

"We'll be away from it in a minute, Father."

Roberto clutched Nevo's wrist. "What is it!"

Nevo sighed and looked down. "It's Calcutta's beggars pounding their empty cups on the pavement. It's their way of cursing a heartless world."

"God."

The night air cooled as the taxi turned right and drove past an elegant domed structure nestled inside a forested park.

"Victoria Memorial, Father. And Saint Paul's Cathedral. A touch of jolly old England in the middle of hell."

Roberto stared at the cathedral's belltower silhouetted against the moonlit clouds. "The pounding's stopped."

"Not really." Nevo's face twisted in a frown. "Strange, the difference a mile can make in Calcutta."

The taxi pulled to a stop in front of a beautiful estate.

"We're here, Father."

"Here?"

"My home."

Roberto stared at the sweeping white-marble structure. "This is your home?"

"Yes."

"It's incredible."

"I'm glad you're pleased." Nevo opened the taxi door and stepped out. "We can dine here, if you like." He backed away and gestured toward the white mansion.

"Yes—of course." Roberto crawled out of the taxi and followed his host across the estate's moonlit lawn to a flight of white-marble steps.

When they reached the top step, a white-uniformed servant swung open two black, wrought iron doors and bowed. "*Namaste*, Mr. Chandola. You are well?"

"I am well, Cheema. *Namaste*." Nevo pressed his hands together and nodded toward Roberto. "This is my friend, Father Santiago. He has traveled many miles."

Gary Naiman

The servant turned toward Roberto and bowed a second time. "Welcome, Father."

"Thank you."

Nevo grasped his guest's arm. "Come—we'll have a light supper and talk."

Nevo led Roberto into a black-marble foyer with a winding gold staircase and crystal chandelier. Below the staircase stood a large painted statue of a man, his black eyes glaring down at Roberto as if challenging his entrance. A third eye glistened red on the man's forehead.

"He is *Shiva*—the Great Destroyer. If angered, He would burn the world to a cinder with that eye." Nevo pressed his palms together and bowed to the eight foot statue.

Nevo turned to the portrait on the foyer's left wall. "*Brahma*—Creator of the Universe." He bowed a second time and turned to face the portrait on the right wall.

Nevo stared at the portrait's handsome, colorfully dressed young man playing a flute. "But there is none greater than *Vishnu*—Sustainer of life." He grasped Roberto's arm and led him to a gold plaque at the base of the portrait.

"I'm afraid I don't understand the writing."

"It's Hindustani, Father. Allow me to translate." Nevo closed his eyes and recited the inscription from memory. "For the protection of good—for the destruction of evil—I come into being age after age."

Nevo opened his eyes and looked at Roberto. "If it weren't for the Compassionate One, the Universe would flash like the lightning we saw this evening. First, coming into being at *Brahma's* hand, only to be destroyed by *Shiva's* anger. Without *Vishnu*, there would be no balance—no order of things."

"Sorry, I'm a bit overwhelmed."

Nevo smiled and led Roberto through two gold-panelled doors into a sprawling white living room furnished in elegant reds, golds, and blues. Above the massive fireplace hung a portrait of a man clad in rags.

"He looks like you."

"He is me, Father. This portrait is my constant reminder that wealth is a gift to be shared with the poor."

"I see. Well—interesting way of remembering."

"I'm a bit eccentric, Father."

They ate a splendid dinner of curried rice and exotic wheat cakes prepared by Cheema in the mansion's ivory-and-gold dining room. Roberto tried to open a conversation, but was abruptly hushed when Nevo explained that food should be enjoyed in silence. Roberto nodded and quietly finished his meal while his stomach settled from the horrifying ride through Calcutta.

Complimenting Cheema on their excellent meal, Nevo led Roberto into his private study where he poured two brandies while gesturing for his guest to sit on one of the white leather chairs facing a large mural of Calcutta.

"That's quite impressive."

"Thank you. I purchased it from a local artist. He painted it sixteen years ago during the great monsoon. You can see the flooded streets glistening in the moonlight." Nevo chugged his brandy. "Many died that year."

Roberto nodded and sipped his brandy. "Excellent brandy."

"Have more." Nevo reached for the bottle on the serving cart, but Roberto waved him off.

"Are you all right, Father?"

"A bit tired. I shouldn't drink anymore."

Nevo nodded and poured himself a fresh glass. "Then we should get down to business. But first a toast." He leaned forward and lifted his bowl-shaped glass. "May your pain be short—Señor Hidalgo."

Roberto stared at his host in stunned silence.

Nevo sighed and looked up at the ceiling, as if searching for the right words. "I'm afraid I have some bad news. At this moment, two agents of Spain's government are enroute to Calcutta on the same train that brought you here. They'll arrive tomorrow with orders to arrest you for treason."

Roberto sank in the chair in disbelief.

"Undoubtedly, they'll also attempt to confiscate your extremely heavy black trunk which I suspect contains a small fortune in gold and international currency."

Roberto shook his head. "How did you find out?"

"It is my job to know these things. When word reached me that your government was offering a sizeable reward for your arrest, I obtained photographs and a character profile. The rest was simple with a little help from my friend in Bombay."

Roberto flinched. "Gideon?"

"Ah, then you've met. I must admit you had us off balance for awhile. I assumed some tragic fate had befallen you when you didn't follow Mr. Collins. I was pleasantly surprised when Gideon informed me you were alive and well in Bombay."

Roberto stroked his forehead. "How did you know I was on the train?"

"A stroke of luck. I was in Jabalpur visiting an old friend when one of my men alerted me that you'd escaped on the midnight train to Calcutta."

Roberto grimaced. "Gombu?"

"Best not to dwell on these things. I want you to enjoy your last hours of freedom."

Roberto's face flushed with anger. "You did it for the money?"

Nevo sighed. "Sorry, my friend. It's my job. Nothing personal."

Roberto rose to his feet. "I think it's time to say goodnight."

"Is anything wrong, Mr. Chandola?"

Roberto turned and saw Nevo's servant standing between the study's parted doors. He held a small pistol in his right hand.

"Everything is fine, Cheema. My guest and I were just beginning a rather deep conversation."

"I'll be outside if you need me." Cheema bowed and closed the double doors.

"Care for another drink?" Nevo stood up and walked to the liquor cabinet. He snatched a bottle of Napoleon Brandy, poured two glasses, and stuffed the bottle under his arm.

Roberto dropped into the leather chair and looked up at the fluted ceiling. "Well done, Mr. Nevo. I never suspected a thing."

Nevo smiled and handed Roberto one of the filled glasses.

He gulped down the other and poured himself a refill. "I'm truly sorry. I was beginning to like you."

"You have a strange way of showing it."

Nevo locked his black eyes on Roberto. "Let's have that little talk."

Roberto ignored him and gazed at the mural.

"When I led you through the streets tonight, I wanted you to know the pain of my people so you would rejoice when I used your wealth to help them."

Roberto glared at Nevo. "You have a gift for words. In ten years, I've met many like you. None of them could be trusted. I was a fool for letting my guard down."

Nevo's black eyes flickered with anger. He seized Roberto's arm and yanked him off the chair. "Come with me, my friend."

Nevo pushed open the study doors and led Roberto past his stunned servant and the towering statue of Shiva. Bursting into the living room, the angered Indian released his grip on Roberto's arm and pointed a trembling finger at the self-portrait hanging over the fireplace. "You think this picture is some self-righteous expression of hypocrisy? I tell you before the gods—every other *rupee* I earn is passed to those beggars in the streets."

"Only every other one?"

Nevo trembled with anger. "How dare you question me! Your Vatican is heaped with gold, and so are the fat pockets of the hypocrites who wander its halls. Is that how your priests care for the poor? Is that how they honor the *Dharma*?"

Roberto forced a smile. "Some of us care, Mr. Nevo. That's why they want to get rid of us."

Nevo glared at him. "The gods have ordered me to be a river to my brothers and sisters in the street. I use all my wealth to strengthen that river."

"You talk like you're one of them."

Nevo looked up at the portrait. "I am one of them. Only a few years ago, I groveled with them."

Roberto shook his head. "You expect me to believe that?"

"Damn your arrogance. Do you think those wretched souls

were crying out to you? A thin-skinned foreigner enroute to his redeeming mission in the sky? No, my imposter friend. I am their *barasahib*. They trust me because I crawled with them."

Roberto eased down on the couch beside the fireplace. "Sorry—I don't believe a word."

Nevo lowered his trembling hand and restrained himself. "Believe what you will—but know this. Before your captors reach Calcutta, I'll break open your steel trunk and fling half its contents into the street. To that woman with the dead child. And that legless beggar who grabbed your feet. And when your captors knock at my door, I'll collect their reward—and do the same."

Roberto looked up at his host. "Frankly, Mr. Nevo, I don't care what you do. If it's all right, I prefer to be alone."

"As you wish." Nevo poured another drink and gulped it down. "May I ask you one question before we say goodbye?"

"I think we've talked enough."

"Please—one last question."

Roberto looked away.

"The profile I received from your government mentioned you come from a rather comfortable life, yet I see great pain in your eyes."

"Do you?"

"I know that pain. It comes from seeing the darker side of life. Perhaps even living it." Nevo hesitated. "I thought you might shed some light on my observation."

Roberto stared at the gold clock on the mantle. "If I could turn back that clock, I'd be in Valencia restoring buildings and chasing women. Instead, I'm in a foreign country waiting execution." He paused and rubbed his forehead. "Not much to show for ten years in hell."

Nevo poured another drink and sat beside him. "Your profile mentioned a touch of instability. References to bleeding religious symbols, whispering shadows, visions of burning cities—that sort of thing. I'm curious. Is that government propaganda—or is it true?"

"Why do you care?"

Nevo looked down at his glass. "Perhaps we can convince

your government that—"

"I'm mad?"

"It might make things easier."

"I'd rather face a firing squad."

"Do you still have these spells?"

Roberto stared blankly into space.

"Tell me about Guernica."

"You know about that?"

"Your profile says you fled Spain after the bombing. You know—Guernica has become rather famous since Picasso's great mural was exhibited in France. I collect art and know these things."

Roberto looked up at the ceiling. "Picasso painted that nightmare on a beach in northern Spain a year before those bombs fell."

"What?"

"He saw it in my eyes when he tried to paint me." Roberto rubbed his forehead and tried to clear the dizziness. "Maybe my father was right—maybe I am mad."

Nevo gestured to his servant. The powerful sedative was taking effect.

Roberto felt a pleasant, warm sensation surge through his veins. He closed his eyes and muttered, "Did you say something, Mr. Nevo?"

Nevo leaned closer. "Tell me about your visions. If I knew more, I could draft a statement that you weren't in control of your senses when I found you."

Roberto smiled through closed eyes. "Do I detect a touch of guilt?"

"I don't want to see you hurt. If it weren't for the money, I'd let you go."

Roberto opened his eyes and glared at Nevo. "Judas."

"What?"

"You're him—aren't you?"

"Him?"

"The one in my nightmare."

Nevo gestured for Cheema to grab Roberto's arm. It would take both of them to carry the unconscious Spaniard to his room.

Roberto's head fell back on the couch. His eyes began to close. "I was lying in a cave. There was no food. Everyone was dead."

Nevo slipped his arm under Roberto's shoulder and started to lift him.

"I saw you there."

"Me?"

"Outside the cave. On a white horse."

Nevo hesitated. "What did you say?"

"You were wearing a hood—but I saw your face."

Nevo gestured for Cheema to ease Roberto back on the couch. He wiped a bead of sweat off his forehead and leaned close to Roberto's ear. "Did I speak to you?"

"You said time was short. And you shouted your name."

Nevo's black eyes locked on Roberto. "Name? What name?"

"Kalki...."

Cheema looked down at Nevo's terrified face. "What is it, sir?"

The lights flickered, and went out. The room flashed with lightning, followed by a deafening thunderclap.

Nevo stood up and backed away from his unconscious prisoner.

"Sir—are you all right?"

Nevo brushed past his servant and walked out of the living room into the darkened foyer. He paused at the statue beneath the staircase and lowered his head.

Cheema stepped into the foyer and eased behind him. "Mr. Chandola?"

"We must arrange for this man's immediate transport to Nepal."

"What?"

Nevo turned and stared at his servant in horror. "He has seen the Tenth Avatar. He thought it was me. If I harm him, I'll burn in hell."

The room shook from a deafening clap of thunder.

29 | Prophecy

"Can you walk?"

Roberto opened his eyes and saw Nevo staring down at him. "Where am I?"

"Howrah Station. Can you walk?"

Roberto clutched his throbbing head. "What happened?"

"There is no time for talk." Nevo slipped an envelope into his hand. "Take this with you. You'll need it when you reach Siliguri."

"Siliguri?"

"Your trunk is on the train. Nothing has been disturbed." Nevo extended his hand. "Goodbye, my friend. It seems we both learned something last night."

Roberto stared at Nevo's outstretched hand. He heard the car door swing open. Someone grabbed his arm and dragged him out of the car. The ground swayed under him.

"You'll be fine, *sahib*. It's from the sedative."

"My bag."

"I have it, *sahib*. Please—come with me." Cheema tugged on Roberto's arm.

"No—wait." Roberto heard the car door close. He turned and saw Nevo peering at him from the window. "What happened, dammit!"

"Be well, traveler." Nevo leaned forward and tapped his driver on the shoulder.

"Wait!" With Cheema clinging to his arm, Roberto made a futile grab for the door as the black automobile screeched away from the curb into the morning traffic.

"Please, *sahib*. The next train to Siliguri doesn't leave until tomorrow morning."

Roberto shook his head and followed the white-jacketed Indian into Howrah Station where they boarded his waiting train, a filthy collection of passenger cars known as the *Darjeeling Mail*.

Cheema led him through the crush of shouting passengers until they reached a musty compartment at the rear of the third car. The Indian pushed open the metal door and helped Roberto into a seat. He leaned over the dazed Spaniard and cracked the window to let in some fresh air.

Roberto watched Cheema lift his leather traveling bag into the storage net above the seat. "Why are you doing this?"

The Indian handed Roberto a rail ticket and bowed politely. "May you find what you're looking for." He slipped through the compartment door and disappeared down the crowded aisle.

Roberto leaned against the window and looked down at the batiste and *sari-clad* passengers rushing through the steam. His ears rang. He couldn't keep his eyes open. He stuffed the envelope and ticket into his jacket pocket and rested his head against the stained leather seat. The train lurched and began to move....

The sun was low in the western sky when Roberto awoke from his drug-induced stupor. Cool air rushed against his face from the opened passenger window. He sat up and took a deep, refreshing breath while studying the rugged hills drifting past him.

He glanced at his watch. Seven hours had passed since the *Darjeeling Mail* pulled out of Howrah Station on its northward journey.

Regaining his senses, he noticed a uniformed Indian seated across from him. He nodded politely and watched the Indian return the gesture.

"A good sleep?"

"Too good, I'm afraid. Where are we?"

The Indian glanced out of the window. "About halfway to Siliguri. If the train doesn't break down, we'll be there in six hours."

Roberto smiled at the Indian's crisp English.

"You're Spanish?"

"Yes."

"Have you visited India before?"

"No." Roberto felt a rush of nerves while recalling his first encounter with Nevo.

"Where are you bound?"

"I'm not sure."

The Indian's black eyes widened. "Darjeeling is beautiful this time of year. Perhaps you'll enjoy it there."

Roberto nodded and looked away.

The Indian leaned forward. "I don't wish to pry, but you must take care not to venture too close to the mountains without an experienced guide. The monsoon is near and the weather can be quite treacherous."

"Thank you. I'll be careful."

The Indian smiled and leaned back in his seat. "Good luck to you, traveler."

Roberto waited for him to drop off to sleep before ripping open Nevo's envelope. He unfolded the four page letter and held it up to the fading light....

My Dear Friend,

I am deeply sorry for interrupting your journey. I hope this belated assistance will atone for my stupidity.

I'm afraid the nightmare is mine. We must never anger the gods. May the gods forgive me.

I never knew my mother and father. They abandoned me to the streets when I was an infant. I would have succumbed if not for the compassion of those hollow-eyed beggars you saw in the shadows. They are my true brothers and sisters.

Before losing consciousness, you described a vision I too have seen. It came to me in an opiate-induced dream while I clung to a floating scrap of wood during the monsoon floods many years ago.

Without food and water, this poor beggar had stolen a few puffs of serenity from an opium den and was preparing to die with his impoverished comrades beneath the Hooley's surging floodwaters.

In my dream, I clung to an ice-covered mountain above the clouds. Suddenly, a great winged horse and rider swooped down from the haze and landed on the rocks beside me....

Puzzled by Nevo's gibberish, Roberto put down the letter

and glanced at the sleeping Indian. A shiver went through him. It was growing colder. He pressed his face against the window and breathed the crisp air.

To the north, a towering wall of clouds glowed yellow in the setting sun. They were so beautiful—like a line of mountains rising into the heavens.

His eyes widened. They were mountains. Barely visible in the haze. A fortress of ivory pyramids blanketing the northern horizon.

He felt his heart pounding. His eyes welled up with tears. After so many miles, he was almost there. In a few days, he'd climb into those mountains to begin a new life.

He stood up and gripped the storage net. Seizing his bag, he dragged it down on the seat and flipped the metal latch while recalling Nevo's promise nothing had been disturbed.

His brown wallet was nestled in his clothing, neatly wrapped with the gold chain and crucifix Pizarro had given him so many years ago. A quick inspection assured him everything was intact. But there was still the trunk.

He closed the bag and returned it to its perch while glancing at the snoring Indian. He sat down and picked up Nevo's letter. He could barely read the words in the dim light....

I was petrified. I felt its hot breath on my face. Its black eyes burned into me. Suddenly, the horse's cloaked rider leaned toward me and spoke in a voice so deep the mountain shuddered with every word.

He warned me that I had been chosen to help the "lowest of low," and that upon awakening, I would come upon great wealth to fulfill my mission on earth.

Unable to speak, I was horrified when the white horse reared up on its hind legs and flapped two enormous ivory wings. As it rose into the haze, the rider peered down from the shadow beneath his gray hood.

I felt a blast of searing heat. A red beam flashed in my eyes, forcing me to look away. The mountain shook from His powerful voice.

He commanded me to use every second rupee of my newfound wealth to feed my brothers and sisters. That this was my Dharma.

Before I could respond, the horse swooped down from the haze, its eyes burning with rage. I curled into a ball and begged for mercy while feeling its hot breath on my neck.

The rider's voice was deafening. He shouted that I must one day help a stranger journeying through India in search of a great mountain to the north. He warned me that the pilgrim had been chosen with three others to fight a holy battle on the "sacred ledges of the five snows." A battle that would decide the fate of mankind.

To ensure my faith, the rider commanded me to look at Him so I would know the truth.

Trembling with fear, I peered into the haze and saw the horse and rider disappear into a shining cloud. In that instant, I saw Vishnu smiling down at me, His long black hair draped across His bare shoulders. And I heard His final words:

"You will help the pilgrim to the great mountain where he will fight an anti-god bent on destroying the Dharma. If the pilgrim fails, I will descend to earth a final time—to burn it to a cinder. If you fail, you will be cast into the eternal depths. Never to be reborn. Never to see Moksha. Do not fail me, Sonam Chandola...."

When I awoke, I was rescued from the floodwaters by a mysterious old man in a small rowboat. The rest of my story isn't important, except to tell you that I believe you are the pilgrim in my dream.

You have seen the Tenth Avatar of Vishnu. I don't know what is to come, but you must reach that mountain—and I must help you.

Your guide will be waiting at the rail station in Siliguri. He is the very best and has served me well since I met him on a trek to Kangchenjunga, two years ago.

He will know you by this letter, and you will know him by his yellow tunic, red sash, and black leggings. But you will know him most by his black eyes, hair, and beard—and the deep scar across his forehead and left cheek. May the gods

Gary Naiman

light your way.
Your humble servant,
Sonam Chandola

Roberto stared at the letter. Spain's haunting memories had suddenly resurfaced in the mystic words of a ruthless man from Calcutta. He crumpled the paper in his fist and looked out at the darkening sky.

The Indian awoke to the train rattling up a steep grade. He stretched his arms and glanced out the window at the starlit sky. "It's grown colder. We must be near Siliguri."

Roberto smiled at the Indian. "Do you live there?"

"My home is in Nepal. I'll trek there from Darjeeling."

"Aren't you worried about the monsoon?"

The Indian smiled. "I grew up in the Himalaya. I've learned not to fear such things—only respect them."

Roberto nodded. "Is that a military uniform?"

The Indian leaned forward and extended his hand. "Allow me to introduce myself. Corporal Akaal Dawa of his Royal Majesty's Gurkha Volunteers."

Roberto shook the Indian's calloused hand. "That's quite a title. You're with the British army?"

Akaal nodded. "Stationed in Dharan."

"You must be very proud."

Akaal smiled and straightened his dark brown jacket.

Roberto glanced at the night sky. "While you slept, I saw a line of mountains. Were they the Himalaya?"

Akaal nodded. "The eastern stretch of the range."

"They're incredible."

"Did you see Kangchenjunga?"

Roberto smiled. "Kang—?"

"The Mighty One. The sacred mountain. Its summit is only slightly lower than the Goddess Mother."

"Goddess Mother?"

"Chomolungma. The highest peak on earth."

Roberto glanced at the dark window. "I don't think I saw it. You say, it's sacred?"

Akaal folded his arms. "To my people, Kangchenjunga is a

The Tenth Avatar

sanctuary of the gods."

"You mean—they live up there?"

"Oh, yes. At night you can hear them singing."

Roberto bit his lip. "Has anyone seen them?"

"The gods cannot be seen, but their descents walk freely among us."

"Descents?"

"Earthly hosts. You see—the gods cannot come to earth in their true form. Instead, they inhabit chosen ones to carry out their earthly deeds."

"Do they have names?"

"Many, but the important ones belong to the trimurti."

"I'm sorry...."

"The holy three—Brahma, Shiva, and Vishnu."

Roberto looked down.

"I see you're skeptical. Please remember, our beliefs are much older and complex than those of your world."

Roberto nodded. "Who's the most important god?"

Akaal shrugged his shoulders. "That's a hard one. The Hindu faith is compassionate to all beliefs. To each his own, as you would say."

Roberto stared at the Indian. "Is there a god known as the Tenth Avatar?"

"Pardon?"

"Is there a god called the Tenth Avatar?"

Akaal looked at him in surprise. "Where have you heard that name?"

"I'm fascinated with India."

Akaal sighed and leaned back in his seat. "He is not a god. He is an incarnation of Vishnu. In the *Vedas*, it is written that Vishnu has visited earth in nine forms, each meant to restore order when evil threatened the *Dharma*."

"*Dharma?*"

"The sacred law, like your bible. Without the *Dharma*, there can be no order. And without order, everything dies." Akaal hesitated and looked out the window. "It is written that the Final Avatar will only come when the forces of evil have triumphed. He will descend to earth as Vishnu's holy messenger, bringing His wrath. Everything will be destroyed. All that is evil—and all that is good." Akaal shrugged. "That is, if you believe such things."

"Do you?"

Akaal smiled at the Spaniard. "I believe in the triumph of good over evil. Man will solve his own problems, and the gods will be content. But tell me, why are you so interested in our ways?"

Roberto smiled. "I'm a man of God."

Akaal's eyes widened. "You're a priest?"

"I'm a missionary trying to reach a colleague in Nepal."

Akaal leaned forward. "He has a mission there?"

"Yes."

"Where?"

"I'm not sure. A guide is supposed to meet me in Siliguri to take me there."

"Then, you have a guide."

"If he shows up."

Akaal stroked his chin. "Strange, you would come this way."

"Why?"

The Indian stood up and reached into a rucksack lying in the net above his seat. He pulled out a map and sat next to Roberto while unfolding it.

"Here is Siliguri." Akaal touched a small red dot on the Nepal-Sikkim border. He moved his finger up the map and tapped a larger red dot. "Darjeeling is fifty miles to the north." He slid his finger to the left. "As you can see, there is nothing west of Siliguri and Darjeeling except some small villages. The terrain is very treacherous. Your friend's mission must be far to the west—perhaps in Kathmandu or one of the hilltop towns. That's a considerable journey from here."

Roberto stared at the map.

"Was the guide arranged for you?"

"Yes."

"And you're sure he knows the way to your colleague?"

Roberto shook his head. "I'm not sure of anything."

Akaal folded the map. "If you like, I'll speak with him. It

will only take a minute."

Roberto smiled at the Indian. "Thank you, Corporal. You're very kind."

Akaal shrugged. "It's our way. Compassion must always be shown to a lonely traveler." He glanced down at the folded map. "How long has your friend been in Nepal?"

"Several months. He's taken over a deserted Buddhist monastery in the mountains."

"A what?"

"A deserted monastery."

Akaal's face twisted in a frown. "And our ruler approved it?"

"That's what I was told."

"I see."

"Is anything wrong?"

"There is something you should know."

"Yes?"

"Last month, I led a French mountaineering team up Kangchenjunga."

"The mountain you described?"

Akaal nodded. "Two men were killed in an avalanche only three thousand feet from the top. My comrade and I managed to escape with two injured survivors."

"I'm sorry."

"So am I." Akaal's black eyes glistened. "Mountaineering carries great risk, but there is no greater risk than defying the gods. I'm to blame for their death. I let them climb a sacred mountain."

Roberto stared at the shaken Indian.

"I'm sure your colleague means well, but he risks your lives by invading a Buddhist shrine."

"But, it's deserted."

Akaal glared at Roberto. "It is not deserted. Your friend can't see the occupants—but they're there."

"Really, Corporal. I don't—"

"Please listen to me. Convince your friend to abandon his mission. Go back to your own kind." Akaal stood up and stuffed the map in his rucksack. "Oh—one other thing. I'm not

Hindustani. I'm Buddhist." He dropped into his seat and rested his head against the leather cushion.

The *Darjeeling Mail* pulled into Siliguri's weatherbeaten rail station at midnight. With Corporal Dawa at his side, Roberto stepped off the train amidst a stampede of elated passengers.

Cries of joy filled the platform as weary travelers searched out their loved ones and swept them into their arms. The rail station swirled with reds, golds, and blues.

Roberto stared at the embracing families while recalling the wonderful moments he'd spent with Ana before that fateful day in Guernica. God, it seemed so long ago.

"Do you have other baggage?"

"What?"

"Do you need to claim anything?" Akaal pointed toward the line of passengers at the baggage window.

"My trunk!" Roberto rushed toward the line with Akaal close behind him.

"Is it a large trunk?"

"I'm afraid so."

"How will you carry it?"

Roberto shook his head. "I don't know."

"My friend, it is nearly fifty uphill miles to Darjeeling, and many more to your mysterious destination in the mountains. You will pay a large sum for porters to carry that trunk."

"Are porters available?"

"For the right price."

Roberto fumbled for his baggage ticket. "I'll empty the trunk and leave it behind—to lighten the load."

"What about the contents?"

"Six leather bags, each about seventy pounds."

Akaal scratched his head. "That's six porters. The daily rate for a decent porter is ten *rupees*. Your journey will cost a great deal."

Roberto glanced at the ticket. "The bags contain valuable artifacts. I'm not leaving them behind."

"It is your decision. Your guide can make the necessary

arrangements."

Roberto's eyes widened. "*Mi dios*, I almost forgot. Please—wait here."

"Do you know what he looks like?"

"I think so."

Roberto milled through the crowd, but saw no one matching the description in Nevo's letter. He was nearly to the station exit when an alarming thought struck him. How could Nevo contact someone so quickly? Had he used a radio? Carrier pigeon? Divine inspiration?

He stopped and stared at the exit. A sudden chill swept through him. He'd been set up! Nevo had claimed the reward and turned him over to the *Falange*! They were with him now! In the station! And that Indian was one of them! Run, dammit! Run while you can!

"I believe you're looking for me."

Roberto spun around and stared at the crowd. The voice seemed to be coming from the shadows on his left. "I can't see you."

"You have the letter?"

Roberto froze as a tall, lean man stepped into the dim light. A deep scar ran across his forehead and cheek. Roberto fumbled for Nevo's letter and extended it toward the shadowed figure.

The man grasped the letter and studied Nevo's scrawled signature. "You have baggage?"

"What?"

"Do you have baggage?" He handed the letter back to Roberto and stared at him with black, glistening eyes.

"A traveling bag and trunk. My friend's attending to them."

"The Gurkha?"

"You saw him?"

"How do you know him?"

"I met him on the train."

"In case I didn't show up?" The stranger smirked under his black beard.

Roberto ignored the remark. "How did Nevo reach you so quickly?"

"We must hurry. The monsoon is only a few days away."

Roberto glanced toward the baggage line at the far end of the station. "Hope you don't mind. I was thinking of asking Corporal Dawa to join us. His village is—"

"We go alone."

"But—what harm can he do?"

"I have two oxen waiting. If we leave now—"

"Now?"

"We can reach your friend in four days and beat the monsoon."

Roberto felt his blood pressure rising. "I don't understand. What's wrong with a little extra company? It will make the trip easier."

The stranger shrugged his shoulders. "Either we go alone or you can rot here with the Gurkha."

"Now just a damn minute—"

"I'll wait behind the station for ten minutes. It's your choice." The stranger turned and faded into the crowd.

When Roberto returned to the baggage line, he saw Corporal Dawa helping two porters lift his heavy trunk onto a baggage cart. He lent a helping hand and backed away from the black trunk.

"You found him?"

"Yes—he's waiting outside the station."

"Would you like me to speak with him?"

"No need. I'll be fine." Roberto extended his hand. "Thank you for your kindness, Corporal. Perhaps we'll meet again."

Akaal clasped Roberto's hand. "Please consider our discussion on the train. May the gods protect you." He slung his rucksack over his shoulder and slipped into the crowd.

"I see we have an agreement."

Roberto turned and saw the stranger peering at him. "If you want to call it that."

"Good, then we'll be on our way."

"We can leave my trunk behind, but the contents go with me."

"No problem."

"The bags are heavy."

"My oxen are strong."

Roberto studied the stranger's bearded face. The black eyes had softened a bit. "You said we're leaving tonight?"

"As soon as we load your belongings on the animals."

"And your fee?"

"There is no fee. I have been paid by Mr. Nevo." The stranger gestured toward the baggage cart. "Come—we're wasting time."

It only took a few minutes to transfer the six heavy packs from the trunk to the oxen. They abandoned the empty trunk in a nearby ditch and headed up the dirt road toward Darjeeling....

Roberto held his watch up to the moonlight and focused his tired eyes on the dial. After trekking uphill for four hours, he could hardly lift his legs. Fighting for breath, he sank to his knees and cried out to the stranger. "Can't we rest a few minutes?"

The stranger looked back at the exhausted Spaniard. He frowned and nodded at the flickering southwestern sky. "The monsoon is in central India. In two days it will be here. In two more, it will flood the river valleys below Kangchenjunga."

"Kangchenjunga?"

The stranger ignored him. "After we reach Darjeeling, we must cross the Terai, a dense jungle below the foothills. We won't be safe until we climb out of it. There is no time for rest." He turned away and headed up the road while Roberto staggered to his feet.

The sun was rising above the eastern hills when Roberto finally collapsed in a clump of tall grass. "Please—I can't go on."

The stranger turned and walked toward him. He reached down and seized Roberto's arm with an iron grip. "You can rest at high noon." He jerked him to his feet and headed up the road.

The next few hours were blurred. Roberto remembered sucking water from his canteen until it went dry. Twice, he collapsed on the soft ground, only to be yanked to his feet by the stranger's powerful grip. He stripped off his soaked jacket and shirt, and tied them around his waist while staggering forward. He was on the verge of sunstroke when the stranger stuck a fresh canteen in his hand.

"I'll make some food."

Roberto collapsed against a tree. He gulped down the water and gazed at the dense wall of palms and ferns lining the road. Orange and blue butterflies danced above his head. The surrounding hillsides were blanketed with conifer, birch, and poinsettia.

"Eat this rice. It will give you strength." The stranger shoved a bowl of curried rice into Roberto's trembling hands and sat on a stump across from him.

"How much further to Darjeeling?" Roberto reached into the warm bowl and scooped a wad of rice into his mouth.

"We're halfway there. We'll sleep until sunset, then move on."

Roberto was about to speak when a bloodcurdling roar echoed through the trees. The air filled with screams of scurrying monkeys, but they were quickly drowned out by a deep rustling sound as thousands of multicolored birds flapped their wings and rose into the sky above the trees.

The stranger scanned the jungle. "A tiger has our scent."

Roberto spotted the rifle tied to the packs. He started to get up but the stranger snared his arm. "Forget the rifle. The tiger has learned to fear us. He won't risk his life for our spoiled meat." The stranger finished his rice and stood up. "I'll stand watch while you sleep."

"What about you?"

"I've already slept."

"When?"

The stranger ignored him and reached into one of the packs. He pulled out a blanket and spread it on the ground beneath a tree. "Sleep on this."

Roberto put down his empty bowl and stretched out on the blanket. He was about to close his eyes when he noticed the stranger spilling a foul-smelling liquid around him. "What in God's name is that?"

"Ox piss."

"What?"

"It will keep the ants from picking your flesh while you sleep." The stranger watched Roberto squirm. "Welcome to the jungle, traveler."

Roberto was awakened by a violent shake on the shoulder. He sat up and rubbed his eyes. The air had cooled a bit and a quarter moon beamed down on him.

"Time to move on. Tomorrow, you will enjoy a cup of tea in the cool hills of Darjeeling."

Roberto stumbled to his feet and watched the stranger adjust the packs on the oxen. "We walk in the dark?"

"And then some." The stranger reached into his pack and pulled out a russet-colored cloth and small brown bottle. "Rub on the oil and wear this tunic. The mosquitoes carry disease." He handed the tunic and bottle to Roberto, and continued to adjust the packs.

"Where are we going?"

"I told you—Darjeeling."

"No—after that."

The stranger hesitated and looked down. "My orders are to take you to Pangpema."

"Pangpema?"

The stranger tugged on the cinch. "I think your friend is mad."

"Mad?"

"He toys with the gods. Pangpema is near the great mountain. He shouldn't be there."

Roberto restrained himself. "He's a missionary—like me. He's doing God's work."

"He is a pilgrim?"

"You could call him that. He's bringing God's word to the people."

The stranger shook his head. "I see you're not a very smart man."

"What?"

"You have much to learn about your friend. He is

mad—and so are you for going up there." The stranger glared at Roberto. "I warn you, traveler. Don't go near the mountain. Don't be a fool like the Gurkha. He was lucky to escape with his life."

Roberto's eyes lit up. "Are you telling me my friend's on Kangchenjunga?"

The stranger smirked through his beard. "Enough talk. It is time to move on." He turned and headed up the road.

"Wait!" Roberto ran alongside the stranger. "Where's your home?"

"In the mountains. I am a hunter and trader. And if the fee is right—a guide."

"Are you Nepali?"

The stranger shook his head. "My home is far from here."

"Where?"

"In Baltistan. Below Nanga Parbat."

"Nanga—"

"A mountain lying to the west."

"Do you have a name?"

The stranger stopped and locked his glistening, black eyes on Roberto. "Karak." He turned and headed up the road.

30 | The Charas Bar

Franz Hessler slipped the ticker tape through his fingers and read the smudged words. He lowered his head and handed the tape to Eric.

"What's wrong?"

Hessler pushed out of his leather chair and stepped to the window. He raised the blind and peered at the falling rain. His voice was barely audible. "It's almost eight in New York. We should call Frank."

Eric stared at the tape in disbelief. A one foot strip of paper had just torn out his heart....

> ....no contact with kh since April 2.........feared lost or captured..........chinois guerilla raid on hangchow prison revealed nothing..........this will be final transmission on kh.........

"No."

"I'm sorry, Eric."

"It's a mistake. Things were going so well?"

"Too well, I'm afraid."

Eric crumpled the tape in his fist. "I could have stopped her."

"No—she wanted it too much. It was her way—living on the edge. That's why she was so good."

Eric glared at the crumpled tape. "It was you, dammit."

Hessler turned around in shock. "What?"

Eric flung the crumpled tape on the desk. "You killed her. You're a goddamned murderer."

Hessler's face reddened beneath his white hair. "Are you crazy? You think I wanted this?"

"Murderer!"

Hessler restrained himself and dropped in his leather chair. He picked up the crumpled tape and slipped it into an envelope. "Stop feeling sorry for yourself and help me make this call."

Eric stepped toward the desk, his eyes blazing, but Hessler

wasn't about to back down. He locked his blue eyes on the enraged Swede and pointed a trembling finger at him. "Snap out of it, dammit. There's a war coming. We don't have time for your self-pity."

"Bastard!"

The Austrian stiffened. A deep frown swept across his reddened face. "Never mind the call. I'll take care of it. Just get back to work. That's the way she'd want it. Her husband too. Now get the hell out of here!" Hessler slammed his fist on the desk, knocking over a calendar. It read June 1, 1939. It was one p.m. in London. In Bombay, it was nearly six hours later....

Lightning flashed across Bombay's darkening sky, followed by a blast of rolling thunder. The heavens ruptured, releasing torrents of warm rain on the suffocating city.

Beneath the deluge, Bombay's streets and garbage-strewn alleys became raging rivers of sewage. Waves of rats scurried from the flooded drains, swarming over everything in their path as they fled into the hills.

Inside the *Charas Bar,* Sir Devin Blakely gave his perspiration-soaked collar a nervous tug while the lights flickered from a nearby lighting strike. "Blast, can't someone turn up the overhead fan? It's stifling in here."

A pudgy Indian folded his arms and leaned against the parlor wall. "Sorry, *sahib*. The government won't give us more electricity."

Blakely threw an angry glance at the Indian and closed his five card hand. He understood the barbed response. The government was British.

Blakely reached into his dwindling stack of chips and counted out a dozen blues. He dropped them on the pile of pound notes, *rupees*, and multicolored chips in the center of the table. "I'll see your raise—and hold."

Without batting an eyelid, Bonaventure spread his cards on the table and leaned back in his chair while Blakely and his three stunned comrades glared at three sixes and two deuces.

Blakely flung his cards at the table and pushed back his chair. "If you ask me, your luck is highly questionable."

Bonaventure smiled politely and scooped up his winnings. He was about to dump them in a large wooden bowl when Blakely reached out and snared his wrist.

"Did you hear what I said?"

"I did." Bonaventure dropped the winnings in the bowl.

"Then answer me, dammit."

Bonaventure seized Blakely's wrist with his free hand and began squeezing it.

"Damn you, let go of my wrist."

"After you let go of mine." Bonaventure smiled and squeezed harder.

"Blast!" The trembling Englishman released his grip and clutched his numbed hand while Bonaventure looked at him with the same unemotional smile.

"That's better. Good sport and all that. Come on, I'll buy you and your friends a drink."

"Swine!" Blakely yanked his jacket off the chair and stormed through the gambling parlor's beaded curtains, followed by his friends. They pushed through the crowd of drunks at the bar and barged through the *Charas'* swinging doors into the falling rain.

The plump Indian snatched a loose chip off the floor and dropped it in the bowl. "I don't think Sir Blakely cares for the *Charas*."

"No—but he has been generous." Bonaventure reached into the wooden bowl and dug out a fistful of *rupees*. He dumped them into the Indian's cupped hands.

"The gods were with you tonight."

Bonaventure forced a smile and patted Jawa on the shoulder. "Were they now. From the look of things, they've given me enough wealth to last another month in this hellhole." The khaki-clad Englishman stood up and stuffed the pound notes in his pocket.

"What about the chips?"

"Put them on my account." Bonaventure pushed through the beaded curtains.

With the rain coming down in torrents, the *Charas'* inebriated patrons fled the bar in a frantic effort to reach their homes and tenements before the waterlogged streets became impassable. Unlike them, Bonaventure was in no hurry to return to his leaking, second-story room near Crawford's Market. He stepped to the bar and purchased a warm bottle of English ale, then headed for a quiet table at the entrance to the gambling parlor. He sat down and brushed away the cigaret ashes with his evening edition of *The Bombay Times*.

Almost a week had passed since Akaal shook his hand and boarded the *East Indian Express* for Calcutta. It had been a tough five days, forcing him to revert to earlier, less palatable skills learned in London's slums.

His fingers were gnarled from twenty years of climbing, but there was still enough dexterity to snatch a rich man's wallet from his inside coat pocket without applying more pressure than a gentle breeze.

As for gambling, he was amazed how quickly old tricks returned after only a few tries. Simple enough to mark a card with the flick of a fingernail, but the hard part was sensing that fine indentation with fingertips calloused from years of climbing. He adapted by dragging that same fingernail along the card's edges until the notch was detected.

He opened the newspaper and scanned the pages for word of a mountaineering expedition looking for guides. After a few minutes, he closed the paper and flipped it on the table.

Was he dreaming? No one in their right mind would venture into the mountains during monsoon season. Difficult enough scaling a twenty thousand foot peak without having to deal with blizzard-force winds and avalanches.

He reached into his pocket and grasped the wad of pound notes. If he could keep at it another month, he might hoard enough pounds to leave India and head for....

He hesitated. Head for where? His home in Switzerland was gone, repossessed by the bank after too many gambling debts and some well-placed political pressure by his enemies at the Royal Society. Anything to drive the renegade mountaineer into oblivion.

He leaned back in the chair and recalled the final dramatic moments on Aconcagua. The wind in his face. The biting snow. The final rush to the top. His victory pennant flapping in the sixty-mile-an-hour gale. Maybe that was it. Maybe he should go back to South America and offer his services to idealistic novices trying to fulfill their fantasies on the mighty Andes. That's it. He'd go to South America.

Bonaventure's thoughts were interrupted when an attractive young woman pushed through the *Charas'* swinging doors. She paused and scanned the deserted saloon as if looking for someone, then slumped against the bar, her blue eyes staring into space.

Bonaventure wasn't the only one noticing the sudden improvement in scenery. An aroused drunk at the far end of the bar grabbed his near-empty whiskey bottle and staggered toward the *Charas'* attractive visitor. He plunked down on a vacant stool beside her and boldly wrapped his arm around her waist while trying to strike up a conversation. His bloodshot eyes locked on the two bulges straining against her rain-soaked, khaki shirt.

Content to let nature take its course, Bonaventure sipped his ale and picked up the newspaper. He was about to immerse himself in the latest Indian protest against British rule when he heard the woman cry out.

He lowered the newspaper and saw the young lady trying to pick herself off the floor from a vicious slap to the face. The drunk cursed and zeroed in for the kill. He seized her by the waist and lifted her body tightly against him while burying his face in her breasts.

She screamed and kicked wildly at the air. "Let me go! What the hell's wrong with you!"

"Nothing you can't fix, bitch! That's it—struggle. I like it when they struggle. God you smell good. Lemme see what's under that skirt. Oh baby. Oh—"

The drunk's head exploded with broken glass as the partially stripped woman dropped to the floor. Enraged, he turned around just in time to see a wooden chair converging on his nose. The chair shattered against the drunk's face, driving him backward against the wall where he crumpled in a heap of dripping blood.

Jawa scratched his bald head and leaned over the bar. "I think you hurt him pretty bad. Maybe you should go home now."

Bonaventure crouched down and placed his hand on the woman's bare shoulder. "Are you all right?"

She gasped and slid back in horror.

"It's all right. Come on—looks like you could use a drink."

Taking care not to send her into hysterics, Bonaventure helped the trembling woman to her feet and escorted her to his table while snapping his fingers for Jawa to bring them a bottle of whiskey.

It took a few seconds for the double shot of whiskey to calm her down. Bonaventure offered her a second double which she chugged down like water. When she reached for a third, he jerked the bottle away while she glared at him with two of the most beautiful blue eyes he'd ever seen.

The young woman's face was smeared with dirt and her tousled black hair was cut very short, but her striking features easily made up for it.

Her soaked khaki shirt was torn at the neck and shoulder, barely covering her breasts. Her frayed skirt was split just enough to reveal a set of shapely legs that seemed unending. After twenty years of mounting towering peaks and loose women, Bonaventure was unprepared for this kind of thoroughbred.

"My name's Bonaventure—Julian Bonaventure."

She ignored him and stared at the whiskey bottle.

"Listen—we need to get out of here before the police pay their nightly visit. I hit that drunk pretty hard. I'm afraid his chum over there will turn me in." Bonaventure nodded toward a half-conscious sailor sprawled on a chair across the saloon. "Are you waiting for someone?"

"Waiting?"

Bonaventure looked into her eyes and noticed they were glassed over. He touched her shivering hand and leaned forward. "Do you want to come with me?"

She didn't respond.

Bonaventure pulled off his khaki jacket and slipped it over

her trembling shoulders. He eased her out of the chair and wrapped his arm around her.

"How is she?" Jawa stared at him from across the bar.

"I'm not sure. I'm gonna try to make it to my place. If you see us float by, throw me a scrap of wood. See you tomorrow night."

"May the gods be with you."

Bonaventure stuffed the whiskey bottle in his shirt and led her past the unconscious drunk. He lifted his jacket over the young woman's head and pushed through the swinging doors into the flooded street.

Bonaventure flicked on the wall light and stared at the two leaks dripping from the faded yellow ceiling. The two metal pots on the floor had overflowed, leaving a small flood in the corner.

He guided his attractive guest past the pots and helped her into a bamboo chair beside the shuttered window. "I have a burner and some fresh water. How about some tea to go with that whiskey?"

She nodded and forced a smile.

Bonaventure picked up the pots and set them on the window ledge. He pushed open the shutter and dumped the rusted water into the flooded street. "If this bloody rain keeps up, the whole bloody ceiling will come down on our heads." He closed the shutter and repositioned the pots under the twin leaks.

He walked around the bed to a table where a brass teakettle rested on a small metal tripod. Striking a match, he lit an alcohol burner and adjusted the knob until its pointed blue flame touched the base of the kettle. "The tea will only take a minute."

She ignored him and stared at the blue flame.

"I guess you're not in the mood to talk."

"Karen—my name's Karen."

Bonaventure brushed back his wet hair. "It's none of my business, but it looks like you've had a bit of a rough time."

She continued to stare at the flame.

"Well—I'll brew that tea."

After letting the tea steep for a minute, Bonaventure poured it into a cup laced with a strong shot of whiskey. He handed it to her and knelt down beside a canvas sack lying next to the chair. He dug into the sack and pulled out a khaki shirt and pair of khaki pants. "You can wear these if you like. I'll cut you a piece of rope for a belt."

She lowered the emptied cup and glanced at the clothes. "Where can I change?"

"I'll go out in the hall until you're finished."

She nodded and stood up. "Not very stylish."

"Afraid not."

"Thank you, Mr. Bonaventure."

Bonventure nodded and left the room.

They spent the next half hour sipping spiked tea and devouring chocolates and crackers from Bonaventure's mess kit. She appeared to be calming down.

"There's a piss poor shower down the hall if you'd like to clean up. I have a towel and soap in my kit."

She leaned forward and stared at him with those soft blue eyes. "Can I ask you something?"

"Sure."

"Are you trying to seduce me?"

Bonaventure's face flushed. "I don't know. Maybe."

"Not just now, Mr. Bonaventure."

He forced a smile. "You're welcome to sleep here if you like. I'll camp out on the floor. You can have the bed."

She looked at the bed and smiled. "Maybe I'll take that shower now."

After showing her how the contraption down the hall worked, Bonaventure returned to his room and spread his sleeping bag on the floor. Feeling exhilarated for stumbling on such a beautiful roommate, he sprawled on the floor and thought about her standing naked in the shower. Above him, the ceiling had turned dark brown from the leaks. Not the best setting to entertain a beautiful woman, but it would have to do. Bonaventure closed his eyes and listened to the rain patter against the shuttered window.

He was nearly asleep when he heard the door close and the light click off. He felt a warm hand on his chest. A pair of soft, moist lips kissed his stubbled cheek.

"Goodnight, Mr. Bonaventure. Thank you for caring."

Rotten luck. Instead of dreaming about his beautiful guest, the god of sleep had arranged something a bit more unsettling for Mr. Bonaventure....

Cartier leaned against the slope and squinted at the blowing snow. "What the hell is that?"

"Don't know. Sounds like a freight train." Frueger crawled next to his friend, followed by Cormier, Angstrom, and Corporal Dawa.

Cartier looked down the slope and saw Bonaventure climbing toward them. "Do you hear it, monsieur?"

Bonaventure scrambled beside him and dug his boots into the ice. They were just below the north ridge, trying to shelter themselves from the blizzard's fifty knot winds. Three thousand feet overhead, Kangchenjunga's invisible peak screamed at them like an angered woman.

Frueger glanced at Cartier. "There it goes again."

Bonaventure was about to speak when he heard a deep, cracking sound and felt the slope shudder beneath them.

"What is it, monsieur?"

"Quiet." Bonaventure peered into the whiteout. An ominous rumble was coming from the summit.

Cartier tugged at Bonaventure's parka. "Monsieur?"

Bonaventure yanked his arm away and pointed at the ridge. "We've got one chance. Climb for the crest."

"What?"

"Now, dammit! We've gotta get up there!"

"But the equipment?"

"Fuck the bloody equipment! We've only got seconds!" Bonaventure seized Cartier's arm and began dragging him up the two hundred foot slope toward the ridge crest. He glanced over his shoulder and saw Akaal and Frueger crawling up behind them.

His eyes locked on Cormier and Angstrom. What were they doing? They were just standing down there. Staring at him from the campsite. "Fools! The whole bloody summit's coming down! Climb, dammit! Climb!"

"Mr. Bonaventure?"

Bonaventure opened his eyes and saw Karen peering down at him.

"Are you all right?"

He sat up and wiped away a bead of sweat.

"Are you a climber?"

"What?"

"You were mumbling something about an avalanche."

He rubbed his forehead and frowned.

"It's stifling in here." She walked to the window and flung open the shutter. The rain had stopped and the moon was breaking through the clouds.

Bonaventure pushed his cramped body off the floor and staggered beside her. He rested his hands on the sill and took a deep breath of Bombay's humid air.

"Looks like it's clearing up."

He shook his head. "That little deluge was just the beginning. We'll probably have a few good days before the heavy stuff moves in. Maybe I'll be out of this bloody hole by then."

She leaned against the shutter and looked up at him. "You're British?"

"How did you guess? Bet it was the tea." He watched her hold back a smile. "From that dialect, you must be American."

She nodded. "And plenty homesick just now."

He looked at the moon flashing between the clouds. "Can I ask you a stupid question?"

"Stupid?"

"If you're so homesick, why are you strolling around bloody Bombay at the beginning of monsoon season?"

"Do you have a cigaret?"

Bonaventure walked over to his canvas bag and dug out the pack of *Lord Pembroke's* he'd lifted from Sir Blakely. "I stumbled on these today. Keep them if you like." He handed her the pack and watched her pull out a cigaret and place it between her lips. He struck a match and touched it to the tip while she took a deep, satisfying drag.

She rested her head against the shutter and blew the smoke at the moon. "I didn't expect to end up here."

He watched her take another deep drag. "Where did you come from?"

"Nanking."

"China?"

"Yes."

"But Nanking's in Japanese hands? It's a bloody slaughterhouse?"

"I was their guest."

Bonaventure's eyes widened. "You were a prisoner?"

She took another drag and looked down at the flooded street. "It's a long story, Mr. Bonaventure. Not a very pleasant one."

"But, you're an American? Things might be a little strained, but they have no right to arrest you?"

"Don't they?" She smiled and puffed the cigaret.

"How long did they hold you?"

"Two months."

"Blast. How did you get out?"

She looked down at the street. "I crawled under a barbed wire during a Chinese guerilla raid. I just kept running and never looked back."

"You escaped?"

"I guess you'd call it that."

He rubbed the back of his neck. "We're three thousand miles from Nanking. How in God's name did you make it all the way here?"

"A few kind people. If it wasn't for them...." She took a final puff and flicked the sparking butt into the flooded street. "I'd rather not talk about it."

Bonaventure walked to the table and grabbed the whiskey bottle. "Interesting who you meet in Bombay." He took a hefty swig and gulped down the burning liquid. "So—now what?"

"I don't know. The Japanese took everything. Passport. ID. Everything."

Bonaventure shrugged. "Go to your embassy."

She shook her head. "Can't trust them. They might turn me over to the Brits."

Bonaventure dragged the bottle off the table and sat on the edge of the bed. "What do you have against the British? I'd think you'd want their help after what you've been through?"

She turned to face him. "I have something the British want as badly as the Japanese. I can't trust them. Hell, I can't trust anyone."

Bonaventure took another swig. "What are you—a thief?"

"I guess you could call me that." She walked to the bed and sat beside him. "Can I ask you something?"

"Sure."

"Are you one of them?"

"Who?"

"Are you working for the British?"

His face flushed. "You mean—the government?"

"Something like that."

He took a swig of whiskey and looked away. "I'm not working for anyone. If I was, it wouldn't be the British."

"I don't understand."

"Good—now we're even."

She looked into his eyes. "I'm at the end of my rope. I need someone I can trust. Can I trust you, Mr. Bonaventure?"

He cracked a smile. "Sorry for being blunt, but I think you have to."

She took a deep breath and looked at the moon shining through the window. "I'm a reporter."

"Reporter?"

She grabbed the bottle and took a gulp. "I was assigned to investigate Japanese atrocities in Shanghai and Nanking. My contact was a missionary helping Chinese civilians escape through Japanese lines. I was told he had a journal of victim testimonies and photographs that might shake things up if I could get it out."

"Sound's suicidal."

A deep frown swept across her face. "Maybe—but it was the chance of a lifetime. If I could pull it off, it might make a difference."

"Ah—glory. Now I'm beginning to understand."

She glared at him. "It was more than that. If I could get that story, it would finish what my husband started."

Bonaventure flinched. "Husband?"

"My husband was killed by German agents when he tried to bring out a secret communiqué containing plans for Hitler's '38 and '39 campaigns. From what I was able to decipher in his notes, he'd also found a link with the Japanese. Something called NI."

Bonaventure shook his head. "Sorry—you just lost me."

"I told you it was a long story." She lit another cigaret and took a puff. "Call it coincidence, fate—whatever. The missionary in Nanking had found the same link."

"NI?"

She nodded. "That's why I volunteered to put my neck on the block."

"Because of a coincidence?"

"No—because I smelled a bigger story. And that missionary was the key to it."

Bonaventure shook his head. "You said you had something."

She hesitated and puffed on the cigaret. "I was working on instinct until Vasquez showed me the journal."

"Vasquez was the missionary?"

She nodded. "Instead of testimonies, the pages were filled with code. Instead of atrocities, I saw photographs of Japanese diplomats and military officers. When I tried to question him, Vasquez stuffed the journal in my hand and warned me to get out before it was too late."

Bonaventure nodded. "You have the journal?"

She looked down at the smoldering cigaret. "I was boarding an international charter at Nanking's airport when the Japanese arrested me. They confiscated the journal and my belongings."

He looked down at her trembling hands. "Are you all right?"

"This is hard."

"Maybe we should stop?"

She shook her head. "They locked me in a cell and promised I'd rot there unless I told them about Vasquez. When I refused—" Her eyes widened. The cigaret rolled out of her fingers. "—they released rats."

"We're gonna stop."

She clenched her fists. "I still feel them—and the pain."

He tried to speak, but the words wouldn't come out. A church bell rang in the distance. The sky had begun to brighten.

She took a deep breath and brushed the tears off her cheeks. "Chinese guerillas stormed the prison before my execution."

"Execution?"

"They didn't need me anymore." She lowered her head and listened to the clanging bell.

"You talked?"

"I couldn't take it. The damn things squirming over me. The teeth...."

"Hell—anyone would break after that."

"They brought Vasquez to the prison and made me watch his execution. I'll never forget the look in his eyes. I tried to turn away, but they grabbed my hair and jerked my head toward him. He kept staring at me with those cold, brown eyes." She clenched her fists. "They beheaded him."

Bonaventure poured a stiff shot and placed it in her hand. He watched her gulp it down, then poured a refill. She chugged the second shot and stretched out on the bed.

She sighed and rubbed her forehead. "I'm so damn tired."

"Mind if I join you?"

"You're such a gentleman, Mr. Bonaventure. I could use a hug."

He laid down and took her in his arms. "Get some sleep. It's over."

"Is it?"

"You're safe now."

She shook her head. "Before I escaped, I lifted the journal off my dead interrogator."

"You have it?"

"It's hidden here in Bombay. I need to get it home before the Japanese find me."

Bonaventure sat up on his elbow and looked down at her. "You think they'd come this far?"

"They want that journal, Mr. Bonaventure. It's bigger than we know."

"Hell, you can't even read the bloody thing. Turn it over to the British and get out of here."

Her exhausted body relaxed in his arms. "I'll take it to Frank. I can trust Frank. He'll know what to do...."

"Who?"

"What a story. Biggest story...of all time...." She closed her eyes and dropped into deep sleep.

Bonaventure spent the next hour sitting in a chair across from the beautiful creature in his bed. If she was right about the Japanese, they could both end up losing their heads.

He stood up and stretched his cramped legs. A beam of sunlight radiated through the opened shutters. He'd just spent the night with a beautiful woman and had nothing to show for it but a bad case of nerves and throbbing headache.

He dug into his pack and pulled out a folded piece of paper. "Well, old friend. Looks we'll be rendezvousing sooner than expected."

He covered Karen with a blanket and slipped through the door. The telegraph exchange was only ten minutes away.

31 | Unexpected Orders

Akaal lowered the wooden cup and breathed a sigh of pleasure. "It has been many days since I tasted butter tea."

The red-cloaked monk smiled and poured more of the steaming yellow brew into the Gurkha's empty cup. "Where are you bound?"

"Dhoban."

"Ah—I know it well. Your home?"

"And my heart." Akaal lifted the cup to his lips and gulped down the warm tea.

"Please—have more." The monk reached for the steaming kettle.

"Thank you, Holy One. I've had enough." Akaal bowed his head and extended the empty cup. "You have made a weary traveler happy."

"Then we're both happy." The monk grasped the cup and rose to his feet, followed by his guest.

Akaal glanced at the dark band of clouds in the southwestern sky. "I should be on my way. The rains will come soon."

"They already have. The first storm reached Kangchenjunga this morning. I watched it through our telescope. It was quite a blizzard. A fierce time in the Himalaya." The monk reached down and picked up the kettle.

"May I ask you a question, Holy One?"

"Of course."

"Have you seen a foreigner on this road?"

The monk smiled and shrugged his shoulders. "Many pilgrims pass this way."

"This one is different. He wears black and carries a gold cross on his neck."

"Ah—a man of the Christian God. He goes to Darjeeling?"

"His mission is in Nepal."

"Nepal?" The monk's smile faded. He locked his brown eyes on Akaal. "I've not seen him."

"If you do, please tell him that his friend Corporal Dawa

458

said a prayer for him today."

"I'll say one for him too. May the gods be with you, traveler." The monk bowed his head and turned away.

Akaal watched the monk shuffle up the hillside toward the red and gold monastery overlooking the road. A gentle breeze brushed across his face. He heard birds chirping in the trees. It was a good time. A peaceful time. He lowered his head and said a prayer for his nameless friend on the train.

Refreshed by two cups of his beloved butter tea, the Gurkha picked up his pack and slung it over his shoulder. A few miles to the north, the city of Darjeeling lay nestled in the haze, its quaint yellow and white buildings straddling an emerald ridge above the tea plantations and jungle. He took a deep breath and headed up the road toward the British *Raj's* favorite hill station.

The sun was falling to the west when he dropped his pack and stretched his aching arms and legs. He was standing on a forested hillside overlooking a dense jungle of palms, bamboo, and wild flowers. He could hear bees humming in the bright clusters of orchid, primrose, and bougainvillea. Gold and blue butterflies fluttered above his head.

He shaded his eyes and spotted the Tista, a lazy brown river winding southeastward through the jungle. A lonely, white cloud drifted overhead. He stared at it and listened to the bees. Everything was still and peaceful. Then he looked north.

Rising into the heavens fifty miles away, Kangchenjunga sat on the clouds like a proud yellow fortress, its massive ridges warning all mortals to stay away. On a clearer day, one could also see Yalung Kang and Kangbachen, but the monsoon was coming and the air was thick with haze.

He turned and studied the black clouds boiling up in the southwest. With Dhoban still two days away, every minute was precious. A brief rest at the army compound, and he'd be on his way. He snatched his pack off the ground and headed up the road.

In the distance, a steam engine's muted whistle cut the silence. The *Darjeeling Passenger One* was nearing its hilltop destination after the tedious nine hour climb from Siliguri. He

Gary Naiman

paused and smiled. Taking the Darjeeling "toy train" would have spared him the fifty mile uphill trek, but it also would have deprived him of this glorious walk through the hills. And besides—he was broke.

As he approached the cluster of villages known as Darjeeling, he spotted a familiar red-white-and-blue union jack flapping above the trees. He veered toward it and walked into a ragged column of *dhoti-clad* laborers headed down the hillside toward the tea plantations. They shuffled past him, heads bowed, their burnt bodies glistening in the midday sun. Such was the way of the *Raj*. The lowest of low sweating in the filthy plantations so their English masters could relax in rattan chairs, sipping their afternoon tea atop the cool, breeze-swept hills. He frowned and marched up the hill toward the flag.

"Corporal Dawa!" Colour Sergeant Craven jogged across the compound toward the exhausted Gurkha.

Akaal snapped back his shoulders and jammed his chin against his chest. "Corporal Dawa, present and accounted for."

"At ease, Corporal. How was the trip up?"

"Uneventful, Sergeant."

"I was worried about you with this bloody weather coming in."

"I'm fine, Sergeant."

"Well—I'm afraid I have some bad news."

"Sergeant?"

Craven reached into his pocket and pulled out a folded piece of yellow paper. "This afternoon, I received this transmission from Major Pierce. I'm afraid your rest and recovery has been shortened a bit."

Akaal took the telegram from the sergeant's outstretched hand and read it…

From: Major Rutherford Pierce / Commanding Officer /
      His Majesty's Dharan Brigade
To: Colour Sergeant Perry Craven
Essential that upon reporting to Darjeeling Hill Station, Corporal Dawa be flown to Dharan for immediate assignment. Upon notifying Corporal Dawa, please contact

Dharan for dispatch of aircraft to Tiger Hill. Corporal Dawa will proceed there to await flight to Dharan.
Respectfully:
Major "Rudy" Pierce

Akaal handed the telegraph message back to Sergeant Craven. "I had hoped to see my family."

"Sorry, Corporal. Maybe you can catch a few winks in the barracks. I'll have one of the men run you over to the airstrip in a jeep."

Akaal looked at him with desperate eyes. "I could walk to Dharan. I'll leave now."

The sergeant's eyes hardened. "Sorry, we have our orders. Get some sleep. I'll wake you when it's time to go." Craven turned and walked away.

Akaal staggered toward the barracks while trying to grasp the message. He paused on the steps and looked to the southwest.

They were waiting for him in Dhoban. His mother was preparing his favorite curry. His sisters and brothers were camped in the hills, waiting to catch a first glimpse of him coming over the crest, the sun shining on his khaki uniform.

In a few days, his father would return from the hunt expecting to see his son standing beside his family and friends. It would be a very proud moment for the old man—and for his son. They would embrace and exchange gifts while the others lit the bonfires. It would be a wonderful time. They would hum the ancient chants and dance the night away. His sisters and brothers would hug him and beg for the first story of mythical battle against robbers and brigand armies. And gallant feats of courage atop the clouds. Yes—a wonderful time. And now, it was only a dream.

He last saw them three months ago when his expedition passed through Dhoban enroute to the sacred mountain. How proud he must have looked standing with the team and his friend Bonaventure. They were going to assault the Great Lady and become famous when his friend planted a victory pennant in the ice, only a few feet from the summit. Must not anger the gods. The summit would remain untouched.

He clenched his fist and looked at the approaching clouds. Fool—did you think it was that easy? Your father warned you to turn back, but you didn't listen. After the disaster, you were too shaken to see him. You walked past Dhoban like a scared child. You should have stopped and cried in your father's arms.

A tear rolled down his cheek. There was no time to reach them. No time to tell them he wasn't coming. *Buddha—please forgive me. Please help them understand.* He frowned and walked through the door.

The barracks was empty—of Indians that is. The British "noncoms" and officers had separate quarters at the far end of the compound. Just as well. He preferred it that way.

Akaal stripped off his uniform and doused himself with cold water from the barrack's makeshift shower. He toweled off and stretched out on a cot beside the window. The soft mattress felt strange after sleeping on rocks, dirt, and ice.

He looked up at the weathered ceiling and recalled the day he met Major Pierce. Pierce had replaced Dharan's former commanding officer, Major Camp. Upon his promotion, Pierce immediately requested Akaal's reinstatement as mountain guide and instructor. Unlike Camp, who had blamed Akaal for his embarrassment in England, Pierce respected Akaal and his Gurkha comrades for their skill and tenacity.

Akaal sighed and closed his eyes. It would hurt not to see his family. After the pain of Kangchenjunga, he needed their love more than ever. But he was a corporal in His Majesty's Army, and Major Pierce had stuck his neck out for him. Compassion was a precious thing, deserving loyalty and respect. And Colour Sergeant Craven was a good man too—because he let his exhausted corporal sleep for two hours....

The jeep ride to Tiger Hill was uneventful except for the ominous rumblings in the southwestern sky. The monsoon had picked up speed and was racing across India toward the Himalayas. This morning, its vanguard had given the region a taste of what was to come, dumping tons of snow on the

Himalaya's southern slopes. In the valleys below the mountains, torrents of rain would soon turn gentle streams into raging rivers—and heaven help anyone stupid enough to be in their way.

The sun was dropping behind the clouds when Akaal's jeep skidded to a halt at the edge of Tiger Hill's dirt airstrip. He climbed out of the jeep and pulled out his binoculars. A faint drone was coming from the southwest. He focused the binoculars on the thickening clouds and spotted a twin-engined aircraft approaching from above the trees.

"That's him, Corporal." Private Mallory jumped out of the jeep and snatched two white flags off the floor. He ran onto the airstrip and began waving them over his head while facing the approaching plane.

The aging *Vicker's Victoria* tipped its dual wings and came in low over the airfield to check landing conditions. Climbing into the haze, it made a steep bank to the left and circled for a landing.

"Must be pretty important to send a plane to fetch you." Mallory smiled at the stunned Indian as the twin-engined biplane screeched onto the dirt airstrip.

Akaal felt a queasy feeling in the pit of his stomach. Clinging to a treacherous mountain was one thing, but flying through the clouds with two whirring fans was not normal. This would be Akaal's third flight since rejoining the Dharan regiment, and he hated the thought of it.

As the olive drab plane rolled to a halt, the pilot looked down from his open cockpit and shouted over the engines. "Hurry, Corporal. We want to beat that storm."

"Good luck, Corporal." Mallory pulled open the nose hatch and handed Akaal his pack.

Akaal nodded and seized the pack. He said a prayer and climbed through the hatch.

The flight to Dharan took less than an hour, but to Akaal it was eternity. When the plane touched down on the dirt airstrip beside the Dharan compound, Akaal praised the gods for restraining their anger at the plane's arrogant intrusion into their domain. Crawling out of the hatch, he sprawled on the

Gary Naiman

ground and said a prayer while kissing the dirt. When he looked up, Major Pierce was staring down at him, his hands grasping a swagger stick.

Akaal jumped up and snapped to attention. "Corporal Dawa, reporting as requested, sir."

The gray-haired officer returned Akaal's salute and broke into a grin. "Welcome back, Corporal. How was your time off?"

"I was going to Dhoban when your orders came."

"I'm sorry about that, Corporal. I'm afraid we have a rather sticky situation on Kangchenjunga."

"On the mountain?"

Pierce nodded and gestured toward the compound. "Come with me, Corporal." He turned and headed for the barbed-wire gate, followed by the exhausted Gurkha.

The major's office was in a one-story building at the far end of the compound. It only took a minute to reach the front steps, but in that short time Akaal was besieged with pats on the back from Lieutenants Cook and Langley. Even Sergeant Flynn saluted him. It was good to be respected.

Pierce led Akaal past the telegraph operators into his office. He closed the door and stepped to a large map of India on the wall behind his desk. Using his swagger stick, he tapped a small red triangle between Nepal and Sikkim. "Today, at twelve hundred hours, we picked up a transmission that an aircraft has crashed on Kangchenjunga."

Akaal's eyes widened. "Aircraft? Was it civilian or military?"

"Civilian aircraft don't venture near the Himalayas, especially at this time of year." Pierce rested his swagger stick on the desk. "We have strong reason to believe the aircraft was Japanese."

Akaal stared at the map in disbelief. "Reconnaisance?"

"That was my first guess, but now I'm not so sure. Before the plane crashed, our man in Pangpema intercepted its emergency transmission. I can't disclose the content, but I can tell you the plane was headed east toward China."

Akaal stared at his commanding officer. "We have a man in

Pangpema?"

"Never mind that. We all have our jobs. He has his—and you have yours."

Akaal felt a sudden chill. "You want me to climb the mountain?"

"Yes—to bring back any survivors and recover the plane's cargo."

Akaal stared at the red triangle. It was coming at him too fast.

"Tomorrow, you'll be flown to Pangpema for a briefing from our contact there. We'll use one of the *Vickers*. It'll be a bit tight with the altitude, but the new engines should squeeze you in. I've asked Sergeant Mariner to volunteer. He's an excellent pilot and decent climber. Two for one, so to speak. Who else do you want?"

Akaal felt his stomach tighten. He frowned and stepped to the map. He ran his fingers along the Nepal-Sikkim border until they touched the red triangle. "Private Nemi."

"And?"

"That will do."

Pierce shook his head. "Only two men besides yourself?"

Akaal nodded. "Do you know where it crashed?"

Pierce looked down. "North ridge."

Akaal's hand slid off the map. He stared at Pierce in disbelief. "Sir—that's twenty three thousand feet. Six thousand above Pangpema. The monsoon is closing."

Pierce fixed his blue eyes on the shaken Gurkha. "We have no choice, Corporal. It's extremely important you make it up there and recover that cargo."

Akaal hesitated. "May I speak freely, sir?"

"Go ahead."

"I doubt anyone is alive up there."

The major forced a smile. "We have to be sure, Corporal. And we need that cargo."

"Yes, sir."

"You'd better get some sleep. Nemi too. You leave at nine hundred hours. Good luck." Pierce returned Akaal's salute and watched the Gurkha turn toward the door. "Oh—I almost forgot."

"Sir?"

Pierce held out a yellow piece of paper. "This was transmitted from Bombay this morning."

Akaal returned to the major's desk and took the telegraph message from his extended hand.

"It seems this Bonaventure knows you rather well."

Akaal read the message and handed it back to Pierce with puzzled eyes. "We're close friends, but I don't know the woman he speaks of."

"Apparently, she's in hot water. Sounds like your friend is asking for help. Maybe we should accomodate him."

Akaal's black eyes lit up. "Sir—Julian Bonaventure is the finest mountaineer I've ever known. When I told you three men would be sufficient, I had no idea my friend was still in India."

Pierce broke into a smile. "Then you recommend including him?"

"Absolutely—if you can find him."

"We already have—and the young lady too. From Mr. Bonaventure's description of her, she's either daft or in possession of some important information." Pierce reread the telegram while stroking his gray moustache. "Sounds daft to me, but we have to be sure. That's all, Corporal. You're excused."

After exchanging handshakes and friendly barbs with a dozen English officers glad to see their "Gunga Din" come home, Akaal walked into the "non-English" barracks and watched twelve slumbering Gurkhas scramble to attention in their underwear.

"At ease, you marmots." Akaal dropped his pack and stretched out on an empty bunk while his stunned comrades besieged him with questions he had no patience for.

Akaal took a tired breath and locked his black eyes on Private Nemi. "You better get some rest. We're climbing tomorrow."

Nemi's eyes widened. "But the monsoon?"

"Afraid of a little snow, Private?"

"No, but——"

"Good—then go away and let me sleep."

Akaal waited for Nemi and the others to clear the barracks before stripping off his uniform and sliding under the blanket. He laid back on the pillow and stared at the ceiling.

What was a Japanese plane doing in Nepal? Didn't they know where they were? They must be mad to flirt with the gods.

A chilling thought struck him. Was he any better? After defiling the mountain two months ago, he was going back to do it again.

He reached into his pack and grasped the prayer beads. "Oh, Buddha—please forgive me. I'm surrounded by madmen." He closed his tired eyes and dropped into exhausted sleep....

"Can you hear me, White Lion?" Pierce leaned closer to the microphone and pressed his fingers against the headset. He shook his head and glared at the radio operator who was nervously adjusting a large black knob.

"Sorry, sir. It's the damn weather. The haze is causing—"

"Blast the bloody haze! This is where you're supposed to prove how good you are. Now get this bloody static out of my ears."

Shaken by the major's stinging words, Private Gage locked the black knob on a tiny white dot and began fumbling with a smaller dial to its right. "I think we're getting it, sir."

Pierce nodded and raised his finger for silence. He flipped the microphone switch and spoke crisply. "Nepal Gateway calling White Lion. Are you there, White Lion?"

The static faded, replaced by an oscillating signal that became a steady whine.

"Got him, sir." Gage looked up and smiled.

"Well done, Private. Now please leave the room."

"Sir?"

"Get the hell out of here and shut the bloody door!"

Pierce watched Gage scramble out of his chair and bolt for the door. He dropped into the vacated chair and flipped the transmission switch. "Nepal Gateway calling White Lion."

"White Lion here."

Pierce dragged the microphone closer. "Listen closely—before we break up. Dispatching four monkeys at nine hundred hours to climb tree. Will advise before take off."

"Message received. Critical to climb tree and retrieve bananas."

Pierce pressed his fingers against the headset and listened to the whine. He flipped the transmission switch and spoke crisply. "Are you there, White Lion?"

"I'm here, but I have some bad news."

"Go ahead."

"I've been in contact with zookeeper. My instructions are to terminate all monkeys after retrieving bananas. Sorry about that. All for now. Will await your confirming transmission at nine hundred hours. Please hurry. Over and out."

Pierce stared at the amber dial while White Lion's words echoed in his ears....

32 | To Dharan

It was lunch time at the Taj, and the *Rendezvous Restaurant* bustled with smartly dressed ladies and gentlemen. The heat and humidity had reached the unbearable stage, but that was no excuse to abandon traditional white cotton suits, long sleeve blouses, and full-length skirts. Not so bad. The iced drinks and whirring ceiling fans made it quite comfortable for the Taj's unflappable guests.

Atop the steps leading into the restaurant, a gold grandfather clock chimed one p.m. As if on cue, several patrons glanced at their watches and folded their napkins neatly in front of them. Rising from their chairs, they strolled out of the plush restaurant for an afternoon turn along the steaming dock leading to the Gateway of India.

From there, it might be a cruise to Elephanta Island for a guided tour of the ancient Hindu temples. Or perhaps a quiet stroll through the cool shadows of the Prince of Wales Museum, followed by a light round of shopping. And if action was in the cards, nothing like dropping in at Queen's Club for the afternoon cricket matches.

When the sun set, a quick nap and sponge would be followed by dinner and bridge at one of the Malabar Hill estates overlooking the city and back bay, accompanied of course by generous rounds of gin and tonic.

With so much pageantry and tradition, it's no wonder the *Rendezvous'* patrons turned a harsh eye toward the khaki-clad couple easing down the marble steps below the grandfather clock.

Karen scanned the shocked faces and leaned against her tall escort. "The *maitre d'* spotted us. I don't like the look on his face."

"Just act regal and let me do the talking."

"What?"

"Quiet."

The white-suited *maitre d'* approached them while eyeing their dishevelled clothes. He paused and clasped his hands in front of him. "Can I help you, sir?"

Bonaventure scanned the crowded restaurant. "Two for lunch."

The *maitre d'* leaned forward and spoke softly. "I'm afraid you're a bit casual, sir."

Bonaventure ignored him and nodded toward a vacant table beside the window. "We just came from the morning polo matches. Lady Bulsworth is terribly hungry. Can't you seat us at that quiet table in the corner?"

The *maitre d'* frowned. "I'm sorry, but I'm sure you know the dress code."

Bonaventure looked at him in shock. "Of course we do. Just this once. I promise—next time it's tie and tails." He reached into his pocket and pulled out a five pound note.

The *maitre d'* glanced nervously at the vacant table. "You'll eat quickly?"

"Absolutely. We're famished."

Hesitating, the *maitre d'* lifted two menus from the reception desk and slipped them under his arm. "Very well—only this once." He tugged on his jacket and took the note from Bonaventure's hand.

Bonaventure nodded and took Karen's arm. Ignoring the gawking eyes and whispers, he followed the *maitre d'* to the table and eased into a chair across from his beautiful companion.

The *maitre d'* opened the menus and placed them on the table. "Please hurry then." He forced a smile and stepped away.

Karen fumbled with the breast pocket of her khaki shirt. She pulled out a cigaret and carefully positioned it between her lips while a uniformed Indian waiter stepped forward with a gold lighter in his hand.

"Allow me, Your Ladyship." He flicked the lighter and touched it to the cigaret.

"Thank you." She took a slow drag and noticed an elderly English gentleman smiling at her from a table across the aisle. She plucked the cigaret from her lips and blew a soft trail of smoke in his direction, much to the dismay of his shocked wife.

Bonaventure leaned forward and smiled. "Well done—Your Ladyship."

"And you too—Sir Bulsworth."

He picked up his water glass and extended it toward her. "You know—behind all that smoke you're quite the looker."

She smiled and clinked her glass against his. "I bet you say that to all the young ladies."

"Hardly."

She leaned back in her chair and took another slow drag. Tilting her chin upward, she blew a soft stream of smoke toward one of the Taj's overhead fans. "I take it you're turned on by women dressed in men's clothing?"

"Only when they look like you."

She lowered her chin and smiled at him with soft blue eyes. "It's been three months since I ate a decent meal. Hope you don't mind if I indulge?"

"Be my guest."

She reached out and touched his gnarled hand. "Looks like you've done quite a bit of climbing."

"I've done my share."

She hesitated. "Tell me about your dream."

"Dream?"

"In the room."

His smile disappeared. "It's not a pleasant story."

She rested her hand on his. "Neither was mine. Please—I'd like to know what happened."

"There's not much to tell."

"Is that why you woke up in a cold sweat?"

He frowned and looked into her blue eyes. "A few weeks ago, I led a team up a mountain in the Himalayas. Things were going well until—"

"Yes?"

Bonaventure wasn't listening. His eyes had focused on the two military policeman that had entered the restaurant and seated themselves at a nearby table.

"Are you all right?"

Bonaventure leaned forward. "I think we have company."

"What?"

"Sitting behind you. Two military police." Bonaventure glanced over her shoulder and saw one of the MP's staring at him.

Karen's eyes lit up. "They want the book, dammit!" She pushed away from the table and rushed toward the marble steps.

"Wait!" Bonaventure stood up to go after her, but a firm hand gripped his arm.

"Mr. Bonaventure, I presume."

Bonaventure turned and looked into the MP's piercing blue eyes.

"Dharan received your message, Mr. Bonaventure. We have a plane waiting at the airfield."

"Plane?"

"To take you to Dharan. Your friend, Corporal Dawa, is anxious to see you."

"What does he mean?"

Bonaventure turned and saw Karen glaring at him. A second MP stood beside her, his hand grasping her arm.

The MP's grip tightened. "I'm sorry, Mr. Bonaventure, but things are a bit close. We should be going."

Bonaventure frowned and walked past the stunned patrons, followed by Karen and the two MP's.

They stepped into the steaming afternoon sun and headed for two olive drab jeeps parked along the dock. The blond MP nodded toward the first jeep.

Bonaventure glanced back at Karen. "What about—"

"Miss Halberton will follow us in the second jeep. Please hurry, old chap. Just protocol."

"Halberton?"

The MP looked at him in surprise. "You don't know your friend's name?"

Bonaventure fumbled for words. "My bag's back at the room. It's all I own."

"It's in the back seat of your jeep, Mr. Bonaventure. Please—we need to move quickly."

They made the fifteen miles to the airstrip in record time after nearly running over a line of pilgrims trekking along the roadside north of the city. When their jeeps approached the converted *Vickers,* its twin engines burst to life, spewing a stream of mud rearward from the thrust of the props.

The two jeeps dodged the flying mud and screeched to a stop in front of the plane's snub nose where two armed British soldiers stood beside an opened hatch. One of the soldiers stepped forward and shook the blond MP's hand. "That's them?"

"In the flesh. How does it look?"

"Not good. The weather's closing. Let's get this over with." The soldier stepped away from the hatch and gestured toward Bonaventure and Karen.

"Time to go, ma'am." The second MP gripped Karen's arm, but she jerked it free.

"I don't need your help." She climbed out of the jeep and walked toward the plane. When she passed Bonaventure, she paused and glared at him. "Funny, who you meet in Bombay."

"Karen, I—"

She climbed the ladder and disappeared through the hatch, followed by the two soldiers.

"Okay then." The blond MP patted Bonaventure on the back and nodded toward the hatch. "Have a good flight, Mr. Bonaventure. From the look of that sky, you're getting out just in time."

Bonaventure glanced at the black mass of clouds moving in from the Arabian Sea. He was halfway up the ladder when he heard the MP shout at him above the roar of the engines.

"My father was a climber! He thinks they gave you a rotten deal! He says you're the very best! Good luck, Mr. Bonaventure!"

Startled, Bonaventure climbed through the hatch and stepped into the plane's dimly lit cargo bay. One of the soldiers pointed to a fuselage seat across from Karen. The seats faced each other. Great—she could glare at him the whole way.

The soldier closed the hatch and strapped himself in the front seat across from his comrade. He rested his hands on a Thompson submachine gun and glanced at his two guests. "Hang on, it'll be a bit bumpy until we're airborne."

Bonaventure heard the engines rev and felt the plane rolling. His body rocked against the straps as the *Vickers* rumbled down the mud-soaked airstrip toward its takeoff point.

When the bi-winged plane reached the end of the runway, it spun around and began to vibrate from its fully throttled engines.

Bonaventure leaned forward and looked into her eyes. "Are you all right?"

"Bastard."

The plane surged forward. Bonaventure had gotten his wish. He was leaving Bombay—but in the wrong direction.

The *Vickers* splashed through the mud and lifted into the stiff southwest wind. With its engines at full throttle, it rolled into a steep right bank and leveled off on a northern heading toward the Narmada River. The flight would take seven hours, with a brief stop in Jabalpur—weather permitting.

Bonaventure unstrapped his belt and eased through the empty compartment toward the two seated soldiers.

"You shouldn't be walking around, sir. It's gonna be a bit rough."

"So I gather. How long to Dharan?"

The corporal glanced at his watch. "If we can skirt the monsoon, we should land at twenty-one hundred. Now please sit down and fasten your belt."

Bonaventure nodded. "I thought these planes had comfortable seats and windows."

The corporal frowned. "This is a military plane, sir. There's nothing out there you want to see. Now sit down."

Bonaventure walked back to his seat and fastened his belt. The *Vickers* was already bouncing around in the turbulent air. He looked across the aisle at Karen and noticed her knuckles were white from gripping the seat. He leaned forward and tried again. "They say we should land in Dharan about nine."

She ignored him and looked down at the floor.

"Things will work out. Blast—they'll probably send you back to the states. Isn't that what you want?"

She didn't move.

"Karen?" He reached out to touch her hand, but she yanked

it away.

"Come on—I'm trying to help you."

She glared at him. "Do you know what you've done?"

"Done?"

Her blue eyes glistened with anger. "Do you think the British care about me?"

"Hell, they're better than the Japanese."

"Are they?" She clenched her fists. "They want that journal, and they'll do anything to get it."

He shook his head. "My friend's in Dharan. He wouldn't steer me wrong."

"Maybe not you—but what about me?" She turned away in anger.

"Come on, you're overreacting to all—" Bonaventure felt a firm hand grasp his shoulder. He looked up and saw the stern-faced corporal staring down at him.

"Sorry, Mr. Bonaventure. My orders are to keep you from conversing. Please come with me."

Bonaventure's shoulders drooped. He undid his belt and followed the corporal to a seat at the rear of the compartment.

"Well—you wanted a window." The corporal pointed to a small window beside the seat.

"Thanks a bunch." Bonaventure plunked down in the seat and secured his belt. He folded his arms and peered through the smudged glass. Through the haze, he could see the plane's shadow dancing along the gentle coastline above Bombay. Suddenly, it disappeared into a thick bank of clouds. He felt his eyes closing. A sweet numbness filled his brain. He hadn't slept for days....

When his eyes opened, the plane's shadow was racing across rugged hills. They'd followed the Narmada River eastward through the Satpura and Vindhya mountains, refueled in Jabalpur, and started a gradual descent to the Ganges Plain.

He glanced at his watch. Six twenty. He'd slept four hours.

"Care for a smoke?"

Bonaventure looked up and saw the corporal extending a pack of cigarets. "No thanks, but the young lady would probably like one."

"She bloody near slapped them out of my hand." The corporal glanced at her and raised his eyebrows. "Quite a looker."

"That she is."

"Say—are you two involved or something?"

Bonaventure looked up and frowned. "She's my mother."

"Sorry—just trying to be friendly." The corporal walked back to his seat and strapped in. Below them, the hills had given way to a sweeping carpet of pale-green grasslands. In a few weeks, that carpet would turn silver from the monsoon floods. When the waters receded, it would turn the darkest of greens as the Ganges gave new life to India.

The *Vickers* banked north and began its final run toward the small fort below the Siwalik foothills.

They touched down at seven thirty after making excellent ground speed with the help of a powerful tail wind. Unfortunately, that same wind would soon bring the next wave of monsoon rains to northern India.

The *Vickers* splashed across the mud-soaked airstrip and rolled to a stop alongside a second *Vicker's Victoria*—the plane that had brought Corporal Dawa to Dharan.

They were met by a jeep and told to hop aboard. Soaked from the stifling humidity, Bonaventure and Karen climbed in, followed by the corporal. The driver spun the jeep around and sloshed across the airstrip toward an open barbed wire gate leading into Dharan's military compound.

Bonaventure brushed back his black hair and studied the drab cluster of barracks, tents, and barbed wire. "Lovely place."

The corporal shrugged his shoulders. "It's home."

The jeep stopped in front of a one-story wood building at the far end of the compound. The corporal hopped out and gestured toward a door where a guard was standing at attention with a rifle slung over his shoulder. "This way please."

Bonaventure climbed out of the jeep and reached for Karen, but she brushed his hand away.

They followed the corporal into an office area where two

khaki-uniformed privates were feverishly decoding telegraph messages while trying to cool themselves with a rotating fan.

The corporal snapped to attention and saluted a crisply uniformed sergeant who was seated at a small desk in the corner.

The sergeant stood up and returned the salute. "Tough flight?"

"Not bad, Sergeant."

"Well done. Get some rest." He watched the corporal do an "about face" and walk out the door.

The sergeant eyed the two civilians and gestured toward a bench against the wall. "Please, sit down. Major Pierce will be with you shortly."

"What—no tea and scones?"

The sergeant frowned at Bonaventure and picked up a pen. He was about to resume his writing when the door swung open and a gray-haired officer stepped into the room. The sergeant jumped out of his chair and snapped to attention. "Sir!"

The officer paused and stared at his seated guests. "Thank you, Sergeant. That will be all for now."

"Yes, sir." The sergeant saluted and stepped back a pace.

The officer smiled and and extended his hand. "Pleasure to meet you, Mr. Bonaventure. I'm Major Rutherford Pierce." Pierce shook Bonaventure's hand and eyed Karen. "And you must be Miss Halberton. Please—come into my office." He nodded toward the opened door.

Pierce led them into a small office with a desk and two chairs. A large map of India covered the wall behind the desk. To the right, a rotating fan hummed atop a file cabinet beside a shuttered window. The only light came from a green-shaded lamp on the desk.

Pierce closed the door and gestured toward the two wooden chairs facing his desk. "Please—make yourselves comfortable." He walked around the desk and waited for them to sit down.

Pierce slipped into his chair and folded his hands on the desk. "Welcome to Dharan. We're a bit pressed for time, so I'll dispense with the usual formalities." He reached into a drawer and pulled out a brown folder. He opened it and lifted out a photograph while glancing at Karen. "Your friends at *Reuters* will be overjoyed when they discover you're alive and well in Dharan."

"Will they?"

Pierce ignored her remark and turned his attention to Bonaventure. "Your friend, Corporal Dawa, spoke very highly of your mountaineering skills."

Bonaventure shrugged his shoulders.

"If it's all right, I'd like to spend a few minutes with Miss Halberton."

Bonaventure hesitated and looked at Karen.

"Please—we won't be long." Pierce pressed the intercom on his desk.

Bonaventure pushed out of the chair and leaned toward her. "I'll be within earshot."

Karen glared at him and turned away.

The sergeant swung open the door and snapped to attention. "Sir!"

"Please take Mr. Bonaventure to his friend." Pierce stood up and extended his hand. "Thank you for sending that message. Your country won't forget it."

Bonaventure hesitated and clasped Pierce's hand. "Let me correct you, Major. My message was intended for Corporal Dawa—not you. I sent it because I was concerned about my friend here—not the British Empire." His grip tightened. "But if you mean what you say—give me back my chalet."

Pierce smiled and glanced at a second folder lying on his desk. "Yes—I heard about that. Most unfortunate. I'll see what I can do."

Pierce watched Bonaventure disappear through the opened door, followed by Sergeant Flynn. He waited for Flynn to close it before extending a pack of cigarets to Karen. "Smoke?"

"No, thank you."

"Interesting—your dossier says you're a chain smoker."

Karen ignored him and stared at the map behind his desk.

Pierce lit a cigaret and took a puff. He sat down and placed the smoldering cigaret in an ashtray. "Where's the journal,

Miss Halberton?"

"Journal?"

Pierce's face reddened. He leaned forward and folded his hands on the desk. "Normally, I'd enjoy a game of repartee with *Reuter's* sharpest reporter, but I'm afraid we have no time for that. I need that journal."

Karen shrugged. "Is this where you bring in the master torturer?"

Pierce's shoulders slumped. "Please—we're not like the other side. It's just that the journal is very important to us."

"Why?"

"You don't know?"

Karen caught herself and leaned back in the chair. "I have some theories."

Pierce forced a nervous smile. "Don't play games. We both know it's encrypted in code."

"How do you know I haven't broken it?"

"I seriously doubt it." He picked up his cigaret and took a puff. "Be reasonable, Miss Halberton. That collection of hieroglyphics is useless to you, but it means a great deal to us."

Karen reached for the pack of cigarets and pulled one out. She placed it between her lips and picked up Pierce's lighter while her host stared coldly at her.

She leaned back and blew a stream of smoke at the ceiling. "I love *Dunhills*. Milder than the others."

"I prefer *Camels*, myself."

She took a puff and rested her arms on the chair. "What makes you think I have it?"

"Your friend told us you did."

She glared at him. "He's no friend."

"I see. My mistake—sorry." He took another puff. "Now—about the journal."

She frowned, as if in deep thought. "It seems we have a problem."

"So it seems."

"Tell you what. I'll give you the journal if you explain what's going on."

"Now really—"

"You have to appreciate what I've gone through for that little book. I'm not giving it up without a story."

Pierce snuffed out his cigaret and looked at her with sharp blue eyes. "You drive a hard bargain, Miss Halberton."

"It's my job, Major Pierce."

He leaned back and folded his arms. "If I were to give you something, how could I be sure you wouldn't break the story without our authorization?"

Karen shrugged. "If it remains our exclusive, *Reuters* will guarantee it."

Pierce looked down at the photograph lying in the folder. "Would you put that in writing?"

"If necessary."

He leaned forward and shoved a piece of paper in front of her. "Then do it." He plucked his pen out of its ink well and rested it on the blank paper.

She smiled and lifted the pen off the paper. Hesitating, she positioned the paper and began writing. A small desk clock chimed eight p.m.

She slid the paper toward him and waited.

"Sign it." He slid it back to her.

Karen scribbled her signature on the paper and dropped the pen.

Pierce picked up the paper and locked his blue eyes on her. "Remember the consequences of lying, Miss Halberton. You've signed this as a *Reuter's* representative."

Karen smiled. "I believe it's your move, Major."

Pierce took a deep breath and pushed out of his chair. He turned toward the map and snatched his swagger stick off the desk. "This morning, an aircraft crashed on this mountain." He tapped the red triangle north of Darjeeling. "We believe there's a linkage between that plane and the journal Vasquez gave you in Nanking."

Karen stared at the triangle. "Linkage?"

Pierce shook his head. "We can't be certain without seeing the journal. Our decoders could decipher it in a matter of hours—and we'd know." Pierce placed the swagger stick on the desk and sat down.

"That's it?"

"That's all we know."

Karen jammed her cigaret in the ashtray. "Well, it's not enough. I think you're holding something back."

"What?"

"There's too much urgency, Major. You may not know everything, but you're certainly working on a hunch or two—and I need to know what they are."

Pierce's face reddened. "That's quite enough."

"Cut the bullshit, Major. Do we have a deal or not?"

Pierce pointed a trembling finger at her. "I warn you, it's best to leave this matter alone and return the journal now."

Karen slumped in her chair. "Well—so much for our little agreement. Please have one of your goons direct me to my cell."

"Damn you!" Pierce slammed his fist on the desk. "I'm trying to do you a favor, you bloody fool! Give me the bloody book and you'll be on a plane to Bombay in the morning. We'll even pay your way back to America."

Karen stood up and smiled. "Thank you for the cigaret, Major."

Pierce wiped a bead of perspiration off his brow. "Sit down!"

She didn't move.

"Please."

She shrugged her shoulders and slipped into the chair.

Pierce lit another cigaret and took a puff. For a moment, the only sound was the fan whirring on the file cabinet.

He placed the cigaret in the ashtray and leaned back in his chair. "In a few months, war will break out in Europe. We believe Asia will follow within a year." He hesitated. "For the past five years, the Germans and Japanese have been working on a secret unification plan that involves a joint thrust to link their forces through Tibet and the Middle East."

She felt a sudden chill. The major was echoing the words Eric had spoken that night in her apartment.

Pierce hesitated and took a deep breath. "By skirting the Soviet Union, Hitler will eliminate Stalin as a thorn in his side.

Once the Germans and Japanese link up, they'll pour divisions of troops and equipment into the breech and become an impregnable force. To be blunt, our strategists believe the Germans and Japanese will conquer the world three years after linking up."

Karen stared at him and struggled for words. "What about the United States and England?"

"Your country has fallen seriously behind militarily and my country can't cope with a two-front war."

"But—"

"Please, Miss Halberton. We don't have time to debate military strategy." He reached for his cigaret and took a puff. "We have reason to believe the aircraft was carrying detailed agreements and plans for a joint Axis offensive through the Middle East, Tibet, and China. We also believe it was transporting a load of gold bullion from so-called neutral countries funding the effort. If we can retrieve the gold, and any survivors, it will strike a serious blow to the Axis' timetable for starting the war. And it might buy the free world enough time to stop the bloody bastards."

Karen stared at the map in disbelief. "My God, Jim."

"What?"

"Go on."

"The journal contains photographs and dossiers of Japanese and German operatives working on the plot throughout the world. I've been told some of them are rather surprising."

"Surprising?"

"Well-connected people in Spain, Sweden, and Switzerland. Even in your country and mine. Pretty sad if you ask me." Pierce leaned back in the chair and rubbed his sweating forehead. "Well, that's it."

Karen studied the shaken commander. Major Pierce was about to learn a painful lesson about obsessed reporters.

"What about NI?"

His face reddened. "Never heard of it."

"I see."

"Where did you pick that up?"

She shook her head. "Not important. So—how do you get

up there?"

"Tomorrow morning, a small team will fly to our listening post below the mountain and launch an assault on its north ridge. From what I've been told, it should take them a week to reach the plane, and another two to climb down with anything salvaged. It's risky, but we have no choice."

"Risky?"

Pierce grimaced. "That bloody aircraft is lying on a twenty-three thousand foot ridge with a bloody monsoon knocking on the door. How's that for openers?"

Karen's eyes locked on the red triangle. "The journal's secure in Bombay. I'll be happy to return it after we come down."

"What?"

"I need to go up there with your team to corroborate all this. And that includes photographs."

Pierce stared at her in shock. "Are you crazy? Kangchenjunga's the third highest mountain in the world. You'd be committing suicide."

"Sorry—that's the deal. Let me know your decision before the plane takes off." Karen picked up Pierce's cigarets and stuffed them in her shirt pocket.

Sergeant Flynn looked up at the flickering black sky. "Bloody monsoon."

"Yes—bloody." Bonaventure folded his arms and squinted at the falling rain. He flinched when a familiar voice cried out to him.

"Bonaventure!" Akaal ran through the mud and skidded to a stop in front of them. Beaming from ear to ear, he embraced his friend while the sergeant looked on in shock.

"Watch it, he'll get the wrong idea." Bonaventure gripped his friend's arms. "Good to see you, old man." He backed away and studied the rain pouring off the barrack's roof. "So this is Dharan."

"Yes."

"I prefer Chowpatty Beach."

"It can be a little confining." Akaal patted his friend's

shoulder and led him away from the sergeant. "Who's the young lady?"

"Long story. She's in quite a mess. Needs protection. Lucky for me you stopped here before seeing your family. By the way, I didn't care for the way your MP's picked us up."

Akaal stared at Bonaventure. "You don't know?"

"Know what?"

"The Major didn't tell you?"

Bonaventure shrugged.

Akaal swiped the rain off his face and glanced at the front gate. "Are you up for a little walk in the rain?"

Bonaventure nodded and followed his friend past a slicker-clothed sentry who snapped to attention when they passed through the barbed-wire gate.

"Interesting—they're not supposed to salute noncoms."

"I saved his life once."

Bonaventure glanced back at the sentry. "How?"

"On the mountain. He was training and fell into a crevasse. I pulled him out."

"Always the hero." Bonaventure followed Akaal through the rain toward a makeshift tent where one of the *Vickers* was being serviced by mechanics with flashlights.

"What are they up to?"

Akaal paused and stared at the plane. "They're readying it for tomorrow's flight."

"Back to Bombay?"

Akaal hesitated. "To Pangpema."

"Pangpema?"

"A Japanese aircraft crashed on Kangchenjunga this morning. There may be survivors."

Bonaventure stared at his friend in disbelief. "How far up?"

"The north ridge."

He wiped the rain off his face. "Is someone on drugs? If the crash didn't finish them, the altitude and weather will."

"Maybe, but the Major said the plane was carrying important cargo. He wants me to go up there tomorrow."

Bonaventure gripped Akaal's arm. "That idiot wants you to go on a fox hunt at twenty three thousand? What kind of officer sends his men on a suicide mission like that?"

Akaal shrugged. "They're my orders. Climb the ridge, search the wreckage, and bring down anything valuable."

"Bloody insane."

"I could use your help. The others don't know what it's like up there."

"Blast!" Bonaventure tugged Akaal's arm. "Come on—we're going to have a little chat with the Major."

"No!" Akaal planted his feet in the mud. "It will be very bad for me if you argue with him."

"Better than losing you to a bloody mountain."

"Listen to me!" Akaal yanked his arm away. "When Major Pierce took over, he came to my home in Dhoban and begged me to come back to the regiment. Do you know what that meant? An *angrezi* lowering himself like that?" He took a deep breath and looked at the plane. "I owe him a great deal."

Bonaventure brushed back his wet hair. "You're my only friend. We've been through hell together."

"And glory."

"Yes—that too. I won't lose you to something like this."

"Major Pierce is doing his job. I trust him. He wouldn't send me up there if it wasn't important." Akaal brushed the rain off his face. "I was wrong to bring you here. I'll talk to the Major. It's better you return to Bombay."

Bonaventure frowned and looked at the rain dripping off the tarp. "Funny, how you end up."

"Funny?"

"All this because I saw some drunks beating up a wog in a pub. Come on—we better get some sleep. The only thing I've climbed in the last two months is a barstool."

"What are you saying?"

"Can't let you kill yourself without a witness." Bonaventure turned and headed for the compound.

Pierce stroked his moustache and watched his radio operator fumble with the black knob. He took a slow, calming breath and listened to the rain pound on the roof.

"Got him, sir." Private Gage stood up and handed the

headset to his commanding officer.

"Well done, Private. Go grab a smoke and call it a night. I'll shut down the radio."

"Yes, sir." Gage saluted and walked out of the stifling radio room.

Pierce sat down and stared at the glowing amber dial while positioning the headset over his ears. He dragged the microphone next to his mouth and flipped the transmission switch. "Nepal Gateway to White Lion. Are you there White Lion?"

"White Lion here."

"How's the weather?"

"Snowing like hell, but the wind's died."

"Understood. Lifting off at nine hundred hours with five monkeys."

"Five? I thought you said four?"

"One of them is the reporter missing in Nanking."

There was no response—only crackling static.

"Do you copy, White Lion?"

"You have the missing reporter?"

"Affirmative."

"How?"

"Pure luck. We flew her in this evening."

"What about the journal?"

"Reporter concealed it in Bombay. Insists on climbing tree with others for news story. I think she knows about NI."

Pierce's headset crackled with static. He flipped the transmission switch and pressed his mouth to the microphone. "Should I repeat, White Lion?"

"I heard you. Can't you squeeze it out of her?"

"I tried."

"Try harder, dammit! She's more dangerous than the enemy. If that book hits the newspapers—"

Pierce flipped the switch. "Sorry, Lion. I'm a soldier—not a butcher." He flipped the switch and waited for a response.

"All right—send her along. I'll take care of it."

Pierce felt a cold chill. "What do you mean?"

"Send her with the others. I'll get the information."

Pierce clutched the microphone. "And then?"

"That's for butchers only. Over and out."

Pierce stared at the radio dial and listened to the static....

At eight a.m., a dozen soldiers dragged the soaked tarp off the *Vickers*. The rain had stopped, but the dark sky was laden with low-hanging clouds. Taking positions behind the wings and tail, the soldiers turned the plane northward and helped the mechanics attach a pair of skis to the wheel struts.

Bonaventure slipped on his blue anorak and followed Akaal and Private Nemi through the barbed wire gate leading to the airstrip. They were within a hundred feet of the olive drab plane when Bonaventure stopped and grabbed Akaal's arm. "Those skis are great for snow, but how the hell do we get off this mud?"

Akaal sighed and looked at his friend.

"Great."

"Here, *sahib*." Private Nemi handed Bonaventure a full supply pack.

"What about climbing gear?"

"It's on the plane, *sahib*—including weapons."

"Weapons?"

"We have to be prepared, *sahib*."

Bonaventure broke into a smirking grin. "Unless you believe angels carry rifles, there's nothing crawling around up there but cliff spiders."

"Mr. Bonaventure!"

Bonaventure glanced over his shoulder and saw Major Pierce and the pilot shuffling toward him. He was about to look away when he spotted Karen walking behind them. She was dressed in military fatigues and was carrying a full pack.

"I owe you an apology, Mr. Bonaventure. Things are looking up." She smiled and tugged on her pack.

Bonaventure locked his blue eyes on Pierce. "Why is she here?"

"She's going with you."

"What?"

Pierce shrugged his shoulders. "It's her privilege as a

reporter."

Bonaventure glared at him. "Are you nuts?"

"Sorry—she's in."

"Then you can count me out." Bonaventure dropped his pack in the mud and started to walk away.

"Now really, Mr. Bonaventure—"

Bonaventure spun around and pointed a menacing finger at the shocked officer. "Listen to me, you idiot. I've put up with this bloody game long enough. If Miss Halberton wants to commit suicide, it won't be on my watch."

Akaal grabbed his friend's arm and tried to pull him away, but Bonaventure shrugged him off.

Pierce scowled at the mountaineer. "Well—I wish I'd known this yesterday. It would have saved a lot of work." He reached into his pocket and pulled out a telegram. "If you want to go back to Bombay, I'll arrange it immediately. But I suggest you read this first." He unfolded the telegram and handed it to the enraged mountaineer. "You see, I didn't forget. That transmission was relayed this morning from our London command. If you help us retrieve the plane's cargo, your Swiss property will be returned immediately."

Bonaventure gazed at the paper. "Why should I trust you?"

"Let me be blunt, Mr. Bonaventure. I don't give a damn who you trust. We could use your help, but we're going up there either way."

"What do you mean 'we'? I don't see a pack on your back?" Bonaventure watched the major turn red. He shook his head and yanked his pack out of the mud.

"Well—it seems we all have a reason to go." Karen smiled and headed for the plane.

Sergeant Mariner looked down from the open cockpit above the nose. "Clear!"

The two mechanics stepped back from the plane and raised their hands.

"Contact!" Mariner felt the plane shake as the port engine coughed and roared to life, followed by the starboard engine. He slipped on his goggles and shook his fist in the air.

They knew what he meant. It was less than a hundred miles to Pangpema, but the terrain was the world's worst, and it was monsoon season.

Mariner gripped the wheel and jammed the throttles forward. The *Vickers* lurched through the mud and began to pick up speed. He pressed against the seat and stared at the speed indicator. The only sounds were the roaring engines and skis sloshing across the soaked ground.

Karen clutched her rattling seat and forced a nervous smile. "Why so glum, Mr. Bonaventure? I thought your type relished this stuff?"

He looked away and noticed Akaal staring into space with desperate eyes, his hands clutching a string of prayer beads.

"Up, dammit!" Mariner pulled back the wheel and felt the plane surge upward, then splash back in the mud. He glanced to the left and saw a red pennant flash by. It was the thousand foot marker. He gave the fully engaged throttles a good luck shove and yanked the wheel back a second time. "Come on, Vicky!" He pressed his back against the seat and stared at the approaching rocks.

Pierce watched the mud-drenched plane lift into the air, accompanied by cheers from the waving mechanics and troops. The *Vickers* banked to the left and disappeared into the thick haze above the Siwalik foothills.

For a moment, Pierce stood there listening to the fading engines. He lowered his head and walked toward the barbed-wire gates. It had begun to rain.

33 | Betrayed

Karak shaded his eyes and squinted at the tan and white buildings on the emerald ridge. "Darjeeling."

"Thank God." Roberto dropped his pack and collapsed in the middle of the road.

"The *angrezi* come here to escape the heat. They enjoy the cool breeze—and other things."

"Other?"

"The women."

Roberto uncapped his canteen. "I take it you don't like the British."

Karak glared at the British flag waving over the town. He brushed back his shoulder-length hair and looked down at his companion. "I know a place where you can rest while I get supplies."

Roberto nodded and forced himself up. "It will feel good to sleep in a bed again."

"It's not in a bed."

"We're not going into the town?"

"I hate Darjeeling." Karak turned away and headed up the road, followed by the two oxen.

They were rounding a bend in the road when Roberto heard a rumble and saw a jeep skid in front of him.

"Watch it, idiot!"

Roberto dived into the brush and felt a blast of hot air as the jeep squealed by.

"Damn wogs! Stay off the bloody road!"

Roberto scrambled to his feet and squinted through the dust. Two uniformed men were seated in the jeep's front seat. One of them waved a bottle in the air while grasping his officer's cap with the other hand. The jeep swerved around the bend and disappeared in a cloud of dust.

Karak stood up and brushed the dirt off his tunic. "They're full of liquor."

"Idiots."

"Maybe they'll crash and break their necks."

The Tenth Avatar

"Tempting thought."

Karak looked at him in surprise. "Strange words for a white."

"Strange? The damn fools nearly killed me."

"They thought you were Indian. They would have stopped if they knew you were one of them."

Roberto shook his head. "I'm not one of them."

"But—you're white?"

"That doesn't make me one of them."

"Then—who are you?"

"I don't know."

They pushed through the trees to a shaded spot covered with pine needles. Karak tied the oxen to a tree and nodded at the brown carpet. "You can sleep here." He disappeared through the moss-covered branches.

Roberto collapsed on the ground and stretched his aching arms and legs. A cool breeze rustled against his face. The air smelled from pine. It reminded him of the forest near Guernica. He closed his eyes and thought of Spain. So many years had passed since that warm, summer day in Valencia. So much pain. So much hatred. And still no answer.

He dreamt of the day he plunged into the Turia's cool waters. The day he waved at Sancho and crawled into the groves for a quiet afternoon siesta. The day he ran across Viveros Park to his home beneath the trees. And saw Maria standing at the door. A wonderful day. A happy day.

He was about to bite into a ripe Valencia orange when a jarring slap on the shoulder snapped his eyes open.

"Time to move on."

"What?"

"We need to reach Yoksum tonight."

Roberto sat up and rubbed his eyes. "But we just got here?"

"Time is short. The monsoon is only a day away. We must cross the Terai before it floods."

"Terai?"

Karak looked down at the thick, green jungle stretching toward the hills. "I warn you, traveler. It will be hard. The mosquitoes swarm before the monsoon—and the leeches thirst for blood."

Roberto grimaced. "Isn't there another way?"

Karak shook his head. "After we clear the jungle, we'll climb the foothills to the Sandakphu plain. When we reach Pangpema, you will be seventeen thousand feet above your world. It will be cold—and hard to breathe. All this in three days." Karak looked him in the eye. "Do you still want to go on?"

Roberto popped open the canteen and splashed some cold water on his face. "We're wasting time." He stood up and snatched his pack off the ground.

"So be it." Karak turned and headed down the hillside.

The next twenty-four hours were pure agony. Hacking through the dense undergrowth, they dodged swarms of darting mosquitoes while rubbing on a foul-smelling brown oil to ward off the disease-carrying insects.

With the sky rumbling, they plodded north toward an obscure line of hills. There were no rest stops. No idle conversation. They were like the two oxen at their side. Desperate creatures trying to escape the oppressive heat and humidity.

The rain began falling at sunset. First, a few harmless drops on the leaves. Then, a sudden deluge as the monsoon swept across the jungle.

Roberto looked down at the mud oozing over his boots. "Maybe we should find some high ground."

"There is no high ground. Tie this rope around your waist."

"Rope?"

"Do it!"

Roberto secured the hemp rope around his waist with trembling hands. He was about to speak when he felt a jarring tug. He sloshed forward behind his tenacious guide. He had become the third oxen.

His watch stopped at one a.m. The intense weather had finally taken its toll on the delicate mechanism. Just as well. Better not to know the time. He clutched the rope and struggled through the ankle-deep mud. Ahead of him, Karak's streaming black hair flickered with unearthly light.

The Tenth Avatar

The water was touching his knees when he felt the first wave of dizziness. He looked up at the flashing sky and felt the rain stinging his face. His head was spinning. A ringing sound echoed in his ears.

He ripped open his shirt and clutched his stomach. There was something there. Something clammy—like wet leaves. The rope tugged at his waist. He felt his legs giving way. The foul-smelling water surged against his hips and waist. He tried to stand, but the dizziness engulfed him like an invisible wave. He slumped forward and felt the water rush over his chest, shoulders, and face. Everything was going black. He couldn't breathe.

A powerful hand seized his arm and lifted him out of the water. "On your feet! Do you want to die here!" The voice faded into the ringing darkness....

Something warm pressed against his lips. He gagged from a burning sensation in his throat. "God—what is it?"

"Better you don't know."

Roberto sat up and blinked his eyes. He was sitting on a stone floor inside a cave. A small wood fire crackled beside him, filling the cave with flickering orange light. The supply packs were piled against the rock wall. He could hear rain falling outside the entrance. "Where are we?"

"In your high place."

Roberto's eyes lit up. "The hills?"

"Close."

He pushed back his wet hair. "How did we get here?"

"I carried you."

"Carried? But we were in the middle of the jungle?"

Karak crawled to the entrance and peered into the rainswept darkness. "You will have some pain. The leeches were up to your chest when I burned them off."

"Leeches?"

"Enough to suck you dry."

Roberto ripped open his shirt and gasped. His chest and stomach were covered with burn marks.

"They jumped all over you when you fell in the water.

They never miss a chance for fresh blood." Karak locked his black eyes on him. "I warned you it would be hard. Now it's too late to turn back."

Roberto slumped against the cave wall and stared at the fire....

They crept out of the cave at daybreak. The rain had stopped, but the sky was thick with low-hanging clouds. Refreshed by a bowl of steamed rice and two cups of tea, Roberto slung his pack over his shoulder and looked at the ox standing beside the cave. "Where's the other one?"

"Dead."

Roberto looked at Karak in shock. "Dead? What happened?"

Karak shrugged his shoulders. "He died. It is the gods' way. Only the strong survive." He crawled into the cave and dragged out one of the heavy packs. Grunting, he slung it on the ox and secured the straps.

"What about the load?"

"I lightened it. Quit talking and lend a hand." Karak gestured toward the cave's entrance.

It only took a minute for Roberto to realize his guide had shed more than supplies in the jungle. He dragged the last pack out of the cave and rested a hand on the ox. "Where's the other bag?"

"In the jungle."

"What!"

"Five bags are better than none."

"Damn you!" Roberto turned and bolted down the hillside.

"Where are you going?"

"To get that bag."

"Are you mad? Your damn gold is under two feet of mud!"

Roberto skidded to a stop on the slippery rocks. He looked up at Karak with stunned eyes. "You know?"

Karak shrugged. "I broke the lock and checked the bag. If it were food or medicine, I would have saved it. But gold is worthless here. Let the snakes have it."

"No!" Roberto took a careless step and felt his right foot

slip out from under him. He slammed against the mud-covered rocks and careened down the slick slope into the quagmire.

He cursed the knee-deep mud and stood up in the steaming undergrowth. There were no sounds. No signs of life. Nothing but low-hanging moss and green water. It was as if everything had died.

Going further was hopeless. Nothing out there but mud. He started to turn away and froze. Something slithered past his knee. Something in the mud. "Shit!" He lunged for the slope and began clawing out of the mud. He'd climbed a few feet when he felt a stinging pain in his ankle. He grimaced and ripped off his boot.

Karak shook his head and looked down at the cursing Spaniard. "This time you burn off the leeches."

They cleared the jungle and headed up the muddy slope with the ox trailing behind them. When they reached the ridge crest, they veered west into a field of high grass that led to the village of Yoksum, a cluster of mud and wood huts nestled beneath a wall of towering green hills.

Roberto was about to exchange greetings with the village's *dhoti-clad* elders when Karak pulled him back.

"I'll handle this. You'll slow us down." Karak brushed past him and stepped boldly toward the frowning villagers. Nodding respectfully, he pointed toward the overburdened ox and sat cross-legged on the ground.

Roberto spent the next hour sitting on a rock while Karak engaged in a fierce shouting match with the crouching elders. When they finally stood up, Karak had successfully traded his ox for a fresh one. To sweeten the deal, he'd thrown in a pouch of tobacco, an axe, two russet tunics, and two blue sashes.

After transferring the packs to their new beast of burden, the two travelers passed through the village while receiving the elders' blessings. A few pats on the back and they were on their way.

Roberto eyed the ox and scratched his head. "Why do that? He looks smaller than the other one."

"The other ox is dying. The jungle was too much for him. He reminds me of you." Karak pulled away from him and marched into the haze.

That afternoon, they climbed into a breathtaking forest of pines, orchids, and moss-covered oaks. They'd gone a few hundred yards when Roberto froze from a deafening screech. It seemed to be coming from the sky. He looked up and saw hundreds of monkeys swinging through the branches above his head. One of them dropped on the ground beside him and chattered wildly while shaking its tiny fist in anger. "What's wrong with him?"

"He doesn't like you. He warns you to turn back."

Roberto backed away from the enraged animal. "Where are we?"

"In the hills above the Terai." Karak nodded toward the purple-gray clouds in the southern sky. "We must clear the valleys before the rain floods the river beds."

"They're dry as a bone."

"So was the Terai." Karak adjusted his pack and brushed past him.

Two hours later, the sun disappeared behind a line of fast-moving clouds. A stiff breeze picked up from the southwest, accompanied by distant thunder.

Karak stopped and looked back at his struggling companion. "Enough for today."

Roberto collapsed against a rock and yanked at his collar. "Hard to breathe."

"We're at ten thousand. It will take time for you to adapt."

Roberto ripped open his collar and gulped the air.

Karak pointed to a line of black boulders on the slope above them. "Beyond those rocks is a village called Tshoka. I know a cave where we can sleep."

"What about the village?"

Karak pushed back his hair. "Tshoka is near the entrance to Nepal. Foreigners aren't welcome. Especially white ones."

"More good news."

They climbed above the tree line onto a windswept slope of brown grass and blackened tree trunks. Their boots grated against the jagged gravel as they approached the fortress of black boulders.

They were within a hundred yards of the village campfires when Karak stopped and pointed into the darkness. "The cave is in those rocks."

"Where?"

"You ask too many questions." Karak tied a rope around Roberto's waist and headed into the shadows. Time to be an ox again.

Ten minutes later, he dragged Roberto into a smelly cave.

"We're sleeping here?"

"Quiet." Karak crouched down and lit a flare. He held it forward and crawled toward a pile of dried moss heaped against the cave wall.

"What's wrong?"

"A bear slept here."

"Bear?" Roberto backed toward the entrance.

"No—it's safe. His litter is decayed. He lives in the forest now." Karak nodded at the floor. "Sleep."

"What about you?"

"I have things to trade." He crawled past Roberto and disappeared through the dark entrance.

Roberto unrolled his blanket and eased down on the cave floor. He stared at the pile of moss until the orange flare faded, and went out. The only sound was water dripping in the darkness.

A frightening thought struck him. What if Karak was wrong and the bear suddenly burst through the entrance? He frowned and closed his eyes. He was too tired to care.

He fell into a deep sleep. In his stupor, he heard thunderclaps and pouring rain. It seemed so far away. Everything seemed so far away....

Roberto felt a sharp slap on the shoulder. He sat up and shaded his eyes from the bright sunlight beaming into the cave.

"Come—we're wasting time." Karak crawled through the entrance, dragging his pack behind him.

Roberto rubbed his eyes and looked around. The cave was empty except for a few smoldering coals from a small fire. He took a deep breath and crawled into the bright light. A disgusting odor stopped him. "What's that smell?"

"Smell?"

Roberto blinked his eyes and froze. A hairy, four-legged creature peered at him, it's shaggy face and brown eyes only inches from his nose. "*Mi dios*—what is it?"

"You have never seen a yak?"

"A what?"

"A yak. I traded the ox for him while you slept." Karak tightened the cinch around the animal's hairy belly. "We'll need him where we're going."

Roberto stood up and eyed the reddish-brown creature. He reached out and snared a clump of its matted hair.

Karak backed away from the animal and handed Roberto a pouch of dry food. "If the snow holds off, we'll reach Pangpema tomorrow morning."

"Snow?"

Karak nodded at the bank of gray clouds on the southern horizon. "When those clouds come back, we'll be at fifteen thousand. It doesn't rain up there."

Roberto jammed a handful of dried barley and lentil beans in his mouth. Minutes later, the two men and their shaggy beast were climbing the ridge above the tree line.

They stumbled past mysterious rock piles and wood poles tied with strips of brightly colored cloth. The humidity was gone and the air had turned cold. A stiff, dry wind blew in their faces.

When Roberto asked Karak the meaning of the stones and cloth strips, the scar-faced guide frowned and shook his head. "You won't understand. You're not one of us."

They staggered over the ridge at high noon. Roberto knelt down and stared at the carpet of yellow grass stretching in front of him. He shook his head and gasped for breath. "This is inhuman. There's no end to it. I can't go on."

"You don't have a choice. I told you, there is no turning back. We'll reach the glacier tonight."

"Glacier?"

Karak dug his hands into one of the packs and pulled out a fur hat, coat, leggings, and boots. "Put these on over your rags.

The next day will be very hard." He dropped the clump of fur on the rocky ground and headed down the ridge toward the yellow grass. A light snow had begun falling.

Three hours later, they scrambled over another ridge and spotted what appeared to be a small village on the snow-streaked plain. Karak shuffled into the cluster of huts and yanked open the hides covering the entrances.

"What's wrong?"

Karak backed away from the huts and retreated toward Roberto. He paused and sipped some water from his canteen.

"Well?"

"It's deserted. They left quickly for the high passes." Karak studied the approaching clouds. "Time is very short. A great blizzard is coming."

They headed north across the Sandakphu Plain toward a towering fortress of white clouds. Roberto didn't realize it, but they weren't clouds. Gasping for breath, he looked down at his lengthening shadow while stumbling across the snow-patched rocks.

Two hours later, his shadow disappeared as a line of black clouds blotted out the sun. He looked over his shoulder and froze. A white haze was falling toward him from the clouds. No—it wasn't haze. It *was* the clouds.

He heard a roar. A blast of chilled wind slammed into him, driving him to one knee. He raised his hand in front of his face to block the blinding snow.

"This way!" Karak's powerful hand seized his parka and dragged him toward a black mass of rocks barely visible through the howling whiteout. He clung to Karak's sleeve and staggered forward.

They were climbing into the rocks when a crushing wind gust buckled Roberto's knees. He sprawled on the ground and clutched Karak's wrist. The wind ripped at his parka, its invisible talons trying to claw him into the blizzard.

"On your feet, fool! Lean into it!"

Roberto stood up and leaned against the wind. The ice tore at his face. He couldn't breathe. He staggered forward and felt the rocks brushing against his legs.

"Get down!"

Karak pulled him down behind the rocks. He could hear the wind whistling over his head. Something brushed against his face. He looked to his left and saw the yak peering at him.

Karak led him into a foul-smelling cave. Striking a flare, Karak scooped up some dried moss and wrapped it around a stick. He jammed the stick between the rocks and lit it with the flare.

Roberto collapsed against the wall and yanked down his hood. "You saved my life."

Karak ignored him and crawled next to the yak. He dug his arm into one of the packs and pulled out the pouch of dry food. He handed it to Roberto. "If the gods are with us, the storm will pass by morning."

"And if they're not?"

Karak shrugged his shoulders. "We die—like the ox."

Roberto devoured a few handfuls of the bland food and washed them down with some water. He huddled against the cave wall and stared at the burning torch.

"What is in your mind?"

"My friend."

"The shaman?"

"He's a priest."

"You worry about him?"

Roberto nodded.

"Don't. Your friend is a survivor."

Roberto looked up. "You know him?"

Karak leaned against the cave wall. "I saw him in the hills. He looked like a tired old man. Then I saw his eyes."

"Eyes?"

"They were evil."

"Eammon?"

"I don't know his name—but I know his kind." Karak lit a black pipe and took a long puff. "He has two faces—like the jackal."

"You're wrong."

Karak shook his head. "Don't trust him. Some night, he'll slit your throat." Karak put down the pipe and rolled on his

side. "If the gods are with us, you'll see your jackal tomorrow."
"Can I ask you something?"
"You can ask."
"Who are you?"
"Your guide."
"No—I mean, where do you live?"
"In the mountains."
"In a village?"
"I live alone."
"You have no one?"
"You wouldn't understand."

They set out at daybreak. The blizzard had passed, but the drifting snow created near-zero visibility.

Exhausted by the thin air, Roberto stumbled forward clinging to the memory of his friend. Eight months had passed since they parted in Bern. In a few hours, they would meet again.

The sky brightened and the sun broke through the haze. From the angle of their shadows, it was high noon. Roberto squinted at the dark silhouette shuffling through the snow ahead of him. He tried to lift his foot, but it wouldn't move. He tried again and felt the ground sway under him. His ears rang. The ground surged up at him. He collapsed in a heap and cried out for help.

Through the vertigo, he heard Karak's boots crunching toward him. A gloved hand reached down and pressed a wood cup to his lips.

"Drink this."

He sipped the burning liquid and gagged.

"Again."

He gulped it down and sat on his haunches.

"Put these on." Karak dangled a pair of leather goggles in front of his face

"I've had it. I can't go on."

"You don't have to. We're here."

Stunned by Karak's words, Roberto dragged off his fur hat

and slipped the snow goggles over his eyes. He squinted into the haze and grimaced from a blinding flash of light.

"Kangchenjunga." Karak pointed toward a windswept peak flashing through the clouds.

Roberto shaded his eyes and tried to get a glimpse of the mountain, but the intense light made him look away. He clutched his throbbing head and slumped in the snow. "Where's the village?"

"Village?"

"Pangpema?"

Karak shrugged. "There is no village."

"What?"

"Your friend is there." Karak pointed to a sunlit ridge.

Roberto looked up at the ridge in disbelief. Something was up there—an ice-covered structure shimmering through the haze. "Where are the people?"

"People? You think everyone is mad like your friend? This land belongs to the gods. There are no people."

Roberto couldn't speak. He stared at the frozen monastery on the ridge. He'd come six thousand miles for this? To live in a deserted wasteland three miles above the earth? This was his brave new world?

Karak unstrapped Roberto's packs and watched them drop in the snow.

"What are you doing?"

"My job is done. I'm leaving."

Roberto looked at him in shock. "You're what?"

"I'm leaving." He grabbed the yak's rope and started to walk away.

"Wait!"

"Good luck, traveler. You've come a long way. I hope you find what you're looking for."

"You can't leave me out here. I'll freeze to death."

"The gods will watch out for you. *Namaste, muzzafer*...."

Unable to speak, Roberto watched him disappear across the snowfield with the yak trailing behind him. A wave of panic swept through him. He looked down at the packs and felt his heart pounding. Better to deal with the *Falange* than freeze to death in this godforsaken place.

He looked up at the monastery. There was only one direction now—and it was up. He jammed a ski pole in the snow to mark the packs and headed toward the ridge.

He was within a hundred feet of the weathered structure when he detected a faint pinging, barely audible above the rustling snow. He struggled up the slope and collapsed on the monastery's frozen steps.

The pinging grew louder, sounding more like intermittent bursts of energy. He lifted his snow goggles and stared at the wooden doors. He'd heard that sound before. On the radio in Guernica's town hall. The screech of a racing telegraph key.

The pinging stopped. He staggered up the steps and grasped the carved door handles. Six thousand miles, *torero*. Six thousand miles for this moment. And now—finally—the truth. He pulled open the doors and stepped inside.

He was standing in a deserted prayer hall. A beam of sunlight radiated through a crack in the roof, striking a large statue of Buddha on the altar in front of him. On each side of the altar, rusted candelabra stood guard like worn sentinels, their broken candles strewn on the stone floor.

He stepped forward and felt his foot strike something. A piece of broken tile. The floor was covered with it. He looked up at the sagging roof and backed away. The ancient building was on its last legs.

He leaned against the wall and stared at the altar. The pinging had started again. It seemed to be coming from the shadows behind the altar. He glanced at the unsteady roof and edged closer.

His heart jumped. Light was coming from a door behind the altar. He edged closer and grasped the latch. So many miles. So much pain. And it was finally about to end.

"What the hell!" Eammon spun around and pointed a forty-five automatic at the figure standing in the doorway. His face was crimson beneath his white beard. His green eyes flared with anger.

"Eammon?"

Eammon stared at the bedraggled creature in disbelief. "My

God—am I dreaming?"

"I wish you were."

Eammon lowered the pistol. "Roberto?"

"It's me."

"How did you get here?"

Roberto reached into his parka and pulled out the frayed letter. "Nevo."

Eammon shook his head. "Nevo? When?"

"I don't remember. Maybe a week ago."

"But the climb? My God—you barely made it up the hill in Bern?"

"I had help."

"Who?"

"A guide named Karak. Do you know him?"

"No...." Eammon sank in the chair.

"He knows you."

"What?"

Roberto stared at the radio. "What's going on, Eammon?"

Eammon was about to speak when the radio began crackling with static. He spun around and snatched a headset off the table. He pressed it against his ear and scribbled down the incoming telegraph message.

Roberto scanned the dimly lit room. A small cot was jammed against the wall beside the radio. He felt a surge of warmth from a cooking stove on his left. A teakettle sat on a grate above the glowing coals.

Eammon tapped the telegraph key and put down the headset.

"Orders from the Vatican?"

"Afraid not."

Roberto stared at the wall above the radio. He brushed past Eammon and touched one of the photographs. "Is that me?"

Eammon nodded. "Remember? I took it just before we came down. Look at your eyes, Roberto. Like a child getting his first toy."

Roberto nodded and backed away.

"How about some boiled rice?" Eammon pushed out of the chair and crouched next to a metal tank beside the stove. He

The Tenth Avatar

snatched a pot from a hook on the wall and placed it under the tank's spigot. He twisted the handle and watched a stream of water trickle into the pot. "Hope you like rice because it's all we've got until the next drop."

"Drop?"

"The supply plane comes once a week. Parachutes in everything I need."

Roberto watched Eammon place the pot on the grate above the coals. The Irishman scooped some rice out of a sack and sprinkled it into the water.

"Only take a minute. Not bad with a cup of strong Irish tea."

"We need to talk."

"I know." Eammon brushed past him and opened a small cabinet beside the radio. "How about a good shot of Irish whiskey to warm you up?"

Roberto watched his friend fill two shot glasses to the brim. He sat on the cot and took one of the glasses from Eammon's outstretched hand.

Eammon raised his glass. "May the wind be always at your back." He smiled and chugged down the shot of whiskey.

Roberto swallowed the stinging whiskey and placed the empty glass on the table.

"Well—that rice should be ready."

"Dammit, Eammon! I just crawled halfway around the world and you almost shot me!"

Eammon took a deep breath and spooned the rice into a wooden bowl. He extended it to Roberto with a trembling hand. "You'll feel better after you eat."

Roberto brushed the bowl aside and glared at him.

Eammon placed the bowl on the table. He poured two cups of tea and laced them with shots of whiskey. "Maybe this will help." He placed one cup next to Roberto and eased into the chair facing him. "Well—how should I begin?"

"With the truth."

Eammon sipped his tea and placed it on the table. He leaned forward and rested his hands on his lap.

"What is this place?"

"A deserted monastery—like I told you."
"And the radio?"
"It keeps me in touch with the outside world."
"Who do you talk to?"
Eammon shrugged. "Lots of people."
"Like Gideon and Nevo?"
Eammon's smiled disappeared. He sat up and glared at the Spaniard.
"Who do you work for, Eammon?"
"You're asking a lot."
"I deserve it, dammit."
Eammon leaned back in the chair. "Do you now."
"What?"
"Since I'm about to bare my breast, let's make it a twosome. Where's the gold, Padre Santiago?"
Roberto stared at Eammon in shock.
Eammon's green eyes locked on him. "You heard me. Where's the gold, you lying bastard?"
"You know?"
"I have well-informed friends."
"Gideon?"
"And he's no priest. And since we're down to the short strokes—neither am I. Hell—I don't even believe in God."
Roberto couldn't speak. Karak's warning echoed in his ears.
"I'm really sorry about this, old man. At the time, it seemed a good idea. You know—a two man show."
"What are you saying?"
Eammon shook his head. "I tried to recruit you, dammit. You seemed so perfect. Disillusioned and all that. I figured you'd bite. You know—a better world and all that." He hesitated and sipped some tea. "I was stunned when you didn't come. Then I got the word from Gideon. You sure had me fooled. The innocent padre turns out to be a thief with half of Franco's agents searching for him. Quite a bit of gold too." Eammon gulped down the tea. "Say—what did you do with all that gold?"
Roberto slumped against the wall. "Are you telling me

you're a spy?"

"I resent that word. I'm a member of British Intelligence. Have been for years. When I met you in Bern, I was waiting for orders to set up this listening post."

"My God."

"Now don't get religious on me."

Roberto glared at the bearded man seated across from him. "You expected me to help you?"

"Gradually."

"Bastard!" Roberto picked up the empty shot glass and flung it against the door, shattering it to smithereens. The tea cup followed close behind.

Eammon looked down at the broken glass and pottery strewn across the floor. "You know—you're making quite a mess of things. That's good Irish whiskey on the floor."

"I hope you choke on it."

Eammon slumped in the chair. "Well—now that we've gotten that off our chests, what do we do about it?"

Roberto looked down at his trembling hands. His mind flashed back to Spain. He recalled his father's reddened face the night they fought in the study. The cold hand pressing against his shoulder in Corpus Christi. The bitter argument with Ordoña. The fierce beating in Granada. Lorca and Picasso. Ana's final words of love before she died in his arms. The brutal crossing on the *Mephistopheles*. Calcutta, and the terrifying night with Nevo. The kind stranger on the train. The mysterious guide called Karak. And above it all—Eammon's promise of a better tomorrow. A chance for a new life at the roof of the world. All of it—a bitter lie. Ten years of a man's life sacrificed to a frozen wasteland and goddamned spy! He pushed off the cot and burst through the door.

"Where are you going?" Eammon picked up the forty-five and charged after him.

Roberto dodged the altar and stormed across the debris-strewn floor toward the monastery's wooden doors.

"Dammit, Roberto, I'm not kidding!" Eammon released the safety and aimed the forty-five at the back of the Spaniard's head. He hesitated and shifted the target to the door handle.

Roberto froze from a deafening crack as the door handle splintered in his hand.

"Quit acting like a madman and talk to me."

Roberto turned and glared at him. "Get it over with, dammit!"

"I'm not a murderer, Roberto. If you would just listen."

"To what—more lies?"

"Believe this. You won't last an hour out there."

Roberto glanced at the forty-five. "From the look of things, I won't last a minute in here."

"Eammon lowered the automatic. "I'm just asking you to listen. Then—you can leave if you want. I won't try to stop you."

Roberto took a deep breath and leaned against the door.

Eammon slipped the gun in his belt. He brushed back his thinning white hair and groped for words. "Something rather serious has happened. Tomorrow, a plane's landing here with a climbing party."

"A what?"

Eammon trained his green eyes on the Spaniard. "This morning, a plane crashed on a mountain near here. I picked up its emergency radio transmission before it went down." He hesitated. "The plane was carrying secret documents and a load of gold bullion. We need to get up there and retrieve that cargo."

"You expect me to believe that?"

"You don't have to. Just hang around until tomorrow and you'll know the truth."

"I already know the truth."

"Listen to me, Roberto. Whatever you think about me—listen."

"Go on."

"For weeks, our agents in China and Europe have intercepted Japanese and German radio transmissions concerning something called NI. I think it has to do with that plane." Eammon frowned and went on. "In a few months, war will break out in Europe. We have reason to believe the Japanese will soon follow in Asia. It's only a matter of time before the English and Americans get pulled in."

Roberto looked down at the floor. "So it's finally come."

"Yes—and my job is to make sure the right side wins."

"Right side?"

Eammon glared at him. "How can you say that? You of all people. Do you want that mess in Spain to spread all over the world?"

"Sounds like it already has."

"No, dammit. We can stop them. Right here. Right now."

Roberto pushed away from the door. "Are you done?"

"Not quite. We believe the documents on that plane contain plans to link Germany's and Japan's armies through Asia and the Middle East. Do you know what I'm saying? If they pull it off, the pigs will rule the world." Eammon raised his open hands. "I didn't plan it this way, but I need you, Roberto. You've come so far. Don't walk away now."

Roberto shook his head. The Irishman's words were taking effect. "If I help you, will you arrange my transport out of here?"

"If that's what you want. All I need is someone to man the radio while I'm on the mountain."

Roberto looked at him in shock. "You're going with them?"

"Have to. It goes with the job."

"How far up is the plane?"

"Twenty-three thousand."

"Are you crazy? You'll never make it."

Eammon took a deep breath. "It's amazing what you can do when you have to. I think you know that."

"I didn't come here for this."

"Didn't you? After what you went through in Spain, it would be a chance to strike back. I thought that's what you wanted."

Roberto's black eyes flashed with anger. "How long will it take?"

"I'm not sure. Maybe three weeks."

"What if you don't make it?"

"We have to make it."

"What if you don't?"

"You'll be the only survivor. That makes you valuable. They'll have to come for you. Either way—you fly out."

Roberto grasped the splintered door handle. He didn't notice Eammon's hand slip over the forty-five.

"Well?"

"My packs are down there. I'll need some help." Roberto opened the door and stepped into the chilled air.

They spent the next hour lugging Roberto's packs up the snow-covered slope. Exhausted, Roberto bedded down against the altar and fell asleep while Eammon peered at him from the door of the radio room.

Eammon's gaze switched to the five padlocked bags lying on the floor. They were too heavy to be supplies. At nearly a hundred pounds each, he figured the gold to be worth at least a quarter million U.S. dollars. He smiled and eased the door closed.

The first telegraph message went to Calcutta....

From: White Lion
To: Nevo
How did he escape? What good are you? If we can't rely on you to follow orders, we're finished. And so are you! No more mistakes!
White Lion

Eammon paused to verify transmission before directing the next message to Dharan....

From: White Lion
To: Nepal Gateway
Please notify Spanish authorities that fugitive priest Hidalgo was robbed and killed by thieves outside Darjeeling. All gold was lost. Hurry with climbing team or I'll climb mountain alone.
White Lion

34 | The Canisters

"Major Tomonaga!"

The voice echoed in his ears like someone calling him in a dark tunnel.

"Can you hear me, Major?"

Tomonaga squinted at the blurred face staring down at him.

"It's Morita, sir."

"Morita?"

"Yes, sir."

"What happened?"

"We crashed, sir. Don't you remember?"

Tomonaga grasped the sergeant's sleeve. "Where are the others?"

"At the plane. I was headed back there when I spotted you."

Tomonaga stared at the blowing snow. "The others made it?"

Morita patted his commander's shoulder. "We're tough marines, sir. Just like you."

Morita slipped a hand under his commander's back and tried to lift him, but Tomonaga's agonizing cry stopped him. He was about to try again when Tomonaga clutched his arm. "No, Sergeant. Too much pain. Everything's broken inside."

"You can make it, sir. The plane is only a hundred yards away." Morita pulled off his belt and slipped it under his commander's waist. "I'm sorry, sir. Better grit your teeth." He slipped the belt through its buckle and pulled it tight.

"Oh—God!"

"Hang on, sir."

Tomonaga didn't hear him. He'd blacked out from the suffocating pain....

It was eight a.m. and Tokyo's wet streets bustled with a queer blend of old and new. Honking cars and buses swerved past horse-drawn buggies, their straw-hatted drivers oblivious to the commotion around them. Kimono-clad ladies brushed against men dressed in business suits and raincoats. In the midst of the traffic jams and scurrying commuters, farmers planted crops in the nearby parks.

A squadron of torpedo planes roared overhead, their powerful engines drowning out the morning temple bells. And there was always the army, its young conscripts strutting through the crowds in their brown uniforms, caps, and gaiters.

Above the busy sidewalks, colorful banners hung from candy-cane poles, all of them displaying the same bright symbols—a red sun, *swastika*, and Italian tri-color. The Tripartite Pact would not be signed for another year, but Japan was wasting no time declaring its alliance with Germany and Italy.

In the distance, twisted columns of black smoke wafted into the powder blue sky above Tokyo's factories. The usual line of trucks and horse-drawn wagons had pulled up to the factories to dump their loads of scrap iron into bins that would begin the tedious process of squeezing out salvageable metal for planes, guns, and tanks. Hard to believe it was possible, considering the contents of those bins. Everything from radiators to lampposts to *Shinto* temple bells.

Yes—it was eight a.m. on April 30, 1939, and Tokyo looked prosperous and happy. What a lie.

The food shortages had become particularly noticeable this year. With the population swelling to crisis proportions, every inch of useable soil was being tilled for food. There was even talk the new Olympic Stadium would soon give up its enormous athletic field to the desperate farmers and their plows. In the slums, green pumpkin vines snaked over the brown, weathered shacks. Pumpkins had become the most plentiful crop in Japan's depleted food reserve. They seemed to sprout everywhere—even in the gutters. The Japanese had learned to survive on them—but how they hated them. The pumpkin had become the nation's symbol of poverty.

And food wasn't the only thing in short supply. In another year, the cars and buses would grind to a halt. There would be no planes or ships. No warmth in the cold winter. No light in

The Tenth Avatar

the darkness. Without oil, the nation would wither and die.

The Americans and British had decided to punish Japan with a cruel embargo on precious oil. After maintaining control of the mineral-rich Far East for a century, the Occidentals had panicked when tiny Japan found it necessary to expand her borders in order to survive.

This was wrong! The Occidentals had no right to intrude. Their embargo was an act of war. In time, the Chinese would learn to accept their Japanese brothers and sisters, and both nations would prosper. The white race had no business meddling in these matters. They were opportunists bent on ruling the yellow race to protect their hold on Asia's rich resources. For this, they would pay a dear price.

These were the thoughts of Captain Schinichiro Tomonaga as he walked through Tokyo's crisp spring air on the morning of April 30. Before entering the Army Air Force's Technical Institute Building, he stopped to watch a line of recruits undergoing bayonet drills at Toyama Military Academy. How determined they looked lunging and parrying their padded poles. Soon, they would be sent to China for the real thing.

Tomonaga sighed while recalling his own bayonet training at Yokosuka Naval Station. It seemed so easy then. How different it becomes when your enemy glares at you and thrusts his metal blade at your face.

He walked into the Institute's black marble lobby and spotted an orderly writing at a desk beneath a spiral staircase. He eased toward the desk and spoke softly. "Captain Tomonaga to see General Yasuda."

The brown-uniformed orderly jumped to his feet and snapped to attention. He bowed his head and clicked his heels. "An honor, sir. We have heard much about you."

"Thank you. All good, I hope."

The orderly smiled and ran his finger down a list of names. "Please—follow me."

Tomonaga nodded politely and followed the young man up the staircase. He glanced at his watch. A parade was scheduled at noon. All businesses would shut down for one hour while the latest weaponry was put on display. Maybe he would get out in time to see the *Zeros* fly over.

Never mind the artillery pieces and armored vehicles. It was the new fighter aircraft that intrigued him. Superbly fast and highly maneuverable. A squadron overflight had been promised for the grand finale. God, what he would give to be a carrier pilot instead of a trench marine.

The orderly led him down a corridor lined with frosted glass doors. Tomonaga listened to his boots clicking across the marble floor. *Kanji* symbols flashed at his eyes as he walked past the stencilled doors. Words like "Research" and "Tactics" made him stiffen a bit, for he had entered the home of the finest military intelligence organization in the world.

They stopped at a frosted glass door at the end of the corridor. The words "Operations Room" were painted on the glass in bold, red *Kanji* symbols.

"Please wait here, sir." The orderly opened the door and stepped inside. He returned seconds later. "General Yasuda will see you now." The orderly swung open the door and bowed politely.

Tomonaga gave his blue service tunic a firm tug and stepped into the brightly lit room.

A large, black conference table filled the center of the room. The surrounding walls were covered with blackboards scribbled with white symbols. The air smelled from chalk dust—like one of his classrooms at the academy.

A bald, slightly built man was seated at the head of the table. He wore a brown uniform with red patches on each collar, each patch decorated with gold stripes and white stars. He stared at one of the blackboards while jotting notes in a purple manual.

Tomonaga heard the door close behind him. He snapped to attention and saluted. "Captain Tomonaga, reporting as requested."

Lieutenant General Yasuda rested his pen on the conference table and pushed out of his chair. He returned the salute and shook Tomonaga's hand while studying the handsome officer with tired brown eyes. "Welcome, Tomonaga. Before I ask you to sit down, let me conduct some official business on behalf of the navy."

"Yes?"

Yasuda reached into his pocket and pulled out a small, blue-velvet case tied with a gold ribbon. He extended it to his guest and broke into a smile. "I believe this belongs to you."

Puzzled, Tomonaga took the case from the general's outstretched hand and undid the ribbon. He popped it open and stared at it in disbelief. The case contained a pair of dark blue patches, each decorated with twin gold stripes and a silver cherry blossom.

"Congratulations, Major Tomonaga. If you ask me, it's long overdue after your excellent record in the China campaign."

Overcome, Tomonaga clicked his heels and bowed smartly. "I am deeply honored, sir."

Yasuda returned the bow and gestured toward the vacant chair on his right. "Please—sit down. We have important business to discuss."

Tomonaga eased into the chair and removed his officer's cap, placing it smartly on the table.

Yasuda resumed his seat and closed the purple manual. He shoved it aside and took a slow, deliberate breath. "What I'm about to tell you is highly confidential."

"Yes, sir."

"I'm sure you have heard rumors that our German allies will soon launch a great campaign on the other side of the world."

"Yes, sir."

Yasuda hesitated. "Assuming things go well, we will undoubtedly follow with major offensives in Asia and the Pacific."

Tomonaga's eyes lit up. "Then— it's come?"

Yasuda paused and lit a cigaret. "I know you don't smoke so I won't offer you one."

Tomonaga nodded, his black eyes fixed on the general.

"When we commit ourselves, I'm afraid we'll inherit two difficult challenges."

"The Americans?"

Yasuda puffed his cigaret. "That's one of them. Once the Americans snap out of their lethargy, they'll surely enter the war and become our most formidable foe."

Tomonaga's eyes flashed. "We can beat them, sir. They're a weak people."

"Perhaps, but even if we defeat them, there is still the second problem."

"The British?"

"No, Major. The Germans."

Tomonaga stared at him. "Germans? But they're our allies?"

Yasuda leaned back in his chair. "Do you honestly believe that moustached maniac will share the world with us after the Americans and British are defeated? The man is a lunatic, obsessed with Aryan superiority and destiny. I'm afraid the Asian race doesn't fit into his long range plans."

Tomonaga grimaced and clasped his hands.

"Good—I see you understand. Now I can explain your mission to Norway."

"Norway?"

Yasuda leaned forward and folded his hands. "Working with friends, I've succeeded in arranging transport of a precious cargo from Norway to Nanking. From there, it will be easy to bring it to Tokyo."

"Cargo?"

"Your mission will be to direct the successful transfer of that cargo from Norway to Nanking."

"Me?"

"You."

Tomonaga sighed and looked down at his clasped hands. "May I ask what the cargo is?"

Yasuda locked his brown eyes on the young officer. "Gold, Major Tomonaga. More gold than you can imagine. Bright, shining gold. Brighter than the sun." He hesitated and puffed his cigaret. "Well—are you up to it?"

Tomonaga glanced at the blue-velvet case lying on the table. He slipped it into his pocket and rose out of the chair. "When will I leave?"

Yasuda stood up and nodded. "There's a briefing in ten minutes. Your submarine departs at seven hundred hours."

"Tomorrow?"

"Time is critical, Major. I'm afraid we'll have to delay your promotion party until after you return."

"What about my naval assignments?"

"I'll take care of that." Yasuda reached out and shook Tomonaga's hand. "Good luck, Major."

"Thank you, sir." Tomonaga slipped on his officer's cap and turned for the door.

"Major?"

"Yes, sir?"

Yasuda forced a nervous smile. "I wish I could tell you more, but rest assured this will be the most important mission of a war not yet started. It will resolve both problems."

"Yes, sir." Tomonaga opened the door and followed the waiting orderly down the corridor.

They stopped at a frosted glass door with no *Kanji* symbols. The orderly pushed the door open and gestured for Tomonaga to step inside.

Two men were seated at a small table. One was dressed in a black business suit and showed no sign of military affiliation. The other wore a brown army uniform with twin silver stars sewn into the red collar patches. The mark of a colonel.

Tomonaga snapped to attention and bowed his head. "Major Tomonaga."

The uniformed man snapped out of his chair and returned the bow. He reached out and clasped Tomonaga's hand. "Colonel Nishina, Major. This is Mr. Noguchi. Please, sit down. We have much to cover and time is short."

Tomonaga exchanged greetings with Mr. Noguchi and eased into the vacant chair. He took a deep breath and glanced out the window at sunlit Tokyo. In the distance, a chorus of air raid sirens practiced their daily melody. Suddenly, Tokyo melted away and the sirens became a whining, merciless wind....

* * *

"He's coming out of it."

Tomonaga blinked his eyes and looked up at Morita's blood-spattered face. "Where am I?"

"In the cargo hold, sir."

Tomonaga gripped the sergeant's parka and pulled himself up. He collapsed against the metal wall and stared at the small fire flickering in the darkness.

Three bandaged marines huddled around the fire, vapor streaming from their mouths. Behind them, a canvas tarp stretched across the twelve foot void that had been the cargo hold's front bulkhead.

Tomonaga closed his eyes and listened to the wind buffet the canvas. A chilled draft swept across his face. He tried to raise his left arm, but it wouldn't move.

"I immobilized your arm with tape, sir. Your shoulder is in bad shape. Looks like broken ribs. I gave you an injection to ease the pain."

Tomonaga squinted at the darkness. "Where are the others?"

Morita looked down. "We were burying them when I spotted you in the snow."

Tomonaga looked at him in shock. "We're all that's left?"

"Yes, sir."

For a moment, there was only the sound of crackling flames and wind. Tomonaga grimaced and struggled to his feet. He leaned against the fuselage wall and stared at the three marines huddled around the fire. "I am deeply sorry. I would gladly give my life if it would bring them back."

One of the marines looked up with glazed eyes. "We'll make it, sir. We'll make it...."

Tomonaga fought the tears and nodded. He took a painful breath and looked at Morita. "Do we have a flashlight?"

"Yes, sir." Morita yanked a flashlight out of his belt.

"Aim it back there." Tomonaga pointed toward the rear of the compartment and winced from the sudden burst of light. It took a few seconds for his eyes to adjust to the bright beam.

Something was there—shining in the debris. He edged closer and felt his heart pounding.

They were intact! Standing at attention like twin columns of soldiers. "More light. Sergeant."

Morita stepped through the debris, holding the flashlight in front of him.

Tomonaga dropped on his knees and patted the metal canisters like a child who has found his missing toy. "I count twenty five. The other five must have broken loose. Did you see anything in the snow?"

"Snow?"

"When you were out there."

Morita grimaced. "Only dead men."

Tomonaga stared at him. "I'm sorry, Sergeant. I meant no disrespect."

"Yes, sir."

"I would like to say a prayer over the men."

"In the morning, sir."

Tomonaga spotted the medical kit lying next to the fire. He slid beside it and fumbled for a syringe.

"Watch that morphine, sir. It can kill." Morita waited for a response, but his commander wasn't listening.

Tomonaga filled the syringe with morphine and plunged the needle into his arm. He slumped against the fuselage wall and felt a warm, numbing sensation ebb through his veins. He closed his eyes and recalled General Yasuda's parting words....

Rest assured this will be the most important mission of a war not yet started....

"Are you all right, sir?"

Tomonaga pulled himself up. "Yes, Sergeant. And so are you. Enough of this wallowing. There's work to be done." He ripped the tape off his left arm.

"Work?"

"Outside."

Morita looked at him in shock. "But—the blizzard?"

"Forget the blizzard." Tomonaga glared at his four stunned comrades. "As long as one of us lives, this mission goes on.

It's more than glory now. It's survival. That gold must get to Japan. Understood?"

Morita snapped to attention and bowed, exposing a deep gash in his scalp.

Tomonaga rested his hand on Morita's shoulder. "How many flashlights do we have?"

"Two."

"And batteries?"

"They're in the flashlights."

"We have flares, sir. A whole case full." One of the marines stood up, holding a red flare in his bloody hand.

Tomonaga stared at the young marine. "You're?"

"Corporal Ishikawa." The marine tried to bow, but his back hurt too much.

"Good man, Ishikawa. Are you married?"

"Yes, sir."

"I promise you, Corporal. We will make your wife proud."

The young corporal smiled and collapsed into his comrade's arms.

"I'll take some of those." Tomonaga reached for the case of flares, but Morita grabbed his wrist.

"Sir, there's nothing out there but charred wreckage and dead bodies. Best to wait until morning."

Tomonaga yanked his arm free and glared at Morita. "If we stay here, we'll be dead in a few days. Our one chance is to salvage enough parts to rebuild the radio."

"Radio? Major—the front of the plane is toast!"

Tomonaga stepped back in anger. He was about to explode when one of the marines stood up and pointed at the shadows. "How stupid of me!"

"What?"

"Private Aikido, sir. We have a radio."

"What?"

Aikido crawled into the debris and dragged out a leather rucksack. He knelt beside it and ripped open the flap. "It's German. They told me it was the best in the world."

Tomonaga frowned. "They said that about the plane."

Aikido reached into the rucksack and lifted out a black

radio and generator box. They appeared intact.

"Well?"

"We'll know in a minute." Aikido connected two wires from the box to the radio. He inserted a small crank in the box and looked at his commander. "I hope it's not like the plane."

"So do I, Private. So do I...."

Aikido spit on his hand and began turning the crank.

Morita eased beside his commanding officer. "I'm sorry, sir. I forgot the spare radio."

Tomonaga wasn't listening. A faint hum was coming from the radio. He leaned closer and stared at the small red light above the dial. The cargo hold filled with blessed static.

Private Aikido looked at Tomonaga and grinned. "They were right, sir. It is the best in the world."

Tomonaga stared at the glowing light. "Can you reach Nanking?"

"Nanking?"

"Look at the good side, Private. We're sitting on the world's highest antenna."

Tomonaga reached into his torn parka and pulled out a small black notebook. He opened it to the first page and handed it to the young marine. "The frequency and emergency hailing code. Give it a shot, Private."

"Hai!" Aikido picked up the headset and slipped it over his ears. "I need some light."

Morita aimed the flashlight at Aikido's bandaged hand. "Be quick, Private. The batteries won't last long in this cold."

Tomonaga watched Aikido trace his finger across the symbols in the notebook. The young private lifted the microphone to his mouth and began reciting a methodical distress call to "Sanctuary."

Tomonaga edged toward the tarpaulin. He nodded for his sergeant to join him.

"I'm sorry about the radio, sir."

"Forget it, Sergeant. We are all shaken men today." Tomonaga placed his gloved hand on the frozen tarp. "We need to go out there."

"Sir?"

"If any of the canisters are salvageable, we need to find them before the snow buries them. We can use those metal rods in the debris. And our *hachimakis*. They'll be easy to spot in the morning." Tomonaga clutched his head and slumped against the fuselage wall.

Morita stared at him in disbelief. "Sir, that wind is over thirty knots. We're four miles up. It's suicide."

"So be it. Now help me with those rods."

"Major Tomonaga!"

Tomonaga turned and saw Aikido staring at him with stunned eyes. He staggered to the marine and knelt beside him.

Aikido pressed the headset against his ear. "I have one of the *Zeros*. He's relaying our message to Nanking!"

The marines broke into cheers, but Tomonaga waved them quiet.

Aikido lowered the microphone. "They're asking our position and condition."

Tomonaga took the mike from the private's trembling hand. He held it to his lips and spoke crisply. "This is Major Schinichiro Tomonaga. Position remains as given by co-pilot Fuchida. Most of cargo is salvageable. We have rations, but are badly injured. Please advise, over...."

Tomonaga took the headset from Aikido and slipped it over his ears. At first, there was nothing but static. "Turn the generator crank, Private. We need more power."

"We must be careful not to burn up the armature."

"Turn it, dammit!" Tomonaga shut his eyes and detected a faint voice through the static.

"Transports leaving Nanking with twenty-four Imperial Marines. Will refuel in Tibet and attempt northern approach. Anticipate landing in twenty-four to thirty-six hours. Use your radio for homing beacon. Activate in twenty-four hours so we can lock your position. Over...."

"Understood. Over...."

"Stand by...."

Tomonaga pressed the earpiece and waited.

"Impossible to reach your position from ground. Can you descend with cargo?"

The Tenth Avatar

Tomonaga looked down at his crippled arm. He held the mike to his lips and pressed the button. "Will descend. Over...."

The air crackled with static. He pressed the button again. "Awaiting rendezvous instructions. Over...."

"Descend ridge to glacier. Relief force will head southeast from landing spot until intercepting you on glacier. Use radio's homing signal on the hour. Over...."

"Understood. Over...."

"See you on glacier. Good luck, Major. Over and out...."

Tomonaga lowered the mike and stared at the marines. "Do we have any equipment?"

Morita nodded toward the pile of broken metal in the shadows. "Whatever we can salvage from that mess."

"They can't make it up here. We have to meet them on the glacier."

Morita forced a smile. "We have to climb down one way or another."

Tomonaga eyed the marines. "We can make it?"

The marines glanced at each other and nodded.

"Good. Then our only problem is finding a way to carry down the canisters." Tomonaga watched their jaws drop. "I know—but we have no choice. There is enough gold in those cylinders to win a war. We can't leave it behind."

Morita eased beside him and spoke softly. "Sir—there are only five of us. It's impossible."

Tomonaga's black eyes flared with anger. "We have no choice." He brushed past him and looked at the marines. "The Sergeant and I are going to search for the missing canisters. If we're not back in an hour, grab some flares and come after us."

Morita grabbed his arm. "Sir, we—"

"Get those rods, Sergeant."

Morita took a deep breath and stumbled into the wreckage. He dragged out five twisted metal rods and stormed past the shocked marines.

They were loosening the tarp when Private Aikido stood up and asked the obvious question. "Sir—how do we bring them down?"

Tomonaga flashed a painful smile. "I don't know. See if you can come up with an answer." He slipped through the tarp, followed by his reluctant sergeant.

It only took a few seconds to know the odds. The biting wind and thin air made it almost impossible to breathe. Tomonaga clutched his sergeant's parka and fought the dizziness sweeping over him. There was no light except Morita's hissing flare. Everything was pitch black. They could barely walk through the knee-deep snow. If hell had frozen over, this was it.

Morita grasped his commander's parka. "Give it up, sir. The flare is useless in this wind. If we lose track of the plane, we'll freeze to death out here."

"Save your breath and reel out that rope."

"But, sir—"

"Move!"

They'd gone a hundred feet when Tomonaga stopped and pointed into the blackness. "Do you see it?"

"Yes—but what is it?"

"Hurry."

"Wait, sir. It's coming from below the ridge. One slip and we've had it." Morita gasped for breath and followed his commander along the windswept ridge.

With the sub-zero wind ripping at their faces, the two crippled marines dropped on their stomachs and peered down at the flickering light.

Tomonaga pulled out his binoculars and pressed them against his goggles.

"Looks like a flare."

Tomonaga lowered the binoculars, his eyes filled with terror.

"What is it, sir?" Morita snatched the binoculars and peered through them. Tomonaga shook his head. "Gold, Sergeant. Brighter than the sun."

"Sir?"

"Come on—let's mark the damn thing and get back to the plane." Tomonaga pushed himself off the ground and headed down the slope, followed by his sergeant. One hundred feet below them, one of the canisters protruded from the snow, its protective metal cap torn away. From its open mouth, a greenish-white liquid bubbled into the snow, sending waves of glowing steam into the swirling blizzard.

The gods shuddered in the heavens. Time was very short....

35 | Face-to-Face

"Mind some company?"

Mariner pulled down his oxygen mask and stared at the bearded face peering up at him from the opened hatch.

"Thought I'd get some air."

"You're serious?"

"Just for a minute—if it's all right."

Mariner shrugged. "Hope you're wearing your woolies. It's bloody cold up here."

Bonaventure held up his gloved hands. "Even got on me mittens."

Mariner nodded at the empty co-pilot's seat and watched Bonaventure climb into it. "Fasten your belt and put on that oxygen mask. And use these." He handed his guest a set of goggles and ear plugs.

Bonaventure leaned back in the leather seat and buckled up. He loosened his hood and slipped on the goggles.

"Don't forget the ear plugs. The bloody engines will drive you mad."

"Won't be here that long." Bonaventure squinted at the vapor streaming off the windshield. "Where are we?"

"About twenty minutes from Pangpema. If you look to the right, you might catch a glimpse of Corporal Dawa's village. We're passing over the Tamur Valley."

Bonaventure poked his head over the edge of the open cockpit. He was about to turn away when he saw Dhoban flash through the haze. "I'll be damned. Never expected to see that again."

"You've been there?"

Bonaventure nodded and slumped in the seat.

Mariner pulled back the wheel and studied the approaching hills. "This is the tricky part. The terrain jumps rather quickly here."

"How high does this thing fly?"

Mariner smiled and pressed the throttles forward.

"Great. Now I know why Akaal's down there playing with

his beads."

"We'll be fine."

Bonaventure glanced at the compass. "Why Pangpema? We should head east to the Sikkim side and land near the Jongsong La. That's the safest route up."

Mariner shrugged. "You'd best discuss that with Corporal Dawa. My orders are to rendezvous with our contact in Pangpema and follow his instructions."

Bonaventure stared at the white peaks flashing through the haze. "Can you land in all that snow?"

"A bit sticky, but the skis work fine and the weather looks pretty decent ahead. Now if you'll excuse me, I have some radio work to do."

Bonaventure nodded and unbuckled his belt. He was crawling through the hatch when Mariner reached down and tapped his shoulder. "One question, Mr. Bonaventure."

"Yes?"

"Corporal Dawa said you're the very best."

"Did he now."

"I saw your little outburst at the airstrip. Can we pull this off?"

Bonaventure smiled and looked up at him. "It depends on the weather and choice of approach. If we try to attack the northwest face, all bets are off." He patted Mariner's wrist and disappeared through the hatch.

Akaal was still fumbling with his prayer beads when Bonaventure plunked down beside him. "Save your prayers for the mountain, old chum. We'll be landing in half an hour."

Akaal mumbled a final chant and stuffed the beads in his pocket.

"Did you see Dhoban?"

Akaal shook his head.

"What's eating you, chum? Maybe I can help."

"I don't think so."

"Try me. You're making me nervous."

Akaal looked at his friend. "This is very hard for me. I owe much to Major Pierce, but this is wrong. We don't belong here. The mountain is sacred. We've already been warned."

"I'm afraid it's a little late for remorse."

Akaal frowned and looked down. "I should have stopped you from coming."

"What—and have me miss all the fun?"

Akaal trained his black eyes on the mountaineer. "You're my friend. We've eaten from the same plate. Drunk from the same bowl."

"Don't forget smoking the same weed."

"I've put your life in danger. If anything happens to you, I'll take it to my grave."

Bonaventure smiled and slapped Akaal's knee. "I think you need a good woman." He started to get up, but Akaal grabbed his arm.

"Did you see how nervous Major Pierce was before we left. It's not like him. He's hiding something." Akaal glanced at Karen. "And that woman. Why is she here? She acts like a child playing with fire."

Bonaventure patted his friend's wrist. "You're just tired. You'll feel better when we land." He stood up and walked to the rear of the compartment where Karen was writing feverishly in a journal.

He sat beside her and waited for a reaction. Nothing—not even a raised eyebrow. Frustrated, he broke the silence. "Can we talk?"

"About?" She continued scribbling in the journal.

"Well—for openers why the hell did you insist on joining this suicide mission?"

Karen frowned and closed the journal. "I'm a reporter, Mr. Bonaventure. I think there's a story here. It's that simple."

"Can I ask you a question?"

"If it's the last one."

"When was the last time you stood at seventeen thousand?"

"That's my business."

Bonaventure glanced out the window. "Don't let those valleys fool you. We're climbing two hundred feet a minute."

"Planes do climb, Mr. Bonaventure." Karen picked up the pencil and twiddled it nervously.

"Have you noticed any lightheadedness? Maybe a skipped

breath or two?"

She shrugged.

"You're lying." He reached down and unclipped a rubber tube from the blue metal bottle under her seat. "Start using this." He held up the tube and turned a valve on the bottle.

She stuck the tube between her lips and took a few welcome gulps of oxygen.

"That's the way it works. You don't notice the deterioration until it's too bloody late. Pangpema's seventeen thousand feet above sea level. It takes a week for a novice to acclimate to that air. We don't have that long. If all goes as planned, we'll be at twenty-three thousand in a week. In case you're slow in math, that's a thousand feet a day. Almost five miles straight up." He smiled and leaned against her. "How are you going to pull that off, Miss Halberton?"

Karen's face reddened. She yanked the tube out of her mouth and glared at him. "Easy. A mountaineer named Bonaventure will guide me up there with tender loving care because it's in his best interest."

Bonaventure locked his blue eyes on her. "When I helped that shaken woman in Bombay, I never thought it would come to this. If you think I'm gonna risk five lives to drag a bloody egomaniac up a wall of ice for a bloody Pulitzer Prize, you've lost your marbles."

Karen brushed back a stray black hair and forced a smile. "You know—I owe you a lot for bringing me here. Whether you planned it or not, this could be the most important story of the decade. Maybe the century. If you were a reporter, you'd understand."

Bonaventure's face reddened. "Excuse me, but I think you've gotten a bit carried away with yourself."

"Have I now." Karen fought back her anger and flipped open the journal. "Before I left Major Pierce's office, he was kind enough to let me read your dossier. Quite a story, Mr. Bonaventure. A delinquent youth is befriended by a Swiss climber who adopts him and shows him the way. Over the next twenty years, the young man becomes the world's finest—and brashest mountaineer. But what drives him? Is it glory, or a deep hatred of the Royal Society that refuses to acknowledge him." Karen paused to let her words sink in. "And now that aging climber is at the end of his career. His reflexes aren't what they used to be. His nerves are worn. For Julian Bonaventure, there's only this final shot at glory leading a party of climbers up the one mountain he couldn't conquer." She closed the journal and stared at him. "You know—I just might write that story."

"I should have let that drunk have his way with you." Bonaventure stood up and walked away. He was about to sit beside Akaal when the cockpit hatch popped open and Sergeant Mariner's voice boomed through the compartment.

"Everyone buckle up and grab hold of something. I'm beginning our descent to Pangpema. We'll be landing on skis, so it could be a bit rough. Good luck."

Eammon pulled off his headset and looked at Roberto. "We better put on our weather gear."

"Did I hear you say Dharan?"

"Right."

Roberto's eyes brightened. "That's Corporal Dawa's post."

"Who?"

"A soldier I met on the train. He's stationed in Dharan."

"Small world." Eammon stood up and snatched his parka off a hook on the door.

Roberto walked into the prayer hall and slipped on his fur jacket and leggings. He was pulling on his hide boots when he heard Eammon's laughter.

"My Lord—you look like a two-legged yak. Where the hell did you pick up that garb?"

"My guide gave it to me."

"The one who abandoned you?"

Roberto ignored him and pulled up his hood."

"I'll see about getting you something to replace that smelly fur."

"Don't waste your time. I won't be here that long."

"Quiet." Eammon raised his hand and looked up at the sagging roof. "Hear it?"

"What?"

The Irishman rushed across the debris-covered floor and barged through the monastery's wood entrance doors. When Roberto caught up with him, he was standing on the ridge with a pair of binoculars over his eyes.

Eammon pointed at the broken clouds. "There! Coming right at us!"

"I don't see anything."

Eammon pulled out a flare gun and popped in a cartridge. He aimed the gun skyward and squeezed the trigger. The ridge echoed with a loud pop as the hissing flare exploded in a shower of red sparks.

"Good, there's hardly any wind." Eammon was too engrossed with the approaching aircraft to notice Roberto drop to his knees when the flare exploded. Guernica had left a scar that wouldn't heal.

Sergeant Mariner eased the *Vickers* into a steep right bank until its nose pointed directly at the sparkling flare. He was levelling off when the cockpit hatch popped open and Bonaventure sprung into the seat beside him.

"Hope you don't mind? I feel better with the wind on my face."

"My God, old chap. You damn near gave me a heart attack."

"Sorry. Last thing we want now. Anything I can do?"

"Buckle up and say a prayer. We're going in."

Mariner pulled back the throttles and stared at the approaching ridge. Five hundred feet. Three hundred. One hundred. The air erupted with blowing snow as the white carpet rushed at the windshield. Ice crystals ricocheted off Mariner's goggles.

"Now!" He cut the throttles and yanked back the wheel, lifting the *Vicker's* nose into a landing stall. For an instant, they seemed suspended in space, floating weightlessly above the white tundra, their faces peering at the blue sky.

The cockpit shook from a jarring impact as the twin skis slammed into the snow at a hundred miles an hour. Mariner clung to the rattling wheel and throttles, his eyes trained on the ridge. He could hear the skis sloshing through the snow. Blowing ice stung his face.

The jostling subsided as the *Vickers* slid to a stop only a few hundred feet from the sunlit ridge. Mariner gave the engines a final "rev" and shut them off. He took a deep breath and turned to his shaken passenger. "Pretty sticky—eh? Say old chap, you can let go of your knees now."

Bonaventure unlocked his frozen hands and took a breath of cold, rarified air. "Well done, Sergeant."

"Thank you, Mr. Bonaventure. Now it's your show." Mariner nodded at the two parka-clad figures scrambling down the ridge. "I believe that's our welcoming party."

Ten years of field experience had taught Eammon Collins the importance of sizing up his prey. He shuffled toward the plane's nose and watched its five passengers climb down the ramp into the snow.

It only took a few seconds to conclude that an automatic weapon would be needed to dispatch the four men "en masse." Unfortunately, the odds dictated they be shot in the back. It was important the young reporter be spared long enough to squeeze out the logbook's location. Once confirmed by radio communication with Bombay, he would end her misery with a shot to the head. Then, a quick burial and—

He glanced at Roberto. He'd almost forgotten the painful part. His gentle friend from Spain would be the hardest kill of all. If the fool had only stayed away.

"Corporal Dawa!" Roberto rushed forward and grasped Akaal's arm. "I can't believe it's you."

Akaal's jaw dropped. He stared at Roberto in shock.

Roberto smiled and shook the Gurkha's hand. "If I'd known this was going to happen, I would have gone with you."

Akaal nodded and forced a smile. "The gods work in strange ways. I'm glad you're safe."

"We have a lot to talk about."

"As you wish." Akaal shouldered his pack and backed away.

Roberto extended his hand to Bonaventure and hesitated. "I'm sorry, haven't we met?"

"Can't say I recall." Bonaventure shook his hand. "Bonaventure—Julian Bonaventure."

"Roberto Santiago. I'm sure we've met before. Bombay perhaps?"

"Don't think so."

Eammon pulled off a glove and stepped forward. "Pleasure to meet you, Mr. Bonaventure."

Bonaventure grasped his hand. "You're?"

"Eammon Collins."

"Ah—the mysterious contact."

Eammon laughed and shrugged his shoulders. "I'm just a radioman in a deep freeze. Nothing very glamorous, I'm afraid." He brushed past Bonaventure and extended his hand to Karen. "You must be Miss Halberton."

Karen clasped his hand. "Pleasure, Mr. Collins. I trust you're our man in Pangpema?"

"You make it sound so dramatic."

"Good copy, Mr. Collins. Good copy...."

Eammon greeted his other three guests and gestured toward the ridge. "I have a warm fire going. Please bring what you need and follow me. We can talk after you settle in."

Sergeant Mariner flipped his pack over his shoulder. "We're carrying what we need, sir. No sense lugging the climbing equipment up there. I'll just shroud the plane and join the rest of you in a few minutes." He glanced at Nemi. "Come on, Private. Four hands are better than two."

Nemi nodded and followed the sergeant up the ramp while Eammon led his guests toward the five hundred foot slope leading to the monastery.

They were halfway up the slope when Akaal hesitated and pointed toward a line of dark clouds on the southern horizon. "I don't like that sky. One good blast of wind from the Bay of Bengal and we'll be buried up here."

Keep moving, old chum." Bonaventure patted his friend on the back and marched up the slope behind him.

They were nearly to the monastery when Bonaventure

heard a yell. He looked down and saw Roberto kneeling next to Karen's crumpled body. "Damn." He scrambled down the snow-covered slope and dropped beside her.

"We were talking and she collapsed." Roberto looked at Bonaventure with concerned eyes.

"I warned her, dammit."

"Warned?"

"Altitude's got her. Come on—let's get her out of this cold."

They carried her into the monastery and placed her on the cot in the radio room. Eammon poured a shot of whiskey and touched the cup to her lips. "Try this, Miss Halberton. I'm afraid you have a touch of altitude sickness."

Karen blinked and looked up at him. She grabbed the cup and gulped down the burning whiskey. Coughing violently, she handed Eammon the empty cup. "Another...."

Bonaventure eased beside the cot and watched Eammon pour a second shot of whiskey. He started to speak, but she cut him off.

"I'll be fine. Just a little lightheaded."

"I'd go easy on that liquor."

Karen looked up at him and smiled. "See what I mean about tender loving care?"

Bonaventure wasn't in the mood for repartee. "Listen to me, dammit. You're on the edge of hypoxia. Your body's starved for oxygen. If you get any worse, we'll have to fly you back to Dharan."

She ignored him and snatched the whiskey out of Eammon's outstretched hand. "When do we climb, Mr. Collins?" She chugged the whiskey and fell back on the pillow.

Eammon rested a hand on her forehead. "I'm afraid Mr. Bonaventure is right. It's six thousand feet to the ridge where the plane crashed. Maybe you should stay here with my friend until we get back."

Bonaventure looked at Eammon in surprise. "You're going too?"

"I've climbed."

"Where?"

"The Alps."

"Alps? That's like an ant hill compared to this."

Eammon's face reddened. "You better get some rest, Mr. Bonaventure. We're leaving at sunrise."

"What if Akaal's right about the weather?"

"We have no choice. It's been twenty-four hours since the plane went down. Another blizzard will bury anything that's up there."

"If the last one didn't do the job." Bonaventure walked to the stove and rubbed his hands over the coals.

Eammon watched Karen's eyes flutter, and close. "Good—just what the doctor ordered." He took the empty cup from her hand and sat down at the radio. "How's the fire?"

Bonaventure glanced at Karen. "I think we should talk."

"Talk?"

"I need to know who's leading this fiasco."

Eammon poured a shot of whiskey and gulped it down. "I'm responsible for the mission, but I have no problem with you leading the climb."

Bonaventure rubbed the seat of his pants and nodded. "Then Miss Halberton goes back in the morning."

Eammon shrugged. "I sympathize with your feelings, but I'm afraid that's not my choice."

Bonaventure stared at the Irishman. "Who are you kidding? I may not be the world's brightest chap, but I know where power lies. You're running this show, Mr. Collins."

"I told you, I'm just a radioman." Eammon handed his guest the whiskey bottle and watched him take a swig. "How much do you know about the mission?"

"Damn little. Akaal told me the bloody plane carried an important cargo."

Eammon leaned back in the chair and took a deep breath. "I don't expect you to understand, but it's critical we recover that cargo."

Bonaventure wasn't listening. His eyes had focused on the photographs above the radio. "That's the Matterhorn, isn't it?"

"What?"

"In the picture."

"Oh—that. Yes—I climbed there last year."

"My home was near the Matterhorn."

"Was?"

"Before the scum took it away from me. Now, it's just a memory."

Eammon rested an arm on the table. He frowned and ran his finger along the telegraph key. "Did Pierce show you the telegram concerning your chalet?"

Bonaventure looked up in surprise. "You know about that?"

"I arranged the deal."

"You?"

"You're right about power, Mr. Bonaventure. I'm the one who decides if the mission is successful. That means your chalet is in my hands. I could use your help up there, but I won't beg for it. Just don't expect any favors in return."

Bonaventure put the whiskey bottle on the table. "Well, at least you're frank."

"Good—then we have an understanding. I'll expect you in full gear at sunrise. Otherwise, your chalet remains Swiss Army property."

Bonaventure walked to the cot. He leaned over and placed his fingers on Karen's wrist. "What about her?"

"Before you left Dharan, Miss Halberton reached a rather tenuous agreement with Major Pierce."

"Agreement?"

"In exchange for her promise to return some missing property, we let her join the mission."

Bonaventure stiffened. "You're helping her commit suicide."

"If Miss Halberton chooses to climb the mountain, it's her decision—understood?"

"Go to bloody hell." Bonaventure stormed out of the radio room.

Akaal watched his friend rush past the firepit below the altar. "What's wrong?"

"I need some fresh air." Bonaventure snatched his gloves

off the floor and pushed through the wooden doors into the chilled daylight.

Roberto picked up a stick and poked the coals. "Your friend seems upset."

"I don't think he likes your friend."

"Hmmm."

Akaal fell back on the blanket and looked up at the statue of Buddha. "The mountains are the only world my friend knows. Soon, he must give them up. It will be hard for him."

"Health?"

Akaal sat up on his elbow and stared at Roberto. "Mountaineering is a harsh battle, best fought by the young. After twenty years of glory, my friend has lost his passion."

Roberto gazed at the fire. "Is Mr. Bonaventure a religious man?"

"Better you ask him."

Roberto nodded and pushed off the floor. "Maybe I'll get some fresh air too."

Akaal watched Roberto slip on his fur parka. "You look like one of us."

"I consider that a compliment, Corporal Dawa."

"You've even adapted to the thin air. That's a good sign."

"Is it?"

"May I ask how you met Mr. Collins?"

"That's a long story, Corporal."

"I'm sorry. It's not my business."

Roberto picked his gloves off the floor. "We met in Switzerland last year. I was searching for something and thought I'd found it."

"You sound disappointed."

"I guess you could say that."

Akaal stared at the coals. "How long will you stay?"

"I don't know. Maybe I'll go back with you." Roberto glanced at Mariner's and Nemi's sprawled bodies. "It looks like your two companions are out cold."

"They're smarter than me. Tomorrow will be very hard."

"Can I ask you something, Corporal?"

"Yes?"

"On the train, I remember you telling me your village wasn't far from here."

Akaal smiled. "That depends on one's condition. Dobhan is forty miles to the southwest."

Roberto was about to speak when Eammon walked out of the radio room and knelt beside the fire. "How are you feeling, Corporal Dawa?"

"Nothing like a warm fire, Mr. Collins."

"Mind if I join you?"

"It's your monastery." Akaal smiled and glanced at the radio room. "How is the young lady?"

"She's asleep. We'll know better in the morning." Eammon looked up at Roberto. "Going somewhere?"

"I thought I'd join Mr. Bonaventure for some fresh air."

Eammon glared at Roberto. "I'd be careful out there. This isn't the Pyrenees."

Roberto frowned and stepped to the doors. He grasped the splintered handle and looked back at Akaal. "Have you ever met a man named Karak?"

"Karak?"

"That was my guide's name."

"Did he mention his village?"

"No—he just walked away and disappeared in the haze."

"Which direction?"

Roberto hesitated. "Toward the mountain."

Akaal stroked his chin. "I've not heard that name, but there is a tale among the villagers about a shaman who lives on the mountain. Some say he's a descent of the gods, sent to earth to protect their treasures on the five peaks. Others talk of a madman who lives on the Kangchenjunga glacier. They say he guards the mountain to protect his sister's spirit."

"Sister?"

"That's all I know."

"And no one has ever seen him?"

"They say he's like a shadow—a wanderer who practices the mystic arts. No one wants to see him. It is bad luck to spy on the gods."

"Then you believe he exists?"

"I believe I am very tired." Akaal fell back on the blanket and closed his eyes.

Eammon stood up and brushed off his pants. "Remember what I said. Don't wander too far. It gets dark early and you never know what might be out there." He turned and walked back to the radio room.

36 | *A Little Chat*

Bonaventure studied the fur-covered figure shuffling toward him. The intruder looked more like a Himalayan brown bear than a human being.

"Mind if I join you?"

"Looks like you already have."

Roberto slapped his arms against his chest. "*Mi dios*, it's cold."

"It's a bit chilly."

"I've never been so cold."

"Try some of this." Bonaventure held out a small metal flask and watched the Spaniard take a sip.

"It tastes like Napoleon brandy."

"Ah—a connoisseur. Nothing but the best when you're three miles up." Bonaventure took the flask from Roberto's outstretched hand and stuffed it in his pocket.

"Sorry about Eammon."

"Sorry?"

'I saw you walk out on him."

"Oh—that." Bonaventure shook his head. "Your friend's a real charmer."

"I had to get out too. He's changed since I met him."

Bonaventure eyed the face beneath the fur hood. "Are you still trying to remember me?"

"No—I gave up on that. I must have confused you with someone."

"It happens. Say—that's quite a pile of fur. What was it before you squeezed the trigger?"

Roberto spread his arms and looked down at the scraggly parka and leggings. "My guide gave it to me. I guess it looks a little odd."

Bonaventure bit his lip to keep from laughing. He shuffled beside the Spaniard and stroked the parka's thick fur. "Can I ask you something?"

"Yes?"

"You won't take offense?"

Roberto shrugged.

"What the hell are you doing up here?"

A frown swept across Roberto's face. "I won't be here long."

"You said your name was Roberto?"

"Yes."

"You're a long way from home, señor."

"Yes—a long way."

"Why?"

"Difficult question."

"Take your time. I'm curious why a man would cross half the world to end up with a bloke like Collins."

Roberto looked down at the snow. "I'd rather hear about you. Sounds like you've had an interesting life."

"Who told you that?"

"Your friend."

"Blast—don't listen to him. He always exaggerates. Besides—I asked you first. And it is my brandy." He reached into his pocket and pulled out the flask.

Roberto eyed the brandy. "I'm from Valencia."

"Ah—best oranges in the world."

"You like oranges?"

"Wish I had one now instead of this damned rice."

"Do you mind?" Roberto reached out and snatched the flask from Bonaventure's hand.

"Go ahead, I have more."

Roberto popped the cap and took a sip. "I left Spain two years ago."

"The war?"

"And other things." Roberto took another sip and looked at the setting sun.

"Snap out of it, dammit!"

Karen squinted at the dark figure crouching over her. She gasped and cowered against the wall.

"Calm down. It's me—Collins."

She stared at the white-haired man peering down at her. "Mr. Collins?"

"It's all right. Just relax."

She slumped on the cot and rubbed her forehead. "What time is it?"

"A little after seven. You were having a nightmare. Something about your father. I tried to wake you, but you wouldn't come out of it. Really had me worried."

She tugged on her sweater. "It's stifling in here. Can't you open a window or something?"

Eammon shook his head. "I wish it was that easy. I'm afraid the altitude's gotten to you."

She took a painful breath and looked up at him. "I'll be all right. Just need some fresh air."

Eammon slipped into the chair beside her. "I think we better talk."

"Talk?"

"He stroked his stubbled chin. "You have me concerned, Miss Halberton. Our little deal doesn't include your premature death. I think it would be better if you stay behind. I'll be happy to share my findings with you. If you like, I'll even take some photos of the crashed plane."

Karen glared at him. She gripped his parka and pulled herself up until their noses were almost touching. "If I don't climb that mountain, your little book will end up on the front page of every newspaper in the world. Is that what you want?"

Eammon's green eyes flashed with anger. He pried her hand loose and watched her fall back on the pillow. "You don't seem to understand. You're dying, Miss Halberton. We can't have that just now."

She closed her eyes and felt the room spinning. His sobering words rang in her ears....

Akaal was half asleep when Eammon tapped his arm. "Where are they?"

"What?"

"Bonaventure and my friend?"

Akaal sat up and looked at the two empty sleeping bags beside the firepit. "They must still be out there."

Eammon glared at him. "Not very smart, Corporal. I'm

relying on you to keep things under control."

"I'm sorry, Mr. Collins."

"Come on—it's time to tighten the reins."

Akaal scrambled off the floor and followed the Irishman into the biting cold.

They were about to head down the slope when Eammon spotted them standing next to the shrouded *Vickers*. "Well—isn't that cute."

"Sir?"

"Go back to sleep, Corporal. I'll take care of it." He brushed past Akaal and stormed down the slope.

Bonaventure flicked his cigaret in the snow and leaned back against the *Vicker's* fuselage. "That's quite a story."

"There are many stories from the war. I'm just one of them."

"No—yours is special. There's only one problem."

"Problem?"

"You talk like someone with deep resolve. Anyone who would give up so much is either a saint or a lunatic."

"I'm neither, Mr. Bonaventure."

Bonaventure glanced at the mountain. "I'll put it this way. I've climbed for twenty-two years. Along the way, I stumbled a few times, but I always got up and kept climbing."

Roberto shrugged. "Not surprising. You seem a determined man."

Bonaventure locked his blue eyes on him. "It's deeper than that, old chum. I didn't want to betray myself. Or my friends. Which leads to my problem."

"Yes?"

"Your actions don't match your words. You talk like a patriot, but that's where it ends."

"Ends?"

Bonaventure folded his arms. "To be blunt, it sounds like you walked away when your country needed you most. When you might have made a difference."

Roberto couldn't speak. He clenched his fists and backed away in shock.

"What's wrong?"

"That's enough!" Roberto glared at the man standing in front of him—and he suddenly remembered. He *had* seen him before. At Victoria Terminus the night he escaped from Bombay. An innocent bump that nearly became a brawl. He disliked him then—but he hated him now.

"Are you all right?"

"Damn you!"

Bonaventure raised his open hands. "Sorry—no offense meant. I guess I got a little carried away."

"You have no right to judge me."

Bonaventure forced a smile. "Watch that brandy, old chum. It's pretty strong."

Roberto looked down at the flask in his hand. He took a deep breath and rubbed his bearded chin with the back of his glove.

"Maybe we should call it a night. We both need sleep." Bonaventure started to walk away, but the Spaniard seized his arm.

"You think I'm afraid to die? I love Spain more than my life."

"Then go back and fight for it. Make your life worth something."

Roberto dug his fingers into Bonaventure's arm. "You think it's that easy? I did fight, and damn near died. But it didn't matter. The fools destroyed themselves. They slashed Spain's wrists and watched her bleed to death."

Bonaventure's patience was running thin. He tried to pull his arm away, but the Spaniard's grip was like iron. "I suggest you let go of my arm."

Roberto released his grip and backed away. "There's something I haven't told you. Something you should know."

"We'll finish this another time."

"No—we'll finish it now."

The mountaineer restrained himself. "Well?"

Roberto took a swig of brandy and slumped against the fuselage. "Before my country went up in flames, I saw it destroyed in a vision."

Bonaventure shrugged. "Just your imagination running wild. Not unusual after what you've been through. I've seen it happen to others."

Roberto glared at him. "I had the vision ten years ago."

"Ten?"

"Since that day, I've been haunted by someone—or something—that keeps warning me time is short." Roberto pulled off his glove and rubbed his forehead. "I've carried this damn thing inside me for ten years. I've lost everything I ever loved. My father. My home. My woman. Even my country. And I still don't have the answer. For God's sake, why doesn't it leave me alone!"

Bonaventure stared at the Spaniard in disbelief. "Blast—the thin air's got you. You need a shot of oxygen."

Roberto shook his head. "I hear voices—and see things I can't explain."

"Come on—let's get that oxygen."

"Last week, an Indian told me I'm supposed to fight a holy war up here."

"I see. Well—how about that."

"Listen to me, dammit! When I had my vision, an eight foot crucifix bled from the hands and feet. When chemists checked the blood, they found it was universal. Do you know what that means? It was the blood of all men. The blood of Christ!"

Bonaventure snatched the flask out of Roberto's hand and took a swig. He rubbed his mouth with the back of his hand. "Well—we all have our little moths in the closet."

"You think I'm crazy, don't you?"

"Maybe a bit eccentric. It's this damn thin air. Have some more brandy." He handed him the flask and watched him finish it.

"Can I tell you something, Mr. Bonaventure?"

"Why stop now."

"After ten years of searching, I think it's come."

"What?"

Roberto shook his head. "I can't explain it, but since your plane landed, I've had this feeling that—"

"Mr. Bonaventure!"

Bonaventure glanced over Roberto's shoulder and saw Eammon shuffling toward them. "Well—speaking of bad visions. Sorry, old chum, looks like we'll have to pick up this up another time."

Eammon barged between them and glared at Bonaventure. "I thought we had an understanding."

Bonaventure restrained himself. "We do, except for Miss Halberton."

"She won't be going. Now please get some sleep. We're leaving at sunrise."

Bonaventure raised an eyebrow and glanced at Roberto. "Guess it's bedtime." He turned and shuffled toward the slope, followed by Collins and the inebriated Spaniard.

They were nearly to the monastery when Bonaventure paused and looked toward the moonlit mountain. A deep rumble was coming from the south.

Eammon edged beside him. "Is it from the mountain?"

"No way of knowing."

The Irishman listened to the rumble fade. "Can we make it?"

Bonaventure stared at the glowing peak. "Two months ago, Corporal Dawa and I led a team up the route taken by Dyrhenfurth's 1930 party. Like him, we believed the northwest face was the fastest way to the top. We were right except for one minor detail—the same one Dyrhenfurth overlooked." He hesitated and looked down. "We were at twenty five thousand when a wall of ice broke off the summit just above us. We lost two good men that day—two more notches in the mountain god's banner."

Eammon forced a smile. "You don't believe that poppycock?"

"I don't know what to believe."

"Get some sleep." Eammon marched up the slope.

The sun was still below the eastern ridges when four weary climbers shuffled down the snow-covered slope toward the *Vickers*. Mariner and Nemi pulled back the frost-covered shroud and climbed through the front hatch into the aircraft's frigid interior. Cursing the extreme cold, they dropped climbing gear into the snow while Bonaventure and Akaal sorted through the pile of ropes, pitons, belts, and axes. It took them an hour to skillfully arrange the hodgepodge into five taut packs.

Inside the monastery, Eammon was feverishly stepping through the radio procedures with Roberto.

"Call me every three hours, starting at noon today. I'll give you our position and condition for relay to Dharan. Write everything down. Don't rely on memory. Short transmissions, got it?"

Roberto nodded.

"Forward my messages to Dharan every evening at twenty-one hundred. That's the best time for transmission." Eammon nodded at a sealed envelope beside the radio. "If anything goes wrong, send them that message. Clear?"

Roberto glanced at the cot. "What about her?"

"Rest, water, and oxygen. Easy on the food."

"What if she gets worse?"

"She'll be all right. Just keep her on that cot until we get back." Eammon slipped on his parka. "Well—that's it. See you in three weeks."

Roberto was about to follow Eammon out of the room when he heard a weak cry. He turned around in disbelief. The young reporter was sitting on the edge of the cot, trying to pull on her boots. "What are you doing?"

"They're not going without me."

"You can't go out there."

"Watch me." She stood up and staggered into his arms. "Let go of me, you idiot. Who do you think you are?"

"Please, Miss Halberton. You're not well. You need rest."

"Take your filthy hands off me!" She grabbed her head and slumped against him.

He guided her back to the cot and eased her down. She collapsed on the cot, gasping for breath.

"I'm really sorry about this."

"Damn you."

He poured some water on a cloth and tried to press it against her forehead, but she pushed his hand away. "Please—I'm trying to help you."

"Go to hell."

He looked down at her and sighed. "You'll feel better after you sleep. I'll be outside if you need me. I'm sorry, Miss Halberton." He covered her with a blanket and backed away. It would be a hard three weeks.

He slipped through the door and rushed across the prayer hall. He was nearly to the entrance doors when Bonaventure barged through them, dressed in full pack.

"How is she?"

Roberto shook his head. "About a breath from total panic. I may have to tie her down."

Bonaventure dropped his pack on the floor. "Can you handle it?"

Roberto rubbed the back of his neck. "I'll manage. I have the radio if anything happens."

Bonaventure cracked a smile. "Sorry about last night."

"Forgotten."

He patted Roberto's shoulder and walked into the radio room.

"How are you feeling, Reuters?"

She looked up at him with bloodshot eyes. "I'm going up there."

"Well—you've got twenty-four hours."

"What?"

"Bloody weather stopped us cold. We're only exploring the glacier today."

Her eyes widened. "You're not going up?"

"You've got a day to heal." Bonaventure reached down and snatched a blue oxygen bottle. "Breathe some of this every few minutes. Slow, deep breaths—got it?"

Karen nodded and rested her hand on the bottle.

"There's another bottle on the floor if you need it. Well—that's about it. We've got a lot of ground to cover before dark. Take care of yourself." Bonaventure patted her shoulder and tried to stand, but she grabbed his arm.

"Thank you for caring, Mr. Bonaventure." She pulled herself up and kissed him on the lips.

"Well—how about that." Bonaventure stood up and walked into the prayer hall.

"Good luck, Mr. Bonaventure."

Bonaventure smiled at the Spaniard. "You're the one who needs the luck. You have the worst job of all."

Roberto nodded and glanced at the radio room. "I gave her some oxygen. It should help."

"Won't you need it up there?"

"We have enough. Besides, I have to keep my reckless reputation." Bonaventure grabbed Roberto's arm and leaned against him. "She has ears like a hawk. I told her we're only exploring the glacier today. It's easier that way."

"I understand."

Bonaventure was halfway out the door when Roberto called out to him. "I'm sorry we didn't have a chance to finish our talk."

"Well finish when I get back."

"Can I ask you a question?"

"Go ahead."

"How can a man with your reputation stop halfway up a mountain?"

Bonaventure flashed a smile. "Good question. I'll have to think about it."

It took two hours for the team to trek across the moraine of broken rock and ice leading to the glacier. A light snow was falling when they finally planted their snowshoes on firm ice.

Bonaventure leaned on his ski pole and looked at Eammon. "Is this where we pass the torch?"

"It's all yours, Mr. Bonaventure. You have the point until we reach the plane."

Bonaventure stepped forward and gave Eammon's straps a violent tug. "Then tighten that pack before you lose it." He stepped back and watched the stunned Irishman adjust his straps.

Bonaventure knelt down and pulled a map out of his

anorak. He unfolded it on the ice and nodded for the small team to huddle around him. "I'll only explain this once, so listen closely."

He pointed to the two red triangles below Pangpema. "The fastest route to the north ridge is around those twin peaks in front of us. Unfortunately, it's the most dangerous."

He paused to let his words sink in. "It'll take a week to reach Kangchenjunga's west wall. We'll be exposed to avalanches every step of the way. When we reach the wall, we'll be at twenty thousand. From there, it's three thousand feet to the ridge crest—most of it straight up."

Eammon backed away in shock. "You're saying it'll take more than a week to reach the plane?"

"If we're lucky."

Eammon's face reddened. "By that time, the damn thing could be buried under ten feet of snow."

"Sorry, it's our best shot. When we reach the west wall, we'll be fully acclimated and ready for a strong push to the crest. We'll also have gained three thousand feet, so the climb will be cut in half. Weather permitting, we should reach your plane in twelve days."

Eammon's eyes filled with anger. "Unacceptable, Mr. Bonaventure."

Bonaventure folded the map and stuffed it in his pocket. He stood up and stared at the Irishman. "It was your decision to launch from Pangpema. If we'd started at Jongsong La, I could have saved us a few days."

Eammon restrained himself. "What about climbing over the twin peaks instead of going around them?"

Bonaventure shook his head. "You're welcome to try, old chum. Only three thousand grueling feet up and three thousand treacherous feet down. What's left of you gets to scale Kangchenjunga's west wall. You'll be lucky to make the first leg."

"Damn!" Eammon flung his glove in the snow.

"Sorry, that's the way you dealt the cards." Bonaventure started to turn away and hesitated. "Almost forgot. For the next few days, we'll be hiking over broken ice slashed with crevasses—most of them concealed. One wrong move and we're dead."

Eammon glared at him.

Bonaventure nodded toward the south. "That band of clouds can sweep over us anytime and dump a load of snow on our heads. That'll increase the avalanche risk when we trek around the twin peaks."

"Enough!"

Bonaventure ignored him and looked up at the haze. "With that soup hanging over us, you'll have to depend on your ears. If you hear a groaning or clicking sound, it's just the glacier moving. But if the sound becomes a rumble, run for your life because the bloody mountain's coming down on your head."

Eammon clenched his trembling fists. His face had turned bright red.

"Questions?" Bonaventure studied the frozen faces. "Good—then let's get this over with." He yanked his ski pole out of the ice and headed toward the twin peaks, followed by his four shaken comrades.

Had Bonaventure looked a little deeper into the haze, he might have spotted the reflection of a rifle barrel pointed at his heart. Twice, Karak had placed his finger on the trigger and applied pressure, only to release it when a gust of snow blocked his aim.

He watched the five man column shuffle toward the twin peaks. Soon, they would reach the mountain's north ridge and begin the climb to his sister's sanctuary on the peak of the rising sun—to defile her spirit a second time.

He stood up and slung the *Enfield* over his shoulder. Time was short. He'd cut across the high passes and beat them to the wall. When they came within range, he'd pick them off like stray goats.

He turned and headed up the glacier. The morning sun had turned the mountains yellow-white. Soon, that color would be blood-red.

Roberto touched the rubber tube to her lips. "Breathe deeply, Miss Halberton. You'll feel better after this." He turned the valve and heard a faint hiss.

She blinked and looked up at him. "When are they coming back?"

"In a few hours. You still have time. Please—breathe some oxygen."

She took a few weak breaths and dropped off to sleep.

He closed the valve and slipped the tube out of her mouth. She looked so peaceful—so calm. In a few hours, she'd awaken to the bitter news they'd gone up without her. He sighed and shook his head. Maybe tying her down wasn't a bad idea.

He grasped her wrist and felt for a pulse. It seemed slower, more relaxed and stable. He glanced at his watch. The hour and minute hands were frozen on ten-forty. He squinted at the military clock on the table. It read twelve-fifteen.

"Damn." He rushed to the table and flipped on the power switch. The amber dial brightened as a soft hum filled the room. He slipped on the headset and leaned close to the microphone. "Are you there, White Lion?" He flipped the transmission switch and turned up the volume.

Eammon's voice was barely audible above the crackling static. *"Idiot! You're fifteen minutes late! Do you want me to drain my power?"*

"Sorry, Lion. Won't happen again. Over."

"Bad news. It looks like a four week trip instead of three. Our position is...."

Roberto pressed the headset to his ear and scribbled down Eammon's coordinates. He flipped the transmission switch and leaned close to the microphone. "Understood. Two weeks to plane. Two weeks to return. Will advise Dharan. Over and out."

He turned off the power and glanced at the military clock. The next transmission would come at fifteen hundred hours. Time enough to get some rest.

He pushed out of the chair and leaned over the sleeping woman. Her breathing had become more relaxed. A good sign. He looked down at her and smiled. She was so beautiful. So much like Ana. God—he missed her. He missed them all.

He shuffled into the prayer hall and collapsed on the sleeping bag beside the firepit. The last thing he remembered was the Buddha staring down at him from the shadows. He dropped into a deep sleep—unaware that his words had been overheard by a very determined reporter.

She climbed out of the cot and steadied herself against the table. The dizziness was intense, but a few sips of oxygen cleared her head.

She stepped to the door and peered into the prayer hall. It appeared deserted except for the Buddha's shadow on the wall.

She crept past the altar and froze. The Spaniard was lying on the floor beside the firepit. He appeared to be asleep. She studied him for a moment before backing away.

She retreated into the radio room and closed the door. A pot of rice was stewing on the grate above the stove. She spooned it into a bowl and wolfed it down. The warm rice felt good spilling into her stomach. She sipped some water from her canteen and dropped into the chair facing the radio.

Roberto's scribbled note lay beside the microphone. She picked it up and scanned the words. Her eyes darted to the opened map. The pencilled "X" below Pangpema matched the coordinates in the note.

She glanced at the military clock. Twelve-fifty. They were nearly four hours ahead of her, but the note indicated they would camp soon because of an approaching storm. By leaving now, she might reach them before sunset.

She folded the map and stuffed it in her pocket. A few gulps of oxygen and she was ready. She slipped on her parka and leggings. Then the boots. She filled the canteen with water from the tank and clipped it to her belt. A quick check of the compass and flares, and the pack was on her back. She clipped the unused oxygen bottle to her belt and glanced at the clock. Thirteen hundred hours. Not a moment to lose. She stepped toward the door. If she could just get past her sleeping guard, she'd be on her way.

She eased into the prayer hall and crept along the wall. He stirred when she went by, but quickly dropped back to sleep. Only a few more feet. With her eyes trained on him, she reached out with her left hand and felt it scrape against the wood door. She groped for the handle, and heard her father's terrifying words....

You stupid bitch! I told you to get whiskey, not bourbon! You can't even read, you good-for-nothing little whore! If your mother was alive, I'd walk out of here tomorrow! You're goddamn lucky I'm willing to put up with you, you little tramp! Now go to bed before I use my strap on you. I'll be in later....

The filthy bastard. She hated him more than the Japanese interrogator who had tortured her in Nanking. If there was a hell, may he be roasting in it.

She pushed against the door and hesitated. A beam of sunlight radiated through a crack in the roof, striking the Buddha's face. She looked up at Him and felt a rush of cold air against her face. It was like a soothing wave, washing away the pain. Her father's bitter words faded away. The years of torment and prostitution. The Halbertons and Connecticut. Frank Gerramino and Times Square. A husband's love and death. Her apartment on the East River. Hessler and *Reuters*. The *China Clipper*. The dark cell in Nanking. All of it faded away.

In that instant, Karen Halberton knew her time had come. Glory was only a few miles away. She could see it jutting through the clouds. A white citadel towering over a petty world. Kangchenjunga—fortress of the gods. Story of the century. This wasn't the end. It was the beginning. Nothing would stop her now. She brushed away a tear and stepped into the sunlight.

37 | Desperation

They'd spent the day dragging cable and spare parts from the wreckage. Tough building a winch at twenty-three thousand, but it was their only hope. With the rescue force only hours away, they had to pull off a miracle. If they could reach the ledge below the ridge crest, they'd camp there tonight and begin their descent at sunrise. There was only one problem. They had to bring down a ton of metal.

Tomonaga let go of the cable and stumbled backward. He clutched his throbbing ribs and watched the four marines secure the final restraining wire to the winch.

"That's the best we can do, sir." Morita rested his hands on his knees and nodded toward the three cables anchoring the winch to the tail section.

"How much cable on the winch?"

"About two hundred feet."

"That's all we have?"

"Yes, sir"

"It's not enough."

Morita pointed down the slope. "We'll lower the canisters to those rocks. That's about two hundred feet. Then we'll disconnect the cable from the winch and drag it down with us. We'll anchor the cable to the rocks and re-use it to lower the canisters the rest of the way. That should do the job."

"You make it sound simple."

"It is—except for one thing." Morita eyed the metal canisters lying in the snow. They'd spent two hours lugging them out of the cargo hold, and another two linking them together with chain. "The winch can't hold that weight. We'll have to leave some of them behind."

Tomonaga glared at him. "We've already lost five. The rest come down with us."

Morita glanced at the black clouds closing from the south. A wind had picked up, sending swirls of snow across the ridge. He edged closer to avoid the marines hearing him. "Better to salvage half the cargo than lose it all."

Tomonaga's eyes flashed with anger. "If any of those canisters stay up here, we stay with them—understood?"

"Yes, sir."

Tomonaga turned toward the marines. "We need to get that gasoline in the generator before it freezes. Then we'll climb off this damned mountain and go home. Now move!"

Shaken by their commander's sudden tirade, the exhausted marines scrambled to their feet and began rolling a dented, red drum toward the winch. It was the only gasoline drum that had survived the crash. The others had broken loose on impact, tumbling through the severed bulkhead into the nose section's fiery wreckage.

It only took a minute to siphon the rust-colored fuel into the generator's tank. Morita grabbed the starter cord and gave it a yank. The generator coughed, and sputtered. "Thin the mixture. The damn thing can't breathe."

Ishikawa twisted the carburetor screw and backed away. He watched the sergeant rewind the cord and yank it a second time. Then a third.

"Let me try, Sergeant." Ishikawa snatched the cord and coiled it around the starter. "I used to repair motors. You have to be firm with these things." He spit on his glove and gripped the rope. "Come on you piece of shit!" He yanked the rope and fell backward.

The generator coughed and chugged to life amidst a round of cheers. The air smelled from burning gasoline.

Tomonaga patted Ishikawa's shoulder and shuffled beside the canisters. "Let's get these little beauties over the edge before the motor stalls in this thin air. Man the winch, Sergeant."

Morita shuffled beside the winch and grasped the shift lever. He watched his comrades drag the first four canisters to the edge of the ridge.

Tomonaga rested his boot against the first canister and looked back at his sergeant. "Ready, Morita?"

"Hai!"

Tomonaga pressed his boot against the canister and shoved it over the edge. It slid a few feet and jerked against the chain anchoring it to number two. He backed away and gestured to Ishikawa. "Over the side, Corporal."

"Hai!" Ishikawa shoved the second canister off the ridge. He watched its chain stiffen as it lined up behind number one.

Nomura and Aikido followed with number's three and four. The four canisters slid a short distance before snapping to a stop, suspended by the chain linking them to the others.

With chilled sweat on his face, Tomonaga gripped number five and pushed it over. Then came six through eight. The four marines fought for breath and looked down at the eight black cylinders clinging to the slope.

When number twelve went over, Morita noticed number thirteen slip in the snow. He pointed to it and shouted above the chugging engine. "Weight's shifting!"

Tomonaga nodded and gripped number thirteen. He took a painful breath and looked back at the three marines. "Ready?"

"Hai!"

He leaned into number thirteen and shoved it over the edge—and he heard Morita's piercing cry.

"There they go!"

Tomonaga jumped back and saw the canisters slide past him like a black centipede. They disappeared over the edge with the cable trailing behind them. Suddenly, the cable stiffened with an ominous twang.

Tomonaga looked back in shock. Morita was staring at the winch, his hand frozen on the lever.

"Too much weight! It's going over!"

"No! Shift the lever!" Tomonaga lunged for the winch, but it was too late. The three restraining cables snapped with sickening twangs.

Tomonaga dived into the snow and covered up as the severed cables whipped over his head. Behind him, the plane's tail section shuddered from the sudden release of weight.

The dislodged winch slammed into him. He leaned against it, but it was no use. The winch's engaged cable was still linked to its seventeen hundred pound load. With the restraining cables broken, the winch was going over—and so was he.

"Major!" Aikido dived at Tomonaga, but he was flung to

Gary Naiman

the side by the skidding winch. He scrambled to his knees and shouted at his commander. "The lever! Pull the lever!"

Grimacing from the pain in his side, Tomonaga reached up and gripped the gearshift lever. He yanked it down and heard a screech of metal. The winch ground to a stop in the snow. With its gears disengaged, the winch's drum spun out of control only inches above his head. He looked up and saw the black cable unraveling in front of his eyes. There was nothing he could do. He buried his face in the snow and listened to the spinning drum accelerate to a high-pitched whine.

The air cracked with a violent whiplash as the disengaged cable flew off the drum like a coiled snake.

"Look out!" Morita spun away from the snapping cable and dived for the snow, but it caught him in the back as it whipped by. He let out an agonizing cry and collapsed against a rock. The cable danced in the air and disappeared over the edge.

Tomonaga wiped the snow off his face and looked up at the spinning drum. Smoke puffed from the chugging generator.

"Are you all right, sir?"

Tomonaga spun around and saw Morita slumped against the rock, his legs extended in front of him. "Do you know what you have done! That was our mission going over the edge!"

Morita shook his head. "Too much weight. It wouldn't hold."

Tomonaga's eyes burned into him. "It was your idea!"

Morita rested his head against the rock and looked up at the haze.

Tomonaga gritted his teeth and stood up. He leaned against the crippled winch and twisted the carburetor screw. The motor coughed, and died. The only sound was the wind.

Aikido stood up and brushed the snow off his parka. "Your orders, sir?"

Tomonaga looked at the black clouds sweeping over the ridge. The wind was gusting and it had begun to snow. In a few minutes, the visibility would drop to zero. He glanced at the skid marks in the snow.

"Sir?"

Tomonaga took a painful breath. "Let's get out of this

wind."

He watched the three marines shuffle toward the crippled tail section. Tomorrow, he would lead them down the mountain in disgrace. He had failed. Thirteen good men had died for nothing. His hand grasped the knife in his belt. *No—not yet. First, get them off this cursed mountain. At least, they'll remember you for that.*

He started toward the tail section and noticed the sergeant still sitting against the rock. "Well—what are you waiting for?"

Morita stared at the summit, his head resting against the rock.

"Sergeant?"

Morita didn't move.

Tomonaga shuffled beside him and knelt down. He waved his gloved hand in front of Morita's eyes. There was no reaction. He yanked back the sergeant's sleeve and felt for a pulse. There was none. "We have a problem here!" Tomonaga clutched the sergeant's wrist and listened to the marines shuffle toward him.

Aikido was the first one who noticed the blood in the snow. He knelt down and grasped the sergeant's back. When he pulled his gloved hand away, it was covered with blood. He stared at the glove in disbelief.

Ishikawa eased the sergeant on his side. "My God." The back of Morita's parka was soaked with blood. The rock was smeared with it.

Unable to speak, Ishikawa stared at the deep gash between the shoulder blades. The cable had sliced through Morita's back, severing a main artery. He had quietly bled to death staring at the summit.

They buried him in the snow beside the plane. With the blizzard sweeping over them, they stood beside his shallow grave and listened to their commander's words.

"Goodbye, old friend. You died a hero—at your post. Good to die a hero. The sun on your face—the clouds at your feet. I envy you, Morita. Oh—how I envy you."

Tomonaga knelt beside the makeshift grave and ripped a silver cherry blossom off his collar. He placed it in the snow and said a silent prayer. No tears were shed. They were too tired to cry.

They built a fire inside the cargo hold and huddled together for warmth. Powerful winds buffeted the shattered tail section, driving the temperature to zero. Someone mumbled a prayer. There were only four now—and the road down looked bleak.

Faithful to his orders, Aikido activated the homing beacon at midnight, beeping signals for five minutes before shutting down the radio to conserve power.

Ishikawa took over at one a.m., managing two bursts before Nomura relieved him at three. Tomonaga finished the night's work with three transmissions.

The sky was brightening when they crawled out of the tail section into the deep snow. The clouds had retreated to the south after dumping a foot of the white stuff on the ridge. Five thousand feet above them, Kangchenjunga's imposing summit glowed yellow-white in the rising sun.

The view to the west was overwhelming—a sea of white peaks that seemed to go on forever. Everything was still, yet there was a feeling of immense power.

Tomonaga looked back at the half-buried tail section. Only the rudder and elevators remained visible above the snow drifts. The next storm would probably finish the job, erasing any memory of "Operation NI."

No words were spoken as they donned their packs and slung coiled rope over their shoulders. Tomonaga's climbing experience was limited to two month's training on Fujiyama. It would have to do. He rigged a belay to a rock and glanced back at his comrades. When they weren't looking, he injected the last of the morphine into his aching side and flipped the needle in the snow. He gave the rope a good luck tug and backed away from the rock while reeling out the brown lifeline. When he reached the marines, he stopped and trained his black eyes on Aikido who was toying nervously with his shoulder straps. "Ready, Private?"

"Yes, sir."

"Watch that radio. It's your ticket home."

Aikido nodded and patted his shoulder strap.

The Tenth Avatar

Tomonaga looked back at the scattered debris. "Let's say a prayer for the ones who aren't coming down." He lowered his head and listened to the snow rustle across the ridge.

"Good luck." Tomonaga coiled the belay rope around his shoulder, waist, and thigh. He gave the rope a hard tug and stepped back onto the forty-five degree slope. He reeled out the rope and backed down the ice-covered slope into the haze.

It only took a few minutes to exhaust the two hundred foot rope. Tomonaga dug his boots into the ice and scanned the cluster of rocks on his right. It was the same cluster Morita had pointed out yesterday. He worked his way toward them and groped for the hammer in his belt. Before leaving Norway, he'd debated abandoning the climbing equipment to store extra fuel. He looked down at the hammer and frowned. At least, he'd made one good decision. He pulled out a piton and hammered it into a crack in the rocks.

He jammed the hammer in his belt and clipped his rope to the piton. Fighting for breath, he cupped his hands around his mouth and let out a painful yell. "Secured! Down in order!"

He watched Aikido scramble down the slope with the radio protruding from his pack. It took the young marine a half hour to negotiate the two hundred foot slope, but he made it without incident. Next came Ishikawa and Nomura. By the time they reached their comrades, the sun was beaming down on them from the summit.

Tomonaga helped the three marines secure themselves to anchor points in the rocks. When they were safely tied in, he unraveled a few feet of coiled rope from Nomura's shoulder and clipped it to the embedded piton. He forced a smile and looked at the young marine. "Well, Private. It gets a little tougher now."

"Yes, sir."

"You go first. I'll stay up here to free the rope. We'll need it for the next leg."

Nomura stared at him with blank eyes.

"Just stay calm and you'll be fine." He patted Nomura's shoulder and looked down at the haze.

Nomura took a deep breath and gripped the rope. He stared

at his commander and backed down the slope.

"You're doing fine, Nomura. Give us a yell when you're on the ledge." Tomonaga watched the young marine fade into the haze.

"Question, sir?"

Tomonaga looked at Ishikawa.

"How much gold in the canisters?"

Tomonaga's face twisted in a frown. "Enough to win a war."

Ishikawa nodded. "Maybe we'll find some of it."

"Maybe...."

Ten minutes passed. Then ten more. Ishikawa cupped his hands around his mouth and shouted into the haze, but there was no answer.

Tomonaga tugged on the taut rope. "Hey, Nomura! What's taking you so long! We're freezing up here!" He listened to the wind rustle across the slope.

Ishikawa looked at him with concerned eyes. "Maybe I should go down."

"Not yet." Tomonaga peered into the haze. He recalled the way Nomura tried to focus his eyes on him when he went down. "How badly was Nomura injured?"

Ishikawa shrugged his shoulders. "He was lucky. Just a mild concussion."

"Concussion?"

Ishikawa nodded.

"How was he this morning?"

"A little dizzy, but we all are in this thin air."

Tomonaga grabbed the rope on Ishikawa's shoulder and uncoiled a few feet. He looped it over a protruding rock and spliced it to Nomura's belay rope. "I'm going to try something. It's dangerous, but we don't have a choice."

"Sir?"

Tomonaga gave Ishikawa's rope a sharp tug to check the splice. He snatched the other end of Ishikawa's coiled rope and tied it around his waist. His black eyes locked on Ishikawa. "I'm going down on your rope. Brace yourself against the rocks and reel me out. When I'm down, I'll signal you to follow."

"What's wrong?"

"I'm not sure." Tomonaga gripped the rope. "Ready?"

Ishikawa nodded and pressed his boots against the rocks.

"You'll be the last one down. Before you come, disconnect Nomura's rope from the piton."

"Disconnect?" Ishikawa looked at him in shock.

"Do it."

"How do I get down?"

Tomonaga pointed to Ishikawa's rope looped over the protruding rock. "That splice will be your belay. I'll anchor you from below."

"Yes, sir."

"See you on the ledge." Tomonaga leaned back and looked up at Ishikawa. "Hold me tight, marine. You're all I've got." He forced a smile and backed down the slope.

Tomonaga was nearly to the ledge when he spotted Nomura lying face down against the forty-five degree slope. Nomura's belay rope was coiled tightly around his back, with a few lengths still looped around his left shoulder. His arms hung limp at his sides. Tomonaga edged along the slope toward the motionless body....

Ishikawa's eyes widened when his commander's voice echoed off the ice. He patted Aikido on the shoulder and nodded at the rope. "Your turn. Watch that radio."

Aikido nodded and headed down the rope.

A half hour later, Ishikawa breathed a sigh of relief when Aikido's voice cut through the haze.

"Secured!"

Recalling his commander's instructions, Ishikawa untied Nomura's belay rope from the piton and watched it drop a few feet until his own spliced rope took hold from the rock above his head. Mustering his courage, he cupped his hands around his mouth and shouted into the haze. "Piton disconnected! I'm coming down!"

His eyes locked on the brown rope looped over the rock above him. He glanced to the right at the spliced extent trailing off the other side of the rock into the haze below. If the splice gave way, or the rope slipped off the rock, he was a dead man.

He took a deep breath and envisioned a spider descending its silken thread. *Be a spider, Ishikawa. Be a spider....* He gripped the rope and backed down the slope, his eyes focused on the rock above his head.

The next few minutes seemed eternal. He thought of his wife and child waiting for him in Tokyo. He'd lied to them about the mission, calling it a routine training exercise. Now, he might never see them again.

A gust of wind blew across the slope, driving ice crystals into his face. He brushed them away with his shoulder and looked up at the rope stretching into the haze. *Be a spider....* He took a deep breath and continued down the rope.

He heard voices coming from the haze. He looked down and froze. Major Tomonaga and Aikido were crouched over Nomura's crumpled body. He scrambled down the rope onto the ledge. "What happened?"

Tomonaga looked down and forced out the words. "I'm afraid he's gone."

"Gone? But he was fine? Just a little dizzy?"

"His brain hemorrhaged."

Ishikawa stared at Nomura in disbelief. He knelt beside him and fought back the tears. "He's like a brother to me. We've been through hell together."

"I'm sorry, Corporal. They were all my brothers."

They covered their dead comrade with a blanket and said a brief prayer. Tomonaga knelt beside the blanket and ripped off a second silver cherry blossom. "I wish we could give our friend the honor he deserves. I'm sure he will understand. May he be at peace." Tomonaga bowed his head and listened to the wind.

They spent the next few minutes reeling in the spliced rope from the rock overhead. It slithered down the slope like a crazed snake before dropping in a heap on the ledge. There was a moment of panic when a rush of snow followed the slinking rope onto the ledge, but the slide quickly subsided.

Ishikawa coiled the rope while Aikido activated the radio's

The Tenth Avatar

homing beacon. They talked about home and watched the sun drop in the western sky. To the south, a bank of purple-gray clouds massed for another assault on the Himalayas.

Ishikawa was sipping some water when he noticed his commander peering over the ledge. He capped his canteen and stretched out on the ice beside him. "How does it look, sir?"

"I make it five hundred feet straight down."

Ishikawa leaned forward and looked down the wall of black rock. Some snow spilled off the ledge, its frozen crystals sparkling in the sunlight.

Tomonaga pulled out his binoculars and focused them on the base of the wall. "The grade eases down there. We'll dig a snow cave and wait until morning. We should do better tomorrow."

Ishikawa nodded and glanced at his watch. Thirty-nine hours had passed since their contact with Nanking. With their rations almost gone, and the weather taking its toll, they couldn't last more than a day or two. Better to die falling off a wall than freezing to death on a ledge. He started to get up.

"Wait."

"Sir?"

Tomonaga lowered the binoculars and looked at him with stunned eyes. "The gods smile on us, Corporal." He passed the binoculars to Ishikawa. "On the slope. Do you see them?"

Ishikawa focused the binoculars on the snow-covered slope below the wall. He scanned a patch of fallen ice, and stiffened. A black cable protruded from the broken ice. He followed it and saw two of the canisters sticking out of the snow. Then four more. They appeared intact.

Ishikawa looked beyond the canisters. A column of vapor billowed from the debris. He pressed the glasses against his eyes and squinted at the bright light flashing through the vapor. "It looks like the sun."

"It is the sun."

Ishikawa lowered the binoculars and stared at his commander's beaming face.

"Gold, Corporal. Enough to win a war." Tomonaga stood up and seized the binoculars. "How is the rope?"

Gary Naiman

"Rope?"
"We're going down."
"But the time?"
"Forget the time."

It only took a few minutes to secure a belay to the ledge. Tomonaga knelt down and lowered the four hundred foot spliced rope down the wall. When it was fully extended, he stood up and backed away from the edge.

His eyes locked on Aikido. "You're first, Private. When you reach the end of the rope, you'll still be a hundred feet from the ice. Hammer in a piton and tie on. We'll be right behind you."

Aikido tried to speak, but the words wouldn't come out. He fought the nausea sweeping over him and clipped onto the rope.

"Ready?"

Aikido nodded and coiled the rope around his shoulder, back, and thigh. He took a deep breath and stared at his commander.

"That's it. Just lean back and dig those heels into the rock. Keep both hands on the rope and let it slide." Tomonaga watched the shaken marine step off the ledge onto the wall. "You're doing fine, Private. One step at a time. Don't look down."

Tomonaga dropped on his belly and watched the young marine ease down the wall. Five hundred feet below them, waves of steam billowed from a boiling lake of melted snow. And in the center of it, a brilliant rod of seething energy glowed brighter than the sun.

He recalled Colonel Nishina's parting words in Tokyo....

Everyone will think it's gold. We prefer it that way. In the end, they will know the truth. We have reached into the heavens and snatched the sun.

Tomonaga stared at Aikido—unaware that the fate of the world was in his hands.

38 | From the Sky

Why was he so dizzy? And that ringing sound? He remembered arguing with Arronategui in front of the hotel. Then the blast of heat and concussion. Now he was lying on a pile of rubble engulfed in thick, choking smoke.

He sat up and rubbed his forehead. His eyes stung from the swirling ashes. He gagged and swiped his hand in front of his face. He couldn't breathe. He had to get out of this goddamned smoke.

He rolled on his belly and began crawling through the debris. A flash of sunlight struck his face. He scrambled toward it and reeled in shock.

The Julian Hotel's front wall had been blown away, its exposed floors sagging on the verge of collapse. Broken bodies lay in the street—some writhing—others still. A few hundred feet away, the rail station and post office were piles of shattered concrete and brick. Across from them, Juan Silliaco's fire station had been flattened, its proud red truck a mass of twisted metal. A hand pushed out of the debris and reached for the sky. It convulsed and went limp.

He was almost to his feet when a terrific blast slammed into him. A rush of intense heat swept across his face. He turned in horror and saw a row of buildings lift off their foundations and crumble in flames. Chunks of concrete and brick rained down from the smoke-filled sky. A severed leg dropped in the debris.

He buried his face in his arms and prayed for the nightmare to end—but it had just begun.

A high-pitched whistle filled his ears. Across the plaza, the marketplace disintegrated in a barrage of deafening explosions. He looked up and saw people running through the flames, some of them screaming in agony, others too stunned to know they were on fire.

A wounded horse lay on the ground, its side spurting blood. Beside the fountain, an old woman rose up on her knees, her hands clasped to the sky, her face twisted in horror. Behind her, Santa Maria's burning steeple buckled and collapsed in *the cauldron of flames that was once a holy city. Guernica had become an inferno.*

"Roberto!"

She was running toward him, her torn blouse smeared with blood.

"Ana!" *He crawled out of the debris and staggered toward her, the ground swaying under him. His arms reached out for her. He could see her face glistening from the searing heat. They were running through a man-made hell, two helpless souls trying to find each other before the flames swept over them. He took her in his arms and felt her collapse against him.*

"My, God, Roberto! My, God!"

He couldn't speak. An ominous whine filled his ears. He looked across the plaza and saw a black, twin-engined aircraft burst through the smoke, its wing guns spouting flame.

He pulled her down and rolled against the fountain. The ground erupted with impacting bullets. Chips of dislodged concrete stung his face as the bullets ricocheted off the stone fountain. He pressed against her and listened to the plane roar over their heads, its guns blazing. When he looked up, it had disappeared into the smoke.

"Now! Before it dives again!" *He tried to help her up, but she didn't move.* "Come on, dammit!" *He lifted her off the ground and froze. She hung limp in his arms, her glazed eyes looking up at him.* "Ana!"

She reached up and stroked his face. "Save yourself, my darling. It's too late for me...."

"No. We'll go to the convent. We'll be safe there."

"Remember me, Roberto. Remember us all...." *Her hand fell away and dangled at her side.*

"Ana! God—no!"

He swept her in his arms and stumbled across the smoke-filled plaza. He could see the Carmelite Convent on top of the hill, its proud cross jutting above the trees. If he could reach Dr. Montero, there was still a chance.

He was almost to the trees when he heard the whine. He turned and saw the plane burst through the smoke, its wing guns blazing. Twin lines of impacting bullets ripped up the ground in front of him. He looked up and saw the pilot glaring at him from the windshield.

"Bastard! You'll burn in hell for this! I'll make you pay! So help me, God! I'll make you pay!"

Roberto opened his eyes and stared at the beam of sunlight shining through the cracked roof. His face glistened with sweat. His heart pounded against his chest. He sat up and gasped for breath.

This had been the worst nightmare of all. He felt her warm blood dripping down his arms when he carried her across the plaza. He gagged on the thick, acrid smoke while listening to the terrified screams of men, women, and children staggering from their burning homes. He stared in horror at the black plane bursting through the smoke with its guns blazing, and felt the chips of concrete sting his face when the bullets ripped into the fountain. And he heard his rasping voice curse the winged-devil and its pilot. The vision of Corpus Christi was no longer a nightmare. It had become a living, breathing terror.

He scanned the empty prayer hall. Everything was still. There were no planes. No bombs. No burning buildings. No screams. The only flames came from the smoldering firepit beside him. Harmless enough. Or was it? He slid away from the red coals and recalled the heat when the candy factory burst into flames and Francesca collapsed at his feet, her body consumed by fire.

He leaned against the altar and looked up at the beam of light. That sun had shone on Valencia today. On the Micalet and Silk Exchange. On Viveros Park and the house he once called home. On the Turia where he escaped the heat so many years ago. On Sancho and his leather-skinned braceros laboring in the fields. And on his beloved orange groves where a young man once tasted life's simple pleasures, and slept in the cool shade above the sea.

He brushed away a tear. Wonderful memories had been destroyed by evil men—demagogues bent on ruling the world. There was no escape. They were everywhere—even here.

He looked up at the Buddha. He would only take four packs

of gold. He couldn't trust Eammon, but Bonaventure seemed an honest thief. Fair exchange—a pack of gold for a safe journey back to Bombay.

They'd part company in Bombay. He'd take a tramp steamer across the Arabian Sea, then work his way through the Red and Mediterranean Seas to the Spanish Coast—and Valencia. If he could pull it off, there would be enough gold to buy arms and ammunition from the Soviets.

It wouldn't be hard to raise a resistance movement. By now, the people knew the truth. Their nation had been seized by a devil. A Napoleonic dictator whose only goal was absolute power. Better to die fighting than live in chains. It would take everything he had, but it was the only way to avenge the ones he loved.

They were gone, but he could still hear their cries in the night. Urging him on. Begging him to remember. Sebastian, Augustin, and Gorka. God, he missed them. And the woman he loved. And the proud old Hidalgo who cried for patriotism when no one listened. The last of the finest that was Spain.

Revolutions need a spark—and he would provide it. He would go to Madrid and the Royal Palace. To have that long-overdue dinner with the portly officer he met in the *Marva Bar* so many years ago. Señor Franco would not enjoy the main course. A piece of hot lead between the eyes. A final gift from the son of Don Felipe Hidalgo.

He rested his head against the altar and looked up at the light. A few more days, *torero*. A few more days and you will go home....

An unsettling thought struck him. That beam of sunlight was striking the Buddha's crown. The sun didn't reach the crown until late afternoon. Impossible, unless—

He looked at his dead watch and gasped. The transmission! He pushed off the floor and ran toward the radio room—and his destiny.

Where was she? His eyes darted around the room. Her gear was gone. And the map. And oxygen!

He slumped against the wall. Bonaventure had warned him she was desperate. She'd lost control of her senses. The thin air had affected her. Now she was wandering out there. Trying to catch them. It was suicide. No—it was murder. And he was the murderer.

He remembered the spare binoculars, compass, and map in the chest under the table. He snatched them out of the chest and ran into the prayer hall. He yanked on his fur weather gear and jammed the map and compass into his pack. With the binoculars dangling from his arm, he flung the pack over his shoulder and burst through the carved doors into the bitter cold.

Thank God, it wasn't snowing. He shuffled along the ridge, searching for a lone set of tracks. To the west, the late afternoon sun dropped toward the white peaks of the Himalaya. In three hours, darkness would swallow her forever.

There! A trail of boot tracks winding down the slope beside the others. He yanked out the binoculars and focused them on the tracks.

It appeared she'd fallen a few times on the way down. It was a miracle she could stand at all. He traced the tracks to the bottom of the slope where they veered south toward the mountain.

"God." He ran into the monastery and charged for the radio room. His heart pounded as he flipped on the power switch and waited for the familiar hum. He backed away and stared at the glowing dial.

Get a hold of yourself, man. You'll only have a few seconds. Be direct. Tell him you'll go after her if he doesn't. Make sure he knows you mean business. He'll have no choice.

He reached for the bottle of Irish whiskey in the cabinet. There was barely any left. He pulled out the cork and swigged it down.

It was four fifteen. Eammon's party had been gone seven hours. It would take them at least three to backtrack to her position. In the young reporter's depleted state, that delay could be fatal, but it was her best chance.

He dropped into the chair and stared at the microphone. A frightening thought struck him. What if Eammon decided she wasn't worth saving? In the past two days, he had learned a painful truth about his scheming friend. Eammon's cold, calculating mind could easily write off someone if the situation warranted it. There was no compassion. No pity. Only a cold-blooded spy focused on his mission.

He grasped the microphone and flicked the transmission switch. "White Lion—are you there? Over...."

The radio crackled with static.

"Are you there, White Lion?" He flicked the switch and listened to the static.

He tried again, but there was no response. He sank in the chair and stared at the military clock beside the radio. Over an hour had passed since the planned transmission. If they'd reached the mountains, his signal might not be getting through. He pulled the microphone closer and started to speak.

No—it was useless. He was wasting valuable time. She couldn't have gone that far. By leaving now, he could follow her tracks before the wind and snow erased them. Dangerous, but he was all she had.

He flipped off the power switch and pushed out of the chair. The military clock read sixteen-twenty.

He was halfway down the ridge when he heard it. A distant hum that seemed to be growing louder. He scanned the bright haze and listened to the hum become a deafening roar.

Was this another nightmare? Was the devil trying to drive him completely mad? Two twin-engined aircraft burst through the haze above the ridge, their black shadows flashing across his face. Flying due west, the planes banked sharply to the left and climbed for altitude. They were nearly out of sight when they suddenly rolled into steep rightward turns across the western sky until they pointed directly at him, maybe two miles out.

Like a skilled eagle, the first plane levelled off and dropped into the snow, sending a spray of white powder to either side. The twin-engined plane slid toward the ridge and came to a graceful stop two hundred feet from the shrouded *Vickers* while its companion landed a half mile behind it in a burst of white powder.

Roberto crouched in the snow and eyed the two unmarked intruders. A wave of fear swept over him. Something was very wrong and he was standing in open terrain like an exposed rabbit. He scrambled toward a cluster of broken ice and dived for cover.

The second plane slid to a stop beside the first, its twin propellers idling. The pilot gave the engines a rev and shut them down. The spinning blades slowed and kicked to a halt.

Everything was still now. The three aircraft sat motionless in the snow. The only sound was the wind whistling across the ridge crest.

A hatch popped open in the first plane's belly. Two men in white parkas dropped into the snow carrying rifles. They fanned out to either side of the aircraft and were followed by two more parka-clad men who assumed covering positions behind them. Within seconds, a dozen armed soldiers had established a perimeter around the twin black aircraft.

With rifles drawn, two soldiers rushed across the snow toward the *Vickers*. They ripped away the canvas shroud and tried to pry open the fuselage door, but it wouldn't budge. Backing away, they crept along the fuselage to the plane's snub nose and began grappling with the cargo door. They were joined by two others who gestured for them to back away while aiming their rifles at the locked door.

Roberto flinched as the soldiers fired several bursts into the plane's nose. They ripped open the crippled cargo door and climbed inside. Behind them, another dozen troops jumped out of the second plane and joined their comrades on the perimeter.

Lieutenant Hiryu slung his machine gun over his shoulder and snapped to attention. "Plane secured, sir."

Captain Yamato nodded and pointed to the ridge. "Take four men up to that temple and check for a radio. That wire on the roof looks like trouble."

"Hai!" Hiryu saluted smartly and started to turn away.

"And, Lieutenant."

"Sir!"

"I want prisoners, not dead men."

Hiryu nodded and shuffled back to the waiting marines. He picked out four and led them across the snow toward the base of the ridge.

Yamato watched the five marines fan out in skirmishing order. With Hiryu at the point, they charged up the slope toward the archaic structure on the ridge crest. The other six marines knelt down and took aim at the monastery from the base of the slope.

Yamato glanced at a second officer who was covering the planes with the remaining eleven marines. "Lieutenant Kirosawa!"

Kirosawa broke away from the marines and shuffled toward his commander. The drawn-faced officer slung his rifle over his shoulder and snapped to attention.

Yamato pulled out a compass and aimed it at the mountains. "Prepare your men for a forced march. From the direction of Tomonaga's signal, our best chance is around those peaks to the south."

Kirosawa nodded. "Should we bring the sleds?"

Yamato pulled back his hood and stared at the mountains. "That's a good man out there. We went through the academy together. He was the finest officer in our ranks. If anyone can pull it off, it's Tomonaga." He locked his black eyes on Kirosawa. "Bring them all, Lieutenant. And be quick. Time is not with us today."

"Hai!" Kirosawa saluted and jogged toward the waiting marines."

"And, Lieutenant...."

"Sir!"

"Set a demo charge in that English kite. I don't want anyone flying out of here except us." Yamato focused his binoculars on the ridge where Lieutenant Hiryu and his four marines were converging on the monastery.

Roberto pressed his face against the ice and listened to the boots crunching toward him. This wasn't the first time he'd cowered in the rocks while an army marched by. He closed his eyes and prayed they wouldn't see his tracks. He could hear their labored breathing when they climbed past him.

Hiryu crouched in front of the carved doors. He eyed the four marines and gripped his weapon. "Now!" He burst through the doors and dived on the stone floor while spraying the prayer hall with bursts of machine gun fire. His comrades sprawled behind him and blasted away at the roof and altar. Chunks of wood and stone crashed on the floor as the ancient walls echoed with ricocheting bullets.

"Hold your fire!" Hiryu raised his arm and glanced back at the prone marines. He popped in a fresh clip and began crawling toward the altar while his comrades trained their sights on the shadows.

"Should we send up another squad, sir?"

"Stand by, Lieutenant." Yamato focused his binoculars on the blackness inside the opened doors. Five minutes had passed since the shooting stopped. He gripped the binoculars and waited.

Hiryu charged out of the temple waving his hands in the air. "Clear! We found a radio and papers!"

Yamato lowered the binoculars and cupped a hand to his mouth. "Destroy the radio and get down here! We're ready to move out!"

Hiryu waved in acknowledgement. He ran into the monastery and ushered out the marines. Grasping his machine gun, he shuffled across the smoking prayer hall toward the radio room.

Roberto flinched from a loud burst of machine gun fire. He peered at the four soldiers standing on the ridge. What were they doing here? They had dropped out of the sky like black birds. Now, they swarmed across the snow like an army preparing for war.

The fifth soldier charged out of the monastery, carrying his weapon and a handful of papers. He barked orders at the others and waved them off the ridge. He was about to follow them when he hesitated and stared at the cluster of broken ice.

Roberto cringed as the officer stood motionless on the ridge crest, his eyes trained on the broken ice, the smoking machine gun in his hand. Suddenly, the officer slung his weapon and headed down the slope toward the planes.

Hiryu ran toward his commander and held out the papers. "I found these in a room behind the altar. They were stacked in a box under the radio."

"Two way?"

Hiryu nodded. "Very powerful."

"Destroyed?"

"Blown to bits."

Yamato shuffled through the papers. "You found no one?"

Hiryu shook his head. "There were signs people had been there. Food, water—even an empty whiskey bottle. And Takawa saw tracks headed toward the mountains."

"Tracks?"

"Yes, sir."

"How many?"

"Five or six—but there could be more." Hiryu pointed to the papers in Yamato's hand. "There's a map in there. It's marked with a route into the mountains."

Yamato grimaced. "Then—they know."

"Yes, sir."

Yamato crumpled the papers in his fist. "Prepare your men, Lieutenant. We must move quickly."

Hiryu nodded and glanced at the slope. "There is one other thing, sir."

"Yes?"

Roberto watched them drag a dozen wood sleds out of the planes. Some of them began linking the sleds together with chain while their comrades spread white shrouds over the twin aircraft.

One of the soldiers climbed into the *Vickers* with a rucksack. Seconds later, he jumped out of the plane without it.

It only took them a few minutes to complete their preparations. With the officers barking orders, they formed twin columns and set out for the mountains with the string of sleds trailing behind them.

Roberto watched them fade into the haze. He had seen enough to know they were on a collision course with Eammon's party.

It would be a massacre. Twenty-four well-armed soldiers against five men with obsolete rifles. He stared at the haze. The young reporter was in their path. He had seen war's horror, and the terrible things soldiers do to women.

He slumped against the ice. Things had become a bit complicated. A week ago, he'd followed a mysterious guide up here to find a better life. Instead, he'd found the same evil that destroyed his country. Spies posing as friends. People scheming against one another. Foreign armies battling for power. After coming so far to find a new beginning, he'd climbed into another war—this one at the roof of the world. An alien war he wanted no part of.

He remembered the radio. If he could get a message to Dharan, they'd fly in troops. It was worth a shot. With a little luck, they might fly him and his five packs out of here. To go back to a war that mattered—the fight for the Third Republic.

He started up the slope and froze. Black smoke billowed from the monastery's sloped roof. He could see flames shooting through the scorched timbers.

The wind caught the smoke and drove it down the ridge into his eyes. He couldn't breathe. The fires of Guernica had spread to the roof of the world.

The gold! He charged up the slope toward the burning monastery. The thick, black smoke became unbearable as he closed on the doors. A blast of heat struck his face. He dropped on his belly and crawled up the steps into the prayer hall.

The rear wall and roof were engulfed in flames. He tried to crawl toward the radio room, but was forced back by the searing heat and smoke. It was hopeless. The monastery had become a furnace.

He looked up at the Buddha. The blackened statue was covered with cinders from the burning roof. The paint on the face had blistered and caught on fire. In a few seconds, it would be too late.

He mustered his courage and slid toward the statue. He had to get up there before the flames reached the Buddha's lap and hands. If he could reach the belly, he might be able to drag out the packs before it was too late.

He cowered against the floor as a section of the burning roof collapsed on the Buddha's face and belly. Chunks of smoldering wood crashed on the floor in front of him, spraying him with sparking embers.

He retreated toward the doorway, slapping at his singed parka. It was no use. The Buddha was bathed in flames.

He crawled out of the inferno and collapsed on the ice, gagging on the foul smoke. Behind him, one of the carved doors burst into flames. Then the other. His only hope was the thin air smothering the fire. If the Buddha could withstand the heat—

The ridge shook from a violent explosion. He rolled over and saw the *Vickers* blow apart in a ball of flame. He covered his head as pieces of flaming wood and metal rained down on the slope. The fireball billowed upward, blackening as it rose into the sky. Below it, the *Vickers* was a pile of burning debris.

The fires died quickly in the rarified air. He pushed off the ice and looked down at the smoldering wreckage that seconds ago was a British transport. Behind him, the monastery's roof collapsed in the furnace of crackling flames and smoke.

His eyes focused on the two shrouded aircraft. They were his last chance. He'd memorized the transmission frequencies. If he could work one of their radios, he might be able to contact Eammon and Dharan.

He charged down the slope, his heart pounding against his ribs. The setting sun flashed in his eyes. In another two hours, it would drop below Everest and Makalu. Time was very short. He must be brief and direct. The words echoed in his head....

This is Pangpema. Two unmarked aircraft have landed carrying armed troops. Your outpost and aircraft destroyed. Twenty-four well-armed troops marching on your team. Will intercept them before they reach crashed plane. Dispatch help immediately....

Had Roberto counted the marines when they set off for the mountain, he would have realized there were twenty-three—one less than the number that had landed.

The bullet struck him in the left shoulder, spinning him around like a top. He collapsed in the snow, clutching at the burning pain in his arm and chest. The bullet had shattered his left humerus bone and ricocheted into his lung, breaking ribs along the way.

He lay stunned in the snow, a black veil creeping over his eyes. He didn't hear the footsteps rushing toward him.

Corporal Nagano lowered his rifle and stared at the unconscious man lying at his feet. He knelt down and felt for a pulse while Captain Yamato and Lieutenant Hiryu rushed across the snow toward him.

Yamato pulled back his hood and bent over the kneeling corporal. "Is he alive?"

"Yes, sir. Bad luck though. He's coughing up blood. The bullet must have deflected into his chest."

Yamato scowled and straightened up. "Take him in the plane and try to revive him. Give him drugs—whatever it takes."

Nagano jumped to his feet and snapped to attention.

"I need to know what's waiting for us out there. If he dies without telling you—you fail."

"Hai!"

Yamato patted Nagano's shoulder. "I'm relying on you, Corporal. We all are." He glanced at his watch. "I'll radio you at twenty hundred."

Nagano saluted and backed away. He watched the two officers shuffle across the snow toward the mountains.

A wave of desperation swept through him. The man lying at his feet was their only link to the enemy force marching on the mountain. Were others coming? What kind of weapons did they have? A British military post lay to the south. If the British were smart enough to intercept the plane's emergency transmission, they might have picked up Tomonaga's messages and set a trap.

He looked down at the wounded man. Fate had dealt him a cruel blow. His comrades lives were in his hands. He slung his rifle over his shoulder and seized the man's fur hood. Two shots of morphine should do the job.

Yamato and his lieutenant had gone a half mile when something caught their eye.

"What is it, sir?"

Yamato stared at the burned temple. "I'm not sure. Probably some Buddhist artifacts melting in the fire. Did you see anything in there?"

Hiryu shook his head.

"They were probably hidden. The monks like to hide things."

"It's so bright."

Yamato shrugged. "The hell with it. We have work to do." He turned toward the twin peaks, followed by Hiryu. A half mile behind them, Corporal Nagano stared at the mysterious light shining from the ridge crest.

The front wall had collapsed, exposing the charred Buddha. Through the fading smoke, liquid gold flowed from the statue's folded hands. It spilled onto the stone floor and spread to the steps where it fanned out like a river opening to the sea.

With the sun's last rays striking the ridge, the melted gold burst into a brilliant beam of reflected light. The ancient statue had become a gold mirror. The Enlightened One had come to life.

Nagano dragged his prisoner toward the shrouded plane. This was no time for distraction. Work must be done. Painful work. Interrogation and execution. The arts of war.

In the years to come, stories would be told of a Buddha below Kangchenjunga that glowed in the setting sun. An ancient statue of gold that lit the way for weary travelers.

The gods had claimed Roberto's gold. To serve a purpose better than revenge. His search was over. He had found his destiny. The gods circled Gold Peak....

39 | A New Record

Eammon shuffled next to Bonaventure and scanned the haze. "Where's it coming from?"

"Don't know."

"What should we do?"

"Say a prayer."

The ominous rumble deepened and grew louder.

Bonaventure tugged at his pack and eased beside Akaal. "Well, old chum?"

The Gurkha stroked his chin. "It's on Kangchenjunga. We're catching an echo off the ridges."

"Sure about that?"

"No."

"Lovely."

The five climbers stood motionless, their eyes fixed on the haze.

The rumble subsided. Everything fell silent except the wind whistling through the peaks.

Bonaventure took a deep breath and turned toward the others. "We were lucky this time. A little warning from the gods. From the look of this haze, we're in for quite a storm. That means more snow on the ridges."

Eammon studied the wall of rock on their left. He couldn't see the ridges through the haze, but he knew what the mountaineer meant. The snow-laden ridges were ripe for an avalanche. Another blizzard could set them loose. He backed away and looked at Bonaventure. "Can't we swing wide of them?"

"Not if you want to reach your mountain."

"There has to be another way."

"Not unless you have wings."

Eammon glared at him and gave his pack an angry tug. "Then let's get on with it." He started to walk away but Bonaventure blocked his path.

"We've gone far enough. We'll camp in that broken ice at the base of the glacier. It's a good hundred yards from the fall zone. Best we can do for safety."

"But we still have an hour of daylight."

Bonaventure shook his head. "You don't walk into a blizzard. That ice will give us some shelter from the wind. Come on—we're wasting time."

"Hold on, dammit!"

Bonaventure ignored him and shuffled down the glacier toward the broken ice.

The storm hit at sunset. They huddled around kerosene burners while forty knot winds tried to pry their tents off the ice. Then came the snow. Biting, swirling, smothering snow. If Kangchenjunga's warrior god couldn't blow them off the mountain, he'd bury them on it.

Bonaventure crawled into the howling blackness and turned his face away from the stinging wind. He pulled out a hammer and pounded the stakes deeper into the ice. He was about to retreat into his tent when Eammon stuck his head into the maelstrom.

"What's wrong?"

"Just checking the stakes. Any luck with the transmission?"

"Nothing. The idiot must have screwed up the radio."

Bonaventure nodded. "Maybe you'll have better luck in the morning. Remember to clear away the snow. Those bloody drifts pile up fast. Pleasant dreams." He crawled into his tent where Akaal was heating a tin of oatmeal on the burner.

"How are they?"

"Peachy."

Akaal smiled and handed his friend a cup of the warm cereal. "Know any good bedtime stories?"

Bonaventure shook his head. "Only one about a bloody climber who was too stupid to say no."

Akaal frowned and turned down the hissing burner. He climbed into his sleeping bag and looked up at the straining canvas.

"Care for a nip?" Bonaventure extended the brandy flask to his friend.

Akaal popped the cap and took a sip. "The wind's getting stronger. Maybe you should tie onto the tent post. Just in case."

Bonaventure nodded and wolfed down the oatmeal. Before climbing into his sleeping bag, he looped a rope around his chest and tied it to the swaying post. Comforting thought. He stretched out on his back and listened to the wind buffet the canvas. "How about some of that brandy?"

Akaal smiled and handed him the flask.

"What do you know about Collins?"

"Collins?"

"The ass in the tent next to us."

"Just what I told you. No one knew about him except the Major."

Bonaventure took a sip of brandy. "I don't trust either of them."

Akaal frowned and stared at the canvas.

"How about his friend?"

"The Spaniard?"

"Bonaventure took another sip. "What do you think of him?"

"A troubled man trying to find answers."

"To what?"

"A failed life. Lost loved one. Who knows? Each man is different."

"I think he's daft. Coming halfway around the world to be with that scum."

"Maybe he's running from something."

"Who isn't? No—it's more than that. The man's lost a screw."

Akaal yawned and rolled on his side. "Why did you tell Mr. Collins it would take a week to reach the wall?"

"To see how desperate he is."

"Desperate?"

Bonaventure leaned on his elbow and looked at his friend. "Don't turn your back on him—not even for a second. I've seen his kind in the streets. They smile at you, then stick a blade between your ribs when your back's turned." He fell back on the sleeping bag. "I wonder what he's really up to." He waited for an answer but only heard snoring.

Bonaventure couldn't sleep. He lay in the darkness, his

eyes fixed on the blue flame hissing in the burner. His thoughts drifted back to the bitter day two months ago when he saw their faces glaring up at him as the wall of snow swept over them. Two brave men standing tall while he scrambled away. God, if he could only have that moment again. Better to die up there than carry that bitter memory to your grave.

At ten, he noticed the wind dying down. Taking care not to wake his friend, he slipped out of his sleeping bag and untied the rope around his chest. He stuck his head through the tent flap and caught a face full of piled snow. He cursed and crawled through the flap into the knee-deep snow.

The intense storm had dumped a foot of fresh snow on the glacier. The air was still except for an occasional gust of chilled wind. A half moon had broken through the haze, flooding the glacier with silver light. He could see Kangchenjunga's ivory summit flashing through the fast-moving clouds.

He shuffled between the half-buried tents, listening for the sound of hissing burners. The loud snores convinced him everyone was well.

He was about to crawl into his tent when something caught his eye. A bright flash in the northern sky. A faint pop echoed off the glacier. He stood up and stared at the flickering red object. Then, it was gone.

Bonaventure burst into the tent. "Wake up."

Akaal blinked his eyes.

"Wake up, dammit. We've got trouble."

"What's wrong?"

"Red flare. Maybe two miles behind us."

Akaal sat up and rubbed his face. "Flare? We better wake the others?"

"No. They'll slow us down. Bring the oxygen. I'll take the stretcher assembly."

"You don't think it's—"

"I don't know what to think." Bonaventure dragged his pack out of the tent and headed across the moonlit glacier, followed by his stunned friend.

* * *

Karen jammed the flare into the chamber and snapped the gun closed with trembling hands. She pointed the flare gun at Kangchenjunga's glowing summit and said a prayer. Hours had passed since the blizzard erased their tracks. She was working on instinct now. With the sky clearing, the flare should be visible for miles—if anyone was watching.

Don't think about it. Take the shot and pray. She squeezed the trigger and felt the gun lurch. The flare rocketed skyward, exploding in a burst of red, hissing sparks. It floated down and faded into the darkness.

Everything was spinning. She collapsed in the snow and felt the ground sway under her. *Oh, God—not this way. Crawl, dammit! What kind of reporter are you!*

She cursed the vertigo and began crawling up the glacier toward the glowing summit. The deep snow brushed against her face. It was becoming hard to move. An ominous chill ebbed through her arms and legs. She couldn't breathe. She dropped on her side and clenched her fists. She could hear the wind whistling through the peaks—and her father's voice cursing her from the shadows. She rolled on her back and looked at the stars.

Akaal lowered the binoculars and handed them to his friend. "Nothing."

"It was a bloody flare. I saw it drop near that ice." Bonaventure pointed to a cluster of ice towers above the glacier.

Akaal glanced at his watch. "We've been gone over an hour. They won't know what happened to us."

Bonaventure wasn't listening. He'd focused the binoculars on a shadow in the ice.

"What is it?"

"I'm not sure. I think that shadow moved." He shoved the binoculars in his pack and charged up the slope toward the ice towers.

* * *

She heard another voice. A powerful voice. Strong hands slipped under her back and legs, lifting her off the snow. She opened her eyes and stared at the bearded face looking down at her.

"My God, Karen."

"Julian...."

"You're bloody insane."

She smiled and passed out in his arms.

"Hurry, man." Bonaventure watched his friend assemble the stretcher. He eased her down on the meshed rope and slipped the oxygen tube between her lips. "Breathe, dammit. Slow and deep."

He watched her gulp the life-saving oxygen. When she started coughing, he yanked the tube out of her mouth and gestured for Akaal to grab the stretcher. "We have to move fast. I don't like that cough."

They lifted the stretcher off the snow and began a forced march to the encampment. Forty minutes later, they stumbled between the tents and lowered the stretcher into the snow.

Eammon scrambled out of his tent and gawked at the stretcher. "What the bloody hell?"

Bonaventure slipped the oxygen tube between her lips. "I saw her flares. Found her on the glacier two miles from here. She must have followed us for hours."

"Why didn't you wake me?"

"No time. We had to move fast."

"What about Roberto?"

Bonaventure shook his head. "She's been delirious the whole time. Keeps mumbling about her father."

Eammon's eyes flashed with anger. He lunged past Bonaventure and dropped beside her.

"What the hell are you doing?"

"Stay out of this." He pushed Bonaventure away and seized her arms. "Wake up, dammit!"

Bonaventure grabbed his arm. "Are you crazy?"

Eammon yanked his arm free and started shaking her. "What happened back there? Snap out of it!"

The Tenth Avatar

"Sonofabitch!" Bonaventure grabbed Eammon's parka and dragged him away from her. He shoved him in the snow and glared at him with ice-blue eyes.

"I warned you!" Eammon pulled out the forty-five and pointed it at Bonaventure's face.

"Don't miss, you bloody bastard." Bonaventure gripped the ice axe in his belt and took a menacing step toward the enraged Irishman.

Mariner and Nemi scrambled out of their tents and reeled in shock at the scene unfolding in front of them.

Akaal backed away from the stretcher, his hand resting on the kukri in his belt. If that gun went off, he'd slash the pig's throat in the flick of an eyelash—and the hell with the consequences.

The five men stood frozen in the moonlight like actors on a stage, vapor streaming from their mouths. The only sound was the wind whistling through the peaks.

Eammon looked down at the forty-five. One squeeze and the mountaineer would be history. And so would the mission. He took a deep breath and lowered the pistol. "Sorry—guess I'm a little on edge."

Bonaventure released his grip on the axe and felt it drop in his belt. He took a deep breath and walked back to the stretcher. Akaal was about to join him when Eammon called out to him.

"Corporal Dawa."

"Yes?"

"A moment."

Akaal shuffled beside him.

"I noticed you grasping that knife. I take it your friendship with Mr. Bonaventure runs very deep."

"Deeper than your heart, *sahib*." Akaal glared at the Irishman and walked back to his friend who was kneeling beside the stretcher.

Eammon fought the anger boiling inside him. *Think of the mission, idiot. Don't blow it when you're so close. You need these puppets. Save the bullets for later.* He took a deep breath and shuffled beside the stretcher. "How is she?"

"We're taking her back."

"We're what?"

"You heard me."

Eammon backed away. "And whose decision is that?"

"Mine."

Eammon stuffed the forty-five in his pocket. "Sorry, Mr. Bonaventure. These men are under my command. They do what I say. We've come too far to turn back."

Bonaventure's face flushed. "Then I'll take her back."

"Will you now." Eammon looked down at the wheezing reporter. "Forgive me for saying this, but I think you've missed something."

"Missed?"

Eammon forced a sick smile. "I may be wrong, but I think this little surprise was Miss Halberton's idea. I'm afraid she doesn't want to go back. Tough dragging an unwilling woman all that way—wouldn't you say?"

Bonaventure stood up and clenched his fists. "What kind of animal are you? She's got hypoxia. You know what that means?"

Eammon shrugged. "Let me know when she's conscious. I need to find out what happened back there." He turned and shuffled toward his tent.

Mariner shuffled beside Bonaventure. "Sorry, old chap. Orders and all that. Is there anything I can do?"

"Go to hell."

Mariner shook his head and retreated to his tent.

Bonaventure looked at Akaal. "What about you?"

"I think she's coming out of it." He nodded for Nemi to help them.

A warm breeze rustled against her face. She opened her eyes and saw a pale blue flame hissing in the darkness. Something warm and firm pressed against her rear end. She remembered the night in Bombay. "Is that you, Mr. Bonaventure?"

"Sorry about that. Just wanted to keep you warm."

She pushed against him. "Feels good."

The Tenth Avatar

"What are you up to?"

"Just staying warm."

"Hmmm."

"How high are we?"

"Nineteen thousand."

She rolled on her back and looked up at him. "How far to the mountain?"

Bonaventure reached down and brushed back her hair. "I don't like that wheezing. You need to stay on oxygen." He reached for the bottle, but she grabbed his arm and pulled him close. Before he could speak, her warm lips were on his.

She pushed him away and smiled. "Thank you, Mr. Bonaventure."

"For what?"

"Being there."

Bonaventure had not known a woman like this. Fiercely independent, yet possessing a sensual warmth he'd not felt before. Maybe it was his approaching fortieth year. Maybe a fear his best days were behind him. Maybe more....

She squinted at the darkness. "Where's your friend?"

"He crawled in with Private Nemi. It's getting a bit crowded up here."

"We're alone?"

"Quite."

She rolled against him. "Want to break a record?"

"You mean—"

"Shut up and get in this sleeping bag."

He crawled into the sleeping bag and took her in his arms. "Are you sure about this?"

"You ask too many questions." She pressed against him and buried her lips on his.

It was tough making love in all those clothes, but they found a way. With her warm body grinding against him and her soft tongue darting between his lips, Bonaventure knew this was a woman he wouldn't easily forget.

It was more than sex. Karen burned with a passion that stirred his soul. A drive to go on when others turn away. To escape life's pain and reach for the stars. To touch the face of

God. Sound familiar, old chap?

There was only one problem. How many men had this queen spider seduced before stinging them to death? Too late, old chum. You should have known better when you lifted her off the floor in the *Charas*. You've fallen in love with an ambitious, neurotic reporter from across the sea.

He looked up at the beautiful face staring at him in the soft light.

"No complaints?"

"None."

She pressed her lips against his ear and whispered softly. "When do we climb?"

Bonaventure felt the hairs prick up on the back of his neck. He pushed her away and crawled out of the sleeping bag.

"Where are you going?"

"Get some rest. You'll need it for the hike back to Pangpema."

Karen glared at him. "You still don't get it. I'm going up there if it kills me."

"It will."

She hesitated and studied the rugged face staring at her. "You have beautiful eyes."

"What?"

"They're blue—like mine. We're alike in a lot of ways, but don't read too much into it. I enjoyed making love with you, but that's where it ends."

He felt the black widow's stinger pierce his heart. So much for tender moments. He reached for his boots and yanked them on. "I need some fresh air." He slipped on his anorak and pushed through the tent flap.

Eammon stretched his arms and scanned the horizon. The band of storm clouds had retreated to the southwest. He looked up at Kangchenjunga's ivory summit jutting into the crystal blue sky.

"When do we climb, Mr. Collins?"

Startled, Eammon turned around and saw the reporter crawl out of Bonaventure's tent.

The Tenth Avatar

"Looks like the weather's improved."

"Eammon stroked his stubbled chin. "How do you feel?"

"Much better. Just needed some rest and oxygen."

Eammon watched Bonaventure crawl out of Mariner's tent and stagger to his feet. "You look tired, Mr. Bonaventure. Rough night?"

Bonaventure frowned and looked away. He slipped on his pack and helped Mariner, Akaal, and Nemi disassemble the tents.

Eammon pulled out his binoculars and focused them on the narrow pass stretching toward the mountain. "Well—are we ready?"

Karen adjusted her pack and forced a smile. "I feel fantastic. Lead the way, Mr. Bonaventure."

Bonaventure lowered his head. "Akaal, give our ambitious reporter a fresh bottle of oxygen. We'll be at twenty thousand by sunset."

Eammon's eyes widened. "Sunset?"

"If the weather holds, we'll reach the northwest face tonight."

"You said it would take a week?"

"I was wrong."

An ugly frown swept across Eammon's face. "I don't like surprises, Mr. Bonaventure."

Bonaventure ignored him and helped the others pack the tents. Minutes later, they headed into the debris-filled pass winding toward Kangchenjunga.

Bonaventure and Akaal took the point, followed by Karen, Mariner, and Nemi. Eammon drifted into the rearmost position, his eyes focused on the blue-anoraked mountaineer and his friend.

40 | Know the Truth

"I've got Tomonaga!"

Yamato dropped his ration can and scrambled beside the trembling marine. He watched Private Genai fumble with the radio dial while pressing the headset to his ear.

Genai shook his head. "He keeps fading. His battery must be going."

Yamato snatched the headset and held it against his ear. He squinted at Genai and listened to the static. "Can you strengthen the signal?"

"I've got it cranked all the way. The problem is on the other end."

The static surged and receded like an ocean wave. Yamato closed his eyes, trying to detect the sound of a human voice. "Turn the crank."

"But, sir—"

"Turn it!"

The marine turned the generator crank until the hiss became deafening.

Yamato's eyes widened. Something was out there. A faint voice in the static. He grabbed the microphone and pressed the transmit button. "Schinichiro, can you hear me? It's Yamato. Purple code—one-two-four-fuji. Operation—NI." He lowered the microphone and waited.

His eyes lit up. "Yes—it's Yamato. With twenty-three marines to take you home. Give me your position."

Yamato pressed his fingers against the earpiece. "Repeat, Schinichiro. I need coordinates. Give me coordinates."

He lowered the mike and stared at the marine. "He doesn't have a map. They're working on instinct."

Lieutenant Hiryu eased beside his commander. "The beacon, sir. Tell him to leave it on."

"But his battery?"

Hiryu shook his head. "It's all he has."

Yamato hesitated and raised the mike to his mouth. "Listen to me, Schinichiro. We're only a few miles from you. Leave your beacon on. It's the only way we can lock your position. Do you read?" He pressed his finger on the earpiece and waited. "Good. We're coming, old friend. Give us a day."

Hiryu touched his shoulder. "How many men?"

"How many with you, Schinichiro?"

Yamato's face went blank. He lowered the mike and listened to the static in the headset.

"Captain?" Hiryu knelt beside his commander. By now, the entire force had gathered around them, their eyes fixed on the radio.

Yamato dropped the headset and took a deep breath. "Major Tomonaga is on the mountain's northwest face with two marines."

"Two?" Hiryu looked at him in shock. "What about the others?"

"Dead." Yamato listened to the rush of stunned whispers. "They've salvaged most of the canisters, but they're too weak to go on. No food. No shelter. They can't last long." He grimaced and stared at the ivory mountain rising through the haze. "We're a day's march away. Bad weather is coming and we have an enemy of unknown strength out there." He hesitated and glanced at Genai. "Any luck raising Nagano?"

"None, sir. The mountains must be blocking our signal."

Yamato stood up and glared at the marines. "Our brothers are up there. They've gone as far as they can. It's up to us now. If it takes all our lives, those canisters must reach Tokyo. Prepare to move out."

The shaken marines scrambled for their packs and equipment. They had longed for a shot at glory—and it had come. They formed twin columns and marched into the narrow pass leading to Kangchenjunga—and the battle of Armageddon.

Corporal Nagano slumped in the pilot's seat and stared at the frosted windshield. The shroud was gone, ripped away by the powerful surface winds.

Fourteen hours had passed since his comrades set out for the mountain. When no transmission came last night, he began hourly attempts to hail them on the purple frequency, but the only response was crackling static.

Was it the weather? Radio? Terrain? Or was something wrong out there? What if they were in trouble? And him sitting on his ass in this frozen tin can. What kind of marine is that?

He noticed a wisp of vapor coming from his mouth. It was getting colder. Better throw a blanket on your prisoner before he goes into shock. Must keep him alive for the interrogation.

He slipped off the headset and draped it on the pilot's wheel. The first rays of morning sun were striking the windshield. Maybe it would warm up soon. He flipped the mike over the wheel and climbed out of the seat.

He pushed through the bulkhead door and stepped into the deserted cargo compartment. The only light came from two small windows near the exit door.

He shuffled through the compartment and spotted a boot protruding from the shadows. He pulled out his flashlight and shined it on the pile of brown fur crumpled against the fuselage wall.

Why did Yamato pick him for this dirty work? He was no butcher. There was no honor in this. A wounded man waiting to die. His master-torturer ready to squeeze the last breath out of him. This was work for a pervert, not an Imperial Marine.

He fought back a wave of nausea. The prisoner had rolled on his back, exposing a black shirt soaked with blood. A small object dangled from a chain on the man's chest.

Nagano stepped closer and looked down at the flickering object. A cross. The man was a priest. He slumped against the wall and felt his stomach churn.

He shoved the flashlight in his belt and knelt beside the wounded man. He yanked away the fur parka and pressed a finger against the man's exposed neck. The pulse was very weak. He placed a thumb on the man's eyelid and lifted it to check the pupil. Maximum dilation. He didn't need to press an ear against the man's chest to know time was short. The labored breathing told it all. An ominous, crackling wheeze from blood seeping into the air passages.

He rubbed his stubbled chin and studied the man's blood-spattered face. Was this the face of his enemy? An unarmed missionary lying helpless at his feet? Ready for slaughter like those pitiful souls in Nanking and Shanghai? Was this the glory he'd been promised? The glory of the rising sun?

His stomach heaved. He scrambled to the cargo door and shoved it open in time to vomit in the snow. He doubled up in pain, praying for the nausea to end.

A gust of chilled wind struck his face, dusting him with snow. He took a deep breath and yanked the door closed. He collapsed against the fuselage wall, his eyes fixed on the man lying across from him.

If this was the enemy, it would be a quick war. These people had no stomach for fighting. They were weak and would fall like cattle before the bayonet.

He recalled Yamato's words before they took off from Nanking. The canisters must be retrieved at all costs. To assure victory in a war not yet started. To break the shackles of the white race and bathe the world in the light of the rising sun.

He stood up and gritted his teeth. *Enough of this. Be strong, Nagano. Remember your oath of bushido. Your comrades are depending on you.*

He glanced at his watch. Seven hundred hours. Damn morphine. Why did he give it to him? This was no time for compassion. Pain was the only way to snap this decrepit creature out of his stupor.

He lunged for the prisoner and seized his fur parka. "Wake up, pig. I want to get back to my men!"

He raked his hand across the man's face and waited for a cry of agony, but there was only the sound of labored breathing. The man slumped against him, his mouth dripping blood.

"Bastard! White bastard!" He dragged the prisoner against the fuselage wall and propped him up. That would slow the blood's deadly seepage into the air passages and keep him alive long enough for the morphine to wear off. He crouched on the floor and stared at the man's bleeding face.

The plane shuddered from a gust of wind. He listened to it whistle against the rudder—and he heard the cries of women being raped in the fields while their husbands lay dead at their side. And the screams of children skewered by bayonets. He smelled the putrid smoke of gasoline-soaked bodies burning in the darkness—and felt the searing heat of villages put to the torch until their flames lit up the night sky.

And now he was going to torture a priest. And when he had what he needed, he would kill him, and drop him in a frozen grave.

He clenched his fists. *Snap out of it, Nagano! This is war! In another hour, the morphine will wear off. A little pressure in the right places and your prisoner will squeal like a stuck pig. Then, you'll put him out of his misery, and it will be done.*

He looked down at his trembling hands. They were covered with blood. Blood from the China campaign. From slitting young throats and bayoneting soft flesh.

He wiped the blood on his pants and stared at his hands. Yamato was right. They were the hands of a butcher. Calloused and scarred from war's reality. From cutting down innocent people in the bloodbaths of Nanking and Shanghai. From strangling young women when they cried out for mercy. From lighting the funeral pyres that burned through the night. They were brutal hands. Killer hands.

He clenched his fists and pounded them against his legs. Only three years ago, those same hands had healed the sick and comforted the dying. They were softer then, the hands of a medical student. Caring hands. Compassionate hands. Trained to save lives and take away pain. To give hope when there was none.

Nagano rested his head against the metal wall and closed his eyes. He felt the tears trying to break through. *What's happened to you, doctor? What's happened to the doctor who has become a butcher?*

Aikido switched on the radio's homing beacon and stared at the pulsing red light.

"How does it look?" Tomonaga rested a gloved hand on Aikido's shoulder.

"Not good, sir. The weather's taken a toll on the battery."

The Tenth Avatar

"Keep your eyes on that light. We need every minute we can get." Tomonaga patted Aikido's shoulder and looked up at the fortress of ice towers.

The last avalanche had nearly finished them. If not for the buttress of rocks at their backs, the collapsing ice would have swept them off the forty-five degree slope like rag dolls. Helpless against the mountain's power, they cowered behind the rocks while waves of debris spilled over their heads, plunging into the haze below.

Ishikawa cleared the snow off the first canister and dropped against the rocks. "Best I can do, sir. If they spot this one, they'll find the others."

Tomonaga nodded and sat beside the young corporal. He leaned against the rocks and stared at the black canister. Five feet of chain extended from the canister to a snow drift below their feet. The second canister was buried in that drift, and five feet below it, the third. And so on, down the slope twenty-one more times. An enormous black centipede buried beneath the snow.

Tomonaga stroked his frost-covered beard. The wind had picked up, sending swirls of powdered snow across the slope. An ominous gray cloud was closing on them from the west. He could hear the wind howling inside it—warning them to get off the mountain before it was too late.

He pulled off a glove and studied the black frostbite on his swollen fingers. God, what his feet must look like. He grimaced and slipped on the glove. "How is the beacon, Private?"

Aikido glanced at the fading red light. "Still transmitting, sir."

Tomonaga gestured for the young marine to huddle beside him. He leaned back and felt Aikido's shoulder press against his arm. The pain in his side and shoulder was gone, replaced by chilled numbness.

He pressed against Aikido and felt something crack in his shoulder. No pain, just an ominous crack. He ignored it and stared at the incoming blizzard. There was no shelter. No warmth. Only three bodies huddled together at twenty-two thousand.

Tomonaga took a labored breath and chose his words. "I want you to know how proud I am to have served with you." He hesitated and fought back the tears. "It is important for good men to know why they die. I have always believed that. We are trained to give our lives without question—and we do. But I think it is good to know why."

He rested his head against the rocks and recalled the fateful morning at the Army Air Force Technical Institute. He'd sworn an oath of secrecy that day, but these were his men—and they were about to die. They should know the truth.

"Before I left Tokyo, I was briefed by three men. Their names aren't important, only their words." He turned away from a blast of subzero wind. A wall of blinding snow swept over them. He clenched his fists, and revealed the secret of NI.

"When war comes, there will be great celebrating in Tokyo. The English and Americans will suffer crushing defeats because of our lightning attacks and superior forces. The Germans will sweep across Europe while we ravage Asia and the Pacific."

"Our generals are convinced nothing can stop us. In secret meetings, they promise we will land on American soil in two years." He turned his face to the wind, his eyes fixed on the blowing snow.

"But they are wrong. America's industrial might is awesome. In time, they will turn the tide against us. It will be too late to negotiate."

"Our generals will grow desperate. They will command us to fight to the death like *samurai* until they are forced to face the truth. In the end, we will surrender in disgrace. A broken nation. A humbled nation."

Ishikawa pulled away in shock. "What are you saying? You're talking treason."

Tomonaga shook his head. "These aren't my words. They were spoken by the three men in Tokyo. Three very wise men who saw the future, and tried to change it."

"They are traitors!"

"No, Corporal. They are not traitors. They are *samurai*. And they're trying to save our nation before it's too late. That's why we were sent on this mission. That's why I lied about the gold."

Ishikawa glared at him. "You tell us this now?"

"Brave men should know the truth before they die."

"Truth?"

Tomonaga reached out and grabbed his arm. "That fluid in the canisters isn't glowing steam. It's the sun, Corporal. We've bottled the sun."

Ishikawa backed away in horror. "You're mad. You've gone mad. Stay away from me!"

What was happening? The ground was shaking. An ominous roar filled their ears. Tomonaga grabbed Ishikawa and pulled him down against the rocks. He wrapped his arm around Aikido and pulled him close. He could hear the ice towers giving way above their heads.

Tons of dislodged snow slammed into the rock buttress, exploding over their heads. Tomonaga grabbed for the radio and dragged it beside them. He glanced to his right and saw one of the ice towers crash into the slope, its jagged crown slashing at them as it careened into the haze.

The canister! If it went over, the others would never be found! He lunged for the chain and felt something slash his arm. He screamed in agony and clutched his bleeding wrist. "The canister! Get the canister!"

Aikido gripped the chain and dragged the black canister toward them. He collapsed in the snow and listened to the rumble fade away.

Ishikawa pulled back his commander's bloody sleeve and stared at the three inch gash in his wrist. A chunk of razor-sharp ice had severed an artery. He pulled off his belt and wrapped it around the major's arm. "Hang on, sir. This is all I have." He looped the strap through the buckle and gave it a yank.

There was no cry. Tomonaga stared blankly into space.

"Major!" Ishikawa gripped his commander's parka and looked into his eyes. "Give me a hand. He's going into shock."

Gary Naiman

Aikido didn't hear him. He lay against the rocks, his eyes fixed on the radio's fading power light. He watched it flicker, and disappear. He was so tired. He closed his eyes and listened to the wind....

Ishikawa felt a deep chill ebb through his bones. A strange calm settled over him. He fell back against the rocks and looked up at the falling snow—and he heard his commander's final words.

"We're alone. The world is against us. The Germans will use us to keep the Russians at bay until they defeat England and America. Then they'll turn on us. We're not like them. We're not their color. They shake our hands and spit at the ground when we walk away. We're alone, Corporal. We always were."

Ishikawa's eyes closed—and he knew the truth.

"The three men in Tokyo were *samurai*. They saw the future and chose to change it. That's why we flew to Germany and Norway. To steal the sun before the arrogant pigs knew what they had. If we could get the canisters back to Tokyo, Nishina could carry on where the others left off. And we could unleash the greatest force the world has ever known."

Tomonaga felt the snow covering his face. The wind echoed in his ears. A black veil closed over his eyes. With his last ounce of strength, he reached out and rested his bloody hand on the canister. And he felt the power of the sun....

41 | For Love and Glory

Bonaventure stuffed the flask in his pocket and stared at the four glowing tents. He could hear Mariner fumbling with the radio while Collins barraged him with the usual meaningless questions. There were no other sounds except the hissing burners. No conversations. No shuffling. Not even a groan.

After crawling through the worst terrain on God's earth, his exhausted team had reached Kangchenjunga's northwest face. At twenty thousand feet, it would take time to cope with the thin air and steepening terrain. Time they didn't have.

It had been a grueling day. A punishing day. Fresh snow had made the rugged glacier even more treacherous, blanketing its fissures and crevasses with a foot of white powder that concealed the gray, rotted ice underneath. One wrong step could be fatal. A five second plunge to oblivion.

Above them, the ridges rumbled from avalanches triggered by the warm afternoon sun. Twice, crumbling walls of snow and ice nearly swept them off the glacier. But they survived because of a brandy-sipping cockney and his Gurkha friend. Two mountaineers who had learned a bitter truth. Kangchenjunga was more than a pile of granite. It was a living, breathing creature that despised man's touch, and struck out viciously when he came too near.

He shuffled along the glacier, studying the enormous cirque of snow, ice, and rock that was the northwest face. To his left, a wall of ice jutted three thousand feet into the darkening sky. Below its crest, a narrow trench curled rightward toward the fortress of rock defending the north ridge.

His eyes followed the trench to the rock fortress, then beyond it along the north ridge's windswept crest as it rose toward the majestic summit in front of him. He focused on a snow-packed terrace three thousand feet below the summit, the fatal spot where Andre Cartier's team had camped before attempting their final ascent.

He pulled out his flask and took a swig. Two months ago, he had stood on that terrace peering at the untouched summit.

He recalled how close it seemed, and the surge of elation from knowing he would soon drive his victory pennant into that ivory peak—and stick a twenty-eight thousand foot dagger into the Royal Society's black heart.

He would stand where no man had stood. The sun on his face. The clouds at his feet. His eyes sweeping eastward from Tibet's purple-brown ridges to Sikkim's lush green hills. Then south to the steaming jungles of the Terai. And west toward Everest, Makalu, Annapurna, and the mighty Himalaya. And he would be free.

Then he heard the roar and felt the ice shudder under his feet. And he listened to Akaal's piercing scream.

Avalanche! The whole mountain's coming down!

He remembered shouting at Cartier and the others while pointing to the ridge crest above their heads. If they could scramble high enough, they might escape the tidal wave of death spilling off the summit.

He clawed at the snow, his eyes locked on the crest. The roar became deafening. He looked down and saw Akaal, Cartier, and Frueger crawling up the slope behind him, their faces frozen in terror. He heard the screams, and saw Cormier and Angstrom standing dumbfounded in the camp. *What the hell are you doing? Run, dammit! Get out of there!*

Everything was shaking. A huge shadow blotted out the sun. He pulled out his axe and drove it into the ice above his head.

He felt Akaal's hands clutch his ankle. He looked back and saw the camp disappear under a blast of white powder. Angstrom had slipped and fallen. Cormier was kneeling beside him, trying to help him up. *Run! For God's sake—run!*

But Cormier didn't run. He stood up and rested a hand on his friend's shoulder, his green eyes locked on Bonaventure. And they were gone....

He gulped down the brandy and wiped his mouth. He would never forget Cormier standing there, his hand on Angstrom's shoulder. So calm. So proud. The snow sweeping over them.

He felt a deep pain in his gut. They were his men. His team.

He should be with them now. Comforting them. Consoling them. Lying with them.

He jammed the flask in his pocket and stared at the black and white cliffs beneath the ridge crest. How many had died trying to climb that impossible gauntlet of rock and ice. To reach a ghostlike summit that seemed to drift away with every step. Luring them higher until it was too late.

A line of shadows crept up the cliffs toward the summit. He glanced over his shoulder at the sun setting behind Wedge Peak. It would be dark soon. How quickly it came. Like an ominous curtain closing over them.

What were they doing up here? Did Collins think they'd find a silver plane lying in the snow? Was the fool on drugs? If a plane had struck the ridge, the biggest piece of wreckage would be a melted belt buckle or charred rudder pedal.

And what if there was no plane? Or huddled survivors? Or mysterious cargo? Only treacherous slopes and deadly avalanches. Hell—what could be so bloody important to risk six lives on a lunatic's hunch?

He heard shuffling and spun around. Akaal was standing in the snow, his black fur hood draped on his shoulders. The Gurkha eased beside him and looked up at the mountain. "I gave her something to help her sleep."

Bonaventure glanced at the tents. "She needs to get down before that fluid builds up."

"She won't go."

"She'll go—with a little help from that sleeping powder in your pack."

"What?"

"I've lost enough people to this bloody mountain."

"But the weather?"

"The hell with the weather. Just give me enough powder to keep her out a few days. I'll rig a sled and take her back to Pangpema."

Akaal stared at him. "Are you crazy? We're too far up. You can't drag her across a glacier in a blizzard."

"Watch me."

"I won't let you do it."

"Sorry."

Akaal backed away. "Give it another day. The powder's full of herbs. It'll work if you give it a chance."

Bonaventure shook his head. "Can't risk it."

"Risk? You call dragging an unconscious woman across a glacier safe?"

Bonaventure started to walk away, but Akaal grabbed his arm. "If anything happens to you, I'll carry it to my grave. This is my doing."

"Bull. I'm the one who telegraphed you—remember? Now let go of my arm before I flatten you."

Akaal's hand slipped away. "If you go—I go. I won't let you kill yourself—and her too."

Bonaventure glared at him. "You call me crazy? You're the one who's crazy. You're in the bloody army. You were lucky the first time, but this is different. They'll court-martial you. Know what that means? Abandoning your post? Disobeying orders? They'll stand you in front of a bloody wall."

Akaal shook his head. "I don't think so. They have enough trouble without executing locals."

"They'll do it, dammit. That's crossing the line."

"Mr. Bonaventure!"

Bonaventure turned and saw Eammon waving at him from the tents. "What the hell does he want?" He started to turn away, but the second shout set him back on his heels.

"We picked up something!"

Bonaventure looked at Akaal in disbelief. He patted his friend's shoulder and ran toward the tents.

Eammon knelt in the snow watching Mariner tilt the radio's whip antenna toward the mountain. "Well?"

Mariner shook his head. "It's tough without a detector. I think it's coming from those rocks on the left. Maybe two thousand feet up."

"You think it's the plane?"

Mariner shook his head. "I don't know what to think. The signal's very weak. It comes and goes. Like a beacon."

Eammon looked up at Bonaventure. "We were trying to raise Pangpema when we picked it up. It has to be survivors from the crash."

Bonaventure watched Mariner position a compass on the map. The sergeant picked up a pencil and jotted down coordinates while sweeping the antenna left to right.

"Did you hear me, Mr. Bonaventure?"

"What?"

Eammon stood up and brushed back his white hair. "It's too late to go up there now. We'll climb at sunrise. That should give you enough time to figure a direct route."

Bonaventure looked at him in shock. "Direct? Are you nuts? Take a look at the snow on those cliffs. If we climb up there, we're finished."

"Sorry, we have no choice."

"No choice? Hell, I know a bloody good one."

"We climb at sunrise, Mr. Bonaventure." The Irishman turned and shuffled toward his tent.

Bonaventure stared at Akaal. "He's not only nuts—he's bloody dangerous. That's the way Dyhrenfurth's expedition bought it. And ours! You don't crawl up those ledges. The only shot is to climb that ice wall on the left. Then head up the trench and swing out on the face. And get the hell off as fast as possible."

Akaal folded his arms. "That will take four days. If there are survivors, they'll be dead by then."

Bonaventure's face reddened. "My God, man—they are dead! It's been four days since the bloody plane went down. No one could survive a crash like that. It's hell up there. Don't you remember?"

"We have to be sure."

"It's bloody suicide."

Akaal reached into his pocket and pulled out a small leather pouch. "Give her a pinch of this every few hours. It will keep her sedated until we come down. It shouldn't take more than two days to reach those rocks. We should be back in four."

Bonaventure felt the pouch slip into his hand. "Don't do it, man. For God's sake, not up the face. Take the trench."

Akaal patted his shoulder. "Stay well, old friend. See you soon. And by the gods, don't do anything rash. You know how rash you can be. She'll be all right. In four days, we'll take her down together."

"There's nothing up there. You're gonna kill yourselves for nothing."

"*Namaste*, friend." Akaal shuffled toward his tent.

"Got it!" Mariner dropped the headset and stood up with the map dangling from his hand. He scanned the mountain and pointed to a buttress of rocks below the ridge. "Right there, Mr. Bonaventure. In that haze below those rocks. That's where the signal was loudest before it stopped."

"Stopped?"

"Probably a dead battery."

"You believe that?"

Mariner stroked his blond hair. "We have to try. Orders and all that. How high do you make it?"

Bonventure shook his head. The sergeant hadn't heard a word with the headset on. He rubbed his beard and looked down at the radio. "Don't know, Sergeant. Don't know...."

Why was everything so dark? And that odor? Like the smell of decayed meat? She remembered the interrogation officer screaming at her under the bright light. And the sharp pain on her thighs when he whacked them with his swagger stick. The hands pinning her to the chair while he fondled her breasts and probed between her legs. The scissors snipping at her hair. His calloused hand waving clumps of it in front of her eyes. The stinging crack when he slammed his hand across her face. The ringing blackness.

She tried to turn over, but she couldn't move. Her wrists and ankles were bound to stakes pounded into the dirt floor. It was so cold. And that foul, rancid stench.

What was that? Something furry brushed against her ankle. She froze, her eyes locked on the darkness.

"Oh, God!" It was on her bare leg. Crawling up her thigh. Over her hip. Onto her stomach. She tried to twist it off, but it clung to her flesh with tiny, clawlike feet.

"No!" She struggled against the ropes, twisting her wrists and ankles until they bled. Something cold and wet touched her

breast. She heard a squeaking sound, and felt a stinging pain. She tried to scream, but the terror trapped it in her throat.

She heard others scurrying across the floor. Brushing against her ribs with their whiskers. The scream ripped out of her throat. She cursed them and tried to twist free, but they kept coming. Nipping at her flesh. Clawing at her with those tiny feet. Scampering across her bare body in the chilled darkness.

"Help me! For God's sake, help me!"

"Karen!"

Her eyes snapped open. Bonaventure was staring at her, his face twisted with concern.

"You bloody near scared me out of my britches. The way you kept swiping at the air."

She rubbed her eyes. "I feel drugged."

"Akaal gave you a sedative. Must be pretty strong." He reached for the oxygen bottle. "Take some of this."

She took a few deep breaths and pulled the tube out of her mouth. "What time is it?"

"Middle of the night."

"Where are we?"

"You don't remember?"

She grasped her forehead. "Don't play games."

"We're below the northwest face. It's clear out there if you want to take a look."

"How high are we?"

"Twenty thousand."

"Shit."

He helped her out of the tent and wrapped an arm around her. The black sky was full of stars.

"No moon?"

"Come and gone. It'll be daylight soon."

She leaned against him and stared at the black silhouette blotting out the stars. "That's it?"

"That's it."

"God—how will we find it up there?"

Bonaventure hesitated. Time for a tough decision. He

reached into his pocket and felt the pouch of powder. A pinch in her water and she'd sleep for a day. He'd already rigged the sled. It would only take a few minutes to tie her in. By the time she woke up, they'd be halfway to Pangpema.

He bit his lip and helped her toward a rock. "You better sit down for this."

"What's wrong?"

He backed away and looked down at her. "We picked up a transmission. It's coming from up there."

Her eyes lit up. "They're alive?"

"If you believe in ghosts."

"My gear!" She jumped up and nearly passed out in his arms.

"For God's sake, Karen." He helped her down on the rock and sat beside her.

"I'll be all right. Just need some oxygen."

"Sure. And the bloody queen's up there with tea and crumpets. Have you completely lost your marbles?"

She rubbed her forehead. "How high is it?"

"Mariner thinks it's coming from a rock cluster below the ridge. Maybe two thousand feet up. I think he's daft. Probably hearing an echo from his own radio."

She looked at him with bloodshot eyes. "When do we climb?"

He frowned and shook his head. "I want you to listen. Just this once. You owe me that."

"Don't waste your breath."

"You've got hypoxia. Your cells are dying. If we don't get you down, it'll be too late. Once it takes hold, it's irreversible. Your lungs are filling with fluid. It's like pneumonia, only worse. Not a pleasant way to go. No story's worth that."

"It's my choice."

"No—it's not that simple." He ran his hand through his black hair. "This is my last climb. Can't mess it up."

"Your what?"

"You heard me." He leaned forward and rested his arms on his knees. "Remember your little speech about the mountaineer who's lost his stuff? Well—you were right. Simple as that.

Only I was too proud to face it. Until it cost me."

"Cost?"

He looked up at the mountain. "I lost two men up there."

"I know about that. It was in Pierce's dossier."

He looked down and sighed. "I could have saved them. Instead, I turned my back on them. Left them on the ice with half a mountain coming down on their heads."

"But the others? You saved them?"

He shook his head. "They had Akaal. They would have made it without me."

"You're wrong. It wasn't your fault."

"Know how they died?"

"What?"

"Proud. Standing tall with a wall of snow coming down on them. They spit in its bloody eye. Now that's the way to go. With the sun on your face and your fists clenched. Not cowering on a ridge with your friend clutching your boot."

She rested a hand on his shoulder. "You had no time. You were trying to survive. Anyone would do the same."

He shook his head. "We don't get that luxury. When you head a team, they're your responsibility. You might hate each other, but up there you're family. And you're the father. If they starve—you starve. If they hurt—you hurt. If they die—you die."

"I see. Well—you sure picked an interesting hobby, Mr. Bonaventure."

He looked up at the mountain. "I love it, dammit. It's all I know. All I've ever known, except the streets. The only thing that ever mattered. And now, it's over. Only why did it have to end this way? I killed them, Karen. I might as well have shot them."

Her hand slipped off his shoulder. "You're not alone. I've lost a few good souls too. Lost them because of blind ambition. I'll carry that to my grave—just like you." She brushed away a tear. "But that's the price we pay for our dreams. That plane's my dream. It's what I've lived for. A chance to make a difference. To be there when something important happens. To record it. Photograph it. Live it. I'll never have this chance again."

"What—chasing a pile of wreckage up a mountain?"

She shook her head. "If my husband was right, that plane is the biggest story of the century."

"Bull."

She gripped his arm. "Pierce told me it was carrying gold."

"Gold?"

"Tons of it. Enough to build a supply line across Asia and the Middle East. To buy out any resistance and overwhelm the rest. Think of it, Julian. A seven thousand mile bridge linking the two most powerful armies in the world. Making them one."

"And you believed him?"

She yanked her hand away. "Now you listen to me. I'm a reporter, dammit. A good one. An editor once told me that, and he was the best. He taught me everything I know. Like never to rely on one source."

"I don't get it."

"That's why you're not a reporter. It wasn't Pierce's little speech. It was the link between his words and my interrogator's in Nanking. And Vasquez' log book. And my husband's final journal entry. Words like 'Nishina,' 'Noguchi,' and 'NI.' And 'gold,' 'Norway,' and 'purple code.' Too many connections. It's real—and it's important." She sat up and looked at him. "And I'm part of it."

He shook his head. "I think you've been sniffing too much oxygen."

She glared at him. "No, Julian. It's real, and we're right in the middle of it. We can make a difference. A real difference. Right here. Right now."

He cracked a smile. "Wish you were right. I'd get my chalet back and you'd get your bloody Pulitzer. Peaches and cream, and all that. Who knows—we might even become friends."

She reached up and kissed his stubbled cheek. "We are friends, Julian. We'll always be."

He slipped his arm around her. Her lips were parched, but they still drove him mad. And that firm body pressing against him. Well, Mr. Bonaventure. You've really made a mess of things. First you throw in the towel. Now you've fallen in love. What a milksop you turned out to be.

He felt her body relax. Her head drooped against his chest. Her labored breathing slowed. Everything was still. A shooting star flashed across the night sky. It was a moment like none other. A moment on the roof of the world.

Damn—why couldn't she be right. After forty years of struggle, he had finally found something more important than mountains. A person so much like him. Someone he could cherish for the rest of his life. A reason to go on.

He looked up at the black summit. Who was he kidding? It doesn't work that way for people like them. People obsessed with their dreams. Fighting to break the shackles of a confining world. Reaching for the stars until one day they slip and fall. Yes—life is short for dreamers. But what a ride.

He stood up and lifted her in his arms. Not so bad, Mr. Bonaventure. You lose a life, but gain something back. Something far more important. Something eternal. Something called glory.

He carried her back to the tent and eased her down on the blanket. The only sound was the blue flame hissing in the burner. He sat in the darkness, his eyes fixed on her.

In a few hours, they'd strap on their packs and head across the glacier to the first barrier, a thousand foot gauntlet of rock and ice. If they survived the treacherous climb up that wall of granite, they'd scramble into the deep snowpack—just in time for the next blizzard. Forced to dig in, they'd lose precious time while the upper ledges swelled with fresh snow.

The storm would pass quickly. With only an hour of daylight left, they'd trudge up the snowpack toward the second barrier of ice and rock leading to the north ridge. With the sky darkening, they'd camp on the exposed icefall, only a few hundred feet below the source of the mysterious signal.

The clouds would clear away, exposing a magnificent bowl of stars. Everything would be still. So calm and beautiful. And the rumble would begin.

There would be no escape. Nowhere to run. The wall of collapsing snow and ice would sweep over them like a giant wave while they stood helpless on the exposed slope. Helpless like Cormier and Angstrom on that fateful day. And it would be done. And Julian Bonaventure would lose the only two people he ever loved.

He kissed her on the cheek and crawled out of the tent. "Not this time, Reuters...."

"Mr. Collins!"

Eammon sat up and shaded his eyes from the bright sunlight pouring into his tent.

"It's Mariner, sir. We've got problems."

Eammon squinted at the sergeant staring at him through the open flap. "Well—spit it out."

"It's Bonaventure, sir. He's gone. I think he's on the mountain."

"What?" Eammon scrambled out of the tent and stood up in the thin air. He grabbed Mariner's shoulder and fought the dizziness sweeping over him. When his head cleared, he saw Corporal Dawa and Private Nemi standing a few feet away, their eyes fixed on the northwest face. "What is it? What's that fool up to?"

Akaal pointed to a line of tracks fading into the mountain's shadow. "He must have left before sunrise."

"Damn him!" Eammon retreated to his tent and yanked the scope out of his pack. He shuffled past the dazed Gurkha and popped it open.

Akaal shook his head. "There are too many shadows. We won't see anything until the sun clears the summit."

Eammon slammed the scope shut. "Pull the gear together. We're going up." He turned for his tent.

"What's wrong?"

Eammon looked down at Karen peering through her open tent flap. "Your friend's trying to beat us up there. Did you tell him about the gold?"

She looked at him in shock. "My, God. He's alone up there?"

"Not for long." Eammon swung his pack over his shoulder and grabbed his rifle.

"Wait—you're not going up without me."

"You're on your own, Miss Halberton. Just don't slow us down." He gave his straps a tug and shuffled toward the others.

Everything after that was a fog. She remembered slipping on her pack and reaching for the oxygen bottles. That's when she realized her camera was gone. In its place, a small note protruded from the brown leather case. She snatched it and read the firm script:

Sorry Reuters,
Guess this is my choice. If I find anything, I'll try to keep my hands steady for that Pulitzer winning photo. Get well....
Bonaventure

"Bastard!" She took a gulp of oxygen and staggered after Collins and the others.

42 | Glowing Steam

Bonaventure ran his fingers along the crack in the granite. Not the best anchor point, but it would have to do. He pulled a piton out of his belt and pressed the razor-sharp point against the crack. His free hand groped for the hammer.

The next few seconds would be critical. If the rock fractured, he would have to climb along the sixty degree wall until he found another anchor point. Easier said than done with quivering arms and legs.

He had been climbing almost five hours. The first four were a blur, an exhilarating charge up the ice between the jagged rocks. By nine, he'd scrambled nearly eight hundred feet. At that pace, he would reach the snowpack by ten and have a shot at the target before the sun dropped behind the western peaks.

A quick search of the area and he'd be on his way down. A little risky with only the moon to light his way, but there was no choice. He had to intercept Akaal and the others before they followed his trail into the mountain's deadly avalanche zone.

It was a good plan, but the mountain had its own. An hour ago, his frantic climb came to an abrupt halt below a two hundred foot wall of granite. With the sun's rays creeping over the summit, he was suddenly cut off from the snowpack and upper slopes by a wall of glazed rock.

There was no way around it. No benevolent traverse. Only a hard stretch of unfriendly granite. The choice was clear. Either turn back or climb the damn thing. Some choice. He seized a handhold and sprung onto the sixty degree face.

Things were going well until a few minutes ago when the cramps began. First, a tightness in his upper back. Then, a wave of agonizing contractions in his arms and legs. After five hours of relentless assault, age and fatigue had begun to take their toll. He slumped against the granite, his body quivering with pain. The ledge was only a hundred feet overhead, but it might as well be a hundred miles.

He'd felt this anguish before. On Aconcagua when he

closed on the twenty-three thousand foot summit with an ice axe in each hand. But that was seven years ago, and that brash mountaineer was no more. The lungs and muscles were weaker now. The back and limbs not as supple. Even the eyes had blurred a bit. No longer sharp like an eagle's, but straining to focus on the rocks overhead.

But the greatest loss wasn't physical. Where was the fierce tenacity that had conquered forty-two peaks in twenty-two years? And the relentless courage that saw him through those brutal days and nights in Whitechapel's violent streets? And the rage that humiliated the Royal Society and its pompous hypocrites?

Tenacity. Courage. Rage. Ripped from his heart two months ago when the mountain crashed down on his team. Replaced by new, unfamiliar feelings. Fear and doubt. Remorse and guilt. Dreaded emotions more dangerous than any adversary.

He clutched the piton and recalled the plaque Hans Furgler gave him on his nineteenth birthday. A simple wood crest with five scrawled lines....

> *Oh, God...*
> *To stand on virgin ice again,*
> *and feel your presence in the wind.*
> *To reach up and touch the sky,*
> *and see your face before I die....*

This was his one chance to make up for what had happened two months ago. If he could reach the source of the signal and retrieve whatever was up there, he might intercept the others before they climbed into the fall zone below the north ridge.

If he couldn't pull it off, they would march into that exposed ice and become the mountain's latest victims. And Julian Bonaventure would lose the only friend he ever had, and the only woman he ever loved.

By now, they had followed his tracks to the ice barrier and spotted his yellow pennant flapping in the wind. With a thousand foot climb looming over them, Collins would order Akaal to take the point, the first good decision the idiot had made since leaving Pangpema.

With Akaal leading the way, the five climbers would reach the granite wall by mid-afternoon. Akaal would spot the yellow strips streaming from the pitons hammered in the wall. He'd crack a smile while recalling the yellow scarf he'd given his friend on his thirty-ninth birthday. His smile would turn to a grin when he noticed the belay rope dangling from the first piton. An invitation to the dance.

It would take them the rest of the day to scale the wall. With the sun setting, and a new storm coming in, they'd dig a snow cave and spend the night at twenty-one thousand. When they set out in the morning, he'd be descending toward them with a camera of exposed film and a report of what he'd seen. Who knows, he might even have a souvenir from the phantom plane.

He felt a rush of anger. What if the Irishman didn't believe him? What if he insisted on going up? Akaal would be forced to follow. And Karen!

"Bastard!" He slammed the hammer into the piton, sending sparks flying in all directions. The recoil drove him backward, nearly throwing him off the wall.

He gave the piton a few more whacks and jammed the hammer in his belt. Good—it was holding. Like the four below it. He rested his head against the granite and took a slow, deep breath. Only a hundred feet, Bonaventure. Can't stay on this bloody rock forever.

He groped for a fresh handhold and felt his arm quiver. A cramping pain shot through his shoulder and back. Ignore it, man. You can't stay down here. Gotta go on. He gripped the rock and pulled himself up.

What was that? An ominous rumble coming from the sky? He leaned back and squinted at the ledge.

The rumble became a deafening roar. The same roar he heard two months ago. There was no escape. Nowhere to hide. His only chance was the snowpack above the ledge. If it didn't give way, it might absorb the slide before the deadly cloud of snow and ice reached him. It was all he had. He stared at the ledge and waited.

His heart jumped as a blast of white powder exploded off the ledge into the blue sky. He pressed his face against the granite and braced for the deadly impact.

Snow splattered against his shoulders and back. He clung to the rock, fighting the deluge of cascading snow.

The roar faded, replaced by an eerie calm. When he looked up, the air was filled with ice crystals. They were everywhere, floating in space like tiny, flickering diamonds.

He brushed the snow off his face and looked up at the blue sky. Was he dead? Was this heaven? Impossible—he wasn't going to heaven.

He collapsed against the wall. The cramps had spread to his stomach and ribs. In a few seconds, he'd double up in pain and plunge to his death. The headlines would be quite a gift for the Royal Society....

Renegade Mountaineer Perishes on Kangchenjunga
Lost in Avalanche on Northwest Face

Fear and doubt. Remorse and guilt. Not much to show for forty years of struggle. His crumpled body sprawled on the ice while their laughter echoed off the Royal Society's hallowed halls.

He'd almost forgotten their laughter. Their fat bodies shaking with it when they read the newspaper headlines. And why shouldn't they laugh? The renegade was dead. No more insults. No further embarrassments. Things would be normal again. Everything in its proper place again. Time for a toast.

No, goddammit. He owed Hans Furgler more than that. And his two friends. And himself.

He dug his fingers into the granite and sprung upward. The pain was excruciating, but he gritted his teeth and went on. He was too mad to die.

Eammon reached down and plucked the yellow pennant out of the ice. "What's he up to?"

"He's marked a route. Like you asked."

Eammon scowled at the Gurkha. "The idea was to help us climb the damn thing. Not lead us on a wild goose chase."

Akaal's face flushed with anger. He turned away and studied the boot tracks leading up the ice.

"Well?"

"Time is short. We must clear the barrier before dark."

"You mean, we have to climb it?"

"It's the only way up."

Eammon stared at the gauntlet of granite and ice rising into the sky. "How?"

"Up the ice between the rocks. I think we'll find more pennants up there."

The Irishman shook his head. "Well—get on with it."

Akaal nodded and pulled out his ice axe while Nemi helped the others tighten their packs. He was about to start up the ice when he noticed the reporter slipping an oxygen tube in her mouth. He could hear her wheezing while she gulped the life-giving gas.

"Well, Corporal?"

Akaal looked down at Eammon and nodded toward the reporter.

The Irishman's face reddened. He jabbed his ski pole in the ice and turned toward her. "I warned you, Miss Halberton. It's not too late to turn back. Plenty of food and oxygen at the camp. You can rest there until we're down."

She yanked the tube out of her mouth and glared at him. "I think that's enough whining for today—don't you?"

Eammon turned away in anger. He snatched his ski pole out of the ice and charged past Akaal with Sergeant Mariner on his heels.

Nemi shuffled beside her. "Please, memsaab. He is right. You can't go on. That's a thousand foot climb."

"Get moving, Private. I'm fine." She gripped her ski pole and brushed past him.

Nemi watched her stagger up the ice. He backed away, but Akaal grabbed his arm.

"Stay close to her."

"What?"

"Stay close. She's your responsibility."

Nemi looked at him in shock. Those were the last words he wanted to hear. A hopeless task. When the young reporter died, it would be his fault. The English would be enraged. He'd be court-martialed and found guilty of murdering a white. They'd hang him from the flagpole in front of the barracks.

He rubbed the back of his neck and watched her stumble up the ice. Oh—how he hated these people. He never should have left his village for a fancy uniform and few *rupees* a month. Nothing was worth this grief. He shook his head and headed up the ice.

Karen jabbed her ski pole into the ice and leaned forward. Her lungs were on fire. Her heart pounded against her ribs, pleading for oxygen while struggling to carry its insane host to an insane destination four miles above the earth.

No one spoke. There were no words of encouragement. Just labored breathing as they staggered up the twisted ribbon of ice. She remembered reaching for the oxygen bottle, but giving up when she couldn't lift it out of her belt. Hell with it. Just keep climbing.

The cramping pain subsided. She couldn't feel anything. She was floating in space. Time meant nothing. Hours were minutes. Minutes—hours. She remembered covering her mouth and coughing violently. When she pulled her gloved hand away, it was spattered with blood. She dropped on the ice.

A firm hand grasped her shoulder. "You can rest now, memsaab."

She looked up and saw Nemi peering down at her through the haze.

"You can rest a bit."

She slumped on the ice. God, she was tired. The hell with it. Just close your eyes and go to sleep.

Nemi jabbed a rubber tube in her mouth. "Please, memsaab. Don't sleep. You will never wake up."

She heard a hissing sound and felt the oxygen rush into her throat. She gulped at it and felt a searing pain in her chest. "No—take it away."

"Breathe, memsaab. Please...."

She forced another breath and felt the pain subside.

"That's it. More...."

She clutched the tube and took slow, deep breaths. The dizziness subsided. Feeling returned to her arms and legs. The pounding in her temples slowed—and she suddenly knew how close she had come.

She slipped the tube out of her mouth and forced a weak smile. "Thank you, Private. That's one I owe you."

"You will be fine, memsaab. Everything will be fine."

They moved out a few minutes later. She managed a few steps before collapsing against the rocks. What was wrong? Her legs wouldn't move. She leaned on the ski pole and lunged forward.

Damn! She was lying on the ice. She tried to stand, but her legs wouldn't respond. A wave of panic swept through her. She could see Eammon and the others climbing into the haze. The bastard was leaving her behind!

No, goddammit! She'd come too far to die like this. She jammed the pole in the ice and tried to stand, but it was no use.

Strong hands grasped her waist and lifted her off the ice. She reached out and grabbed Nemi's parka. "I'll be all right. Just give me a minute."

"Try to walk, memsaab. I'll pull you the rest of the way."

Nemi tied a rope around her waist and gave it a firm tug. "Can you walk?"

She nodded and grasped the rope.

"Hang on, memsaab. Don't look down." He attached the rope to his belt and headed up the ice.

She felt the rope yank against her waist. A smile cracked her lips. Now she knew how a cow felt on the way to the slaughterhouse. The only thing missing was the ring in her nose. She stumbled up the ice, her hands clutching the rope.

She heard a familiar voice echo off the rocks. He'd been dead fifteen years, but she would never forget that drunken, rasping voice. And those filthy, calloused hands. Touching her. Violating her.

Oh—he was up there all right. Cursing her. Threatening

her. Humiliating her. He wouldn't rest until she was lying with him in that rotted coffin. His little baby in his bony arms.

She reached down and gripped the ice axe in her belt. If she was going to die, may God grant her one wish. That she could take this razor-sharp axe with her. To split that bastard's black heart when she saw him on the other side. She gripped the rope and staggered upward....

Eammon slipped his right hand inside his parka and clutched his chest. The numbing pain had spread to his left shoulder and arm. The symptoms were unmistakable. He looked up at the checkered slope of granite and ice. A beam of sunlight struck his face. He could see Corporal Dawa climbing through the yellow rays, his supple arms and legs gliding up the ice like a snow leopard.

He leaned against a rock and wiped the stinging sweat from his eyes. Can't quit now. Only a few hundred feet. He yanked off his glove and jammed his hand in his pocket. He grasped a small envelope and groped for one of the nitro capsules while glancing at the others. No danger of them noticing. They could barely lift their heads.

He placed the capsule in his mouth and positioned it between his teeth. It cracked when he bit into it. He closed his eyes and felt a rush of reassuring warmth.

"Are you all right, Mr. Collins?"

His eyes snapped open. Mariner was staring at him, his blond hair glistening with sweat.

"You look a little shaky."

"I'm fine, Sergeant. Just a little winded. Looks like we're almost there."

"Yes, sir. Sure you're all right?"

Eammon nodded and waved him on. He watched him fade into the haze, followed by Private Nemi.

He took a deep breath and pushed off the rock. A rope brushed against his arm. He hesitated and looked down.

She stared at him with exhausted eyes. She could barely speak, but her words found their mark. "Anything wrong, Mr. Collins?"

"I'm fine, Miss Halberton. How about you?"

"I think we're about the same—don't you?" She forced a weak smile and staggered past him.

He reached into his pocket and clutched the envelope. *God—not like this.* He'd always figured it would come from a sniper's bullet or knife in the ribs. But to die like this. An aging spy clutching his heart on a pile of ice and rock. *No, goddammit! Too much at stake.*

Tomorrow, they'd reach the plane and tag the gold. With a little luck, he'd get off a message to that fool in Pangpema, instructing him to contact Dharan for assistance. Within two days, Pierce would fly in a second team with enough muscle to bring down the gold. Then a flight back to Dharan, and a trip home to Ireland. And a "well done" from Ten Downing Street.

He popped a second capsule into his mouth and bit into it. Hang on, you tough old Irishman. There's work to be done. Find the gold, send the message, and pump four slugs into those fools. Then a few unpleasantries with Miss Halberton, and you'll still have a bullet left for your meddling friend in Pangpema. A bit challenging, but a fitting way to wrap up ten years service in the world's finest intelligence organization. A rewarding one too, especially with those five packs of gold stuffed in the Buddha. *So get on with it!* He took a gulp of oxygen and headed up the ice....

Bonaventure leaned on his ice axe and stared at the snow streaming off the ridge. The blue sky was gone, replaced by ominous haze. Behind him, the sun's orange disk had plunged into a bank of storm clouds.

A chilled wind swept across the snow pack, lifting swirls of white powder into the air. He turned away from the stinging crystals and waited for the turbulence to pass.

After climbing through deep snow for four hours, he was within striking distance of the rock cluster Mariner had pointed to. With the storm only minutes away, he had to get up there before the wind and snow erased any hope of finding something.

He pulled out his canteen and popped the cap. Frozen. Just as well. Something stronger was in order. He reached in his pocket and dragged out the flask. The brandy burned like hell going down, but it gave him the boost he needed. He jammed the flask in his pocket and headed up the ice toward the windswept ridge.

He was scaling an ice buttress when the storm hit. A black haze swept over him, followed by a blast of frozen wind. Sheets of wind-driven snow splattered against his anorak. He clung to the ice, fighting to maintain his grip in the fifty knot winds.

A lightning bolt struck the top of the buttress, showering him with sparks. The air smelled from static electricity. He reached for a handhold and tried to lift himself, but his arms and legs wouldn't respond. He collapsed against the ice and looked down at the metal gear clinking in his belt. *Blast, I'm a bloody lightning rod!*

He yanked the axe out of his belt and slammed it into the ice above his head. He tried to lunge for the ledge, but a cramping pain stopped him. He let out an agonizing groan and slumped against the ice. And he heard Han's piercing voice...

What kind of mountaineer are you? Do you want to die down there? All the way, dammit! All the way!

He dug his fingers into the ice and clawed like an animal. He didn't stop clawing until he dropped on his belly in the deep snow above the ledge. The wind ripped at his hood, cursing him for conquering another barrier. The hell with it.

He sat up and tightened the scarf covering his nose and mouth. The storm was at full force now, its winds driving the snow into his face. He had to find shelter before it turned him into a block of ice.

He jabbed the axe handle into the snow and pushed himself up. Straining against the wind, he stumbled up the steep slope toward a shadow of rocks barely visible in the whiteout.

He thought of Karen and the others. *God—don't let them come up here. This isn't a place for human beings. It's for madmen like me. An asylum for insane mountaineers.*

He straightened up and braced against the wind. A bolt of

lightning flashed over his head, followed by a blast of thunder. All hell had broken loose on Kangchenjunga. God, he loved it. Oh—how he loved it.

He looked up at the churning haze. They were up there. Only two thousand feet above him. Asleep under the snow. They were so close. They would never be this close again.

A choking pain welled up in his throat. He clenched his fist and screamed at the invisible summit. "Cormier! Angstrom! It's Bonaventure!"

He scanned the whiteout and listened to the wind. The Spaniard's words echoed in his ears. *How can a man with your reputation stop halfway up a mountain?* Good question, chum. Damn good question. He gritted his teeth and charged up the slope.

What was it? Was he seeing things? He edged toward the three shadows huddled against the rocks. There was no movement. No sign of life. It was like staring at a photograph. He knelt down and studied their faces.

Their eyes were closed, as if in deep sleep. There was no pain. No fear. Just three men huddled together in the drifting snow.

He reached out and touched the center man's frost-covered face. It was a handsome face, appearing oriental. The other two looked younger. All three wore white parkas with the hoods flapping against their frozen faces.

He leaned forward and brushed away the snow. The center man's parka was ripped open, revealing a gray thermal sweater. A blue collar protruded from the neck. Small blue patches were sewn on the collar's points, each containing twin gold stripes. Silver threads dangled from each patch.

He rubbed his finger across the torn patches while recalling his climb up Mt. Fujiyama eleven years ago with a young Japanese officer named Hada—a captain in the Imperial Marines. Hada wore twin blue patches on his sleeves, each with gold stripes and three silver cherry blossoms stitched neatly in a row.

Bonaventure leaned back in shock. What kind of madness was this? He was sitting in a blizzard at twenty-two thousand with three dead Japanese marines.

He squinted into the whiteout. If a plane had crashed on the ridge, these poor souls had descended at least a thousand feet before succumbing to the altitude and weather. Incredible feat, given their condition. They were men of great courage. They deserved a better fate—just like the others he lost two months ago. He lowered his head and said a prayer for the dead.

The wind had eased and the sky was brightening. The fast-moving storm would be gone soon, along with the fading light. *Snap out of it, man. There's work to be done.* He stood up and began probing the snow with his axe handle.

He found a radio buried against the rocks. It was coated with ice and appeared dead. When he tried to crank its generator, the frozen handle snapped off.

The three soldiers carried no possessions except a small black book jammed inside the center man's pocket. It was printed in *Kanji* and contained a series of coded messages. Bonaventure knew enough Japanese to recognize the recurring letters "NI."

When he flipped the pages, a small photograph dropped out of the book into the snow. He brushed it off and studied the beautiful oriental woman holding a small child. He nodded and stuffed the photo in the dead man's pocket. "Sorry, chum. Wonder if they'll ever know."

The two marines clutched automatic rifles, as if waiting for an invisible enemy to charge up the ice.

Bonaventure pried one of the rifles free and checked the clip. It was full. He slung the rifle over his shoulder and picked a second clip from the dead marine's belt. It would be good evidence for the doubting Irishman. And to add a little insurance, he ripped the headset off the radio and stuffed it in his pack. The *swastika* on the earpiece looked a little out of place, but that was Collin's problem.

With the snow trailing off, he backed away from the nightmarish scene and looked up at the thinning haze. In another hour, the sky would clear and the moon would rise over the summit. No sense waiting. Nothing else worth salvaging. Better get down while the weather held out. He gripped his shoulder straps and gave his pack a firm tug.

Something jiggled inside his pack. The camera! He'd forgotten the bloody picture!

He yanked off his pack and pulled out the bulky camera. *Easy, old man. If you break it, she'll kill you for sure.*

He unscrewed the shutter cap and peered through the eyepiece. Too bad he couldn't get a shot of the plane's wreckage. Maybe an insignia off the wing. She'd probably make a million off it. Who knows, she might even buy back his chalet.

He aimed the camera at the three bodies and backed away. *Make it good, Bonaventure. While there's still light. That's it. Just a bit further.*

He stepped back and felt his boot strike something in the snow. Before he could react, he was sprawled on his back with the camera lying beside him. "Damn!" He sat up and yanked the camera out of the snow. If the shutter was damaged—

He hesitated and looked at the spot where he'd tripped. The snow was gouged away, revealing a length of black chain. He crawled beside it and brushed away the snow.

What was it? He ran his gloved hand over the black metal canister. Not very big. Maybe a foot in diameter. He eyed the cap protruding from the cylindrical top. "What the bloody hell?"

He brushed away more snow, revealing a second chain extending down the slope. He ran his hand along the black chain until it struck a second buried canister. He uncovered it and found another chain extending further down the slope. What kind of warped contraption was this? He continued down the slope until he'd exposed three more canisters. The chain seemed to go on forever.

He sat in the snow and stared at the five canisters stretching up the slope toward the dead men—and he recalled Karen's story about the gold. Impossible—three exhausted men couldn't drag a load of gold down a mountain. And why would they stuff it in metal canisters? It would be boxed in dust-catching paper or cloth. Maybe even foil. No—this wasn't gold.

He leaned forward and gripped the fifth canister's metal cap. It didn't budge. Enough of this bloody game. He was wasting critical time. He sat up on his knees and pulled out his hammer. A few good whacks would do the job.

He slammed the hammer against the soft metal, putting a healthy dent in it. Puzzled, he ran his fingers along the dent. Lead? Why would they pack something in lead? He raised the hammer and prepared to give the cap another whack.

What was that sound? A faint hiss coming from the haze? Maybe a hundred feet below him? He looked down at the dented canister. Where the hell was that hiss coming from? Certainly not from these things. Unless—

His eyes lit up. Mines! The damn things were mines! He dived into the snow and buried his face in his arms. The only sound was the hiss.

He squinted into the haze. Something was down there—like steam rising from the snow. He stood up and shuffled down the slope into the haze.

What the hell? A plume of glowing steam billowed from a five foot crater of melted ice. A brilliant white light radiated from the crater's center. He edged closer and peered through the steam.

A small, glowing object lay in a pool of bubbling water at the crater's center. It emitted a blinding white light that made him look away. It was like the sun.

He crouched down and stared at the thirty foot plume of steam. What was it? A geyser? Budding volcano?

His eyes darted to a dark object lying at the far edge of the crater. It was one of the canisters. The cap had broken off, spilling its contents into the crater. A chain trailed from the canister into the snow.

He stood up and backed away from the crater. What kind of hellish creation was this? Lead canisters chained together beneath the snow? Glowing steam? A small rod brilliant as the sun? Burning its way through a mountain? Was this the plane's mysterious cargo? Had good men died for this? Had he climbed twenty-two thousand feet for this? Let it be, Bonaventure. This witch's brew wasn't meant for man's eyes.

Gary Naiman

He slipped on his pack and headed down the slope. He'd forgotten to take the photograph. He'd even forgotten the camera. It lay in the snow beside the first canister, its film clouded with radioactive light.

He stopped once to look back. The moon had broken through the clouds, bathing the northwest face in silver light. All was calm under the canopy of stars. All except a spot below the north ridge where a glowing pillar of steam rose into the night sky. He shook his head and turned away.

43 | The Battle

They dragged him into a shadowed room with mirrored walls and a black marble floor. There were no windows, only a large portrait on the far wall. He recognized the subject.

A crystal chandelier hung from the gold ceiling, its glistening centerpoint suspended over a polished black table. All the chairs had been removed except two black leather highbacks at opposite ends of the elongated table.

Strong hands pressed him into the chair facing the portrait. He slumped against the black leather and stared at the empty chair across from him. There were no sounds except a clock ticking in the shadows.

A door swung open below the portrait and a man stepped into the room. "Welcome, young Hidalgo. It has been too long."

The guards seized his arms and yanked him out of the chair. They clicked their heels and snapped to attention while tightening their viselike grips.

He stared at the portly officer smiling at him from the opened door. The man's brown uniform was plastered with gold and silver medals. His receding charcoal hair had been brushed back, exposing a round face and protruding nose. The brown eyes were a gambler's. Shifting, smirking eyes.

He glanced at the uniformed man in the portrait. Yes—they were the same. One regal and bigger than life on a five foot canvas of red, black, and gold. The other, a rather meek looking man with a bulging belly and squatted frame. Amazing what an artist can do.

"Short for words? Not like you, señor." The portly man smiled beneath his abbreviated charcoal moustache and gestured for his guest to be seated. He waited for the two guards to jam him into the chair before sitting down.

The Generalissimo rested his arms on the table and leaned forward. "Not sure who I am? Maybe this will help." He nodded toward the opened door where a servant held a red candle. The white-haired servant stepped into the room and placed the flickering candle on the table.

"There—a candle for effect. Does it remind you of anything?"

"Remind?"

"You know. Valencia. The Marva Bar. Flamenco music. Lieutenant Campeador and his beautiful fiancée."

"I know who you are."

"Ah—very good, señor. Then you must know why you're here."

"I have an idea."

The Generalissimo leaned back in his chair and placed a finger against his lip. He lunged forward and pointed the stubby finger at his guest. "You're going to die, señor. To join your father and his treasonous friends in a muddy grave outside Madrid."

His hands clenched the chair. "You moved my father's remains?"

Franco shrugged his shoulders. "Traitors don't deserve a grave overlooking the sea. They belong in the mud with the lizards. You'll be glad to know we didn't disturb your mother."

"You separated them?"

"I guess we did."

He lunged out of the chair, but the guards seized his arms and pinned him facedown on the table.

"I see you haven't lost your hatred, señor. That's good. It will help you in the harsh days ahead."

He tried to move, but their grips were like iron. He heard the Generalissimo slide out of his chair and walk toward him, his boots tapping across the marble floor.

"You can make things easier for yourself. Confess now and we'll be lenient. All we want is our gold."

He tried to turn away from the evil face peering down at him, but one of the guards pressed his head against the black table. He looked up in disgust as Franco bent close to him, his face only inches away.

"I won't ask again, señor. After all, I've kept my part of the bargain. A bit late perhaps, but we are having that dinner." Franco reached out and clenched his hair. "Well—what's it *going to be? Or do more of your father's friends have to suffer? Like the old woman in the prison. I believe her name is Maria."*

His face turned red hot. His blood was boiling. He yanked an arm free, but a punch to the ribs stopped him.

"So be it, young Hidalgo. Too bad, I rather liked your spirit. I could have used you."

"Pig! Bastard!" He felt the punches slam into his ribs and kidneys. And that ugly, twisted face sneering down at him.

Oh, God. Not Maria. How could they do this to an old woman? To the only mother he'd ever known. To all that was proud and good in Spain.

He spit at Franco's face and felt a stinging pain in his jaw. Everything went black....

He opened his eyes and saw his breath floating in the air. The gold ceiling and chandelier were gone, replaced by a curved metal roof. It was very cold.

He tried to sit up, but a searing pain stopped him. He fell back and clutched his chest. His parka and shirt had been cut open. Something coarse was stretched across his ribs. It felt like a bandage.

He grimaced and rolled on his side. A bright light struck his eyes. He was staring at a small round window. It reminded him of the porthole on the *Mephistopheles*. He gritted his teeth and propped himself against the metal wall.

He was sitting on the floor of a plane. There were no seats, only twin metal benches running the length of the fifty foot compartment. The benches terminated at a bulkhead where a metal door was swung partially open.

His eyes froze on the door. A voice was coming from the other side. It seemed strained. Almost desperate. Harsh and clipped. Exploding with anguished outbursts. He recognized the dialect.

He rubbed his forehead. It was coming back to him. The two planes. The soldiers. The fire inside the monastery. The sharp force slamming into him. The crushing pain.

He looked down at the white bandage wrapped around his

chest. There were no creases. No separations. Each layer had been carefully overlapped on the one beneath it. A second bandage was wrapped around his upper left arm and shoulder. His left wrist and elbow rested in a sling looped around his neck. This wasn't the work of a soldier. A physician had tended his wound.

The voice grew louder. In a few seconds, someone would push through that metal door. Would it be the physician or the soldier? It didn't matter. He was dead either way.

Fighting the pain, he struggled to his feet and staggered toward the round window. He could see the second black plane sitting in the snow, its engines covered with canvas shrouds. His eyes locked on the cargo door. He would have to jump.

Nagano pressed his fingers against the headset and listened to the crackling voice. The transmission had caught him by surprise. Three days had passed since his comrades marched into the haze. Three days without a word. Three days with bitter memories. Memories better forgotten. Like the faces of Nanking's dead. Staring at him in the darkness, their bony fingers pointing at him. Cursing their murderer.

"I don't care about his coma! We have an enemy of unknown strength dead ahead. Conditions are very bad. Only enough oxygen for a few hours. We need to get this over with!"

"Yes, sir."

"Then interrogate him! Interrogate him now! How many on the mountain? Positions? Automatic weapons? Mortars? Artillery? Now, Corporal! We need to know now!"

Nagano slumped in the seat. "Yes, sir."

"Standing by...."

Nagano looked down at the radio's green transmission light. It was bitter cold, but he felt a trickle of sweat running down his forehead. For a few hours, he had been a doctor again. Digging out a bullet. Removing bone fragments. Stopping a hemorrhage. Cleansing and dressing a wound. It didn't matter his patient was the enemy. A doctor shouldn't care.

He gripped the seat and pushed himself up. His comrades

were out there preparing to fight. If he didn't do his job, they might walk into a trap. Twenty-three good men could die because of his weakness.

He looked down at his trembling hands. The doctor's good deeds were done. It was time to be the butcher again. He grimaced and walked out of the cockpit.

Where was he? Nagano stared at the empty cargo compartment. He ran to the spot where he'd performed the operation. The floor was strewn with strips of tape and blood-soaked gauze. A used syringe lay in the shadows. A cold draft struck his face. It was coming from the cargo door.

He rushed to the curved metal door, his eyes trained on the red restraining latch. It was in the vertical position. The door was unlocked.

"No!" He gripped the metal latch and pushed the door open. A blast of chilled air made him turn away. He yanked up his hood and peered into the swirling snow.

There! Just beyond the other plane. Crawling on his belly in the snow. The coward didn't have the strength to run, so he was trying to slink away like a snake.

What a fool he'd been. Aiding the enemy. Helping him fight another day. He picked up a coiled rope and slung it over his shoulder. The bastard would pay. Oh—how he would pay. He jumped into the snow and charged after his prisoner.

Roberto heard the boots shuffling toward him. He tried to stand, but his legs collapsed under him. *Run, dammit! Stand up and run!* He let out an agonizing groan and rose to his feet, but never took a step. A firm hand seized his parka and pulled him down. He was sliding through the snow, his legs dragging limply behind him. He could hear his assailant cursing him in Japanese while lugging him toward the opened cargo door.

Nagano looped a rope under his prisoner's arms and knotted it behind his back. When the desperate man tried to break free, he slammed his fist into the man's face, knocking him senseless. The incensed marine gripped the cargo door and lifted himself into the plane with the rope trailing from his belt.

Roberto felt the rope tighten around his chest. He struggled to pull free, but it was no use. His body lifted off the snow.

Strong hands gripped his parka and dragged him into the plane. He heard the door slam shut. An angry fist jerked him into sitting position. Through his dizziness, he could see the young man's crazed eyes glaring at him.

"How many?"

"You—speak English?"

"How many!"

The man's hand raked across Roberto's mouth. He reeled in pain and fought the nausea sweeping over him.

"Talk!"

Roberto squinted at the man's sweating face. He coughed and forced out the words. "Why are you doing this? All I want is to get out of here."

"Pig!" Nagano raked his knuckles across Roberto's face. He couldn't stop shaking. He glanced at the cockpit door. Twenty-three lives were in his hands. Time had run out. The prisoner must talk. "How many!" Nagano slammed his fist into the prisoner's face.

Roberto's head was spinning. He had come six thousand miles to find a better world. Instead, he had found twisted men with twisted faces. He slumped against the fuselage wall. The black plane that killed Ana had followed him six thousand miles to the roof of the world. Its pilot was kneeling over him—trying to finish what he started in Guernica. To kill the last man who cared. The last man who might make a difference. The mountaineer was right. It was time to fight. For your father—and the mother who brought you into this hellish world. For Augustin, Sebastian, and Ana. Yes, *torero*. It was time to stop the pain.

"Bastard!" He lunged at Nagano's throat.

The marine was caught off guard. He seized the hand clutching his throat, but it was like a vise. He couldn't breathe. Inhuman power was crushing his windpipe. He looked down in shock at the two eyes glaring up at him. There was no fear in those eyes. No compassion. Only rage. Pure, burning rage. His ears rang. Everything was going black. This was no priest. He was more dangerous than anyone on the battlefield. Kill him! Kill him before he kills you!

He slammed his fist into the prisoner's bandaged wound, forcing an agonizing moan. Again, dammit! Again! He pummeled the wound with his fist until the prisoner's grip weakened, and slipped away from his throat.

Nagano gagged while glaring at the man writhing in pain in front of him. His face was white hot. Rage pulsed through his veins. Fuck Yamato. Fuck the interrogation. This bastard must die! He lunged forward and clutched the prisoner's throat with both hands. He could feel the exposed windpipe and jugular veins. "How does it feel? How does it feel to die?" He pressed down on the prisoner's throat and heard him gag. Just a few more seconds and it would be over. A few more seconds. A few—

The bullet ripped through Nagano's chest, sending him sprawling backward on the metal floor. He looked up in shock at the smoking pistol in the prisoner's hand. The prisoner's dazed eyes stared at him, then closed as the man's head rolled back on the floor.

Nagano tried to sit up, but a knifing pain stopped him. He looked down at the red blotch spreading across his white parka. His hand slipped down to the spot in his belt where the pistol should be. He couldn't breathe. His head dropped back on the floor. He felt the warm blood pulsing out of his chest, each futile beat draining life from his body. His eyelids grew heavy. Everything was so dark....

Yamato yanked off the headset and stared at his radio man. "Something's wrong. I'm getting static."

Private Genai took the headset from his commander and pressed it against his ear. He closed his eyes and twisted the dial.

"Well?"

"He's gone, sir."

"Gone?"

Genai shook his head. "Maybe the weather."

"I don't like it. Keep trying to raise him."

"Yes, sir."

Yamato pushed away from his radio operator and scanned

the line of marines huddled against the broken ice. His eyes locked on Kirosawa who was sprawled on his belly peering through a pair of binoculars. "What do you have, Lieutenant?"

"Two stragglers, sir. A half mile ahead. One looks like a woman."

"Woman?"

"Yes, sir. And in bad shape. The other keeps helping her."

Yamato stroked his chin. "Others?"

"Three more further up. Headed toward the ridge."

"Weapons?"

"Only rifles."

"Anything else?"

Kirosawa hesitated and focused on a small dot below the ridge. "I've got one more coming down the ice. Maybe a mile out."

"Coming down?" Yamato crawled beside his lieutenant.

Kirosawa handed him the binoculars and pointed toward the furrow of tracks winding down the icefall.

"Damn."

"Sir?"

"Get ready to move up." Yamato glanced at his watch and handed Kirosawa the binoculars. It was zero-six-hundred on the morning of June 7. Since uncovering the enemy's camp yesterday afternoon, they had climbed a thousand foot stretch of ice and rock, followed by a forced march up the snow pack. It was a miracle they were still alive.

Yamato looked back at the weary marines. Except for some survival training on Fujiyama, none of them had climbed above five thousand feet. They only had enough oxygen for another few hours. It would take them that long to reach the plane—if they could find it.

It was an impossible task. Even if they found the survivors, Yamato's exhausted marines must lug a ton of cargo down a two mile gauntlet of snow and broken ice, dodging avalanches all the way. If they managed to reach the cliff above the glacier, it meant lowering the canisters down the same thousand foot wall they had just climbed. Then, two more agonizing days across an unstable glacier to reach the twin aircraft that could fly them out of this hellhole—if the British didn't kill them first.

"We're ready, sir."

Yamato nodded. He shuffled past his two lieutenants and faced the twenty marines. "The enemy has found Tomonaga. We've spotted six of them, but there could be more. It could be a trap, but we have no choice." He glared at the marines. "To the death."

"There!" Mariner pointed a trembling finger at the man stumbling down the icefall.

"I'll be damned." Eammon focused his binoculars on the weathered figure staggering through the knee-deep powder. "How far do you make him?"

"I can't tell with the shadows."

"Bonaventure!" Akaal broke away from his stunned comrades and scrambled up the ice toward the flapping blue anorak. He'd known his friend for many years and could see something was wrong.

"Shoot him a flare, Sergeant."

"Yes, sir." Mariner yanked out his flare gun and fumbled for a cartridge.

Bonaventure watched the green flare explode in the morning sky. He dropped on his knees and squinted at the familiar figure rushing up the ice toward him. It had taken him ten hours to descend the icefall. Double what it took to climb it. What was wrong? Why was he so damn weak?

He could see Mariner and Collins crawling up the ice behind Akaal. No one else was in sight. He collapsed on his side and watched the Gurkha close on him.

"Thank the gods." Akaal dropped in the snow and gripped his friend's arm.

"Good to see you, old chum."

"You're insane."

"A little."

Akaal glared at him. "What possessed you? I'm your friend. We're supposed to stick together."

Bonaventure forced a smile. "I could use some water."

Akaal yanked the canteen out of his belt and popped the cap. He handed it to the exhausted mountaineer and watched him guzzle the near-frozen water. "Go easy. You'll cramp up."

Bonaventure fell back in the snow. He yanked off a glove and rubbed his frozen face. "Almost bought it up there. Strangest thing. I was making good time when this bloody weakness came over me. Can't explain it. Just ran out of gas. I feel like a dish rag."

"It's the thin air. And you without oxygen." Akaal unclipped his oxygen bottle and handed him the tube. He opened the valve and watched his friend suck the life-giving gas.

Bonaventure nodded gratefully and handed him the tube. "Where are the others?"

"Coming up behind me."

"No—I mean Karen and Nemi."

Akaal hesitated. "I know what you mean. They're behind Mr. Collins and the Sergeant. Climbing through the shadows."

"What?"

"Couldn't stop her. We begged her to turn back, but she wouldn't listen. She kept falling and sucking oxygen, but she wouldn't quit. When we reached the granite wall, I tried to dig her a snow cave, but she grabbed your belay and started to climb. I tried to stop her, but she fought like a wildcat. There was nothing I could do."

"Dammit, Akaal."

The Gurkha locked his black eyes on him. "What did you expect? Sneaking out like that. Dumping her on me. Things are bad enough without you making them worse. I'm the one who should be cursing."

"What a bloody mess."

Akaal glanced at the two men climbing toward them. "Something is wrong with Mr. Collins. I think it's his heart. He keeps sneaking pills. Almost passed out when we headed up this morning."

Bonaventure grimaced and rubbed his forehead. The sky was brightening. In a few minutes, the sun would clear the eastern ridges and expand the brittle ice on the cliffs—and all hell would break loose. He stood up and brushed the snow off his anorak.

"Mr. Bonaventure! What the hell are you doing!"

Bonaventure ignored the Irishman's tirade and snatched his pack out of the snow. "Getting off this bloody mountain."

Akaal noticed the automatic rifle sticking out of his pack. "Where did you find that?"

"Up there—with this." Bonaventure reached into his pack and handed Akaal the broken radio crank.

The Gurkha's eyes widened. "You found it?"

The mountaineer looked up at the shadows below the ridge. "You don't want to know what I found."

"I heard that!" Eammon shuffled between them and jammed his ski pole in the ice. He could barely stand and was having trouble breathing.

"A little out of sorts, aren't we, old man?"

"Never mind that. What did you find up there?"

Akaal handed him the crank. The Irishman stared at the *swastika* etched on the handle. He looked at Bonaventure with stunned eyes. "You found the plane?"

Bonaventure shook his head. "There's no gold, if that's what you mean."

"You expect me to believe that?"

"I don't care what you believe." Bonaventure looked down the slope. Two figures were stumbling up the ice toward them. He recognized Karen's purple scarf flapping in the wind.

Eammon gripped the mountaineer's arm. "I won't ask again, Mr. Bonaventure. What did you find up there?"

Bonaventure glared at the Irishman. "Three dead Japanese soldiers and some canisters of steam."

"What?"

"Let go of my arm."

Eammon's hand slipped away. He stared at the mountaineer in disbelief.

"Oh—almost forgot. The steam glowed."

Eammon looked up at the ridge, his white hair ruffling in the wind. He didn't notice Bonaventure brush past him.

"He made it, memsaab. He is safe. We can go back now."

Karen ignored Nemi and stared at the blue apparition sliding down the ice toward them. Yes—it was him. She struggled to her feet and yanked the ski pole out of the ice. Bonaventure was almost on top of her when she wound up and took a wild swing.

"What the bloody hell!" Bonaventure dived into the snow, narrowly escaping the razor-sharp point.

She was winding up for a second try when Nemi seized her arms. "Bastard! Trying to ruin my story! You sonofabitch!"

"Karen—wait!"

"Where's my fucking camera!" She threw the ski pole at him and collapsed in the snow.

Bonaventure crawled beside her and lifted her in his arms. Her breathing was labored and her lips were coated with dried blood. "We've got to get you down."

"Damn you...." She clutched his anorak and tried to pull herself up, but she was too weak.

"It's all right. I've got the bloody pic—" He froze. The camera! He'd left it up there! She'd kill him when she found out!

Nemi knelt beside them, his black eyes fixed on the reporter. "I tried to stop her, but she is like a caged animal."

"Can you rig a sled?"

"Sled?"

"To take her down."

"Just a goddamn minute!"

Bonaventure looked up and saw the Irishman stumbling down the ice toward him, his green eyes burning with anger.

Eammon jammed his ski pole in the ice and pointed a menacing finger at him. "This is your fault. She came up here because of you." He grimaced and clutched his chest. "We're not turning back. We need to get up there and you know the way. Now get off your egotistical ass and take the point!"

"Go to hell." Bonaventure started to lift her, but a familiar click stopped him. He looked up and saw Eammon holding the forty-five.

Akaal shuffled down the slope toward the Irishman, followed by the others. "Mr. Collins, this isn't the way."

"Shut up, Corporal!" Eammon flicked the forty-five at Akaal, his eyes filled with anger. "You don't understand. None of you understand. That cargo is more important than us. We've got to get it to Dharan."

Bonaventure stood up and faced the Irishman. "Listen to me, you idiot. She's not the only one in trouble. You think I don't see that hand on your chest. You're dying, old man. Those pills won't help. If we don't get you down, you'll stay up here forever."

Eammon backed away, his eyes suddenly focused on the shadows below them. "Did you see that? Something moved down there." He lowered the forty-five and stared at the shadows stretching across the white slope.

Bonaventure looked at him in shock. The altitude had finally taken its toll on the exhausted Irishman.

"Well?"

Akaal scanned the slope. "Nothing, Mr. Collins. Just shadows."

"No—I saw something. I don't like it. I think—"

A bullet whizzed past the Irishman's ear. The air flashed with orange tracers.

"Get down!" Akaal grabbed Eammon's arm and pulled him down on the ice.

Bonaventure didn't need a warning. He'd seen enough civil strife to know the rat-a-tat of automatic weapons. He dropped beside Karen and yanked out his binoculars.

Mariner and Nemi dived into the broken ice and unslung their *Enfield* rifles. They pointed the obsolete weapons down the slope and squinted at the orange bursts coming from the shadows.

Eammon slid next to Bonaventure and unslung his rifle. "Who are they?"

"You're asking me? How the hell should I know?"

Mariner dug in behind a rock and trained his binoculars on the ice below them. "I've got a dozen armed troops in camouflage white. They're fanned out in skirmishing order, about two hundred yards below us. Looks like they're preparing to charge."

Akaal crawled beside him and squinted at the ice. "Any insignia?"

Mariner wasn't listening. He'd focused the binoculars on the cliff above them. "I've got another dozen in those rocks on the left. Ten o'clock high."

Eammon gripped his rifle and stared at the rocks. "Sergeant, see if you can get off a transmission."

Mariner dragged off his rucksack and pulled out the radio. He was about to start cranking the generator when the ice exploded with incoming tracers.

"Who are they?" Karen tried to stand but Bonaventure pulled her down. "Keep your head down! We've got big trouble."

Mariner drew a bead on one of the approaching soldiers, but Akaal pushed his rifle down. "Wait until they clear the shadows."

Mariner glared at the cliff. "What about them? They'll cut us down before we get off a clip."

"Stay calm. Their backs are to the sky. We'll pick them off like birds."

Eammon gripped the Gurkha's arm. "Are you crazy? They've got us outgunned four to one. We don't have a chance down here. Let's get up to the plane. We'll dig in and try to negotiate with them."

Bonaventure glared at the Irishman. "Negotiate? At four-to-one odds? Are you nuts? Our only chance is to give ground and let them pass. They don't want us. They're after the plane."

Eammon squinted through the broken ice. He could see a dozen parka-clad troops sprawled on their bellies in firing position, their goggled faces peering up at him.

"Get ready, I hear their clips popping." Akaal barely got out the words. The ice erupted with incoming tracers. At least a half-dozen of the enemy were firing down at them from the rocks.

Nemi dived into the open and fired at the orange flashes. He heard a scream and scrambled for shelter. The Gurkha let out a muffled scream as a volley of machine gun bullets ripped into his neck and back. He clutched his throat and convulsed on the ice, his parka smoking with bullet holes.

"Nemi!" Akaal seized the Gurkha's parka and dragged him behind the broken ice, but it was too late. His young friend stared at him with glazed eyes.

"The hell with this—I'm going up." Eammon scrambled past Bonaventure and started up the ice.

"No—you don't know what you're doing!" Bonaventure lunged at him, but it was no use. The desperate Irishman charged up the ice like a madman.

Mariner slid next to Bonaventure, his eyes filled with terror. He looked at Nemi's lifeless body and took a deep breath. "I'm sorry, Mr. Bonaventure. I have to go with him."

"You what?"

"It's my orders."

"Are you crazy? One step on that ice and you're a dead man."

"We have a shot. If we can clear the slope—"

"Clear? You won't go ten feet!"

Mariner brushed back his hood and squinted at the rocks. "We could use you up there, old man. You know—to buy us some time. If I can get off a message to Pangpema, the Spaniard will radio Dharan for troops."

"Troops? Wake up, Sergeant. Pangpema's lost."

"Lost?"

"How do you think those blokes got up here? They landed in Pangpema. The Spaniard's dead, and so's that bloody fool crawling up the ice. It's over, Sergeant. Come to your senses and help us get off this bloody mountain."

Mariner rubbed his chin with the back of his gloved hand. He glanced at Karen and shook his head. "Good luck, Mr. Bonaventure. Hope you and the lady make it." He slid away from the mountaineer and charged up the ice. The enemy had stopped firing.

Bonaventure slumped against Karen and watched the two men climb into the shadows. His eyes drifted to Akaal who was hunched over Nemi with a string of prayer beads dangling from his hand.

Akaal jammed the beads in his pocket and looked at his friend. "We don't have much time. Head for that debris field at the base of the icefall. Stay inside the shadows. It should take about an hour. I'll give you covering fire. Maybe enough to distract them until you're out of range."

Bonaventure's eyes widened. "Are you mad?"

Akaal grimaced. "Can't disobey orders—remember?"

"It's suicide, man. You can't make it."

"You should be on your way, Mr. Bonaventure. You're the only one going down."

Bonaventure looked at Karen in shock. She'd crawled against the ice, her blue eyes fixed on him.

"Biggest story of the century—remember?"

The mountaineer stared at them in disbelief. He was about to lose the only two people that ever mattered, and there was nothing he could do.

Yamato focused his binoculars on the two men climbing up the ice. The first one seemed to be slowing, as if in pain. The second appeared in better shape. Younger. Stronger. More determined.

The battle-hardened officer grimaced and lowered his binoculars. He'd picked the wrong one! Change the orders! He gripped his rifle and waved it in the air, but he was too late.

A loud crack echoed off the rocks. Private Imai had left nothing to chance. Windage. Angle of attack. Distance. Trajectory. His bullet caught Sergeant Randolph Mariner square in the back of the head.

Karen stared in horror at the broken body tumbling down the ice. Mariner's lifeless corpse slammed into the rocks beside them, his face and shoulders covered with blood.

"Sergeant!" Akaal scrambled next to him and felt for a pulse, but there was none.

"Here they come!" Bonaventure yanked the confiscated machine gun out of his rucksack and sprawled on the ice beside Karen. He pulled back the cocking lever and felt Akaal slide against him.

Yamato swept his right arm forward and scrambled up the ice with the marines at his side. Above him, Hiryu's men opened fire on the three bodies huddled in the broken ice.

The marines charged up the ice, their machine guns blazing. They had to overrun the enemy before the lead climber escaped into the haze. If they lost him, they'd lose the plane. There were no options. Take no prisoners.

Bonavanture listened to the deadly rounds thud into the ice above his head. They were pinned down, unable to strike back at the advancing enemy troops. In a few seconds, it would be over. Not a pleasant way to go—clinging to each other while crazed soldiers pumped them full of rounds at point blank range. His friends deserved more than that—and so did he.

The mountaineer gritted his teeth and popped a cartridge in the flare gun. He dived at the exposed ice and aimed the silver pistol at the rocks. The air filled with a deafening hiss as the flare rocketed skyward. Time to be young again. Tenacity! Courage! Rage!

Direct hit! The rocks exploded in a red starburst. A dozen marines scrambled for safety, their parkas smoldering with hot embers.

Now! Before they regroup! Bonaventure aimed the machine gun at the stunned marines and squeezed the trigger. The gun vibrated from its discharging rounds. He heard screams and saw two bodies crash on the ice, one of them writhing in pain. The wounded man convulsed and fell silent.

He ejected the spent clip and jammed in the spare he'd confiscated with the rifle. *Hurry, dammit! Here come the tracers!* He aimed the machine gun at the rocks and started to squeeze the trigger, but a stinging pain stopped him cold. He clutched his left shoulder and crawled into the broken ice.

Akaal fired a second flare at the rocks. He stood up and aimed his *Enfield* at the line of advancing marines. His round caught one of them in the chest, dropping him like a ragdoll. He pulled back the bolt and inserted another bullet, but the ice exploded in front of his face. He dropped on his belly as the ice disintegrated from impacting bullets.

Bonaventure grimaced and reached for the machine gun, but it wasn't there. He looked up in shock and saw Karen leaning against the ice, the machine gun in her hands. She'd pulled back the cocking lever and aimed the lethal weapon at the scrambling marines.

"No—get down!"

She squeezed the trigger and watched in horror as two of the attacking marines collapsed on the ice. She dropped the weapon, her eyes locked on the dead marines.

Bonaventure snared her boot and yanked her off her feet as a volley of bullets ripped into the ice. He pulled her close and felt her tremble against him, her eyes staring blankly into space.

Akaal gripped his friend's wounded arm. "Go! I'll hold them off until you're clear."

Bonaventure glared at him. "No way."

The Gurkha glanced at Karen. "You don't have a choice." He stood up and fired at the advancing marines. They were only a hundred yards away.

"I'm not leaving you here. If you die—we die."

Akaal dropped beside him. "We've had our fun. It's time to say goodbye."

"Akaal—"

"This is my home—not yours. You belong with her." Akaal gripped his friend's shoulder. "We should have stayed on Chowpatty Beach."

Bonaventure couldn't speak. He clasped his friend's arm and backed away.

Everything after that was a daze. He remembered grabbing Karen and sliding down the ice. When he looked back, Akaal was still blasting away with his *Enfield*. Buying them precious time.

He recalled the day he rescued him in that London pub. And the battles fought on God's towering mountains. Two men swimming against the tide. One white. The other yellow-brown. In a world gone mad, a Cockney Englishman and Nepalese Gurkha had found a common bond that made them one. A bond called glory.

The mountaineer brushed away a tear and headed down the ice. He didn't hear the first explosion.

Akaal picked up the smoking grenade and flung it at the charging marines. It exploded in mid-air with a deafening concussion, dropping one of the marines on his knees. The wounded man clutched his face and fell forward in the snow.

They were only thirty yards away. He could feel their bullets thudding into the ice. He popped in his last round and stood up to fire. His hand slipped into his pocket and yanked out the prayer beads. Buddha was with him. He wasn't afraid.

Something thumped in the snow beside him. He looked down at the smoking grenade. He picked it up and flung it over the ice, but another fell in its place. He reached down and grasped the handle. A brilliant light filled his eyes. Buddha was with him....

The marines swarmed over the broken ice, their guns raking the three bodies. There was no time to lose.

Yamato waved his machine gun in the air. He shaded his eyes and watched Hiryu and the others crawl down the rocks to the ice. There were only nine of them.

He grimaced and looked back at Kirosawa who was standing beside the four dead marines lying in the snow. Seven men lost. Only seventeen left to pull off a miracle.

Hiryu slung his machine gun over his shoulder and shuffled beside his commander. "Position secured, sir. We're moving up, but I think we have a problem."

"Problem?"

"Tracks—headed down the icefall into the haze. Let me take two men to finish them."

Yamato shook his head. "We can't lose any more men. Forget them."

"Captain, they might be going for help. It will only take a few minutes. We'll catch up with you below the cliffs."

Yamato looked at the marines crawling up the ice. A rescue mission that should have taken two days was well into its third.

Gary Naiman

He had just lost seven good men in a skirmish with a bunch of rabble. And the worst was yet to come. Damn this place. Damn it to hell.

"Captain?"

Yamato gave a painful nod. He watched his lieutenant gesture for two of the marines to follow him down the icefall.

What a waste of fine men. Fifteen marines killed trying to fly a cargo of black canisters across the world. Seven more killed trying to salvage the same canisters. All because three eccentrics in Tokyo had convinced the Emperor that Japan's fate lay in thirty canisters of glowing steam.

Yamato slung his machine gun and headed up the ice.

44 | Should the God's Warriors Fail

The wind had picked up and a light snow was falling. In a few minutes, the approaching blizzard would dump another foot of white death on Kangchenjunga. But the greatest danger wasn't snow or avalanches. At twenty-two thousand, the winds reached ninety miles an hour, creating sub-zero temperatures no mortal could survive.

Bonaventure slipped away from her and crawled out of the rocks. He stood up in the knee-deep snow and flinched from the wound in his shoulder. The bullet had missed the bone, passing through the flesh without puncturing an artery. He flexed his arm and grimaced. It was getting stiffer. Nothing worse than a frozen arm when you're trying to climb down a mountain.

They'd managed to descend a half mile before the deep snow overwhelmed them. Alone, he might take a shot at the ridge running down the mountain's west shoulder. It was only five hundred feet to the crest. A walk in the park for a decent mountaineer.

From there, he'd descend the ridge to the west wall, staying slightly below the crest to shelter himself from the blizzard's intense southeast winds.

The drop to the glacier would be harder. Not easy crawling down a three thousand foot wall of rock and ice—but he'd find a way.

He glanced at the woman huddled against the rocks. Quit dreaming, Bonaventure. She wouldn't last an hour on that windswept crest. There was only one chance. Say a prayer and retreat up the icefall. If they could reach Akaal without being detected, they'd trek down the snowpack to the cliff above the glacier. With a little luck, they'd make it down the thousand foot barrier before the enemy caught up with them. Then, across the glacier to Pangpema and—

He thought of Akaal. His friend was too good a fighter to roll over to a few tin soldiers. He'd probably waited until they were almost on top of him before firing his last flare. When the red starburst exploded in their eyes, he broke for the shadows and dived into the seracs. By the time the fools recovered, he was gone. Vanished in a flurry of red sparks. Yes—his friend was up there—waiting to lead them down.

Bonaventure reeled from a blast of frigid wind. The air erupted with snow as a black cloud swept over them.

"Julian!"

She was crawling toward him, her eyes filled with terror. He dropped beside her and held her in his arms.

"We've gotta get to the plane."

"Forget the bloody plane."

"Can't quit now. We're so close."

"We're close all right. Close to freezing to death. Come on—let's get out of this damned wind."

Something whizzed past his ear. The whiteout flashed with orange tracers. He heard bullets thudding into the ice.

He dragged her behind the rocks and squinted at the blowing snow. Three shadows shuffled toward them, their white parkas flapping in the wind. He could see machine guns cradled in their arms.

"What a bloody mess." He groped for the ice axe in his belt. It was all he had.

Hiryu waved for the two flanking marines to fan out. Katama would work his way around the rocks on the right until he was behind the enemy. He'd open up on them from the rear while his two comrades blasted them from the front. The lethal crossfire would finish them in seconds.

Hiryu dropped on his belly and waved Kanoy down. He watched the young marine dive into the snow on his left. Katama had disappeared behind the rocks on his right. It would be over in seconds.

"Lieutenant!"

Kanoy's shout caught Hiryu off guard. He wiped his goggles and traced Kanoy's finger to the rocks dead ahead.

Was he seeing things? A man was standing on the rocks, his long black hair streaming in the wind. He wore a brown fur parka and looked more like an animal than a human being. His hands grasped a rifle. He was just standing there, peering down at them through the blowing snow.

Hiryu cocked his weapon. Who was this madman? An enemy soldier? Lost climber? Confused native? The hell with it. Bring him down. He raised his machine gun and opened fire.

The tracers streamed over the rocks, but there was nothing there. The brown specter had vanished. Hiryu jammed in a fresh clip and took aim.

Katama pressed against a boulder and listened to the bullets pinging off the rocks. He clutched the machine gun and glanced back at his trail in the snow. He'd crawled nearly sixty yards since slipping behind the rocks. They had to be in that ice cluster dead ahead. If he could just slide a few feet to the right, he'd have them in his sight. A few quick bursts and it would be over.

The exhausted marine rested his head on the machine gun. In a few days, he'd be in Nanking getting drunk with his comrades. Then, a good woman and—

What was that? A rustling sound on his left? He scrambled into firing position and trained the gun on the shadows. Nothing—only fallen ice.

Something thumped behind him. He spun around in time to see a chunk of ice plop into the snow. First one side—then the other? He's above you, idiot!

Katama rolled on his back and aimed the machine gun at the sky, but it was too late. A terrific force slammed into him. He cried out in pain, but a gloved hand stifled his scream. He tried to jam the machine gun's barrel into the man's ribs, but it was useless. He let go of the gun and grasped the knife in his belt. His heart pounded against his ribs. He dragged out the knife and thrust it into the thick brown fur pressing against him. Too late. A blinding pain radiated through his chest. He gasped and went limp as the stranger's knife punctured his heart.

He couldn't breathe. Everything was spinning. He heard a man's voice whisper in his ear, but he couldn't understand the words.

Gary Naiman

"No one touches my sister."

Hiryu glanced at Kanoy. Twenty minutes had passed since their comrade crawled behind the rocks. The wind and cold were unbearable. They couldn't hold any longer.

Hiryu shook his fist in the air and scrambled to his feet. He charged at the rocks with Kanoy at his side. Thirty feet! Twenty! Ten! He dived into the snow and sprayed the rocks with machine gun fire.

Where were they? Hiryu popped in a fresh clip and scanned the shadows. The only sound was the howling wind.

There! He poked his comrade with an elbow and nodded at the snow in front of them. It was splattered with blood.

Hiryu gestured for Kanoy to crawl around the boulder. It would only take a few seconds for the young marine to get behind them. If his deadly rounds didn't finish them, the pigs would be forced into the open where Hiryu would empty his clip on them.

The exhausted lieutenant rubbed the snow off his goggles. What was he doing here? So many had died for something no one understood. He thought of his young wife in Tokyo. How good it would feel to be in her arms. Making love in a warm bed. Yes—he would be home soon.

He squinted at the whiteout. The man in brown fur was kneeling on a boulder, his rifle pointed down at Kanoy. He was going to shoot!

Hiryu stood up and aimed at the brown fur. He squeezed the trigger and felt a powerful hand grip his shoulder. He spun around with the gun still blazing, and glared at the last thing he would see on this earth. A silver axe.

Bonaventure plunged the ice axe into the marine's chest. He grimaced in pain while his wounded arm blocked the machine gun's discharging barrel. The spent gun dropped in the snow.

The marine let out a muffled groan and stared at Bonaventure with stunned black eyes. For an instant, he seemed frozen like those dead marines on the ridge. He stiffened and fell back in the snow, his eyes fixed on the whiteout.

Bonaventure looked down at the dead marine. He had killed before, but never like this. The young man gazed at the sky, oblivious to the snowflakes blowing on his face. He couldn't be more than twenty five. The poor soul had barely tasted life. What a waste. What a goddamn waste.

A rifle shot cracked the air, followed by a muffled scream. Bonaventure snatched the dead man's weapon and fumbled for a fresh clip.

Something rustled behind him. He spun around and saw Karen leaning against the rocks, her glazed eyes staring at him. He crawled beside her and took her in his arms. "Come on, let's get off this bloody rock." He started to lift her and froze. A man was standing in the whiteout with a rifle cradled in his arms. He wore a brown fur parka. The hood was pulled back, revealing a scarred face and streaming black hair.

Bonaventure jammed the clip in the machine gun, but the stranger was quick as a leopard. He flicked his rifle into shooting position and fired at the machine gun, blowing it out of the mountaineer's hand.

Bonaventure clutched his stinging hand and fought the dizziness sweeping over him. He felt Karen brush past him. She lunged for the machine gun, but the stranger kicked it away as she sprawled in the snow in front of him. The stranger backed away and pointed the rifle at her head.

"You're *Angrezi*?"

She looked up at the scarred face.

"*Angrezi*?"

She brushed the snow off her face. "We escaped. The others are dead. Can you help us?"

The stranger's eyes filled with anger. "You ask my help?" He popped in a bullet and placed his finger on the trigger.

"Wait!" Bonaventure raised his aching hand.

The stranger glared at him. "You killed everything I loved—and you ask my help?"

"What are you saying? I never saw you before."

The stranger sneered at him. "You'll say anything. You're a jackal."

Bonaventure's blue eyes flared with anger. He stood up and pulled out his knife. The stranger stood motionless, his rifle pointed at Karen's head.

"Goddamn you to hell!" Bonaventure lunged at the stranger, but his thrust only found air. He sprawled in the snow, waiting for the deadly impact.

He heard Karen's scream. What was the fool waiting for? Impossible to miss at this range. He looked up and saw the stranger staring at Karen, his rifle hanging at his side.

Was this some kind of sick game? Would he suddenly raise the barrel and squeeze the trigger? Bonaventure looked down at the knife in his trembling hand.

The stranger dropped the rifle and collapsed on his knees, his hands clutching his side. He gasped for breath and locked his black eyes on Karen. "You look so much like her—my little queen of the gods. It is you, isn't it? Come to play a trick on your brother."

Bonaventure stared at him in disbelief. *Snap out of it, man. Move!* He rose to his feet and edged toward the rifle lying in the snow. When he reached down to pick it up, the stranger offered no resistance. He seemed delirious. The snow beside him was pink with blood.

Bonaventure backed away and aimed the rifle at the stranger's head.

"Save your bullet, English. I'm finished."

Bonaventure shuffled beside Karen and gripped her arm. He helped her up and backed away from the wounded man, his finger tight on the trigger.

The stranger tried to stand, but couldn't make it. He stared at Bonaventure with desperate eyes. "Help me, English. She's so alone. I'm all she has."

Bonaventure glanced down at the rifle. One well-placed bullet would put the bloke out of his misery. He lifted the rifle into firing position.

"No!" Karen broke away from him and rushed toward the stranger.

"What are you doing? Are you crazy?"

She dropped beside the wounded man and rested an arm on

his shoulder. "Who are you?"

He looked at her and smiled. "I'm so tired. I want to go home."

Bonaventure shuffled beside them, his eyes glancing nervously at the blowing snow. He bent down and gripped her arm. "The storm's letting up. We've got a shot."

Karen ignored him and brushed back the man's black hair. His face was strong, with a scar running across the bridge of the nose. She looked into his black eyes. There was so much pain in those eyes.

"Karen." Bonaventure squeezed her arm.

She wiped away a tear. "Funny how things turn out. I find the story of a lifetime and no one will ever know. Collins finds his treasure and fades away. The Japanese try to pull off the coup of all time and disappear into the clouds. And this poor soul only wants to go home."

Bonaventure looked down at the dying man. "So do I."

She shook her head. "Time to face the music, Mr. Bonaventure. There's only one direction for us—and it's not down. I don't know what brought us here, but none of us are going down."

"We'll make it." He slung the weapons over his aching shoulder and helped her up. He was about to turn away when he hesitated and looked down at the dying man. "Can you walk?"

"I'll walk."

"Then let's get on with it." He reached down and grasped the man's parka.

The blizzard passed quickly and the clouds cleared above the mountain. With the next storm closing from the southwest, the three mortals struggled up the ice to confront an overpowering enemy. Twelve miles to the north, the Spaniard lay near death on the floor of an abandoned aircraft. It was a dark time. The chosen ones had failed. A thousand suns would soon blanket the earth. Evil had triumphed. The *Dharma* was threatened. The prophecy had been fulfilled.

Gary Naiman

The gods rose into the heavens. It was time to summon Kalki....

45 | *A Better Place*

The pain was unbearable. He couldn't breathe. He ripped open his parka and clutched his chest. Six thousand feet above him, the mountain's summit streamed snow into the powder blue sky.

How long had he been climbing? An hour? Two? He glanced at his watch. Useless—the damn crystal was coated with frost.

He pulled off a glove and rubbed his frozen face. Something snapped across his eyes. The light was blinding. His snow goggles! The damn strap had broken. He lunged for them, but it was too late. They tumbled down the forty degree slope into the haze. He covered his eyes and cursed the light.

Where were the others? They should be here by now. They had to get to the wreckage before the Japanese. Mariner had to get that transmission off to Dharan.

It would only take an hour to fly in a planeload of troops. The *Vickers* could carry a dozen well-armed men. Certainly enough Brits to take care of a few maniacal Japanese. One taste of a belching B.A.R. and the cowards would drop their weapons like frightened children. Forget that crap about *bushido*. The Japs were no match for the Brits.

A smile cracked the Irishman's parched lips. Not bad, Mr. Collins. You retrieve the cargo and capture a platoon of Japanese regulars along the way. The boys at Ten Downing will love it. Nothing like a little interrogation to find out what those bastards are really up to. Especially with a war brewing.

But what about the gold? The mountaineer said there wasn't any. Was he lying? Or was it buried under three feet of snow? Hell with it. If any gold was up there, the Brits would find it. And if not? Well—there were still the five packs in the Buddha's belly. Luck of the Irish, as they say.

And what about those canisters? They hadn't told him much about them. Real secretive when it came to talking about them. And what did Bonaventure mean about that steam? Why the hell climb a mountain for some containers of steam? Gold

Gary Naiman

yes—but steam?

Maybe he'd write about it after this bloody mess was over. Only problem would be getting people to believe him. No matter. He'd make it a novel. He could see himself now, typewriter in hand. Peering out the window of his mansion in Galway Bay. His study facing the water so he could catch the sunset and dream of "times gone by."

His smile became a grin. Mansion, eh? Hell, why not? Might as well do something with all that gold.

He reached into his pocket and clutched the forty-five. It would be easier now. With Nemi dead, only four bullets should do the job. The problem was timing. Gotta keep them alive to fight off the Japs. And don't forget the reporter. If she died without giving up the location of the logbook, he'd never hear the end of it.

He slipped his hand off the gun and rubbed his burning eyes. A little tricky, but he'd find a way.

He thought about Roberto. Tougher to kill him with the Brits swarming over Pangpema. Gotta make it look like bandits finished him—remember?

He recalled their first meeting in Bern. The fool should have stayed down there. If it wasn't for the gold, he'd let him go back to Spain to fight his little war with General Franco. Hell, he was doing him a favor. Better to die up here than rot in a Spanish prison. Closer to heaven, and all that.

Yes...it would all work out. Just a little rest...and he'd...be on...his way....

His eyes snapped open. *Wake up, idiot! Want to die up here!* He rubbed his forehead and tried to clear his head. Come on, you tough old Irishman. Almost home. In another hour, you'll be sitting pretty on the ridge crest. Then, a few flares to mark your position and—

That sound. Boots grating against the ice. Mariner! It's about time. He squinted at the haze. Better fire a flare. The damn limey won't see you in this bloody glare. He fumbled for the flare gun in his belt.

What was wrong? He couldn't grip it. His fingers wouldn't close. A numbing pain radiated through his arms and legs. *The*

The Tenth Avatar

nitro capsules! Hurry, dammit! He tried to reach into his pocket, but his left arm wouldn't move.

What was happening? A wave of panic swept through him. He took an agonizing breath and shouted into the haze. "Here, Sergeant! Up here! Right above you!"

He looked up at the sun. He could hear Mariner's boots crunching toward him. Hang on, you bloody Irishman. Just a few more seconds. Stay calm. It's almost over. You're almost home.

He was breathing easier now. Slow, deep breaths. No strain. No pain. And that sun floating in the haze. Like an autumn morning on the beach in Galway Bay. The waves lapping at his feet. The air fresh with the smell of the sea. The fishermen hauling in their nets. The distant hum of a foghorn. The gulls splashing off the water, their high-pitched shrieks crying out to him. Calling him home.

Mission accomplished, Mr. Collins. We stopped them on Kangchenjunga. Too bad no one will ever know. So be it. Goes with the job. Relax and have an ale. Enjoy the day, and that warm...beautiful...sun....

Yamato gulped some oxygen and stuffed the tube in his belt. He leaned against the ice and stared at the corpse lying beside him.

"Look at his eyes, sir."

Yamato nodded and glanced up at the sun. He brushed the Irishman's eyes shut and fumbled through his parka. He found a gold four-leaf clover, forty-five automatic, and box of capsules. There were no papers or identification. Just a nondescript man lying dead on the ice at twenty-two thousand. Not exactly Galway Bay.

Yamato looked down at the column of marines. He dug his boots into the ice and headed up the slope, followed by his men. They plodded upward toward the hundred foot ice buttress, their eyes fixed on the swirling column of steam rising into the pale blue sky.

With only a half mile to go, the air filled with an ominous cracking sound as tons of ice and snow broke loose from the cliffs below the summit. The helpless marines muttered *Shinto* prayers while watching the avalanche explode down the icefall, only a hundred yards to their rear. They would have to cross that icefall on the way down. They pulled their climbing ropes and prepared to climb the ice buttress.

The sun was dropping to the west when they reached the crater. At fifty yards, it looked like a geyser spewing hot vapors into the sky. But there was something more. The vapors flickered with unearthly light.

Kirosawa started toward the crater, but Yamato seized his arm.

"What is it?" Kirosawa slid up his goggles and peered at the crater.

"I don't know, Lieutenant. I don't want to know."

Yamato deployed his men around the thirty foot crater and ordered them to probe the snow for objects. It only took them a few seconds to uncover the broken canister.

Private Inouye knelt down and waved for his comrades to have a look. He brushed away the snow and ran his hand along the black chain trailing from the canister.

Yamato's eyes lit up when he saw Inouye uncover a second canister a few feet above the first. Yes—this had to be them. He pointed to the snow above the second canister and shouted orders.

The marines headed up the slope and began sweeping away the snow. When they were done, they backed away and stared at the cause of so much pain. Twenty-four chained canisters, all intact except the first.

Yamato eyed his exhausted men. He was about to order the impossible. Thirteen men must haul seventeen hundred pounds of lead down a mountain. He took a gulp of oxygen and peered into the haze. Where was Hiryu and his marines? They'd make a huge difference now. Why did he let them chase a bunch of helpless stragglers down a mountain? He ripped the tube out of his mouth and cursed himself for being so stupid.

"Captain!"

He looked up the slope and saw Kirosawa waving at him from the rocks. He jammed the oxygen bottle in his belt and staggered toward the lieutenant.

Kirosawa lowered his head. "I'm sorry, sir."

Yamato stared at the frozen hand protruding from the snow. He knelt down and brushed away the snow.

"I'll get the men." Kirosawa backed away and headed down the slope.

Yamato yanked off a glove and grasped the major's frozen hand. He lowered his head and spoke softly. "I'm sorry, old friend. We tried, but the gods weren't with us today. I hope the end came quickly." He gritted his teeth and fought back tears. "Well done, Major Tomonaga. You almost pulled it off. Now it's our turn. We won't forget you, old friend. Japan won't forget you."

He rose to his feet and listened to the marines shuffle behind him. "A prayer for our brothers." His black eyes locked on the three corpses. "I salute you, Major Tomonaga. *Banzai*!"

The marines raised their arms and shouted the ancient battle cry. Then again. And again. They lowered their arms and bowed while their commander planted a small rising-sun pennant beside the three dead marines. He bowed and backed away.

Yamato turned toward his men, his black eyes flashing with anger. "We'll finish what they started."

They formed a column and passed back a climbing rope for each man to secure around his waist. With Yamato taking the rear position, they headed down the slope with the chained canisters dragging behind them. Above them, three frozen corpses lay beside the flapping pennant, their gravesite marked with a pillar of glowing steam.

Bonaventure felt her go limp against him. He dropped down and cradled her in his arms. "Almost there, Reuters. I can see the plane."

"Plane?"

"On the ridge. All broken up. Only a hundred feet above us."

She sank in his arms. Her breathing was uneven and strained. Her face had turned ashen gray.

Gary Naiman

"Hang on, Karen. Only a few more feet." He looked up at the broken ice and screamed at the top of his lungs. "Akaal! For God's sake—I need you!"

She looked up at him and forced a smile. "I...should've gone...to...Miami...."

"Come on—the oxygen's up there. A few gulps and you'll be good as new. Only a hundred feet."

She gripped his anorak and pulled him close. Her lips were like ice. She stared at him with soft, blue eyes. "We made it, Mr. Bonaventure. Story of the century."

"Right—we made it. Now come on."

"Is the camera ready?"

"Camera? Sure—all set. Great shot from the rocks. We've gotta hurry to catch the light. Come on now."

"You better take the picture. I'm a little tired just now."

"No—don't close your eyes. We're almost home."

"Home?"

"You know—Switzerland. The Pulitzer. Hiking in the Alps. A new life. A better life."

She reached up and touched his face. "You were right about us, Mr. Bonaventure. We make a good team. Who knows...we might...even.....become......friends........"

"Karen!"

She heard him crying in the darkness. She wanted to hold him. Comfort him. They were so different—yet so alike. Two crazed souls reaching for the stars. Trying to find a better world.

She reached out for him, but there was nothing there. His voice faded away. Everything faded away. She was alone in the darkness.

What was that light? So bright—like the sun? And that silhouette? Like the statue in the museum? What in God's name was happening?

An ivory horse lit up the darkness, its hooded rider peering down at her.

"Who are you?"

"Come, Miss Halberton. You're going to a better place...."

* * *

"She was your woman?"

Bonaventure glared at the man lying beside him in the snow. "She was my hope."

"I'm sorry, English."

Bonaventure lowered his head and clutched the woman in his arms.

"Why did you come here? You don't belong here."

"Go to hell."

"Hear me, English. Don't grieve for your woman. She has found a better world."

Bonaventure pointed a trembling finger at the stranger. "I think you've said enough. It's time for you to die."

The stranger looked up at the peak, his eyes filled with tears. "Yes...I see you. Oh, Nangi...it's a blessed miracle. Thank the Gods."

"I warned you, dammit."

The stranger looked at Bonaventure with shaken eyes. "Forgive me, English. I didn't know."

"What are you babbling?"

"The exchange."

"What?"

"My sister...for you. *Namaste*...mountaineer. *Namaste*..." The stranger collapsed in the snow, his black eyes locked on Bonaventure.

Bonaventure stared at the stranger's glazed eyes. There was no anger in those eyes. Only peace. As if a great burden had been taken away.

He'd cried only once before—when he left Hans on Jungfrau. Time to cry again. He buried his face against her and wept for the life they would never have—and for the mountaineer who had lost his final battle.

He placed the stranger's rifle in the snow beside his lifeless body, a bullet still in the chamber. Good to die with your rifle at your side. He paused and said a prayer for the man whose name he didn't know.

He slung the machine gun over his shoulder and lifted her in his arms. There was still time for revenge.

Gary Naiman

* * *

"Captain!"

Yamato spun around and saw the string of canisters twisting toward him like a giant serpent. He scrambled out of their path and shouted at the stunned marines. "Dig in! The damn things are out of control!"

The marines dug their boots into the ice and gripped the rope as the canisters swept past them. It was a simple equation. Thirteen exhausted men against twenty-three chained canisters. A ton of muscle against seventeen hundred pounds of sliding metal. The ultimate tug of war.

The string of canisters snapped tight with a sickening twang, ripping the marines from their footholds. The desperate marines skidded down the ice, the restraining rope tearing at their waists. There was no breaking free. If the canisters went over, so would they.

The ice grated against their boots as they strained against the overpowering weight dragging them down the slope toward the buttress. A few of them cried out in agony. Some of them fell and were dragged with the others while scrambling to regain their footing.

On the verge of collapse, the panicked marines skidded to a stop on the broken ice. They dug in and glared at the line of canisters resting precariously on the slope. They'd glissaded nearly a quarter mile. They were only fifty yards from the edge of the cliff overlooking the icefall.

Yamato dropped in the snow and eyed the crouching marines. "Everyone all right?" He waited for their weary nods. "Then on your feet. We can't stop now."

Kirosawa pushed back his hood and looked down at the canisters. "How can we get them down to the icefall?"

Yamato grimmaced. He scanned the rocks at the edge of the cliff. "We'll tie them to that cluster of rocks. Then we'll climb down and anchor them from below. We'll use the rocks for a winch to lower them to the icefall. It's only a hundred foot drop."

"Yes, sir."

"It's a quarter mile across the icefall to the snowpack. Then another mile to the cliff above the glacier." He hesitated and looked down at his lieutenant. "Shouldn't be too hard for Imperial Marines."

"Hai!"

"Then on your feet. I don't like that sky." Yamato nodded toward the band of clouds closing from the south. The next blizzard would hit in a few hours. If they could reach the cliff above the glacier, they'd dig a snow cave and sit it out. If not, they'd freeze to death on the exposed snowpack. It was the best he could do. Yamato gave his pack a tug and headed down the ice....

An hour had passed since he spotted them lowering the canisters to the icefall. An incredible effort, given the hundred foot drop and weight. They moved like ants. Without fear or hesitation. Thirteen disciplined men focused on one objective.

They were on the icefall now, their cargo dragging behind them. In a few minutes, they'd reach the snowpack and begin the descent to the cliff above the glacier.

Bonaventure lifted the machine gun into firing position. If he could bring down a few of them, it might signal Akaal to open up from the seracs. Between them, they might do enough damage to stop the bastards. Anything to make them pay.

He took aim and rested his finger on the trigger. He only had a few seconds before they dropped out of range. He squinted down the barrel and squeezed the trigger.

Nothing happened. He lowered the weapon and stared at it. What was wrong? He released the cocking lever and popped out the clip.

Ice! The damn clip was coated with it. His own sweat had done the damage, drenching the clip inside his parka. The chilled air had done the rest. The bloody thing was a block of ice.

He flung the machine gun in the snow. Below him, the soldiers faded into the haze, their cargo trailing behind them.

He slumped against her, his eyes fixed on the haze. The sun had disappeared behind a line of approaching storm clouds. He could hear thunder echoing off the peaks. The wind was picking up. Not much time left. The broken ice was only a hundred feet above him. He still had one flare left. He'd fire it from up there and hope his friend saw it before the storm hit.

He stood up and lifted her in his arms—and he felt his heart break. "Come on, Reuters. We're going home." He leaned into the wind and stumbled up the slope. It only took a few minutes to reach the broken ice.

He eased her down and stared at the three bullet-riddled bodies lying in the snow. Mariner and Nemi were lying off to the left, their faces covered with snow.

He knelt beside Akaal and brushed away the snow. One hand still clutched the spent *Enfield*. The other grasped a string of prayer beads.

He lowered his head and rested a gloved hand on his friend's blood-soaked parka. There were no tears. No cries of anguish. Only memories of two men clinging to a windswept slope. Their faces to the sun. Their eyes trained on the summit. One white—the other yellow-brown. Two comrades reaching for glory. And now—it was over.

A bolt of lightning struck the peak. The ice shook with thunder as the mother of all storms swept over the mountain. Kangchenjunga's fierce god wanted more blood.

Bonaventure dug in behind the ice, his two friends at his side. He clung to them and imagined a world where people are judged by character and deed. Where each person can reach for their dream. A better world. His world.

The storm would pass quickly. With a little luck, he could make it across the icefall before the next avalanche broke loose from the summit. Then down the snowpack to the cliff and—

And what, Bonaventure? A four mile descent to a world gone mad? A world of fear and doubt? Remorse and guilt? A world ready to tear itself apart? What kind of world is that?

Daylight gave way to darkness as gale-force winds ripped at the three shadows huddled in the ice. A bolt of electricity hissed across the black sky, flooding the north ridge with unearthly light.

He looked down at the two bodies lying beside him. What good is life without friendship and love? It had taken him forty years to find something greater than himself. Now it was dead. Lying beside him at twenty-two thousand.

The ice shook with thunder. He stood up against the wind, his blue eyes locked on the flashing peak.

Life is so fleeting. We need something more. Something everlasting. Some call it God. Others call it glory. To Julian Bonaventure, it was granite.

The sky lit up. A blast of wind ripped into him, knocking him backward into the snow. He heard the seracs toppling in the wind. The gods were screaming at him. Warning him to turn back. He had gone too far. He was standing on sacred ground.

Or was it those hypocrites at the Royal Society. Laughing at him, their glasses raised to the renegade's death. Yes—that was it. They were laughing at him. Celebrating his death.

He grasped Akaal's climbing rope and axe. The Spaniard's words echoed in his ears. *Tough to stop halfway, isn't it, Mr. Bonaventure?*

He stood up against the wind, his eyes locked on the peak. "Here's your story, Reuters." He leaned into the wind and marched toward the crumbling seracs. Cormier and Angstrom were waiting for him up there, but he was going further. Much further....

A blast of wind dropped him to his knees. He rose to his feet and glared at the flashing peak. "You're mine, dammit! Mine!"

46 | Face the Devil

"Major Pierce."

Pierce raised his head and saw Sergeant Flynn staring at him from the door. He blinked his eyes and glanced at his watch. Zero-seven-twenty. He'd been asleep since midnight.

"Pangpema, sir. We've got them on the radio."

Pierce's eyes lit up. He stood up and leaned against the desk. "How long have they been on?"

"Only a minute."

Pierce stormed past the sergeant and disappeared through the opened door. The calendar on the wall read "June 8, 1939," but that was yesterday. It was the morning of June ninth. Six days had passed since Dharan's last contact with White Lion. Six long days. Downing Street was in a frenzy. In a few hours, an intelligence officer would arrive from New Delhi with orders to take over Operation White Lion. The implications were clear.

Pierce rushed past the empty officer's desks and pushed through the door marked "Radio Room." Private Gage was hunched over the radio, his fingers pressed against the headset. Pierce closed the door and sat beside him. "What do we have?"

"Pangpema, sir. Sounds like trouble." Gage slipped off the headset and handed it to his commander. "I'd better stay here. He keeps fading."

Pierce nodded and slipped on the headset. He snatched the microphone and flipped the transmit switch. "Nepal Gateway to White Lion. Are you there, Lion?"

At first there was only static. Then he heard it. An unfamiliar voice crying out like an echo. "I can barely hear you, Lion. Can you elevate your power?"

Pierce pressed the headset against his ear and squinted at the radio's amber dial. He snatched a pencil off the table and scribbled something on a pad of paper. "Please repeat. Who are you? What's happened up there?"

Gage watched the major's face go blank. He'd heard the stranger's plea for help when he picked up the transmission.

And the gibberish about the Japanese. He frowned and stared at the radio dial.

Pierce sank in the chair, his eyes staring into space.

"Want me to take over, sir?"

Pierce ignored him and raised the microphone. "How long can you hold?" He pressed his fingers against the earpiece and listened to the reply.

Pierce lowered the mike and looked at Gage. "What's the weather forecast, Private?"

"Clearing, sir."

Pierce glanced at his watch. He took a deep breath and spoke into the mike. "Will send troops. Should arrive your position at twelve hundred hours. Can you mark landing sight with flares?" He leaned forward and pressed the headset. "Can you hear me, Pangpema?" He tapped the earpiece and shook his head. "Something's wrong. I've lost him."

Gage slipped on the headset and turned up the power. He twisted the knob and squinted at the dial.

"Well?"

"Line's open, sir. I think he stopped transmitting."

"You're sure?"

"Pretty sure, sir."

Pierce snatched the notepad off the table. He stood up, his eyes fixed on the private. "Not a word of this to anyone."

"Yes, sir."

"Keep trying to raise him. If you get through, tell him help's on the way. Twelve hundred hours. Got it?"

"What about the morning dispatches?"

"The hell with them."

"Yes, sir."

Pierce burst out of the radio room and gestured for Flynn to follow him. They brushed past Lieutenants Cook and Langley who were coming in for their morning turn on the message desks.

The two officers snapped to attention and saluted smartly. Pierce ignored them and barged out the front door, followed by his sergeant.

Cook lowered his hand and stared at the swinging door.

"What's got into him?"

"Probably got reamed for sending Dawa and Mariner on that bloody goose chase."

"Aah—they're okay. Probably lost their radio. Dawa's the best. He'll bring 'em back in one piece."

"Unless the *Vickers* crashed into the bloody mountain."

"Aah—you're daft. Mariner could land that thing blindfolded."

Langley folded his arms and smiled at his friend. "Care to place a wager on that, old chum?"

"Wager?"

"Might as well make it interesting."

Cook broke into a smile. "How much?"

"Five quid?"

"You're on." Cook shrugged and sat down at one of the empty desks. First thing he'd do with the money is buy Corporal Dawa a drink.

Pierce sloshed across the mud-soaked compound to the front gate. The rain had stopped and the sky was clearing. The air was heavy with the smell of damp earth. He pulled out a cigaret and jabbed it between his lips. "Got a light, Sergeant?"

Flynn struck a match and held it in his cupped hands. He watched the major lean forward and take a puff. When their eyes met, he knew something was wrong.

Pierce backed away and took a deep drag. He lowered the cigaret and exhaled. "We've got trouble."

"Sir?"

"The bloke on the radio said the bloody nips landed troops up there."

"Troops?"

Pierce stared at the second *Vickers* nestled under its camouflaged tarpaulin. "We need to get up there. It's more than a crashed plane now. This could be the beginning."

Flynn's eyes widened. "You mean—invasion?"

"I don't know what I mean." Pierce stroked his silver moustache. "I want you to pick a dozen of your best men. Load them up with ammo and weapons. Tell Corporal Wright to get the *Vickers* ready. You need to be in Pangpema by noon."

Flynn stared at him in shock.

"The weather's clearing. It should give you enough of a window to get in there."

"Sir—if it's an invasion, twelve men won't have a chance up there."

Pierce took a long drag and shook his head. "I wish there were another way."

"That's two of us, sir." Flynn looked down and rubbed the back of his neck. "It doesn't make sense. If the Japs are up there, how did your man get through?"

"He didn't."

"Sir?"

"The transmission didn't come from White Lion. It came from a stranger."

"Stranger?"

"He told me he was transmitting from one of their planes."

Flynn's jaw dropped. "It's a bloody trap. The bloody nips are up there waiting for us."

Pierce flicked his cigaret in the mud. "Take two B.A.R.'s and plenty of ammo. Buzz the landing sight before you come down. I told our friend to mark it with flares, but I'm not sure he heard me. Any sign of trouble, fly the bloody *Vickers* back here. And for God's sake, stay in contact with us."

"Yes, sir."

Pierce looked out at the Siwalik foothills. "Looks like our visitor from New Delhi will get an earful. Wonder what they'll do to me."

"Do?"

"They'll need a scapegoat for this mess—and I'm it. Probably transfer me to some nondescript post in Malaysia."

Flynn shook his head. "If you're right about this, they'll need you up here—and a lot more like you."

"I'd rather be a scapegoat."

"Sir?"

"If I'm right—we've had it. They'll cut through us like a knife through butter." He patted Flynn's shoulder and walked away.

* * *

Roberto dropped the microphone and collapsed in the leather seat. He slipped his right hand inside his torn parka and rested it on the bandage. When he pulled it out, his palm was streaked with blood.

The bleeding had begun during the night, accompanied by sharp pains in his chest and shoulder. He'd seen enough wounded men to know how bad it was. The soldier's pummeling had taken its toll. If he didn't get medical help soon, the trickle of blood would become a torrent.

He looked down at the radio. Thank God, he'd remembered the Dharan frequency. Hard to find it with all those *Kanji* symbols, but he'd gotten through. It was the only way he could help them now—if they were still alive. Just a few more hours and the place would be swarming with British troops. And he'd be on a plane to Dharan.

He'd told them he was a missionary who had stumbled across Eammon's monastery in a blizzard. When they landed, he'd give them a fake name and use Calcutta as his home. By the time they figured out he was lying, he'd be landing in Bombay. A quick check of the steamer schedules and he'd be on his way home, heaving his guts in the Arabian Sea.

There was only one problem. It would take more than a swift tongue to pull it off. It would take money. Lots of it.

He stared at the frosted windshield. No time to lose. The sun was already above the ridge. It wouldn't be easy, but he had to try. If any of the packs had survived the fire, he could use them to bribe his way back to Spain—and that dinner with *El Caudillo*. One well-placed bullet would do the job. Right between the eyes. And Roberto Hidalgo would die a better man than he had lived.

He tried to stand, but a burning pain stopped him. He collapsed in the leather seat, clutching his side. Shut it out, *torero*. There is work to be done. He gritted his teeth and forced himself up.

He pushed through the cockpit door and stared at the darkened cargo hold. Twin beams of sunlight shined through the two small windows across from the cargo door. One of them struck the dead soldier's ashen face.

His stomach wrenched. How long since he'd squeezed that trigger? One day? Two? He gripped an overhead strap and staggered toward the corpse.

His foot struck something. It was one of the discarded ration tins he'd pulled from the dead soldier's pack. He looked down at the rusted tin and kicked it away. The stuff tasted awful, but it had kept him alive. Like that blanket lying against the fuselage wall. Without it, he would have frozen to death in the subzero darkness. Two gifts from his enemy.

He stood beside the body, his eyes fixed on the gray, lifeless face. There was so much anguish on that face. So much pain. Like those strained faces in Picasso's mural.

He knelt down and rested a hand on man's blood-soaked parka. His eyes drifted to the medical bag lying against the fuselage wall. How could it be? The man had tended his wounds, then tried to kill him? What kind of sickness turns a healer into a murderer?

He looked down at his bloodstained hand. Was he any better? Killing another human being to save his own life? Is that how it would finally end? The human race annihilating itself in the name of self-defense?

He wiped the sweat off his face and glanced at the flare gun in the man's belt. There was still time. If he could get to Spain and put an end to *El Caudillo*, it might ignite the revolt that would turn the tide. Maybe even spill into Italy and Germany. God knows, it was all he had. A final chance to make up for a wasted life.

He stood up and leaned against the cargo door. He could see the other plane through the windows, its black wings caked with ice. His hand gripped the red release lever. One chance, *torero*. One chance. He gritted his teeth and yanked the lever. A blast of chilled wind struck his face. He lunged for the overhead strap, but it was too late. The door gave way. He swiped at the air and plummeted through the opening.

Paralyzing pain shot through his chest and shoulders as his body slammed into the snow. He cried out in agony, but the pain took his breath away. He clutched his side and felt the blood ooze through his parka. His ears rang. Everything was going black. *No! You've come too far!* He tried to stand, but the dizziness overwhelmed him. He collapsed in the snow, his black eyes locked on the ridge.

What was that light? A blinding radiance like the Matterhorn? The sun's rays were reflecting off something in the ruins? Beneath the charred Buddha?

His eyes brightened. Yes—it was up there. Buried in the rubble. His ticket home. His last chance at glory. He gritted his teeth and pushed off the snow.

They'd marched all night. Ten weary men trying to pull off a miracle. A day had passed since they lowered the canisters down the thousand foot gauntlet of rock and ice. Tense hours clinging to belay ropes. Straining against their seventeen hundred pound cargo. Hemp and muscle stretched to the breaking point. Burning, cramping pain. Lungs gasping for breath. And when they were down, a twelve mile trek across treacherous ice. Twenty-four agonizing hours without sleep.

The grueling march across the glacier had taken a terrible toll. Kobayashi, Imai, and Ito were gone. Victims of a collapsed ice bridge. Yamato could still hear their screams when they plunged into the darkness, their hands clawing at the severed lifeline. He would never forget the rope's sickening twang when his knife sliced through it. The desperate cries. The sudden silence. The anguish. Three men sacrificed to save ten others. Better to have gone over with them. Another bitter memory to take to his grave.

Only ten left. Ten exhausted marines on the verge of collapse. Their fingers blackened with frostbite. An ominous chill eating at their bones. No food. No rest. Each step more painful than the last. But they plodded on. Proud soldiers dragging their cursed sleds behind them. Driven by an obsession to finish what their dead comrades started.

Their weary minds turned homeward. To the morning sun above Tokyo Bay, its golden rays striking Fujiyama. The fishing fleet headed out to sea. The sweet smell of cherry blossoms in the wind. Families embracing their returned warriors, their eyes wet with tears. A hand-clapping prayer beneath the *Shinto* shrine. A warm meal and bottle of *saki*. The rush of wind chimes in the soft darkness. A loved one's tender kiss. Warm thoughts of home. It was all they had left.

Lieutenant Kirosawa ripped off his goggles and peered into the haze. "Tell me I'm not dreaming."

Yamato yanked out his binoculars and focused them on the drifting snow. He heard the others shuffle behind him. There were no words. Only the wind and rustling snow.

"Do you see them?"

Yamato swept his binoculars across the white landscape. He hesitated and swept them again. He lowered the binoculars and shook his head.

"But I saw them. Dead ahead."

"Just shadows, Lieutenant." Yamato stared at the blowing snow. He was about to look away when something caught his eye. A flash of reflected sunlight. Probably just ice, but it could be something more. He lifted the binoculars toward the haze.

"Sir?"

Yamato's eyes widened. He lowered the binoculars and stared at his lieutenant in shock. "They're out there. Sitting in the snow. Just like we left them." He turned toward the marines. "We made it. We're going home."

The air erupted with cheers as the marines converged on the two stunned officers, their eyes straining to get a glimpse of the twin aircraft sitting in the blowing snow.

There was no time to lose. Yamato backed away from his beleaguered men. "Lieutenant Kirosawa."

"Sir!"

"Take four men and form a skirmishing line. We'll wait for your green flare.

"Hai!"

"And, Lieutenant."

"Sir!"

"If it's red, we'll come in shooting."

Kirosawa nodded and clenched his fists. He knew a red flare meant the end of them.

"When you reach the planes, check for trip wires. They could be mined. We're not out of this yet."

"Hai!"

Yamato watched Kirosawa and his marines shuffle across the snowfield toward the two planes. He waited until they faded into the haze before turning to the others. "Corporal Tenai."

"Sir!" The young marine snapped to attention.

"If we come under attack, your orders are to place grenades against the canisters and detonate them."

"Detonate?"

Yamato locked his black eyes on the marine. "Mark me well, Corporal. At all costs, blow them up. We can't let them slip into enemy hands. Understood?"

"Yes, sir."

Yamato saw the anguish on the marine's face. How much more could they take? If it was a trap, they were all dead men. He knew it, and so did they. He turned away and trained his binoculars on the five men closing on the planes.

"Captain!"

Yamato spun around and saw Tenai pointing toward the ridge where the monastery had stood.

"Someone's up there. Near the top."

Yamato focused his binoculars on the ridge crest and swept them down to a small shadow on the ivory slope. A man was staggering toward the ruins, maybe a hundred feet below the crest.

Yamato lowered the binoculars. "Forget him."

"But, sir. He might be trying to warn the enemy."

Yamato glared at the corporal. "Forget him!"

"Yes, sir."

The next ten minutes were eternity. The wind had picked up and it was turning colder. The sun had faded behind a veil of thickening haze. Another storm was closing from the south. If they didn't get out soon, they'd stay up here forever.

Kirosawa cocked his machine gun and crept toward the first plane. He was within two hundred feet of it when Corporal

… The Tenth Avatar

Tamura grabbed his arm and pointed to the opened cargo door.

"I see it. Stay behind me." Kirosawa lifted the machine gun into firing position and crept closer.

He was within fifty feet of the opening when he spotted the tracks in the snow. He knelt down and pulled out his binoculars.

Was he seeing things? Someone was on the ridge, climbing toward the ruins. He stood up and shouted at the top of his lungs. "Nagano! It's Kirosawa! Where the hell are you going!"

He pointed the machine gun at the sky and started to squeeze the trigger. No—it might alarm the others and bring them in shooting. He took a painful breath and waved the machine gun in the air. "Nagano! Come down! We made it! We're going home!"

He waited for a reaction, but the man kept climbing. What was wrong with him? Was he deaf? He lowered the machine gun and stared at the opened cargo door.

He backed away and glanced at the four marines crouching behind him. "I'm going in. If anything happens, fire a red flare and pull back."

Tamura nodded at the slope. "What about Nagano?"

"That isn't Nagano." Kirosawa lifted the machine gun into firing position. He said a prayer and crept toward the opened door.

Yamato lowered his binoculars and stared at the green flare. He breathed a sigh of relief and listened to the men's cheers. Corporal Tamura and three marines were running toward him from the whiteout. But where was Kirosawa?

Tamura stumbled beside his commander and gasped for breath. "We found Nagano."

"Yes?"

"He's dead, sir. In the first plane. The Lieutenant's with him."

Yamato's face twisted in a scowl. "How?"

"Bullet through the heart. Close range."

Yamato stepped back in shock. Operation NI had claimed its thirty-second soldier. Thirty-two battle-hardened marines killed by a mountain and handful of rabble. And what did they have to show for it? Four dead enemy soldiers and twenty-three canisters of glowing steam. All because a few crazed scientists had convinced the Emperor to go forward with an insane mission called "NI."

Yamato felt the blood pounding against his temples. He glared at the man crawling up the ridge. They had spent five days in hell to bring back an unexplained cargo. Ten Imperial Marines were going home, but thirty-two of their comrades would stay up here forever. Thirty-two families had sacrificed their hopes and dreams to a mission without honor—and that pig was getting away.

Yamato ripped the machine gun off his shoulder and stormed toward the ridge.

"Where are you going, sir?"

"To kill that pig. Take the sleds in. I'll see you at the planes."

The stunned marines watched their commander shuffle into the whiteout, the machine gun dangling from his hand.

Roberto collapsed in the snow, his hand gripping his side. The slope swayed under him. He looked down at the ominous trail of splattered blood. He could feel its warm wetness oozing through his glove.

He tried to stand, but his legs wouldn't move. He was so tired. If he could just close his eyes....

He looked up at the charred Buddha. He could almost touch it. He pushed off the snow and fought to keep his balance. He was so dizzy. So weak. He jammed his fist against his side and staggered upward.

Ten years ago, he had climbed another slope. The sun was warm that day. The air sweet with flowers. Instead of snow, the hillside was covered with orange groves. Behind him, a beautiful fortressed city stood against the sea, its domed mosques jutting proudly into the crystal blue sky. It was a wonderful day. A happy day. His mind danced with thoughts of love and home. Of the caring father who had sacrificed everything for his son. And the beautiful mother who had given her life to bring her only child into the world. All of it—gone. Destroyed by an evil that had spilled beyond Spain's borders to threaten the entire world. And there was nothing he could do. He collapsed in the snow, his eyes fixed on the Buddha.

What was happening? Something whizzed past his ear. His legs exploded in pain. He cried out and buried his face in the snow. The air rattled with machine gun fire.

He looked down at the haze. A man was standing at the bottom of the ridge, a smoking gun in his hands. The man lowered his weapon and stared at him.

Why wasn't he afraid? He should be afraid? He looked down at his bleeding legs and felt a deep anger well up inside him. An anger he'd known only once before. In Guernica's burning town square. When the plane burst through the smoke, its wings belching fire.

The time had come. The voice in Corpus Christi. The blood on the cross. His tortured life driven to this moment. He gritted his teeth and pushed off the snow, his eyes glaring down at the man in the haze. He had found his demon. The evil that took away everything he loved. The cancer that turned brother against brother, and destroyed a nation. And he was the last one in its path. He had found his destiny.

He heard the cocking lever snap back. The air shook with a deadly rat-a-tat. A terrific force slammed into his chest, throwing him backward into the snow. He couldn't breathe. He clutched his chest and felt the bullets rip into him. And he remembered the nightmare. The bullets striking his chest. The searing pain. His hand clutching the crucifix. The voice whispering to him in the darkness.

A bullet tore into his leg. Then another. My God—the animal was still firing at him. Like that plane diving at the bodies in Guernica's town square. Raking the dead with machine gun fire. What kind of beast shoots the dead? Only one, *torero*. That thing at the bottom of the ridge was more than a demon. It was the Devil himself!

He staggered to his feet, his black eyes burning into the stunned man and his smoking weapon. Yes—it was him. The Devil had come from Guernica to put an end to the last one who cared.

He raised his trembling fist and screamed in agony. "Bastard! You'll burn in hell for this! I'll get you! So help me, God. I'll—"

Yamato popped in a fresh clip and pulled back the cocking lever. He aimed it at the raging madman and squeezed the trigger. The bullets tore into the man's brown parka. Blood spurted in the air. The man clutched his chest and stumbled forward. His bullet-riddled body plunged into the snow and tumbled down the slope, arms and legs flailing like a ragdoll.

Yamato popped in another clip and shuffled beside the blood-soaked body. He looked down at the ashen face. It was the same man Nagano had shot five days ago. He poked at the body with the smoking barrel and backed away, his eyes fixed on the small gold crucifix on the man's chest.

So this was the enemy. An unarmed missionary clothed in animal fur, his only weapon a tirade of indecipherable curses. Thirty-two men dead because of a missionary and his band of rabble. What would he tell them in Tokyo? How would he explain it to Tojo? The first skirmish of a war not yet started. A bitter defeat. He turned and shuffled across the snow....

47 | So Help Me God!

They buried Nagano in a shallow grave marked with a rising sun pennant. It would be hard to leave him behind, but there was no choice. Everything possible must be done to lighten the load. At least he wasn't alone. Thirty-one of his comrades were with him. They would not be forgotten.

Time was short. The storm clouds had already reached Kangchenjunga's southern slopes. In another hour, a fierce blizzard would rake Pangpema with subzero winds and blinding snow. If Yamato and his nine marines were still on the ground, it would be the end of them—and Operation NI.

Yamato split the marines into two work groups. The first loaded the canisters into the untouched plane while the second siphoned gasoline from the other. With only one pilot left, they could only take one plane, and that meant carrying as much spare fuel as possible.

While they worked, Corporal Tamura climbed into the cockpit and began the critical struggle to start the engines. The fierce winds had shredded the protective tarps, exposing the wings and engines to the bitter cold. Their only hope was a blast of intense heat to melt the ice on the wings, and that meant using the welding torch they'd brought from Nanking.

Kirosawa pulled Private Nissei from the work groups and ordered him to strap on the heavy contraption. Nissei bowed while cursing his prior training as a welder. He slung the red fuel cylinder on his back and climbed onto the right wing, the nozzle tucked in his belt. If it worked, the flames would melt the ice and thin the oil. If not, the explosion would blow him to eternity.

The marines backed away as Nissei turned on the gas and ignited the nozzle. He said a prayer and aimed the hissing nozzle at the wing while slowly tightening the gas jet.

A blue flame shot out of the nozzle, striking the ice on the wing. Nissei stepped forward, sweeping the pointed flame in front of him. Just enough to melt the ice without setting off the gasoline in the tanks. Minutes seemed like hours. A treacherous walk across wings of ice, the torch's blue flame hissing in front of him, invisible death churning under him.

Twenty minutes later, the shaken marine crawled off the wing and dropped the empty cylinder in the snow. He looked up at the cleared wings and heaved a sigh of relief while his comrades swarmed over him. Now it was Tamura's turn.

Yamato looked up at the cockpit window. "Well?"

Tamura poked his head into the cold. "Maybe we should wait a few minutes. Another blast of heat on the cowlings."

"We don't have minutes. That storm is almost on us. The mountain is already covered. It's now or never."

Tamura felt his stomach churn. He dropped back in the seat and stared at the instrument panel. His turn to be the hero. Ten lives in his hands. If not him—who? He took a deep breath and stuck his head out the window. "Stand clear! I'm starting the engines!"

The marines backed away, their eyes locked on the *Nakajima*'s twin propellers.

Yamato leaned toward Kirosawa. "Cargo secured?"

"Anchored with chain."

"And the spare fuel?"

"As much as we could load." Kirosawa looked south toward the approaching storm. "Damn, why did it have to be Kobayashi?"

Yamato grimaced. Kobayashi was the senior pilot who had led the flight from Nanking. Now he lay at the bottom of a crevasse with two of his comrades. With only one pilot left, their chances had been cut in half. Too many blunders. Too much desperation.

Tamura primed number one and opened its throttle. He gritted his teeth and grasped the magneto switch. "Contact!" He flipped the switch and listened to the engine groan.

He slumped in the seat and glared at the motionless rpm needle. More air, dammit. Let the bitch breathe.

He adjusted the mixture and glanced out the window. Nine desperate men were staring at him—waiting for the sound that would take them home.

"Contact!" He flipped the switch and felt a rumble. The

propeller rotated and died.

A bead of sweat trickled down his forehead. He pumped the priming knob and grasped the switch. The wind was picking up. In a few minutes, the crosswinds would make it impossible to take off.

"Contact!" He flipped the switch and listened to the engine groan. The propeller whined and coughed to a stop.

He slammed his fist on his lap. "Come on, you bitch! Turn over!" He flipped the switch and felt the plane vibrate. Black smoke and flame shot out of the exhaust at the rear of the engine. The propeller roared to life, engulfing the cheering marines with blowing snow.

No time to waste. Tamura adjusted the throttle while glancing at number one's dancing rpm needle. He primed number two and opened its throttle. His fingers grasped the second magneto switch.

"Contact!" Number two groaned and sputtered. He adjusted the mixture and flipped the switch again. The right propeller kicked on amidst a cloud of black smoke and blowing snow. The plane shook from its fully-engaged engines.

Yamato waved the men aboard. His last act was to fling a demolition pack into the other plane. The timer was set for ten minutes. He ran to the cockpit window and shouted at Tamura. "Do you need help turning it around?"

Tamura shook his head and waved his commander aboard. He'd never executed a "one-eighty" on skis, but he felt lucky today. He stared at the ridge through the cleared windshield. About six hundred feet of space. More than enough.

Kirosawa stepped into the cockpit and rested a hand on the young pilot's shoulder. "All secured."

Tamura nodded and placed his hand on the throttles. "Strap in and say a prayer."

Kirosawa gave him a reassuring pat. "Good luck, Corporal. We're with you." He backed away and disappeared through the cockpit door.

Tamura placed his feet on the rudder pedals. He stared at the ridge and jammed the throttles forward.

The plane shook from the sudden roar. He heard a dull,

cracking sound as the skis broke free of the ice.

The plane lunged forward, its skis sloshing through the snow. Twenty knots. Thirty. His eyes locked on the ridge and charred Buddha. He was almost on top of them.

Now! He pulled back the right throttle and pressed the right rudder pedal.

A powerful force pushed him to the left as the plane's nose veered sharply right. The ridge and Buddha raced across the windshield and disappeared. In their place, he could see the snowfield leading to the distant western ridges. The plane had done a perfect one hundred eighty degree turn.

Tamura pulled back the left throttle and released the right rudder pedal. They were facing due west with a mile of snow between them and the ridges. He slumped in the seat and heard the cockpit door swing open. Yamato brushed against his shoulder and dropped in the seat beside him.

"How does it look?"

"The wind is behind us, sir. I'll taxi out a mile and turn again. We'll take off into the wind."

"Well done, Corporal."

Tamura felt a gust of wind strike the plane. He glanced to his left and saw a gray haze sweep over the glacier. Only minutes left. He opened the throttles and felt the plane surge forward.

Yamato stared at the snow blowing against the windshield. The plane was rocking now, its nose pointed at the western ridges.

"Better strap in, sir."

Yamato nodded and leaned back in his seat.

With lightning flashing above the glacier, the *Nakajima* executed another perfect turn, this time coming to rest with its nose pointed at the east ridge and ruins.

Tamura stared at the gusting snow. One mile should be enough, but what about the load? Seventeen hundred pounds of lead. Seven hundred pounds of spare fuel. Two hundred pounds of weapons and ammo. Fifteen hundred pounds of flesh and blood. Two tons of weight pressing the twin-engined aircraft into the snow. He set the flaps to "FULL" and leaned back in the seat.

"Ready, Corporal?"

Tamura nodded and took a deep breath. He rested his hand on the throttles and jammed them to the stops.

The cockpit shook from the sudden roar as the *Nakajima* surged forward. Tamura listened to the wind whistling against the glass. The plane rocked from side to side as the young pilot fought to hold a straight course against the increasing crosswinds and blowing snow. He could see Kangchenjunga to the right, its summit protruding through the gray clouds.

Sixty knots. Seventy. Tamura's brown eyes locked on the ridge. The charred Buddha stared down at him, its black silhouette jutting into the sky. It was like a magnet. Drawing him closer. Pulling him into its protective arms.

One hundred knots. One ten. Now!

Tamura pulled back the wheel and felt the wings strain against the wind. The skis lifted into the air and skipped off the snow. "Come on you bitch! Take us home!"

The marines broke into cheers as the plane skipped off the snow. Next stop, Tibet and a waiting squadron of *Zeros*. Then east to Nanking, and north across the China Sea to the Sea of Japan. They were going home! Mission accomplished!

Kirosawa's eyes drifted past the cheering marines to the canisters. How useless they looked straining against their chains. Worthless metal cylinders. So many dead for so little.

Oh, Lieutenant—if you only knew the truth. You were staring at the future. A future brighter than the sun—yet darker than hell itself. A future you would never see.

Yamato leaned forward, his eyes locked on the windshield. "What is it?"

"A man. Standing in the snow. It can't be. I'm seeing things."

"The hell with him." Tamura pulled the wheel against his stomach and felt the nose rise into the air. The Buddha fell away from the windshield. Only a few more seconds and they'd be on their way home.

It was coming at him through the haze, its twin engines churning up clouds of snow. He felt his legs giving way. His knees struck the snow. Everything was growing dark. Only seconds, *torero*. Seconds to stop the pain. For the patriots! For Guernica! For Spain!

His ears filled with a deafening roar as the black bird rose into the sky, snow streaming from its wings. It was escaping! To kill again! Maim again! Destroy again! He raised the flare gun and squeezed the trigger. A tremendous blast of wind slammed into him as the plane roared over his head.

He fell backward in the snow, his eyes glaring at the black shadow climbing over the ridge. The air swirled with white powder—and it was gone.

He felt the gun drop out of his hand. Everything was so still. A gust of wind brushed his face. Or was it a soft hand caressing his cheek?

He looked up at her. She was so beautiful—like in the portrait.

"Mother?"

"I'm here, Roberto."

"Is it over?"

"Yes, my son."

He closed his eyes and felt her warm hand stroke his forehead. "I'm so tired. I want to go home."

"You are home, my son."

"Home?"

"Yes, Roberto. You've come home."

He could see the mosques jutting into the azure sky, their multicolored domes gleaming in the bright sun. And the Micalet rising above the ancient gates, its bells ringing in a new day. Beneath it, the Turia wound through the great city, its calm waters flowing past the Cathedral and Palace—and Museum of Art—and Silk Exchange. The shining fortress that was his home.

Beyond it, the blue Mediterranean stretched across the horizon, its waves splashing against the fishing boats returning with their day's catch.

The air was sweet with the scent of spring flowers—and the groves. Oh yes—the groves. A tapestry of orange stretching across the fertile green hills.

He ran through the Torres de Serranos Gate into the bustling city. It was market day and the streets were jammed with shouting vendors and artists. He ran past the Silk Exchange and Museo de Bellas Artes. Past the Palace and Great Cathedral. Past Corpus Christi and the University. Across the Puente Del Real Bridge and swirling Turia. And into Viveros Park where he paused and stared at the beautiful home nestled beneath the conifer trees.

The sun had set and darkness had closed over the great city. He took a breath of warm night air and headed across the park toward the light in the window. He could see Maria standing at the gate, hands on hips. He hesitated and smiled. He was late again, but his father would understand. He always understood....

"Something's wrong! I can't get any lift!"

Yamato stared in horror at the young pilot struggling with the wheel. He felt a blast of heat against his face. Flames were spewing out of the right engine. "Fire in number two!"

Tamura pumped the extinguisher while trying to level the wings. He closed number two's throttle, but the flames had spread to the wing. The right propeller sputtered and kicked to a stop.

"What happened?"

"I don't know. It sounded like an explosion."

"What should we do?"

Tamura shook his head. "We've got to turn back and land while we can."

"Are you crazy? We can't go back now. We're so close."

Tamura looked at him with terrified eyes. "It's all we have."

"You mean—"

Tamura jammed his foot on the left rudder pedal and turned the wheel hard left. There was no response. He tried a turn to the right, but nothing happened. He fell back in his seat and stared at the monolith blotting out the sky, its towering summit rising into the heavens like a mighty fortress. Kangchenjunga.

Gary Naiman

Home of the gods. Defender of the human race....

48 | Kalki

The storm had cleared the mountain, but powerful gusts still raked the summit and north ridge. Another foot of snow had fallen on the great lady—and it was just the beginning.

To the south, an armada of purple-gray clouds prepared for the next onslaught. To the north, Pangpema was being hammered by seventy-mile-an-hour winds. Nothing could withstand that inhuman pounding—nothing except a madman.

Bonaventure looked up at the white powder streaming off the ridge crest. He turned away from the stinging ice crystals and collapsed against the sixty degree slope. He could see Wedge Peak jutting through the haze, its twenty-two thousand foot summit barely touching his boots. And Yalung Kang, just a bit higher at twenty-three thousand, its ivory peak below his waist. Only Kangbachen rose above him, its twenty-six thousand foot peak glaring down at him like an offended giant.

He couldn't see the others through the bright haze, but he knew they were out there. Everest. Annapurna. Makalu. A hundred towering peaks. Watching him. Cursing him. Waiting for him to fall.

He'd managed to dig in below the ridge crest before the blizzard struck. A wise choice, picking the western side. The deadly storm had hammered the mountain's eastern slopes with ninety-mile-an-hour winds before moving on. He could still hear the winds pummeling the crest above his head.

He pulled off a glove and rubbed his throbbing head. He was so dizzy. Hard to breathe. He ripped open his collar and gulped the thin air.

He fumbled for the brandy flask, but it was gone. It had slipped out of his hand and fallen down the ice. But when? Yesterday? Today? A moment ago?

He pulled out his canteen and popped the cap. Frozen solid. Not even a drop. He flung the leather canteen down the slope and watched it carom into the haze. He'd have to eat snow. Not very safe, but it was all he had.

He scooped a handful of frozen white powder and bit into

it. Damn, what he'd give for a warm bottle of beer. He took another bite and rested his head against the ice.

How long had it been since he left them on that broken ice? Since he held her in his arms and kissed her for the last time? Since he stroked his comrade's blood-soaked hair and said goodbye? How long, Bonaventure? How long?

He had seen the moon twice since then. Or was it a dream? Could two days pass so quickly? Could a wounded mountaineer survive that long at twenty five thousand?

He closed his eyes and recalled the climb to the ridge crest. An agonizing struggle against frozen granite and waist-deep snow, the relentless wind ripping at his face. He remembered collapsing against the ice, his tired eyes closing, sweet numbness ebbing through his bones. Then that sudden rush of snow against his face. And those flapping wings.

He never saw the bird, but the shadow was unmistakable. An enormous creature rising into the starlit sky, its powerful wings churning up the snow above him. Spilling it down the sixty degree wall into his face. Just enough to snap him back to consciousness.

Was it a falcon? Condor? Not at twenty five thousand. Just a lucky dream. Good to dream. So quiet and peaceful. No pain. No sorrow. Just soft...numbing...sleep....

His eyes snapped open. He pushed away from the slope and grasped his forehead. Almost did it, old chum. Another few seconds and you'd dream forever.

He felt a warmth on his face. The morning sun was creeping over the ridge crest. He pushed back his hood and ran his hand through his hair. Well, old man—what's it gonna be? Close your eyes and dream? Or do we go a little further? He dug his boots into the ice and lunged upward.

He crawled onto the ridge crest and collapsed in the deep snow. A blast of frigid wind slammed into him. He buried his face in his arms and waited for it to pass. Come on, mountaineer. You're not dead yet. On your feet. Only a mile to go.

He stood up in the waist-deep snow and glared at the summit. How beautiful it looked spilling snow into the blue sky. So close he could almost touch it. And that ivory crest winding toward it like a heavenly path. Leading him to another world.

He gripped his ski pole and turned away from another blast of wind. The snow swirled up at him, its crystals stinging his face. A final warning from the angered mountain god.

Oh—how it hated him. Clinging to its white shoulder like an unwelcome parasite. Threatening to soil its untouched crown with his unclean hands. It would use every trick to stop him. Every step would be more treacherous than the last. It was war now. The ultimate struggle between man and granite.

He looked north toward Twin's Peak. Beyond it, Nepal Peak gave way to the Jongsong La and Tibet. He had stood here before. Only two hundred feet down that slope on the right, his eyes gazing at the untouched summit. Then he heard the roar and saw the wall of snow explode through the haze. And he heard their screams and saw them disappear beneath the white tidal wave.

He leaned against the ski pole and felt a chilled breeze on his face. Yes—they were here. All come back for a final round. He wasn't alone. They were at his side.

He looked up at the peak. Only a mile to go. A mile up that winding crest. It would be the longest mile. The hardest mile. The last mile. He jammed his ski pole in the snow and stumbled forward.

What was that sound? A high-pitched whine coming from the haze? The wind? No—too steady. He leaned against the ski pole and scanned the surrounding peaks.

His eyes widened. That choking and sputtering. He'd heard it before. Two years ago in Shanghai during the bombings. The sound of an aircraft in trouble.

Impossible. He was hallucinating. His mind had snapped. He crouched down and peered into the haze.

There! Low on the northern horizon. A mile below him. Smoke streaming from its engines. Its black wings flashing in the sun. He watched the wounded aircraft fly past Twins Peak, its coughing engines struggling to keep it airborne. It surged upward, its wings straining to lift it over Kangchenjunga's north ridge.

He could see it more clearly now. The flames had spread to the wings and tail. It looked more like a dying flare than an aircraft. It rose higher, black smoke trailing from its burning engines.

The plane lunged upward in a final act of desperation. It was almost to him, maybe a half mile away. It seemed to be floating in space, clawing at the air in a valiant, last gasp effort to clear the ridge.

The air shook with a violent explosion as the plane's burning right wing ripped away from the fuselage. He could see bodies falling into space as the flaming aircraft rolled over into a deadly, screaming spiral.

He watched it plummet into the haze. For a moment, there was no sound except the fading whine. Then he heard it. A sickening thud as the black bird plowed into the glacier.

He pushed up his goggles and stared at the spiralled trail of black smoke, and he recalled the soldiers dragging their heavy cargo down the mountain.

Was it possible? Could they have survived the treacherous descent for this cruel end? No—it wasn't real. This wasn't happening. You're hallucinating, dammit! Imagining this whole bloody mess! The damn thin air's got you!

His eyes brightened. He felt his heart pounding. Maybe a lot of things weren't real. Maybe Karen and Akaal were still down there waiting for him with Collins, Mariner, and Nemi. Maybe there were no Japanese or skirmishes on the ice.

He straightened up and stared at the haze. The plane's smoke trail was gone. Vanished like a mirage.

Of course! Because it never existed! That's it, dammit! Don't you see? You never came down! The thin air got you! You've been wandering up here for days! Turn around, man! Get off this goddamned mountain! They're alive, Bonaventure! Down there waiting for you! It was all a bloody dream!

He winced from a blinding flash. Everything was so bright. The sky glowed with silver light. He could see the Himalayas stretching before him, their peaks shining like mirrors. And that rumble. Deep and powerful. Like a volcano about to erupt.

A terrific blast of heat slammed into him. He felt the ski pole fly out of his hand. He dived off the crest into the snow on the eastern slope, his head buried in his arms.

What the bloody hell was going on? The mountain was shaking. The rumble had become a deafening roar. The air crackled with thunder. He could hear the seracs toppling off the cliffs as tons of dislodged snow exploded off the summit. The air smelled from static electricity. Bolts of lightning flashed across the sky. All hell had broken loose at twenty five thousand.

A second blast slammed into the crest, blowing away the snow like a giant's breath. He pushed away from the slope and looked up at the barren stretch of rock. What in God's name was happening?

He turned and looked up at the summit. It was glowing bright orange against the silver sky, but the sun was still behind it? What work of the devil was this? He crawled up the slope and peered over the barren crest. And he saw the face of hell.

A seething, orange mushroom cloud churned into the sky above him, its flickering stem rising from the glacier. If he was dreaming, it was the mother of all nightmares.

No, Bonaventure. You weren't dreaming. It was all coming together now. The urgency in Pierce's voice. The Irishman's frantic rush up the mountain. Glowing steam rising out of a bubbling crater. Unexplained lead canisters. Desperate soldiers sacrificing themselves to retrieve a mysterious cargo. Their exhausted comrades risking their lives to haul it down the mountain. And they almost made it. Almost pulled it off before going down in flames. My God—if they only knew their epitaph.

He turned and looked up at the summit. It was white again. The sky had returned to blue. The sun was striking the ridge crest, its rays lighting his path.

Julian Bonaventure had gotten a glimpse of the future. It would be more than armies this time. More than artillery and planes. Hellish new weapons had been discovered. The fools were out of control. Before it was over, they'd blow themselves to kingdom come and burn the world to a cinder.

Gary Naiman

He spotted his ski pole sticking out of the snow. He shuffled beside it and grasped the shaft. Behind him, the orange cloud faded into the heavens, its mushroom top distorted by the high altitude winds. Good riddance to it, and to the world he'd left behind. He was going to a better place.

Bonaventure locked his blue eyes on the peak and staggered upward—and he remembered the words....

Oh God...
To stand on virgin ice again,
and feel your presence in the wind.
To reach up and touch the sky,
and see your face before I die....

49 | *Silver Light*

"TWO MINUTES...."

Major Kogio Yamashita looked up at the trumpet-shaped loudspeaker, his face strained with tension. To his right, two dozen officers and scientists scrambled for shelter in their sandbagged trenches. They were too pressed to notice Corporal Hisei Tenagi climbing the sixty foot tower behind them.

Tenagi stepped onto the tower's platform and peered at the black sky above the Sea of Japan. He glanced at his watch. It would be daylight soon. The young corporal pulled away the canvas tarp covering the signaling beacon. He fumbled for the power switch and flicked it on. A white beam shot through the darkness, lighting up the sea.

"ONE MINUTE...."

Tenagi aimed the beam at the island. He grasped the signaling lever and began flipping it in staccato bursts. The water flashed with reflected light.

Yamashita leaned against the sandbags and raised his binoculars. All was still except the waves lapping against the shore, and the beacon's flapping shutters.

He stiffened. A white light flashed in the darkness. It was coming from one of the ships circling the island. "The signal, Nishina San. Everything is in order."

"I see it, Major." Yoshio Nishina pushed away from the sandbags and sat up on his aging knees. He studied the five men sprawled on his right. How innocent they looked peering through their binoculars. Like children watching a shooting star.

Four years had passed since they first met at the Rikken Institute of Physical and Chemical Research in Tokyo. Asada. Yazaki. Suzuki. Kikuchi. Sagane. Honorable, brilliant men. The very best Japan could muster. How hard they had struggled since that fateful meeting at the Rikken. All for this moment.

"FORTY SECONDS...."

Nishina grasped the welder's goggles hanging from his

neck. He took a deep breath and spoke in a calm, steady voice. "Put on your goggles and remember to look away for the first five seconds."

They lowered their binoculars and turned toward him, their faces showing the strain of the moment. Sagane forced a reassuring smile. Suzuki nodded and muttered a prayer. The others could only stare at him, their eyes filled with anxiety.

"Well—it's good luck then."

Time stood still as the exhausted scientists slipped on their dark goggles and dug in behind the sandbags. To the north, the darkness shook with artillery thuds. The Soviets were wasting no time. In another day, they'd sweep through Konan like a scythe.

"TWENTY SECONDS...."

Yamashita pointed a trembling finger at the brightening band of light on the eastern horizon. "The rising sun. A good omen."

Nishina ignored the officer's exclamation. He placed the goggles on his forehead and listened to the crackling voice begin the final countdown.

"FIFTEEN SECONDS...FOURTEEN...THIRTEEN...."

Nishina leaned against the sandbag and aimed his binoculars at the flashing light. He could barely make out the small island silhouetted against the brightening horizon. For two days, the navy had worked around the clock towing obsolete warships, junks, and fishing trawlers into position around that nondescript piece of rock and sand. Exactly one hour ago, an unmanned launch was ferried through the cluster of ghost ships and beached on the islet's western shore. Now it rested quietly beneath the brightening sky, the water gently lapping at its stern while an on-board timer ticked away the final seconds.

"TEN...NINE...EIGHT...."

Nishina placed his binoculars on the sandbag. He slipped the welder's glasses over his eyes while reflecting on the past week's horror. How quickly things had changed. Four days ago, his team was on the verge of reversing the tide of war, only to see their four year struggle vaporized in the fires of

Hiroshima and Nagasaki. Now, he was being called a traitor by the same militarists that had rejected his pleas for funding. Through the darkness, he could hear Tojo's shrill voice demanding proof such an enormous investment would work. Proof Colonel Yoshio Nishina couldn't provide because of an obscure plane crash six years ago.

"THREE...TWO...ONE...ZERO...."

A strange quiet filled the darkness. Nishina clenched his fists and listened to the water washing against the shore.

"What's wrong? Nothing happened?" Yamashita draped himself on the sandbags, his binoculars focused on the horizon.

"Stay down!" Nishina grabbed the officer's pants and pulled him down.

"I don't understand? It's zero plus five and nothing—"

Yamashita froze in horror. The sky blazed with silver light. He could see the clouds shining overhead. And the glowing faces of the scientists staring at each other through their dark glasses. The sun had burst from the sea. Thunder was coming from the east.

"Yes!" Kikuchi sprung to his feet and draped himself on the sandbags, followed by his four colleagues. "Look at it, Yoshio! Genzai bakudan!"

Nishina blinked his eyes in disbelief. An orange ball of flame reflected off Kikuchi's dark glasses. The air shook with thunder. The aging scientist rose to his feet and looked eastward in stunned silence.

Nine miles across the water, a seething orange and black fireball churned into the heavens. The Sea of Japan rumbled with thunder. Below the rising mushroom cloud, the islet and ships had become an inferno of boiling gases and flame.

Kikuchi clutched his binoculars with trembling hands, his eyes locked on the funeral pyre of burning ships at the base of the mushroom's spreading stem. "The fireball's at least a thousand yards across! Eighteen thousand tons of TNT!"

"Congratulations, Nishina San."

Nishina lifted his goggles and saw Yamashita glaring at him, his hand extended.

"Congratulations—you are vindicated."

Nishina looked down at the major's outstretched hand. He was about to clasp it when a blast of hot wind swept across them. The ground shuddered under their feet.

"Incredible! Even at nine miles we feel it. I'll get word to Tokyo immediately." Ecstatic, Yamashita turned toward the swaying communications truck.

"Wait, Major!"

"Sir?"

Nishina stepped toward the excited officer. "There isn't much time. Charges must be set. Your men must destroy the factories and equipment before the Russians break through."

Yamashita stared at the aging scientist in disbelief. "With all respect, Nishina San. We must notify Tokyo to delay the surrender. If we can hold on a few more weeks—"

"Hold on?" Nishina locked his brown eyes on him. "Ten divisions of Russian troops will be here by midnight. We can't leave anything intact. Everything must be destroyed. It's over, Major. We've lost."

"How can you say that?"

"Listen to me, Major. The Emperor has given his word. In four days, a document of surrender will be submitted to the Americans. The war is over, Major Yamashita."

Yamashita's face flushed with anger. He restrained himself, his fists clenched at his sides. "I lost two brothers at Okinawa and Iwo Jima. Until this moment, I thought they died in vain. Look at the sky, Nishina San. Genzai bakudan! We can still win!" He wheeled around and ran toward the communications truck, his hand clutching his sheathed sabre.

"Will they listen to him?" Ryokichi Sagane eased beside his friend.

Nishina shook his head. "They think Hiroshima and Nagasaki are enemy propaganda. A ploy to trick us into surrender. They need to know the truth. Someone must tell them the truth."

Sagane nodded. "They should have walked with us through the rubble. Two flattened cities. Two hundred thousand dead. The others dying from radiation. All from a speck of unleashed energy."

The Tenth Avatar

Nishina felt his stomach heave. He clutched the loudspeaker post and began vomiting. He saw the burned bodies lying in the ruins. And heard the screams of the dying. And that smell. The sickening stench of decaying flesh. All because of two bombs. Creations of desperate men in a world gone mad.

Sagane rested a hand on his friend's shoulder. "You should see a doctor, Yoshio. I think you picked up some radiation."

Nishina wiped his mouth and took a deep breath. He leaned against the loudspeaker post and looked up at the fading orange cloud. "Remember today, Ryoki. The day we looked toward home and saw two rising suns. One beautiful, the other deadly." He turned to his friend. "Which one rises tomorrow?"

Sagane grimaced and looked toward the burning island.

"I would like to speak with the men before I go."

"You're leaving now?"

"No time to lose. Yasuda must see the photograph. To know how close we came."

Nishina turned and walked toward the communications trailer where Yamashita had just received a stern reprimand from Tokyo. He paused to rest his hand on the stunned officer's shoulder. "I'm sorry, Major. There are things you don't know."

Yamashita jerked his shoulder away. "I know this, Nishina San. You're a traitor. I hope you burn in hell."

Nishina lowered his head and walked away. He headed toward the dirt airstrip where a twin-engined plane waited to transport him across the Sea of Japan. When he arrived in what was left of Tokyo, he would submit a report to Lieutenant General Yasuda on the successful August 10, 1945 detonation of Japan's first—and last—atomic bomb near the remote Korean industrial complex known as Konan.

Nishina was about to board the plane when he saw his five comrades rushing toward him in the morning sunlight. He stepped off the ladder and turned to face them. The warm breeze felt good on his face.

The five scientists gathered around their technical and spiritual leader. For a moment, nothing was said while they

Gary Naiman

glanced nervously at each other.

Sagane broke the ice with a joke. He tugged at Nishina's brown army fatigues and stepped back, hands on hips. "What will Yasuda think when he sees you dressed like this? At least comb your hair, Yoshio. And see about some black dye to cover those gray spots."

Asada took the hint and chimed in. "Maybe you will visit the Emperor tonight. Very impressive, glowing in the dark at the Imperial Palace. What will he think?"

Yazaki smiled sheepishly and scratched his head. "Don't you know? That's why the Emperor likes Yoshio. He glows like a lantern. Saves oil for the lamps!" He broke into nervous laughter, followed by his four comrades.

Nishina gave them the evil eye and joined in. It felt good to laugh again.

The air erupted with dust as the transport's twin-engines kicked on with a sudden roar. Nishina glanced at the cockpit window and saw the pilot looking down at him, his finger nervously tapping his watch.

"Well—it's goodbye then. Perhaps we'll see each other again." Nishina stepped forward and clasped each man's hand, his brown eyes glistening with tears.

He backed away and forced a smile. "I'll miss you. I won't forget you. Good luck." He turned and stepped on the ladder.

Tatsutsiro Suzuki couldn't restrain himself. He rushed forward and grasped his friend's wrist. "We came so close. If we had a few more months, we could have beaten them."

Nishina looked down at his distraught colleague. "It's over, Tatsu. Be glad it's over."

"But—we could have won."

"No, Tatsu. Impossible."

Suzuki stepped back in shock. Had the radiation affected his friend's mind? "You're not well. You don't know what you're saying."

Nishina looked up at the orange haze. "You haven't seen what I've seen. Two great cities wiped out in the blink of an eye. Almost two hundred thousand dead. A half million more dying from radiation. No, my friend. A few months would have meant nothing."

Seishi Kikuchi stepped forward in anger. "Then why did we build the damn thing? Why waste four years on a hopeless cause?"

Nishina shook his head. "We had no choice. It was our only chance. If the fools hadn't delayed the funding, we could have deployed the bomb last year and scared off the Americans."

"You mean—destroyed them."

"No—I mean scared them. These weapons must never be used again. They're a curse on us all." Nishina swept his eyes across them. "Hold your heads high. We did our best and it worked. We lit the sky today."

The pilot gunned the engines and stuck his head out the window while angrily pointing at his watch.

Nishina looked down at his colleagues and uttered a final warning. "I don't trust Yamashita. He has suffered too much pain. If you have to do it yourselves, those cyclotrons and separators must be blown up today. Nothing must survive. If the Russians capture that equipment, it won't be the end. It will be the beginning of the end. We will all live under a dark shadow for years to come. The Americans are dangerous enough, but Russian nuclear weapons will bring us to the brink. There is too much hatred in the world. We are not ready for these things. Blow them up. Blow them up now. It will be your finest hour." Nishina turned and headed up the ladder.

Nishina's plane reached Yokohama's Atsugi airstrip at two o'clock that afternoon. A Tokyo landing had been ruled out because of the devastation wrought by the B-29's.

Not that Yokohama was in better shape. Tokyo's sister city had been flattened by months of firebombing, as had neighboring Kobe, Nagoya, and Osaka. Usable airstrips were scarce these days.

The prevailing winds forced Nishina's transport to fly over Tokyo on its final approach. Five months had passed since he last saw the beleaguered city. Better not to have looked down.

Through his window, he could see the green parks and hills surrounding the Imperial Palace. They appeared untouched except for a few black smudges.

The palace hadn't been so lucky. An entire wing had been reduced to black ash by the hideous firebombs. He stared at the palace's protective moat. It seemed so out of place in this era of modern warfare. So useless against the napalm falling from the sky. They had used the moat's water to combat the fires. A medieval bucket brigade struggling against fires that wouldn't die. It was a miracle the Emperor survived.

The hardest part was flying over the rivers that flowed through the crippled city. Five months ago, he had stood on their banks, his stunned eyes glaring at the charred bodies piled against the shore. Thousands of innocent men, women, and children burned beyond recognition in the March ninth firebombing, the water washing over them. He would never forget that horrid smell.

His forehead pressed against the glass. Where were the bridges? The quaint, arched passageways where he had spent so many wonderful days and nights gazing at the Sumida's gentle waters with colleagues and loved ones. The Omiya, Nobashi, and Hajima. The Kiyosu, and Ki along the Jikan River. The Iida near Yanagicho Hill. The Ryogoku, Itsu, and Asakusa. All of them gone. Only the rivers remained, their gentle waters sweeping the gray ash from the banks, carrying the ghosts of the dead to their final resting place at sea.

The shipyards and factories were gone—consumed in the first raid. The harbor district and Koto section—melted. The Kiba district—blackened. Fukugawa—scorched beyond recognition. Tokugawa—erased. Honjo—a smudged memory. Mukaiijima—charred. Kojima—a patch of scorched earth. Tokyo's districts and wards wiped out in the first night of fire bombing.

But the Americans weren't satisfied. Night after night the bombers returned—until nothing was left to burn.

He had evacuated Tokyo before the bombings, only to be summoned back by the Supreme Command after the first incendiary raid. It seemed the military wanted a scientist's appraisal of America's newest terror from the sky.

What was wrong with them? Didn't they have eyes? Ask

the people, you fools! Ask the poor souls who spent that horrible March night clinging to their loved ones in the boiling river while super-heated typhoon winds burned off their clothes and blistered their skin. Ask the petrified citizens wading through sewers to escape the spreading firestorm. The desperate mothers clutching their babies, unable to breathe in the searing heat, their eyes cauterized shut, their hair crackling. Ask them instead of an old man building an atomic bomb.

Better to have stayed in Tokyo and perished with them. Instead, he had lived to see his beloved city die, incinerated by three hundred American B-29's dropping fifty thousand M-47 and M-69 incendiary bombs from the night skies. Sixteen square miles burned black by the creeping napalm. Two hundred sixty thousand homes lost, their bamboo frames and rice-paper windows consumed like kindling. A hundred thousand screaming civilians cremated. And that was just Tokyo. In five months, more Japanese citizens had died in the firebombings than in Hiroshima and Nagasaki combined. Three hundred thousand human beings fried in the night.

Nishina clenched his fists. What kind of victory was this? These animals were no better than the *bushido* militarists who butchered Shanghai and Nanking. Was their hatred unquenchable? Was their quest for revenge insatiable? How far would they go? Where would it end?

He closed his fountain pen and stared at the papers in his lap. He had spent the last two hours drafting his final report to General Yasuda. It spoke of a blinding flash above the Sea of Japan, followed by rolling thunder. Then a fireball billowing into the heavens, its flickering stem seething with uncontrolled energy.

The U-238 conversion had worked, unleashing a blast equal to Hiroshima's. There was enough U-235 and deuterium in Konan to build a dozen bombs like it. The new missiles were close to readiness. And the submarines. Three more months, and they could launch.

But it was too late. The Russians would swarm into Konan's industrial complex within twenty-four hours. They must not be allowed to capture it. Everything must be destroyed, even if it meant disintegrating the cyclotrons and separators in a second mushroom cloud.

He had written these words in the final paragraph of his report. A warning that must be heeded.

Nishina felt the plane descending. He glanced out the window at devastated Yokohama. Tokyo's sister city was a mass of rubble. Eighty percent of the great city had gone up in flames one terror-filled night two months ago when thousands of firebombs rained down from the sky.

Ironic they were landing at Atsugi airstrip. Planes rarely landed at Atsugi. It was here the *Kamikaze* pilots received their spiritual and technical training before taking off for the last time. To throw themselves at the Americans in a final, desperate attempt to turn back their approaching armada. So futile. So cruel. Nishina closed his eyes and said a prayer for the thousands of young men who would never know life's beauty.

The twin-engined plane touched down on the scarred airstrip, barely missing an enormous bomb crater. The pilot cut the engines and jammed on the brakes in a frantic attempt to bring the aircraft to a stop before it plowed into the next cluster of bomb craters. The black *Nakajima* skidded to a stop, its wing flaps pointed at the ground.

The rough landing snapped Nishina's eyes open, or was it the frightening thought flashing through his mind?

What if Yamashita didn't obey orders? What if he formed a defense perimeter around Konan and fought the advancing Russian troops? He still had two divisions at his disposal, and the Russians were known for their hesitance. If it came to a stalemate, the Russians might dig in and wait for more divisions. They wouldn't shell Konan. It was too valuable.

He reached down and gripped the briefcase. Once the Supreme Command received word of the successful detonation, they might change their minds and reinforce Yamashita with enough divisions to hold off the Russians. It would be an easy decision. They hated the Russians as much as the Americans. And now, with renewed hope....

God—what if the fools decided to sacrifice the homeland

for those dozen bombs. To launch a final, glorious strike at America's mainland. To burn San Francisco and Los Angeles. Yes—it was possible. And they were mad enough to try it. How many other Japanese cities would go up in flames before it ended? How many world cities?

He jammed the papers into his briefcase and peered out the window. A jeep had pulled up to the plane and two officers had hopped out. He felt a hand on his shoulder. The pilot was looking down at him.

"Ready, Nishina San?"

He nodded and pushed out of the seat, still clad in his brown fatigues.

A stiff breeze struck his face when he stepped out of the plane. It was coming from the west. Had it been an easterly wind, it would carry the acrid odor of smoke from Yokohama and Tokyo. He stepped off the ladder and returned the officers' bows.

"Greetings, *Sensei*. Your flight went well?"

Nishina nodded politely. "How long will it take to reach Tokyo?"

"Our orders are to drive you to a farmhouse only a few miles from here."

"Farmhouse? We're not going to the Army Institute?"

The officer hesitated. "I'm afraid it has been destroyed. General Yasuda felt this would be safer. Please...." The officer gestured toward the jeep.

Nishina stepped into the jeep and rested the briefcase on his lap. One of the officers hopped into the rear seat while the other jumped in beside him and gunned the engine. They sped away from the plane in a cloud of dust and picked up a dirt road leading into the countryside.

It was a typically warm August day with the afternoon sun shining down on them from a clear blue sky. The jeep bounced along the dirt road, weaving through rice paddies and fields.

Nishina spotted a few straw-hatted farmers tilling the soil with their primitive hoes. There were no signs of war out here. It was as if nothing had happened. He clung to his bouncing seat and felt the warm breeze tousle his hair. It was good to be home.

The farmhouse looked quite innocent from the dirt road. Just a small, wood shack shaded with shrubs and overhanging trees. Nishina stepped out of the jeep and followed the two officers toward the weathered front door. He passed a small barn and iron plow lying tilted in the dirt. No animals were visible.

The first officer pushed open the farmhouse door and gestured for him to go inside. Nishina nodded and brushed past him into a dimly lit room.

"*Sensei!*" Lieutenant General Takeo Yasuda rushed around a makeshift conference table and grasped his friend's arms, his black eyes dancing with excitement. "Is it true?"

Nishina nodded. "The sun rose early this morning. It lit the skies above the Sea of Japan."

"How powerful?"

"Equivalent to Hiroshima."

The short, stocky general backed away, his eyes gleaming.

"Well done, *Sensei*." Jun Noguchi stepped out of the shadows and clasped Nishina's hand, his black eyes glistening with pride. It was his money that had built the mighty complex at Konan. Money raised from fellow profiteers throughout the world. Men who didn't care about causes or nations. Only financial return.

Noguchi gestured toward an empty chair. "You must be exhausted."

"I won't be staying. I must find my family."

"Of course."

Nishina rested his briefcase on the table and lifted out his report. He turned to Yasuda and extended the scribbled papers and hastily developed photograph.

Yasuda took the report and gestured toward the table. "Please, Yoshio. Sit for a moment." He returned to his chair and waited for his longtime friend to sit across from him. Noguchi took the remaining chair.

Nishina noticed a bottle of plum wine on the table. He couldn't resist. He hadn't tasted plum wine since leaving for Konan five months ago. He poured himself a glass and gulped it down. When he put down the empty glass, Yasuda was smiling at him, his hand grasping the photograph.

"I'll have a case sent to your residence."

"Residence?"

"In the hills north of Kyoto. Lovely home. I had your books and papers sent there from the institute. We cleared everything out before the firebombings."

Nishina rested his hands on the table. "Have you heard anything from my family?"

"They are well, my friend. Waiting for you in Kyoto."

"Thank God."

Noguchi reached out and clasped Nishina's wrist. "It was the least we could do. No harm will come to you there. When the Americans occupy the country, you will be left alone except for some visits by their scientists. Just routine, you understand."

Nishina looked at him with puzzled eyes. "How do you know these things?"

Noguchi smiled. "Let's just say I've made some contacts in high places. Convinced the right people that you're much too valuable to place against a wall." He forced a smile and eased back in his chair.

Yasuda leaned forward, his eyes locked on the aging scientist. "Tell me, Yoshio. What were the conditions when you left?"

"Conditions?"

"The Russians."

Nishina sensed a sudden tension in the room. He took a deep breath and composed himself. "I could hear their artillery. They couldn't have been more than thirty miles away." He glanced at his watch. "By now, they've reached the Chosan and Fusan Rivers."

Noguchi pushed out of his chair. "There is no time to lose. I must get word to them."

"Word?"

"That there will be no resistance."

Nishina looked at him in shock.

Noguchi glanced at the general. "Shouldn't he know?"

Yasuda nodded and spoke softly. "Listen to me, Yoshio. The war is lost—but we can still strike a blow for our country. We can't let the Americans dominate the world. They are no better than the Russians."

Nishina's eyes widened. "What are you saying?"

"A deal has been struck."

"Deal?"

"With the Russians."

Nishina fell back in his chair.

"It was for the best, Yoshio. That way, the Americans will be held in check. Once they learn the Russians have the bomb—that's good for us. They'll be forced to help us rebuild. You know—to keep the Russian Bear at bay."

Nishina stared at his friend. He felt Noguchi brush past him. The door swung open and closed.

Yasuda reached for the bottle of plum wine and filled his friend's glass. He set down the bottle and leaned back in his chair. The only light came from the hastily rigged lamp dangling above the table. "It was the only way, Yoshio."

"But—the Russians are our enemies."

"And the Americans aren't? Desperate times call for desperate acts. Don't you see? We'll have them at each other's throats while we rebuild our nation. Who knows—we might even make a profit."

"Profit?"

Yasuda forced a smile. "Relax, Yoshio. It's over. You have done your job. Go home to your family. Smell the cherry blossoms. Write your memoirs."

Nishina brushed back his graying hair. "This is wrong. I left orders for my men to destroy the cyclotrons."

Yasuda nodded. "We expected that, old friend. A man of your genius would naturally think that way. No harm will come to the complex."

"But what about Sagane? Suzuki? The others?"

"They're safe."

"Then get them out of there. Bring them home now."

Yasuda looked down. "I'm afraid they're part of the deal."

"What?"

"The Russians will need more than equipment and raw materials. Knowledge is critical." Yasuda stood up and rested his hands on the table. "I'm sorry, Yoshio. It's for the good of our nation."

Nishina sank in the chair. The radiation had sapped his strength. He stared at the table and shook his head.

"Oh—I almost forgot. It seems Major Yamashita has committed *hari-kari*. Can't blame him. Relieved of his command. Nothing left. Better to die in the field than come home in disgrace."

Yasuda eased around the table and rested a hand on his friend's shoulder. "The jeep will take you back to the plane. A quick hop to Kyoto and you'll be with your family. I've arranged for a doctor to visit you. You need rest and care. In a few months, you'll forget all this and your life will be back to normal."

Nishina rose to his feet. He reached into his pocket and pulled out a worn photograph.

"You still carry that silly thing?"

"It lifts my spirits when I'm down."

Yasuda reached for the frazzled photograph. "Hard to believe that's us. Only six years ago. Look at us, Yoshio. We look so young. Two drunken idealists posing with Tomonaga beneath the great Buddha the night before he left. We could barely stand from all the *saki*."

"They were better days."

Yasuda shook his head. "Strange thing—fate. If Tomonaga had made it through the mountains with that uranium and heavy water, we would have pulled off the greatest coup of all time. So much for the master race. When their scientists gave Tomonaga the U-235 samples in exchange for the gold, they had no idea how close we were. Hell, the plane was packed with enough deuterium and green gas to take out Berlin. A little gift from their unsuspecting comrades in Norway." His frown became a sneer. "Hitler would have shit his pants if he'd known what we were up to. Hell—the fools even loaned us their best transport to get us home. And two of their lunatic scientists. How kind of them. They wanted to be so kind to their inferior yellow brothers."

Nishina took the photograph from his friend's hand and stuffed it in his pocket. "I think we came too close. I think the gods turned against us."

"Nonsense, Yoshio. Just a twist of bad luck. A few hundred feet and Tomonaga's plane would have cleared the mountains. Tojo would have gotten his proof and we would have gotten the money. Hell—we would have deployed the first bomb last year. We could have used it on their carriers. Or blackened one of their occupied islands. Then—east toward Hawaii and San Francisco." He gripped his friend's arm. "We would have won, Yoshio. We would have pulverized the bastards and sent a warning to Hitler and Stalin they wouldn't forget. Let the Occidentals have the west. The East belongs to the rising sun."

Nishina's face flushed. "You don't understand. None of you understand. You think a year would have made a difference? That the Americans would have surrendered? That our bombs would have broken them? That our missiles and submarines would have brought them to their knees? No, Takeo. They would have built their bombs while we rained death on them. Until they could strike back. Their hatred would have kept them alive until they levelled our cities."

Yasuda glared at him. "And what about our hatred?"

Nishina nodded, his brown eyes glistening with anger. "Yes—I think you're beginning to understand. Two nations at each other's throats. Atom bombs falling out of the skies. Cities aflame. Don't you see, Takeo? Don't you see?"

"What—the end of the world?"

Nishina glanced at Noguchi's empty chair. "Stop that madman before it's too late. Blow up those cyclotrons now."

Yasuda stiffened. "I'm sorry, Yoshio. I'm afraid it's you who doesn't understand. This damned war has taught me a hard lesson. One you should learn. The world isn't driven by nations or causes. Only by powerful men like Jun. Without them, there would be no order. Forget your gods. They couldn't care less."

Nishina lowered his head and turned toward the door. He lifted the latch and hesitated. "If Jun and his kind control our

The Tenth Avatar

future—we're doomed. Goodbye, Takeo." He stepped through the door into the sunlight, and said a prayer for the human race.

Yoshio Nishina died six years later, his body racked with cancer from the radiation picked up at Hiroshima and Nagasaki. But his prophecy lives on—and it remains unheeded.

When the Soviets occupied Konan, they found the cyclotrons and separators intact. They also found five dead scientists huddled together on the beach facing the Sea of Japan, victims of their own hand. Nishina's comrades had honored their *sensei's* final request in the only way left to them. Without their knowledge, the bomb couldn't be built. It was their finest hour.

But it was only a temporary setback for the Soviets. Using captured Nazi scientists and agents in the United States, they exploded their first atom bomb in 1949, launching a nuclear terror that lives today. A cancer that has spread to lesser, unstable nations. A radioactive cauldron that threatens to boil over with each new border conflict.

The gods have returned to the heavens, but the Tenth Avatar remains on earth in its final form—to await man's decision. Will he purge himself of the evil in his heart? Or perish in flames? Will compassion replace hatred? Will love triumph over avarice and greed? Will the priests open their vaults of grain to feed the hungry? Will the kings care for their people? Will the armies put down their weapons and embrace each other as brothers?

Man's fate has been placed in his own hands—and time is running out. The Tenth Avatar has taken its final earthly form. *Kalki* has become the nuclear sun. Which sun rises tomorrow?

The four warriors had not failed. They had come to the great mountain and confronted the anti-gods—and perhaps bought the world a few precious years. As mere mortals, they could do no more.

For their sacrifice, the reporter and mystic would be rewarded with rebirth through *Karma*. To carry their enlightened spirits into a world more threatened than ever before. And if necessary, to be called a second time.

And the Spaniard? He would be reunited with his loved ones in a better world. To swim in the Turia's swirling waters with the sun on his face. To climb the fertile hills and taste the sweet nectar again. To run across the park toward the beautiful home nestled beneath the conifer trees. A fitting reward for the tormented man who heard a voice whispering in the darkness, and gave his life to stop the pain. For this, he would be granted *Moksha*—and everlasting peace.

But what of the last one? Lying beneath the snow only five feet below the mighty one's ivory crown, his bleached fingers still clutching the tattered blue and orange pennant he'd jammed into the summit with his last breath of life. He differed from the others because he saw the Tenth Avatar six years before its eruption above the Alamogordo, New Mexico desert.

Julian Bonaventure could have climbed down that day, but he chose to follow an ivory ridge into the clouds, the sun on his face, the world at his feet. He died an honorable death because he was strong enough to conquer the mighty lady, but wise enough to leave her ivory crown untouched. For this, he must be rewarded.

The night sky filled with stars and the Himalaya glowed with silver light. There would be no storms tonight. No wars. No pain. The mountain was going to sleep. Mr. Bonaventure was going to sleep. For now—they were one....